KINGDOMS OF DEATH

Also by Christopher Ruocchio:

The Sun-Eater
EMPIRE OF SILENCE
HOWLING DARK
DEMON IN WHITE
KINGDOMS OF DEATH

Christopher Ruocchio

KINGDOMS OF DEATH

THE SUN EATER: BOOK FOUR

DAW BOOKS, INC.

DONALD A. WOLLHEIM, FOUNDER

1745 Broadway, New York, NY 10019

ELIZABETH R. WOLLHEIM

SHEILA E. GILBERT

PUBLISHERS

www.dawbooks.com

First Printing, March 2022
1st Printing

DAW TRADEMARK REGISTERED
U.S. PAT. AND TM. OFF. AND FOREIGN COUNTRIES
—MARCA REGISTRADA
HECHO EN U.S.A.

PRINTED IN THE U.S.A.

TO ELGIN AND DARLENE,
MY SECOND PARENTS.
I LOVE YOU BOTH.

CHAPTER 1

TWILIGHT

NIGHT.

Night had fallen on Eikana and clung about the rooftops and bristling antennae that crowned the old refinery like weathered tombstones. No light of moon was there, and the stars kept silent vigil, distant and cold as the gray sands that flatly stretched to the horizon all around.

"The Pale won't know what hit them," Crim said, whispering despite the relative safety of the ship around us. I sensed the anticipation in the man—sensed it in all the men about me, the soldiers huddled like the Achaeans in the bowels of their wooden horse. Each one of them seemed to be holding his breath.

"They better not!" groused Pallino. "The fleet's still three hours behind."

"Heat sinks are holding, my lord," said the pilot officer, reassuring. "Only way they'll see us coming is if they sight us out a window."

I knew the pilot was right. The *Ascalon* was the fastest ship in our fleet, a Challis-class interceptor whose massive heat sinks made it possible to mask its sub-light emissions for days, thus making it invisible to heat and light detection and perfect for such stealth missions as ours. It was a small ship, a mere five hundred feet from end to end, its hydroponics and life-support systems designed to support an active crew of perhaps ten men and fugue creches to sustain another forty. A small complement, but enough— I prayed—for our task.

Three hours.

We had three hours to secure the Yamato Fuelworks at *Virdi Planum*.

Peering out the slit window, I could clearly see the silver line of the bundled hadron colliders. Fully operational, the machines produced kilo-tons of antimatter a day, iron hearts synthesizing the volatile substance from the collision of the smallest quanta to fuel the sector's starships. In the distance, I could make out the silvered domes where containment silos waited to be hauled from Eikana's surface to high orbit.

Without antimatter, our starships could not travel faster than light's slow speed.

Without Eikana, the local capital at Nessus—and by extension, the great mass of the Imperial navy in the Centaurine provinces—was as good as crippled. It was a cunning target.

It was not like the Cielcin to choose cunning targets.

Not like *most* Cielcin.

Something of my disquiet must have registered on my face, for Pallino asked, "You all right, Had?"

I snapped my attention to the other man, found him watching me with shrewd eyes. When I'd first met Pallino on Emesh centuries before, he'd been a grizzled old soldier, one-eyed and scarred. Decades of loyal service to myself and to the Imperium had won him a new eye and a second youth, while I—whose palatine genetic advantages promised me centuries—had grown older. Pallino had slept for more nearly a hundred years on ice aboard the *Tamerlane* while I had served as counselor to the Magnarch on Nessus. I had passed him by, but even still there was a spark of almost paternal concern in the once-older man's face.

"This attack has Dorayaica's name all over it," I said, sure I was right. *The Scourge of Earth,* they called it. *The Prophet.* Prince of the Princes of the Cielcin, great enemy of man. While most of the great Cielcin war fleets migrated from system to system, burning and pillaging entire worlds as they went, Dorayaica moved deliberately. Its alien mind had grasped our own strategy with a vision none of its fellows possessed. It burned ship-yards, disrupted supply chains, captured legionary transports.

Pallino made a face. "You don't know that."

"I do," I said, eyes flitting over the masked and armored soldiers of our cadre. My Red Company. Raising my voice, I addressed them all. "I want the refinery cleared before our fleet arrives!" I leaned away from the bulk-head, one hand grasping the loop on the padded arch above my head to steady myself. "I want clean knife-work, lads. We must not alert their ships to our presence." It was imperative we seized the Fuelworks by hand. It took one errant shot from a ship's tactical maser or misplaced photonic explosive to detonate the huge AM reservoirs beneath the outlying domes, and there was enough antimatter on Eikana to transform *Virdi Planum* from plateau to crater and crack the planet's crust.

"Clean as can be, lord," said Crim, one hand checking the set of knives in the bandoleer he wore.

The *Ascalon* banked into a low arc, its knife-like body cupping the air as we slid lower. The silver line of the foundry's colliders swung into place beneath us.

"Prepare yourselves!" I exclaimed, and pressed the trigger on my suit's neck flange, which triggered the helmet to rise. Metal panels rose about my face, unfurling like the petals of a flower, and closed about my head. The suit's augmented vision flickered on a moment after, twin cones of light projected onto my retinas. Pallino and Crim had done the same. A sea of armored soldiery stared back at me: featureless ivory masks with the pitchfork-and-pentacle of the Red Company painted over the spot where their left eye should be.

We had to move fast. The few seconds where the *Ascalon* hovered above the top of the collider were the most risky. It would be all too easy for any of the xenobites in the refinery ahead to spot the vessel crouching like a vulture above the pipeline.

"Venting the cabin in five, four, three . . ." The end of the pilot officer's countdown vanished beneath the rush and thunder of blood in my ears. Almost seventy years I'd been trapped on Nessus, my punishment for surviving the trial on Thermon. That trial had cost another twelve years. It had been more than a century since I'd faced the Cielcin in battle.

So long . . .

The shudder of my own heart was drowned by a violent hissing as the *Ascalon*'s rear compartment was vented of air. Eikana had none, and so the ramp opened on grim silence. All the better—there would be no wind to carry our voices or the clangor of our feet.

I led the way down the ramp, Pallino close at my side. Ahead, a few hundred yards of covered pipeline marched toward the squat and brutish buildings of the refinery complex. Not far ahead to either side, the rails of ladders rose, and with a gesture I ordered that my men should fan out. I paused to let them filter past, and turning back, watched the black blade of our starship rise on silent repulsor fields, ramp closing. Then it was gone, a darker shadow against the dark of night.

"Lord Marlowe."

The man who had spoken was a common trooper, the last in line.

I realized then that I'd been standing atop the collider for far too long. My gaze lingered on the silver expanse of the machine where it marched out to the horizon. The refinery's hadron colliders girdled the entire planet, so if I'd wanted I might have followed the track of that machine about the planet's equator until I came upon the complex from the far side. A single road, unbroken—a ring around the world.

"Lord Marlowe?" the man said again.

Stirring at last, I followed him down the ladder.

The men ahead of me moved in triases, in knots of three darting cover to cover. We progressed quickly along the ramparts that ran along the outside of the great machine, and for the better part of a minute the only sound in my universe was the noise of my own bootheels reverberating through my armored suit.

"Contact," one of the soldiers said. "On the left."

A horned figure stood upon the roof of the nearest building, black against the darkness, an unearthly gargoyle crouched upon the heights above. It had not marked our approach, and I caught myself wondering if our inhuman adversary had fallen asleep at its watch.

One of our hoplites raised his lance. Invisibly, a laser flashed, smote the gargoyle. No sound. No cry. The horned figure toppled, fell.

"Two more," came the voice of one soldier over the line.

"Nice shot, one-three!"

"They're down," came the first voice again.

"Sure seems like they weren't expecting us," said another. "There's almost no guard!"

And why would there be? The Cielcin were counting on their long-range sensors, were counting on us to launch a full-frontal assault on their orbital blockade. They were not expecting the attack to come from men on the ground—and therein lay our advantage and our hope.

Ahead, the central building loomed. There the newly created antimatter was extracted from the collider and funneled through magnetic coils to storage in one of the outlying silos. There too were the controls for the whole refinery. Our goal. If we could shut down the collider and clear the refinery of the volatile substance, we'd be able to bring ships and troops down with impunity when the fleet arrived.

We would need them.

A hatch cycled on the wall to our right, and a figure in gnarled black stepped out. Eight feet tall it was, and it had to stoop to clear the airlock.

At a glance, the xenobite might have been human. Two arms, two legs, a slim torso. The horns atop its head might have been only some feature of its cruel helmet. But I knew the Cielcin well, knew the subtle differences, the way the uncanny horror of the creatures unrolled itself the longer one looked at them. The arms were too long, with grasping hands possessed of too many fingers with too many joints. The legs were bowed and crooked, the torso at once too slim and too short. And the crown of horns was not a feature of any helm, but a part of the inhuman creature's own flesh.

It hadn't expected us, betrayed surprise in the way it flinched as its white-masked face turned and saw us, the circular black lenses over its eyes wide and staring. Crim's hand flashed, and a moment after, the creature folded, ichor black as ink spraying from a wound in its throat. Crim leaped upon the body, tugging the slender blade free with a motion that tore the inhuman neck open.

Crim hardly broke stride, signaled two knots of men to retrace the creature's path into the still-open hatch. "Check inside. There may be more," he said, voice void of expression. We'd studied schematics of the Yamato refinery on route to Eikana, and a three-dimensional projection of the plans floated in the periphery of my vision.

"I don't like this, Had," Pallino said, speaking over a private connection so as not to upset the men. "It's too bloody quiet."

"That'll change soon enough," I said. "Door's not far."

Crim had reached the door as I spoke, a heavy, square portal of solid steel. Not an airlock. The areas of the refinery surrounding the hadron collider's collection ports were kept in vacuum to better isolate the antimatter in the event of a leak. Another layer of security, futile though it perhaps was. One of the men hunched over the control panel and in a moment had the entire unit off the wall. He drew a thin wire from his armor's gauntlet terminal and inserted it into the new hole he'd made.

"Can you open it?" Crim asked.

I could hear the tech's frown through his mask. "Yes, sir, but they'll know the minute we do. Working on override."

"We should backtrack through that side hatch that one came out of," Pallino suggested, jerking his head in the direction of the creature dead upon the catwalk behind.

"No good," I said, double-checking the map to be sure. "We'll get tangled up in fuel collection. We need to get up to central control, lock the building down."

The tech swore. "No good. I can't cycle the door without lighting up security."

"Can you disable the sensors?" Crim asked. "We'll burn our way in."

"They're sure to pick up the temp spike," the fellow said.

"Then we'll have to cut our way in," I said, shouldering men aside. My hand went to the magnetic hasp at my right hip, armored fingers finding the familiar Jaddian leather grip of my sword. "Stand aside, soldier."

The technician did as he was told. "All clear, my lord."

Fingers tightened on the dual trigger, and the highmatter blade flowered like a ray of moonlight on that world that had never known a moon. The exotic material rippled like quicksilver in the air, gleaming like a spike of liquid crystal. I checked my advance, sword casting ghostly highlights on the catwalk beneath us and the metallic wall rising at our side. My left hand went to the catch that activated my suit's body shield, and I prepared myself for whatever was to come. I had been so long removed from the fighting that I'd forgotten the charge of it, the harp-string tension in the air. Almost, I felt a boy of thirty again, not a man of three hundred thirty.

I plunged the point of the sword into the door. The metal cut easily. The atom-fine edge of my weapon sheared between molecules, and in short order I'd carved a ragged hole in the steel. I stepped back, blade humming in my grip as Crim and two legionnaires stepped in and pushed on the door. It fell with a muted bang that reverberated up from my boots, a noise felt—not heard.

Crim went first, one hand still clutching his bloody knife, the other grasping the hilt of the ceramic sword in his belt. He moved like a stalking panther, head down between his shoulders, footfalls delicate. The men behind moved like chess pieces, stiff and precise, sweeping the gray hall with the points of their short lances, ready to fire at the first signs of life. No alarm sounded, no guard sprang to alert.

"All too easy," I heard Pallino say. I silenced him with a look and followed our men across the threshold, my shadow stretched before me by the torch beams of the men at my back. The moment I entered the hall I saw a flash of light reflected on the polished walls and heard the hoarse shouts of men.

"Contact! Contact!"

One of the men staggered back into the hall from a side passage, lance raised as he wrestled with something silver that wound itself snakelike about his weapon arm.

"Nahute!" I exclaimed, lurching forward.

The alien drone coiled tight about my soldier's arm. He screamed, panic flooding the comms channels as the metal serpent *tightened*. I saw the man's arm break as the snake bent his elbow backward. The soldier hit the ground, his cries turned to shrieking.

"Hold still!" I said, trying to straighten the ruined arm.

Nothing in the man's response indicated he had heard me. He screamed as I steadied his arm. The serpent drone twisted its tail around my own wrist. Lifting my sword, I slashed the snake in half, felt the machine die and tumble to the floor.

"Can you stand?" I asked, offering my hand to the injured man.

I never heard his answer. Two more of the silver drones spiraled out of the dark from the side passage, drill-bit teeth whining. One shot over my head as I turned and the other caromed off my shield—so fast did it travel in its eagerness to reach me. The second fell in the flash of my blade, and I stood square to face the dark opening of that side passage, waiting.

A white face hovered in the gloom, sharp-chinned and featureless but for its gaping black eyes. Horns. Talons. A wicked white sword. The Cielcin berserker launched itself at me, elongated body seeming to materialize as if condensed from the shadows. I knew then who had thrown the serpent drones at us and lunged forward to meet it, praying the beast had not put out the alarm. The white sword flashed over my head as I ducked, alien ceramic notching the steel of the door frame. The creature had not seen highmatter before, I guessed, for it seemed not to realize its danger. Nothing would stop a highmatter blade short of the long-chain carbons of adamant of which starship hulls are made, unless it was highmatter itself. The rubberized polymers of the inhuman's body suit were no obstacle.

Rising from my crouch, I dragged my sword through a rising arc that sliced through door frame and foe alike. The creature fell in two pieces.

"They must know we're here by now," Pallino said, coming to my side, weapon raised.

I kicked the fallen xenobite's sword from nerveless fingers, spurned the body with my toe. Dim red lights flickered from pockmarked recesses in the slashed breastplate, made black blood shine. Suit diagnostics? Or the indicator of some distress signal? I knew Pallino was right. "We have to move."

The first half hour of our window was gone, and our secrecy with it. I told myself the Cielcin had no way of knowing if they faced an army or a last desperate survivor of the refinery work crew, but that did little to allay my concerns as we climbed square spiral stairs. Nearly five hundred work-ers had lived on-site—the only permanent inhabitants of airless and arid Eikana. I shuddered to think of the fate that had befallen them.

Refinery control was not far, up several levels and along a gallery over-looking fuel collection and the maintenance tram. The chamber itself lay at the end of an accessway that ran out above the refinery floor so that the techs might peer down at their complex machinery.

It was sure to be guarded.

As I mounted the third landing the stairs shook, and above I saw the flash of energy-lances as men shouted over the line. The lack of air may have afforded us silence as we entered the fortress, but it had its disadvan-tages, too.

We had not heard them coming.

"Stay back!" Pallino said, throwing an arm across my chest to stop me climbing. Above, I saw the horned shapes of the enemy vying with our men in the entrance, a half dozen at least. The steel runners rattled beneath my feet, and looking down I saw more horns behind, black shapes moving on the stairs.

"No good!" I shouted.

The whole stair fell by inches, its bolts torn loose. Pallino and I lurched against the rail, and looking down I saw the white-and-silvered jewel scarab shape of a Cielcin chimera. The alien brain inside the machine re-garded me a moment through optic sensors. Little of the creature it had been remained, and the body the Cielcin's human allies had built for it was stronger than any flesh. Its jointed iron hand clutched the bottom of the stair, rail crushed like paper in its fingers.

"Climb!" I shouted, shoving Pallino on. We made the landing just as the creature tore the steps free. They tumbled a dozen feet and hit the steps below with a resonant *boom* that echoed up my feet. Two men fell with them. They'd been too slow.

The chimera flexed its mighty thighs, pistons firing, and leaped. Pallino fired, but his lance was absorbed by the monster's shield. The magi who had crafted the thing's new body had lavished all their art upon it. Jointed white fingers closed on the lip of the landing at our heels, but the beast had forgotten elementary physics. The tremendous weight of its body bent the metal of the platform, and I felt a grinding beneath my feet as mighty bolts scraped against the poured stone wall of the stairwell.

We ran, spurring our men ahead of us. I followed them through the open door onto the gallery above, stepping over the bodies of man and xenobite alike. Crim's sword drew a black line across the throat of one attacker and moved smoothly to parry the strike of the next. Flowing like water, the Norman swordsman punched his assailant under the arm with one of his knives, drew it out wet. The ink-dark substance boiled in that airless place, and the desperate creature tried to return the favor, only to be skewered on the bayonet of the nearest soldier's lance.

The gallery ahead was filled with horned devils, white-masked, black-armored, wielding scimitars the color of bone or else grasping *nahute* coiled in hooked hands like silver whips.

Nothing for it.

No way out but through.

"Seal the door!" someone called, and the bulkhead closed behind us. Through sloping windows at our left a man might look down upon the cluster of hadron colliders where they passed collection and the magnetic siphons that channeled the volatile fuel out towards the silos. I had a fleeting glimpse of the control room through the window, hanging like an inverse mushroom above the refinery floor, but the shouts of men over the comm line filled my ears, and I came crashing back to myself.

There must have been a score of them in the hall between us and the airlock to access refinery control. The space between us was filled with the snarling of flying drones and the slashing of blades. Energy lances fired, shield curtains gleamed. Men died and Cielcin, too. Crim's sword sketched a bloody maze through the bodies of those who fell upon him until his red and white armor was stained black. I slew two of them myself. The sword Sir Olorin had given me so very long ago made short work of the enemy. A *nahute* had gotten through the shield of one of our hoplites and chewed between the plates of his armor. Red blood ran and boiled like the black, and I saw three men cut down where they stood.

But we were gaining ground.

Doom.

The floor beneath us shook, and looking back I saw the heavy steel of the bulkhead warp inward as though some mighty fist were knocking. The chimera had reached the door.

"Into the airlock!" Crim shouted. Those doors were double the strength of the ones we'd just closed and electromagnetically shielded, for what little good that would do in the event of a critical failure to the refinery systems. With antimatter—there is no containment, no shielding. Annihilation will out.

Doom.

Another blow dented the far door. I stood on the threshold of the air-lock, looking back across a river of dead men and monsters. We were almost there.

"Lord?"

"Close the door," I said.

CHAPTER 2

TRUTH

"HOW LONG WILL THE door hold?" I asked the room at large, surveying the control chamber and the dozen or so inhuman bodies we'd left slumped in chairs or over consoles. Despite the size of the Cielcin fleet in orbit about Eikana, they had left remarkably few defenders in the refinery station itself. I supposed they must have concentrated their efforts on the fuel silos, preparing to offload the valuable material up the gravity well.

I didn't know the man who answered, voice flattened by his helmet in the stale air of the control room. "Long enough, unless they brought something bigger than that giant."

"They might blast their way in," suggested another.

"Not this close to the collider!" Crim objected. "They're not suicidal."

But I had seen the Cielcin throw themselves to their deaths on foot and in space, and I wasn't so sure. Eyes locked on the tangle of magnetic coils that spiderwebbed the chamber below. "Can you shut it all down?"

The man hunched over the central console paused and looked back at me. "I think so, lord. It's more complicated than the fuel shunt on the *Tamerlane*, but I've nearly got the collider down. It should be a simple matter of letting the siphons funnel the AM out to storage." He was a junior engineer—one of Ilex's men.

"Should be?" Pallino asked. The chiliarch glanced up at me from his place by the central console. I did not need to see his face to feel the disbelief and exasperation wafting off him. I raised a hand for quiet, locked eyes with my thin reflection in the alumglass. My reflection peered back, black mask fashioned in the shape of an impassive human face touched with labyrinth tracery about the eyes. The armor still fit after so long, breastplate shaped in Roman fashion after a muscled human torso, the pitchfork-and-pentacle cartouche of my house set amidst eight mighty wings resplendent in enameled crimson in the center of my chest. This over a tunic of matching red, strapped pteruges at shoulder and waist, leather intricately embossed. The gauntlets and greaves were richly shaped, decorated with sculpted ceramic vines and faces. And above it all the cape: black above, red below; fastened at the right shoulder.

Lord Hadrian Marlowe stared at me from my reflection, not really seeing.

In the momentary calm I saw—he saw, we saw—the infinite manifold *us*. A thousand Hadrians stared back me from that glass. A thousand thousand eyes, ten thousand thousand black masks . . . all the infinite versions of myself spread out across the infinite versions of that instant, each one slightly different, and more different the further those reflections stretched from me. As I watched, I saw countless versions of myself vanish, wiped out in a flash of light as the tech at the console failed. Whole parallel worlds vanished from my sight as his mistakes killed us. I did not understand the choices the fellow was making, do not understand the mechanics of particle accelerators or electromagnetic siphons, but I understood their consequences well enough.

It is said that in the presence of an observer, the particles of light collapse from waves of energy into the beams our eyes understand, that the presence of consciousness alters reality itself. The Quiet changed something in me upon their mountain. I felt then as I imagine a blind man must feel, opening his eyes for the first time—as if I'd been blind all my life. As our eyes make straight the waves of light, my new vision straightened time. I had only to look. To concentrate. To choose.

I chose for us to live, focused on a path through time where containment did not fail.

"I've done it," the technician said, unaware of my influence.

The vision faded, reflections dripping back together, infinity collapsing until I stared at my solitary reflection once again, eye to eye.

"Very good, soldier," I said, screwing my eyes shut inside the helmet. Calling on the vision was never easy. "How long until the fleet arrives?"

Crim had removed his helmet and ran a hand through his shaggy mane of curling dark hair. "One hour. Thirty-seven minutes. We can hold here." He squinted, peering through the windows back toward the gallery whence we'd come. I followed his gaze to the gallery we'd so recently vacated. Cielcin soldiers moved hurriedly along it, back and forth, relaying orders or else carrying equipment. "They won't dare blast their way in. They'll use plasma cutters."

"Most like," I agreed. Still more of the creatures were moving on the floor of the refinery below. Evidently the bulk of the force remaining on the station had found us. There must have been two . . . perhaps three hundred of them. Not for the first time, I wished I were a scholiast, able to subitize their precise number at a glance.

As we spoke, a faint mechanical whining—almost unnoticeable from the moment we'd passed through the airlock to the command center—began to slow. Below us, the great engine that wrapped about the planet began to shut down. With the collider stopped it would not be long before the siphons emptied the refinery of its volatile product and funneled it to the storage silos miles off. It was possible the Pale would not notice, standing in vacuum as they were. If they did, they might opt to blow the control center entire and abscond with the fuel already in the outlying silos. They had no notion that the fleet was coming or when it might arrive.

But I thought not. It was not like Syriani Dorayaica to waste an asset, and the Yamato Fuelworks was an asset. No, the Pale Prince of Princes would try to squeeze it for all its worth. The Cielcin would not risk trying to destroy the refinery until they were sure they could not hold it. That was why it was imperative the collider be powered down. Active, a single shot might trigger a runaway annihilation. Inactive, it might sustain damage, but damaged was not destroyed.

Stalemate. For the moment.

"I don't like this," Pallino grumbled. "Not having a way out."

"We have a way out," Crim said, removing something from a pouch on his belt. Despite decades in Imperial service, the former Norman mercenary still wore his striped red-and-white Jaddian kaftan over his armor.

The old soldier rounded on Crim. "Sitting on our ass is not a way out."

Crim leaned against a console with the ease of one lingering in a city park. He peeled the wax paper off the candy he'd taken from his belt and popped it into his mouth, chewing thoughtfully. "They'll be here." He tossed the paper on the floor. "Want one?"

Pallino shook his head and turned away, letting the silence stretch awkward between them. I did not intervene. The other soldiers all stood in knots in the doors, one man bent over the security terminal that monitored the airlock and the gallery doors. Presently, one of the junior men—another who'd removed his helmet—cleared his throat and said, "Can I . . . can I have one, sir?"

Wordless, Crim reached into his belt pocket once more and tossed the fellow a candy. No one else asked.

"Collider should be fully powered down in another nine minutes," the tech said. "Magnetic siphons cleared in thirteen."

I allowed the man the barest nod and touched him on the shoulder as I passed toward the door. "What are they doing?" I asked the man at the console.

He flinched as if struck. "I'm not sure, my lord. They've run a cable from downstairs, but the cameras are out all along the gallery. Didn't want us watching . . ." He glanced up at me and away. "I think they're gone for some kind of plasma bore. Cut their way in like the commander was saying. It's hard to tell at this angle." I peered over his shoulder at the holograph plate. It showed the feeds from four different cameras within the airlock, only one of which peered out through one alumglass panel toward the outer door. The massive chimera stood stolidly outside the door, blank face staring fixedly at the command center, unmoving. It must have tried its luck on the airlock door and been defeated by the cubit-thick steel. Its comrades busied themselves with a heavy black crate, its surface ribbed and gnarled, as thought it were the rotting carcass of a box.

It was definitely some sort of weapon. Plasma cutter, possibly. Some kind of drill.

"It's a pity we can't talk to them," I said, wincing inwardly. Seldom had I spoken truer words. Without air in the outer hall, I could not speak to our attackers in the gallery, unless . . . "Can you access the public address system?"

The soldier fumbled on the controls. "I think so. Yes."

"You're one of the new ones, aren't you?" I asked. We'd taken on new men for the expedition. So many of the Red Company's technical and support staff had been stripped from the *Tamerlane* after my trial on Thermon. Ship technicians and engineers were always in short supply, and with the *Tamerlane* in mothballs with its crew for almost a century while I languished in a gilded cage on Nessus, they had been needed elsewhere. I'd been given new men when the crisis on Eikana had ended my seventy years in purgatory.

The man stopped fussing with the security terminal. "Yes, Lord Marlowe. First tour."

"What's your name, lad?"

"Leon."

"Leon," I said, studying the fellow's rank insignia. He wore a hoplite's heavy plate, but his shoulder panels bore the red circles of an ensign. "That's a very old name."

"Aye, my lord. It's been in my family for a very long time."

"You've never seen the Cielcin before, have you, Leon?"

"Only in the holos." I could hear the pained expression he wore in the stain in his voice. "I didn't think they'd be so big." He turned his masked face to look at mine. "Is it true they . . . eat people?"

Beneath the mask, I smiled, thinking of a dinner conversation more than three hundred years gone, and of my brother, Crispin. "Do you doubt it?" I asked.

"No."

"I did," I said. "When I was a boy. I believed it was a story the Chantry told to frighten us into war." Why was I unburdening myself on this young man so? Had I been so long out of the world of battle? Was it nerves? Or had I become an old man in truth beneath my body's still-youthful appearance? "But some stories are true. That's a terrible thing. Better to believe nothing is true, then you're free to make what you want of the world."

"My lord?" Leon's frown was as audible as his pain had been.

"I won't lie to you," I said. "It doesn't get any easier. Fighting." I clapped him on the shoulder. "But we'll fight together, eh?"

The junior man stood a little straighter. "Aye, sir."

"Put me through public address and step aside," I said.

Leon did as I asked, and I marked how much surer were his fingers on the controls, though privately I was glad it had not been him in charge of depowering the matrix of hadron colliders.

A blue light pulsed in the corner of the holograph plate, indicating the feed was live. Most of the refinery was airless, but there were pockets like the control room that were conditioned for the comfort of the work crew. Though most of the address system would wind silently in vacuum, I was sure to be heard somewhere, and I was doubly sure the chimera would hear with its internal radio—along with any more of its kind on the base.

"*Bayarunbemn o-ajun!*" I said, speaking the xenobites' own tongue. *You have us surrounded.* "I would speak to your leader." My likeness was sure to be displayed on every holograph plate in the refinery, black and red. Even in places where my message would not be heard, my face—my mask— would be seen. I had fought the Cielcin for hundreds of years on dozens of worlds, battled them from the far Expanse of Norma and up and down the Centaurine provinces: Aptucca and Oxiana, Berenike and Mettina, Comum and Senuessa.

My face and mask were known.

The inhuman reply came slowly, as if our foe were waking from long sleep or deep focus. No image appeared on the plate. The voice that spoke was higher and colder than any human tone, and flat of all affect. "You are the Devil," it said.

"In the flesh," I answered it. "You have the command here?"

"Daratolo ne?" the creature said, strange flat voice crackling as the signal faltered. "You live? After all this time . . . I had almost lost hope of meeting you."

I stood stock still, glad of my suit's mask for fear the xenobite would have understood the look of surprise that colored my face. It was not the greeting I'd expected. After a moment's hesitation, I managed to say, "Who are you?" I did not know the voice.

"You killed two of my sister-brothers," it said. *"Raka'ta ude ti-wetidiu."*

We are four now. The answer clicked into place like the mystagogue's last fortune card.

"Iubalu," I said. "Bahudde." A wordless snarl answered me, grinding like the noise of sawblades. It was no natural sound, as though the voice were generated on some sound board and not the product of any throat. Those names had riled it. "You are one of the *Iedyr.*" The Iedyr Yemani—the White Hand—were Syriani Dorayaica's generals, its concubines and sworn servants. Each one had been given a machine body by its master, no two of them alike. I had killed one fighting on the road to Nemavand, and with the help of the Irchtani, we had slain another on Berenike.

"You dare speak their names!" the creature said.

"They're moving in the gallery!" Pallino's voice cut across my attention, and I spared a glance through the window to where the Cielcin massed by the outer door of the airlock. They'd removed the lid of their box, though what lay within I could not tell from my vantage point.

The flat, cold voice was not finished. "I will bring you to my master," it said.

"You may try." A taut smile pulled one corner of my mouth. "Might I know the name of my destroyer?" I asked.

The creature made a high keening sound, like a woman wailing. It was a Cielcin laugh. "I am Hushansa the Many-Handed, *vayadan ba-Shiomu,* and I will enjoy watching him break you. My master has . . . desired you for so long."

It took every effort to stop my stomach turning over. I knew all too well what the Cielcin were capable of, but I said, "You haven't won yet."

"Siajenu ti-saem yu kianuri!" Hushansa exclaimed. *You have nowhere to run.* "You cannot escape. You will be ours."

"That is what your brothers thought," I said, matching the alien coldness, and cut the transmission.

Turning, I found Pallino watching me through his helmet. "What was that for?"

"I wanted to know who we were fighting," I answered him. "And I wanted it to see me."

"Why?" my old friend asked. No other soldier would have dared question me in front of the others.

"Because now it wants me alive," I replied. "They won't try anything that's sure to kill us all."

Pallino fell silent, seeing the logic in this. I could almost hear the man's teeth grinding like gears beneath his helmet. "We're still stuck here."

"No, we're not," I said, moving to the window and looking down on the refinery floor. Groups of Cielcin still hurried about or else stared up at us with their hideous white masks. They had no firearms, and I took the fact that none had trained explosives on us as evidence that my hypothesis was correct. I checked my wrist-terminal for the time. "Seventy-nine minutes 'til our fleet arrives. We'll drag this out so long as we can."

In the gallery beyond the airlock, the Cielcin had readied their machine. Hoses and cables ran from the stair and the lower halls, and the machine itself rose on three spindly legs. It *was* some manner of plasma bore, a bit of repurposed mining equipment retrofitted to melt through the reinforced metal of the door. That the machine's alien makers had built it for hollowing out the asteroid warrens they made their home, I did not doubt.

"How much time do we have?" I asked, watching them clamp the device to the airlock door.

To my surprise, it was Leon who answered. "Those doors are eighteen inches thick. If that burner of theirs is close to one of ours? Fifteen minutes? Twenty?"

"For each door . . ." I mused. It wasn't enough time. It was barely half the time we needed. "Remind me: how much longer until we're sure the siphons are clear?"

The tech who'd powered down the collider cleared his throat. "They're clear already."

"Good," I said. They must have cleared while I was speaking with Leon or with Hushansa. "Mine the door. Use the biggest charges you have."

This order was met with dumb silence. The men all looked at me. None dared speak. I knew what they must be thinking. Even with the refinery cleared of antimatter, setting off high-powered explosives in so confined a space was a death sentence. I ignored them.

"Lord?"

"Move!"

The end came in time. The Cielcin succeeded in melting through the outer airlock door, and after a few minutes' careful fumbling transported their plasma drill through the glowing hole they'd made. The chimera followed, leading ranks of Cielcin troopers as they set to work on the inner door.

It was going to be close.

I explained my plan and stood waiting, watching as the doors began to glow dull red, then golden.

"Fifty minutes 'til the fleet arrives," Crim said. He'd been counting off the time in five-minute intervals. "We should move." The Norman had donned his helmet once again and stood with one hand on the hilt of his sword.

"Almost there," I said. Every second was a gift. The moment I made my move the Cielcin below would be all over us. I did not think the chimera from the stair was this Hushansa. There would be others where the first chimera had come from, and worse. "Get ready," I said, watching the steel begin to flow like melting ice.

It was time.

I drew my sword and cut my circle.

The floor fell away beneath me, and I rode it down. Forty feet straight down to the level of the refinery floor. My suit's gel-layer took the impact, protected my bones and delicate joints. Still, I winced as I rolled clear, shield up, sword in hand but unkindled to protect myself from the fall. Men fell after me like a heavy rain until all forty-two who remained of the three score we'd brought were down.

I gave the signal, and the control room above erupted in oily scarlet flames. A secondary explosion followed as the plasma bore detonated. I pictured the chimera and the scores of inhuman soldiers packed into the airlock turned to cinders and winced, imagining the whole factory erupting from some overlooked sample of the precious fuel.

No annihilation came.

Only the enemy, circling like sharks.

CHAPTER 3

THE RED AND THE BLACK

WHAT IS THAT CLASSICAL English expression? *Out of the frying pan, into the fire.*

We were surrounded, but we had struck a mighty blow against the enemy, and we had less than an hour before our fleet arrived. We could make it, but only if we could win free to some better position. My stunt in the control room had bought us time and taken out an entire enemy platoon, but I'd thrown us from one desperate position to another.

All the air in the command center had rushed out when I'd cut the floor out from under us, and the lances of the men about me fired mutely at the approaching foe. Bright spots flashed against their rubberized armor and smoked as they fell.

"There's no way they can power on the refinery again, after that," Crim said, looking up at the ruins of the control room. "We should radio the *Ascalon* for evac. It can get here before the fleet."

"They know we're here now," I said. "They'll be on guard . . . shoot it right out of the sky. We need the fleet for cover!" As I spoke, I slashed one of the enemy's *nahute* in half, ending its murderous flight. A lone Cielcin berserker leaped down from a catwalk over our heads, the point of its sword thrust down to skewer me. I jumped aside. The xenobite's ceramic blade bit the floor and splintered. It rounded on me, abandoning its broken sword. The creature was strangely puppet-like with its face hidden, like one of the full-scale marionettes one sometimes saw perform at the courts of Nipponese lords.

Pallino's voice dominated the line. "We can't stay here!"

"The tram!" someone shouted.

The tram. There were a set of maintenance tram cars that ran along the exterior of the collider beltway, making it so that workers could ride all around the massive machine if necessary to affect repairs. There were way-stations placed at regular intervals about the track for those repair missions that took station techs thousands of miles from the compound on *Virdi Planum*. They relied on magnetic accelerators, and in the airless environs of Eikana, could reach speeds of nearly three hundred miles per hour.

"Will it work?" I asked.

A thin voice rose in answer. "Should do! The trams should be on a separate system."

"They're not far!" said another.

"We still have to get there," said a third.

"Then move!" I ordered, brandishing my sword in the direction of the platform.

Another trio of Cielcin screamers clambered down from atop the housing of one of the magnetic coils. Pallino shot one and ran the second through with the bayonet of his lance. The other's sword clanged against his armor, and another soldier shot the creature before it could try again.

The nearest tram platform was not far: straight ahead and down a short stair beneath the track of the hadron colliders where it ran clear through the refinery. Crim was already at the steps, locked in combat with one of the Pale. Another of the *nahute* flew past my head, braided metal body rolling against my shield like a passing eel. I heard a man scream, and to my left I saw him fall, writhing as one of the alien drones chewed through his suit's underlayment and burrowed in the flesh beneath.

Something huge and white landed on the nearest catwalk, and thin strand of metal buckled beneath its weight and crashed to the floor in eerie quiet. Huge as a bear, the chimera loomed over my men, dull white armor and thin limbs making it seem like the skeleton of a giant. The half-machine creature seized one of my men with fingers long as daggers and snapped him like a rag doll. Without breaking stride, the giant hurled the body of its victim at another of our men, who hit the deck and skidded beneath the weight of his dead comrade.

"Keep moving!" Pallino shouted, taking aim at the giant.

Cielcin crashed into our company from either side. They had the numbers and the superior position, but we were shielded, and the light of our energy-lances tore through their line like a hot knife through wax. The giant lashed out with its arm, sweeping two of my men off their feet. They hit the wall and bounced off, tumbling down the stairs after Crim.

I drew up, sword in hand.

I was on the wrong side.

The chimera's turret of a head swiveled toward me.

"Found you!" The flat, mechanical voice sounded over my suit's built-in comms, and I knew it was no ordinary chimera that stood before me. Twice the height of a man it stood and narrower, as though it were an evening shadow cast back across the earth. Its white armor was of adamant, proof against even my sword. All the villainous art of MINOS lay in the shape of its graceful arms, the wicked curves of its knife-like fingers, and in the faceless terror it called a head crowned with metal spines. Here was no mere lieutenant, no servile creature. Here was the general itself, the *vayadan* Hushansa.

"You're smaller than the others!" I said, taunting it in its own tongue. It wasn't even *Many-Handed* . . . "Was there nothing left when they built you?" I watched over the general's shoulder to where the front half of our forces hurried around the bend for the tramway.

Hushansa's fingers all lengthened. A hatch opened in its shoulder, exposing the silvered head of some projectile. The grapnel lanced out, fast as an arrow—slow enough to pierce a shield. Time stretched, and at once there were countless millions of grapnels arcing toward me. So accurate was the general's machine-assisted aim that most struck the soft joints of my armor and skewered me like a fish on a line. Many more bounced off, and others . . . I raised my sword and slashed the grapnel in half, severing the line before the awful spike could strike home.

"*Gennuthar ne!*" Hushansa said. *Impossible.*

I said nothing.

"Hadrian, we need to move," Pallino said from his place at my shoulder.

"I know."

A flash of violet light smote the metal giant, and Hushansa lurched to one knee. I knew that tell-tale shade, the color of hydrogen plasma.

"Grenade!" the cry went up a moment after, and a second flash of light followed as superheated plasma blossomed against the back of the staggered giant. Hushansa fell face-forward, scrabbling against the floor like some manner of crab. I saw Crim standing at the top of the stairs, Jaddian robe flapping strangely in that airless place. Two legionnaires bracketed him, each aiming the short grenade launchers at the slumped metal monster. The plasma grenades were suspended in a colloidal gel that made them stick to whatever they impacted. The launchers themselves were only air-fed, relied on gas cartridges to fire them slow enough to bypass any personal shield. Hushansa rose, rounded on them.

"*Talaq!*" Crim exclaimed. That was *fire* in his native Jaddian.

The grenadiers fired again, and again twin rosettes of violet fire bloomed. The metal monster lurched backward, fired a barrage of pin missiles from a hatch in one wrist. They impacted against Crim's shield and those of his men, useless.

"Forward!" I shouted to the knot of men who stood with me, pointing toward the stairs with my sword.

The next barrage of grenades struck home. Pale shards of the general's white armor flew in all directions. The crowned head fell and hit the metal floor with what would have been a mighty clangor had there been air to hear it.

I had no time to reflect upon the death of so great a captain of our enemy. I followed Pallino down the steps, spurring our men before me. Crim stopped to help one of the injured to his feet and carried him with one arm wrapped about his shoulders. We hadn't far to go: down the steps and around a bend to the left, then down a hall that ran along just beneath the main body of the colliders' housing to the tram platform.

Cielcin stood in our way, but we cut them down as we came jogging and limping down the stairs. Twice I slashed *nahute* from the air, and when one of the Cielcin dropped from the collider track above, I took its legs out from under it with a single sweep of my blade.

The tram lay dead ahead now: two short cars hanging from the overhead magnetic rail bracketed to the underside of the colliders. Without concern for aerodynamics, they were ugly, square things wrought of the same gunmetal as the refinery itself. My eye followed their track in a straight line past where it exited through an open arch in the refinery's outer wall and vanished to a point on the horizon.

"Almost there," Crim said to the man he carried.

"Get the men on board!" I said, gesturing sharply to Pallino. We had perhaps forty minutes until the fleet arrived. If we could get as far as the nearest waystation along the track of the hadron collider, we would make it. The foremost of our men already had the doors open and were piling inside. Crim made the threshold and pushed the injured man into the arms of two of the others and doubled back to hold the door.

The voice of the tech who'd powered down the particle accelerator chimed in. "We're ready to go here."

"Take the first car and go!" I said to Crim, who nodded and ducked through the hatchway. Reaching the level of the second, I turned back. A full dozen of our men still came, stretched out across half a hundred yards of hall. Behind them rushed a small army of the Pale. The nearest Cielcin whirled *nahute* above their heads like bolos, their brethren loping behind, long arms trailing almost to the ground.

Then came a scream, a cry like grinding metal, so loud I felt it in my chest and through the soles of my boots. I froze where I stood, knowing the sound heralded some new evil. The Cielcin hurled their metal serpents, and the men at my side fired. One of the *nahute* caught fire and bricked itself, crashing to the plated floor. Another caught the hindmost of our running men and dropped him. I felt my muscles spasm as I made to leap forward, but Pallino caught me. "It's too late, Had!" he said, fingers tight on my arm.

Behind me, a loud *bang* heralded the disengagement of the braking mechanism on the first car. The whole hall shook, and a faint hum and vibration shook the ductwork all around as electromagnets powered on. I had a brief glimpse of Crim as I looked back over my shoulder and watched the hatch of the first tram car slide shut. The old assassin did not salute, only gave a perfunctory little wave with the first two fingers of his left hand—the rest still clutched one of his beloved knives. Then he was gone, and fully half our men slid away on silent accelerators, launched near-instantaneously to three hundred miles per hour. They cleared the wall of the refinery in seconds, and soon they were little more than a black dot shrinking as it rocketed toward the horizon . . . and safety.

The metallic shrieking resounded through the superstructure all around, and even the onrushing Pale drew up short.

"Hurry! Damn your eyes!" Pallino spat, waving the other men on.

In the distance I discerned a pale shadow moving amidst the coming horde. Like the Cielcin it was, but greater—taller and narrower, its featureless turret of a head capped with a crown of silver spines.

It was my turn to say, "Impossible."

The *vayadan*-general Hushansa parted the ranks of its men like a rock in the course of a black river, its clawed hands outspread. "You are not the only one who can't be killed!" it said. The same flat voice. The same cold laughter.

"Another one?" Pallino asked.

I shook my head. "The same one."

I felt the chiliarch grow tense. "Crim's boys blew that fucker away, man."

"Evidently not."

The Cielcin general must have given some signal to its men, for the other Cielcin drew back, allowing their master to pass them and come nearer me. It had to stoop beneath a stanchion that buttressed the colliders as it came, lest the points of its crown scrape the metal.

"*Marerose o-okun,*" it said, straightening. "I told you: you cannot escape."

"Hadrian . . ." Pallino tugged my arm. The general's intervention had allowed our men the chance they needed to clear the last few dozen yards to the tram. We were nearly free. "Hadrian!"

Something in the force behind that second *Hadrian* made me turn my head. Another of the crowned chimeras stood at the far end of the hall moving slowly toward us, identical to the first—and to the one Crim had slain upon the stair.

Two Hushansas.

"Hushansa the Many-Handed," I said, looking from one copy to the other, understanding growing in me like a cancer. The creature Crim's grenadiers had dispatched above was not Hushansa, nor were either of the creatures before us in the hall. Neither—I guessed—was the thing that had attacked us on the stairs and died in the airlock when we blew the door of the command center. The *true* Hushansa lay elsewhere, safe on some grounded shuttle or even in the fleet above the refinery. These bodies—these hands—were its shadows, its puppets, emanations of its vile will. There was nothing of the original flesh in them, as had been true of its brothers. They were no two alike, these *vayadayan* of the White Hand. The human magi who served the Cielcin had fashioned each according to its need. Iubalu had been a crawling horror, Bahudde a giant thirty feet high. This Hushansa was a ghost flitting between bodies, possessing one or several at will. Turning my head so I could see either creature by turn, I said, "I see."

"You cannot hope to win," it said, spreading its hands. "What did you hope to accomplish coming here? We will take the fuel stores and destroy this place from orbit. What have you achieved?"

Beneath my mask, I smiled. *"Sim yadanolo ne?"* I asked it. *Can't you guess?*

The right thigh of the first of Hushansa's bodies opened up, and the general reached in and drew out a sword. The blade hinged open, unfolding to its full length. It looked short at the end of the creature's too-long arm, but it was easily seven feet from pommel to point. Every fiber in me screamed to make a move for the tram car, but I knew the instant I turned my back it would be on me, and if I knew one thing about the metal demons those traitorous scientists had crafted in the bowels of Arae, it was that they were fast.

Instead, I willed my mind to calm, to find that clear space beneath feeling—that Quiet space within. The first Hushansa lunged at me with its sword. I twisted sideways, shoving Pallino out of the way. As I'd expected, the second Hushansa had leaped as well, hands outstretched to seize me. Each moved faster than any mortal man could react, but slow enough to skate beneath the energy threshold of my shield. The blade should have pierced my chest, at least impacted my armor. Those taloned hands should have seized on me thigh and shoulder.

But for every potential state where they succeeded, there were as many quantum positions where they failed. The blade that should have pierced me passed through me instead, and the taloned hands that should have seized on me closed on empty air. Understand: I was not insubstantial. I only interposed one reality on the other. Hushansa's blade and my chest occupied the same place in the universe, but with the power the Quiet had given me, I willed the two not to meet. For a moment, the universe recognized a paradox.

I ended it by stepping aside—stepping out of the blade and talons. My sword flashed, shearing up through the ceramic of the giant's blade and down deep into the joint at the back of one knee. The chimera's armor may have been proof against even highmatter, but the common metal of its joint was not. The metal leg buckled and one giant stumbled, crashed into the other.

"Go!" I shouted to Pallino, and almost shoved him onto the tram car. I staggered against the doorframe, head swimming with the cost of what I'd just done. I felt sick, felt that I must vomit there in my helmet.

It will pass, I told myself, and clambered after Pallino.

Behind us, the two Hushansas struggled to untangle themselves. The Cielcin soldiers behind them hurled *nahute* at us. I spun on the threshold and hit the red button that slammed the tramway door on silent hydraulics.

"Launch, damn you!" I hissed into the comm. Already my ill spell was passing, head and vision clearing, leaving only the dull tattoo of blood in my ears.

The soldier at the tram controls did as he was ordered, and I felt the faint hum as the car's electromagnets powered on. We started moving, smooth as a ship on a mirrored pool. Through the alumglass window, I saw the uninjured Hushansa find its feet. That crowned-turret head swiveled, found us with unseen optics. We were surely moving half a hundred miles an hour already.

The chimera *ran.*

Using its long arms like legs, the unholy thing bounded after us, tearing along the edge of the tram platform at speeds no living creature could match. We accelerated. Still it gained.

"Black Earth . . ." I heard someone swear.

The beast was running out of platform. The arched opening in the refinery wall was dead ahead, we would pass it in seconds. Beyond, the laser-straight track of the collider ran out above the desert and airless wastes of *Virdi Planum* and vanished over the horizon.

"Get back!" I shouted, shouldering my way to the rear of the car.

Hushansa leaped. Its great mass and velocity carried it through the air like a missile, and the whole tram car rattled like a bell. I fell sideways against the wall of the compartment, and had a brief glimpse of the thing's white torso through a rear window. Hushansa had *caught* onto the rear of the tram car, clung to it like an insect.

A muffled *bang* reverberated through the tram car, and the whole thing shook. Beyond the windows, black desert swept by. We had cleared the refinery, and the tram car was rocketing toward its top speed, putting distance between us and the Cielcin horde in the refinery.

"Where is it?" I ground my teeth, trying to figure out where our enemy had gone. I craned my neck, peering wildly out the windows.

Another *bang* echoed up from my feet. An image of the chimera clinging to the bottom of the tram pod flashed in my mind, and for a moment I considered thrusting my sword through the floor. Lights bracketed to the underbelly of the collider above flashed by, marking out the miles as we streaked farther and faster from the refinery.

I couldn't afford to miss.

The whole tram began to rattle then, and an awful squealing whine conducted through the superstructure all around us.

"We lost power!" the man at the controls shouted. The magnets that ran along the overhead rail had been switched off. We were grinding to a halt then, bleeding speed as we squeaked along the last stretch of rail. The waystation was not yet in sight, and behind, the refinery had been reduced to a pale blur of light on the far horizon. The pilot slapped the controls, cursing.

Yet another *bang* resounded through the car . . . and we were falling, hurled from the rail above like a stone skipped across the surface of the lake. The low gravity worked in our favor, and someone somewhere in the car screamed at us to brace for impact. The car struck stone and sand and bounced, tossing us head over heels. I caught a rail and held it, glad my suit's gel-layer hardened to protect my joints. Still, I hit the ceiling, my body and the others all hurled like fish in a barrel. The tram car tumbled wildly, throwing up sand and dust as it tumbled across the desert.

We ground to a halt across hundreds of yards, rolled far out from the silver track of the hadron collider.

"Open the doors!" I barked. "We have to get out before it gets here!"

If the chimera made it inside the crashed pod, it would carve us all to ribbons in seconds.

Fully a third of the men sprawled on the tram seats or on the gray floor; dead or dazed I was not sure. Each's man armor ought to have saved him as I'd been saved, but there was no telling—and there was no time. We'd settled on an angle such that we had to climb toward the exit. Two of the men had the hatchway open, and one had leaped out onto the sands, his lance primed.

Where was Hushansa?

"Radio the others," I snapped at one of the men. "Tell them what happened." I lingered a moment on the lip of the tram car, gaze sweeping the sands. The track of the hadron collider shimmered above us like an oversized aqueduct, its line of graceful arches marching toward eternity in each direction, the only monument to civilization in sight.

How far had we traveled in so short a time, and how quickly?

My head still rang from the fall. I'd lost track of how much time remained before the fleet arrived . . .

. . . and where was Hushansa?

I leaped down onto the sands—glad of Eikana's gentler gravity. It had made what might have been a disastrous crash that much safer.

"Do you see it?" one of the men asked another, scanning the horizon with lance at the ready.

The other legionnaire's reply was almost casual. "Maybe it fell somewhere nearer the track?"

The other men were slowly pulling themselves out of the crashed car, the hale helping the injured. Several appeared to have broken limbs in the crash, pure chance or some failure of their suits, I guessed. Our fall had carved a mighty wound in the face of *Virdi Planum*, a black scar dozens of yards long. It felt wrong for there to be no wind. No fires. No smoke or stink or burning.

"My lord!" One of the men raised his voice and pointed back toward the collider.

A white shape stood tall beneath the arches, and even at this distance I could make out Hushansa's crown. Across those many hundred yards my eyes met its optic sensors, and I knew it had seen me, too.

Beneath the mask, I grinned again.

"Everyone, get back!" I raised my left hand to underscore the order. Fast as it was, Hushansa might kill any number of them on its way to me if they got in its way. "It's after me." It would not kill me, if it could. Its dark master wanted me alive. But it would come for me first of all the men in the company.

Straight for me.

The metal monster moved, bounding toward us across the level ground, loping on all fours like an ape in the lost jungles of Earth. I settled into a low guard, the hilt of my sword unkindled in my right hand.

Quiet as it was and still, my vision came easily, blood hammering still harder in my ears.

Hushansa splintered as my reflection had, became not a creature, but a quantum wave barreling toward me like the changing of the tide. I watched it come, watched lines of potential converge like a holofilm of glass shattering in reverse. The *vayadan*-general's body was armored in adamant, proof against even the edge of my Jaddian blade. Impenetrable, save for those rare, soft places where the titanium endoskeleton lay exposed. I might strike at my enemy a billion times, and a billion times I'd fail.

My options narrowed as my enemy boiled closer, crossing a dozen yards for every bound. My focus wavered, a white pain flaring behind my eyes. Whole pieces of the spectrum vanished from my sight, blotted out as I struggled to stretch my still-too-human senses to encompass infinity. *Let this be quick,* I thought, and waited, fingers on the twin triggers that would kindle my blade, hand back, toe forward. There would be a way—*one* way in a billion—for my blade to strike true.

The demon captain was upon me then and leaped, claws outstretched to seize me.

Fingers tightened on the triggers, and liquid metal blossomed and shone brighter than the watchful stars. I lunged, all my possibilities collapsing in that clarion instant to a single, perfect reality.

The blade connected with Hushansa's leg on the outside of the knee, bit, and cut. Sliding upward, it found the ball-and-socket joint of the chimera's hip, and, rising, sheared through the left leg from groin to hip—and caught the left arm inside the elbow. The giant fell to pieces and tumbled to the dust about me. My blade completed its arc, and I stood unmoved. Triumphant.

All about me, the men cheered.

"Halfmortal!" they called, and "Marlowe! Marlowe!"

I turned slowly, found the remains of Hushansa's torso trying to right itself with its one remaining hand. There was no point trying to threaten it—it had no life in that body to lose. No part of the creature's brain or organic body was there. Only an echo, a copy of its ghost. Desperate, a panel opened in its shoulder and the harpoon lanced out, but its balance betrayed it in its crippled state and the shot went wide.

"It doesn't matter!" the *vayadan* said, voice sounding in my suit speakers. "We will have you in time. The *Shiomu* will have you in time."

The Prophet.

I stopped five paces from the ruined hulk. Hushansa leaned upon its one remaining arm. It angled its faceless head defiantly. "And you have failed here. *Kianna!*" It made that flat, shrill sound that passed for laughter among its kind. "Run back to your Emperor and tell him you failed. This world is ours."

"Is it?" I asked. I took one more step forward to show I was unafraid. "Run back to *your* master. Tell it I'm coming."

Hushansa laughed again. *"Tsuareu suh cadolo ni ne?"*

You still think you can win!

I took a few steps back, made a gesture with my left hand.

My men got the message. Two grenadiers fired on the ruined general. The puppet body blew apart in a rosette of violet flame that cast my shadow far across the level sands.

The rest was silence.

We had nothing to do but wait. Not long after, a new sun flashed in the middle of the sky and faded. Another. A third that banished the stars. Each faded in turn. Our fleet had come, right on schedule. Before long, shuttles and lightercraft streaked across the sky and fired on the refinery. While we waited in the desert, we watched the lightning of their war play out as the brief Battle of Eikana unfolded. With the collider neutralized, our forces were able to safely take the refinery.

At last, the arrowhead shape of the *Ascalon* appeared on the horizon just as the true sun was rising over *Virdi Planum*, and only when it landed and Crim emerged with the medical staff from two adjoining shuttles did young Leon approach.

"How did you do . . ." he gestured at the ruins of Hushansa's third or fourth body, at the collider standing in the middle distance, at the spot where the distant refinery still lurked, ". . . all that?"

No *my lord,* no *sir.*

"I told you," I said. "Some stories are true."

CHAPTER 4

NESSUS

SINCE THE DAY I died aboard the *Demiurge*, my dreams have haunted me, even in fugue. Since Annica, since those days upon the mountaintop of that other world, I dreamed of what I'd seen. The Quiet had revealed all of time to me, poured past and present and possible futures into my head. Universes of events so unlikely they were indistinguishable from dream. I had supped of those waters like a man who drank the ocean—and though I'd swallowed it all I could not hold it, and spat it back again.

Pieces of that total vision came back to me, sounds and images, sensations remembered by the unconscious mechanisms of my all-too-human brain. Chains bound me wrist and ankle, forced me to hobble like an old man. The Cielcin surrounded me, watching with unmasked faces, their black glass fangs glimmering as the guards at my back spurred me on with their spears. Ahead, a black dome rose like half an enormous egg, and upon its steps awaited a figure in black and azure, silver-crowned.

"You knew it would come to this, kinsman," said Syriani Dorayaica, black eyes on me. It raised one clawed hand and pointed at the sky. "Time runs down."

I followed the gesture skyward—and cried out.

"Hadrian!"

Darkness.

Light.

A hand on my cheek, cool and dry. The scent of smoke and sandalwood.

"Valka . . ."

We were in bed. She'd turned on the lamp, a baroque piece of stained glass, and propped herself on one elbow. It took me a moment to remember where I was. My eyes wandered among the richly carved beams and plastered ceiling, soaked in the wood paneling and Jaddian carpets and the high, narrow windows that overlooked the balcony and the gardens.

Maddalo House. Sananne. Nessus.

The old villa had begun its life as an abbey for Cid Arthurian monks in the years before the Empire came to Nessus. It perched on a bluff overlooking the villages that surrounded the great city of Sananne. By night, the sky-spires and the cyclopean outlines of the mile-high drydocks glowed with artificial light, and the air was thick with the song of cicadas. Gentle winds blew the pencil cypresses that fringed the bucolic grounds, reminding me of home.

Home.

It had been my prison for seventy years, and though it was a gilded cage, a cage it remained. For twelve years the Chantry tried me for treason and for heresy, and for twelve years they'd proved nothing. Recordings they'd collected and suppressed on the galactic datanet of my miracle on Berenike could not be proved undoctored, and the scholiasts who had served in my defense fought the Inquisition tooth and nail. In the end, in desperation, the Chantry tried to kill me, just as Augustin Bourbon and the Empress had tried on Forum. They failed, and botched their trial in the process. For their pains—and because I'd caused the Emperor too much pain—I'd been sent to Nessus, capital of the Magnarchate of Centaurus. With the Veil of Marinus lost, Centaurus had become the center of our war with the Cielcin, and so it was to Nessus I'd been sent. The *Tamerlane* sat in orbit, its crew on ice save for Valka, who'd been allowed to live with me in my comfortable prison for the past several decades.

The Emperor had shuffled me off here to keep me out of trouble, to keep me away from Forum and out of the public eye. It might have been a good life, were I not bounded in a nutshell.

Were it not that I had bad dreams.

"Are you all right?" Valka asked, stroking my cheek with tattooed fingers. When I didn't answer, she added, "The dreams again?"

I nodded and sat up, swung out of bed and, naked, crossed the thickly carpeted floor to the basin to fill a glass with clear water.

When still I didn't speak, Valka asked, "'Tis not Eikana, is it?"

"No," I rasped. It had been three weeks since we'd returned from Eikana aboard the *Ascalon*. I'd finished my reports to the Magnarch's people and to the Legion Intelligence Office, and was enjoying a brief furlough on the villa's estates. "Eikana was nothing."

I did not have to turn to know Valka was shaking her head. "What was it?"

"Nothing new," I said, and thought, *Time runs down*. I'd had the dream a thousand times over the years, seen myself marched toward the black dome in chains, seen the Cielcin Prince of Princes standing there.

The scholiasts say that memory exists to impart lessons that protect us from injury. The memory of burning our hands teaches us not to play with fire. What then can be said of my memories of the future? If that was what they were?

"You've hardly slept since you got back," she said.

"You can take responsibility for some of that," I said, turning, the crooked old Marlowe smile firmly in place.

She matched that crooked smile with an asymmetric curling of her lips. It was not her old smile. The worm Urbaine had loosed upon her mind had done its damage, and though Valka had recovered from her ordeal, she had never fully healed. Here and there the scars of what the magus had done showed in the asymmetric stillness of some muscle or the faint tremor of a hand.

"Something *is* bothering you," she insisted, pushing untidy red-black hair from her face.

"It's been so long," I said at last.

"Since you fought?"

"Since I had the dream," I said, and conceded, "but that, too." I had slept for the nine-month return journey from Eikana, and for once my dreams had not followed me into cryonic fugue. "And I keep thinking about something that . . . general said. *'We'll have you in time.'"*

A crease formed between Valka's winged eyebrows. "Dorayaica's been after you since before Berenike. 'Tis not news, Hadrian."

I looked down at the water glass cradled in my hands, at my ghostly reflection in it—then to Valka. Time had been kind to her—if Urbaine's worm had not been. The long decades had made but few marks upon her face and body. Yet she was Tavrosi and no palatine. Faint creases marked the corners of her eyes, and the lines that marked the perimeter of her smile were set more deeply. But there was no frost in the dark fire of her hair, and when she smiled—and this time it was the full smile, not the uneven one—it was with the old electric spark that lit my own face.

"You're right," I said, eyes wandering the length of her. "Of course you are." I drained my glass to disguise the moment necessary to gather my wits. "But I can't shake these . . . visions."

Valka arched one eyebrow. "Perhaps they are only dreams now." My smile flickered. She was right about that, too. If I was right—if the Quiet had showed me all of time when I stood upon that mountaintop—then much of it would never be. Much of what haunted me might be as good as fiction. I dreamed myself seated on the Solar Throne with Princess Selene at my feet, or toiling in a field in chains alongside a girl who looked very much like Siran. Sometimes, I saw myself standing naked on the auction block while men bid on me for the fighting pits, sold by that pirate, Demetri. Other times, I dreamed my first encounter with Uvanari, only we were standing amidst the green sea of a plantation and not in the tunnels of Calagah. A boy named Switch died in my arms beneath Emeshi skies, but he was not the Switch I knew. And I died beneath Gilliam's blade. Beneath Uvanari's.

Things that had never happened—that *could* never happen. I saw them all.

"Hadrian." Valka's voice reached me where I sat at the bottom of my thoughts. "Come back to bed."

I did not answer her at once, but turned over all these thoughts and un-memories one after another. Valka was right, too many of the dreams were impossible. They would never be.

Why then did I wake sweating in the night to this particular nightmare?

My eyes flickered to the antique clock that glowed above the cold hearth. It was nearly dawn. "I think I'll stay up," I said. "I have to meet the Magnarch later this morning."

Karol Venantian was far from the picture of the Sollan Magnarch one imagines. Not the barrel-chested former officer or stuffed-shirt politico. The Supreme Lord of every system in the Centaurus Arm of the galaxy, one of three men in all the human universe to hold the office of Magnarch and speak with the Emperor's own voice, had the bearing of a scribe. Rapier-thin and stooped somewhat by his nearly six centuries, old Lord Venantian would not have looked out of place in the green robes of a scholiast. He wore the violent purple of his rank instead, a half-toga that left both arms free pinned at the left shoulder of his long white-and-gold jacket.

"The Consortium delivered the uranium for Ramannu Province on schedule," he said, surveying the landing field out the window of our flier. "Once the fuel barges arrive from Eikana, the whole caravan will be ready to launch. Commandant Lynch tells me our Nipponese friends were quite pleased to find their refinery more or less intact."

Talk of the Wong-Hopper Consortium and uranium put me in mind of home. Had some of that latest uranium shipment been mined on Delos or in its system? I supposed I could ask the Magnarch, but it was better not to know, better to imagine.

"Yamato estimates it'll be about eight months before the Eikana Fuelworks are operable again, but that's much better than the timeline we were looking at before."

Through the porthole at my right, I could see the gray-white face of the nearest Sananne shipyard building rising more than a mile into the sky. The tallest towers of the city seemed meager things beneath it. Pale as it was, it reminded me of an old painting in the Peronine Palace of the city of London burning in the shadow of the colossal pyramids of the Mericanii. Discomforted by the comparison, I turned to the Magnarch. "There's always the possibility the Cielcin will return. We beat them, but their general escaped and doubtless will have carried word of its defeat back to its master."

"Yes, quite." The Magnarch stroked his pointed chin. "The Yamato are doubling their in-system security, but we will dispatch a legion to support them."

"You'd best dispatch a legion to every refinery in Centaurus," I said.

The Magnarch's brows contracted. "Has your time offworld made you forget your place so quickly, Lord Marlowe?" Lord Venantian's tone betrayed the iron in the man, and for a moment he seemed no scribe at all. "You're quite correct, of course. There's no telling what intelligence the Pale might have collected when they ascertained the location of the Eikana Fuelworks. Possibly our entire refueling infrastructure is compromised."

"Possibly," I agreed.

"You heard the news about the Jaddians, yes?" Venantian asked.

"What news about the Jaddians?"

"Prince Aldia has promised us an army."

"Again?" The Jaddians had been promising support since I was a boy. A dozen times it seemed the Principalities were on the verge of sending an armada—thousands of ships and millions of soldiers—but every time the princes had seemed on the verge of launching their fleets, they'd pulled back, preferring instead to send a token force, a fact-finding expedition such as the one the Satrap governor Kalima di Sayyiph had led to Emesh so long ago.

From the look on his seamed face, I could tell the old Magnarch was thinking the same thing. "So it would seem," he said, a touch of acid in his tone. "I had word from Forum that our Jaddian friends have launched a fleet of some twenty thousand warships under the command of Prince Aldia's grandson, Prince Kaim."

"Kaim du Otranto?" I said, arching my eyebrows. *"Al Badroscuro?"*

Venantian snorted. "Darkmoon," he said. "What a truly ridiculous nickname."

"He is not a ridiculous man," I said. I had never met the young Prince of Jadd, nor seen a proper holograph of him. The men of the *eali al'aqran*, the Jaddian palatines, wore masks for all their public appearances, painted porcelain prostheses that moved with their expressions. They were meant to separate the man from his station, to symbolize the divide between personal and political—though whether they succeeded in this was a question for men other than me. The result of this was that though men like Aldia du Otranto and his warrior grandson were known across the galaxy, their faces were not, whereas the face of our holy Emperor and his predecessors peered at us from official portraits and from the observe of every golden hurasam.

The Magnarch seemed to chew something a moment, said, "No indeed. The War Office says he's bringing an army of two hundred *million* mamluk clones."

I felt surely that I was wearing one of those Jaddians masks then, and that the jaw had fallen off. "Two hundred . . . million?" I repeated the figure, throat at once very dry. It was a staggering figure, nearly the equal of all the Imperial legions and the armies of the greater and lesser houses in the Centaurine provinces.

It was easy to forget why cloning—*duplication*—was one of the Chantry's most grievous sins. The illegal construction of clone armies had allowed the Jaddians their independence in the first place, and before the Cielcin Wars, it had been their militant maintaining of those same clone armies that had kept the eighty-one Principalities of Jadd free of Imperial control. But if the Jaddians were willing to commit their not-inconsiderable resources to the war effort for true—their clone mamluk slaves could be precisely the weapon we needed to turn the tide on the xenobites for good and all.

"They ought to have the demons quaking in their boots!" Venantian said. "Though they'll not arrive in these parts for *decades* yet."

Still reeling, I nodded. Jadd lay on the outermost edge of the galaxy, on the far side of the Sollan Empire, tens of thousands of light-years from Nessus and the front. "Are you sure we can trust them?" I asked. I of all people had no reason to mistrust the Jaddians—Sir Olorin Milta and his satrap master had been instrumental in ensuring the launch of my ill-fated expedition to find Vorgossos—but the mere mention of such *staggering* numbers was enough to chill the blood.

"Prince Aldia and His Radiance have been friends for centuries," the Magnarch said, leaning back in his seat as our flier slowed over the landing pad high on the exterior of the shipyard dry docks. "I do not think we've anything to fear. We've increased levies across the outer provinces. It is the Emperor's wish we match that number by the end of the century, and that's to say nothing of the new of naval personnel we'll need to train up for all these ships we're building."

Our shuttle landed the moment after, and presently Lord Venantian rose. I was to join him in surveying the progress our shipwrights were making on the construction of components for the new dreadnought. When it was completed, the *Huntsman* would be among the largest battleships in the Imperial service, a hundred-mile rival even to Kharn Sagara's *Demiurge* and the Sojourners of the Exalted. The ship's superstructure was being assembled in orbit above one of Nessus's five moons, but many of the mighty vessel's component parts were being assembled on the ground where gravity was more boon to the construction worker than bane to the construction process. In time, the components would be lifted into space on impossibly long cables for final installation.

The Magnarch's aides—silent for the duration of our flight—scurried down the open ramp ahead of us, gray-suited logothetes and scholiasts alike. I followed on behind, keeping to the great lord's side.

"How did you find your reprieve, Lord Marlowe?" the Magnarch asked, pausing at the base of the ramp.

"Your Grace?" I stopped beside him. The day stood fair, the wind quiet even so high above the ground. My black hair floated in the air between us, and I combed it back behind my ear.

"Eikana," he said. "You're been with us, what? Seventy years?"

"Sixty-eight, before Eikana," I replied. Old though he was, white-haired and wizened, the Magnarch of Centaurus yet looked down his nose at me. I have always been short for a palatine, if tall by the standards of common men. I raised my chin, certain that our entire meeting that morning existed so the Magnarch—my jailer—could ask this one question. I squeezed the hem of my black cape in my left hand until ordinary bones would have ached from the strain. "I have served the Empire all my life," I said. "I will continue to be of service."

The Magnarch smoothed his porphyry-colored toga with one ringed hand. "There are those on my council who expected you to run."

Despite the warmth of the white sun, I felt a chill creep into my bones, freeze my blood and soul. A flicker of the old Marlowe anger passed through me, and I said, "I am sorry to have disappointed them."

"I'd not have relished siccing my dogs on you."

That was as much a lie as it was not a figure of speech. On his rare off days, the Magnarch was famous for taking his wolfhounds into the highland forests north of Sananne to hunt foxes and the ten-legged fur salamanders who called the planet home.

"I'd have given them a merry chase, I'm sure," I said coolly, allowing a small smile to hint that I only meant it as humor. It was only desperation that had prompted Lord Venantian to send me to Eikana in the first place. Mine had been the only company with the force necessary to liberate the refinery within rapid-response distance, the only one with ships fast enough and soldiers waiting.

"I'm sure!" the Magnarch agreed with equal coolness.

I could have hit him. The bastard had insisted Valka remain at Maddalo House when I left precisely because he knew it prevented the very scenario he was describing. To suggest I would have fled *without* her was an insult I'd gladly break teeth to set right.

"I remain the Emperor's faithful servant," I said, effecting a short, punctilious bow my dancing master had taught me long, long ago.

"Good!" Lord Venantian said. "He will be delighted to hear that when he arrives."

CHAPTER 5

THE SUN DESCENDING

THE MUSIC OF SILVER trumpets filled the air about the landing field. To either side stood our countless soldiery, armored red and white, their horsehair crests and feathered plumes rippling in the wind. They might all have been statues, so still they stood beneath their white banners and their staffs tipped with the wrought icon of the Imperial sun.

Might have been statues, were it not that I felt the pressure of their eyes on me and on the rest of the train that followed the old Magnarch up the aisle toward the gilded frigate that like a dragon crouched upon the plain before us.

The Emperor's *Radiant Dawn*.

Karol Venantian led us, bracketed by two lictors armored in the bronze and white of his house, their cloaks fringed in violet to mark them as servants of the Magnarch. Valka walked beside me in a formal gown of dark lace that covered her plain right arm to the wrist but bared the tattooed left. Behind us came the high lords of the Magnarch's court, his chancellor and scholiast advisors, among them Commandant Anders Lynch and the director of the Sananne Shipyards. Behind us all marched two double lines of guardsmen armored and shielded, alternating columns of Imperial legionnaires in white and red and Venantian house soldiers in the white and bronze.

Dressed as we both were in black, Valka and I could not have looked more out of place. The only other figures in black were the Chantry clergymen, distinguished by their tall white Egyptian crowns and matching stoles. These watched from stands in the rear like a line of vultures perched upon a rail, craning their stiff necks to see.

The Emperor had come.

Coolant jets sprayed the hull of the Imperial frigate, and great tongues of steam rose toward the eggshell sky, and amidst those trailing fingers marched forth the Knights Excubitor like mirrored scarabs, white crests tall and silk capes floating in the warm breeze. They moved in perfect synchrony, and I watched our approach reflected in their breastplates as they formed ranks amid the steam beneath the golden shadows of the landed vessel.

Valka's nails dug into my arm. "'Tis necessary, all this?" she asked, muttering in her native Panthai, a language none of the others understood.

I patted her hand in lieu of a reply. Valka was Tavrosi, and neither our lifetime together nor the torments her own people had put her through exorcising Urbaine's daimon from her head had changed that. All our Imperial ceremony, the pomp and pageantry and martial awe, were nearly so alien to her as the Cielcin themselves.

As if in answer to her question, the trumpets sounded again, and distantly the Legion band took up the Imperial anthem.

And there he was.

No float palette or similar machine bore the Imperial person upon his throne. Instead, His Imperial Radiance, the Sollan Emperor William XXIII of the Aventine House, rode atop a palanquin supported by two dozen androgyn homunculi in Imperial livery, all in white wigs and white uniforms. The Emperor himself wore a suit of armor in Roman fashion, muscled breastplate embossed with the Imperial sunburst set amid a design of folded wings and lesser stars. Every inch of his armor was exquisitely sculpted and patterned of the purest, snow-white ceramic—and his hands were red. The Emperor wore no gauntlets, only the scarlet velvet gloves of state, each finger—save one—bedecked with a ring of yellow gold.

A cloak of scarlet samite hung on his shoulders, red as his flaming hair, and the circlet set upon his brow was fashioned of living gold. Behind him trailed the usual cluster of attendants and advisors: scholiasts in green and logothetes in the dull gray of civil service trailed the throne, like flotsam pulled by the passage of a great wave. I was pleased not to see the face of Prince Alexander among them. I had been told my former squire was among those who had traveled with his father from Forum, but discretion or care on the part of the Emperor or his staff had seen fit to leave the prince aside for this very public audience.

The music swelled as he approached, fell silent as the Magnarch knelt, dropping to both knees before his lord. As though a wave passed through our train, we knelt, though I had to half drag Valka down after me. The homunculi brought the mobile throne to a halt and lowered it to the earth. Three times the Magnarch pressed his face to the rich carpet that had been unrolled to greet the Son of Earth. "Earth bless and keep you, Radiant Majesty!" he exclaimed, not at all the same creature who had threatened me on the landing pad outside the shipyards a little over a month before. "Welcome! Welcome to Nessus. We pray your voyage from Forum was an easy one."

The Emperor raised a hand, two fingers extended in salute and benediction. "Well met, Magnarch. We must say, the courtesy of your world is greater now than in our memory." Here Caesar swept his emerald gaze across the gathered forces, the band and clergy. "I trust construction of the new fleet is proceeding on schedule?"

Karol Venantian straightened as much as he could without standing. "We lost time dealing with the Eikana affair, Radiant Majesty, but we expect to recoup those losses over the next five years." The Magnarch kept talking, and as he did, I scanned the retinue behind the Imperial throne, looking for familiar faces among the drab ministers and green-robed scholiasts. I spied square-faced Sir Gray Rinehart, the man who'd replaced the disgraced Lorcan Breathnach as head of Legion Intelligence, as well as mustachioed Lord Haren Bulsara, Director of the Colonial Office. I noted the Emperor's Confessor, a dour Archprior called Leonora, stalking the Emperor like a shadow sewn to the hem of his robe. Beside her, carrying that very hem in two gloved hands, was a man I had often seen but never spoken to—if *man* were the proper word. The butler was one of the Imperial androgyns, a eunuch homunculus bred to serve as the Emperor's bodyservant and batman. Its face was utterly hairless, as all of the androgyns were, but it wore no wig, and its white uniform distinguished itself from those of the others by the bloody sash it wore cross-wise like a baldric before it wrapped about its slim waist.

"Lord Marlowe." The Imperial voice cut across my examination of the retinue, and I bowed my head. "It is our understanding that we are once more in your debt. It seems that even in exile your usefulness knows few limits."

It took every ounce of Gibson's stoic instruction to smooth the smug smile from my face at the thought of what must be going through the Magnarch's mind in that moment. I did not bend to kiss the earth—it was not expected of me—but neither did I raise my eyes as I said, "Thank you, Honorable Caesar."

From the way the shadows moved, I guessed the Emperor had stood, and indeed a moment after a pair of white boots entered my vision, and a red gloved hand that glittered with rings. I took the offered hand and kissed it, conscious—and self-conscious—of the statement the Emperor had just made. He had bypassed his own Magnarch and had risen to greet me first of all the nobiles in the company.

"We regret we were unable to render assistance in the matter of your trial. It pleases us to find you well."

Lifting my eyes, I released the Emperor's hand—it would not have done to touch his royal person a moment longer than the forms required. I found myself unsure as to how to respond to this statement of His Radiance's. It had been his own order that delivered me into the Magnarch's tender care. When the Chantry's assassins failed to kill me and so end my years-long trial, it had been William Avent's own seal and signature beneath the order that mothballed the *Tamerlane* and locked me into an advisory role here on Nessus. *For your own protection,* the Emperor had said.

To keep me out of trouble seemed more like it.

In the end, I settled for a neutral, "Thank you, Radiance."

That seemed to satisfy the Emperor, whose attention turned away like the beam of a searchlight. "And this must be your paramour. I don't believe we've been introduced."

I blinked. I had met with His Radiance the Emperor more than a hundred times over the centuries, and on almost all of those occasions, I'd been alone. It seemed impossible that Valka and the Emperor would not have crossed paths, and yet. . . . The red velvet glove descended once again for Valka to kiss. She did not. I felt her eyes burn the side of my head an instant, but held my tongue. At last, seeing no alternative, Valka kissed the Imperial rings.

"Honorable Caesar," I said, already imagining what Valka would have to say about this exchange when we returned to the villa at Maddalo House, "this is Doctor Valka Onderra." I did not add the *Vhad Edda* toponym. Valka and I had journeyed to her home after the Battle of Berenike, seeking a cure for her affliction. We found one, but Valka's clan had forced her into *reeducation,* hoping to cure her of the outlander pollutants that her long sojourn amongst us *barbarians* had put in her mind. In the end, the demarchists had opted to *reconfigure* her entirely, to wipe her mind with the aid of the machines that impregnated her brain and build a new woman on her ruins.

She'd barely escaped with her mind.

Still, something in the name must have jogged the Emperor's memory, for he said, "The Tavrosi! Of course!" Taking a step back, the Emperor surveyed the whole of the Magnarch's party. "Rise," he said. We stood, Valka once again taking my arm.

Just then one of the androgyns—the thin butler who had held and tidied the Emperor's cloak—approached and whispered a word in its master's ear. Caesar gripped the homunculus by the shoulder and nodded. "Thank you, Nicephorus," he said, and looked round for the kneeling Magnarch. "On your feet, Magnarch Venantian. You must show us your great city and this fleet you are building for us! Please!"

"Your Radiance," the Magnarch said, rising with the help of one of his lictors. "I've the tram prepared to bring us to the palace, if you will allow me."

"Of course, dear Magnarch. It is your world, after all. Lead on!"

The Emperor and the Magnarch drew aside then as the Emperor's escort went ahead, paving the way back down the central aisle toward the train meant to carry us to the Magnarch's palace for the welcome feast.

His Radiance had traveled far, would travel farther still. Throughout the wars, the Emperor had seldom stirred from his halls in the Eternal City. He had made brief expeditions to various Legion fortresses, to some of the provincial capitals, and once or twice so far as Nessus—but the last such trip had been before Vorgossos, before my knighthood. Centuries had passed since last the Firstborn Son of Earth had come to the outer provinces, and never like this.

Nessus was but the first stop on a tour of some thirty worlds: Vanaheim, Aulos, Carteia, Perfugium . . . some of them strategic assets, some of them sacked by the Pale. After the fall of Marinus and the loss of control in the Veil, the reinforcement of Imperial territories in Centaurus had taken on a critical importance. Marinus had been a mighty blow, cutting off the newly minted Norman conquests.

Dozens of worlds lost.

"We mean to set the frontier to order," His Radiance said.

"We've prepared reports on the state of the frontier," said Karol Venantian.

The Emperor was nodding, but there was a stony weight to his tone. "Very good. But it is our understanding that you are undermanned, Karol."

Though his back was to me, I heard the Magnarch's frown. "Not undermanned, Radiance, but our fleets have suffered greatly. We have the men ready in Legion stores—Gododdin, Perfugium, and so forth—but without the vessels to field them they are of little use. We are building as fast as we can." As he spoke, the pale monolith of the shipyard docks rose its mile into the sky beyond the landing field, remote as the distant mountains in the way it impressed itself on the mind. "The Cielcin have grown cunning in their war against us. They've destroyed two of my shipyards across the sector in the last eighty years. They might have destroyed fuel production had I not acted quickly in the matter of Eikana."

"Khun," Valka swore in my ear. Still in her native tongue, she added, "What did he do, exactly?"

"Leave it," I said gently.

"Marlowe!"

The sound of my name turned my head around.

The rest of the Emperor's party was disembarking from the frigate behind the sovereign. The usual panel of logothetes and scholiasts and Chantry clergy had taken their places in the Emperor's train, leaving the military advisors to bring up the rear in the red or white berets and formal dress blacks of naval officers. I thought I recognized a face or two from the Eternal City—two of the strategoi had sat on the Intelligence council with Augustin Bourbon and Lorcan Breathnach. The legates were almost unknown to me, Centaurine commanders come on the Emperor's invitation.

But Tribune Bassander Lin I'd have known anywhere.

The Mandari patrician officer leaned heavily on an ashwood cane and grimaced as he limped nearer. The man had broken nearly every bone in his body battling the *vayadan*-general Bahudde on Berenike, and not even the best Imperial medicine could put him back together as he was. That he was back together at all was a testament to medical science. That he was still in service was a testament to Bassander Lin.

"Lin." I offered the man a short salute. "I'm surprised to see you here. I understood the 347th was out past Sete."

The tribune returned my salute. "The 347th was reconfigured after Berenike. Hauptmann's replacement had Leonid Bartosz reassigned and gave the legion to some legate from the Perseus I'd never heard of. I've been moved to the 409th."

"And promoted, I see," I indicated the double star and oak clusters that marked his new rank. I did not offer any congratulations. Lin and I were not friends, had never been friends. I'd known the prickly officer since he was lieutenant, had served with him on the quest for Vorgossos. It was thanks to him and the late Titus Hauptmann that peace talks with the Cielcin clan Otiolo had broken down—though not the reason they'd failed. I'd not been able to admit it at the time, that peace with the Cielcin was impossible. Lin was a constant reminder that I'd been wrong.

Lin touched his rank insignia with his free hand. "Yes. Small blessings." His eyes found Valka a moment later, and he said, "Doctor . . . I was glad to hear you'd been healed of your affliction." He bobbed his head in greeting.

"And I yours," she said.

"Shall we walk?" Lin asked, indicating the procession back across the field to the tram platform. I gestured for Bassander to take the lead, and Valka and I fell into step beside him, moving slow to keep pace with Lin's limping gait. After a moment, the tribune cleared his throat. "How do you find Nessus, Marlowe?" No *lord*, no *sir*. Bassander Lin never been able to reconcile his holy terror of whatever I was with his contempt for the boy I'd been. He had seen me die aboard the *Demiurge*. And seen me return.

"*Trying*," I said, staring daggers at the back of Magnarch Venantian's head.

"I would have thought it suited you," Lin said. "So near the action, and in a position to do something about it."

"In a position to tell other men what to do about it, you mean," I said.

Valka interjected, "And the rest of our companions have been in frozen orbit since we arrived. 'Tis lonely here."

I nodded my agreement with her. "After what happened on Thermon, the Emperor felt it was wiser that I be put somewhere where I'd not make a spectacle of myself."

"He ought to have put you on a flight bound out of the galaxy, then!" Lin said, causing Valka to choke back a laugh.

"Don't give His Radiance any fine ideas," I said. "I'm sure he has plenty of counselors lined up saying much the same." When Lin did not reply at once, I asked, more pointedly, "Alexander is with you, is he not?"

"The prince?" Lin's dark eyes caught mine. "Aye. His Radiance ordered him brought along for seasoning."

"Seasoning?" Valka echoed the word, and I knew from the pointed quality of her tone that she was thinking the same thing I was thinking.

Alexander was still the heir apparent. Or not-so-apparent. He was one of the *afterlings*, the one hundred seventh child of the Emperor, a child of his age. The elder children, like the Crown Prince, Aurelian, were old almost as the Emperor himself. Should any of them come to rule, their reigns would be short as they were old. Alexander was young—though how young he was by then, how many years he'd spent in fugue I could not say. And so it seemed he still was the Emperor's favorite to succeed him.

And he had seen my miracle at Berenike, had seen me weather a direct blast from the Cielcin's orbital laser without so much as scratch on me. Did he still fear me as his mother did? As did the Lions of the Imperial court?

As did Mother Earth's Holy Terran Chantry?

Lin seemed to hesitate before asking his next question. He leaned in and whispered beneath the blaring of the trumpets. "Is it true the Chantry tried to poison you?"

I glanced at him and said nothing, which was answer enough, though not the whole answer. The Chantry had sent an assassin to my cell. I'd made him take his own poison. The facts had not survived their journey across the stars. I'd heard it said that Hadrian Marlowe had taken poison, had drunk it on the stand before the praetor and the jurors and had *refused* to die.

The tribune seemed to get the message.

"You'll have to come visit us at the villa," Valka said, speaking to cover the awkward silence for fear we might be heard. She lay a hand on Lin's shoulder. "Nessus is much nicer the farther you get from the city." It was not safe to have any conversations of that sort anywhere in the city, too many ears pricking and cameras prying.

"I may take you up on that," Lin said. "But I expect we'll be tied up in committee for some time, Marlowe and I. You heard about the Jaddians, I assume?"

"Prince Kaim and his army?" I asked. "Yes, I did."

Lin leaned in conspiratorially. "The Emperor has not come here simply to check on Venantian's progress with the fleet. He was slated to do that on the end of his tour of the provinces."

That piqued my interest, and I leaned in, too. "This stop wasn't on his itinerary?" That would explain the suddenness with which Venantian had sprung the news on me, and the venomous mood he'd been in the day we'd inspected the shipyards together.

The tribune shook his head. "He diverted the fleet five years out of its way to come here first."

"Five years?" Valka asked. "Why?"

"It's only a rumor. I overheard Sir Gray talking to my commander."

"Who's your commander?" I asked, not sure if it was relevant.

"Sir Sendhil Massa, Legate." Lin said, tone increasingly hushed.

I didn't know him, though there was another member of House Massa on the Intelligence council—I couldn't remember his name, an acquaintance of Lorian Aristedes. "What did they say?"

"That's just it," Lin said. "They said the Emperor was here for you."

CHAPTER 6

OLD SCARS

OF ALL THE PLACES I have lived, Maddalo House was among the most perfect. Had it been on Colchis and not Nessus, it might have been the very best. The Cid Arthurians who'd built it millennia before had done so on the edge of the bluffs that overlooked the riverlands and hedged pastures that rolled over hills and ran between them toward the capital on the horizon. The exterior was all of lime-washed stone, and the peaked rooftops were each supported by wooden beams intricately sculpted in the geometric style so closely associated with that chivalric cult.

It was not the grand palace of any great lord of the Imperium, but beautiful in a way balancing humility and pride. The two wings of the former abbey enclosed a courtyard and a rock garden that once had encircled the customary anvil and sword of the Arthur-Buddha. The Chantry had had that cult icon removed and melted down when Nessus was conquered by the Imperium, and here and there the villa showed the signs of the Inquisition: a rough patch in the wood where a lotus or a grail had been chiseled off, a petrified stump where the sacred fig tree had been cut down. There were places on the walls where traditional artwork had been removed and replaced with artifacts that clearly did not belong: a stuffed bull's head, the nude portrait of palatine woman reclining on a leather couch, and a sculpture that seemed to me no more than a gnarled mass of bronze, shapeless and ugly.

I'd had the bull's head and the ugly sculpture removed, replaced with a bat-winged angel in the style of those gargoyles who'd protected my childhood home of Devil's Rest. Valka—not surprising me—had insisted on keeping the painting. It made me uncomfortable, and she found that amusing.

The place was filled with the signs of our long occupation. Twin battle standards of the Red Company stood on pennon-staffs bracketed to either side of the grand staircase. Each bore the pitchfork and pentacle of my branch of House Marlowe bordered by the twisting labyrinth pattern that recalled my mother's family's Greek heritage. The library—a square tower on the southwest corner—contained nearly all the books that had traveled with me for so long on the *Tamerlane*. There too were housed the dozens of journals—white-paged and black—that I'd filled with sketches and snatches of poetry and favorite quotations over the long centuries.

Valka had claimed one of the upper halls for a study, and there filled the place with phototypes and print-outs of maps and scans of the various Quiet sites she'd visited in her life. The revelation that the circular anaglyphs that covered the Quiet's ruins were no glyphs at all, but the fingerprints in three-dimensional space of the higher-order dimensional mechanisms the Quiet had left behind, had broken her for years. But she was a xenologist, and language or no she would unravel the mystery she'd set out to solve.

I'd been given a small staff along with the place, of whom only old Anju remained after seventy years. She'd started as a scullery maid when Valka and I first took up residence at Maddalo House. Now she was the cook, and had been for nearly thirty years. She was terribly ancient for a plebeian, but was first to awaken every morning to prepare breakfast for myself and for the rest of the villa's small staff: the groundskeeper and two housekeepers. Often I would eat with them before taking my exercise in the vaulted gymnasium in the east wing. Once, the place had rung to the sound of steel as the Cid Arthurians sparred with one another.

The fencing gimbals with their target dummies and the holograph well were the only vestige of the monks that had not been scratched or painted over in some capacity. As I so often had in the morning those long decades—while Valka slept after a quiet night's labor—I stood in the center of the fencing round, targets dancing about me on the end of articulated metal arms. Holograph projectors painted the images of men over those targets. The Cid Arthurians had designed and programmed the images of medieval knights in Gothic plate, their visors down, tunics bright and richly patterned.

I felt shabby by comparison, barefoot, bare-chested, clad only in close-fitting trousers, the sword in my hand a weighted fiberglass rod. There were four of them, circling with blade or mace in hand, holographs mapping neatly over the armatures at the end of each of the gimbal arms, so that each knight appeared connected to the circular device on the ceiling above us by an umbilical of elbowed steel. How the device could pass Chantry inspection I was not sure, nor could I guess at how the machine's iron will operated without recourse to artificial intelligence, yet operate it did, never once repeating itself. I had toyed with the thought of removing it—its jointed arms too much recalled the limbs of the Exalted and of the chimeric half-machine soldiers that formed the core of the Prophet's armies—but I never did. The Chantry had done enough harm to the old place when it tore out the old religious icons—I would do it no more harm. Moreover, I confess a certain attachment to the machine. The holographs recalled the images my own mother would paint in her holograph operas, and so—standing against those ancient knights in their metal armor—I felt I stood in one of her stories.

The first knight lunged, red plume dipping as it thrust out the point of its sword. I parried the blade, slid the point of my sword inside and up under the knight's visor. The holograph faded, and the padded automaton withdrew, dummy blade drooping as the gimbal retreated, pulling it into the air. One down. I leaped aside in time to dodge a blow from the next knight, whose false image wore a surcoat of blue and gold with what looked like the fleur-de-lis of House Bourbon stitched upon it. The others came on, one in black and gold with a huge mace and the other in lobstered steel with a helmet like a barrel and bristles beneath the eye slits in imitation of a mustache. I parried a blow from the black knight and swung wide to put it between me and the other two. I had to control them, to try to isolate one opponent at a time.

My bare feet slid on the glassy floor as I backpedaled, retreating before the ferocious onslaught of the black knight. The blue one darted round toward my left, hoping to pincer me. I charged the black knight, batting its mace aside and striking it a blow that rang its armet like a bell. The knight staggered, metal umbilical whining as it went to one knee, according me the time I needed to turn and parry an overhead cut from the knight in blue. The mustachioed knight raised its great sword like an executioner.

I lunged, kept the point of my weapon forward through a careful parry that pushed my enemy's blade aside. It struck the floor as I extended, the tip of my training sword passing through the illusion of plate to strike the target at center mass. The knight vanished, dummy skeleton lifting back into the air, circling round even as the first dummy deployed again, holograph painting the image of an ancient Nipponese samurai in lieu of the knight with the plume.

By then, the black knight had recovered its feet, and both it and the blue moved together, working as a unit. Their ghostly feet made no noise where they trod over the laser-smooth stone, nor did their armor rattle. They struck together, and though I struck the black in the head, the blue one's holographed sword walloped me across the back, leaving an angry welt.

Snarling, I blocked the blue knight's sword arm with my left, felt little pain as my false bones bore the brunt of the impact. I whirled, blade whistling round to strike my mock opponent in the side of the head. It fell and faded, beaten. Knocking out three in such rapid succession had earned me a reprieve from respawning opponents, and I stood facing the samurai, sword raised in the forward *line* that had been my preferred guard since my days in the fighting pits of Emesh. The antique knight had a demonic mask that hid its face beneath the sloping *kabuto*. It advanced, blade flashing. I parried, side-stepping in a way that forced my point nearer the samurai's eyes. The simulacrum retreated, changing its guard. The curved blade came up, slashed down. I slackened my grip, allowed my sword to dip and flow out of the way as my opponent overcommitted, momentarily offering me its shoulder.

As a boy, I had so often hesitated to strike when Sir Felix pitted me against my brother.

I struck.

The fourth drone's holograph faded, and all four of the gimbal arms rotated above me, dangling their combat dummies like evil fruit. I slowly rotated in the midst of them, watching as the automata touched down on the stone about me, brandishing padded batons that turned into the steel swords of ancient knights as the holographs flared back over their metal skeletons.

I gritted my teeth, swept my attention round in a circle to assess my situation. I had a moment, crooked Marlowe smile reflected in the mirrored breastplate of the knight before me, knife-edged face a determined mask. I was great, then, great as I had ever been. Great—perhaps—as I would ever be.

The lead knight tapped its blade against its open palm, image producing no sound. Its fellows fanned out, circling about me like sharks in bloody water. Surrounded, no man could fight four at once. No ordinary man. I turned on the spot, knowing I could not keep all four in my sight— within the scope of my vision. Four became eight. Became sixteen. Thirty-two. Sixty-four. Hundreds. Thousands.

They struck, and vanished as they struck, their possibilities snuffed out by time's relentless flood. One blade whistled by as I turned my shoulder, and I turned another aside as I pivoted, bringing my own weapon around to chop into one golem's shoulder. I did not stay still, but hurried back, escaping the center of the knot my enemies had made, blade held between myself and them.

How many times had that hall rung to the clashing of our blades? How clearly I remember the color of the sunlight through the wrought-iron grates in the windows, how clearly I recall the smooth chill of the glassy floor beneath my horned feet. So many thousand such mornings lay behind me, so few were yet to come. Silence was coming to Maddalo House. Silence, and a shadow called Hadrian Marlowe who would one day face smiling Sir Hector on that very glass and struggle even to hold his sword.

The silver knight thrust its weapon at my eyes.

"Pause simulation."

With a dopplered whine the servos in the gimbals and in the metal puppets ground to a halt, the silver knight's holograph sword inches from my face. I relaxed, turning to see Valka standing in the circular arch of the door, dressed in a loose, sleeveless shirt and flared jodhpurs. Tribune Lin stood beside her, leaning on his cane and studiously looking anywhere but at the hideous, deep scars that striped my left hand and arm, relic of the highmatter sword that had nearly killed me in the Grand Colosseum on Forum.

Still surrounded by the holograph knights, I said, "Lin! I'd not realized the time."

The tribune wore undress blacks beneath his greatcoat, and carried his white tribune's beret beneath the arm opposite his cane. "I'd not realized you kept *that*," he said, using his cane to point at the yellow flag that hung on the far wall of the gymnasium. It showed a black, eight-winged angel with a skull for a face. It had belonged to Marius Whent, the self-styled *Admiral* whose dictatorship we'd toppled on our quest for Vorgossos.

Looking up at it, I said, "It's the one that flew above the state building. Jinan . . . Lieutenant Azhar cut it down during the celebration." Jinan and I had climbed the spire ourselves.

"I still have his sword," Lin said, and patted the weapon through his coat. Though not an Imperial knight, Lin had carried the weapon ever since the Pharos affair. I was surprised no one had ever challenged him over it. "Are those from the arena?"

"What?" I turned distractedly, midway through the motion of handing my training sword to one of the automata. The antique knights flickered, and the drones withdrew, pulled up toward the arched ceiling like puppets exiting the stage. He meant my scars. Ordinarily, I wore a black leather glove buckled to the elbow to hide the worst of it. "Yes. Relic of the time *before* the last time the Chantry tried to kill me. They're bound to succeed if they keep going on like this."

"Don't say that!" Valka said.

I shrugged. Thanks to Valka's demarchist implants, we were quite certain the house was not bugged. Part of the reason I'd selected Maddalo House for my own was its antiquity; its one-time status as an abbey meant the old place's connection to the planet's datasphere was thin at best. There were no electronic locks on doors and windows, no security cameras, no integrated comm systems. If anything in the vicinity had been transmitting, Valka would have sensed it with her neural lace.

"How do *you* find Nessus, Lin?" I asked, toweling myself off. "Enjoying your meetings with the Magnarch?" I'd sat in on several of Lord Venantian's advisory sessions with the Emperor, discussing the logistics of His Radiance's tour of the outer provinces. Frightfully dreary work.

Lin shrugged. "It's not so bad. You seem to be quite comfortable."

"The house?" I looked round at the gymnasium, at the tall, narrow windows that overlooked the grounds and the English garden, safe within its high hedge walls. "The house is the only part of my cage here that's any good—except my cellmate."

Valka rolled her eyes.

"Still," Lin said, stumping over to the windows to get a better view of the garden, "you could do worse. I was surprised to get the invitation, truth be told."

"We mentioned it when you arrived," Valka interjected.

"Yes, but . . ." He did not turn to face us, but squared his shoulders as he surveyed the world below, drummed his fingers on the head of his cane precisely as old Raine Smythe had done, "we have not always seen eye to eye." As he spoke, it occurred to me those drumming fingers belonged to the hand I'd once cut off. After an uneasy silence, Lin added, "It has been a long campaign . . ." His voice sounded drawn, tired—every note of it betraying the tribune's several hundred years. I had to remind myself that he was patrician, that though we were close in age, his less nobile blood was wearing on him more than mine. Lin was not a young man. "I am grateful that we are on the same side, Marlowe."

Where was all this coming from?

"As am I, Lin," I said, not sure what else to say.

"I never thanked you for getting me off that field on Berenike."

"You don't have to," I said, draping the towel about my shoulders.

The tribune turned on his heel, inhaled sharply. "I do."

Receiving Bassander Lin's gratitude was not the most comfortable experience of my life, so I stepped around it. "Berenike was hard."

"Whatever happened to those Irchtani soldiers of yours?"

Nearly two-thirds of them had died in the final assaults against Bahudde and the drill the Cielcin had sent against our fortress. "Reassigned," I replied. "Their commander, Barda, went to a Legion fort on . . . Zigana, I think it was. Took his men with him." I shifted posture, folded my arms almost defensively. "They're training more of their kind to fight for us." At the funeral for Udax and the hundreds of dead Irchtani, I had promised Barda my loyalty to his people. It was a promise I'd done little to keep. Shaking myself from such guilty reflections, I said, "Please, let me dress. I'll be back shortly."

I withdrew to the safety of the bedchamber then, and quickly washed and clothed myself: a white tunic with loose sleeves belted above my customary black trousers and high boots. I lingered a moment to fuss over the silver fasteners of the leather gauntlet I wore to conceal the scars on my left arm, violet eyes studying their own reflection in the mirror. An antique laving basin stood on the vanity before the mirror. It had belonged to Jinan, who had used every morning and evening to perform the ablutions her Jaddian fire god asked of his faithful. She had left it with me when I left her. I had used it to hold certain valuables ever since. My rings lay in it: one of ivory, one of rhodium, one of yellow gold. Nestled amongst them was the piece of white shell the Quiet had given me and whose radiance had guided me out along the rivers of time from the Howling Dark, and the silver half-moon of the genetic phylactery Valka had made for me. There too was the silver cylinder that housed the inert pentaquark reservoir of the highmatter blade that Augustin Bourbon had given to his picked assassin for that day in the Colosseum. I'd removed it before sending the empty hilt back to its owner so that he knew who it was that had encompassed his fate. I'd kept the core ever since.

A reminder of what I was and what I should not become.

This reminder I tried to square with the vision of me Bassander Lin had, his gratitude, his holy terror. The last buckle tightened on the cuff of my gauntlet, and I shook the white sleeve down over the glove. As I stepped away, the light reflected on the silver solder that held the smashed basin together. I had broken it moving into my quarters aboard the *Tamerlane* when the Emperor gifted me the old battleship, and its scars shone bright as my own did, without a glove to hide them.

I thought of Lin, his bones smashed and stitched back together with worn-out tools, and of Valka, her mind burned by MINOS's virus. The war had left its marks on each of us, as all Time's servants must.

I found Lin and Valka in the main hall, and coming down the grand staircase between the Marlowe banners, I led Lin on a tour of the house and grounds, the three of us talking of little things, old memories. We spoke of Raine Smythe, of Vorgossos and of the time before Vorgossos. We spoke of Emesh and of Sir Olorin, and of Otavia Corvo and the others who slumbered in icy crypts in the *Tamerlane* above.

"I've not seen any of them properly since before Thermon," I said. "Pallino and Crim were with me on Eikana, and I spoke to Lorian and Corvo on comm after, but I've been cut off a long time."

"We both have," Valka said, reclining in her seat. The three of us had absconded to a table the housekeepers had brought out into the garden for the evening meal. "Wine?" She proffered the bottle of Carcassoni blue.

Lin refused the vintage as he had refused it at the start of the meal. "Just water." He refilled his amethyst glass from a matching pitcher to underscore his refusal. "I imagine it's not been easy, cut off from your people."

"And the Magnarch is not my greatest admirer," I said, cutting through what remained of my quail.

Seeing Lin's raised eyebrows, Valka put in, "He is very . . . devout."

"So am I," Lin said coolly.

"She means that Lord Venantian considers me guilty of heresy and witchcraft and . . . everything else the Inquisition brought against me at Thermon." I swallowed my bite of quail and watched Lin closely for a reaction.

The Mandari officer betrayed little feeling in his face, but shook his head furiously. "Impossible. I saw what you did on Berenike, and on that ship . . . if you were machine or some *experiment*, the Inquisitors would have found out. They'd not have needed an assassin."

I felt a frown slice across my face. Lin's point was one I'd made to myself many times in the dead of night when the dreams came swift and silent. If I were anything but human, the Chantry would have found it. I was myself alone, and whatever the Quiet had done to me, they had not changed me as Kharn Sagara had changed, trading his body for another.

A wind tousled the pencil cypresses and walnut trees beneath whose boughs there came the spark of fireflies in the fresh gloom of evening. "That's the problem," I said at last. "It would almost have been better if I *was* guilty. They would at least have known what to do with me in that case. I'd not be trapped here." I gestured at the garden, at Maddalo House, at all of Nessus unrolled beneath the darkling sky.

"There are worse fates."

"Maybe," I agreed, and sipped my wine.

"You said the Emperor was here for us?" Valka interjected, one hand settling on my arm. "On the tarmac. You said you overheard Sir Gray Rinehart and your legate talking?"

Despite having told us so much already, Bassander Lin looked uncomfortable. The man was Legion to his aching bones, and for him to engage in hearsay like a newly minted academy cadet was more than passing strange.

Bassander set his amethyst drinking goblet on the table, eyes darting back beyond the garden and across the lawn to where his flier cut a knife shadow against the sunset, as if afraid it might hear him.

"Sir Gray believes the Emperor means to name you an auctor of the realm."

I was glad I'd set my wine glass back on the table, for surely I would have dropped it.

"Auctor? Me?"

"What's an auctor?" Valka asked, gold eyes darting from the tribune to me.

Bassander answered for me. "It's an old office, one which hasn't been invoked since the Jaddian Wars."

"Since the Aurigan Wars," I corrected. I'd read Impatian's histories of the Empire a dozen times over the centuries. Turning to face Valka, I put a hand on her knee. "You can't be serious." But Bassander was never unserious. In decades of knowing him, I'd hardly known him to smile.

"If you two don't answer my question . . ." Valka put her own glass down and hid her left hand in her lap. I recognized the tension in her shoulder as she masked one of the occasional tremors.

I raised a conciliatory hand, but it was Bassander who spoke. "The auctors were Imperial proxies, co-Emperors in all but name. They speak with the Emperor's own voice, issue commands, draw up laws, command the Legions."

"They were surrogates," I added. "The old Emperors used to appoint them and send them out in their stead to carry out their will. Hand-picked men, trusted. They'd exercise the Emperor's office until their mission ended and then be done. After the Aurigan Wars, the Emperor—I want to say it was one of the Tituses—created the system of Magnarchs and Vice-roys instead. That was a little more stable, a bit less centralized."

Valka was nodding along, right hand massaging the left. "You really think he'd resurrect this old office?"

Lin shrugged. "Like I said, he diverted the fleet five years off schedule to make this extra stop. Why do that if not for something like this?" The tribune leaned over the ruins of his meal. "Making you auctor would set you above the Chantry. They'd not dare move against you. You'd be safe. Safe to leave this place."

My eyes narrowed reflexively. "What makes you so sure the Emperor wants me to leave this place?"

"To hear Rinehart tell it, the Emperor didn't want you sent here in the first place, said you were wasted here." Lin lifted his amethyst cup and drank.

I dwelt on this. Sir Gray Rinehart was Director of Legion Intelligence and by extension a man mere footsteps from the Imperial Council. Hearsay this auctor business might have been, but hearsay from the Imperial spymaster was something much closer to fact than lesser rumor.

For the first time in a long time, I felt an absurd twinge of hope, and suppressed the lopsided smile, concealed its spread by looking down at my plate. "Auctor," I said, *"auctor."* It made sense. There were few things that would drive the Sollan Emperor to divert his escort—to divert an entire battle fleet—over a hundred light-years out of its way, adding years to the time His Radiance was away from Forum. The appointment of an Imperial auctor was one. The first auctor in over nine thousand years.

Valka laughed suddenly, a bright sound in the twilit air. "Oh, your friend the Magnarch won't like this at all!"

CHAPTER 7

THE KING'S DEMON

WEEKS PASSED BEFORE THE summons came. I spent most days in the Magnarch's palace, more often than not a silent accessory to the reports and inspections of the shipyards and the great cubicula where slept our waiting thousands, our soldiers awaiting the trumpet blast. The Emperor spoke but little through all this, taking in Lord Karol Venantian's news with the studious quiet of the lifelong monarch. Good rulers—in my experience—listen more than they speak. It had been so with Raine Smythe, and indeed with my father, who for all his callousness ran his prefecture with the ruthless efficiency of a thinking machine.

As the days ran by, I began to imagine that Bassander's rumor was only that: a rumor. But for the odd remark in council, the Emperor made no more special notice of me than of any other member of the council, as if I were not the man who had delivered him the heads of two Cielcin clan chiefs and cut as many fingers off Syriani Dorayaica's White Hand. As if I were not the man who refused to die in the Grand Colosseum, as if I were not the man who stood unburned beneath laser fire before the gates of the Storm Wall on Berenike. That itself, I realize now, was a statement in itself, a reminder from His Radiance that whatever I was, *he* was Caesar.

But the summons *did* come.

"Just this way, please," said the Emperor's manservant, the androgyn whom Caesar had called Nicephorus. The homunculi's bald pate shone in the lamplight as it led the way up the narrow stair to the viaduct approaching the Chantry sanctum where the Magnarch had his private chapel. "His Radiance asked I bring you to him directly after you arrived."

"He's in the chapel?" I asked.

"His Radiance is in the custom of taking these private moments for prayerful contemplation come evenfall," Nicephorus replied. "Particularly of late. The disposition of the provinces weighs heavily on his mind, you understand."

I paused a step to permit Valka to go ahead of me up the narrow way, and said, "I do."

"I trust your time here on Nessus has been satisfactory, my lord?" the servant asked, apparently just filling the silence.

"Save the part where we can't leave, yes!" Valka replied.

I caught her hand, and she glared down at me, mouthed the word *What?*

A servant Nicephorus might have been, but a servant with the Emperor's ear—meaning the butler *was* the Emperor's ears. Every word that passed between us, I felt sure, would be passed back to Caesar with no distortion.

"It is bittersweet to be back having been so briefly away," I said, thinking of the mission to Eikana. Siloed as I was aboard the *Ascalon*, I had not seen Otavia Corvo, or Lorian Aristedes, or most of my Red Company. They had fought the battle in orbit, and our Imperial minders had made it quite clear we were to return directly to the provincial capital. Coming back felt like a man dreaming thrust back into the gray and waking world. Or perhaps Nessus was the dream, a dull nightmare, and Eikana true wakefulness. The old house—which had become home despite the unseen bars of the cage Venantian and his ilk maintained for Valka and for me— had become *like* home, but Eikana—and the brief time I'd had with Pallino and with Crim—had reminded me that my home lay cold in orbit, its occupants once again immersed in icy dream.

Nicephorus stopped at the top of the stair for Valka and me to join it. The androgyn smiled, but the light did not quite reach its Imperial emerald eyes. "It brought His Radiance no joy to order you here."

It was as close to an Imperial apology as any man in the galaxy might hope to get.

Nicephorus extended a hand along the viaduct toward the sanctum—a tall, square building beneath a verdigris dome surrounded by its nine fluted prayer towers. "Come. Caesar should not be made to wait."

The Excubitors parted and two of the mirrored knights pushed the carved oak doors aside to admit me to the chapel. I had seldom entered the place in all my years at the palace, attending only those ceremonies which necessity compelled me to attend.

The Emperor knelt before the altar, his back to me, arms outstretched in prayer. About him stood his various attendants and hangers-on, the logothetes and scholiasts, heads bowed in mingled prayer and respectful silence. The Archprior Leonora stood to one side like the watchful queen beside the king on his chessboard, though with her black robes and white miter it was impossible to say whether she checked the Emperor or protected him from check.

The altar stood beneath the chapel's central dome, whose plastered surface was frescoed with the green and blue cloud-streaked face of Earth. The scent of myrrh rose from thuribles hung in the arches that opened round the circumference of that dome, and the smoke of candles burning before the icons in their graven niches twined about the scent of food left before those same icons in offering to the virtues and powers that shaped mankind and her world. Prudence and Justice, Time and Space, Temperance and Fortitude and Bloody-Handed Evolution. There were Icons of Death and Fate and Fury, too, and dozens more less well-known and less prayed-to.

I sensed Valka's unease boiling off her at my side, and understood it. She was a daughter of the clans of Tavros, a witch in the eyes of the Holy Terran Chantry for the machines that spiderwebbed her brain. Stepping over the threshold of the chapel was like a sheep stepping into the lion's den, or a lion leaping in among armed shepherds.

Of Bassander Lin, there was no sign, nor did I see Sir Gray or Sendhil Massa, the legate.

The Emperor did not turn, and before Valka and I could make it five paces along the minutely tiled space between, a logothete in the red-piped charcoal of the civil service stepped in and—throwing out an arm— whispered, "Lord Nicephorus! The Emperor is at prayer."

"We can see that," Valka said, unable to curb the acid in her voice. She softened it with the sharp V of her smile. Too sharp. The man's eyes narrowed, and in lieu of answer I bowed my head and waited, twisting the ring of yellow gold upon the first finger of my right hand.

The Emperor's ring. The ring that belonged on the conspicuously blank spot on his right hand. The ring he had given me before banishing me from the Eternal City after Bourbon and the Empress's failed plot in the Colosseum.

The Dragonslayer's ring.

Moving with the smooth grace of a lifetime's courtly training, Nicephorus interposed itself between Valka and logothete. "Please wait here," it said.

His Radiance did not stir for another several minutes, nor did his arms waver, red-gloved fingers spread wide to either side, the line of his shoulders straight and proud despite the weight of centuries. It was only then I saw the violet togaed form of Lord Venantian bent not far off upon a velvet-cushioned kneeler, head bowed and hands clasped. On the altar before them, the figure of William the First—the God Emperor—knelt himself beneath the painted dome of Earth, knelt as he had upon the Aventine Hill of ancient Rome in the ashes of his victory over the machines. The statue held aloft a crown of twisted wires, prepared to rest it upon his sainted brow.

In time, the red hands clasped above the Emperor's red head, and making the sign of the sun disc, he stood, gathering his scarlet-and-gold cape over one arm as he turned. "We had thought you would come alone."

I did not bow, but went to one knee as was my right as a soldier and knight of the Imperium. I turned my face down, and so could not see if Valka bowed or knelt or gave any sign. "Honorable Caesar," I began, using the address that, too, was my right as a soldier, "my companion has been imprisoned here beside me these seventy years. She is not your subject, but I had hoped she might add her voice to mine in pleading for our release." I risked a glance upward to see how the Emperor would respond.

His Radiance turned fully as two attendants hurried forward and adjusted the drape of his cloak and straightened his regalia. He planted one foot on his kneeler and said, "Is that why you are here? To plead? Was it not we who summoned you?"

I felt Valka's hand on my shoulder, and from its angle guessed that she was standing. She did not speak, but that contact gave me the strength necessary to raise my head entire. I may have been the Emperor's favorite servant for a time, but that time was long ago, and if Lin's rumor was wrong, there was great risk in boldness. And yet . . . "Your Radiance," I said, "I am your faithful servant, but I cannot well serve you here. I accomplished more for your Empire in a single day on Eikana than I have in all these years on Nessus. If I must plead to better serve you, so be it." Reasonable as he was, the Emperor was not immune to flattery. Few great lords are.

The Emperor's emerald eyes showed no emotion as he studied me for what felt the life-age of a sun. "Rise, Sir Hadrian," he said at last, gesturing with one hand. His eyes swept the assembly in the chapel about us, and speaking to the congregation, he said, "Leave us."

At once the scholiasts and logothetes took their silent leave, slippered feet scraping over tile. I remembered the way cold dread used to ooze down my spine as my father's counselors filtered from his conference chambers, the way anticipation had clamped iron fingers about my heart. But I'd been young then, was young no more, and though the Emperor should have filled my veins with ice, I found there was little fear left in me.

It was a dance, nothing more.

Leonora and the Magnarch evidently exempted themselves from the Imperial order to vacate themselves, as did the watchful Excubitors, who stood by with highmatter swords blazing and active in attentive hands. Even the Emperor's androgyn servants departed, save only hairless Nicephorus, who stood with head bowed beside a candlelit altar to two-faced Time. When all the rest were gone, His Radiance said, "I do not know what to do with you, Lord Marlowe."

No royal *we*. I did not know if I should take that as a good sign, or a very bad one.

He continued, speaking as if the Magnarch and Archprior were not present. "Do you understand what you've done?" I did not answer, but stood in the aisle with Valka, hands clasped before me, the gloved hand twisting the Emperor's ring. The Emperor began pacing, circling the great altar where the God Emperor's statue knelt amidst ten thousand burning candles, their bases all blurred into one, their points blazing like a little galaxy. "Four times now you have performed miracles. At Vorgossos, they say you returned from the dead. At Aptucca, you won a victory without spilling a single drop of human blood. In my Colosseum, you defied death again, and again on Berenike. I do not believe the first story. I *know* the second is not true. The third my Inquisitors have disproved—your false bones—but this . . . fourth one. Berenike. I have seen the recordings."

I was especially glad, then, that I'd confiscated the suit camera recordings from the Battle of Eikana. It would not have done to add to my list of crimes.

The Emperor had vanished around the rear of the statue then, and against my better judgment I approached the altar where the Magnarch and Archprior stood. "I have tolerated these stories for so long not because I believed them or disbelieved them, but because I believed their usefulness was greater than the threat they posed. The people believe almost anything, and if what they believe is useful to our fight—I call that good." The Emperor reemerged from the far side of the altar, continued pacing with hands clasped in front of him. "My Chantry," here he nodded toward Leonora, "believes differently. They believe you are a charlatan and a threat to *me*. In pursuit of their belief, they have acted in accordance with what they believe to be my best interest and the best interest of the Imperium and of mankind as a whole." He spread his hands. "Know this: in acting against you, they have acted without orders from me."

"'Tis reassuring," said Valka, arms crossed.

I felt my heart leap into my throat, but the Emperor ignored her.

"Do you understand the situation you have put me in?" the Emperor asked.

"Will no one rid me of this meddlesome priest?" I intoned, speaking in Classical English.

The Emperor evidently understood that ancient tongue, for he arched one eyebrow. "Just so. My left hand strikes at my right, and I have need of both. Understand: if I order you somewhere—here, say—for a period of some years, know I do not act without reason. I have kept you and my Chantry apart. Kept you from those agencies who believe they know my mind even when I do not." He came to a halt before the statue of his ancestor, noble face creased with long care. "When last we spoke face to face, you told me you had visions. I did not quite believe you. But as I say, I have seen the recordings from Berenike . . . *millions* have seen them."

He turned away, stared up into the graven face of the God Emperor. "They say you are the Earth's Chosen. That these . . . *miracles* of yours prove as much." The Emperor stood straight as a laser beam, so still he might have been a statue himself but for the motion of his jaw. "Perform your magic for me."

"I am not a sorcerer," I said carefully. Talk of magic and witchcraft conjured thoughts of forbidden machines, and it was important that I distance myself from such things as quickly as possible. "And you told me once that you do not believe in sorcery."

"Are you not my servant?" the Emperor asked. "I gave you an order."

"Eikana," I said. "Berenike. Nemavand. Aptucca. Vorgossos. I gave you victories, Radiance. Is this not magic enough?" Valka choked back derisive laughter.

"Curb your tongue, man!" Karol Venantian spat, unable to contain himself.

"You address the Earth's Anointed!" added the Archprior Leonora.

William XXIII raised one ringed hand. "Wisdom Vergilian and the Chantry Synod would have me kill you, Sir Hadrian. And there are those on my council who believe it would be best if I banished you to Belusha to live out your days, rotting in exile." He turned, and for the first time I discerned the fractal gleam of the body shield he wore flickering against the candlelight behind. It was no idle threat. Belusha was the most famous of the Empire's prison colonies, a frigid world beneath a dim and failing star where so many Imperial embarrassments met their end.

"You wouldn't dare!" Valka said, unable to stop herself. "Do you know how much he has given to you? How much he has fought?"

I held out a hand to stop her, heart swelling with love and gratitude even as it leaped into my heart with fear.

The Emperor's lips pressed together.

"Silence, witch!" Leonora raised her hand to point at Valka.

"You're one to talk!" Valka thrust out her chin. "Hadrian has done everything you've asked of him. Everything! And this is how you thank him? Threats of execution? Imprisonment?"

"Valka, that's enough," I said, too aware of her danger.

"No, 'tis not."

The Emperor's compressed expression had transmuted into a papery smile. "In nearly six hundred waking years, madam, I cannot recall the last time anyone has taken such a tone with me."

"Perhaps they should start," she said.

"Valka!"

Silence found its place among us. I offered no apology, begged no pardon.

The Emperor's smile had not vanished. "The female of her species *is* more deadly than the male," he said, speaking in Classical English. Valka made another derisive noise. Returning to Galstani, the Emperor said, "You two may be more dangerous than the Cielcin . . ." He inhaled sharply through his nose, eyes shut in what I recognized was a scholiast technique for clearing the mind. "Which brings us to our present concern."

"Radiant Majesty, this cannot stand!" Leonora said. "The woman must be punished!"

"The woman is not my subject, nor am I yours, Reverence. Be silent."

The Archprior bowed and retreated a step, though I caught the spark of flint in her black eyes.

"Besides, this is a private conversation. No public offense has been given. Lord Marlowe is fortunate to be blessed with so zealous a defender."

Not knowing what else to say, I said, "Thank you, Radiance." I could sense the danger Valka and I were in too acutely. Another Emperor might have ordered Valka killed then and there for such an outburst. I glanced at the score of Excubitors who yet held their posts about the chapel's perimeter.

"No matter. I have thought of a better use for you, Lord Marlowe."

The Emperor fidgeted a moment with his rings. "I shall be frank. You have remained here on Nessus so long for one reason: I do not waste tools that are of use to me, and you are of use. Charlatan or sorcerer, you *have* gotten results. You say your victories are magic enough. I agree. And while I have kept you here to keep you out of trouble, I believe you are right: you are more use to me off Nessus than on it."

Earth and Emperor, Bassander Lin had been right. Sir Gray and the legate were right.

Auctor.

The Emperor meant to name me an Auctor of the Imperium after all. I braced myself for the news, for the tide of outraged fury that was sure to come from Magnarch and Archprior alike.

"I want more victories from you," the Emperor said. "And so you will take your ship and go to Padmurak as our apostol. You will head a delegation to the Lothrian Grand Conclave."

"What?" I could not help myself. It was not at all what I'd expected. "Padmurak?"

Visions of Hadrian, Auctor of the Sollan Empire, faded in a twinkling.

I ought to have been relieved, and yet I felt a perverse melancholy, not because I'd wanted the honor, but because it would have upset the Magnarch and the Chantry's representative far more than any outburst from Valka ever could.

"The Commonwealth has stood apart from this conflict for too long now," the Emperor said, brows raised at my outburst—though he withheld comment. "With Prince Kaim committing the Jaddians to the war effort, it is right and just that the Commonwealth should join us as well. You will secure their support. Our people have bled enough for mankind on their own. If the Scourge of Earth insists on changing the nature of this war, than we shall insist as well." The royal *we* had returned, and with it the stoic impassivity of the Emperor's visage.

It made sense. The Lothrian Commonwealth was—after the Sollan Empire—the largest human nation in the galaxy. Their Grand Conclave—a body of Party officials nominally elected by the people but really appointed from on high—ruled more than a hundred thousand worlds spread across the upper reaches of the Sagittarius Arm of the galaxy, nearer the core in the galactic west. Each planet was ruled by its own conclave of Party appointees, and each conclave nominated one of its members to represent it to the Grand Conclave on Padmurak.

I smiled. "This is another form of exile, isn't it?"

"Another impossible task." The Emperor glanced at Venantian, and I wondered if the Magnarch had put him up to it. But no, the Emperor had still diverted his fleet years out of the way to come early to Nessus on his tour of the far provinces. This *was* important. "And yes. I will not risk another Thermon. That is why I sent you here. That is why I am sending you to Padmurak. The Commonwealth can no longer be allowed to play the hermit. You will go to them and secure their military support. You will be empowered to make concessions to them: lift trade embargoes and so forth. My counselors will get you all you need. Magnarch Venantian?"

The old man nearly stumbled in his hurry to approach the Imperial person. "Radiance?"

The Emperor's eyes never left my face. "See to it that Lord Marlowe's ship is brought out of space dock and outfitted for its journey. I want him on his way at once."

"That's it, then?" I asked.

"Those are your orders," the Emperor replied. "Go and perform your magic, sorcerer."

CHAPTER 8

SHATTERED GLASS

"HOW LONG 'TIL RENDEZVOUS, pilot?" I asked, wasting no time as I came through the portal to the bridge of the *Ascalon*. The Challis-class interceptor hummed beneath my feet as I took in the narrow bridge and the three men crewing it. The *Ascalon* could run with as few as one man at the controls. It had been designed to transport small numbers at great speed and in great secrecy. I'd added it to my list of assets before the Battle of Senuessa, some years before Thermon, when the need to travel between the relatively close-knit worlds at the edge of the Veil had been great and the *Tamerlane*'s speed was insufficient.

"Ten minutes, my lord," said the chief pilot officer, a reddish woman with a shock of white hair.

Her navigator spoke up. "Should be able to see the old girl in about three though, sir. She's coming round the day side."

Valka entered as he was saying this, and said, "Be sure to put it on screen, please. I'd like to watch our approach."

"Aye, ladyship."

I felt Valka bristle at the honorific, but she did not rebuke the man. Centuries spent among us Sollan barbarians had worn down her defenses, and at any rate, our sojourn among her people had not more endeared her to the demarchists' way of life.

A moment passed in professional silence as the three officers went about their work. The helmsman sat forward-most of all, strapped into a chair thrust out into the midst of an alumglass geodesic blister, glass above and below and to all sides. It was the only true window on the bridge, used mostly to allow the helmsman to communicate by body language with ground crew whenever the ship was in dock. In space it was . . . less useful, though it eased the claustrophobic bottling effect common on so many starcraft, especially the smaller ones. The other seats—those of the chief officer and the navigator—stood farther back beneath the low, sloping roof. It was between these I stood, ungloved hand resting on the back of the navigator's seat at my right, the Emperor's gold ring shining on my finger. I'd half-expected him to demand its return, but before I'd left Nessus I'd seen His Radiance the Emperor one more time. He'd insisted I keep it as a sign so the Grand Conclave on Padmurak knew I represented him personally.

"'Twill be good to see Otavia and the others again," Valka said. "It has been so long . . ."

That was an understatement, but after so many decades any statement would be.

"She said they'd all be waiting for us," I said. I'd spoken to the old mercenary captain earlier that very same day to coordinate our pickup. The *Ascalon* had landed in the meadow outside Maddalo House, and old Anju had overseen the house staff work to carry the crates Valka and I had earmarked for transport to the *Tamerlane*.

"Don't suppose I'll be seeing you again, master," the cook said, peering up at me with eyes half-veiled with age. She'd been but a girl when she'd started, all elbows, those eyes sparkling with laughter. I'd watched three generations of her family come and go. Her great-grandson had just passed his examinations and entered the civil service, working for the Magnarch's office. Anju said he aspired to patrician uplift, and I'd promised to put in a good word. How strange the passage of time is. Generations for the old chef, a lifetime.

And my hair had yet to gray.

Stranger still, as for Otavia Corvo and the others aboard the *Tamerlane*, it had been no time at all. Sixty-eight years had passed them by in less than a dream, and the familiar faces we rode to meet, whom we longed to see again after so lengthy a separation—had seen us merely yesterday.

"No man ever steps in the same river twice," I murmured, quoting. "Everything flows."

"My lord?" the chief pilot officer looked round. I had spoken in Classical English, and that dead language was alien to the young man.

I caught Valka looking at me, one brow raised. She'd understood me perfectly. "Nothing," I said, and shut my eyes, thinking of the shimmering rivers of time, of whose strange waters and stranger shores I dreamed each night.

The navigator cleared his throat. "We have line of sight, lordship. On the overhead."

A false window blinked on the canted ceiling above the three officers, showing a contrast-boosted and greatly magnified view ahead.

I had not seen her at Eikana, had not seen her in so many years.

The *Tamerlane* crested above the cloud-streaked green and white face of Nessus like a city sailing. She flew inverted to us, her armored dorsal hull facing the planet we orbited so that the spires and geometric holds and the organic swell of engine clusters that hung beneath that armored top layer seemed the black towers and bastion of a dark castle wrought of steel. My castle. The five great cones of her fusion engines were dark, and only the faint points of ion drives shone like stars across her stern. She was flying away from us, and we were overtaking her, our own ion drives sparking, pushing us to higher and higher orbits.

More than a dozen miles she stretched from pointed forecastle to the arrowhead of her stern. Between the naval crew and officers, the infantry who slept frozen in her holds, and the aquilarii who manned her lighter-craft, more than ninety thousand men called her home—none more than me.

Not speaking—not needing to—Valka wrapped an arm about my waist.

I smiled.

We were home.

In time the hangar doors were opened and we passed through the static field into the launch bay. On approach, the pilot officer inverted the *Ascalon*, flipped it head over heels so that we slid into the launch bay backward, relying on the ion drives and on common repulsors to bleed the momentum from our burn. Magnetic clamps embraced us, and the great bay doors slid closed.

Valka and I were aware of this only as a distant clangor, for we waited by the hatch. She squeezed my hand and kissed me, hooked an arm around my neck to draw me down and close. The seventy years of our exile melted then and dripped away—and more than those years. The odorless, recycled air and the brisk chill of the starship brought back the sense of ages past, and the Valka who kissed me was not the dark lady of Nessus, but the young xenologist I'd met on Emesh when I'd been little more than a boy.

"Back on the road again," she breathed, forehead pressed to mine.

I matched her grin and kissed her in turn.

The hatch opened, pale light streaming in.

"Good to see some things haven't changed," came a familiar voice. "Hasn't it been like a hundred years for you two?"

Otavia Corvo stood at the end of the gangway, seven feet of corded muscle in her captain's blacks, floating coils of bleached hair twisting about her dark face. She uncrossed her arms and grinned.

Valka and I sprang apart as First Officer Bastien Durand said, "Welcome back to the *Tamerlane*, Lord Marlowe. Doctor Onderra." He bowed, adjusted his arcane spectacles, tried his best to hide the wry amusement he shared with his commander.

"Seventy years," I said in answer, striding forward to clasp Otavia by the arm.

She grinned wolfishly. "You haven't aged a day."

"Otavia!" Valka pushed past and embraced the taller woman.

"Valka!" The captain returned the embrace, surprised by the fierceness of it. There is a part, I think, in those of us with augmented lifespans, which has never adjusted to them. It is as if our memory and our cells expect only to live the three score and ten of our mythic past, and so seeing Corvo and Durand again after so long a separation was meeting again a friend from childhood in the twilight of deep age and finding them unchanged.

When Valka and the captain had come apart, Corvo said, "White and Koskinen are prepared to take us out-system as soon as we get clearance. The Commonwealth? Really?"

"Have you ever been?" I asked.

Corvo shook her head. "Heard stories."

"I sailed with a woman who came out of there before Pharos," Durand said, his old composure restored. The First Officer had been distant and chilly before Annica and Berenike, but after he'd been almost remote as the stars. If my experiences with the Quiet and my *magic*—to borrow the Emperor's term—had converted Bassander Lin from adversary to friend, they had alienated Durand. I had forced the officer to shoot me and watched the blood drain from his face when he saw the bullet had done me no harm. I am not sure he had so much as looked at me since. "She was strange. Laconic. Sort of spoke around what she wanted."

"The Lothrians don't have ways of referring to individual people," I said. "No names or titles. No identity, no property."

"Sounds like hell!" Pallino said, appearing from round the corner at the end of the gangway tunnel, Elara in tow.

"Pal!" I clapped the man on the shoulder. I'd seen him far more recently than the others, but it was still too long. Elara I embraced. They were—besides Valka, and I supposed Bassander Lin—the last link I had to what I considered the true beginning of my life on Emesh. "How long have you two been out of freeze?"

"Only since yesterday," Elara said. "We'd have called, but the captain here said you were busy with the Emperor." She smiled in an almost motherly way. Elara had fallen into the role of quartermaster when we'd stolen the *Mistral* and left Bassander and Jinan above Rustam. She and Pallino had never married. They'd both been older when I'd met them in the fighting pits on Emesh, and though both of them had entered a second youth when I'd named them my armsmen and members of my house, I suppose neither of them felt the need to formalize their entanglement, as Valka and I had never done.

Valka and I moved out of the gangway umbilical and into the hall overlooking the launch bay. Through high, narrow windows I could see the black and silver knife-shape of the *Ascalon* clamped into its moorings. As I watched, the three nacelles and the wing on the near side folded against the hull of the ship.

"The Emperor?" asked a small, pale-eyed man with long hair so blond it was nearly white. "What's this, then?"

"Good to see you, too, Aristedes."

Commander Lorian Aristedes returned my acknowledging nod, toyed with one silvered brace that kept his too-long fingers in their proper places. "Is the Emperor here?"

Valka interjected. "He's on tour, visiting worlds across the front."

"He's who ordered this mission to the Commonwealth," I said.

Lorian's skeletal face composed itself into a frown. "Straight from the top, eh?" I could hear the gears in his head starting to turn. "Are they trying to push you out of the action again?"

"It does certainly seem that way," I agreed. The little man had an unnerving habit of cutting straight to the heart of things. Turning to Corvo and Durand, I said, "Will you have someone take our things to our quarters?"

Durand tapped his chest in salute and moved off, pressing past the others to find the stevedores. When he had gone, I asked Corvo, "How long will it take us to reach Padmurak?"

The captain chewed the inside of her cheek. "A little over forty-three years standard."

"Is Halford out of freeze?" I asked, referring to the night captain, the man whose job it was to tend the *Tamerlane* while she sailed between the stars with her primary crew in fugue.

Corvo shook her head. "I figure the ship's been offline so long we ought to take the first leg to shake her down. It's seven years to Gododdin at top speed. We'll refuel there and cross the rest of the way to the Sagittarius before we turn core-ward and make our way up the arm."

"Good," I said. *Seven years.* "I'll stay awake as well; that way I'll be around if anything arises that requires my attention. Besides, it will be nice to have some time with everyone. We'll wake Halford and the rest at Gododdin; he can take us on to Padmurak." The thought occurred to me that traveling up the Sagittarius Arm would mean passing near Colchis. Even if it were not possible to set into port there, I made a note to leave a message by inter-system relay for Siran and Gibson—assuming they were still alive.

"This will probably be Roderick's last voyage," Corvo said, meaning Commander Halford. "He's over two hundred years active time now. Three hundred by the time we make it back from the Commonwealth."

Half his palatine life . . . I thought. I seldom thought of the night captain. Despite all the years he'd put into our company, I had spent but little time getting to know the man who had saved us all from pirates off the coast of Nagapur. "I can hardly believe it's been so long."

"I know!" Pallino exclaimed. "Seems like just yesterday we were dealing with that stick old Lin kept up his Mandari ass."

"Tribune Lin sends his regards, by the way," I said to Corvo, who accepted this news with a nod. Everyone was quiet a moment, and I said, "On the bright side, this is a diplomatic mission. We're moving away from the fighting for once. I don't expect there'll be much call for shore leave in the Commonwealth, but see we spring for the good stuff when we resupply in Gododdin. You've all been under the ice a long time. Do you good to live a little."

"All they've got on Gododdin's *bromos*," Pallino groaned. "I've eaten enough hyper-oats for a hundred lifetimes."

Valka laughed. "'Twill do you good."

"Believe me, Valka, I've had enough *good* done me by that shite to last 'til Earth comes."

I caught myself grinning, looking round at all the others. My friends. "I have missed you all."

"Wish I could say the same, lad!" Pallino barked. "But they keep us nobodies froze up, so I saw your ugly mug day before last."

"Good!" I snapped back, and for an instant I was not Hadrian but *Had* the myrmidon again. "That way you won't forget it. Old man like you needs reminding."

Pallino pointed a finger in my direction. "Think that's funny, do you? I'll teach you to respect your elders, lad."

"You're not my elder anymore, Pal," I said, and felt my grin die a little as Durand returned with the porters to take mine and Valka's effects to our cabin. I found new life for it again and continued, "Maybe it's you who needs teaching."

The old soldier beat his chest. "Try that in the ring, son."

"It's a deal!" I said, laughing along with the others. "What's ship time?"

"Fourteen hundred hours," Lorian answered.

I took this information in with a curt nod. "Good. Corvo, would you walk with us? I want to see everything gets set up in the cabin proper and we'll all reconvene for dinner, yes?" I paused, realizing only then that we were short. "Where are Crim and Ilex?"

"Still in medica," Durand answered. "Started the thaw later than the rest of us. Okoyo says they'll be clear by end of day."

"Let's push dinner, then!" I said, brushing past Lorian with a gentle hand on the short intus's shoulder. "I'd rather see everyone together!"

The air felt dry and lifeless as the doors cycled and the ventilators kicked quietly on. The lights bloomed from dark to orange to golden. All was as we had left it. The wall was bare where Whent's flag had been removed, and the bookshelves on the curved gallery on the level above yawned their emptiness. The books had all been taken to Maddalo House, and in Maddalo House they remained. Valka had gone with Corvo to the bridge and left me to oversee the reordering of our lives.

I drifted toward the couches and the low table that made up the central sitting area in the center of the room, taking in the old dining table beside the wine cabinet and refrigeration unit and the pocket-door that led to the dumbwaiter that descended to the officers' mess. There, too, were the old coat hooks above the sideboard where once I'd kept Jinan's laving basin.

Something on the floor caught my eye, and I crossed to the sideboard, crouched beside it.

Shards of glass littered the floor, shone in the soft overhead light.

It took me a moment to realize what they were from.

It was the remains of the glass bubble I'd ordered made to preserve my Galath blossom from the predations of time. When I'd left the *Tamerlane* at the start of my exile, it had seemed wrong somehow to take the flower with me. Perhaps it was because it was a symbol of the Empire, and the Empire had spurned me. Or perhaps it was only that it had come to mean little to me, like the Nipponese woodcuts that hung on one wall.

The globe must have fallen with the motion of the ship, or perhaps one of the porters who had helped empty the chamber had shattered it by accident as we sealed the rooms. I'd no way of knowing, for surely security logs so old were purged from the ship's database. I poked through the smashed glass and found what I was looking for.

The white flower had withered at last, its silver-edged petals wrinkled and gray. I lifted it by its desiccated stem, twirled it in my fingers, a frown coming unbidden to my face. My reflection glowered at me from out of the glass front of the sideboard. I might have been the same young man who'd first taken ownership of the *Tamerlane*. The pointed nose and high cheekbones were the same, as were the violet eyes and curtains of ink-dark hair. My age betrayed itself only in the deepened permanence of the creases at eyes and mouth, and in the tiredness of the spirit that clung to me.

In the quiet of the chamber, and unwatched, I reached for that second sight. I saw the flower across infinite variations. Dead. Dead. And dead. Here a petal was missing, here the stem snapped. There I found it flattened, and in too many places . . . found it not at all. I reached further and further, casting my eyes toward the very edges of the cone of light that described the boundaries of my sight—the boundaries of the possible. In not one of them were the flower and the glass made whole. They had broken long ago, and it was only the present I could change—and the future with it.

Only the past is written.

"Lord Marlowe?"

I crushed the flower in my fist, looked round to find the stevedores had arrived with the first of mine and Valka's luggage on a float pallet.

"Yes?" I stood, let the dust of the flower fall. "What is it?"

"I . . . where would you like this, sir?"

"By the stairs." I pointed with my gloved hand. "Unless it's earmarked for our personal quarters. Carry that through."

"Yes, my lord." The men shunted their float pallet over the Tavrosi carpets and set about their work.

"And someone clean this up!" I said, indicating the shattered glass as I swept from the room to join Valka and Corvo on the bridge, my original task forgotten.

CHAPTER 9

KINGS AND PAWNS

"HAVE YOU LOOKED IN all the creche lockers?" asked Lorian Aristedes, lounging on one of the crash seats that lined the walls of the *Ascalon's* small hold.

I paused midway through the act of searching through the crates that stood clamped to the floor in rows down the middle of that long, narrow chamber. The walls slanted in at either side, narrowing toward a roof supported by raw metal struts like the ribs of an iron whale. With most of the little ship's systems powered down while it remained safely tucked away in the *Tamerlane's* hold, the air was cold, and our breath frosted the air. Little more was being done than to maintain the atmosphere and the ship's little hydroponics garden.

Unable to mask my irritation, I asked, "Why would *my* necklace be in someone else's fugue locker?"

The younger man shrugged.

Valka's phylactery—the silver half-moon pendant she'd given me before the fighting on Berenike—had not been among the items brought from Maddalo House. The pendant contained a complete copy of Valka's genetic and epigenetic information etched in quartz alongside a crystallized sample of her own blood. Among her people, such things were given as gifts when a clansman earned enough esteem in the eyes of his or peers to be allowed the right to have a child. They had no families but the clan, and every man and woman parented alone. Marriage was forbidden, for to marry was to privilege one partner above all others, which the clansman called the vilest sort of prejudice. The Tavrosi forbid even the exchange of phylacteries, fearing that the existence of siblings would create something too like the exclusive family unit.

Valka had made two phylacteries. She kept the other—wore it always on a chain about her neck. That one contained all that I was, as mine contained her. Such a trade would have had the both of us imprisoned where Valka came from, packed into the Demarchy's reeducation centers. It had been her compromise: not a marriage as I'd wanted for us, nor the dissolution of ties Valka's culture expected.

How much of life consists of such mutual surrenders?

"I don't suppose it was simply *left behind*?" Lorian asked, tucking his thin arms tighter across his chest. "Earth and Emperor, it's cold."

Standing, I shut the heavy metal lid of the crate I'd been examining and shoved hands into pockets. "Possibly." Some of mine and Valka's possessions had yet to be sorted through, and the crates all rose about me. I'd sifted through most of the boxes already, found little but clothing and copies of Valka's many notes. Two armored crates each contained suits of combat armor that had been crafted for me on Forum. These we had not seen fit to transfer up to our quarters, and doubtless much of it would remain in place through to journey's end. "It should have been in with my old washbasin. The one I keep my effects in."

"I haven't seen the basin, either," Lorian said, unhelpfully.

"I know!" I snapped, tossing back the tails of my greatcoat to sit upon the crate facing the smaller man. Lorian looked half a child huddled in his cape, his knees drawn up to this chest in the crash seat. Voice sour, I added, "I *had* noticed it was missing, too, thank you."

Not uncrossing his arms, Lorian shrugged a second time. "You asked for my help. I'm helping."

I grunted. "I'll telegraph Nessus from Goddodin; I'll sleep easier on the trip to Padmurak once I know where it is." That meant enduring years of quiet anxiety about the phylactery, but it was not possible to send or receive quantum telegraphs while the *Tamerlane* remained at warp. "I'm sorry."

Lorian waved this aside. "I hope it turns up, but like as not there's a crate or two still sitting on Nessus somewhere, collecting dust."

"I just have to hope the Magnarch doesn't sell the villa while I'm away."

"He'd not do *that*, surely," Lorian scoffed.

There was nothing to say to that. Lorian was probably right, and if the basin and Valka's phylactery were sitting beneath the mirror in our bedroom beneath the carved beams of the roof, it would be all right. Anju and her people had probably already overseen the mothballing of the old place: dropcloths like funeral shrouds draped over furniture and statuary, systems powered down, only the gardener still haunting the emptied grounds, tending the hedges and the fish.

When we'd been quiet for the better part of a minute, Lorian—not a man known for his ability to keep from talking—said, "Are we really going to Padmurak?"

I blinked at him once, twice, not sure how to interpret this question. "As opposed to?" I had the sudden suspicion that this was why Lorian had volunteered to accompany me as I searched through the boxes.

"I thought perhaps we might be going off-book."

"Going renegade?" I arched one eyebrow. "What gave you that impression?"

The little man chewed the lining of one cheek a moment. "Well, this is obviously another punishment mission. I don't know all that happened while I was taking the ice nap with the rest of the crew, but I thought there was a chance you had something in mind. Like after Colchis."

"You mean the Annica mission?" I said, at last letting the eyebrow relax. "No, Lorian, we're going to Padmurak."

The good commander seemed to deflate a little at the news. Lorian let his legs down, feet dangling just above the floor. "I only thought there might be something. Perhaps you and the doctor unraveled some mystery about your Quiet friends and the Cielcin."

"Lorian, I spent about the last seventy years under house arrest because the Emperor couldn't trust the Chantry or his own wife not to try and kill me again. I spent the decade before that in custody, in case you've forgotten. There's no *play* here. No plan. We have a mission and a duty. I mean to perform that duty and remind the Emperor of the debt he owes me and my company." Here I gestured at Lorian. "The Chantry believes I threaten their religious power. They think I think I'm some kind of prophet. False prophet, I suppose. And they saw what happened on Berenike. There's no hiding it anymore."

Alarmed, Lorian sat forward. "Do they know about your . . . ?" He drew a finger across his neck, miming decapitation.

I'd almost forgotten Lorian had seen Pallino's recording of my death aboard the *Demiurge* and my apparent resurrection. "If they did, I'd be carved up on a slab on Vesperad or . . . somewhere. As things stand, I think they believe I fabricated Syriani's orbital strike."

"They can't be that stupid."

"On the contrary," I said. "They think their doubt makes them clever."

It was my turn to cross my arms then, fingers agitating one of the clasps on my glove through the thick wool of my sleeve. "The Emperor knows better."

"Does he?" I swore if Lorian leaned any further forward he'd tumble right out of his chair.

"When one is enmeshed in a web of intrigue, my friend, the best course is often to tell the truth to the highest authority who will hear you and cling to his protection."

Lorian combed one lank strand of almost white hair back behind one pointed ear and said, "Cut through the swamp, eh? I guess that explains what we've been doing for the last century."

Something in the tactical officer's tone sent a spasm of irritation flickering across my face. "The Chantry nearly killed me, Lorian. The Empress and her Lions nearly killed me. This isn't a punishment mission—or it isn't *only* a punishment mission. There is no Chantry in the Commonwealth. We are going somewhere we can do some good. We have managed to slip the political net a while longer."

"All the more reason to turn renegade," Lorian said, circling back round. "When this is done, I mean. You've three legions worth of men in this company. You have the ship, and there's not a one of the officers who'd gainsay you. If we go back to Nessus, they'll put us on ice again and put you back in that villa. Emperor will probably make you Magnarch or something . . ."

The words tumbled out. "Bassander Lin said Director Rinehart thought the Emperor meant to name me auctor."

"Auctor!" Lorian *did* fall out of his chair then, bounced up on his feet like a downed boxer eager for another round. I rose sympathetically, worried the intus had hurt himself in his fall. The idiosyncrasies of his condition had Lorian's joints often slip out of place or caused him to lose function temporarily in whole branches of his peripheral nervous system. "Auctor? Black planet! Are you serious?"

"Are you all right?" I asked.

Lorian glared scathingly up at me. "I'm fine, Marlowe. Don't fuss!" He leaned back against the edge of the seat he'd so suddenly vacated. "Auctor? That would do it . . ." He massaged one hand with the other, colorless pale eyes fixed suddenly far away. "This is a *test*, then."

"Got it in one," I said. "Assuming Lin's rumor is accurate." The realization had been Valka's, had come to her about two months into our trip, and I'd not been able to shake the certainty of it ever since. Important as our envoy to the Commonwealth was, it was insufficient to explain the urgency of the Emperor's presence on Nessus. He had wanted to see me, to get a measure of me after so many decades apart.

On the edge of his seat, Lorian had crossed his arms again, using the gesture to draw his cape even more tightly about himself. "Damn. And Lin heard it from Rinehart himself?"

"So he says."

Lorian's skeletal features sagged. "He's Director of Legion Intelligence. Surely he'd *know*." The intus rubbed his jaw. "By damn."

I turned away from the other man and walked a few paces beneath the ribbed ceiling. At length I turned back. "When the Emperor diverted to Nessus early, Lin thought it was to make the appointment."

"But you got Padmurak instead?"

"We got Padmurak instead."

"It could be a play for time on the Emperor's part," Lorian mused, still stroking his chin. "Sending us all the way to the Commonwealth buys the Emperor nearly another century of real time—time he's spending in the freeze on this tour of his."

I stopped in my pacing. "He's taking his tour to extend his life," I said, realization flashing over me. "He's not young. He's been Emperor more than a thousand years. There's no telling how old he is biologically— someone must know, keeping track of all his fugue time . . . but he must be . . . six . . . seven hundred?" We palatines did not age like ordinary men. Our artificially lengthened telomeres held back the slow decay of age, pushed it off until the very end, when—as in the lab rats of uttermost antiquity—cancers and other mutations accumulated more and more rapidly in the absence of ordinary decay. Rare was the palatine nobile who lived to see white hair and failing eyesight such as old Gibson, and so despite the Emperor's outward vitality, I felt sure I must be right.

I am old, cousin, the Emperor once said to me. *I would see this war end before my reign does.*

"That's probably right," Lorian agreed. "This could all be preparation for the transition. Has he named a successor? I've been out of it for a little while."

"No," I said. "I'm sure the plans have been made, but . . . no." The Emperor had more than a hundred children. The eldest, Aurelian, was nearly so old as he—his birth ordered on the day of William's coronation more than a thousand years ago. The very youngest—I'd lost count— couldn't be more than ten years old. The Aventine House had a habit of producing new reserve heirs to a schedule, of spreading them out across the Imperium to protect against dynastic collapse.

Lorian chewed his tongue. "If he names our friend Alexander—which I still think he will—this auctor business *would* make sense. He'd essentially be setting you up as co-Emperor."

The hollow that had formed in my stomach when Lin first shared his rumor grew deeper and more sour. I had never forgotten the look in Alexander's eyes when I'd returned from the field of fire on Berenike. Unburnt. Like his father, Prince Alexander of the House Avent knew the stories they told of me were true, and he feared me for it. I had made an enemy of the young prince, treated his admiration with contempt.

"Co-Emperor . . ." I repeated, hands clenching and unclenching at my side. "Going renegade doesn't sound so bad now."

"What doesn't sound so bad?" came a new voice.

Both Lorian and I turned our heads in time to see Elara ducking though the hatchway from the access umbilical leading out of the *Ascalon* and back onto the *Tamerlane* itself, Pallino in tow. She smiled, and by way of explanation said, "Valka said you were down here. Looking for something?"

"It's starting to look like a box or two of my things were left on Nessus," I said, relaxing against a tower of crates bracketed together along the central aisle of the hold.

Pallino frowned. "Did you check the fugue lockers?" Catching sight of Lorian, he tapped his forehead in approximation of salute. "Little man."

"Triclops," Lorian said, returning the salute.

I didn't ask.

"Whole crates wouldn't fit in the fugue lockers," I said. "I was just saying: I'll telegraph Nessus once we reach Gododdin, just to be sure." Inwardly, I'd resigned myself to be separated from the phylactery until we could return to Nessus, though it pained me.

Elara seated herself beside me and placed a reassuring hand on my arm. "It'll turn up."

I could feel her smiling at me, and looked down at my hands in my lap. I felt a sudden warmth bud in my chest, and all Lorian's dire predictions about the course of empire and my place in it seemed at once very far away. Smiles are catching, and glancing at Elara, hers sparked mine. "I am glad to have you all back," I said. "I missed you."

"We missed you too," Elara said, squeezing my arm. Empty words, but kind ones. She and the others had slept the long years since Thermon. They had missed much, but not been aware of it.

Pallino barked a laugh. "I didn't!"

Elara threw him a glance. "Shut up, you."

The old chiliarch saluted, more properly this time. "Yes, ma'am."

Clearing my head, I looked from Elara to Pallino, the last of the myrmidons who had come with me out of the lands of Emesh. "Did you need me for something?"

"Like we said," Elara replied. "Valka said you were searching for something. We thought you might like some help."

The warm feeling spread a little more. "I suppose it couldn't hurt to check out those fugue lockers anyway . . ."

CHAPTER 10

PARADISE

THE WORLD BENEATH US shone gray and white as a holograph plate tuned to a dead signal. What air Padmurak had was stale and lifeless, and Vedatharad, the *Great City*, sprawled across snow-streaked tundra that had never known the touch of life. Each of the Great City's districts stood sealed beneath mighty domes of common steel and alumglass, reminding me of nothing so much as the demon-haunted city of Vorgossos.

Even from the air, the effect of the Commonwealth's capital was one of crumbling utilitarian efficiency, of brutal concrete blocks and right angles beneath mighty domes of glass. Soulless monuments to a godless scripture that made cogs of men and claimed to set them free not by breaking their chains, but by labeling those who forged the chains and held them as *fellow workers*. The Commonwealth claimed its wealth in common, and claimed there was no class, no hierarchy, no division between one man and the next. Its people had no names—so it was said—no stations. They dwelt in empty cells in the great hive towers that rose like the stacks of Satanic mills about the perimeter of each of the vast city's domed arcologies.

"Hell of a place," Crim said, peering through the slit window in the side of the shuttle as we prepared to disembark. "This is their capital? They couldn't put it on a world people can breathe on?"

"It is rather telling, isn't it?" I asked, peering out beside him.

The sky above was gray as the planet, white clouds matching white snow. One of the outlying domes filled the sky before us, the lines of its black skeleton carving its order against the heavens. So unlike the Eternal City it was, fencing out the sky.

"Helmets on!" Pallino ordered, taking charge of our little procession. I thumbed the trigger that deployed my helmet from its hiding place in the neck flange of my armor. The whole thing unfurled and clicked into place above my face with jewel-like precision while the others lowered their helmets into place. I heard the whine of pressure seals and hiss of air systems as the suit's air began to flow. Tor Varro wore his scholiast's greens over the black environment suit, his face hidden behind a mask of featureless black glass. Valka's helmet was similar, black alumglass and jointed steel above the padded matte underlayment, but the rest more resembled my own: the breastplate she wore over her blood-red tunic was sculpted to evoke the female torso, the pitchfork-and-pentacle embossed over the sternum—just as mine. She was no soldier, and so wore no pteruges at shoulder and waist, nor any armor upon arms or legs. But the polymer of her left arm bore the fractal pattern of her *saylash*, her clan tattoo—exact to the minutest detail—black against black.

I hadn't seen her wear it in decades, and smiled beneath my mask. She carried her old Tavrosi service repeater strapped to one hip, partially concealed by the heavy brocade of her short cape—cousin to my own.

What a pair we made.

"Helmets secure?" Pallino went up the line. His inspections complete, he rounded on the pilot officer and said, "Go to equalize cabin pressure."

A louder hiss accompanied the venting of the shuttle's air to balance the less wholesome air without, and an instant later the shuttle hatch opened on the ramp. The first of our guard went out, dressed in armor of Imperial ivory, their lances tall and keen, shaming the shabby guards of the Commonwealth in their drab grays. Varro followed, then Crim and Pallino ahead of Valka and myself, leading the knot of more heavily armored hoplites who made up the core of our guard.

We'd been instructed simply to march straight ahead across the field and toward the low, wide slit of the receiving bay that stood open across half a hundred yards of open tarmac. Why we had not been directed or permitted to taxi directly into the bay was a mystery to me. Perhaps the Commonwealth intended a subtle insult in the way they forced us to march.

The Lothrian soldiery lifted their lances in salute on either side. There must have been two hundred of them, armor hung with medals and dripping with braided cords.

"Looks like they sent their best, eh?" Pallino asked, whispering despite the private comms channel.

A thin wind cast about us, so insubstantial it barely lifted the heavy brocade of mine and Valka's capes.

Varro answered him. "It is an unusually high concentration of decorated men."

"They're trying to impress us," I said. As if the soldiery could compensate for the decaying urbanity of the starport.

Above the rectangular lintel of the hangar mouth was carved a stylized relief of the Lothrian people working arm in arm, two columns marching toward one another to meet in the middle beneath the graven image of a book. Their postures were rigid, artless, and mechanical—and their faces were carved with empty expressions aping joy and determination both, an unnatural mixture that I can't recall having ever seen on the faces of living men.

Nodding at the graven book, Valka asked, "'Tis the Lothriad?"

I returned her nod. "Yes. I'm told we'll see it everywhere."

The Lothriad formed the foundation of the Commonwealth. More than a code of laws, more than holy scripture, it contained the list of approved statements, the phrases and ideas which were permitted by the Grand Conclave for use by the people. Once, the peoples of the Commonwealth had spoken freely, it was said. But as the partisans tightened their grip, they revised their dictionaries shorter and shorter, pruning out dangerous and *unnecessary* words. In the end, they outlawed even names and other words by which one man was identified from the next—for it was said that to recognize distinctions was to foster inequity. If the clansmen of Tavros feared to prejudice one partner over another in questions of love and marriage—the men of the Commonwealth feared prejudice itself.

In time, they published no dictionaries. In their place was printed not a list of approved words, but of approved thoughts. There would be only one way to express hunger, or pain. Only one way to request assistance, or address a comrade. Where once had been a language, there was to be set of ideologically approved sentences, like hieroglyphs. Unchanging.

Or so it was said, so we were asked to believe.

We passed beneath that graven lintel, and steel doors ground behind us, shutting out the pale and jaundiced sun. The light that shone from the flat ceiling overhead was utterly without color. Indicators in the periphery of my vision told me that air was being pumped into the cavernous hangar, and on the receiving platform ahead I saw a portal open and admit a man in a gray suit without emblem or device, bookended by men in armor of unassuming black.

As we drew nearer the platform, the gray-suited man raised a hand. *"Dilijatja vatajema,"* he said, speaking the guttural Lothrian tongue. *The delegation is welcome.* "On behalf of the Conclave, a representative bids the delegation from the Sollan Empire welcome to Padmurak and the People's

City." I marked the earpiece the man wore, and guessed that a panel of advisors—if not the machine itself—was feeding the man his lines, ensuring he stayed on-book.

I returned his bow. Curious, I tested the air and spoke in Galstani. "Thank you for your warm welcome, representative. I am Lord Hadrian Marlowe of the House Marlowe-Victorian, apostol from His Radiance, Emperor William XXIII. I am sent to treat with your masters, the Chairs of the Great Conclave, that we might respond to the Cielcin threat in a way mutually beneficial to our two peoples."

As I expected, the man paused a long moment before answering, waiting for his machine or the puppet masters behind it to censor and translate my meaning. I might have spoken Lothrian, but I sensed that to do so was a risk. I knew the language, but not the list of stock phrases approved by the Conclave and its various ministries, and sensed that to try was to stagger blind and drunk into a minefield.

"That which is for the good of all men is good for each," the minister replied, this more clearly a quotation. He offered a weak smile. I wondered at the enormous complexity required to converse with an offworlder not bound by Lothrian speech codes. I did not envy the fellow his task, for surely the firing squad or the guillotine awaited failure.

"Let us hope so," I said, and realizing my helmet was still on, reached up and removed it with a button press, the whole apparatus folding away like some Nipponese paper sculpture. "Are you one of the Conclave?"

The man shook his head. "Each man must serve the good of the People in fullness of ability. Even the smallest contribution to the good of the People is a benefit to all." I took that to mean that no, he was not one of the Chairs—though I did not doubt he was some manner of logothete or secretary high in their service. The Lothrians could pretend to have no hierarchy, but that did not mean one did not exist. The man bowed, ushering us forward. Still speaking his native tongue, the man said, "Cars have been brought for the delegation."

We passed through the drab streets of Eleventh Dome and along gray boulevards unrelieved by the green of trees or grass. Nothing seemed to grow in that dreary city, and great stacks vented steam into the air, where it condensed and dripped from the glass overhead like sad rain. I had the distinct impression—peering out through rain-streaked glass from the rear of the representative's motorcar—that we were being taken down streets cleaned especially for our visit, for we saw few people, and the brutal stone and concrete facades of buildings shone where hydraulic cleaners had scrubbed away so many years of grime. Bronze reliefs that showcased the virtue and exploits of the People were everywhere in evidence, and everywhere shining without patina or rust.

"Where are all the people?" Valka asked, watching two men and a woman in identical gray suits hurrying along the street beside us.

The representative peered out the window of the car, blinking. He seemed to be looking for the very people Valka asked after, but he was only waiting for his prescribed reply. It came after but a second. "Let each toil for the good of all."

I could feel Pallino longing to say something, and directed a glare at the captain of my guard. The patrician fellow looked pointedly out the other window, watching the other cars of our motorcade following on behind.

At length, we passed out of Eleventh Dome and along an underground highway that ran beneath the blasted tundra toward another of the domes. This journey only reaffirmed my suspicion that the city had been emptied ahead of our arrival, for six lanes stood open for our motorcade, and I guessed on any other day the traffic would be fierce. I found I had little desire to question our host, who had nothing of his own to say.

Lights pulsed by, orange and sickly.

They gave way to the pale yellow sunlight of another dome, this one mightier than the first. We'd come out under the heavy arch of steel gates that might be shut to isolate the dome should necessity arise and onto a high bridge that ran across a churning reservoir. A mighty dam rose to one side, its sluices open to let forth the flood in thunderous cataracts.

Across that long bridge rose the crowded geometry at the heart of Vedatharad. Pile upon pile of cyclopean stone rose into the yellowed day. The air about seemed thick with some haze—as of the steam that wafted from the stacks in the outer dome—and through the glass curtain of the dome itself I saw the windowless hulks of the blockhouses rising like factories. There were the people of the Commonwealth, I knew: sealed in their hovels.

There were more people as we approached the core of the city, men and women in the same dull gray uniforms hurrying about beneath First Dome's bottled sky, some alone, some huddled together beneath umbrellas to shield against the drip of water from the glass above. Still more wore medical masks over their faces, and everywhere there were guards. I was not unused to seeing military police—we had prefects on every Imperial world—but the sheer *number* of them! A black-armored man stood on every street corner, reminding me once more not of any Imperial city, but of the city above the palace of Kharn Sagara on Vorgossos.

And like Vorgossos, there was a darkness underneath.

The People's Palace stood behind an encircling wall of concrete and steel half a hundred feet thick and three times as high. Within its bounds, the central ziggurat rose in great steps like the pyramid of some false, forgotten god. Outbuildings, windowless and unadorned as tombstones, stood about the perimeter wall: barracks and arsenals and the offices of the secret police. Water played from abstract fountains or jetted in arcs above the main road, leaping from one pile to the next. Soldiers in the matte black of the Conclave Guard or in the highly decorated gray and red of the formal service stood at mechanical attention before doors and fountains, or looked out from the steps of the ziggurat that rose a thousand feet toward the apex of the dome above.

The cars circled around the last fountain and came to a halt before the great stair. A red carpet flowed down those steps like magma, like the incarnadine rug Klytaemnestra unrolled beneath the feet of Agamemnon the Great when Earth was young. Two armored guards opened the clam-shell doors, and the representative made a gesture to indicate that I should lead the way out. Pallino went first—Crim was in the car ahead of us—and offered me a hand up. I returned the gesture to Valka, who took my arm.

"It reminds me of home," she said in Panthai.

I hadn't wanted to say it. Where she had come from, beauty was subjective—and the world was subjective. At home among her people, Valka had seen what she wanted to see, what her implants painted over her world, illusions in her mind's eye cast like shadows on the real. She had seen rich gardens where I had seen bare stone, imagined rich wooden floors and hand-carved furniture in place of laminate tile and nylon upholstery. The demarchists imagined riches and papered over ugliness, but the Commonwealth embraced that ugliness and imposed it on all they possessed.

"Are you all right?" I asked her, leaning in. It seemed unlikely that any of the Lothrians about us should speak Valka's relatively obscure language, but there was always a chance.

She smiled bravely. "Fine. 'Tis nothing."

A trio of camera drones took holos of us as we mounted the stairs. Security, perhaps, or perhaps the organs of some state propaganda broadcast eager to spin some yarn about our visit. I flashed one a crooked smile, acknowledging the salutes of the pikemen on the stair. Ahead, Crim marched with the signifer who carried the diplomatic staff aloft with its red banner, white-striped where the red Imperial sun shone bright. As we mounted the steps and passed beneath gargantuan square pillars toward false doors forever open and carved like the open pages of a book, I saw ranks of shadowy figures standing to receive us: gray-suited men and women, pale-faced and dark of hair.

I expected us to be stopped and welcomed at the doors, but we were marched instead through security, scanners glowing. They would know about my sword and shield projector, and about the sidearms strapped to one thigh. They'd know too about my parrying dagger, and about the loadout of each and every one of the forty men in my guard down to the smallest of Crim's knives. Even the adamantine bones of my left arm were laid bare to them.

Only Valka's implants might escape their notice, that and the monofilament coil Crim kept hidden among his dark hair.

Our representative waved a stiff salute to two others—a man and a woman—who hastened across the atrium to greet us. Each was so like the first that I thought they must be brothers, gray-skinned, black-haired, and hollow-eyed. The three of them each seemed propped up by stimulants, though whether it was verrox or amphetamines or simple caffeine I could not say. Both wore earpieces identical to that worn by the first.

"The delegation is welcome," they said in unison, waving their short salute. It was the precise phrasing the first man had used to welcome us in the hangar.

"We are honored," I replied, allowing them time for a translation to be heard and read to them. "When will the Grand Conclave hear us? I am eager to meet with your masters."

The woman bowed slightly, hands clasped before. "There are neither kings nor masters in the Commonwealth." She spoke with the chiding edge of a schoolmaster, of a scholiast correcting a slow learner. "The Conclave is not in session this day. The delegation will be summoned when the Chairs arrive."

A frown threatened to storm across my face, and I looked from Valka to Tor Varro. "Is there to be no reception? I had hoped to begin at once."

The two men and the woman exchanged glances, each waiting for words to be put into their mouths by the correct authority. Already I felt my patience wearing. Silence I could endure, but this empty-headed passivity that passed for civic virtue was more than I could bear.

"I come on a mission of special significance from the Sollan Emperor himself. Am I not to be received?"

The woman—clearly the senior of the trio, though doubtless that observation would be met with the paean about each man serving the good in fullness of ability—fixed me with a stare and taut smile. "Let each toil for the good of all. Let there be bread, and board, and good order for all who toil."

"Busy, eh?" I hooked my thumbs through my belt and surveyed the cavernous blank space we had entered. Here the floor was not plain concrete or laminate, but marble tile, a white and black grid. Ahead, a low pool gleamed, lit from beneath, its surface perfectly smooth above dark stone. A black mirror. I felt the child's impulse to disturb that stillness, to shatter the illusion of perfect order all around.

I knew what was happening.

They were posturing, pretending as all lords must that such great matters were of little moment to them. Pretending that the arrival of an apostol from the Sollan Empire was not a sign of the end of their world.

War had come to Padmurak, whether its dark lords willed or no.

CHAPTER 11

THE GRAND CONCLAVE

NIGHT AGAIN, AND DREAMS.

Dreams of drowning and deep water. Pale hands trailing in the dark, caressing, dragging me down. I was dead, or nearly so, sealed inside my armor. Time ran backward, and I fell, fell *upward* toward red light and sound and the chaos of battle. I stood upon a bridge of crumbling stone outside a city of gray towers. Groundcars burned about me, and ragged men held guns.

If, as some believe, time is without end, then in time all things are made true. I believe there must be a final end, as there are endings for so many lesser things: empires, planets, men. But even the centuries of a man's life are time enough to make truth of mistruth. I had told Lorian once that I did not dream the future. I had not known I could.

The guns fired, muzzles flashed.

I woke.

Dawn had come to Padmurak, and the pale yellow sun shone sickly through the horizontal slits of window glass in one wall, showing cross sections of the brutal, cyclopean city. From our penthouse atop the sky-spire that housed the Imperial embassy, I could make out the shapes of the other domes in the distance. Somewhere miles off lay the shuttleport. Beyond that lay the freight starport: twice the night before I'd seen rockets flare across the sky. Beyond that was only tundra. Tundra, and the endless factories and barracks and labor camps that made up the foundation of Lothrian society.

I let Valka sleep, and washed in the waterless shower, scraped myself beneath the sonic jets and watched as the shower pod flash-incinerated whatever material remained within the stall. I donned my diplomatic best: white shirt and the trousers with their double blood-red stripe along the seam. Over this I belted a tunic jacket in paisley black-on-black brocade lined with crimson. I took my time fitting the leather gauntlet over the sleeve, clicking the fasteners into place. I screwed the Emperor's sovereign ring onto the first finger of my right hand, and tucked the pendant with the white shard of the Quiet's shell onto its chain. The boots fitted themselves, tightening about my calves. The sword clicked into place.

The Grand Conclave awaited.

Varro, Valka, and I crossed the antechamber's black-and-white-checked floor, bracketed by our guards and led by new representatives of the Commonwealth government. Each day we saw new ones, and never again the old faces. We were led round the reflecting pool and up an angled stair to a gallery that ran left and right along the width of the palace ziggurat and overlooked the antechamber and the lower halls or out upon the palace grounds. Ministers and functionaries in identical gray with the black star of government service above their hearts milled about. These were the *pitrasnuks*, the partisans who ruled the Lothrian Commonwealth in the name of their *zuk* People.

The inner wall of the gallery was all one mighty frieze depicting the People in triumph. Straight ahead of the main gates stood a square arch. Through this we marched past security, past more gray murals and down a narrow hall whose ceiling was so high above it was lost to darkness. No side passage appeared, and I sensed that we approached the very heart of the ziggurat. The place reminded me of the unforgiving concrete fastnesses of the Chantry bastille on Thermon, or the cell blocks in Borosevo on Emesh. I wondered if the Commonwealth had taken their inspiration from the Chantry so many thousand years before, had stolen their cold architecture for the terror it evoked.

The hall opened on a round chamber, and looking up I found that we had walked out upon the pit of an amphitheater. A coliseum. Sheer walls encircled us, ten feet high, and above that lip, behind an iron rail before us were seated the thirty-five Chairs of the Lothrian Grand Conclave, forming an arc before us. The central chair stood empty, but the others—seventeen to either side—held the assembled gray-faced and gray-robed lords and ladies, each black-haired or white. Lesser functionaries sat behind and above them and all around above that central floor, faces half-veiled in the dingy shadows of that hall of power.

"The Conclave recognizes the delegation from the Sollan Empire," said an elderly man seated to the right of the central seat, whom I took for their speaker. "On behalf of the Conclave, it is hoped that the delegation's presence marks the beginning of a new era of cooperation between the Empire and the Commonwealth. The good of all is the good of each."

He spoke these words with the weight of a priest at his ceremony, and indeed no sooner had he finished speaking than the other Chairs and the congregation of lesser functionaries all intoned, "The good of all is the good of each." After each pronouncement, a device embedded in the wall beneath the vacant chair in the center of the Bench above repeated their words in awkward, stilted Galstani—presumably for my benefit.

In the dim air, I detected the shimmer of a prudence shield between us and the upper level, and without having to ask I understood how it was we'd been admitted with our guards. No hand weapon we might bring to bear could penetrate that energy curtain.

Sensing my cue, I stepped forward and bowed, one hand over my heart, the other thrown wide in the courtly manner expected for planetary rulers. "Honorable Chairs," I began, straightening. "I am Sir Hadrian Marlowe, knight of the Royal Victorian Order. I am sent by my Imperial Master, William XXIII of the House Avent, to request aid in our war against the Cielcin xenobites who have ravaged our worlds and the human universe for so long." I paused, allowed the lords' earpieces time to translate my words, allowed time too for a response, but the Chairs of the Grand Conclave all watched me with impassive eyes.

I took a step forward. "Our Empire has borne the brunt of this offensive for more than a thousand years." Again I paused. I'd known in my heart that the war had raged so long, but to speak the words aloud was something else entirely. Inhaling, I pressed on. "For more than a thousand years we have fought and bled—and died—to keep the enemy at bay. For more than a thousand years we have held the line. It is the blood of *our* people that has bought safety for your own. But the Cielcin have crossed the Expanse in force. Their navies burn planets along the Centaurine frontier. We are attacked on more fronts—in more systems—than we can defend. We need ships. We need more men." This pronouncement met with stony silence from the men and women on the bench above. With a sidelong glance to Varro, I said, "My Imperial master asks that you join us in defending mankind from this unprecedented threat."

Still the Chairs made no sign. The elderly man at the right hand of the empty seat glanced about at his compatriots, looking for some sign from them. Presently, the man in the Ninth Chair shifted forward in his seat. So young he seemed by comparison to the other, his short black hair oiled and neatly combed, gray eyes flinty above hollow cheeks. "Who names others *master* or *slave* cannot know a man as *comrade*. Ask how equality may be practiced by one who knows it not."

I said nothing, turned this response over in my mind. I understood the Lothrian perfectly, but the machine-translated Galstani repeated his words as I stood there. It was not a direct answer, but then I had not expected one. Was the Ninth Chair asking a question of me? Or admonishing against the Conclave for granting this audience? I marveled at his age, and wondered how so young a man might rise to such a height in the Commonwealth. Perhaps mastery of the Lothriad was a greater asset than experience in the eyes of the Grand Conclave? Perhaps the young man was a scholar of some kind, a theologian of their godless faith.

A moment passed, and I decided the Ninth Chair must have meant his statement for his fellows on the Bench, for another—the woman in the Thirteenth Chair—raised her nasal voice. "A yearning for equality lies in the heart of all." Was she encouraging dialogue? I looked again at Varro. The scholiast's dark features were as ever entirely void of emotion, evincing none of the frustration I felt.

"They don't trust us," Varro said, leaning close to whisper into my ear. "The gentleman on the left does not expect us to deal fairly. I believe he thinks we mean to capitalize on the situation. The woman disagrees."

Nodding, I surveyed the Chairs of the Grand Conclave, each minister overshadowed by the high, square back of his or her seat. A camera drone tracked through the air, sketching a circle about the rail that hemmed us in on the lower floor. I watched it go, staring down its lens. "I am empowered to make concessions to the Commonwealth in the Empire's name, starting with this." I drew a crystal storage chit from a pocket on my belt, a card perhaps an inch wide and twice as long. I held the device aloft for the Bench to see.

At a gesture from the elderly man in First Chair—that to the right of the empty seat in the middle—a plinth rose from the floor at the focus of the arc of seated chairmen, and I laid the crystal atop the glass surface. An instant later a projection flowered in a cone of light cast by a holography suite lost in the darkness above and behind the seated lords.

Embedded beneath a layer of fractal security stamps that confirmed the holograph's validity as an Imperial document marched line upon line of legal text. "As you can see," I began, one hand behind my back, the other raised as if offering something up on my palm, "we're prepared to offer an immediate end to our embargo on the sale of refined uranium and anti-matter. We will even allow certain corporations operating under Imperial charters to deal with your colonies. There is no reason an arrangement between our peoples cannot be mutually beneficial."

A murmur went down the line, and above and about the main Bench where sat the group of thirty-four, the various lesser functionaries mut-tered and stirred. Presently, the woman in the Sixth Chair raised her hand. "A man requests the Voice!" she said.

Once more, I looked to Varro, eyes inquiring. The scholiast's pinched brows rose, and he shook his head. Slowly—very slowly—the various chairs turned to watch each other, variously leaning in or peering one to the next. Sixth Chair kept her hand raised. At length, another joined hers, that of the square-jawed man in Seventeenth Chair—him at the leftmost extreme of the Bench above us, the furthest at the right hand of the center. The ice thusly broken, more hands rose. Ninth Chair folded his arms, and seeing this a number of the others did likewise. The old man in First Chair went up and down the line, counting. "Twenty-one!" he exclaimed. "To thirteen. The Voice is granted."

I wondered what they did in the case of a tie.

The Sixth Chair stood, one hand steadying the drape of her gray robe. "Why now? The Empire has been an enemy of the People for thousands of years. The Empire has blocked trade. The Empire has blocked the es-tablishment of colonies. The Empire now begs the People for aid. Why?" The translator repeated her words in the same flat, sexless voice as it had the others.

Thirty-four gray faces looked down on me. Sixth Chair did not seat herself, but waited. I stared up at her, astonished.

A man requests the Voice, she'd said. She had requested the right to speak her mind, to speak off-book—and the others had voted on it. Would she have spoken had they voted against her? I guessed not, for who in all the Commonwealth would be watched more closely than this group of thirty-four?

I glanced at Ninth Chair before responding to Sixth. "Worlds are burn-ing across the Centaurine," I said. "Hundreds of worlds. The Cielcin are moving now in numbers unlike any they've sent against us before. The front is too long—in too many systems—for even our forces to adequately defend. The regional governors and feudal lords are overrun." I spared a glance to Valka, who offered me the smallest smile of encouragement as I plowed ahead. "The Centaurine has acted as a bulwark against the enemy for centuries. If it is overrun, the Cielcin will be at your door. Our people have been a shield for yours since the war began. Even should we maintain control of the region, it is entirely possible the Pale will burn channels through our territory to yours. I tell you: the war has changed."

Sixth Chair seemed to mull this over a moment before answering. "If the *Rugyeh* come here, it will be costly. The *Rugyeh* fleets will be overextended. Weak." This remark elicited nods from several of the other Chairs on the Conclave's Bench, including both the Ninth and Seventeenth Chairs.

Rugyeh was *Others* in Lothrian. It was their word for the Cielcin.

"The Cielcin will be fat on plunder, their numbers replenished by so many years spent in transit," I said. The various studies Legion Intelligence had conducted on the few Cielcin ships we'd taken intact over the years had revealed no fugue creches, and the many dissections and gene sequencings performed by scholiasts and their lay technicians on the bodies of the Pale had hinted at monstrously long lives. The Prince Aranata Otiolo had once hinted to me that it was over a thousand years old—though how long a Cielcin year might be relative to our own was a mystery I'd yet to solve. The Cielcin were not idle as their migratory fleet clusters plied the Dark between the stars. Generations were born, lives lived, so that the armies of the enemy were bred anew and stronger with each flight between worlds. Between battles. It was thanks in no small part to this fact that the army Bahudde had led when it razed Marinus had been so strong when it flew to assail Berenike. For humanity, a long flight across the stars meant stasis, meant sleep—but for the Pale? For the Cielcin it spelled flourishing and strength.

"You do not understand them as I do, Honorable Chair." I locked eyes with her, willing her to understand. "The Commonwealth is not prepared. And should it come to fighting in Lothrian space, my Empire will not be in a position to fly to your aid."

"A threat!" shouted one of the other Chairs, a reedy man far up the left side of the Bench, speaking out of turn. "The delegation threatens the People!" The mechanical translator piped his words into the ensuing silence without translating his tone. His objection played out dead and spiritless on the air.

First Chair's quavering voice intervened, saying, "A man who speaks without correct speech elevates individual will above the will of the People." The elder placed a hand on something in the vast empty seat in the center of the Bench. "On behalf of the Conclave, the Twenty-Fifth Chair is to be censured."

The Twenty-Fifth Chair blanched and regarded the hands twisting in his lap. He had spoken out of turn. In a small voice, the fellow said, "A man requests the Voice." To my surprise, he did not raise his own hand, though Sixth Chair—still standing—raised hers. As before, Ninth Chair crossed his arms, his lackeys with him, and again as before First Chair counted hands.

"Seven!" the First Chair proclaimed. "To twenty-seven. The Voice is withheld."

Twenty-Fifth Chair frowned but said no more.

The Sixth resumed her line of questioning. "The delegate says the Commonwealth is not prepared, but the delegate asks for the assistance of the Commonwealth. This is confusing."

Unable to help myself, I said, "The good of each is the good of all." This evinced a rumble from the Chairs and a muttering from the robed and suited congregation in the stands about and above us. "What is good for my people is—in this case—good for yours. Or are we not people in your opinion?" When the Sixth Chair had no response to this, I took a rhetorical step forward, underscored by a literal one. "I assure you, the Cielcin will make no distinction between yours and mine. Their dietary preferences are *quite* apolitical."

To my surprise, Sixth Chair had no reply for this, but sank back to her seat. That broke the spell—or rekindled it—for she said, "The good of all men is greater than the good of any one."

Varro spoke for the first time. "Does that mean you agree to our terms?"

I hadn't dared to think it would be so easy. Were the Lothrians so hungry for want of resources? I understood that—like my father—they worked their *zuk* serfs to the bone, though unlike my father they paid them only in bread and protein base.

Seventeenth Chair interjected, "The actions of the Commonwealth shall never be decided by one." He studied his compatriots thoughtfully, resting his chin on one fist, appearing almost bored. "On behalf of the Conclave . . ." He paused, waited for a nod from two or three of the others before proceeding. For the first time, I realized that phrase was a kind of marker—like the request for the Voice—an indication that what followed adhered to no line of their beloved book. I supposed there must be unique statements required for such groundbreaking proceedings as ours. Indeed, this whole audience stretched the endurance of Lothrian *correctness*; we were on the borders of politically approved truth. Hence the requests for Voice, hence the censure of the Chair who'd spoken out of turn. "On behalf of the Conclave, this will not be decided at once. The Conclave must review the delegation's proposal." As he spoke, his fellows nodded along. Abruptly, Seventeenth Chair cleared his throat. "A man requests the Voice." He raised his own hand. Again the hands went up; again Ninth Chair and his coterie crossed their arms, the only ones not to raise their hands.

Again First Chair tallied. "Twenty-nine," he said. "To five. The Voice is granted."

Seventeenth Chair smiled thinly before proceeding, standing as the Sixth had done. It struck me that the fellow was very tall, and wore his judge's robes with the air of a king, lordly and imperial. He did not seem the representative avatar of an equal *People* at all. "The Sixth Chair raises a fine point. The Empire's sudden clemency speaks of desperation. The delegation claims the power to make concessions. Further considerations beyond those drafted in this proposal from the Sollan Empire must be considered. Amendments must be made."

"Amendments?" I asked, relieved to once again be speaking to a man and not a mouthpiece.

"Such as?" Varro put in.

Valka remained quiet between us. She was no representative of the Imperium and had no right to plead on its behalf. She was my eyes, for the machine eyes her Tavrosi clansmen had given her so long ago missed nothing, and the nematodes that ordered the gray matter of her brain forgot nothing, just as Varro—with his centuries of mnemonic schooling—forgot nothing. As witnesses, they were indispensable.

"Settlement rights in the Upper Perseus," he said, smiling as the auto-translator played out its message in the only tongue they knew I understood. That the Seventeenth Chair did not hesitate for an instant told me that this had been planned from the start.

I cast my eyes downward. Had I been sent to the Commonwealth to fail? Had the Imperial Council expected the Grand Conclave of the Commonwealth to make a request I could not grant? A request they would never grant?

Had the Emperor given me another impossible task? Surely the Imperial Council and their advisers would have known this possibility would arise. We had blocked Lothrian expansion into the Perseus Arm of the galaxy for millennia. Our last war with them had been fought to decide that state.

"Settlement rights . . ." I shook my head. "I will have to telegraph my Imperial masters." Had I indeed been made auctor, I might have granted it on the spot. "It will take time to communicate properly. In the meantime we may discuss the details of an arrangement."

"On a purely hypothetical basis," Tor Varro added, ever the champion of precision.

Another voice sounded in that dark hall. "A man requests the Voice."

All heads turned to the speaker.

The Ninth Chair raised his hand, a single finger extended. Having thrice voted against his compatriots' right to original speech, it shocked me to see him raise a hand so. Several hands rose at once—those of his coterie—and the hands of the others.

All the others.

I was ignorant of the inner workings of Conclave politics, and so dared not guess at what this might mean.

"Thirty-four," First Chair rasped. "To zero. The Voice is granted."

The man called Ninth Chair did not stand. Like an Emperor himself—lordly as the still-standing Seventeenth Chair—Ninth Chair sat back against the smooth granite of his seat, the high back like a grave monument. "Why does the Sollan Emperor send *this* man? Hadrian Marlowe is known. The delegate is a warrior. Why does the Red Emperor send a warrior to Padmurak?"

"Because each man must serve the good of the People in fullness of ability," I said tartly, speaking for the first time in perfect Lothrian.

The Ninth Chair clapped. "Very good! And quite correct," he said. "But the question remains unanswered: why *this* delegate?"

The Lothrian habit of indirectness—of the erosion of all identity save role or function—was starting to grate on me. The Lothriad may have liberated the serfs from their masters, but in the Empire even the meanest slave had the dignity of a name. I had had a belly full of Lothrian collectivism, but I clenched my jaw, let the frustration ebb away as I exhaled through my nose and reflected on one of Gibson's stoic aphorisms. I sensed a great many things hung upon my answer, though why I was not sure. I held Ninth Chair's gaze for several seconds before examining the others: the elderly First Chair, the noble Seventeenth. The multitudes of near-faceless men rising in higher orbits behind the Grand Conclave's bench, microphones and holographs on the tables before them, all of them clad in gray like a college of sorcerers.

"I know the Cielcin," I said, and for effect repeated myself in the tongue of the Commonwealth, working around the awkward, impersonal nature of their language. *"Din konraad vedajim Rugyeh."*

A man knows the Others.

"There is no one in the Imperium better acquainted with the enemy," I said. "I have killed two of their princes myself—a claim no other man may make. I have fought three fingers of the White Hand who serve the Scourge of Earth. It was I who negotiated the first surrender of the enemy at Emesh. The Emperor has sent me that I might advise your admirals in the tactics and nature of the enemy. Of *our* enemy." Addressing my next words to the Twenty-Fifth Chair, I said, "My presence is not a threat, sir, nor are my words. They are a warning. The Cielcin are coming, and should we fall, they will come for you. They will crack the domes of your Great City and use your People for meat. Aid us, and we will aid you."

Ninth Chair smiled through my words, but when I had finished speaking, he said nothing, only leaned back in his seat, his piece apparently said and done.

The First Chair spoke instead. "The Conclave will review the delegation's proposal. This audience is at an end." When he'd finished this declaration, the First Chair reached down into the empty throne beside him and slammed something. Craning my neck, I could just make out the black leather cover of a book, a volume perhaps a foot wide and a cubit tall, a little larger than one of my own folios. Standing, he lifted it above his head, showcasing the black star embossed upon the cover. I knew then that I was looking at a copy of the Lothriad itself.

I had never seen one printed. I'd read it as a boy, of course—every child of every great lord does, if only to understand the evils of it—but like so many of the texts I'd been given as part of my education on Delos, I'd only interacted with holos. Seeing it somehow in its proper place it struck me as an object of horror.

A black book.

The *only* book permitted in the Commonwealth.

A fitting emblem that, a fitting contradiction. They were a people who called slavery freedom, a nation that called narrative truth, a culture that glorified its People by destroying the very concept of personhood.

How could they be anything but a nation of book burners founded on a book?

CHAPTER 12

COMMONWEALTH

NEGOTIATIONS WERE LONG.

I shall not rest on the weeks of hearings and conversations, nor mire you in the details and double-think and the quagmire that was negotiating with the Lothrians. Whole days were spent waiting for the quantum telegraph drip to transmit documents to the Imperial Council—data flitting one bit at a time across the thousands of light-years between Padmurak and Forum. Days more passed while the Council communicated with the Emperor, who had long since left Nessus on his tour of the frontier. I gathered he had stopped on Vanaheim and would remain there for some months.

The Council and Emperor both were unwilling to cede unsettled territory in the Upper Perseus. The Commonwealth had spread across the upper reaches of the Sagittarius, forming a bulwark that kept our own settlers from lighting out across the galactic west. It was their presence in the first place that had forced Imperial settlements to cross the Second Gulf by way of worlds like Gododdin into the Centaurine in the first place. Access to the Perseus would not only open up new expanses for settlement by the Commonwealth and give them access to the Outer Arm and the galaxy's edge, but would bring the Lothrian frontier dangerously close to the Durantine Republic and the Principalities of Jadd, a development that would not endear us to the Durantines or our Jaddian allies.

The Cielcin were the greatest threat humanity had known since Columbia and her daughters, but no threat justified such a betrayal of our allies.

At the same time, we could not refuse. We needed Lothrian support, and I could not afford to return to Nessus and Caesar in anything but triumph. And so I too circled the subject of our arrangement with Lothrian imprecision. Other concessions were made, the possibility of Lothrian settlements in a reconquered Norman Expanse were floated as a possibility, and new borders were drawn across the Rasan Belt, the no-man's-land between Empire and Commonwealth across the Sagittarius.

It was dry work, and the details of it bear little on this accounting.

Valka grew tired of the whole business in a matter of days, and I could not blame her. She had insisted on coming down to the city with me—she would not be left behind. I had long ago learned my lesson. Since Berenike, she and I were seldom parted, and then only because some other agency mandated it—such as had happened with Eikana—or because we agreed to go our own ways. She ceased to sit in on my talks with the various Chairs after the first few days, preferring to remain in the lavish apartments in the palace complex our hosts had set aside for us. We spent many an evening dining with the various members of the Imperial consulate's staff.

The chiefest of these was Lord Damon Argyris, Chief Consul to Padmurak. Argyris had spent the better part of the last fifty years in Vedatharad—nearly all of it within the walls of the embassy tower. "They don't hold with foreigners in their cities, these Lothrians," he said. "It's gotten worse. In my predecessor's day, there was a foreign market past Eleventh Dome where offworld merchants were allowed to trade. Not ours, of course. Not since the Persean Wars. But offworlders all the same." The consul rested his head against the minutely tiled wall of the sauna, dabbed at his forehead with a corner of the towel he wore draped about his muscled frame like a toga. "Truth be told, I'm almost surprised the Grand Conclave had any interest in the Emperor's material concessions. The fuel, maybe—you never can have enough—but I almost expected them to refuse the offers of trade. Perhaps things are different in the other Commonwealth systems, but Padmurak had become nearly so inaccessible as the Earth itself."

"I suppose we should be grateful," I said, admiring the high-resolution mosaic that dominated the wall behind the consul. It depicted the God Emperor as a hero of classic antiquity—muscled and nude—crushing an iron serpent beneath his heel. One hand clutched the mechanical demon about the throat, the other raised a flaming sword. So small were the individual *tesserae*, each as small or smaller than a grain of rice—that the mosaic appeared no mosaic at all, but a painted image that glistened with the steam of the baths.

From the way Argyris's eyes had wandered, I knew he was admiring the other bathers. When the consul remained silent, I added, "Since the Emperor will never allow Lothrian settlement of the Perseus, we should take what we can get."

Still Argyris said nothing. I cleared my throat. "No indeed!" he said, smoothing his mustache with one hand. "To do so would be to undo the work of centuries." His black eyes focused on me again, wrenched from the sight of so much nude flesh at great personal cost. "I'm not comfortable with the potential re-drawing of the borders in the Rasan Belt, either." The Belt had formed a neutral zone between the Commonwealth and the Empire since the Persean Wars, a hundred-light-year-wide space that both powers agreed to leave unsettled. The new arrangement—if agreed upon—would close that space by half entirely on the Commonwealth's side, allowing them to settle and prospect rank thousands of new solar systems. It was not access to the Perseus and the Jaddian border, but it was something—a clear loss and concession on the part of the Empire.

"Nor am I," I said, falling silent. I gripped the edges of the stone bench on which I sat as Argyris gestured for his serving girl to lave more water on the hot rocks between us. Her gold collar marked her for a slave, and I reminded myself that for my moral outrage at the strictures of the Lothriad, the Empire committed its own sins. Steam flowered between the consul and myself, and as the girl leaned forward to collect more water, Argyris reached up to touch one bare breast. The girl said nothing, but flinched when the consul pinched her nipple.

"Enough!" I snapped.

Argyris glowered at me, but let her go.

"Give me the ladle, miss," I said to her, extending my left hand. Unintended, the hideous, deep scars on my arm stood out silver-white in the yellow light from the lamps floating overhead. I saw her eyes go to the old injuries, felt the consul's gaze too. Impatient now, eager to get her gone and away from Argyris—if only for a time—I snapped my fingers at her. Wordless, she passed the instrument over. "You may go."

"Hold on just one moment!" Argyris said, glowering at me. "You can't just!"

The girl was caught between her master and myself, and stood, visibly torn, barefoot and wearing nothing but a silken breechclout and the gold costume jewelry the consul had dressed her in. "Lord Argyris, we are having a serious conversation," I said dryly, brandishing the ladle like a schoolmaster's baton. "Do try and focus." Both of us being palatine, I had no way to know Damon Argyris's age, or even if he were my junior or senior. After the first hundred years of living, I've found diminishing returns on maturity to be the rule, not the exception. Whether he was two hundred or five, Argyris was a creature of habit as surely as I was; it was only that I found his appetites grotesque. As a boy, I had nearly pressed one of my own servants to service me before realizing what it was I was doing. I had thought it possible that she might love me. I'd hoped she would. But there exists a gulf between master and servant—even more so between master and slave—that is wider than the Rasan Belt, wider than the Gulfs where no stars shine, and the only avenue across it is coercion.

And love does not coerce.

I had realized my mistake in time. Had I not, I supposed it might have been me harassing slave girls in the consulary bathhouse. Reflecting on this, I ladled more water over the rocks. Amid the steam I said only, "Let her go, Argyris."

Remembering that I was the Emperor's apostol and a knight of the Royal Victorian Order—and the *Halfmortal* besides, as my scars too obviously attested—Argyris swallowed and waved the girl away. Swaying, she hurried off, and in her wake, the consul shrugged. "Have it your way, then."

Smiling my crooked smile, I circled back. "You said things have changed here?"

"Oh yes," the consul grimaced. "Like I say, they shut down the foreign market before my time here, but even when I was new it was possible to walk down the street without a Lothrian escort . . . now . . ." He stretched luxuriantly, craning his neck to continue his observation of the room. "Now Padmurak is a world of tunnels. Shuttle to motorcar to building to tram to next building, chaperones all the way."

"I assume they don't want us to see their way of life?"

"They don't want us to see how dirt poor they are," he said, dismissive. "For all their talk about the *good of the People*, their perfect order is *good* for very few." Argyris wiped his face again with his towel. "You can see it driving around if you look. They do their best to paper over the parts we get to see. But every now and then an accident on the highways will put you through the next block and you'll see it: crumbling roads, broken windows, shuttered hives."

"Hives?"

"Those blockhouses the *zuk* workers live in around the perimeter of each dome. Call them *vuli*, hives."

I could not help but stare at this. "Like . . . bees?"

"Aye, like bees." The consul chewed his lip, "Damn it, Marlowe. You sent my girl away and the steam's going." Obliging the fellow, I poured water over the black stones between us. "That's better," he said. "City's not crowded like it used to be. I've heard talk of the Conclave redistributing the population. They're always worried about a mob here—the domes, you know. Very susceptible to sabotage. And there's the revolutionaries to mind."

That caught my attention. "I've never heard about Lothrian revolutionaries."

"That's how they like it," Argyris said coolly. "But there *are* liberalist revolutionaries, if the Commonwealth broadcasts are to be believed."

"Liberalists?" I raised one eyebrow. "Republicans?"

"Not sure if they've thought so far ahead." The consul groaned as another wave of steam rose about us. "Not sure they *exist*, to be honest. Our intelligence boffins think they might be a party bogeyman. Pure propaganda."

I felt myself getting confused and again set the ladle down. "I thought you said they feared the mob."

"Of course they do. There are—best guess—one point three billion people on Padmurak. Maybe twenty . . . twenty-five million in Vedatharad? But fewer than a million of those are proper *pitrasnuks*. The Chairs and their ilk are outnumbered, and that makes them hostages to their own people." That at least was not so different from how things were in the Empire. A lord ruled only by consent of the governed, even if that consent was not enshrined in law. The threat of popular revolt was an eternal problem, one only solved by just rule. Lords who ruled harshly, as my father did, had no choice but to rule more harshly day by day to keep their people in line. Machiavelli had it wrong. Far better to be loved than feared—and better still to be both loved *and* feared.

But of the obligation of kings I'd seen little in the Commonwealth. Beneath its veneer of fresh paint and buildings sprayed clean of grime, the city—and perhaps the entire Commonwealth—was crumbling with neglect.

"You should hear their broadcasts," Argyris continued. "Pure poison. If it's not their *liberalists* blamed for stealing rations or blowing the air supply, it's *us* for blockading trade routes."

"Bread and circuses," I said knowingly, arms crossed.

"Mostly circuses. The bread goes to the partisans," Argyris assented with a sigh. "Of course, they're the ones who closed the trade routes in the first place, we just won't reopen them. Always accuse the enemy of what you're doing."

Into that pregnant silence I laved another cup of water, struck by the cosmic irony of our circumstances: two nobiles of the Imperium—rich men by all accounts—enjoying the consul's lavish appointments while the city outside the embassy tower fell into neglect and disrepair. I mollified myself with thoughts of Anju and the staff at Maddalo House, and of the pension I'd left for them. A small thing measured against the grinding poverty of the Commonwealth, but something.

A young logothete emerged from a nearby pool and collected his towel from a stone bench, bare feet slapping on the tile floor. Argyris watched him go with something like approval. I waited him out, and when at last the object of his interest had gone from sight, I said, "The Eleventh Chair invited Doctor Onderra and myself to witness the ice harvest down south end of the week—and we're to visit the city farms tomorrow. Will you be joining us?"

"No, my lord," Argyris said. "Ghastly business, those ice mines, but it will give you a sense—I think—for what this place is *really* like. Likewise the farms. Built like a fortress! I will be with you for the First Ballet, however." That was three days before the polar expedition. "I'm told they'll be performing Ademar's *Earth Afire* in our honor."

"I can't say I expected theater from the Lothrians," I said.

"Void as they are of color?" the consul asked, a knowing edge in his deep voice. "No, they'll still find ways to surprise you. Don't tell anyone on Forum I said it, but the Lothrian First Ballet are the best I've ever seen. Better than anything the Emperor puts on."

Circling back to the more immediate subject, I said, "I'm surprised the Lothrians don't have a better source of water. Don't they recycle what they bring in from the ice?"

This return to less aesthetic pursuits clearly dimmed the light in Damon Argyris's eyes. "Yes . . . well, they do, Sir Hadrian. You saw the dam and the sluice gates on your way in?"

I told him I had.

"The domes are not the original city—or so my predecessor said. The Lothrians have been on Padmurak a long time. They dug tunnels first, whole networks below the surface. It's where they got the notion of hives, I'll warrant. After the domes went up, the tunnels were converted to infrastructure. Highways, ventilation, waterworks. But it's not enough. Even with the City shrinking—as I say—they still use more than they can take in. Padmurak lacks for water, aye, but what she really lacks . . ." he gestured round at the baths, "is air."

CHAPTER 13

STILL THE ORCHESTRA PLAYS

DAMON ARGYRIS HAD NOT exaggerated. The Lothrian First Ballet was sublime. I have little understanding of dance, perhaps less of music. But *beauty is*, and even the poorest poet among men knows it by its signs. A line of women in pale leotards moved like crystal clockwork upon a stage of glass, their ghostly reflections chasing them as they danced to music sweet and clear.

The music swelled, filling the auditorium with the opening strains of Ademar Giallo's *Earth Afire*.

I counted the dancers.

There were fifty-two.

Watching them dance and spread across the star-strewn glass, I wondered if Ademar knew the significance of his figure, or else if the association between the Mericanii and the number fifty-two was lost even in his remote day. But I knew it. The answer was one of many things we'd learned in the Archives Emperor Gabriel II had left beneath the Great Library on Colchis. There had been fifty-two daughters of Julian Felsenburgh's revolution, fifty-two distinct artificial intelligences bred by his chief creation, the Columbia system that had ruled Old Earth as the sun set on her Golden Age. In allegory they danced before us, each daughter played by a Lothrian girl so like the next they might be clones of another: lithe, high-breasted, black hair pulled up.

We could not see the audience beneath our box, and sat in whispering quiet—Valka and I—alongside Lord Argyris and certain of the consular staff. Our hosts sat about us, politely attentive. The Ninth Chair had not spoken all evening, leaving the duties of host to the gallant Seventeenth Chair, who leaned in to inquire, "Is the delegate pleased?"

I was unclear on what subtle change in Lothrian protocol allowed the man the right to speak more freely, or if it were only that for him the rules were more flexible. A more cavalier attitude toward the niceties from the Seventeenth Chair might explain the stony silence on the part of the Ninth, whose dedication toward Lothrian's brand of progress he guarded with an almost religious zeal.

Valka answered for me. "They're marvelous!"

"They are impressive," I said, watching as the fifty-two daughters of silicon each in their own circle of light seduced male counterparts in red leotards with gold circlets about their foreheads. They were, I knew, the great kings of men who ruled the offworld colonies before their fall. "They must train all their lives."

"May all who excel in one avenue of life offer that excellence to the People," the Seventeenth Chair agreed, shifting back to the stilted language of formal Lothrian, perhaps responding to the silent pressure of the Ninth Chair not five seats away. "May each bend that excellence to the service of the People. May each offer a life entire."

Yes, I translated to myself.

The white-clad girl in center stage danced about one of the men, but he rebuffed her while all about the others fell. Nodding at him, I said, "That's our God Emperor." The first Sollan Emperor had—when he was but a petty king in exile on Avalon—rebuffed the advances of the Mericanii. They had wanted his world. On the other colonies they sublimated or built—as on Earth herself—mankind had been seduced by his own creation, and from that incestuous union had sprung all the horrors of machine rule: the great pyramids that rose above the cities of Earth and her colonies. The dream worlds into which the machines led mankind and trapped them. The cancers whose ceaseless growth kept those men alive so the machines might crouch spider-like in their unused brains. The homunculi grown to replace the few who died and to swell the ranks of captive man, to replace him, and to serve the machines he'd made to serve himself.

I doubted that Ademar had known any of it when he'd composed his ballet. What had been history had turned to legend over the long millennia, and legend to fable and scripture. Few were the men who knew the names of Felsenburgh and Columbia, and fewer still those who knew the horrors they had wrought. And of those who knew the God Emperor of old had received his visions and his authority from the Quiet, the same alien *thing* whose unseen hand guided me, the same being who had redeemed me from the dead, two were seated in that box.

"I've never seen such precision," Valka admired.

I leaned toward her and whispered, "Because they kill the ones who fail." By then, we were certain that neither Chair understood Valka's native Panthai, and I thought I'd spoken soft enough not to catch the ear of any of their retinue.

Valka scratched me gently with long fingernails. She spoke Galstani to forestall reply and so end the conversation there. "And your lot don't?" Even an exile and a fugitive from her clan, she was Tavrosi to her bones. I felt certain that some great lord of the Imperium had killed performers before, but I felt equally certain that the Chantry had punished many lords for such excesses.

"Of course we don't!" I said, never one to back down from her challenge. "And what do you mean, *my lot?*"

"I don't see much difference," Valka said.

"They don't even have *names*, Valka!" I hissed, squinting at her in the dark of the box.

She waved this aside. "As you like, but I . . ." She broke off suddenly, her machine eyes unfocusing.

"Are you all right?" I feared she was having another episode, another flashback caused by Urbaine's worm. Her hand tightened on my arm, and she shook her head as discreetly as was possible.

"'Tis nothing," she said. When I did not back down she glared at me more intently. "'Tis *nothing.*"

Wholly unaware of Valka's distress, Lord Damon Argyris exclaimed, "Did I not tell you they know their art here in the Commonwealth?" He leaned around Valka to look at me, missed Valka's nails like claws digging into my gloved left arm. "You should have seen the display they put on for the Durantine Doxe. The holography alone shames anything in the Eternal City!"

"You have been too long apart from the Empire, my lord consul," I said, eyes still watching Valka. Whatever had bothered her, it had not been *nothing.* "You are too quick to discount the achievement of your countrymen."

The Seventeenth Chair, overhearing this, cut in, "Is the performance not to the delegate's liking?"

I realized I'd not answered the question myself when he'd first asked, and turned from contemplation of the stage to regard the man who seemed so lordly and imperial in that place which professed hatred for lords and empires. "Oh, the delegate is quite impressed," I said in Lothrian, sparing a glance at Ninth Chair, who sat stone-faced to the far side of his associate. Before speaking, I drank from the nearly flavorless spirit our hosts had poured for me. Not knowing how to express myself with the limitations of Lothrian, I switched back to Imperial Standard. "I only mean it is an Imperial ballet you perform for us, however impressive the performance. My friend the consul forgets this."

Beneath his bushy mustachios, Damon Argyris frowned. "Fair point, Lord Marlowe, but mine stands. These Lothrians are capable of quite the performance."

"I should have liked to see the show you put on for the Doxe," I said to the Seventeenth Chair. Privately, I was surprised the ruler of that most serene republic had come to a place like the Commonwealth. On the stage below, the dancers had traded white for red, and the women writhed in artful tumbles across the floor before the advance of the men—now in white with the dancer playing the God Emperor at the center. I had never seen a performance of Ademar's rendition of the Burning of Earth before, but I did not think the composer intended the way each male dancer—dressed in *Imperial* white, I realized—stood above the female dancers like conquerors in a captured harem. I smiled at the implied insult, at the Lothrian ability to say so much without words. "I'm sure it was quite a show."

In time the curtains fell, and in the space where an applause ought to have been there was only the awkward clamor of *our* hands. The Lothrian audience below did not clap or give any sign. Uncomfortable—having stood to clap as was the Imperial custom—I bowed and thanked our hosts.

"Here is a People without masters," the Ninth Chair intoned, staring up at me with flinty eyes, "without gods, a People whose every action glorifies itself."

I looked down at the little man in his gray robes, his eyes as gray beneath his cap of oiled black hair. Studying him, I was struck again at just how similar these Lothrians were to one another.

The Ninth Chair kept watching me, and when I did not respond, he continued, quoting, "Let there be hard labor for the strong. Let there be deep learning for the wise. Let there be great trials for the just. Let the skill of each be turned in service to the good of all."

"Your dancers served well," I said. Not asking, I wondered what service a man with no name might offer, not knowing himself or what he was worth.

"Let each be loyal to the Conclave," the Ninth Chair replied. "Let then the Conclave be loyal to the Book. This is order and justice."

I bowed again. "I know something of loyalty and of service myself."

CHAPTER 14

GHOST OF THE MACHINE

DINNER WAS SERVED AT a long, black table in the middle of an empty room. We'd ridden a lift from the levels of the People's Palace to the marble terraces I'd spied from the streets below. The architecture of these rarefied climes was just as brutal and cyclopean, but here the blocks shone white in the starlight that fell through the veined dome above.

The floor of the dining room was of marble, too, and the walls were faced with it. No curtains hung on the horizontal slit windows, nor was there any rug to relieve the pale utility of that chamber. Its only furnishing—besides the table and its attendant chairs—was a mighty globe of the planet Padmurak in magnetic suspension slowly turning above its stand in one corner. The walls bore little decoration. No paintings or artwork relieved the dour sconces. One wall held a holograph plate disguised as a mirror. There'd been one in every room of the Chair's apartments. I guessed they were a part of the man's security and communications network.

The food itself was plain, but good. As Third Chair had said, there was no meat to be found in Lothrian cuisine. The meal centered instead about a stew of white beans and carrots in tomato sauce. There was bread, and roast garlic to spread on it, but no butter. No eggs. No cheese or any other byproduct of animal life. There were not even their imitations, grown in vats or synthesized.

"Are there not servants?" I asked in Lothrian, where there was no word for servant. *Manyoka*, I said. *Helpers.*

Seventeenth Chair deposited the last platter on the table. "An idle hand is ever turned against the People." He brushed his hair back from his face as he took the seat opposite us. "Let no hand be idle. Each must serve each." He gestured at the door through which he'd entered, indicating the direction of the kitchens, where I was certain that for all his civic piety, Seventeenth Chair had done nothing to aid the preparation of the meal.

I translated this for Valka, whose Lothrian was limited. "It all looks lovely." She smiled at the Chair. Valka had worn her diplomatic best for the ballet, an understated black and ivory gown as much business as fashion, her red-dark hair pulled up and pinned. The nearly black lipstick she wore called attention to that smile. "You must be very proud."

Our host returned the smile, pouring water for us each from an unassuming but well-made metal pitcher, serving me first, then Valka, then himself. "The only true pride," he recited, "is pride in the People." He lingered a moment, studying the spread. It struck me that without meat or fish, the meal was an oddly uncentered affair. There was no true entree, with the other dishes supporting it or otherwise accompanying it, no sense of what should be eaten first or how.

"It is a pity the Ninth Chair could not join us," I said, noting the empty seat at Seventeenth Chair's left hand.

Our host's progress slowed as he contemplated his answer. "Let no hand be idle," he said again.

Unseen beneath the table, Valka nudged me with a toe when I leaned in to whisper to her. I understood her all too well. I did not fancy the prospect of an evening spent with so limited a conversation partner. Talking to the Lothrians was like trying to roll a stone uphill, only to have it roll back again, as though I were poor, doomed Sisyphos.

Fortunately, unlike Sisyphos, I was not alone.

"Chairman," Valka began, ladling a measure of the bean stew into her bowl, "I wonder about your language. Hadrian tells me you speak entirely by reciting quotations from your people's codex. Can that really be so?"

I translated this from Galstani into Lothrian for our host, using sentences that were doubtless not approved by the Lothriad. The Chair still wore an earpiece, but I felt the need to editorialize.

Seventeenth Chair replied, "Only correct speech serves the will of the People."

"Correct speech?" Valka asked. "What is correct speech?"

"That which is for the good of the People," Seventeenth Chair replied. It was a deftly employed fragment of a sentence, used void of its original context.

Failing to translate this for Valka, I said, "The Lothrian taught in the Empire lacks this emphasis on quotation." I had to struggle to fit my thoughts into the Lothrian pattern. It was difficult to describe how my tutor had taught me in a way that referenced neither the tutor nor myself. I was sure I sounded half a fool. I'd had little occasion to practice the guttural language since I'd left Devil's Rest. Strange to think I spoke Cielcin better than this tongue of man.

"It is incorrect," the Chair said. "Only the Lothriad is correct."

"Surely that has limitations," Valka said when I translated this for her. "Or are there correct ways to ask for the toilet?"

Seventeenth Chair only laughed.

"Or supposing you encountered something you have no words for, how could you discuss it?" Valka leaned over her plate, eager to have answers to these questions after so many weeks in the Commonwealth—and to have the opportunity to grill a *pitrasnuk* of the Grand Conclave at last. "Suppose you encountered a race of xenobites. What then?"

"Rugyeh," I said, reaching her answer. To Valka, I added, "It only means *the Others.*" To the Lothrian, ordinary words were forced to carry the weight of a dozen others. There was so much context, so much subtext depended on for clarity of communication.

Valka toyed with her spoon. "But that doesn't address the problem. You have no way to discuss new things if your words are written out in advance. You can't adapt."

Our host nodded along as I translated this, and paused to chew a mouthful of his stew. He tore a piece of bread off his portion and dunked it in his bowl. "The will of the Conclave is the will of the People. A good man is to the Conclave as a son is to a father. A father gives voice to a son."

"How?"

"By teaching," Seventeenth Chair replied, and again I suspected his answer was the fragment of some other sentence.

"Voice," I said, repeating the word I'd seen used to such grave effect in the Conclave's arena. *Halas.* "The Conclave writes new sentences as time goes on. And you're the only ones permitted use of the Voice?"

"Da," our host replied.

"And why *man?*" Valka asked. *"A good man is to the Conclave . . .* what of women?"

The Seventeenth Chair studied her a moment before replying. "There are no women," he said, though the word he used for *women, samkanka,* was more precisely rendered as *females.* "Nor men." This of course was untrue; the Third Chair and the Sixth were women, and several of the others besides. We had seen women by the dozen in the urban farms, and the ballerinas had been women as well. "There are no females," Seventeenth Chair repeated, "no males. There is only the People. Only *man*."

I had wondered at the Lothriad's aggressive sexlessness. Their word for man, *ovuk*—which showed clear ties to the word for worker, *zuk*—meant only *human*, implying neither sex. Thus their language was half-like our own, where *woman* has no true companion, and the word *man* means *man* and *human* both. How we survive such confusion is difficult enough to fathom. How the Lothrians theirs I could not begin to comprehend.

"But your eyes know the difference, whatever your words," I said, encouraged by Valka's objections. "There are things stronger than our words, sir. Language cannot change reality. Only stretch it."

"And it only stretches so far," Valka appended, evidently as confounded by this Lothrian way of thinking as I was.

Seventeenth Chair studied the both of us over his half-eaten meal for a long moment. He lifted his water cup to his lips—there was no wine, nor any of that colorless spirit we'd been given at the theater—and drank. Not answering, he rose and plodded over to the globe of Padmurak revolving in its magnetic field. He gripped the rail that encircled the display, fiddling with his hair.

Not his *hair*, I realized an instant later, half-turned in my seat.

His earpiece.

Seventeenth Chair *removed* his auto-translator and set it—dead—on the lip about the globe. "Perhaps for now it is so, Lord Marlowe. My Lady," he said, speaking perfect Galstani. "But in time, even this will change."

"You speak the standard?" Valka asked, dark lips twisting into something neither smile nor frown.

"The standard!" the Chairman barked. "That too is true only for now. But we all speak your language. I was schooled in your Empire. At Teukros. So many are."

I took this sudden change in stride. Often I had seen palatine lords disable their own security systems to speak unobserved. My own mother had done it in her Summer Palace as we planned my escape from home so long ago. I had done it myself aboard the *Tamerlane* time and time again, and so this revelation came as little shock. I had expected that beneath the rigid adherence to Lothrian civic scripture was an agnosticism little different than the false piety of so many Imperial lords. "So it *is* all an act," I said. "The Lothriad. Your speech codes. All this talk of equity and community, and yet you are governed by different laws than your *zuks*."

"As in your Empire."

"My Empire does not pretend to be something it's not," I said, eager at last to have someone I could hold to account for the world I'd been witness to then for the better part of a month.

"Nor do we," the Chairman said. "I am only a handmaid. When the Lothriad is perfected, the Conclave will no longer be necessary."

"Perfected?" Valka echoed, glad—I think—to no longer be barred from direct conversation by her ignorance of the Lothrian tongue. She turned fully in her seat to look at the stately man in his plain gray judicial robes. "Perfected how?"

Our host's smile did not falter, and there was a light in his black eyes such as I had seen in the *vates* who pray naked atop pillars in city squares and howl at the sky for Earth's return. "The Old monsters shall be swept away: Old Customs, Old Culture, Old Habits, Old Thoughts. But the ancients did not go far enough. They kept their language. They kept their names. These things tied them to the past. True progress—true perfection—demands more."

"You sound like the Extrasolarians," I said.

"The Extrasolarians have vice, not vision. They shape themselves in accordance only with the disorder of their natures. We impose *our* nature on nature," the Chairman declared.

Uncomfortably half-turned in my seat, I stood. "Is hubris not vice, then? You can only push men so far . . ." With eyes for Valka, I added, "And women."

"Old Thoughts. Old Bodies. Old Natures too will be swept away." He shut his eyes, recited in Lothrian as though it were a mantra. "How shall Old Thoughts be expunged? By eliminating Old Desires. How shall Old Desires be expunged? By eliminating Old Natures. How shall Old Natures be expunged? By eliminating Old Bodies."

Still Gibson's keen disciple, I asked, "New bodies are . . . what? Neither male nor female?"

"Of course," the Chair replied, slipping back into his native Lothrian to quote, "Where there is distinction, there is disparity. Where there is disparity, suffering. How shall suffering be overcome? By overcoming disparity. How shall disparity be overcome? By overcoming difference."

I met him quotation for quotation, saying, "Each angel knows his place. It is in hell that all are equal." My gloved hand went reflexively to the Red Company pentacle pinned to my lapel, my mind to the old Marlowe devil I had not worn in centuries.

"Hadrian!" Valka put a hand on my arm. *"Var rawann."* Be careful.

"Why have you not done it, then? There are hermaphrodite homunculi among the Mandari. The technology exists."

Seventeenth Chair did not answer, only narrowed those black Lothrian eyes.

"I see," I said after a moment's silence, believing I understood. "Your people fought back."

A brittle smile creased the bureaucrat's handsome face. "They are not yet ready."

"To be replaced? No, I think not."

Valka tightened her grip on my arm.

The Chair had called himself a *handmaid*, and so I imagined him, pictured him standing in a stark surgical theater to watch his children being born. A new generation to replace the old, to supplant nature. They had already removed the words for man and woman, but that was not enough. They had introduced their New Bodies, their new men, but the *zuks* had not accepted them. The Conclave could not replace the trillions of people in their Commonwealth, not from an assembly line. Not even the great clone manufactories of Jadd were up to that task. Had the Conclave expected its people to breed with its new men? To breed the old out of existence?

It seemed they had been disappointed. The Lothrian people had rejected the Conclave's new men, if I understood the Chair correctly.

"We will try again," Seventeen said into the silence.

"Old Natures die hard," I said.

"You are Sollan," Seventeen said. "You are a creature of the Old. It is in your nature to think this. Doubtless you were schooled by a scholiast. Scholiasts are creatures of the Old, too. They have no place in the future."

One hand on the back of my seat, I lifted my water glass to the Chairman. "And yet you yourself were schooled in the Imperium. By scholiasts. Sweeping away the old is like knocking the foundations of a tower out from under your feet. Tradition grounds a man. Even for you Lothrians it is so." I took a short drink. "You've been building your *new* world for thousands of years."

The Seventeenth Chair barked a laugh. "I am but a steward. I will not live to see my paradise made real, but I will die building it."

"I say it is the cruel law of art that all things must die, and that we ourselves must die after we have exhausted every suffering so . . ."

". . . so that the grass, not of oblivion but of eternal life should grow," the Chairman said, finishing the old quotation, his polished voice sliding over mine like a fencer's blade. *"Fertilized by works.* I see you know your Proust."

"I had a good teacher," I said in answer.

"Indeed you must have done," he said. "You understand me perfectly."

Did I? I wasn't sure. The whole meal I'd felt as though the Chair was trying to teach me a lesson. No, it was more than that. He was trying to *impress* me, to impress *upon* me the total superiority of Lothrian resolve, just as the ballet had been designed to convince me of the superiority of Lothrian art, as it had so evidently convinced Lord Argyris. But Argyris was a fool.

"Me . . ." I echoed the little word. It was a word no Lothrian—certainly not one of the Grand Conclave—should ever use. "Do you have a name, sir?"

"I am a steward of the Lothriad."

"I'm serious," I said. "Do you still have names? You must have used one when you studied in the Imperium. Shall I call you *Steward*?"

"Talleg," he said. "Lorth Talleg."

Valka cut in. "I knew you all must have names. 'Twas simply no way . . ."

Talleg's tight smile returned, "Only those of us in the Party have proper names." He toyed with the discarded earpiece on the table. "The *zuks* have none."

"How is that possible?" I asked.

"We *make* it possible," came the reply. Four words. Just four words. So little . . . to fill so many graves.

"You hypocrite!" Valka said, taking her hand from my arm. So strange for us both to be on the same side of an argument. Despite her Tavrosi collectivism, Valka's people still valued the individual—still valued the human soul.

Lorth Talleg's smile vanished. "Not at all. As I say, I am a handmaid of the Lothriad. A shepherd. It is my role—the Conclave's role—to bring humanity under the *Lothriad*, not to live under it myself."

"And to reduce mankind to *Eloi*," I said.

"To what?" the Chairman asked.

Having established the Chairman was only a middling student of literature, I joined him by his globe. Padmurak was a sad, pale world of ice and snow and naked stone, its airless surface unrelieved by seas or lakes, gray face scarred by glacial action in the planet's far past. It did not want for water, but what it had lay frozen in massive caps to either pole. Mountains were short and uninspiring, for the planet—while not tectonically dead—was unenergetic in the extreme. Examining the artifact, I was unsurprised to find the coastlines and lines of latitude and longitude were inlaid with platinum wire, a subtle mark of wealth. I had to remind myself that despite the apparent spartanness of the man's apartments, here was one of the men who commanded the Commonwealth. Talleg was one of a group of thirty-four who presided over a hundred thousand settled worlds.

"It doesn't matter," I said. "It's an old word. From an old book." The word *old* hung heavy on the air between us, twisting like a knife.

"Are you always like this?" Talleg asked, eyeing me intently.

"Oh yes," I replied, glancing up from my study of the globe, "ask anyone who knows me."

Talleg's eyes must have shifted to Valka for confirmation, for her clear voice answered a moment later. "Try spending a century with him."

Our host's smile—vanished in his transition from Seventeenth Chair to *Lorth Talleg*—returned for a trifle. "You hate us, don't you?"

"I do," I said, sitting straight, feeling myself almost on trial. "We have slaves in the Empire, to our shame. But here all men are slaves."

"Is that what you think of us?" the Chairman asked, leaning against the window frame. "A nation of slaves? But you forget, Lord Marlowe. I studied in your Empire. You keep whole armies in chains, imprison entire worlds. You yourself were *ordered* to come here. Are you then a slave?" He scoffed, a look of disgust coloring his handsome face. "Speak not to me of freedom. Freedom is like the sea."

I froze, eyes pulled to Valka, who sat watching still half-turned round in her high-backed seat. Lorth Talleg had said he was schooled on Teukros. That could only have been at Nov Senber, the very athenaeum *I* had failed to reach when I fled Delos as a boy. His teachers had been scholiasts. It was a scholiast aphorism he quoted at me.

". . . to be truly free is to be like one who is adrift on a raft in the middle of the sea. One can sail anywhere, in any direction . . ." It was Valka who had spoken, quoting Imore in the *Book of the Mind*.

No, I realized. *Not quoting Imore.*

She was quoting *me*—quoting my own imperfect rendition of Imore's words as I'd recited them in that chilly dungeon beside the lake where Brethren slumbered beneath the ice and the gardens of Vorgossos.

Talleg was smiling again, nodding along with her. "But what good is that by itself?" he asked, finishing the quotation. "Freedom is no virtue,

Lord Marlowe. It is an obstacle to it." Had I not argued that same thing to Valka so long ago when I'd defended the Empire from her attacks?

I had *not* argued that same thing to Valka.

"So what?" I asked our host. "You have drained that ocean dry?"

"We have given the People one voice, one goal, one golden path to follow," Talleg answered me. "And it is one where man is *free*. Free from poverty, free from pain. No gods, no kings, no masters."

"Except yourself," I said.

Talleg came off the wall, one finger pointed squarely at my chest. "I told you, I am only a handmaid. *The purpose of the Conclave is to dissolve the Conclave.*" This last he said in Lothrian, and I knew whence it must come. Only the Lothriad could contain so bald a contradiction.

"That day will never come," I said, and released the globe, thus setting Padmurak to spinning once again. "Your Commonwealth is a desert, and a desert is nothing. Everything in it has turned to stone."

"And what of your Empire?"

"The Empire is a river," I said in answer. "It has currents and a course. And while our movement may be limited—we are always limited. By our bodies, as you correctly noted. By our minds, by nature itself. Freedom is accepting those limitations and responding to them with humility. We cannot change nature."

"We can!" Talleg said, and his eyes were the eyes of a fanatic, bright and deadly as the eyes of his cohort, the Ninth Chair.

"Not all of it," Valka said, voice cutting across our back-and-forth as a gunshot stuns the duelists to stillness. "Time does not run backward, Lord Talleg. Nor entropy."

Lorth Talleg rounded on Valka. "I am no lord, lady." The title had clearly rankled him.

She shook her head. "I am only a clanswoman of the Wisp," she said. "Both your worlds are strange to me, but I would sooner die in Hadrian's Empire than live in your Commonwealth." She stood then, and came round her chair, leaning heavily on the arm. Only then did I notice the tension in that face I loved best in all the worlds, mark the dilation in the left pupil unmatched by the right. "Why did you invite us here, Chairman? Or do you insult all your guests?"

We never did get the answer to that question.

Valka collapsed in the next instant, and no answer Talleg might have given would have mattered a steel bit to me. Too late to catch her, I hurried to her side, cradled her head. "It's all right," I said, brushing her dark hair from her brow. Her left pupil had fully dilated, tracked independent of the right, and she'd begun sweating. "You're all right."

But she wasn't.

The worm Urbaine had set loose in her mind had woken up, triggered by elevated stress perhaps, or some special feature of the conversation, or by nothing at all. She had gone so long without an episode that I had almost begun to hope they were behind her. Too well I remembered those black nights on Edda, when I had first taken Valka to seek the help of her people. The way she would bite her cheeks, her lips. The way her fingers scratched at her face, tore at her flesh until the doctors had to restrain and sedate her. Too well I remembered how that hand had reached for her throat while she ate. She hadn't even noticed it, as if it were some other will that moved the tattooed fingers—not her own.

"What's wrong with her?" Talleg asked, shadow falling over us.

Not answering him, I seized her left hand in mine, squeezed unfeeling fingers. On Edda, the Tavrosi had done all they could—short of destroying her mind entire—to destroy Urbaine's virus. Their efforts had neutered the worm, dismembered it, stopped it trying to kill her. But they had failed to wholly purge the thing from her mind. What remained was only a shadow of what had been before, a chronic but fading terror that came upon her in bursts.

"What's wrong?" Talleg asked again.

"Seizure," I said flatly, not wanting to explain.

Talleg took a step back. "I will send for my physicians."

Your physicians, I thought. *Yours.* Not a lord, indeed. But I said, "No need. She's quite safe. But I must take her back to the embassy. I am sorry, but I must cut our conversation short."

Valka shook as I helped her into the groundcar Argyris had sent for us, an ugly black Lothrian vehicle whose native driver did not so much as nod at us as I helped Valka inside. Sheltering her head to keep her from striking on the door frame, I bundled her into the rear compartment, noting the inch-thick alumglass of the window and the starship-grade adamant and titanium armor in the door itself.

I lingered a moment in the damp, peered up at the soft fall of mist in the streetlamps and out at the spray of the abstract fountains on the approach to the People's Palace. Talleg's words lingered, and the dome above pressed closer and closer still. We'd made so little progress in months of negotiating, and no wonder. The Lothrian Commonwealth was not a nation, but an experiment in human lives.

"Hadrian, get in." Valka's voice came from within, thin and thready.

I climbed in after her, and held her left hand as it shook. She lay her head on my shoulder, the other fist clenched in her lap. We did not speak for some time after that, permitting the driver to take us on in silence. The car was of Imperial make, red leather seats and gilt fittings. It was like a raft of home in that sea of unmixed gray. Condensation dripped like rain on the windows and ran down.

"I can't believe this place," Valka murmured, speaking Panthai. "I thought your Empire was bad enough."

Matching her language, I said, "So did I, once. Really." I could feel her skeptical eyes without having to turn back. The muscles in her arm spasmed, and she clenched them to keep them under control. "I did. But I every time I leave it, I realize I was wrong. The Extras. The Commonwealth. At least the Empire protects *humanity*." I turned to study the rainy city through the windowpane, and thought, *Humanity. And mankind.* The Commonwealth's ideals were as toxic to the human animal as the surgeries and augmentations the Extrasolarians enjoyed. Each people saw *humanity* as a problem to solve.

"What do you mean?"

I told her, and added, "The Empire isn't a solution. It accepts the human condition, ugliness and all, and does not force its idealism onto the world."

"Doesn't force its idealism?" Valka repeated, nestling closer against me. Her tremors were dying down. Whatever vestigial processes the MINOS virus had left in her were running down their programming, or else were being blocked by subsystems in Valka's neural lace. "What do you call you palatines?"

"Firstly, I thank you for the compliment," I said smilingly. She turned her heard away with a groan. "And secondly, the High College has not made us something other than human, only stretched our humanity a little further. You heard what Talleg said. They tried to replace their whole people with homunculi, just like the Mericanii."

Valka shuddered, though whether it was with remembrance of the images and the monographs we'd seen in Gabriel's Archives and the revelations Horizon had made or only another of her tremors I could not say.

I peered out at the city with its stark, monolithic architecture, watched blockhouses and spiritless government buildings slide past like mountains in the early dark of Padmurak's long night.

"This whole place is like a dream," I said, still reflecting on Talleg's words, "and the dream's fading."

"A nightmare, more like," Valka answered, peering past me. "Like I said, it reminds me of home once you strip away . . ." She tapped her forehead with black nails, indicating the illusory world the Tavrosi painted over the utilitarian starkness of their lives. In Tavros, they lived a kind of waking dream, painted their personal artificial utopias over their colorless lives.

"Or a memory," I said. The Commonwealth and the Demarchy were—each in their own ways—reflections of the Mericanii Empire that had ruled man's first stars. It was their dream I saw when I looked out the window at the Great City of Vedatharad, their dream I had seen reflected in the canyon cities of Edda and in the sanitary halls of the asylum I'd rescued Valka from. I had even seen its vestiges in the state cult of the Chantry, whose Mericanii antecedents had venerated Felsenburgh as we venerate the God Emperor and who placed mankind at the center of the universe.

Ghosts of the Machine.

"I think 'tis passing," Valka said, but did not take her head from my shoulder. So long together, we were slow to part.

"You're all right?" I squeezed her hand, and remembered. "Are they getting more frequent? Your seizures?"

Valka paused, consulting some mental record. "No. The last was when we were on the *Tamerlane*, before we stopped at Gododdin."

"Then . . ." I paused, not sure exactly what to say. "What was that in the theater?"

"What?"

"You froze up at one point. Told me it was nothing. I thought you were having another of your . . ." I trailed off, feeling I had used the word *seizure* enough for one conversation.

Valka opened her mouth, eyes glassy as she ran back. "Oh! I thought . . ." she shook her head, "I thought for a moment I sensed another neural lace. But it must have been another flashback."

"Another neural lace?" I asked. "The Lothrians don't use them, do they?"

She shook her head. "I don't think so. I haven't sensed anything like since we arrived. Not even with the Conclave. I imagine if anyone here had one, one of their secretaries must." She raised her right hand to shade her eyes. "'Twas nothing, Hadrian. Truly. The virus just manifests . . . fingerprints. Sometimes." She swallowed. "'Tis like he's still in my head."

I did not not have to ask to know that *he* was the Extrasolarian magus, Urbaine.

"Let's go back," she said, and said again, "'Twas nothing. I'm all right. I promise."

CHAPTER 15

BY FIRE

MY TOUR OF THE water-harvesting facility in the south polar regions had been unremarkable. Valka had remained in our suite in the Sollan Embassy under the watchful eyes of Damon Argyris and the consular staff; her seizure had been one of the worst in recent years. She'd recovered, but the thought of traveling from the Great City and across the wastes by train to a place the Lothrians called *Lahe Uenalochta,* Everfrost Station, was more than she could bear. The journey had taken nearly two days by train, packed into spartan accommodations with Pallino and Crim and twenty guards for company.

Of the camp itself I shall say little. But I saw a *zuk,* a woman, forced to stand naked on the ice beneath the station's dome for some crime—they would not tell me what it was, or let me approach. She had no hair, and little flesh on her bones. Her feet were turning blue.

But I could not have seen it.

There are no women on Padmurak, I was told. And no men either.

I am no prophet. The visions of all our futures that the Quiet poured into my head are unsorted, and I lack the wit to sift wheat from chaff. I know only what can happen, what may happen—and only a little of that. So I shall not prophesy. But I *know* the Commonwealth will fall. Whether by sword or by beast, by famine or thirst, I know not, but I know it will. What Gods there may be—mine or any other—cannot long tolerate such crimes. So too our Empire will fall. It is falling already. I have knocked its pillars down, torn out its heart with the heart of my star. The world is changing, and as Valka said: time does not run backward, nor entropy turn back.

We remained at *Lahe Uenalochta* for but two days. I dined with the Commandant, who was indistinguishable from every partisan and military person of the Commonwealth I had met. I cannot even recall his face, though I recall every line of the woman's. It was her face I drew in the little sketchbook I secreted in a pocket of the heavy coat I wore.

The train put in near Thirteenth Dome, near the southernmost tip of Vedatharad. Our representative escort chivvied us from the train into a fleet of black motorcars that seated five men each. With traffic cleared along the route ahead, we were expected to pass along the underground highway through Eighth Dome on our return to the Imperial Embassy. Our drivers were Lothrians; only their partisans were allowed to drive vehicles in the Great City. It simply would not do to give outsiders much latitude in exploring the capital in all its ruined splendor. Besides, only those raised in Vedatharad stood a chance of navigating the circuitry-dense streets that honeycombed the bedrock beneath the domed arcologies of the city.

"You heard from her?" Pallino asked, eyeing me with his customary paternal concern.

"No signal yet," I said in answer, realizing as I spoke why the Lothrians had decided on a metal skeleton for their great domes. Each bubble was a Faraday Shield, an iron net that blocked standard radio and tight-beam transmissions. The denizens of each of the city's domes were cut off from the next, unable to communicate, unable to coordinate.

Pallino chewed his lip and looked for all the worlds like he meant to spit in the Lothrian vehicle. "Thought she was getting better."

"She was," I said, sparing a moment's notice for our Lothrian representative and the three other hoplites of my guard who'd joined us. I did not wish to discuss Valka's condition in front of any Commonwealth partisan, or to give any details about her implants, for such things were frowned upon even in that far country. Nor did I wish to discuss her reference to the other neural lace she'd sensed in the theater—assuming it was not only Urbaine's shadow. "But it's not the sort of thing that ever really heals."

Beyond the window, gray towers rose almost to the level of the dome three thousand feet above. Vaguely I recalled this stretch of highway from our journey out to Everfrost Station. Our track skirted the perimeter of the dome past bridge after bridge that turned inward and ran across the lower district and the dense network of canals and waterways that shot through it toward the towers in the dome's heart. We had only to follow the perimeter and this road would dip back and braid itself into another of the underground thoroughfares that would carry us direct to First Dome and the embassy.

"Only wish her people'd done more to actually help instead of tried to fry her head," Pallino said.

"She's all right," I said, unwilling to agree. To say that Valka was *damaged* was to betray her victories. My mind went to my old basin, its shards held together by silver solder. Was I too not scarred? Valka had never spurned my wounds—not even my death—how could I not return what she had given me?

Over the rail to our left, the road fell off quickly, plunged a thousand feet or more to streets and water channels where fresh floods newly arrived from places like Everfrost burst from sluices below us into the city.

"I'm surprised there's any open water here," I said.

"Let there be provision for all the People," our representative intoned, responding to the translation of my remarks through his earpiece. "Let there be water and food and rest for all that labor."

Pallino leaned across to me. "The hell'd he say?"

Our Lothrian escort had of course spoken in his own native tongue. "Nothing," I told Pallino, and that was true. Pallino sat a little straighter then. He was seated facing forward and so had a view of the road ahead. He leaned against the window, trying to get a better view of something. "What is it?"

Gone was the fellow's casual air, and from the way his lips moved I could tell he was subvocalizing with his lieutenants in the other vehicles. I craned my neck to look, but whatever Pallino saw I could not see.

"Military police in the road. Flares." Pallino looked round at our Lothrian escort, who sat blinking at the sudden change in my lictor's demeanor. "The hell is this?"

I felt certain then that our Lothrian friend understood Galstani perfectly, for he looked round like a man in pursuit of an answer even as his earpiece murmured its translation. "The enemies of the People are everywhere," he recited.

"Details, man!" Pallino hissed when I'd rendered this translation. "How do these braindead fuckers get anything done?"

"When our backs are turned," I said dryly, not caring what our host might think, and made the thumb-and-pointed-forefinger gesture that meant *stay alert*.

No sooner had I said this did our car begin to slow. Through the heavy doors and armored windows I heard shouting in Lothrian, though the specific words and quotations used were lost.

"They're directing us over the bridge," Pallino said. "Road must be out." He glowered at the Lothrian sitting beside me. "Hey. Grayface. Why is the road out?"

The Lothrian only blinked at him.

Pallino leaned across the compartment, blue eyes flashing. "I asked you a question. Why is the road blocked?"

Laying a hand on Pallino's arm, I repeated the question in the Lothrian's own language.

The Lothrian representative tilted his head, listening to some message from the powers that held his strings. "On behalf of the Conclave," he said, marking his next words for an actual response, "there has been a disturbance along the N4 connecting to First Dome. A collision has blocked traffic in the tunnel. The delegation and escort must reroute to the C7."

Pallino turned to me for translation. "Traffic accident in the tunnel," I said. "They're sending us another way."

Peering out the window, I watched the black beetle shapes of the Lothrian motorcars marching along behind us as we began to roll again. Despite the inconvenience and the faint thrill of concern—after so many years a soldier and so strange a life, any deviation from the plan was an occasion for worry—I could not help but feel a spike of curiosity at the prospect of turning off the carpet which the Lothrian government had unrolled for our arrival. I half-expected the windows to turn opaque, but they never did. Not as we turned across the bridge over the lower district toward the gray towers at the heart of the dome, nor when we reached the far side.

Like the other *kupa*, the other domes we'd passed through, Eighth Dome's most developed urban spaces lay in the center, where the steel-and-glass false sky was highest. In First Dome, the central buildings were all Party government buildings, with the ziggurat of the People's Palace standing above all. There was no comparable central structure here, only tower after square tower rising dark and nearly windowless into the gray and misty air.

"Seen better days, eh?" Pallino asked, watching broken glass facades and crowds of men in tatty gray overcoats clustered about oil drum fires. I saw more men, more *zuks* here than in the parts of Vedatharad we'd been meant to see, but the impression was still of emptiness. "If this is their capital, I'd hate to see what the colonies must be like."

Thinking of the woman I had seen standing barefoot on the ice, I said, "More like Everfrost Station, I imagine."

"Reckon they blame us blocking trade," Pallino said, speaking as though our Lothrian tagalong were not present. "Figured they'd be happier with your terms. Dunno why it's taking so long."

Our talks had not been going well. Like the Cielcin, the Lothrians were limited by their language. They struggled to express or incorporate novelty into a system so frozen by the need for correct thought, and the process for approving new thoughts outside the limited context of the use of Voice was a slow and arduous one.

"No one ever said it would be easy," I said, spotting a line of men and women standing in line outside the busted front of a dispensary marked with a black star and the word *Paishka—Rations*—marked in phosphorescent letters.

We came through the inner district, past the rusted hulks of long-abandoned groundcars. Down one street, a black-armored personnel carrier slowly rolled, blue klaxons flashing but silent. In silence then we skirted the perimeter of the inner district, traveling counter-clockwise toward another bridge that would carry us over the watercourses and canals and squat buildings of the outer ring. Turning to peer out the window, I had a clear vision of its gray span where it rose on concrete pilings, the tallest of which rose nearly a thousand feet above the canals and the rooftops below.

Our line of cars slowed as we approached, for the Conclave's careful scrubbing of the streets had come too late, and the traffic ahead of us thickened with the trucks and groundcars of the Great City's everyday life.

"On behalf of the Conclave, this route will add some eighty minutes to our travel time."

"Great . . ." Pallino said. "More of this."

In time we pulled out onto the bridge and into six lanes of traffic.

"They're clearing the way ahead, Crim says," Pallino said, two fingers to the comm patch behind his ear. Crim was riding in the foremost car, with the rest of us strung out between the other five vehicles. "Pushing the cars to each side."

Still our progress was slow. A klaxon blared from the foremost vehicle, and an amplified voice rang out in flattened Lothrian. "Clear the way," it said. "Clear the way."

We ground to a halt.

Pallino swore under his breath.

Uncomfortable silence filled the cab like water, my hoplites shifting in their seats. The Lothrian man sat there unmoving as a stone, eyes fixed on a point out the far window, mind lost somewhere in the curling mist above the low district hundreds of feet below us. I watched with him, looking back at the gray towers like headstones beneath the center of Eighth Dome.

It looked strangely familiar to me, as though I'd been there before. Was it Vorgossos again? The memory of Kharn's ancient city has never left me, so powerful was its first dark impression.

We'd sat there unmoving for the better part of ten minutes before the shouting began.

"What's that?" I turned to see.

Pallino's craggy, revitalized face turned down in an expression of grave alertness. Turning to our escort, he barked, "What's going on?"

The representative shook his head and did not answer.

Pallino seized the man by the front of his drab, gray tunic.

"Let him go!" I hissed. When Pallino did not, I reached out and laid a hand on his wrist once more. "I won't have you starting an international incident over a traffic jam, Pallino. Stand—"

Down.

But the last word caught in my throat, canceled by a soft and distant popping.

The crack of gunfire.

Pallino's grip tightened on the representative's lapels. "What the *hell* is going on?"

Seeming to understand his meaning if not his words, the representative replied, "The . . ." He froze, clamped his jaw shut.

"The liberalists," I said, stringing two and two together. I turned to the representative and repeated the statement. *"Bodanukni. Paustanni?"* Rebels?

Before he could think about an answer and self-censor, the representative nodded.

"Tell Crim and the others to get sharp," I said, and worked the elastic coif free of my suit's collar baffle. I pulled it over my head and tucked my long hair in and away from my face before I keyed the command to don my helmet. The segmented casque unfolded and closed about my head. The entoptics flicked on a moment later. All the while I heard distant gunshots. Screams.

Crim's voice came over the line then, ". . . won't be getting far in these cars. Anyone have eyes on the enemy?"

"None behind," said one.

"Not yet," said another.

The Norman-Jaddian commander replied. "Eyes forward. Watch the cars on either side. I don't want us outflanked."

"*Tohn! Tohn!*" came a distant cry. That was *quickly* in Lothrian.

Another gunshot. Not the crackling discharge of phase disruptors, nor the blaze of plasma.

"Is that a shotgun?" Pallino asked.

I could only nod. Rounding on the Lothrian representative I said, "Summon your prefects. Where are the Conclave Guard?"

The man's frown deepened, and he said, "On behalf of the Conclave, the delegate is requested to stay in the vehicle. Help is on the way."

"Bah!" I pressed the comm patch behind my own ear. "I want men posted on either rail. We need to outflank *them*, Commander."

Crim's reply was terse. "Aye, lord."

He relayed the orders down-chain, tagging two men from each vehicle, ordering one right and one left. The two in ours moved to open the door, and the representative shouted, "The delegate is requested to stay in the vehicle. Help is on the way!"

The second hoplite out the door made a rude gesture. A shot rang out the moment his boots hit the pavement, and his shield flashed, making him stagger. He slammed the door, dropped into a half crouch as he snapped his short-stock plasma burner to attention, and moved for the cover of the stopped cars. What the gray-faced Lothrian peasantry must have thought to see Sollan Legionnaires in ivory plate and red tabards spilling from their Party's groundcars was any man's guess. The men moved with quiet efficiency, signaling for the *zuks* to abandon their vehicles and run. Many did, spilling back along the bridge for the inner portions of the district.

I remember being remarkably calm.

"Can we get word to the embassy?" I asked.

"Not through the fucking dome," Pallino said.

More shouting. A gunshot shattered the window of the car opposite us.

"Help is on the way," the Lothrian stooge repeated. "Stay in the vehicle."

Something whistled on the air, and a moment later the whole car shook and lifted into the air, flipped clean over. Relatively safe in my armor, I threw an arm across the Lothrian to help pin him in place as the armored vehicle skidded upside down along the road.

"Rocket!" Pallino swore, escaping his restraints and falling to the ceiling beneath us. He kicked the door open.

"You have to stay!" the Lothrian man exclaimed, speaking Galstani as I dropped to follow my guards.

I was not shocked to find he spoke our language—I guessed every man the Conclave set to watch us must. "*You* stay," I said, and slammed the door behind.

Mist and smoke mingled, and orange flames lit the gray day from places where cars were burning. Men and women in the dull gray coveralls of the *zuk* class ran past. Two cursed at me as they went by, still more went wide-eyed with fear.

"*Ne bahovni, ne panovni!*" one shouted and spat. *No gods, no masters!*

Still more shouted, "*Zara! Zara!*" That was *king*. Caesar. On their lips, it had the weight of a slur.

"They blame us for this," I said, and flinched as a bullet broke against my shield.

"Fuck them! Earth rot their bones!" Pallino hissed, and raised his disruptor to fire.

One of the liberalist guerrillas had appeared from behind one of the cars. She fell in a tangle of limbs and gray fabric, her allegiance to some other order betrayed only by a red and white armband. I stared at her body a moment, wondering what lies or desperation had led her mutinous hand to turn on me.

I had no time to dwell on it.

"Where's that grenadier?" I asked.

"No sign," came Crim's reply. "Pallino, get His Lordship under cover." The swordsman tugged one of his throwing knives from its bandoleer and drew his ceramic sword. It shone white as milk as he turned. I drew my own sword, but did not kindle it. A hail of bullets fell about us, pockmarked the face of the upturned car. More men in gray with armbands or headbands striped red and white appeared, not charging but advancing slowly, methodically between the cars ahead. They did not move like revolutionaries, like anarchists or liberalists or whatever they called themselves, but like professional soldiers.

One of my guards fired, and his disruptor bolt caught—not on a shield—but on some insulating garment worn beneath the gray coveralls. The man flinched and turned under cover. Crim caught another as he emerged from the sidelines, having evidently dispatched one of our men by the rail. The white Norman sword flashed as Crim shoved the man's rifle up and out of the way. The off-hand knife flashed. Blood flowered. Crim spun away, hurled his knife in a tumbling arc that caught another man behind the eyes. He fell like a Nipponese marionette, his shotgun discharging with a noise to shame the thunder.

The others opened fire, bullets tearing the air between us. Car windows shattered, and the fleeing people cried out and fell bleeding. We returned fire, hoplites crouched behind the government motorcars for added protection.

"We need to find whoever was behind that rocket!" I said to Pallino, gripping the old soldier by the upper arm.

Pallino nodded once, relayed my order over broad-band comm to the rest of my guard.

Where were the Lothrian prefects? Surely they had fliers inside the dome for rapid response. They should have been there already, filling the air to either side. Pallino fired around the rear of the car and hooted as he felled one of the enemy.

A bullet pinged the glass between our heads, and looking up I saw nearly half a dozen of the liberalists closing in from the *other* end of the bridge, each with a pistol leveled at our heads. Grateful for my shield, I almost laughed. It seemed innocent bystanders had not been the only people streaming past us.

"Well done . . ." I muttered under my breath.

Not waiting to allow Pallino the chance to gainsay me, I leaped away from the vehicle and pounded down the road toward them, crossing the empty space between the rear of our motorcade and these new assailants. The liberalists were picking their shots carefully, mindful of their fellows on the other side. A shot pinged off my shield, bullet dashed to flinders. I kindled my blade, highmatter flowing like mercury as I reached the nearest man. He'd stood bravely through it all, hoping my body shield might fail with each successive shot.

The fellow's eyes were wide by the time I reached him, conviction shading to panic. He must have had little experience with Royse fields, had hoped to break my guard with so small an effort. An energy lance might, *might* have depleted the barrier in time, but common bullets?

He fell in two pieces.

Five men swiveled and fired on me, the shrapnel of their rounds filling the air around. I threw a hand over my face and dove sideways behind a parked van, still venting steam from its fuel cell. I felt the crunch of sheet metal and crack of glass as bullets riddled the hulk. The civilian vehicle lacked the armor of the government motorcade, and I feared a stray shot—or an expert one—might breach that fuel cell. I could not stay still.

One of the gunmen came round the side of the van, a shotgun in his hands. He wasn't of the five—those all had held small arms. He must have come down the side by the rail. He thrust the muzzle forward like a bayonet, hoping to get the aperture inside the energy curtain of my shield before I could react. I slammed his head into the car beside us. Dazed, the fellow pulled the trigger by reflex, shots flashing off my shield and peppering the street beside us.

The man staggered back, bleeding from his head. Another shot pinged off my shield above my head, and I turned, distracted. Another of the liberalists had taken cover behind a low-slung car, had fired over the hood. Seeing his chance, the shotgunner darted forward with a yell.

Too slow.

The highmatter sword flashed once through a rising arc that cut the stock of the weapon in two and severed both the man's arms. He fell back as a shot from one of my hoplites claimed the man who had shot me. I saw another target among the vehicles by the rail and ran toward him, heedless of the shots falling all around, the way they smote the concrete about my feet. At my back, Crim held the bulk of the liberalists at bay, knives flying and blade flashing.

I plunged toward the rail, blade hewing through a lamppost that toppled and fell with a splash into the waterway a thousand feet below. Another mighty explosion shook the bridge, and a nimbus of red flame flared where the fuel cell of one van stood burning. Scarlet light cast all the world in bloody colors, and I turned back to see black figures framed against the flames. Once more their precision struck me. Not a ragtag collection of desperate freedom fighters. No. These were soldiers trained and outfitted. I remembered what Damon Argyris had said.

Our intelligence boffins think the rebels are a Party bogeyman, a scapegoat . . .

A scapegoat. *Or a puppet . . .*

As I stood there at the rail, I saw Pallino and his men make short work of the last of the liberalist rear guard. They turned to join Crim. We were winning. I thrust my sword up and raised my voice to rally the men for the final effort. "Earth and Empire!" I shouted, not for piety or patriotism, but as a pronouncement of identity in that hideous place.

And then I understood.

I remembered.

Remembered why the bridge looked so familiar.

The gray towers that rose from the heart of Eighth Dome seen from that spot on the bridge were precisely those I'd seen—those I'd remembered from a future that had not happened—in my dream the night before I first met the Grand Conclave.

A future that had not happened, *yet*.

If memories exist to instruct us on past failings, my memories of the future are signposts to warn me off future errors. As a familiar scent or sound triggers memories, so my arrival in Vedatharad for the first time had triggered nightmares of things which *might* happen there, things my body and brain remembered from that day upon the mountain when the Quiet poured all of Time through my head.

I remembered falling a second too late.

The third rocket struck the car nearest me. I had no time to focus my sight, no time to cry out. If Pallino swore and Crim shouted, I did not hear them. I flew back and struck the rail with enough force to drive the air from my lungs. The last thing I remember was the headlong rush of air and darkness that came before the crash.

CHAPTER 16

VULTURES

IN THE DREAM I fell again, saw again the bridge, the burning. Heard again the guns, the shouting. My head rang like a temple bell. I clenched my teeth, even though that motion brought pain. Arms moved. Legs moved. Nothing was broken. My suit must have saved me, the gel-layer hardening to protect my limbs as I fell. Something sticky and sucking pulled at me.

Mud.

I was lying face-down in mud.

Something jabbed me in the ribs. Not hard. Feeling it, I felt certain I'd been jabbed already once before, that it was that jab which had awakened me.

"Zhivon!" came a hoarse whisper. My brain was as muddy as my suit, my head throbbed. It took me the better part of a minute to remember that *zhivon* was Lothrian for *alive.*

Lothrian, I told myself. *I am in the Commonwealth.*

I was on Padmurak.

"Valka!" I tried to rise, but my hands carved deep furrows in the mud, and I fell back into the mire with a wet smack. How long I lay there was any man's guess.

That something jabbed me again.

"Zhivon?" This time a question. I tried to turn. Mud caked the optic threads in my suit's mask, and it was a struggle to smear it away.

A tall, gray-faced man loomed over me, leaning on a long wooden pole. He had the bald pate and hollow cheeks common to nearly every *zuk* I'd seen, though he wore rubberized boots that went to mid-thigh over his faded coveralls.

"The drowned man breathes, Carry!" said another voice, this one higher, the voice of a woman or young boy.

"Quiet!" the man said, nudging me with his pole. "The drowned man is not drowned." The big man crouched, both hands still on his pole. "Where is the drowned man from?"

They were not quoting the Lothriad at all, though they spoke the tongue of the Commonwealth. "A man is of the Sollan Empire," I managed to croak.

The other straightened and staggered back a step. *"Solnechni?"*

"The drowned man is a knight!" the other voice said.

Again I tried to rise. Again I fell. My head swam and pounded, and at last I settled for rolling over in the muck. I'd lost my cape in my fall . . . and my sword. "My sword!" I felt for the magnetic clasp at my hip. There was nothing.

I had lost Olorin's sword, and the feeling drove my head deeper into the mire.

Two faces peered down at me. One was a man's. The other was as indeterminate as the voice that belonged to it, that of either a strong-jawed girl or an effeminate boy. "What should be done?" the second asked, glancing at the taller man. The child could not have been older than fifteen standard. "Living men are not salvage."

"Quiet, Looker!" the man said, thudding his stick into the mud after each word. "A man thinks."

"A man visits Padmurak," I said, my Lothrian halting in my current state. I prayed I did not have a concussion. "A man was attacked by the *bahovni*."

"A man fell into the river!" the child called Looker said.

The man, Carry, frowned. *"Bahovni?"* His frown worsened.

"Are you . . . rebels, too?" I asked, looking from one to the next.

"Rebels?" Looker repeated. "There are no rebels, drowned man. Everybody knows this."

A small *ah* escaped me, and I felt myself sink even farther into the mud. That explained the absence of the Lothrian prefects. They'd been called off. Snatches of the battle on the bridge rebounded across the dark interior of my mind, the way the rebels had disguised themselves among the retreating mob, the precise way they'd moved, their disruptor shielding.

They'd been as Lothrian as our escort.

Why would the Lothrian government want me killed? They must know that to kill an Imperial apostol was to court war. They could not seriously want war with the Imperium, and over what? The Rasan Belt? Persean expansion? They could not hope to win. Though the Commonwealth commanded great territory, they surely lacked the hardware and the manpower necessary to stand against our Legions. Nothing in the crumbling brutalism of Vedatharad spoke to a nation that was master of a war machine to shake the stars. The Lothrians were ragged, starving, poor.

Unless that too were a posture carefully cultivated, a moth-eaten cloak to hide tempered steel. With so much of the Empire's might concentrated in the Centaurine marches, the Conclave surely imagined our defenses in the Outer Perseus and across the Rasan Belt would be diminished, that in dividing the Imperial attention between two fronts, the Commonwealth might stand a chance at victory.

They may have been right.

That they would buy their victory by allowing the Cielcin to grow stronger in the galactic east turned my stomach.

"The drowned man is dead?" the man, Carry, asked.

I realized I had been still and quiet a long time. The child prodded at me with something short and silver, body tense as if to leap away at the slightest moment. Recognizing the weapon, I seized Looker by the wrist and half pulled myself into a seated position.

"Let go!" Looker cried out. "Let go!"

The big man struck me across the head with the butt of his pole, but my suit took the impact. Still, my rattled skull ached from the blow, and I held on tighter, slipping my hand from Looker's wrist to the hilt of the highmatter sword.

My sword.

My fingers found the twin triggers, and the pentaquark baryons that made up the blade lanced out, blue-white in the gloom. Looker yelped and let go, and it was only a mad backward scramble that kept the Lothrian from falling. Before Carry could strike me again, I pointed the blade up at him. It was a nearly empty threat. I could hardly hope to stand as I was. From the pain in my head and the blurriness of my vision, I guessed I had a concussion. "Stand down," I said, struggling with Lothrian's stilted grammar. "A man is not another man's enemy."

"Liar!" the child shouted, clutching a bruised wrist.

I unkindled my weapon, but kept the hilt ready in my hand. With the same hand, I thumped my chest. "Hadrian," I said. There was no way to say *My name is* . . . I did it again. "Hadrian."

Apparently my point had gotten through, for the big man pointed at his own face and said, "Carry." He pointed at his counterpart, who—wild-eyed and tight-fisted—looked now more like an angry boy than a young lady. "Looker."

"You have names . . ." I said, slipping into Galstani by reflex. It was all I could do not to laugh. What I'd have given to see Lorth Talleg's face in that moment, to know for all his intellectual utopianism, his dream of a perfected Lothriad, that humanity was like a weed in cement. His ideals and ideal future may have been a boot stamping on human nature and dignity, but man's roots ran deeper still and would not be ground out.

"*Stoh?*" Carry asked. "What?"

There was no Lothrian word for *name*, no word for *you* or *your*.

I pointed up at the man with my empty hand. "Carry." I pointed at myself. "Hadrian."

"Ha . . . drian?" he repeated.

My head swam badly, and I half-fell back against the earth. I stayed that way a moment, vision clearing, my surroundings swimming themselves into sharper and sharper focus. I lay upon a kind of artificial shore, my feet still trailing in the brown water. There was no sky above, only a rust and lichen-streaked concrete roof bracketed with pipes. What light there was came in the form of antique diode lamps, dull and orange.

"A man's words are . . . *ne lothtara*," I said. *Not correct.* The relation between the word *lothtara*, *correct*, and the word *Lothriad* were plain to see. I hoped whichever enterprising partisan had rewritten the Lothrian dictionary to form that particular association had been rewarded handsomely. More likely he had met a firing squad and so transmuted his revision to eternal truth.

To my astonishment, Carry *spat*.

"*Lothtara! Lothriad!*" he said. "These are for the *pitrasnukni*."

"The partisans," I said. "These men . . ." I gestured to Carry and Looker both, "are *zukni? Zuks?*"

Carry nodded. Looker padded around to stand beside the bigger worker. "Let no man be idle!" the big man said, a pathos and a bitterness in his tone that astonished me. It was the first line of the Lothriad I'd heard pass his lips. He gestured to a vehicle equal parts boat and sledge—laden with what looked like scrap—that lay half-mired in the slime in which I myself lay caught. "Looker and Carry run salvage in waste-water tunnels."

Scavengers.

"Waste-water?" I looked round at the muck I lay in, glad then my suit's integrity had held.

In sterquilinus invenitur. In filth it will be found.

I tried to laugh. The bottom of the world indeed.

"Can the drowned man stand?" Carry asked.

I tried again, and Carry threw out a hand to steady me. He was stronger than he looked, not bulky, but wiry. It was enough to free me from the filth, but my vision blurred again, and I staggered forward up the concrete slope. I collapsed again. Hands and knees. Blood pounding in my ears. I clutched Olorin's sword tight, mindful of the way the twin shadows of the man and his child loomed over me.

I had to get back to the embassy, had to get back to Valka, to Crim and Pallino. But I couldn't stand. I could hardly see. "Must warn . . . the others," I said, struggling to shove my thoughts into Lothrian's limited vocabulary. How could I explain that my friends were in danger if I could not express our relationship? "People will die."

"Hadrian will die," Carry said, crouching next to me. "Hadrian is hurt."

Looker spoke up then. "Magda could help."

"Magda?" the big man echoed, almost thoughtfully.

"Who is Magda?" I asked, twisting to look up at my newfound companions. My vision swam. I was certain by then that I had a concussion.

Carry extended a hand. "Doctor."

Had I been fully conscious, I might have marveled at how the method these *zuks* had devised for working around the limitations of their language—the elimination of pronouns and direct address, of identity itself—was to give one another names. I would have wondered, too, at *Magda.* Looker and Carry both were simple names, almost job descriptions. *Magda* was something else. It had an antique sound to it, not Lothrian at all.

I took the big man's hand and—leaning on his staff for leverage—he hauled me to my feet. I tottered, forced him to steady me as I nearly swooned again, my right hand desperately clinging to Olorin's sword.

"Must find water valve and hose drowned man off!" Carry exclaimed, laughing. "The smell is foul."

Safe inside my helmet, I could not smell it, but I was sure he was right. The slime that caked my armor and clung to me was—I felt certain—equal parts oil and sewage. Strangely, the big *zuk* seemed not to mind, but then I supposed he and the child spent their time in these tunnels and waterways, poling for scrap.

We were beneath Vedatharad, deep in the tunnels that connected and predated the building of the domes. The ancestors of the ancestors of the Lothrians who had first settled on Padmurak during the great outward expansion of mankind millennia ago had carved these tunnels with explosives and cutting lasers and great machines. They had filled them and smoothed them with cement and steel and packed into them like ants—like the Cielcin in the dark dawn of their existence. Perhaps the very harshness of the tunnels and Padmurak's airless environment had forced them to turn to so extreme a set of social controls. Reflecting on those tunnels now, I cannot help but think of the *vuli*, the blockhouses that dominated the cityscape, wherein dwelt the Commonwealth's uncounted trillions on this and a hundred thousand colony worlds.

Hives, indeed.

Empty now, those tunnels were little more than bones, the fossilized remnants of what the Commonwealth had been in its beginnings, its only inhabitants the grave beetles and vultures like Looker and Carry who fled there to escape the world above. Better to pick the bones of that awful place than live beneath the boot of the Conclave and the Lothriad.

There are no rebels, Carry had said. That was not strictly true. He was one, his child another, though they fought no battles.

"Magda will help," Carry said, wrapping one of my arms over his shoulder to help me toward his boat-sledge. "Magda will help you."

CHAPTER 17

THE ADORATOR

CARRY MADE GOOD ON his threat about the water valve. After he poled us down the channel for some time, he took us up another, slower waterway—relying on an outboard motor for thrust and his long staff for steering. There we stopped long enough for the big man to douse me in the jet from a fresh water main, to spray my armor and tunic clean of filth. I remember falling as the jet hit me. I do not remember being hauled back to Carry's boat. In my damaged state, I drifted, addled mind confusing the dark sewer pipes for the rivers of light and Time.

There was another jet, another series of pipes. Water draining. An ocean draining. A lake. I lay on the ground at Carry's feet, feeling the torrent wash over me. I felt bones crunch beneath my feet, remembered hurrying down a slope as the tide retreated before me, heard the awful screaming of some monstrous creature of the deep. Its bloated mass loomed before me, tendrils flailing as it died. Innumerable bleary eyes focused on me, and a trembling hand reached out, imploring. I reached out to take that hand, and knew the monster in that moment.

I blinked, gasped as Looker turned the wheel to stop the flood and the vision-memory alike. Carry hauled me to my feet. It was his hand I'd taken, and no monster's.

I was on Padmurak.

Padmurak.

I had to tell Valka and the consul, had to warn them. Had to save them.

The Conclave was trying to kill us. They wanted to start a war.

Would they be safe in the embassy? Would the Commonwealth risk so flagrant an assault?

"Is not far now," Looker said, crouching near me by the gunwale. "Not far."

Dimly I was aware of the boat, of Looker watching me and Carry looking down as he guided us down another channel. Twice we passed other *zuks* working on the pipes, or else plying their own way in the dark and doubtless foul-smelling waters. Jinan glared at me from across the small boat, eyes white with fury, the azure ribbon in her hair. I sat upright, tangled in the sheets of my bed aboard the *Tamerlane*, the smashed myrmidon's helmet watching me from the bedside table. The woman beside me moved, and looking down I saw the bronze length of Otavia Corvo tangled at my side, naked as I was.

She blinked blearily up at me. "Can't sleep?" She rested one warm, strong hand on my thigh. Corvo rose and kissed me. So startled was I that I sat there, paralyzed, her tongue in my mouth, her floating hair all about my face.

I awoke again, this time blearily, my vision thick and fuzzy as my thoughts.

Other memories. Other lives.

Dazed as I was and damaged, my mind flickered from memory to memory. Things that never happened and never would. I feared I would never find myself again, would wander lost in the memory of those other lives, other Hadrians, and never come back to that little boat.

I needn't have feared.

"Help take this mask off," came a gentle, feminine voice. I felt my helmet hiss open, felt warm, wet air on my face. A bright light tracked left, right across my eyes. "Concussion," the voice said. "Carry says you are . . . offworlder?"

She was speaking Galstani.

"I am," I said. "I am an emissary from the Sollan Empire. We were attacked by . . . by liberalists."

"There are no liberalists," the voice answered.

"I know that now."

A woman's face—smiling and matronly—emerged from the harsh, pale light. She had a round face beneath a cap of short, graying black hair—not shaved like the other *zuks* I had seen. But she *was* a *zuk*. She had the familiar Lothrian black eyes, the same gray pallor. She wore the same gray coveralls. "You must rest."

"I *must* get back and warn the others. Valka . . . the consulate . . ."

She pushed me down with firm hands. "You *must* rest, by God." She kept a hand on my chest. "It will take days before you're fit to go anywhere."

"I don't have days!" I said. "Valka doesn't have days!"

"If you go, Carry and Looker will be fishing you out of the drains again before sunrise." She turned away and busied herself spraying down a series of tiny, exquisitely sculpted fruit trees that stood in stepped rows beneath lamps. Despite their diminutive size, the fruit borne by a few of the trees was ordinary. Two apples ripened on one, and three oranges on another. A third held a single pomegranate. "Not that there is a sunrise down here."

The room—blurred though my vision was—was not much larger than a city tram car. A line of cots, each little more than a foam roll and a plank atop a metal frame, marched down one side. All but mine were empty. The side opposite was given over to the trees, which glowed beneath their pointed lamps. The walls were concrete buried beneath layers of overlapping metal pipe and rubberized conduits. There were doors at either end. The place gave the impression not of a hospital ward, but of a power station or steam tunnel.

"What is this place?"

She looked at me, all Lothrian terseness. "Clinic."

"You're . . . Magda," I said. She did not deny it, nor had she really answered my question. Words slow and stumbling, I tried again. "Why *this* place?"

The Lothrian woman cradled her spray bottle. "Why down here, you mean?"

It hurt to nod.

"The Guard don't come here," she said. "Too deep. Too old. They don't know the ways." As she spoke, she busied herself with a black plastic crate that had lain beneath the next cot. "People come down. Nowhere else to go on Padmurak. They all drain down here. Some of them washouts like you . . . some of them outcasts like your friends. Some of them just . . . run away."

"Which were you?"

"I was called," she said, and stopped fiddling with the crate to touch something through the front of her gray tunic. From the look of things, she had altered the Lothrian fatigues common to all the *zuks* I'd seen into a long tunic or loose dress that hung on her stick frame like burlap to a scarecrow. She reached into the box and drew out a white pill bottle. Magda opened it and shook three small pills into her hand. "Take these."

Olorin's sword was still in my hand. "What are they?"

"Painkillers," she said. "They'll help." I held her gaze so long as I could, but had to shut my eyes. I extended my free hand, and palmed the pills dry the moment she gave them to me. "You're . \. . palatine, yes?"

My eyes opened to mere slits, cautious. I decided a moment later that it was too late for caution—I had taken the woman's medicine, after all. "I am. My name is Hadrian."

"Palatines heal fast. Two days. Maybe three. You'll be right as rain."

Unable to help myself, I echoed, "Right as rain?" It was an old idiom, one that had survived to our time from the days of Classical English. It had no place on this world that had never known English or rain. "Are you Lothrian?" She had the look. The Lothrians were so distinctive, so mono-lithic an ethnic group with their black hair and ashen skin, that I knew the answer before she said it.

"Yes."

"Where did you learn Galstani?" I asked. The Grand Conclave could not possibly want many of its people learning languages not censored and pruned by their ministries.

Magda glanced toward the door in the back of the little ward. "Father Dias," she said. "God rest his soul."

Twice now she had mentioned *God,* a word I'd never thought to hear from a Lothrian, and certainly not a word I ever thought to hear on Pad-murak, not least so deep in the warrens of the Great City. "Your father?" I asked.

"No." She reached down the front of her dress and drew out a pendant on a thin chain. It was a cross made from two nails crudely welded to-gether. "He was a priest. Came here to . . . to help us. To help *me* help us."

"A priest?" I asked, uncomprehending. Why would a Chantry priest come to Padmurak? And what had he to do with a cross? I thought perhaps her Galstani was not so good. I remembered only slowly, recognizing the antique symbol for what it was: the emblem of an ancient cult, one of the adorator faiths protected in the Empire by ancient law. "You're . . . a Mu-seum Catholic." There were Museum Catholics back home on Delos, but I had never seen them, never encountered their symbols in the flesh. I knew a little of their faith, had read the Books of Dante and Milton on Gibson's orders as a boy, and though I knew enough to recognize the cross for what it was, I knew little of their ways then.

Magda shook her head. "I try to be. Father Dias was."

Here was truly a marvel, that twenty-five thousand light-years from Earth and twenty thousand years hence should be found beneath the domes of Vedatharad a single, solitary devotee of a god who had been old when the God Emperor was young. By ancient decree, made to dwell on reserves like that which stood in the mountains above Meidua. The Empire had long tolerated—long segregated—such pagan mystagogues as the Catholics, the Vaishnavites, and the Theravada. The accords which protected them in the Empire ran back to the Great Charter, millennia before the formation of the Holy Terran Chantry, though why the Chantry had not moved to abolish these adorators, I dare not speculate.

But we were not in the Empire.

"He's dead, then?" I asked, too abruptly in my addled state.

Magda nodded. "He built this place. Saved me. Baptized me. Gave me my name." She indicated the clinic all around. "So I carry on. Help the poor rats Carry and his like drag in. Helped Carry, too. Him and his . . . child." Her reticence as good as confirmed my guess that Looker was one of the Lothrian *new men*.

"Aren't you afraid you'll be . . . found out?" I asked.

Magda fixed me with a flinty gaze, all iron. "I'll not be the first to die in His Name."

I could only assume she meant her old god.

"Like your priest?"

"Father Dias was baptizing us. Giving us names. Teaching us to speak the standard. Conclave didn't like that. Caught him when he went above to treat the sick." She glanced down at the crate beside me. "They rounded him up. Sent him away with the others."

"To the camps?" I asked, thinking of Everfrost Station. "He was a physician?"

Magda chewed her lip. "He was. And I guess. People disappear all the time. Families. Entire hives. Could be the camps." She studied my face carefully, as if gauging me for my reaction. "Could be they sell them to your Empire. They say you palatines drink blood, that that is how you live so long."

"What?" I almost burst out laughing.

"They say the blood of children keeps you young."

"It doesn't!" I did laugh then, and regretted it instantly as pain flowered in my skull. "Genetic engineering does that." But Magda was smiling. "Were you having me for a laugh?"

She bared crooked teeth, her smile lighting up her aging features. "There are those who think the Conclave sell us offworld."

"They *do* take people, then?" I asked, thinking of how empty Vedatharad had seemed.

"All the time," she said. "More and more. But it is only to settle new worlds. If he was not killed, Father Dias was sent to a *lahe* offworld. A camp colony." She laughed softly. "I do not think you a blood drinker."

I winced, touched my exposed face with my gloved hand.

"You should let me take that armor off," Magda said, rising from the next cot to lean over me, her hands seeking my suit seals. "Let me have a look at you."

Acting almost without thought, I seized her wrist—it took me two attempts to succeed—and pointed the emitter of the highmatter sword at her. "No."

Magda only blinked at me. There was little fear in her eyes. "You may have other injuries."

"No," I said, voice flat, final. "I'm fine." I'd have known by then if I had broken any bones, would certainly have known if I was bleeding into my suit. There would have been alarms, notifications on my helmet's display and on my wrist-terminal. There were none. I would have seen them when I tried to signal the others.

"Let me help you."

"I'm fine, damn you!" The strain of half-sitting up set the blood to pounding in my head. My vision blurred and I fell backward, felt the sword tumble from fingers suddenly nerveless.

I whited out.

Lost in white darkness, I could sense nothing. Even the pain was gone, muted—the effect of Magda's painkillers, I don't doubt. I existed as little more than one of Descartes's sad solipsists, aware of nothing but myself. It was like being dead, like nothing so much as my experience of the howling Dark through which my soul had wandered before the Quiet sent me back. How long I lay like that in Magda's clinic I dared not guess. Hours? Days? Time meant little through that pale haze. Once or twice I woke and found the Lothrian doctor watching me from the next cot, or else tending to her little fruit trees.

Once or twice I heard her sing, though she thought me dead to the waking world.

> *From all that terror teaches,*
> *from lies of tongue and pen;*

From all the easy speeches
that comfort cruel men;
From sale and profanation
of honour and the sword;
From sleep and from damnation,
Deliver us, good Lord.

The words were in English—that was the strangest thing. "Did he teach you that?" I think I asked her. "Your priest?"

He must have done, though I cannot remember her reply. It seemed an appropriate song for the Lothriad. A prayer for a world that knew too much of lies and terror. Too much . . .

I awoke screaming, clutching my side. Blood soaked my fingers where I'd torn crude stitches open, sheeted down my side. When had I been wounded? When had I been stabbed? Magda emerged from the back room, already rolling her sleeves back.

"Lie flat!" she shouted, slipping into her native Lothrian with panic as she scrambled for the plastic medical kit beneath the next bed. "A man will die if not."

It took an act of will to prize my hand away from the wound in my side, the wound I had been sure was not there a moment before. I pressed my head back against the pillows, jaw clenched, the fibers in my neck straining.

Magda paused as she approached. "What did you do?" She peered at the wound.

"Nothing!" I said, honestly. I had no memory of her removing my armor, but I felt certain I'd have remembered so deep a wound in my side.

"This wasn't here before!" she exclaimed, applying pressure.

I yelled.

"You tried to close this yourself?" she said, examining the sutures. She looked around, face drained of color.

"What have you done to me?" I asked. Remembering her story about the palatines drinking blood, I rasped, "What did you take?" The pagan adorator meant to harvest my organs, that much was plain. Looker and Carry had not brought me to Magda to save me, but to kill me instead.

Magda stepped back, hands bare. "Nothing! I was in the back. I heard you scream."

My sword lay on the bedside table, just at the edge of my reach. Why hadn't she taken it? I reached out to seize it, causing an ecstatic flash of pain to spasm through me as torn muscle pulled apart. Magda's hands seized me, tried to steady me, but it was too late.

"Mother of God . . ." I heard her swear.

But I was already fading.

When I awoke next, Magda was nowhere in sight. Carry sat against the wall beneath the ranks of little trees, arms crossed, head tucked against his chest. He was snoring. Fresh bandages wound about my chest from sternum to navel, so tight it hurt to breathe.

I must have made a sound, for Carry cracked an eye. "A man wakes," he said. "Magda says a man cut himself."

"A man did no such thing," I managed to grunt out, looking round. My sword still lay on the bedside table. Why hadn't they taken it away? If they meant to hurt me—as I thought—surely they would have taken away my arms as they had my armor.

But there was my armor on the next bed. Catching me looking at it, Carry said, "Carry had Looker clean a man's armor."

Forgetting my Lothrian, I nodded weakly. "Thank you."

That, too, was not the action of an enemy. What was going on? Stiffly, I moved a hand to my wounded side, felt for the injury. What had happened?

"Magda says a man must stay longer. A man is unfit to travel."

I took my hand away from my side and stared at it as though I'd never seen it before. "What?" I hadn't properly heard the man. His words caught up to me a moment after. "No. No, I can't stay."

I'd been speaking Galstani again, and Carry hadn't understood me. He shook his head, ran a hand over his prickly scalp. "Magda brings food. A man has slept now for three days."

"Three days?" I managed to prop myself on my elbows, and was surprised when I felt no pain. Anything could have happened in three days. Had Crim and Pallino made it safely to the embassy? Was Valka safe with Damon Argyris? Was the *Tamerlane* safe in orbit?

Carry moved swiftly to my bedside and helped me to sit up. I waved him away. "I'm all right," I said, and switched to Lothrian. "A man must bring a man to the surface. To First Dome."

"Not until Magda says," Carry said.

I seized him by the front of his gray fatigues, all bleariness and pain forgotten. "Please. A man's people will die."

The big *zuk* peeled my fingers off his clothing with steady hands. "A man must wait." He stumped away, vanishing through the outer door with a shout. "Looker! Come and watch the drowned man!"

Alone a moment, I felt my dressings again, fingertips parting the pale linen. I expected to find the black tape of a medical corrective beneath, or sutures such as I'd found when last I'd woken up, but I was mistaken.

There was no wound on the umblemished flesh.

There was nothing at all.

CHAPTER 18

UP ACHERON

"NEVER SEEN A MAN heal so quickly," Magda said, finding me already in my suit and sitting up when she returned. Like its father, Looker had dozed off while it kept watch, snoring softly beneath the fruit trees. It had been time enough for me to don my suit's black underlayment, the garment tightening into place as I activated its seals, smart material contracting until it formed a second skin.

Thus the healer found me when she returned with four cups of egg noodles in some brown and subtly fungal broth. These I ate gustily, discovering I was starving—and small wonder! I had not eaten since the morning of the battle on the bridge, and not eaten well since we left the embassy for Everfrost Station more than a week before.

"Like I said," I said around an eager mouthful, "we palatines are genetically engineered to be . . ." I almost said *superior*, but stopped myself. "Well, to heal quickly."

"I wish you'd let me look at it," she said, pointing at my side with her plastic fork.

"I'll survive," I said, mindful of the uncertainty in the woman's black eyes. She'd been watchful ever since I'd awoken her screaming with a fresh wound in my side. I knew she believed I'd harmed myself, as I had at first suspected some foul play on her part. When pressed, she'd produced a medical scanner, proved my kidneys and liver, my spleen and all the rest were where they ought to be. Ever after, she acted as though I'd struck her, as though her fears were ludicrous and cause for offense. I'd apologized so much as I could, but maintained a careful distance.

I could not let her examine my wound. I could not let her know it was gone, vanished as readily and as without warning as it had appeared. I would have thought it only another product of my damaged brain and fevered dreams—like my vision of myself with Otavia—were it not for the bandages and the dried blood on my sheets. Unthinking, I felt my side with my hand. My *right* hand. The hand I'd lost and regained. Had something similar happened? Had my consciousness, my *will*, reached out across the parallel bands of time and seized another? Had I shut my eyes on one universe and opened them on the next? I imagined consciousness like the beam of a torchlight swept back and forth along a bookshelf, stopping to select one title, one narrative—and then the next.

It was how the Quiet had saved me aboard the *Demiurge*, trading the dead Hadrian for the living one; the man who had lost right arm and head for the man who had lost the left. My memories remained constant. I remembered my death not because the past had changed—the past cannot be changed—but because the present had been. The Quiet had conjured up a state of *Hadrian* lost to entropy and cast it back into the world, produced it from *behind the stage*, from a potential state the universe would never have seen otherwise. The Quiet had only nudged probability, altered the wave function about me until what had been lost in potential replaced what was. I had lived again. So too had I traded the concussed Hadrian for the wounded one, called out in my delirium, and found my wounded self.

I'd made a mistake. That was how I knew I was responsible. The Quiet did not make mistakes. When it left me without my left arm, it had known I would need bones of adamant there to survive my duel with Irshan. It had showed me all of time, but my human mind could not encompass it. But it had left me with a measure of its power and a fraction of its sight, however limited I was by my body.

Seeing the gesture, Carry asked, "A man is all right?"

I took my hand away from my side. How had I done it? Was it some feature of the medicine I'd taken? Or had my trauma brought it on?

"I . . . ." I realized I was speaking the standard and switched to Lothrian. "*Da.*"

Let them think it was my palatine biology that had saved me. It was so much easier that way. There was too much I did not understand, and more they would not. Turning to Magda, I spoke again in Galstani. "Long ago, another woman helped me as you have. I had nothing to give her. I have nothing to give you now. But I am grateful." I set the empty box of noodles down. How had this woman obtained them? Extra rations could not be easy to obtain, and despite the opulence of the greenhouses Third Chair had shown me, I found it difficult to believe all those beneath the Conclave's Bench ate well. "Thank you."

"It was the right thing to do," Magda said.

I stood suddenly, head clear. There was no pain. Whatever I had done in my delirium, I had escaped concussion and injury both—though I was not sure I could do it again. My suit gauntlets lay on the little metal table, and I clicked them into place.

"God sent you to me," Magda said, and touched her cross, "as He has sent all the others." My tunic was a total loss, but my armor was clean again. I looked smaller reflected in the glass front of a medicine cabinet without tunic or cape, with only my armor and the form-fitting combat skin beneath it. But I looked like myself at least. Magda was not finished. "You say you are a great lord of the Empire. Perhaps you are why He called me here to serve. To save you."

"I do not believe in your god," I said, too harshly.

But Magda did not balk or so much as blink. "He does not need you to."

"Magda." I looked down on the pagan woman with a sad smile. "I have not come to destroy your Conclave. I am here to save my own people, to stop the *Rugyeh*."

"The what?" she cocked her head.

In spite of myself, I laughed. A weak, hollow sound in that place of metal and stone. She had not even heard of the *Rugyeh*, of the war that raged across nearly a third of the settled universe. And why should she? The Conclave would not wish the People to know what passed beyond their borders, for to them there was nothing beyond their borders, could be nothing. The Lothriad was all, and though they knew of the Sollan Empire, of Jadd and the Durantines, they understood these places only as fictions written by their *pitrasnuk* masters. How could I begin to explain?

I decided not to even try.

"I must go," I said, and taking her hands in mine stooped and kissed them. "You saved my life. I will not forget you."

She accepted this without despair, and as I turned to follow Carry out the side door, she said, "Lord Hadrian?"

I froze and turned to look back. I said no word.

"He has a plan for you, I think. My God."

Why should those words haunt me so?

There were bodies in the water. The slow current moved them toward us as Carry's little boat carried us upstream. Once or twice, the big *zuk* lifted his pole and shunted one aside as it drew near. Some were men, others women, others too far gone to say. One wore a black skin-suit beneath torn gray fatigues. There was a band tied about his arm, white and red. I fancied that here was one of my attackers from the bridge, but he could have easily been from some other altercation in the city above.

"Conclave Guard," Carry said, jerking his chin at the man. "Secret police. Often such men are wearing the colors of liberators."

"Why?"

"*Panovni.* Rebels shoot people. Party protects. People love Party." He shrugged.

We sailed on quietly for some time after that, the only sound the faint whine of the boat's engine. Looker trailed a length of pipe in the water, watching its little wake. Once we passed a pair of men wading across a broad waterway on stilts and carrying large nets on the end of poles. Carry saluted with his staff, and they returned the gesture, but no words were exchanged.

Mean though their existence was, there was hope in it, in people like Magda and in her faith to her old god. Hope that all that mighty edifice of cement and brutal steel might one day come crashing down. For all their ingenuity, the architects of the Commonwealth and authors of the Lo-thriad had not broken the human spirit. Their boot might tramp on men's faces for a day, a year, or an age—but in the end it would be the foot that broke.

"How many live down here?" I asked the ferryman.

Carry thought about this a long while. "No man knows," he said. "Thousands. More. Many." He shrugged again, his usual gesture when frustrated by the limitations of his crippled tongue. "Less than when Carry was young. Patrols come through main tunnels, clear men out. Take men away."

"Magda said the patrols take people to the work camps."

"More and more," came the reply. "Patrols used to take one man, two. For reeducation. For offworld." Shrug. "Now patrols take ten. Twenty. Take men from above, too."

I nodded, ran a hand over my eyes. Little could I remember being so tired or so sick with worry. I prayed—to Mother Earth or Magda's god or to some other power I could not say—prayed that Valka and the others were safe. Pallino and Crim might have won the battle on the bridge, might have driven the convoy back to the embassy themselves.

They might be dead, said another, softer voice.

It was all too easy to picture the embassy tower afire, all too easy to imagine the telegraph broadcast by a fleeing *Tamerlane*:

Lord M missing, presumed dead. Embassy destroyed. Consul dead or captured.
War.
War.

"War," I muttered. A truly ancient word, unchanged from the Golden Age of Classical English, and hardly changed since the Hyperborean times when man was young and dragons ruled the Earth.

"*Stoh?*" Looker asked, turning to look at me.

"*Voyn,*" I said in answer. "If the Conclave has attacked the Sollan embassy, it is war." I reflected that despite my words to Magda, my visit might spell the beginning of the end of the Commonwealth. Another accidental prophecy.

The child frowned at me and asked in broken standard, "Your . . . people. Kill Conclave?"

I looked at the hermaphrodite in surprise. It was the first time either Looker or Carry had shown any signs of speaking Galstani. Perhaps Magda had shared a word or two. I studied Looker's face for a moment. The child still trailed its length of pipe in the water, but was not looking at it. Looker's Lothrian black eyes blazed with a light I had not seen there before, the fires of revolution and of hope.

"Maybe," I answered.

"Maybe not," Carry grunted, having evidently understood enough of the standard. His voice was thick with the pessimistic realism of age, in stark contrast to that of his child. He pointed then over our heads up the dark tunnel before us. Slipping back into his native Lothrian, he said, "First Dome is not far." Ahead a low, broad arch opened on a broader watercourse, and the darkness seemed more gray than black. Wall sconces flickered dull and orange, and the slime of eons shone wet and black on the walls and on the curved ceiling above.

"A man must watch for patrols," Looker said, shifting to look back at me. "On the surface, eyes will be everywhere."

It would be no easy feat finding the embassy once I was in the city proper. The Lothrians had done all in their power to obscure the plan of their city from foreign visitors. I envied Valka her perfect memory, and wished terribly that she were with me. I dared not try to contact her, for any transmission I might send was sure to be overheard by the Lothrian police—and if what Carry and Magda said were true, if it was the Lothrian government itself and not their liberalist bogeymen who had attacked my party on the bridge—I could not afford to be overheard. I would have to move quickly.

I knew the look of the embassy tower—it was one of the tallest buildings in First Dome, and close to the People's Palace in the center of the district—but the nature of the streets was strange to me, and I had no way of knowing if I were climbing up right beneath it or on the dome's far side. Almost I thought I should abandon my armor, travel in the grays of a common *zuk*. But to pass for one of the low-caste workers I would need also to shave my head, and I'd no way of doing that then and there.

As Carry poled us closer to a rickety metal strand on the far side of the arch, I tugged my suit's coif up over my grease-matted hair. It cinched tight.

The bigger *zuk* killed his boat's motor, and he poled us the rest of the way to the dock. Rope in hand, Looker leaped onto the dock and tied the boat in place. I clambered over after the child, less steady on my feet. My boots clanked on the metal decking, and I looked round. Not far beyond our little dock the water came rushing down the gentle incline of a spillway through an opening far above that might have been a hundred feet wide where the waters of the artificial lakes of First Dome drained below.

For a moment I stood there, looking to neither Looker nor Carry. I was remembering another waterway, another city.

Another life.

Tell me a story, would you? One last time.

Wet cement. Lichen. Rot. Refuse.

The smell was the same, the same as that awful culvert in Borosevo where Cat had died. For the moment I stood there, the stench drew a bright, straight line from Padmurak to Emesh, and I was a boy again, and Cat was dying in my arms.

"Hadrian-man!" Carry's voice intruded, and looking round I saw him pointing along the narrow path that chased the wall of that vast culvert to the base of the spillway. "There is a door. The stairs will take a man to the city."

"Thank you!" I replied in Galstani, certain then the man knew that much at least.

The big fellow raised a hand. "Peace be with you."

Those words were English, and were certainly words he'd learned from Magda, or from her priest. I had not stopped to consider the man and his half-homunculus child were members of the doctor's ancient faith.

I suppose they must have been.

Not knowing what to say—knowing there was little peace on my road—I only echoed him, saying, "Peace be with *you*."

Then, alone again, I turned away and made my way back to the world above.

My own story was not yet done.

CHAPTER 19

THE TURN OF THE SCREW

GRAY DARKNESS LAY ON the Great City, and the sky beyond the arcology dome was thick with cloud. Compared to a Norman or an Imperial City, it was remarkable how dark that darkness was. Few lights shone in windows, and fewer on street corners. Here and there a ground-car trundled past, or one of the military police vans. I took to the shadows, never stopping, never standing still. I felt certain it would be only a matter of time before city security noticed me, and I felt more certain still the *zuks* and *pistrasnuks* alike were the subjects of a curfew whose threshold was long past.

Carry's stair had brought me to a kind of park on the edge of the dome. I hurried along the edge of the reservoir lake beneath the shadows of block monuments carved with relief images of the People at their work, farmers with hand scythes and builders with mallets, factory workers with wrenches and welding masks. The mouth of the spillway yawned behind, a literal gate to the underworld, to the old world whence the Commonwealth had sprung.

Two times patrolmen saw me. I lost the first one leaping down a stair between two hive buildings, and the second by hiding myself among bags of refuse that lay in a back alley awaiting the street sweepers. There I hunkered a long time, not wishing to kill the man who'd seen me. I knew I needed to move toward the palace ziggurat in the center of the dome where the greatest towers stood. But in the dark and at that distance I could not recognize the Sollan embassy.

It was going to be harder than I thought. I could not risk the use of my suit's comms. Someone was bound to intercept and overhear, and to back-trace my signal to its origin. To me.

Hiding among the trash, I remembered another night in Borosevo. I remembered rain, and Cat calling out to me from the rooftop. Memories so remote, so ancient they felt almost to have happened to someone else, as though my own history were the life of some character on a page. At length I hurried on, jogging through the dark. My helmet sealed once more, my suit forced air into my lungs. I half-crouched as I moved from the shadow of one pillar to the next, one hand ever on the catch to activate my shield.

An unmarked car slowed on the road beyond the colonnade, and two men got out. They weren't revolutionaries in red and white, but Conclave Guardsmen in matte black, armored and faceless.

They were hunting me, I knew. City security had got its bead on me at last. The cameras were everywhere. It was possible they did not know it was Hadrian Marlowe they hunted, possible they thought me some true insurgent in breach of curfew on some seditious errand.

Possible, but not likely.

Fear is a poison, I told myself, tamping down my quickening heart.

Adrenaline. Cortisol. All the toxins of fear and stress. Perhaps they could not see me, veiled as I was in the shadow of the square columns.

A shot flared, disruptor fire fizzling against the stone at my left ear.

Too much to hope for.

I thumbed my shield catch and ran. Shouts in Lothrian chased me, echoing down the colonnade, and shots crackled against the stone as the guardsmen pursued.

The streets ahead stood empty as I burst from the end of the colonnade, though barriers high as a man divided the two sides of the highway from each other. I skidded to a halt in the end of the colonnade, scanning frantically to either side, spied a step bridge at my right that crossed the highway and led deeper toward the heart of the central district. Booted feet pounded up the walkway behind me, and I took the stairs two and three at a time, stumbling in my exhaustion and ill-fed state. Making the top of the bridge, I slumped a moment against the rail, and looking back saw the black shapes of three Conclave Guardsmen approaching from the other end.

Not truly having a plan, I tugged Olorin's sword free of its hasp and hurried across the narrow bridge, long shadow flapping on the empty highway below. The bridge comprised a single span of paved steel, without arch or pillar to support it. As I neared the far side, I kindled my Jaddian blade, highmatter throwing white-blue light in the lamplit gloom. The police had made the top of the bridge behind. A disruptor bolt caught on my shield and died. I raised the sword and slashed through the narrow span, carving through rail and paved top and the steel beams that supported it.

The Lothrian prefects yelled as the bridge bent and crashed to the highway below. I wasted no time. I leaped the stairs entire, fell thirty feet to the street on the far side of the highway. I unkindled my sword without flourish and padded on.

Dead ahead, the Palace rose like Bruegel's Tower, level upon level until it touched the glassed-in sky, its marble heights ghostly pale in the cloud-bound night. Water dripped from gutters and collected on the naked masonry of buildings. Litter papered the streets. Here was part of the district we offworlders were never meant to see. Unlighted signs promised coffee and liquor rations. Above another somber door was writ the word *Loth-tarsemya*, Right-Birth. A board beside the door promised obstetrics, state prostitutes—women and *new men*—and disposal.

I did not linger to dwell on these questions. Ahead the buildings grew taller, square towers windowless or with flat slits no more than a handspan wide. A broad avenue arced round to either side, encircling the palace. The embassies were all on such a circular avenue, though I had no way of knowing if it were this street or any other. How I wished then that I might run my vision forward, following some other Hadrian from my place to the proper door. When I had stood upon the Quiet's mountain, I had seen all of time, every moment possible and actual. Standing there, I must have seen the way I had to go through that gray city, but I had only memories left—broken and insufficient—and though various storefronts or street corners felt familiar, I did not know the way.

I was not on the Quiet's mountain. I was in Vedatharad . . . and the clear path was lost. What visions of the future remained to me were buried in unconscious memory, fragments burned there by amygdala and prelimbic cortex—as my vision of the battle on the bridge had been—by memory of expected crisis.

I turned left, tore across the beltway at an angle. Before I'd gone a hundred yards I heard a siren wail in the distance, and the streetlamps flared brighter, shading from orange to vivid white. They were meant to blind me, but my suit's entoptics cut the glare. Nowhere to run. Nowhere to hide. Every shadow was banished by that blinding light, as though I stood upon the margin of an atomic's blast radius.

They'd found me.

Which meant one thing: I'd nothing to lose. "Marlowe to embassy, Marlowe to embassy. Valka, Argyris—anyone!" I kept running, fingers fumbling with the controls on my suit's wrist-terminal. It was possible the Lothrians were jamming all signals, but I felt certain that so near the embassy, inside the same dome, I had to get through. "Marlowe to embassy. I am on Avenue . . ." I spied a passing sign, "J! Avenue J and 138th Street, moving clockwise. Pursued by the Conclave Guard. Is anybody there?"

The wail of the siren came closer. I kept running, waiting, straining for a friendly word on the comm. *They're all dead,* a little voice whispered. Ahead, two of the prefect vans swerved into sight.

"Lord Marlowe?" a clipped tone sounded in my ear, the Legionary polish clear in his voice. "Turn right next chance you get, we're at Avenue H and 137th. You're close."

"Close!" I almost laughed, and seizing the next lamppost used it to sling-shot myself around a corner. I heard the grind of the police vans' spherical wheels as they yawed round, overshooting my street. The empty fronts of what looked like cafes yawned at my side. Here, I imagined, were false shops and eateries propped up for foreign visitors, more fresh paint tossed over decay. But the buildings all were empty.

I reached Avenue I as one of the riot vans skidded to a halt before me and a half dozen Guards spilled out, grasping disruptor wands in armored fists.

I didn't stop, only changed angles to run round behind the van. One of the lawmen moved to block my path. I leaped, pointed my knee to slam him in the chin. He toppled back, and I tumbled into a messy roll and regained my feet before the other Guards could close. The other vans barreled after me, sirens screaming in the night.

I wasn't going to make it.

Images of being rammed from behind by the Guard's van played in me, and I hurled my shoulder at the nearest door. The plate glass cracked, shattered on the third attempt, and I fell over the threshold into an empty cafe. Scrabbling to my feet, I staggered round the bar and into an empty kitchen. White floor, white walls, steel counters and benches. There had to be a back door.

There!

Shouting and the sound of feet filled the room behind, but I burst out through the door and turned left along the back alley toward Avenue H. Strange to see a back alley in such a city so clean, but there would be no trash, as there had been no people. Magda's and Carry's words about how many had vanished into the camps or into starships bound offworld played in my head, and I steadied myself against the wall of the far building as I limped on. I had only to turn right on the avenue and hurry back coun-terclockwise several blocks.

"Valka!" I rasped. "Is Valka . . . ?"

"I've sent a man to fetch her, lord," the embassy man said over the comm. "Lord Damon's on his way down to the lobby. You have to run."

"Thank you, soldier," I said, unable to keep the razor's edge from my tone. The man went quiet.

I turned right. A solitary light shone at street level six blocks away along the bend of the avenue. I broke into a dead run. Not far! There were ar-mored soldiers in the white and red of Sollan legionnaires in the door. I did not stop or turn back.

"Here!" I shouted, voice amplified by my suit's chest speakers. "Here! Here!"

The men hurried forward, their lances tucked and ready as they moved to meet me. I thought I heard the sound of feet on the sidewalk behind, fancied I heard the squeal of wheels as the Guard's vans swerved onto the avenue. I clapped one of our men on the shoulder as I hurried by, and I stumbled climbing the short stair to the doors of the Sollan embassy so that I fell across the threshold, chest heaving, burning from the effort. Rolling over, I looked back out through the open doors.

There was no one on the street behind save our door guards. The vans were nowhere to be seen, nor any man of the Conclave Guard. Avenue H stood empty, as if there'd been no pursuit at all.

"My Lord!" came the unctuous tones of the consul, Argyris, his words an address and an imprecation both. "What in Earth's Holy Name is going on?"

"Ask the Conclave!" I gasped, finding my knees again. "We were at-tacked returning from the ice mines."

Argyris put his hands in the pockets of his velvet robe. "We know. Your man Pallino told us all."

"Pallino's alive?" I asked, "and Crim? And the others?"

"Six dead in your guard, but the two officers are here. More came from your ship when you went missing. We've been trying to coordinate with the Conclave Guard to search the city, but they've been stonewalling us."

"They would," I said, triggering my helmet to unseal. "They're behind it." I peeled my coif back from my hair and glowered up at the man, ragged in my fury.

Argyris stuttered. "Lord Marlowe! That is . . . that is a dangerous ac-cusation."

"You're damn right it is, Argyris. Now be silent!" I bellowed, and such was the force of my voice and my conviction that the hairy giant of a man stepped back as if I'd struck him. Even gasping on the tile, my reputation could freeze the blood. In much quieter tones—a trick I'd learned from my lord father—I said, "I know what this means. But I know I'm right. They were trained men on the bridge."

The consul waved this away. "The liberalists."

"There are no liberalists!" I sneered. "You know that as well as any on this planet, and don't play the fool!"

"Hadrian!"

I looked up at the familiar voice in time to see a black streak speed across the checkerboard floor. Valka went to her knees beside me, arms about my neck. I embraced her in return. "You're alive!" she said, and kissed me full on the mouth. "We thought . . ."

"I know." She did not have to say it. I returned her kiss, more gently, on the cheek. Squeezing her hand, I said again, "I know."

Looking over her shoulder, I saw more figures standing in the arch that led to the lift lobby. Pallino stood there in Red Company fatigues, looking tired and more like the old myrmidon I'd met on Emesh than the patrician soldier he'd become. Crim stood beside him in matching undress reds, his black boots half-fastened. The swordsman had evidently just woken up. Between them in red and black, her tunic jacket over one shoulder, her floating yellow hair its customary cloud above her chiseled face, was Captain Corvo.

"Brought in the cavalry, I see," I said to the room at large.

Valka nodded and sat back on her heels. "When you . . . when we thought . . . I called Otavia down. We've been trying to work with the Lothrians to find you, but like Argyris said, they wouldn't let us out to search."

I chewed on my tongue a moment, deciding how best to carry matters forward. I realized I'd bent so much of my efforts on returning to my people that I'd left little thought for what I'd do if I made it there. I had no proof the Conclave was behind my attack. Except . . .

"The Guard followed me all across town. Shot at me . . ." It was all I could do to find my feet then. Valka helped me rise. "And they drew back before I got in sight of the embassy." It was evidence of a kind, if not a kind satisfying to men like Damon Argyris. Yet it was a tacit admission of guilt. If the Guard had thought they were pursuing an ordinary breach of curfew, they would have pursued me to the gates of the embassy. And would they have sent such force? Would an ordinary jaywalker or young lover out for a tryst merit so many men? "They knew it was me they were chasing."

"You can't be serious!" Argyris said, taking a few steps nearer. "What earthly reason could they have for such a thing? Attacking an Imperial apostol . . . it's an act of war!"

I fixed Argyris with my flintiest glare. I'd had time to ruminate on this and more on my boat ride through the waterways beneath Vedatharad, and I'd reached no true answer, only more troubling questions. "War . . ." I said, patting Valka on the arm to extricate myself from her embrace. "If they wanted war, Lord Consul, they'd simply firebomb this building and send a fleet across the Rasan Belt." I turned away. "They may still do that."

"There'd be no cause for this ruse with the terrorists if their object was war," said Otavia Corvo, pushing into the lobby. "Why bother?"

I shook my head. "I was meant to disappear. This is about me."

Valka and the others were silent. Argyris held my attention with wide eyes, as if waiting for me to say more. When I only stood there, letting the silence stretch, the consul—ever the sort of man uncomfortable with quietude—cleared his throat. "About you? What possible reason could the Grand Conclave have for kidnapping you?"

"Perhaps they've heard the stories about me," I said, thinking of the footage of my miracle at Berenike. "Perhaps they believe they are true."

I felt certain that recording had found its way across the light-years to Padmurak. In the Empire, it was said that Lothrian scientists were ever prying into the secrets of the human mind, chasing sensory mechanisms whereby the ancient dreams of telepathy and psychokinesis might be realized. The scholiasts were quick to deride their efforts as pseudoscience, but all the same, it was no stretch to imagine the Lothrian *Navkaburo*, their science ministry, might be all too happy to dissect my body and brain in an effort to learn my secrets. Had not the Emperor himself told me—after Thermon—that much of his reason for sending me to Nessus in semi-exile was to prevent me meeting a similar fate under the knives of the Chantry's Choir and its cathars? For a moment, I wondered if the Chantry itself might be behind this latest attempt as well. It was said they had some influence even in the Commonwealth—though how that might be I could only guess. Perhaps they traded secrets with the Conclave, acting in their role as scientists and researchers, not as priests and judges.

Or perhaps I'd become paranoid in my old age—if it was paranoia to suspect the hand of an institution that had conspired to kill me on no fewer than four occasions of abetting a fifth.

But no, suspecting the Chantry's hand in this so far from Earth and Forum did not pass Occam's Razor. I recalled Ninth Chair's question from our first meeting with the Grand Conclave. *Why does the Sollan Emperor send this man?* he'd asked, his voice given the unanimous consent of the Chairs. *Why does the Red Emperor send a warrior to Padmurak?* How could I have been so blind?

Damon Argyris dabbed at sweat beading on his forehead with a silk kerchief produced from one sleeve. "What are we to do?"

"My mission is a failure," I said simply, turning my gaze on Otavia. "We will make sail for Nessus immediately."

"You mustn't!" the consul exclaimed.

I only glared at him. "I will telegraph the Emperor myself. The Commonwealth will not help us. They are not to be trusted. Pallino!" I turned my attention to my old companion, who stood straighter, his training taking over. "Have your men pack our effects. We return to the *Tamerlane* at once."

"At once!" Argyris said, taking a step nearer. "My lord, it is the middle of the night! At least wait 'til morning!"

"*My lord,*" I said, repeating the style not out of politeness, but with an edge to emphasize our difference in rank, "I will not wait on this world a moment longer than necessary. You would be wise to do the same."

Argyris threw out a hand to stall Pallino's departure. Ever obedient, the old soldier lingered in the marble arch that led back to the lifts. "But this is madness! We must speak with the Conclave. Surely there is some explanation for all this."

"Go, Pallino," I said, overriding the consul's objections. The one-time myrmidon saluted and vanished through the arch to the lifts. Turning to Otavia, I said, "How many men did you bring with you?"

She did not hesitate. "Twenty."

"The remnant of my guard makes thirty-four, plus Crim and Pallino. Then you, Valka, myself . . . where's Tor Varro?"

"Returned to the *Tamerlane*," Corvo answered. "With two guards."

I did the arithmetic. "Lord Consul, you will arrange vehicles for thirty-seven. Now."

"But my lord! This is *so* irregular. It's the middle of the night! You've only just returned! You're still rattled from your experience on the bridge. Shell shock . . ."

"*Shell shock?*" I repeated, and might have spit acid on the tile there and then. "Shell shock? Hear this now: you will find me those transports,

Argyris, and you will find them now." I stopped just short of threatening the man; Argyris was already shaking and sweating furiously. Had I put so great a terror on the man?

The Lord Consul began nodding, but changed to start shaking his head as he started to speak. "But my lord . . . we have no vehicles. The Commonwealth does not permit offworlders free travel within the city! You know this!"

Rage is blindness, I told myself, and checked my breathing. "You mean to tell me . . . that you've no vehicles? No groundcars. No fliers. No chariots *at all?*"

"Commonwealth law does not permit it!" he said. "I told you! No one travels in Vedatharad without an escort."

I had to shut my eyes, hooked my thumbs through my shield–belt. "Then it seems you get your wish after all, Lord Consul. Contact the Lothrians. Tell them we need transport." I drummed my fingers against the belt and the hasp that held my sword in place. I did not hear feet. "Now!"

From the shuffle of slippers on tile, I knew Lord Damon Argyris had gone.

"You're sure it was the Lothrians behind the attack?" Valka asked.

In answer, I gestured Crim close and said, "I want your men ready. We may have to seize their vehicles."

"If they don't attack us first," the assassin replied.

"Siege the embassy?" I said. "How many men are on station here?"

"In the embassy?" Crim frowned. "Five hundred legionnaires on staff, another fifty in Argyris's personal guard."

I felt myself shaking my head. "They'd not try anything so flagrant. Certainly not with the *Tamerlane* in high orbit." Though saying that aloud, I felt certain the Lothrian home fleet would be more than sufficient to overmatch one Imperial battleship, even one so formidable as the *Tamerlane.*

Something of that thought was written in Captain Corvo's face.

Crim rummaged a moment in a pocket of his fatigues and handed me a slim, black phase disruptor, its firing slit dark and quiescent.

"What's this?" I asked.

"You lost your sidearm, boss." He cocked one canted brow and glanced at the empty gun holster on my right leg behind the sword hasp. I hadn't even noticed.

"Must have lost it in the fall." I took the offered weapon. "Don't you need it?"

Crim tapped the side of his nose. "Oh, I've spares." Before I could holster the weapon, the former mercenary proffered a dark red *something* wrapped in wax paper. It was one of his gel candies. "Cherry, boss," he whispered conspiratorially. "For your breath."

I'd of course not been in any condition to care for my teeth, not in several days. Suddenly self-conscious, I took the candy. "Argyris will be back before long," I said. "Crim, roust the men, and help Pallino get everything in order. I want the whole party ready to move in twenty minutes."

When he, too, was gone, I sank into a high-backed chair at the base of a fluted column.

"Are you all right?" Valka stood over me. She was dressed plainly: loose trousers and an old pullover shirt blazoned with the marks of some Tavrosi musical act in faded phosphorescent color. She'd not been sleeping.

"You should get ready to move," I said, and spread the injunction over her and Corvo alike. "You'll need your suits if we're to make the shuttles."

"I'll go," Corvo said, laying a hand on Valka's shoulder for a moment.

Valka gripped it with a strained smile. "Thank you, Tavi." The captain vanished after Crim and Pallino. Alone a moment, Valka said, "I thought I'd lost you this time."

Reaching up, I tugged on the chain that held Valka's phylactery about her neck, the one that contained a sample of my own crystallized blood. "Never."

Pallino returned first with our luggage and five of our men. No longer alone, Valka returned up the lift to ready herself. More of the soldiers reported in, with Crim and Corvo bringing up the rear. "Typical civil service," Pallino grumbled, "always bringing up the rear. Figures we'd have the whole unit ready to roll before the consul flounced back down here."

"It won't be long," I said.

"You're sure it were the Conclave on that bridge?" Pallino asked.

Rather than answer him, I said, "Something's not right here. Can't you feel it?"

"There's a lot not right here," the old myrmidon replied.

With a sigh that betrayed every one of my three hundred and forty years, I found my feet. "Where is Argyris? He's been gone long enough."

We hadn't long to wait for the answer to that question. The consul emerged from the lifts still sweating and puffing like a man three times his weight, a trio of aides in tow. He seemed surprised to find my people together and outfitted for the journey so quickly, but took it in stride, pausing only to dab at his beaded forehead. "The Lothrians are sending a convoy. They'll be at the back gate in twenty minutes."

I checked the time. It was nearing the fifth hour past midnight. The sun would be rising before long.

"The back gate?" I asked.

"City curfew ends in about ten minutes. Traffic is about to pick up. They don't want us blocking the road while we load up so many." Damon Argyris cast his eye over the assembled Red Company legionnaires.

Otavia Corvo spoke up. "We'd best get down there, then."

Crim and Pallino took charge of organizing our retreat through the lobby of the embassy, past the reception desk—empty at that hour—and the blast doors to the guard station behind. The men were grumbling and making jokes the while, carting the luggage or shouldering packs of their own.

"Ain't nothing to see on this rock, Otho!" said one.

"Would have liked some fresh air is all," said Otho.

The first answered him, "Ain't you heard? No fresh air, neither. That's recycled Lothrian wind you're huffing."

"Shut up, Galba! Not in front of his lordship and the lady."

Valka hid a smile behind her hand.

"Can it! The lot of you!" Pallino barked when we'd descended an escalator and passed through the broad main hall of the conference center. We'd arrived at the embassy following our first visit to the People's Palace and the Conclave's arena by the same route. Ahead stood a series of glass doors that opened on an underground carport accessed by a winding ramp that allowed vehicles on and off the avenue above. Past the last conference rooms to either side, the hall split left and right and ran the length of the great building, leading to lavatories and side stairs that fed back to the lobby above and to the higher floors.

"I've radioed your shuttle pilots and alerted them," Argyris was saying, shuffling along just ahead of me in his slippers. "They'll be ready for you when you arrive." He paused a moment, turned back, nearly causing me to slam into him. "Are you sure I can't persuade you to stay, Lord Marlowe? You've hardly been here a month. Progress is slow on Padmurak. I'm sure the Chairs can be brought round."

I did not stop, but brushed past the consul toward the glass doors. "I will not stay on Padmurak a minute longer than I need," I said. The Conclave had tried to capture me—had tried to kill my men. I hoped by hurrying to leave quickly, I could clear the City before my enemies had time to act. I was being reactionary, I knew that, but whoever had ordered the attack on the bridge and my arrest as I crossed Vedatharad that night had not counted on me reaching the embassy. They would be reacting, too.

"But there must be some explanation for all this!" Argyris exclaimed. "My lord, I have lived here for decades!"

At the head of the column then, I was nearly to the door, Valka and Corvo at my sides, Pallino just behind. I rushed past the last set of conference room doors and reached the carport lobby. That was when I heard it.

The unmistakable whine of stunners being primed.

I felt iron fingers tighten about my heart and squeeze adrenaline into my system. Thus heightened, I looked to either side in disbelief. Thirty Sollan legionnaires stood in either branch of the hall, disruptors set to stun. They were fully shielded.

Knowing I was trapped in the crossfire, and worse, knowing Valka was, too, I did the only thing I could.

I raised my hands.

"I am sorry," said Lord Damon Argyris, Imperial Consul on Padmurak. "I have my own people to think of. They said if I didn't turn you over, they'd torch the building."

Without turning, I said, "They're still going to torch the building, Argyris, you damn fool."

"They won't," Argyris said. "Tell your men to put their guns down."

Very slowly, I rotated on the spot, found the bulk of my men armed and shielded and drawn into defensive triases in the hall behind. Not in the direct line of fire as I was, they'd had more time to react. But even as I turned I saw more legionnaires in embassy livery hurrying down the hall from the front lobby. We were well and truly surrounded.

"You're dead, traitor," I said to the consul. "The Emperor will not stand for this."

"The Emperor need never know," Argyris said, strangely less nervous now his deception was in the open air. "I will write Forum and say that you were killed in a terrorist attack. Nasty bunch, those liberalists."

Through the doors behind, I heard the rumble of groundcars, knew the sound well enough by then to know it was not the quiet purr of diplomatic vehicles. It was the heavy grind of Lothrian armored vans.

"They're early," Argyris said, almost brightly. He clapped his hands once and advanced for the doors.

"What did they offer you, Argyris?" I asked, turning to follow the sybarite's path, dropping my hands. "All this for your harem? Your slaves? Your comfortable little life?"

Argyris spread his hands. "Not *so* little. I told you, I've lived here for decades."

I understood. This was no spur-of-the-moment betrayal, no mad scramble of the desperate civil servant to safeguard his position and his life. "How long since they bought you?" I asked, looking round at the consul's men. "Do they know? What did you tell them?"

"Don't talk about things you don't understand, my dear lord," he said, but gave neither answer nor excuse. Beyond the glass doors, Conclave Guardsmen came pouring out. There must have been a hundred of them—at least so many as there were soldiers in Argyris's retinue. "You are a dangerous man, Lord Marlowe. Is it true you wish to seize the throne for yourself?"

So that was it, that was how Argyris had convinced his men to turn on the Emperor's own apostol. He'd convinced them I was the traitor, not himself.

Always accuse the enemy of what you're doing.

I snarled, and moving with palatine agility faster than the consul's plebeian guards could track, I drew Crim's pistol and fired. The disruptor crackled, its red bolt striking Argyris full in the face. The energy burned his nerves to carbon, tore skin and scorched it. The treasonous consul fell dead without ceremony or another word.

"Drop your weapon! Drop your weapon *now!*" a dozen of the embassy guards cried at once.

Sure that the stunner bolts would start flying at any moment, I did just that, and placed my hands on my head as a knot of the soldiers hurried forward to secure me. Near enough to the traitor's corpse, I spat on it.

CHAPTER 20

THE AMAZON

THEY FORCED ME TO my knees. One soldier stripped me of my sword while another stood with the slit of his stunner pressed to the back of my head. Beside me, Valka was similarly relieved of her plasma repeater and made to kneel. Corvo sank to both knees without protest, hands on the back of her head.

"I thought this mission was taking us *away* from the combat, Marlowe," she said dryly.

"So did I." I could not imagine what the Lothrian government would want with me, but I felt certain it was me they wanted. I supposed they could have sent my corpse and footage of my execution back with a declaration of war, but like I'd told Argyris—realizing it all too late—if war had been their aim they'd have done as well to torch the embassy, and there'd have been no cause to go to all this trouble apprehending me.

"Order your men to stand down," the man at my back said, and jostled me with his weapon. Through the doors ahead, I watched the Lothrians square up, standing at attention while their Imperial puppets attended to their prisoners. "I said order your men to stand down."

Not turning my head, I said, "You're making a mistake, soldier."

"You killed the consul!" the man barked. "Traitor!"

"Traitor? Your consul betrayed the Empire. What I did was justice." While I spoke, I stared at the disruptor-scarred corpse that had been Damon Argyris moments before. I was too angry to regret my actions. I spoke fast, all the while fearing a blow or a stunner blast. "You're the one about to turn a Royal Victorian knight over to the Commonwealth. Look in a mirror, you damn fool!"

That seemed to catch the fellow's tongue a moment, and in his hesitation, I saw a glimmer of hope. Ahead, the glass doors slid silently open, admitting the damp of early morning. A man entered flanked by two of the Conclave Guard. He wore the formal gray and red of the Lothrian military: high black boots, gray tunic and trousers with red piping and cords, and a long gray coat that trailed almost to the floor. He wore a ceramic helm in lieu of a hat, its brow painted with the Lothrian black star. Without having to be told, I knew the man was a Party Commissar, as like to our knights as anything in the Commonwealth.

He surveyed us coolly with those familiar black Lothrian eyes.

"The enemies of the People will be brought low by unity and resolve," he pronounced in his native tongue.

By charade and subversion, more like, I thought.

"On behalf of the Conclave, the delegation from the Sollan Empire is under arrest." He peered down at me, lifted my chin with one hand. Here, I guessed, was the man who had commanded the attempt to catch me that very night. He glanced down at the body of Damon Argyris. *"Koya tranya,"* he said. *What a waste.* The Lothrians had called off their pursuit as I drew too near the embassy, doubtless to maintain an air of deniability regarding my account, but when Argyris had called and made his offer—my head for his continued comfort, I could only assume—he had removed the need for such deniability.

And I had removed Argyris.

The Commissar barked an order to his own men to disarm mine and take us into custody. The Conclave Guardsmen advanced toward Valka and Corvo and myself while the embassy guards still tried to disarm our column.

"Take the delegate and the delegate's companions to the car," the Commissar said. "The Chair will want to speak with the delegate at once." Guards moved forward with manacles for me and the two women.

In Galstani—hoping the Commissar would not understand—I addressed the legionnaire with the stunner to my head. "He's going to have you all killed," I said. The man's stunner dug into the back of my neck, but he did not fire. "The only way you have off this planet is with me."

Lothrian soldiers forced Captain Corvo to stand. Two patted her down, duplicating the efforts of the legionnaires who had disarmed her already. They moved to shackle her even as I was dragged to my feet.

Otavia Corvo was having none of it. Since she joined on Pharos, Corvo had been a bridge officer, captain of the *Mistral* when Bassander had run the Red Company, and captain of the *Tamerlane* after my ascension to knighthood. I had not seen her in a fight since the Pharos affair. The giantess slammed her forehead down into the Lothrian's face with enough force to stagger him even through his helmet. I heard the fellow swear even as Corvo gripped his head in both hands and smashed her knee up into the officer's face with enough force to crack the tempered glass. The man hit the ground before any of the others had the sense to train stunners on the captain.

But Corvo was only getting started. Whirling, she seized a second Lothrian by the throat and lifted him bodily into the air, hurled him squeaking across the tile floor. A stunner bolt struck her—fired by the Lothrian or legionnaire I couldn't say—but Otavia did not stop. She struck another of the Lothrians with a precise elbow to the face. He went sprawling, his disruptor rifle skittering away. The Commissar reached for his own sidearm, but Corvo snapped a kick that caught the fellow's hand as he raised it to fire on her. A second stunner bolt caught her between the shoulder blades, but Corvo only snarled. Turning, she keyed the switch to activate her shield.

I did the same.

I had long suspected that Otavia Corvo was not truly human, that somewhere in her family's Norman past someone had bedded a homunculus, some giant bred for labor or for sport. Here was the proof. No ordinary human could take direct fire from a stunner like that at such close range. I had weathered glancing blows in my time, but not even a palatine could withstand such a shot. The myelin insulating Corvo's nerve cells must have been truly something.

"Shields up!" I shouted to Valka and to all who'd hear me, and I snatched up the disruptor I'd used to kill the consul. Spinning, I rounded on the man who'd taken my sword. "Give it to me!" I said, pointing the weapon. "I don't want to hurt you."

The soldier hesitated, head tracking between me and the Lothrian Commissar locked in a hand-to-hand contest with my amazon of a captain. "I do not have time to argue, soldier. Give me my sword." When still the fellow did not move, I shouted, "They are going to kill all of you if you do not stand with me. Now!" I holstered Crim's sidearm, extended an empty hand.

About us, chaos was circling in wider and wider spirals. Confusion tugged at the embassy guards as they were torn between their consul's final orders and the obvious reality. Between the Empire and the Commonwealth.

"Strel! Strel!" the Commissar exclaimed, staggering back from Otavia's onslaught.

In so doing, he made up the legionnaires' minds for them.

Shoot!

The Conclave Guard trained weapons on the shielded legionnaires and fired. My captor and I stood for a nanosecond in the eye of a terrible storm beneath his cloud of indecision.

It broke.

He handed me my sword. Turning, I keyed the command that closed my helmet up over my face and kindled the highmatter blade.

"Pallino, Crim!" I shouted over the general line. "To the vans! They're our only way out of here."

A Lothrian soldier ran at me and fell dead with a knife in his throat. "Aye, boss," came Crim's reassuring tone, and glancing briefly back I saw the Norman standing fast by Pallino and a knot of our men. He'd drawn his sword.

Ahead, Corvo lifted the Commissar by the lapels of his long coat and tackled him to the ground. Her fists fell like hammer blows, and when she stood again, breast heaving, it was with blood on her hands.

"Captain!" I tossed her Crim's disruptor. Sword in hand, I did not need it. Corvo caught the weapon and offered me a short salute.

"Forward, you dogs!" Pallino shouted, voice lifted above the din.

Side by side, Corvo and I pressed for the door. The Norman giant tugged her suit's coif up over her hair as she went, ducking as shots streaked over her head. The Lothrians pushed forward, shattering the glass with handheld rams. One of the Conclave Guard rushed forward, eager to get inside my shield curtain, his rifle raised. Perhaps he had never seen high-matter before. I raised my sword. He fell.

"For Earth and Empire!" I cried out, seeking to stoke the same flames of patriotism Argyris had abused. "For the Emperor!"

But the Lothrians had made the embassy guards' choice for them. They fired without discrimination, without care, and where before there had been two Imperial companies at one another's throats, there was but one.

"To the right!" Crim said, slicing through the neck of a man who'd come too close. "Front of their convoy!"

"Valka, stay with me!" I reached out a hand for her, afraid the stress might trigger another of Urbaine's seizures. She swatted my hand aside and shot a Lothrian peltast in the chest. She'd recovered her old Tavrosi service repeater, and the weapon chimed as it fired three plasma rounds into the man's unshielded chest. Many of the Lothrians wore no ceramic, but ballistic jackets over anti-disruptor skins. Unshielded as most of them were— a cost-saving measure, I guessed—they were almost defenseless against plasma fire.

Teeth clenched, Valka shot another. "I'm fine!" she gasped, following after me.

"Watch those stunners!"

"Down! Down!"

Shouts in standard and in Lothrian filled the hall and the echoing carport beyond. Corvo, Valka, and I made it through the doors, shattered glass crunching beneath our heels. I took the arm of a Lothrian officer who came too near, stabbed another through the heart as he moved to tackle Valka.

The Lothrians had come in more than a dozen of the blocky, armored vans that had pursued me through the streets. Each was painted matte black and was large enough to field ten men, two in front and eight on benches. Their rear doors all stood open, and a line of soldiers with ceramic tower shields held the ground between.

"I'll take them," I said. Imposing as those shields were, they were no match for highmatter. All around, the Lothrian police were firing gas cannisters, and the air was filled with smoke where plasma had set the building afire.

Corvo grunted and stuck fast by my side. As we closed on the Lothrian line, she ducked her shoulder and struck one of the shield-bearers with such force the man *flew* ten feet and slammed into the nearest van, knocking the wind from him. My highmatter blade sheared through the nearest riot shield and the man behind it. Shock and terror welled in the men about, faceless though they were. They staggered back, realizing their heavy medieval shields were useless before Corvo and myself. One man dropped his and fired on me, disruptor bolts crackling in the air between us.

A shot caught him in the side, and looking back I saw Pallino with a knot of our Red Company men pushing out into the carport. "We need to radio the shuttles!" he said. "Tell them to be on their guard!"

"We can't get a signal out of this dome! We *need* to evacuate the embassy!" I countered. "All these men are dead! Argyris may as well have shot them himself."

"No time!" Pallino replied. "My job's to get you to safety, Had!" The old soldier drew up beside me, and jerking his head in the direction of the foremost van, said, "We have to go."

I lingered, torn as my captor had been between hard choices. "I don't know the way to the shuttle port! Do you?"

"I do!" Valka said, and tapped her forehead. "'Tis all here."

"Where's Crim?" I asked.

As if in answer, a knife felled another of the Conclave Guard not twenty feet away, and looking back I saw a huge wave of Imperial soldiery force its way out of the embassy basement. The last line of Lothrian resistance started to break and run for their vans. A hail of plasma and disruptor fire chased them across the carport.

Corvo seized me by the shoulder. "We have to go! Into the first car, now!" No *sir*, no *my lord*. All business. I unkindled my blade and followed, taking Valka by the wrist. Corvo leaped into the open rear doors of the police van and shouldered her way into the front compartment. I heard a muffled cry and the faint cough of disruptor discharge. Then the body of the driver was booted without ceremony through the hatch to the pavement.

Corvo's coifed head re-emerged from the front compartment as I leaped into the rear of the van. "I'll drive."

"I'll help!" Valka answered, and squirmed through to take the passenger seat beside the captain. I turned to give Pallino a hand up as Crim piled in beside with half a dozen men in tow. "I'll try to raise the ship and the shuttles once we clear the dome. The tunnels may be insulated, but 'tis worth a try."

"Very good!" I said, and lingered a moment at the hatch. Our men were fighting their way aboard several other of the vans, but just as many were in Lothrian hands, and no help was coming for the rest of the embassy. "They're going to die."

"We have to go, boss!" Crim said, reaching out to close the door. "We have to go now!"

I raised a hand to stop him slamming the door, but Pallino put a hand on my shoulder. "There's nothing we can do with a hundred men, lad."

I swore and turned away even as the van surged to life beneath us. "Up and right," came Valka's voice from the front, "then left onto the avenue."

Crim and Pallino slammed the doors on madness and dead men. I had to take hold of one of the straps hanging from the ceiling to steady myself as Corvo took us screaming round the ramp. The van yawed wildly, skewing on its spherical wheels, and slammed into the wall of the ramp as we cornered.

"We're fine!" Corvo insisted, taking us onto the street.

The rear compartment had no windows, though there were firing slits in the back doors: narrow horizontal hatches just wide enough for an officer to poke the muzzle of a rifle or phase disruptor through. I slid one of these back and watched a second police van lumber out of the ramp tunnel and onto Avenue H.

"Take this to 87th street and turn right!" Valka shouted. "That'll take us out to the edge of the ringed district, then left toward the bridge!" I pushed through the press of bodies to peer into the driver's compartment. Corvo sat to the right, both hands on the wheel, Valka half-crouched in the seat beside her, pointing out through the windscreen.

"The others won't know how to get out without us!" I said, meaning the other vans.

"Tell them it's a right on 87th until we hit the reservoir!" Valka shouted.

"On it!" Crim said.

Pallino put a hand on my shoulder and turned me. "What the hell is going on?"

I sagged against the bulkhead that separated the driver's compartment from the rear and removed my helmet. Shaking my head, I said, "The Lothrians want me. I can only imagine it's . . . something to do with . . . with what I can do."

"They know about all that?"

The other man put a hand on my shoulder, steadied me as the van swerved through traffic. I looked from Pallino to Crim to the half-dozen faceless soldiers watching through their helmets. "They asked why I was sent of all the Emperor's men. They must know something, or suspect."

"They might just want to hold you hostage," Crim put in. "Keep you on the table for some counter-offer. Keep negotiating."

"Maybe," I said, bracing myself against the wall as the van shook. "I think their ambitions run deeper than that." I held Pallino's gaze a long moment. The myrmidon had been one of a precious few who had seen me die. Valka and Bassander Lin had been present by that lakeside on Kharn Sagara's ship when Prince Aranata Otiolo had cut off my head. "I think they know what I can do . . . and I think they want it for themselves."

I had no way knowing if the changes the Quiet had wrought in me were something a surgeon could glean from my bones, much less replicate. I had not been willing to submit to medical examination since the mountain on Annica precisely for fear they might discover something too tempting for the Empire or the Chantry to resist. If the Emperor had marginalized me for my own good, exiled me to Nessus, the Lothrians had no cause for similar forbearance.

"Well, we can't let them get you, then." Pallino clapped me on the shoulder.

Bang.

Something struck the van with enough force to hurl us men against the far side. Pallino pushed me off him, swearing as only Pallino could.

"The hell was that?" Crim asked, adjusting his bandoleer.

I pushed my way past the others and slid one of the firing slits open. I could only see directly behind us, but there was the crouching black shape of another police van closing in.

"What hit us?" Crim asked, coming up beside me.

Not the van. I strained to look sideways, caught sight of the rear of a smaller black vehicle keeping pace with ours. It must have rammed us from the side. "Trying to drive us off the road . . ." I muttered.

"What?" Crim asked, straining to see himself.

Before I could answer, a high-pitched whine filled the air outside, and despite the roof above our heads I felt the instinct to duck. Bright light—white and cold—shone through the open slit. I threw an arm across my face and squinted. I could just barely make out the pinpoint diodes of running lights as the small aircraft hove into pursuit. Men stood on flying platforms, hands gripping the control bar, feet bracketed into stirrups.

"Chariots!" I hissed.

The chariots kept spotlights trained on us as they opened fire. The armored van shook.

"We're not going to last long like this," I said. "Half the city's after us."

CHAPTER 21

HEROES END

"HOLD ON!" OTAVIA GROWLED, slamming on the brakes and slewing the van to the left along another of the great avenues that encircled the palace at the heart of the city.

"What are you doing?" Valka asked. "The waterfront was that way!"

"We're not going to last two minutes on the straightaway," the captain said, teeth audibly clenched.

Otavia's gamble paid off. The armored van pursuing us overshot our turn, and only one of the smaller cruisers managed it. The second collided head on with a civilian vehicle. The men on the chariots braked hard, repulsors flaring as they backpedaled and hurried after us.

"Move over!" Pallino said, thrusting the muzzle of his plasma burner through the slit and taking careful aim. He fired, and a shot of violet plasma streaked out, illuminating the still-dark street. For an instant, the nearest flying charioteer vanished in a nimbus of white and gold as the plasma cooled on impact, but the flier came on. "Earth's tits . . ." he swore, firing again. "Bastard's shielded."

The charioteers opened fire, peppering the hull. A stray shot passed through the open slit and blew apart against one of the legionnaire's shields. The man swore and ducked, covering his face.

"Wish we'd brought a lance," Pallino said dourly.

"Next right! Next right!" Valka exclaimed, voice going high.

Two of the men caught me as I turned to peer through the hatch to the front compartment and nearly fell. As I stood, I heard Corvo say, "That was close."

"What happened?" I thrust my head out between Corvo and Valka's seats.

"Hit someone!" came Valka's answer.

I had to brace myself in the hatchway as Corvo torqued us round the bend, feeling the ball-wheels grind underfoot as we rotated ninety degrees onto what I guessed was 85th Street. Except that traffic was rushing *toward* us.

"*Noyn jitat!*" I swore.

"Quiet!" Corvo said, voice dangerously calm.

Ahead of us, the mounting traffic of the early morning's commute panicked and parted to either side. Warning horns filled the air. Rather than argue, I reassured myself that our van's armor would be sufficient to weather any impact.

"Surely they won't fire . . ." Valka said, "they'd hit their own people!"

As if on cue, another hail of bullets fell from the chariots behind us.

Evidently, that *the good of all was the good of each* was a maxim that ran in only one direction. We hadn't far to go. I could see the steel fencing that marked the waterfront and the overlook to the great reservoir that made up the outer regions of First Dome. Ahead, the line of a monorail that connected the *vuli* blockhouses about the outer perimeter to the central district slashed across our street at an angle, and it was only another five blocks to the end.

Another hail of bullets peppered the rear of the van. A stray shot slammed against the inside of the windscreen, making Valka jump.

"Man down!" said one of the soldiers, and turning I saw another of the legionnaires had collapsed with a bullet in his throat, leaving a red streak down the inner wall. His suit had tightened automatically to stanch the bleeding, but it was too late.

"Baro?" said one of the others, crouching over his fellow. In the wounded man I recognized a soldier I'd fought with a dozen times. He'd done time as one of my personal guard on and off for decades.

I crouched beside him and took his hand. "Shield must have failed," said the other soldier, and I recognized the man, Galba. "Anyone got a beta canister? We can stop the bleeding."

But it was too late. The bullet had torn through his windpipe and out the far side—lodged in the far side of his suit's underlayment. He was beyond saving. I tried to calm myself, to find the quiet clarity that allowed me to see time unfolded. For a moment, I saw two Baros, four, eight, sixteen . . . but there was no river of time down which the fellow's life's blood was stanched. I quested farther, looking for something—anything—that might avail. I tried to reach out as I had in my concussed state and change the world entire, to find a Baro who had not been shot.

Each passing fraction of each passing second drove those lines of potential farther from the shores of the real. I glimpsed far off along the shoreline where reality broke like a wave, a point where the bullet had struck just an inch to the left and spared his breathing. I reached for it, but even as I did it slipped away, further and further as the wound set in. I was not the Quiet—only its hand. Small as I was, I could not save him. Like the Galath blossom that withered, Baro's life was gone.

"We need to do something about those damn chariots!"

Corvo's words brought me crashing back to the present—the single present.

Pallino was looking at me, brows drawn down.

"What?" I asked him.

He shook his head.

Another hail of bullets struck the van, and Crim slammed the firing slits shut—too late to save Baro. "If we open the doors, I might be able to get a knife in one," he said.

"No good!" I said, standing. "We'd be wide open." I cast about the rear compartment, looking for something, *anything* to avail us. There wasn't much: benches ran down either side, each with the space to seat five officers. A rack that once had held the Guardsmen's rifles stood behind the driver, but behind Valka's chair—above Baro's body—there were rungs. Rungs and a hatch in the roof.

A terrible idea formed in my mind, terrible but so mad it might work.

"Help me get this hatch open!" I said, nodding to it.

"What are you going to do?"

"I'm going to climb onto the roof and draw fire." I tapped my belt. "My shield's rated for three kilotons. I've got the charge. Should keep them off the van for a while."

Crim threw out a hand to stop me. "What are you going to do, boss? Wave your sword around?"

"Something like that," I said.

Valka poked her head around from the front. "Have you lost your mind?"

"I'm not letting anyone else die over this!" I said, did not say *over me.* Thrusting a finger at Baro's rapidly cooling corpse, I said, "All those men we left at the embassy are dead. Everyone is dead!"

"You don't know that," Valka said. The van shook.

Corvo swore again. "Almost there . . ." She meant the waterfront.

"If they're not dead they'll be shipped to labor camps. The Commonwealth can't leave any witnesses to this. They tried to make me disappear, but it didn't work. They've overplayed their hand. They're desperate. Let me do this." I did not wait for her to object, but leaned forward and kissed her. I paid no mind to the others for a fleeting instant, a single sterling second. For that narrow space of time, everything dropped away. The deaths, the Commonwealth, the Cielcin.

Everything.

I drew back and nodded out the windscreen. "Help Corvo drive. I'll be back." And then I turned and leaped over poor Baro's corpse and opened the hatch. The wind of our passage whipped at me and knocked my coif loose. Black hair streamed in the wind as I tugged myself up onto the broad, flat surface of the roof. Crouching like a boxer to steady myself, I stood tall and defiant as I was able.

I had not said *I love you*. That was the worst part.

A wave of bullets shattered against my body shield, sending fractal coruscations flickering in the gray air. All about us, the roofs of lesser vehicles—gray and white and tan—rushed by. I threw an arm across my face as another barrage flashed about me. Otavia struck a passing commuter and I lurched to one knee. For a moment, all was still, and looking up I saw the two charioteers draw back, contemplating their plan of attack. They knew I was shielded, knew their guns were useless. They'd have to adjust tactics. I had not drawn my sword. I did not want them taking into account the fact that I wanted them to come closer.

I felt sure they'd try.

Where had the other van gone? The rest of the Conclave Guard?

There was no time to ask such questions. One of the charioteers accelerated, swooping toward me. He meant to ram me, to knock me clean off the roof of the van and onto the street below. Precisely as I'd expected. Precisely as I'd hoped. I leaped as my enemy closed and wrapped my arms around him and the control column of his chariot. The impact was enough to knock the wind out of me, but I held on tighter. My feet dangled free, and I fought to overcome the sensation of falling.

My quarry was not so level-headed. The chariot depended on balance, relied on the placement of hands and feet to keep the craft stable and upright. As the charioteer flailed to disentangle himself from my clench, he released the yoke and the whole chariot tumbled down. I managed to land on top, the yoke and control column between us. Only then did I unsheathe Sir Olorin's blade, and moving quickly placed the emitter against the side of the charioteer's armored head. His visor had shattered in the fall. I remember his solitary black eye, shining at first, then dull.

The pedestrians about me screamed and drew back, and it was only then I realized they were there at all. *Pitrasnuks,* to judge by their suits and robes. They watched in horror at the murder in their midst and at the offworlder in his finery. I had confirmed in that moment so many of the fables the Party told of the Sollan Empire. I'd even stooped over the poor fellow like a vampire drinking blood.

I had no time for soliloquies. The other charioteer had not peeled off to catch me, and our van was speeding away at several miles an hour. I kicked the chariot free of its owner's body and got my feet in the stirrups. The repulsors whined as I leaped into the air in pursuit. At rest, a man could stand upright in a chariot, his feet in the stirrups, controlling direction by his lean. At full bore, I leaned forward as on a skiff or bicycle, hands pushing the yoke as far as it would go.

I'd not ridden one in eons, but the things were built to be intuitive. By pointing my toes I drove myself upward, and so came down on the other charioteer from below. The poor fellow never stood a chance. Wounded, he flew at a sharp angle and crashed into the face of the nearest tower. Ahead, Otavia had made the waterfront. I overshot on reaching the end of the street and wrestled a powerful sense of vertigo as I flew out over the reservoir a hundred feet below the level of the street. In the distance, I thought I saw the opening of the spillway by the perimeter of the dome, and beyond that the awful tundra and the wastes of Padmurak.

Above it all, I had a moment to contemplate the lay of things. Corvo had perhaps less than a mile of road between her and the entrance to the tunnel back toward Eleventh Dome and the starport. The bridge was near, the same lonely span of concrete that passed the mighty sluiceways that had run fat with water to impress us when we'd arrived. The water was barely a trickle then, a thin, sad stream like the spit of a long-neglected fountain.

It was not the bridge I'd fallen from, but it was as good as.

Looking back I could see all the way down the radial street to the high wall that surrounded the People's Palace, and I could see the Palace itself—a narrow slice of it, at least—surrounded by the high square towers of Vedatharad. I half-expected to see smoke from the burning embassy, but if the Lothrians meant to firebomb the block they'd not done so as yet. I never learned the fate of the men we left behind. I pray at least one made it to the warrens beneath the city. A man who could speak Galstani plainly might be precisely the kind of man Padmurak needed most.

A man who had a name.

I dove hard after the van, marking as I fell the trio of black cruisers in pursuit. To my astonishment, there were none ahead, nor any on the bridge as Otavia turned. I fired on the cruisers and broke their tight formation. They scrambled over the pavement, struggling to ascertain the source of their threat. I looped around, took aim at their tires. The smaller vehicles had ordinary wheels and not the huge spherical ones the vans relied on. I caught one, and the car flipped, rolling, bouncing like a cast-off shoe. One eye shut, I squinted through the reticle and fired again.

Click.

Empty.

Nothing for it. Spurring the machine forward, I dropped low until I was almost at road level, streaking just above the tops of the passing cars. Corvo had made the bridge, and was turning at last onto that straightaway and the approach to the steel arch and the gates that led to the highway and freedom. Only then did I understand why the Guard had not moved to cordon off our escape.

I had forgotten the gates.

And the gates were closing.

Why they were not *closed* already I could not begin to guess. Perhaps the Guard had been overconfident when their Commissar brought his men to the Sollan Embassy on Argyris's invitation. Perhaps word had been slow to reach the keepers of the gate. Perhaps they had not known how we planned to make our escape until that very moment. I can't say.

But the gates *were* closing.

"Go!" Without my helmet or the ability to touch my wrist-terminal, I could not communicate with the others. "Go, go, go!" I was not sure if I spoke to Corvo and Valka or to the iron horse I rode, but hardly ever in my life had I prayed so fervently for so little.

For so much.

Go.

I was gaining. The mighty portal was grinding shut on mechanisms little oiled and much neglected. I dropped then to the level of the pavement, pushing the chariot hard as it would go to close the gap between the van and me. The Conclave Guard came hard behind, sirens screaming in the pale dawn like the loosed hounds of some pagan hell. The whine of the repulsors drowned out everything. Even my scream.

A thousand feet.

It might have been light-years.

Corvo pushed the van to its limits. The mighty armored beast ground over the pavement, leaving black stripes where it passed. She was so close.

They were so close. The doors were nearly shut, a slim sliver of orange light stood between their jaws, a narrow slit growing narrower still. It was the eye of a giant's needle, but a needle all the same.

And Otavia Corvo *threaded it*. The van scraped by, leaving paint—I felt certain—on either side. They'd made it.

"Go!" I screamed, and knew then I screamed for Valka and the others, because I knew I would not. Still, I leaned almost flat, driving the chariot forward fast as any arrow. I let my vision stretch, blood pounding in my ears as a million million gates ground shut before me. On I stared, seeking one—somewhere in time—that stalled. Faltered. Failed.

My chariot struck the bridge beneath me, jarring me back to myself. The whole platform wobbled beneath me, and I clenched my teeth. The vision collapsed like a pane of shattered glass, leaving only the blood music and a dull ache behind my eyes. *No use,* I thought. *Too late.*

I was going too fast.

A thousand feet remained.

Three seconds.

Not enough.

The door ground shut. I could not turn away in time or tilt to brake. I leaped free of the chariot instead, momentum carrying me into the heavy steel door with a noise like a terrible gong. The chariot struck the door below and a dozen feet to my left. Relatively light without a driver, it bounced and caromed over the side and into the water far below. Dazed, I slid to the tarmac, my back against the door.

I'd taken too long to get my bearings in the air. I'd wasted too much time.

"Damn your eyes, Marlowe," I cursed, keying my terminal. "Valka! Valka, it's me!"

But there was no answer, could be no answer. The dome was sealed. No signal was getting in or out. For a moment, I entertained the thought of leaping into the reservoir again, but I knew that with prefects on chariots, they'd track me before I could swim a hundred yards.

There was nowhere to go, and so I did the only thing that seemed suitable.

I stood up and drew my sword.

Half a dozen of the smaller Conclave Guard cars screamed toward me, one of the riot vans in hot pursuit, and further off I saw the glare of four charioteers knifing through the air above. If I could get to one of them, I might win free. I entertained thoughts of carving my way out through the dome and driving the chariot to the shuttle port.

It was the only way I saw.

"Always forward," I muttered to myself, tugging the coif back over my head and tapping the button inside the neck of my breastplate to tighten the metamaterial before I put on my helm once more. There was no point trying to cut through that gate. I knew its thickness, and knew also that if I carved a piece of it large enough to admit me that I would not have the strength to move it, much less the strength to run the length of that subterranean highway to catch up to Valka and the others. I had only to pray they might escape, and to pray also the Lothrians truly did want me alive. From the *Tamerlane*, Corvo and Valka might launch a true attempt to rescue me with ninety thousand soldiers at their back.

But I would not go quietly. I would not go gentle.

The masks and helms of Nipponese knights were fashioned like snarling demons, like ogres and other fell beasts, with feathered mustachios and eyebrows, their helms bristling with horns. The Cielcin—often as not—wore masks that left their horns exposed to vacuum, for their bony hide was bred to endure the titanic emptiness of the Dark between the stars. On Earth of old it was said a thousand tribes and kingdoms put on the skins of lions and wolves, or painted their faces unholy colors to frighten the enemy.

We Sollans—like the Romans, our forebears—had chosen the serene faces of gods. It was with just so serene a visage that I stood alone upon the bridge, my grim face concealed behind my mirror-black mask. I checked my shield in the corner of my eye. All systems still blue.

Good.

Every second I stood upon the bridge was a second I diverted at least part of their attention from the others. If I truly was the object of their desire . . . then all the better.

The cars all ground to a halt, half turning to fan out across the width of the roadway ahead. Men in the faceless matte black of the Guard piled out, leveling stunners at me. Others pumped gas launchers and fired canisters in arcs over the heads of their brothers. They clattered about me, hissing like a den of snakes, belching their poisonous fumes into the oppressive air in noxious, gray-green clouds.

Safe in my suit, I smiled. One fell at my feet, and I kicked it scornfully aside, kindling my sword with a flourish.

They all opened fire at once.

Breaking left, I charged the line, weathering stunner fire as I came. Two men hunkered behind the right-hand door of the nearest car, using its armored steel plate for cover. I raised the highmatter sword and brought it down like a headsman. The pentaquark blade sheared through steel and ceramic and flesh alike, and the two men fell. Turning away, I dragged my blade through the front of their car, chewing through frame and fuel reservoir. I had only seconds to leap away as the fuel cell ignited, and the blast wave hurled me back—slammed against my shield as the whole vehicle went up in flames. The blast carried me into the bridge's rail, and this time I did not fall over, but stood, shaking off the ringing in my ears. Between the others and myself the flaming hulk of the destroyed car stood burning, belching black smoke to mingle with the white and poisonous green of their gas.

Through that noxious fog, a stray shot caromed off my shield, and I lurched behind the burning car. I heard muffled shouts in Lothrian, but I could not make them out. Crouched behind the rear of the burning vehicle, I saw the shadow of one of the Guards cast dancing on the pavement before me, and with a roar I stood, blade cleaving the stock of his stunner in two and severing his left hand. The man staggered back and fell, and before I could follow through two of his fellows leaped at me. One seized me about the waist and the other grappled with my sword arm, trying to immobilize my wrist.

Struggling thus over highmatter was often lethal to both parties. It was so easy to torque one's hand and drive the peerless blade through self and enemy alike. But my left arm was free, and I drove my elbow up and back and cracked the man who held my waist in the visor, rattling him. With him momentarily stunned, I dragged my knife from its belt-sheath and punched it into the man's padded flank. His armorweave took the brunt of the blow, but the blade was sharp enough and wielded with enough force to pierce the soft flesh beneath the floating ribs. It was enough to slacken his hold, enough to gain a moment to bring the knife to bear on the other man.

There was no armor in the joint of his arm, and the blood ran free as he released his grip on my sword hand. The highmatter fell like the hand of Fate, and spinning I cut through the first man as four more came round to face me. I leaped and slid across the hood of the next cruiser, blade slashing through the windscreen and the far door as I went. The man there avoided being decapitated by mere inches as he fell backward, crawling away. Ignoring him, I cut the car's wheel in half with a single stroke and advanced, half-ducking as another barrage crackled against my shield.

Stunner fire.

They were still not trying to kill me.

I worked my way up the line, moving from the left side of the bridge to the next, sketching a scarlet maze on the drab, gray pavement. Three more men fell and another of the vehicles before the others started to retreat, peeling off down the line, retreating up the bridge. I raised my sword. "Run, you dogs!" I shouted, fury for Baro and the other dead hot in me as my fear for Valka and the others ran cold.

But they had run to a purpose.

A hail of bullets rained about me, pocking the cracked roadtop. The charioteers had closed in, and the shine of their drive lights came so bright my suit's optics had to polarize the glare. I weathered the onslaught a moment and dove behind the nearest parked car. I heard the noise of safety glass crunch and metal deform beneath that heavy rain, then the whine of repulsors dopplered as the charioteers streaked overhead. They would be shielded, and I had no weapon save knife and sword, and neither would avail.

But there was one of the dead men near to hand, his armored fist still clutching his disruptor rifle. Unkindling my sword and sheathing it, I leaped for the dropped weapon and snatched it up, left hand fumbling with the phase settings—still holding the knife. The indicators swapped blue for red, and tucking the thing to my shoulder I squeezed the trigger, aiming the best I could. The charioteer slewed to one side, crimson bolt missing him by whole feet as he returned fire.

My shield's charge indicator shaded blue to yellow in the corner of my vision. I grimaced. Strong though the Royse barrier was, it would not hold forever. The nearest charioteer had slowed, orbiting me as he fired.

I fired back.

The red charge of the disruptor washed over the man's shield. Useless. Swearing, I cast the thing aside. I was never going to defeat four shielded flying charioteers with a disruptor rifle, not in a million years.

But I could still render them impotent. Cavalier though their fellows had been about firing on the People, I felt confident these fine fellows would not fire on their own. Slamming the dagger back into its sheath, I swept free my sword and charged after the retreating members of the Guard. Palatine as I was, I gained swiftly, but before I'd closed half the distance, I drew up short.

Not one, but *three* of the riot vans had parked further down the bridge, their back ends facing me, their doors thrown wide. Thirty members of the Conclave Guard stood firm, advancing as a block behind their tower shields. Though I knew my sword could make short work of them, I could not stop the sense of numb terror that rose in me, so formidable was that sight.

They advanced in lockstep, each man carrying neither stunner nor gun, but a heavy ceramic baton with a head like a medieval mace. These they beat against their shields, creating a din like the noise of drums.

I settled into a low guard and thrust my sword in line. I could not fight thirty men and win, but I might engage them all the same. The words of an oath I'd sworn so long ago floated back to me in the Emperor's voice.

Do you swear to see to its end any course begun?

I do.

I shifted my footing, mindful of the chariots circling me. They held their fire now, operating—I guessed—under new orders. Looking past the block of men advancing toward me, to the white-lit interiors of the van, I saw the jacketed and helmeted figure of another Lothrian Commissar standing arms crossed and admiring. He was indistinguishable from the one Otavia had killed, as though our defiance at the embassy had never occurred.

I was alone.

But I had stood alone on Berenike, on Arae, and—before that—before Prince Aranata.

I had not forgotten how to die.

I had not forgotten how to stand, either. When the battle line had come to within twenty of me, I charged. No Lothrian I'd seen had worn adamantine armor or carried highmatter themselves. The shields I could see were carbon fiber and ceramic as the ones the men in the embassy carport had used. I slashed them to ribbons, but even as I did, the edges of the block rushed forward to entrap me. I was surrounded.

By dead men.

Outnumbered as I was, out-positioned as I was, the Lothrians could not face my sword. They fell around me in awful pieces or staggered back slashed inches deep. The space about me was a charnal house, the pavement slick with gore. Behind me, one of the Conclave Guard smote me with his mace, and so terrific was the blow that I went to one knee, head ringing. My helm had spared me the worst of the trauma, but still I saw double.

There were hands on my arms, my shoulders. Howling, I stood and whirled, and three men fell dead. Still more leaped upon me, and I slipped on the blood-soaked concrete. My blade scored the road top, and I tried to roll.

"Hold the man!" came a distant voice in shrill Lothrian. The commissar? "Hold the man down!"

Boom.

A titanic blow rang my helmet like a bell. Indeed, I heard bells. The deep, temple-hushed tolling of the bells of Devil's Rest. Was I going mad? My helmet's vision sparked and fizzed, entoptics damaged.

"Valka!" I cried out, reaching for that quiet place in my soul.

I couldn't find it.

"Valka!" It took every ounce and fiber to find hands and knees. Where was my sword?

There it was! Still in my hand.

But the act of striking out with it, slashing wildly to strike the foes on my right, only allowed the left wing to crush me to the pavement.

Boom.

Again the hammer fell. My suit's vision sparked again and went dead. I was alone in the dark closeness of my armor, blind and bruised. I prayed for a miracle, but none came.

A boot—I think—stamped upon my face, and all my sinews went numb. I had a dim understanding of hands on me—many, many hands.

"Valka . . ." I said at the last. Or thought. Or screamed.

The boot pressed my armored face into the pavement, and a third blow wiped me out.

CHAPTER 22

THERE IN THE SILENCE

THE WORLD PASSED BY through a cottony blanket. Someone had removed my helm, and the blood pounded like distant tympani in my ears. Only the vaguest sense of my surroundings was left to me. I remember falling, and muffled shouts in Lothrian. Semi-conscious, I sank in and out of that quagmire which lies beneath sleep, here and there rising long enough to catch a glimpse of a black-armored Guardsman or the inside of a van.

Darkness.

Two men dragged me, my arms over their shoulders, feet trailing like those of a puppet. One cursed, and I fell again, knees striking stone. Eyes unfocused, I stared at the ground between my hands. Greenish stone. Pale dust. Something rattled, and abruptly a chain I had not known was fixed to a collar about my neck pulled taut and I lurched gasping to my feet. The creature holding my chain bared glass fangs in a vicious smile.

The Cielcin said nothing, and its brothers at my shoulders pushed me on, their white swords held flat against their shoulders in the crooks of their right arms. I stopped, feeling the wind rip at my hair and snap at the black cape of alien silk they had fixed about my shoulders.

I was not on Padmurak at all.

Padmurak had no wind—not in the domes—and the black pillars that rose like topless trees all around me into the gray, dead sky were like nothing I had seen in the Commonwealth.

Was I dreaming? Had I not seen those pillars before?

"Aeta!" barked an alien voice. *"Aeta! Aeta!"*

A king! A king!

Looking round I saw my danger. A sea of Cielcin stood all around, stretching away to either side, filling what seemed to me a valley between the arms of a mountain, blurry and angular at the margins of my sight. Each of the Pale wore a mask whose slitted eyes blocked the wan sunlight. Many carried staves, spears from which flew the silken banners of a hundred hundred clans. *"Aeta! Aeta! Aeta ba-Yukajjimn!"*

The King of Vermin! The King of Rats! they cried, their voices like the harsh music of crows.

They were pointing at me, I realized. Laughing at me.

I staggered forward, half-dragged by my keeper with its chain.

I knew where I was. Knew what waited in the great black dome ahead. I fixed my eyes forward, deaf to the cries of *Aeta!*

"Oimn Belu!" still others cried. *Dark One.* It was a name Aranata Otiolo had called me, once.

Ahead, I saw the cruel lances and crooked scimitars of the enemy flashing in the sun, and I realized I was being led in triumph as I had led the smashed ruin of General Iubalu through the cloud-crowned streets of the Eternal City. I spied the white armor of the Demons of Arae, the hybrid Cielcin-machines wrought by the traitorous posthuman sorcerers of MINOS, and thought I spied a trio of slender figures crowned and escorting a floating white eye.

Hushansa.

And those other figures—the winged one and the colossus and the warrior with the white crest—those were the other generals, *his* other generals, the other fingers of his White Hand. The Iedyr Yemani, the holy slaves and guardians of the Prince of Princes, Syriani Dorayaica itself.

I knew where I was. Knew that beneath the arch of the black dome my chain would be threaded through an iron loop as the Scourge of Earth clapped its clawed hands. How many times had I dreamed this dream? How many times had I seen what was coming? Heard the screams?

I screamed.

One of the guards at my side dropped me—struck me, or so it seemed. But he was only human. That grim plain with its black pillars set in spirals about the dome vanished, and the Cielcin with it. I was in a cell. There were no Cielcin. There was no black dome, no sea of pillars. Another vision. A waking dream.

The Lothrians had taken not only my helmet but my armor, stripped me down to my underlayment. Before I could rise, a plated knee rose and cracked me in the side of the head. I skidded across the floor and struck the wall, spitting blood and the broken fragments of a tooth. The next blow caught me in the stomach, and it was only grace that kept me from vomiting. Through the next flurry of blows, I slowly managed to get my hands up to shield my head.

It wasn't enough.

My hands ached.

I tried to move them, but I could not. Blearily, I became aware of the fact that they were fixed above my head. I tried to lower them and winced at the pain that coruscated down my arms and shoulders. Chains rattled.

I was manacled, my hands in cuffs attached to a length of chain bolted high in the wall. The rest of me was free so that I might stand and so relieve my arms, but I could not sit or sleep without raising them again and so tormenting myself.

"What a terrible fate," a hoarse voice said. It took me minutes to realize the words my new acquaintance had spoken were Galstani, which would have been unremarkable except that I was sure I was still on Padmurak—had never left Padmurak—sure that this at least was no dream.

It took a force of will to raise my head. I was in the same low-ceilinged cell, the only illumination a single red sconce gleaming in the crumbling mortar by the square steel door. My wrists chafed from my bonds, and even the faintest motion made the thews and fibers of my arms shriek with pain. My body ached, and beneath the underlayment I guessed my flesh was a welter of bruises. I could not blame the Lothrian guards. I had killed so many of their fellows on the bridge alone. I probed the spot where my tooth used to be with my tongue and spat, and only then found my cellmate.

An old man sat in the corner, his bony hands in his lap, unchained. He wore nothing save a ragged breechclout, and his skin was pale and faintly jaundiced, his body covered with scars. His hair fell almost to his waist in oily curtains that shadowed his face, the matted black streaked liberally with white. He had no beard, and I could count each rib and trace each vein through the papery skin. Starvation had withered his muscles, and his nails were like claws.

"This must be," he said. "This *must* be. Remember?"

"What did you say?"

"Thought we could escape . . . thought . . . we were too old already."

His accent was . . . strangely familiar. Beneath the brittle qualities of starvation and pain yet remained the polish of class and old breeding. It was an Imperial accent, the accent of the scion of some antique Imperial house. What such a man was doing moldering in a Lothrian dungeon I felt sure might fill several books. "Do I know you?" I asked.

"Though he slay me, I will trust in him," the stranger replied, and lifted violet eyes to mine. "And he *has* slain us before."

I recoiled. Deep sunken were those violet eyes, and far away their stare, yet I knew them still, and knew intimately then the scars that marred the flesh of the other man's arm. I knew every scar. Remembered the mark beneath his left eye where our father's ring had torn my cheek. Recalled the bright spots on my right arm from the brace I'd worn as a boy, and the marks of war and crime and Colosso. But there were fresh wounds on his left cheek—the mark of talons red and terrible. And he was thin. So thin! And so bruised I thought his skin must burst in places.

"Do you know of whom I speak?" the other Hadrian asked.

I was going mad, or else here was another vision.

"The Quiet?"

Hadrian nodded. "We are on the shortest path now. We *must* be," he said, and screwed shut his eyes to make of his words a prayer. "I'm sorry. I'm sorry . . ."

"Sorry for what?"

He had no answer, though the look in his eyes was enough.

"Find us in you," he said, and pointed a finger at me.

"I don't understand!" I tried to get my feet under me, tried to stand, to approach my other self if I could. What horrors had wrought that other Hadrian in such an image? I thought I could guess. I had walked that path not long before, bound in chains.

A king! A king!

"One way!" said Hadrian Marlowe, raising a hand for emphasis, one finger extended. I recoiled. The last two fingers of that hand were gone. Only scarred and ragged stumps remained. "There is but one way through the needle!" It was one of Gibson's old aphorisms, and the memory of it and of Gibson in that wretched place were like the memory of sunlight on a world without a star. "Always forward, always down. Never left or right." Hadrian said again, "Find us!"

"I said I don't understand!"

The red light beside the door went out, and with a buzzing loud as raid sirens it cycled blue, and the door hissed open. My attention flickered from my counterpart to the scrawny gaoler who entered with a plastic dinner tray. "A man must eat," he said, setting the tray on the floor before removing the control wand to uncouple my wrists from their chain. Still manacled, my hands fell to my lap.

The other Hadrian was gone.

CHAPTER 23

WHO HOLDS THE STRINGS

DAYS PASSED BEFORE THEY came for me. How many I cannot say for certain, for they had taken my terminal with my armor. I had only the coming and going of my gaoler to mark the time. The scrawny *zuk*, hook-nosed, hairless, and black-eyed, never said a word. He never undid the manacles that bound my wrists together, but neither did he chain me back to the wall. Twice daily he entered my cell to deposit a fresh meal tray and to clear away the ruin of the old. He never lingered long nor entertained any of my questions, and no wonder: the fish-eye lens of a camera eye watched from high in one corner, and it never blinked.

The food was foul: every day a brick of white and putrid-seeming protein paste alongside some greenish mush and a heel of stale bread. They had not taken the underlayment of my suit, and its waste processing and water reclamation still worked. Thus I had more water and cleaner than I could get from the greasy tap that thrust from the far wall.

I counted sixty-seven meals before the Guard came for me. Thirty-four days, assuming the meals had come at regular intervals, as they almost certainly had not. Once, I had dined with a junior commandant of the Imperial prison world of Pagus Minor, who told me it was common practice in his profession to stagger a prisoner's meal times, serving meals too close together, and then too far apart. Deprived also of the light of the sun and all other external indicators of the passage of time, the client becomes uncoupled from the basic rhythms that provide his body and mind with the structure upon which his comfort and his sanity depend. This increases his anxiety, triggers a depression response, and robs him of sleep—to say nothing of the disregulation of the bowels and discomfort of the stomach caused by irregular eating and poor fare. These are subtle tortures—and subtler indignities—compounded by the fact that for those thirty-four days, the manacles remained a part of me.

"A man will stand," the Guardsman decreed, his arrival trumpeted by the blast of the alarm. He tapped his truncheon against his thigh.

Standing was an agony in itself. Cramped muscles spasmed from malnutrition, from my beating, and from my month of sleeping on the bare stone floor. They beat me again, more cursorily this time, and took great pains to avoid my head. When they were done, they half-marched, half-dragged me through a maze of corridors so starkly lit I fancied I could hear the buzzing of the lights in their fixtures.

The lift buzzed more loudly still, and rattled to a halt. The heavy door rolled open, and still more of the Guard pulled back the iron grill that blocked the opening. We emerged into a security checkpoint teeming with the black-clad Conclave Guard, and exited behind a bank of security scanners into a marble-tiled hall whose walls bore cement friezes of the Lothrian People marching arm in arm.

I knew where I was.

It was the tunnel that pierced the heart of the palace ziggurat, that ran from the lobby and the fountains to the floor of the Conclave's arena. I was being taken to the very heart of Lothrian power. As we drew near the great doors, I did my best to get my bare feet under me again. I was not going to be dragged before the Conclave a broken man, bruised and freshly bloodied. So I dressed myself in the vestments of Empire—invisible to all—and raised my chin to come in chains before the gathered lords of the Commonwealth.

The lights within were dim, tuned to their lowest, reddest setting. My bare feet slapped against the tile, and the noise of my tread and of the boots of my escort clattered against the vaults and the empty stands that rose in circles all around. Ahead, the tall backs of the thirty-four chairs that stood to either side of the Lothriad on its great throne rose like funeral markers, their occupants watching my approach in ringing silence. I caught the eye of the First Chair, white-haired and solemn, but what he saw in me must have unsettled him, for he looked away. The Third Chair watched me, too, she who had led Valka and me on our tour of the Party's farms. There sat the Sixth, who first of all the Grand Conclave had questioned me under the power of Voice. Of the Ninth Chair there was no sign, but there sat the Twenty-Fifth, who'd been censured by the Conclave the day I'd arrived on Padmurak.

And there was Lorth Talleg, watching from his place to the far left, smiling to see me brought so low.

But for a few lesser functionaries seated immediately behind the great Bench about the square entryway by which the Conclave entered and the guards posted on the perimeter doors, the great space stood empty. The army of clerks and secretaries and logothete-partisans who had filled the chamber like spectators at Colosso were nowhere to be seen. I was, evidently, to be tried with as few witnesses as possible.

When I'd approached within earshot of the Bench, my guards shoved me, and I fell to my knees at the focus of the arc along which the Chairs were seated, and just under half their seats stood empty.

Few witnesses indeed.

"The Conclave recognizes the delegate from the Sollan Empire," the First Chair said, keeping to the proscribed forms, speaking in his native tongue, his voice soft and quavering. *"Ushdim."*

Rise.

I did not move.

"Ushdim!"

At the sound of my guards approaching, I raised my manacled hands and stood. Still, the two guards seized me roughly and held me fast.

First Chair's hushed tones rose again and filled that echoing space. "On behalf of the Conclave, the delegate stands accused of fomenting war with the People of the Commonwealth, of conspiring with revolutionary agencies against the People of the Commonwealth, of traveling and treating under false pretenses with the People of the Commonwealth, of the murder of a foreign diplomat on Commonwealth soil, of the murder of a commissar of the People of the Commonwealth, of the murder of officers in the service of the Commonwealth, of doing violence against the People of the Commonwealth, of destroying the property of the People of the Commonwealth, of stealing the property of the People of the Commonwealth, and of failure to comply with officers acting in the defense of the Commonwealth. *Dya vinatva?"*

These last words were strange to me, though I had studied Lothrian as a boy. Focusing through the pain, I tried to make sense of them.

"Dya vinatva?" the First Chair asked again.

Vinatva . . . Vinat was *fault. Error. Guilt? Vinatva,* then, was *faulty. Guilty.* But *dya?*

"Dya vinatva?" the First Chair asked again, and added, *"Panacca!"*

Confess.

The last piece clicked into place, and I understood. *Dya* was *you.* The Lothrians had—publicly—abolished names, abolished *I* and *we, he* and *she, us* and *them*. They clumsily addressed people by their functions, *the delegate* or *a worker*, or in general terms, *a man*. But they had retained, as an archaism or artifact of legal formality, this solitary word. This singular way to separate the lamb from their flock of goats. *You*. I felt certain I understood correctly.

"Are you guilty?" the First Chair asked. And then the order. "Confess."

They had abolished every identity save guilt. The word *you* remained, atrophied but still potent, as an organ for singling out the enemy for punishment.

I raised my chin, a lord still despite my almost-nakedness. "Let us speak plainly, my lords," I said, and I was pleased to find my voice neither broken nor strained. I spoke in Galstani, in the language of men whose minds at least were their own. The translator did not speak for me. The great room's recording suite was not engaged. There would be no record of my trial, only of my death. I had died upon the bridge, died a terrorist attempting to start a war. "You have done this, not I. Those were your men who attacked us as we returned from our tour of your polar camps. Argyris was *your* man, and it was on your orders that he detained my party in our embassy. You might have let us leave peaceably, but you did not. Your agencies ensured there would be violence. Your orders."

The First Chair slapped his hand against the arm of his throne. *"Dya panacca?"*

"No!" I shouted. "I do not confess!"

A blow caught me in the back of one knee, and I fell with a crash.

"Panacca!" the First Chair commanded.

Steadily, I found my feet once more, half-turning to see the guard who had struck me. He held his truncheon ready at his side. "The question is why!" I raised my hands to forestall the guardsman's blow. "Why bother with this charade? If it is war with the Imperium you desire, you might have done so before I ever came here. Why force this . . . pretext?" I turned then and took two steps toward the Seventeenth Chair. "Lorth Talleg!" The use of the man's right name sent a murmur along the Bench and forestalled any retribution. "Tell me *why*."

Lorth Talleg of the Seventeenth Chair peered down at me. Slowly, he leaned forward in his seat until he peered over the rail like a sentry from between the merlons of his castle wall. He looked out with the air of a man watching the throes of an especially close contest.

"Confess!" the First Chair's dusty voice implored, overriding any response from Talleg.

Another blow caught me in the lower back, and I struck the stone wall beneath the Conclave's Bench. I was permitted once more to stand, though I had to use the wall to lever myself back to bare and callused feet. I understood the game well enough. They did not mean to kill me, as any lord of the Empire might have done. They wanted me to relent, wanted to break me, wanted me to say what they told me to say. By such small surrenders they would secure my compliance, and they meant to secure it by the oldest methods imaginable.

Obedience through fear of pain.

They would send Hadrian Marlowe back to the Imperium not as himself, not as a man, but as their man, a dancer trained as surely as those who performed Giallo's ballet for us upon the stage. They wanted the Halfmortal remade in their image, rebuilt as a Lothrian creature.

"But you did kill our men, did you not, my lord?" Lorth Talleg inquired, confirming my suspicions. Small truths. They would ask me to agree to small truths first, make me speak their words one step at a time. Had Talleg given me his name only to play my friend now?

"I defended myself!" I said, and glowered at the guard that had followed me to the end of the bench. He didn't move. "Hit me, coward. Or do you only strike a man when his back is turned?" Still he made no sign, so I addressed myself to Talleg and the others. "I will not play your games. Kill me or release me. You waste my time and yours with this dumb show."

"But you *did* kill them, did you not?" Talleg inquired mildly, speaking my own language. "And you *did* kill poor Argyris, did you not?"

Talleg had not stirred from his place on the rail.

"What I did, I did for the good of my people." I froze, ready for the guard to charge and strike me. "Where are my people, Talleg?"

"The Sollan embassy has been liquidated," came the response in Lothrian, and turning my head I beheld the speaker standing on the level above the level of the Bench, his hands clasped neatly behind his back, gray suit neatly ordered, gray eyes flashing with triumphant delight. It was the Ninth Chair, his slight figure framed against the blackness of the hall by which he'd entered the congressional arena. "All dead."

He allowed these words to hang in the air like gun smoke while behind him the other absent Chairs filtered in, hovering about the Ninth Chair like satellites to his Jove. What was it about the little man that commanded such terror and obedience in the other Chairmen?

I had but little time to contemplate that question, for the little man's words hung over me. "Dead?" I repeated, thinking of the guards we'd abandoned in the carport, of the hundreds of personnel who lived and worked in the embassy complex, of Argyris's poor slaves.

Of Pallino, of Corvo and the rest.

Of Valka.

When the Ninth Chair did not reply nor any other intervene, I said, "You cannot win. Kill me if you wish. Destroy my people if you can. You will not win the war. My Empire will tear your planets from the sky."

"You should not threaten," the First Chair said, speaking in Galstani for the first time. "Any man who comes to Padmurak begging aid has come in no position to threaten."

The Ninth Chair overrode him, raising one hand. "The delegate's threats are empty. The survival of the Commonwealth has already been assured." He surveyed the floor of the arena, where I stood, barely standing with four guards close about me. He seemed to take notice of my state for the first time, and a flicker of rage moved beneath the gray-paper skin of his face. The Ninth Chair let out an exasperated sigh, and all the wind went out of him. "The Conclave was asked to keep the prisoner in good health."

"The delegate must be punished!" cried one of the seated chairmen.

"The Conclave renders to the enemies of the People what is due the enemies of the People!" declared another, sparking a riot of noise from the seated members of the Grand Conclave. First Chair struck the arm of his throne, but the councilmen did not cease.

Third Chair shouted at the Eighth, and the Eighth at Twenty-Fourth. All the while Talleg leaned forward upon the rail, looking not down on me but up toward the Ninth Chair, who stood above it all as Julian Felsenburgh must once have stood above the mobs of Earth, untouched by the tableau beneath him.

The Ninth Chair raised a hand, and silence fell.

In a soft voice, the occupant of the Ninth Chair said, "I am sorry to have kept you all waiting. Evidently you cannot be left alone with my prisoner even for a day." To my shock, he spoke the words in Galstani, his voice theatrically hushed in the sudden stillness.

"Your prisoner, Iovan?" the Sixth Chair exclaimed in standard, turning in her seat.

"*My* prisoner, yes," the Ninth Chair replied. "Was it not I who arranged for his capture? Was it not I who arranged for the capture of his *ship*?"

"What?" I staggered forward. "You lie!"

The little man looked down on me, but did not answer me. It could not be true. The *Tamerlane* could not be lost. I confess my mind went blank, went white with shock and rage. What had happened to Valka? To Corvo and the others? Had they made it to the ship? Had they lingered to stage some escape? Some abortive rescue? I screwed shut my eyes to block the tears.

No. No no no.

"My master will not appreciate you playing with his new pet," the Ninth Chair said.

"Tell them he is not our master!" the Sixth Chair replied. "We have a deal, Iovan."

"Tell them yourself!" said Iovan of the Ninth Chair.

The Sixth Chair nearly fell against the rail. "Lord . . . Lord Vati is coming here?"

"Indeed I am," came a new voice, deep and sepulchral, as though it issued from the ground. I had heard such a voice only once before—on Berenike—and the black music of it tore the heart from me.

I heard the demon before it appeared, its armor clinking, servos whining in the dark of the tunnel. Everything came crashing together then. Every little piece found its place. The Lothrians had no desire to make me one of their puppets. They had designs on Imperial territory and desires for war, but I was not to be their scapegoat, their casus belli. They had bent all their will to capture me to make me a gift . . . to the Cielcin.

That was why the chamber was empty but for the great lords who knew the Commonwealth's most terrible secret. That was why the lights in the Conclave's arena were turned down low and red.

The creature that appeared in the black arch above the level of the Conclave was decidedly inhuman. It had to stoop to enter the high hall, for the crest of its iron skull stood fully ten feet from the ground. I knew it at once for one of the Iedyr, for its armor and its iron skeleton were of a kind with Iubalu, with Bahudde and Hushansa. The same flanged plating, the same graceful, organic lines. No scrap of the alien flesh was visible, as though it were one of the medieval knights in Maddalo House's combat holos. Featureless and smooth was its opalescent mask, with a braided queue of false hair bound at the nape of its neck to evoke the Cielcin style. Where the others had been fashioned into shapes different from the bodies they'd been born to, this Vati's shape was little different from that of any Cielcin, save that it was taller. Its style recalled that of the Nipponese knights I have seen, with banded pauldrons and two stylized horns above the place where the eyes should be. And on its chest in faded silver was the print of a Pale hand.

Behind it came a dozen *scahari* warriors in traditional Cielcin black and blue, the cloaks above the fleshy contours of their armor embroidered with interlocking circular runes, their white scimitars drawn and held at the ready—as in my vision—in the crooks of their right arms. They dwarfed Ninth Chair Iovan and his coterie, appearing as men among children.

Words fled me.

When Valka and I had eaten with Lorth Talleg, I had accused the Commonwealth of reducing mankind to *Eloi*, to sheep. How right I'd been! Here then were the Morlocks, the dwellers in darkness, the creatures the shepherds were fattening their sheep to feed.

The Cielcin.

At once Argyris's somber ode to the decline of the Great City and Carry and Magda's tales of patrols rounding up men for deportment off-world took on a sinister cast. Fifty years, Argyris had said. Fifty years. How many men had this Conclave sold to its inhuman masters? How many women and children? My bare feet felt fused to the ground, and I watched in wide-eyed horror as the Pale knight descended on cloven feet from the platform to the level of the Bench.

"At last," it said, regarding me with its faceless face. I felt the presence of a million tiny, faceted eyes on me, and took a step backward, skin crawling. "I should slay you for what you have done to my sister-brothers, but my master has forbidden it." The creature's artificial voice seemed to shake the dust from the red lights above, so deep was its resonance. "Do you know who I am?"

Raising my chin, I answered, "You're one of the White Hand."

"I am Vati Inamna, First Slave of the Prophet." Implants the sorcerers of MINOS had installed in the creature's brain translated its native tongue to standard. The general stalked round the circumference of the stands about me, moving toward one of the narrow stairs by which men might reach the floor. "I hoped I would be the one to catch you. The gods have heard my prayers."

Up close, the giant towered over me, its head cocked at an angle. Its heavy black cloak fluttered from pointed shoulders as it raised an arm. I had had occasion to examine the bodies of Iubalu and Bahudde both, and marked the same stamp of handicraft in the design of that arm and hand. The artificers who had designed the metal body had given it the look of an anatomical sketch; the corded texture of the adamantine plate evoked sheets of muscle, the fibrous polymers beneath tendons shifting over metal bones. The segmented and six-fingered metal hand gave the impression of a flayed man.

Vati touched my face, hard fingers closing over my mouth as it turned my head like a buyer examining the teeth of some Norman slave boy on the auction block. The blank white face peered down at me. The sensation of crawling eyes grew stronger. I recoiled, but the fingers only tightened until I thought my jaw might crack.

"He has waited for this," Vati said, "for such a long time." The creature released me and traced the line of my nose with one blunt ceramic fingertip. "They say you are chosen by your god."

"The Quiet," I said.

The giant twitched its iron hand. I barely saw it. The blow caught me beneath the chin and sent me flying through the air to crash against the wall beneath the Lothrian Bench. My head rang, and I had to shut my eyes to keep the world from spinning.

"Only a man," Vati said, dismissing me. The Pale knight's shadow fell across me. "There are no gods but ours."

For once in my life, I did not argue.

Vati had called itself Dorayaica's *First Slave*. The *vayadayan* were slaves, as all Cielcin who were not Aeta were slaves. Here then was the Grand Vayadan, the First Finger of Syriani Dorayaica's White Hand, Chief of the Iedyr Yemani, captain of its armies, master of its hosts. Before it, in chains, I *was* only a man. A rat. *Yukajji*. The pain in me kept my vision cloudy, and even if I could have stood before that metal monster, I could not stand against the Commonwealth, who had placed all their hideous strength at the service of mankind's greatest enemy.

"Talleg!" I shouted. "How can you allow this?"

"The good of all is the good of each, my lord," Talleg replied. "Their sacrifice . . . for the security of the Commonwealth."

Somehow, I'd found the strength to stand. "Your people *are* your Commonwealth, you fool!" I shouted. "A nation is its people, and you sold yours for meat."

The Grand Vayadan threw back its head and let out a sound like tearing metal. It was an inhuman laugh. Vati turned to its escort, and in its own tongue barked, "Gorre! Take our guest to the ship and prepare him for his journey." High above, a Cielcin I assumed was Gorre leaped to obey. The Ninth Chair hurried to join it. Why the little minister should accompany the xenobites I'd no idea, but three of the Ninth Chair's coterie and fully half a dozen of the Cielcin descended to join their master on the arena's floor.

"The desert is nothing, Lord Talleg!" I cried, recalling our dinner conversation. "Nothing!" I had to make him see, to make someone in this republic of monsters *understand*. The world they sold their souls and their people to build would never be. Like every Faustian pretender, they had not realized the very act of purchasing their desire had put that desire forever out of reach. Their pound of flesh might buy a place in the sun from their new masters, but the Lothrians would be only tenants there. The Conclave was selling its own people for food, just as they had accused the Sollan palatines of capturing Lothrian peasants and devouring them to extend their lives.

What was it Argyris had said?

Always accuse the enemy of what you are doing.

CHAPTER 24

THE SORCERER

MY CIELCIN CAPTORS MARCHED me through the palace halls, their clawed hands clamped tight above my elbows, claws pressing against the armorweave of my skin-suit. We moved in stages, the Conclave Guard clearing zones ahead of us, securing doors to preserve their secret alliance with that arch-nemesis of mankind. Iovan of the Ninth Chair marched on ahead of me, accompanied by one of his coterie—a woman. Had she been the Fourteenth Chair? The Thirteenth. My head still swam, and my whole body ached from the blow Lord Vati had delivered me.

"It won't work," I said, lifting manacled hands to test the bruise blossoming on my jaw. "When your people find out what you . . . what you've done . . . they won't accept it."

Iovan halted, turned to my alien escort. *"Dajaggaa o-tajun ne!"* he snapped, ordering the xenobites in their own tongue. *Gag him.* "I'll have no more of his prattle." To my astonishment, the Cielcin obeyed. One produced a length of silken cord and wound it between my teeth. That accomplished, Iovan lay a hand on my shoulder in mock affection. He smiled, gray eyes alight. "Don't want you causing a scene now, do we?"

A short lift ride later we found ourselves exiting onto a loading dock. Members of the Conclave Guard stood at entrances and at vantage points all round, ensuring the place was secure. An armored van of the kind we'd stolen from the embassy awaited us, and it was into its rear compartment the xenobites loaded me, securing my manacles to a length of chain attached to an iron ring in the floor. My inhuman guards seated themselves to either side, neither saying a word. Outside, Iovan shouted orders in Lothrian to the driver and the guards before climbing in himself, the Thirteenth Chair on his heels. I was not surprised when he hove into the seat opposite mine as his men shut the doors.

He was smiling ear to ear, but said nothing as the van groaned to life and began to move.

I could not speak, and so contented myself with a narrowing of the eyes.

We stayed that way for what felt like minutes, the car bouncing and rolling beneath us. Black-robed, armored, and white-masked, the Cielcin officer, Gorre, watched over us from its place by the door, its sword still unsheathed in the crook of its arm. When it seemed the silence might stretch no more without breaking, Iovan said, "You wouldn't believe how difficult I found it giving the order to bring you in." He spoke Galstani, studying my face as though I were some specimen on a slide. "When you escaped us on the bridge, I thought we'd lost you. I almost let you go after that. To lose an adversary like yourself after all these years . . ."

". . . It's a tragedy," the woman finished for him.

Iovan nodded soberly. I kept staring. He spoke as one who knew me, and I was certain I did not know him. Iovan was Lothrian through and through. He had the Lothrian gray pallor, the black Lothrian hair, the blunt features and black eyes . . . but no. Iovan's eyes were gray, and seemed to glow in the dim light of the cabin in the same glassy, reflective way Valka's eyes did in the right light. They weren't real. Seeing confusion writ on my face, Iovan said teasingly, "You don't remember? I'm hurt."

"We've met before," the woman put in, and her eyes were the same flashing gray.

"On Arae," said the man. "Your dog shot me."

Arae. I felt my eyes grow wide as the pieces all ticked into place.

Arae. It was on Arae that we had first encountered signs of any alliance between mankind and the Cielcin. It was on Arae that the sorcerers of MINOS had forged the first Cielcin-machine hybrids. It was on Arae—likely—that the Iedyr Yemani themselves had been designed, their iron limbs manufactured. The sorcerers themselves had all committed suicide rather than be taken alive, each transmitting an image of his or her mind across the Dark to a ship that had slumbered undetected in deep orbit. Siran and I had chased one of their number to a foundry deep beneath the earth, and there battled her and her pet monster, a lesser demon, a prototype of the hybrids that had led the *Shiomu*'s armies ever since. Siran had shot the witch, but *she* had been a woman.

What had her name been?

"You really don't remember?" Iovan asked.

The woman smacked her forehead. "Aah! But that was Severine's memory! It is we who are confused."

Severine, that was her name. The name of the witch on Arae. Urbaine himself had used that name on Berenike as well, in the crawler.

"Oh, but this is no fun!" the woman said, and reaching out tugged the silken cords from between my teeth.

I worked my lips and tongue, tasted blood where the Cielcin bonds had torn flesh. After a long moment, I gasped. "It was you." The two sorcerers surveyed me with sparks in those dead mechanical eyes. "Valka said she sensed another . . ." I spat pink. "Another neural lace. She thought it was a flashback, but it was you."

"Ah, your Tavrosi concubine." Iovan nodded primly. "Her implants do pose a problem, one that . . ."

The woman overrode him. "Urbaine fucked her good, didn't he? I'll bet there are days she still can't walk straight!"

Snarling, I made it halfway out of my seat before the Cielcin restrained me. Even chained, I might have made it across the van and shattered the woman's toothy smile.

"*Adajjaa!*" the Cielcin commander barked. *Restrain him!*

For a moment, I struggled against the xenobites who held me back, but malnourished and beaten as I was, I was not up to the challenge. I collapsed back into my seat, chest heaving. The Thirteenth Chair tittered, and Iovan exclaimed, "Still fight in you! Good. I was worried they'd broken you." Here he reached out and tapped me on the nose with a forefinger. Iovan smiled. "Our employer will be pleased."

"The Cielcin don't have employees," I said. "They have slaves."

"Know them so well, do you?" both sorcerers said in unison.

I blinked. The words, the rhythm, and the inflection had all been identical. My mind went back to Arae, to the circle of corpses we'd found tethered into the transmitter that had broadcast their images across space. Those sorcerers had shed their bodies as a snake sheds its skin. They were not men at all, but ghosts, thoughtform programs that infested and possessed one shell and then another, not so unlike Kharn Sagara himself. I looked from one to the next and wondered if they were sharing thoughts between one another, or if Iovan were both the man and the woman.

Realizing I'd been silent longer than the question really demanded, I answered. "I do." I glanced toward the inhuman commander, Gorre. Unsure if it understood our tongue, I said, "The Cielcin are using you. They will keep you around so long as you are useful." Gorre gave no sign our human babble meant anything, and why should it? Humans were slaves. Vermin. Food.

Iovan leaned toward me and raised his eyebrows. "It is well we are of *much* use."

The Thirteenth shook her head, and watching her do so it struck me how detached, how singular was every gesture, as though each of the two's expressions were the result of careful consideration, as though the mind that animated the puppet flesh were far removed. "It won't matter," I said. "The Lothrian people won't stand for this once they discover what you're doing."

"The Lothrian people are well in hand," Iovan replied. "The Conclave were all too willing to sell their precious proles out from under them if it kept them off the menu. It wasn't even hard. Three generations I've been here—they die so fast! Three generations to subvert the Conclave to our aims." He sat back, a smug expression coloring his gray face as he affected the attitude and severity of the Ninth Chair. "And the will of the Conclave is the will of the People." His solemn mask slipped again. "Like it or not, Hadrian—may I call you Hadrian?—the Commonwealth is suzerained to the Cielcin Prince. You've lost." He lay a hand on the woman's shoulder. "And I was the one who beat you."

The woman's smile flickered into place mere instants behind the man's. "The hour is far later than you know," she said. "Your Empire is doomed."

I blinked at her. "You're doing this . . . to destroy the Empire?"

Iovan pulled a face. "Well . . . yes. Your Empire has *crushed* humanity. The galaxy has changed, but we have not. Or *you* have not. Your Chantry has kept us in a dark age for thousands of years. Thousands of years wasted kneeling to your Red Emperor and his golden throne. No more! It is time for change, do you see?" He shifted eager in his seat, one hand to his breast. With the other, he seized my hands, gray eyes fixed on mine. "The things I've seen . . . you cannot begin to imagine."

"I can imagine more than you think," I said quietly.

Both Iovan and the woman laughed. "Vati did not exaggerate," Iovan said. "Their gods are real. Beings you couldn't begin to comprehend . . ."

"*Caihanarin,*" I said, using the Cielcin word. "The Watchers."

If I had expected this word to ruffle the two sorcerers, I was disappointed. "You know a word and you think you know *them*? You know *nothing*, Hadrian, *nothing* of what is out there." Iovan pointed through the roof of the van. "We shall be like gods ourselves. Like them."

"The Empire will vanish, and mankind will be free," the woman said. "Free to evolve again, to transcend."

"Like you?" I said, inclining my head to indicate the machines that filled their heads.

"We," both the Ninth and Thirteenth Chairs intoned, "are only the beginning."

"Nettan suja wo!" Gorre barked, ordering us to silence. It was unsettled— I guessed—to hear the name of its gods on my tongue. Iovan and his counterpart each fell silent then, peering up at the hulking commander where it stooped just inside the rear of the van.

Noting their meek obedience, I held the man's gray gaze a moment and mouthed a single word:

Slaves.

Still in chains, they dragged me from the van and into the pale light of a hangar cousin to the one in which we'd been greeted when we first landed on Padmurak. Naked steel arched above us, and the bones of catwalks and gantries hung overhead, lending the place an oppressive, industrial weight. The shuttle that awaited us could not have been more out of place in that place of right angles and hard lines, its long fuselage crooked like the head of an old man's cane, its surface striated and ribbed as some anatomical sketch, raw and organic as the design of Vati's body had been.

It had no ramp, but a lift platform lowered into place as we approached.

The commander, Gorre, shouted orders to the two xenobites who manned that lift. It spoke quickly, and with a thick accent that blurred my understanding of the alien tongue. But I caught the word *wananna*. *Prepare.* In response, I saw one of the Cielcin mount a ladder and climb one of the struts on which the lift had descended and vanish back into the ship above. My escort forced me onto the platform, pausing only to hiss at the lift operator.

"Psannaa!" Iovan called, ordering my guards to halt.

The Cielcin forced me into position on the lift platform and turned me round. Iovan and his nameless companion, his fellow sorcerer, stood arm in arm, each wearing identical plastic smiles. "It is a pity I can't go the whole way with you," the woman said, twining her fingers through the man's. "I want to see what the Prince will do to you. He has such interesting ideas . . ."

"We shall have to wait until we can synchronize with the others," the man said, and kissed the woman's hand, his smile hardly faltering. "Say hello to them when you see them." He disentangled himself from the woman and approached, mounting the lip of the lift platform. He made a show of smoothing the already taut shoulders of my skin-suit like a concerned parent adjusting the uniform of a son they meant to send to war. "I meant what I said: it really was difficult ordering your capture. I don't want the game to end. But I am glad—so, so glad—that I was the one who beat you."

"You haven't beaten me," I said.

"No?" Iovan leaned forward and—inexplicably—kissed me on the forehead.

I slammed my face down into the little man's nose, felt the satisfying crunch of cartilage. Iovan staggered back, tumbled off the lift platform to the hangar floor, laughing all the while. I wondered if the sorcerer's fleshly puppet felt pain. Urbaine had not, nor had Urbaine died when Udax had taken his head. The Cielcin held me more tightly, their talons straining to pierce the skin-suit's weave.

Hooting, Iovan found his feet, one hand clutching his dripping nose. "Save some of that spirit for the Prince. You'll need it on Dharan-Tun."

It was the first time I'd heard the name spoken aloud, the dark world and black fortress of the enemy, citadel of the Scourge of Earth. It was a petty victory I'd scored on Iovan. He was right. He had won. He had beaten me, and if what he said was true . . . he had beaten us. If what he'd said was true, if the Tamerlane itself had fallen, then all was lost.

But despair is the deepest sin, and the final failure.

I gritted my teeth and glared down at the little sorcerer.

"Salu'ayan ne?" Gorre shouted to the others. I heard the breathy sound that passed for yes among the xenobites. "Eija!"

The lift rattled as it ascended and pulled me into the stinking darkness above.

CHAPTER 25

REBIRTH

I COULDN'T REMEMBER FALLING, but I was on the ground. I scrabbled hands and knees, tried to kneel, to stand, to *breathe*. Coughed instead, spat gobbets of pink fluid on the stone beneath me. Struck my head. The blood rushed and pounded in my ears like the approach of a stampede, and it was all I could do to weather clenching muscles as every fiber heaved to vomit up the bile in stomach and lungs.

They were supposed to drain you before they pulled you out of fugue.

I could hardly remember ever feeling so cold.

Trying once more to stand, my foot slipped in the amniotic fluid, and I cracked my skull on the earth.

"There, there," a softly musical voice said, "there there, gentle lord. There there."

Those were hands on my face, cradling my head. My chest felt fit to burst or tear from the pain of coughing. Spitting. I couldn't see, couldn't speak. The sound of my coughing and retching was all I knew, all I knew but that angelic, feminine voice.

"Valka?"

The woman hushed me even as my coughing began to subside.

"No, no . . ." the woman crooned. "It's just us. Hush now. Breathe."

It could not be Magda. They could not have got her, too. Was I still on Padmurak? No . . . no. I remembered, remembered Gorre stripping me of my skin-suit, forcing me into the pod. They had taken my shackles, strapped me into the creche. "Valka!" I managed to scream that time, and lurched to my knees. One faltering step set me falling once again, hard. "Where?"

"Dead, I fear," came the reply.

"No," I said, voice hollow and weak. "No . . ."

"Your ship was taken. Destroyed with all hands." I heard the soft slap of feet in puddles, felt again the cool hands. "You are what is left, my lord." Those same hands half rolled me over, and I sensed rather than saw a woman crouch beside me and pillow my head on her thighs. For an absurd moment, I thought it was my mother, and then I remembered my mother was dead, a victim of those long years I'd spent frozen between the stars. Still, I thought I heard her voice.

You are my son.

Another voice—higher and colder than that of the woman—intruded on my blindness and my still-galloping heart. "What is the matter with him?"

When the woman spoke, I could hear her smile. "I awoke him without draining his lungs."

"He will recover?" the cold voice asked. Something familiar in that voice, something I could not quite remember.

"It will pass," she answered, stroking my face. The woman crooned and made gentle hushing noises. "It is more amusing this way."

The sound of hard soles on metal. "I want him alive, doctor."

"I . . ." Another fit of coughing seized me, and the woman pushed me upright. Blue-green sputum spattered my lap, a blur against my pale nakedness. "I can't see . . ." It was not strictly true. The world revealed itself to me as a smear of light and shadow, the only color the bluish-green of the slime that covered me and the floor about.

"It will pass," the woman said again. "Those *jitaten prophanoi* who did your freezing made rather a mess of you, I fear." Something cold pressed against my back, and I heard the faint whine and beep of some medical instrument. "Still some fluid in the lungs. That will take time." A white light shone in my left eye, tracked to my right. I winced. "I hoped Iovan would have put you in fugue himself."

More footsteps sounded on the metal, circling us. I turned my head, tried to point my ears to track the source of that noise. "I asked for Hadrian Marlowe, doctor. Not his corpse."

"He's alive!" the woman replied, and I thought I could hear terror beneath the motherly sound of her voice. "Core temperature is rising. EEG is . . ."

"Is what?" the frozen voice demanded.

"It's . . . strange."

"If your colleague's inattention has caused my kinsman permanent damage, Doctor Severine, I shall be most disappointed."

"Yes, Great One," the woman demurred. "It's not that. His action potential rates are off the charts."

I caught her hand, adrenaline tightening my chest. "Severine?" I squeezed her hand until I thought the bones might break, felt ridges there on the printed bone so like the false bones of my own left hand. Images flickered: A white metal hand punching the armored glass of a tank. The hulking shape of our colossus marching bow-legged across salt pans toward a looming mountain. Men dead and wired to a transmitter. Siran. A shot in the dark. "You're one of them!"

Again I tried to stand, shoving the witch Severine away from myself. Again I slipped. Again I fell, rolling onto my back in the slime of my rebirth. The darkness swam about me, lights orbiting overhead. Slowly, I became aware of the way the fluid plastered my hair to my face, and of the aching pain in my fingers and at my throat.

My rings. They had not taken my rings, had not removed them when they strapped me into their Extrasolarian-built fugue creche. The skin beneath had frozen to the metal and ivory and burned away. As my body warmed, the pain seeped in, and blood dripped from my fingers and ran from similar wounds where the chain and the piece of the Quiet's shell had burned my neck and chest. I could just barely make out my hands, palms and blood-streaked fingers resolving from smears to mere blurs. Shakily, I worked Prince Aranata Otiolo's old ring from my left thumb, biting back a cry as the flesh beneath peeled back, baring meat and cord.

"Your poor hands . . ." Severine said, taking my hands in hers. "We'll have to fix that." For the first time, I realized she was wearing gloves and a medic's shapeless, glossy coveralls. The face behind the transparent visor was not the one I remembered from Arae long ago. She had spoken Jaddian, but the face that looked down on me was Mandari, narrow-eyed and high-cheekboned. She had not been Mandari on Arae, had she?

I snatched my hand away, wincing as the freezing air whistled against the exposed flesh. Not taking my eyes off Severine, I held the injured limb close, red rings seeping blood from thumb and third finger and the first finger of my right hand. They would scar something fierce. I'd had such a cryoburn scar on my left thumb—my original left thumb. That realization sent a laugh—small and fragile—past my teeth. I clamped it back. That I should have lived so long and traveled so far to gain the same injury again was an irony more bitter than any I could then imagine. The absurdity and the horror of my situation impressed itself on me: sitting naked and cross-legged on the floor before my empty fugue creche, covered in blood and bluish fluid.

"I remember you," I said, though as I say the face she wore was not the same as the one I remembered, but she *was* the same witch of MINOS I'd encountered on Arae so long ago. "Thought Siran killed you at first."

Severine smiled thinly. "Had she aimed for the head, she might have succeeded." She extended her hand. "Hand it over." She meant Aranata's ring. I looked down at the bloody thing. The red stone leered at me like an evil eye from rhodium molded—like so much Cielcin art—to evoke naked muscle. Taking advantage of my fugue-sick state, she plucked it from my fingers.

"Let me see that," the other voice said.

The woman stood, left me on the floor and turned, crossing the puddles of slime I'd made falling from my creche, and knelt. I tried to turn my head, but could not see past the kneeling woman. My creche stood in the center of a pool of pale light amidst greater darkness. Faint illumination—red as hell—shone on walls of webbed stone whose organic arches put me in mind of the intestines of some petrified giant.

"So it is true," the voice said. "It really was you who liberated vile Otiolo. I had heard the story, but stories are *lies*." The tap of feet on metal resumed, and a figure in ribbed, enameled armor and black robes emerged from the darkness, pausing to rest a possessive hand on Doctor Severine's head. I felt my breath catch, and cursed my cold-addled brain for not realizing—not recognizing—sooner.

Prince Syriani Dorayaica stepped carefully onto the wet floor, one jeweled and taloned hand clutching the hem of its robes to keep it from the clinging slime. Tall and terrible it was, tall almost as its iron servant, Vati, though in the planes of its face and the lines of its body there was no sign of the machine. Here was a lord of the Cielcin such as had been bred in the dark chasms of their birth, its limbs clean and unaltered by MINOS's electric sorcery. As it moved, silver threads in the black robes shimmered, highlighting the shape of runes that glittered like stars reflected in waters black as space. A silver pin fashioned in the shape of a grasping hand secured the folds of that imperial garment at the left shoulder—in imitation, I realized with growing horror, of the togas of our own Caesars. Its armor was decorated with a motif of twining arms, ornate as any emperor's. Its face was a screaming horror, smooth as glass, white as marble, with eyes darker even than its robes and large as eggs beneath its crown of horn.

Delicate silver chains hung across its brow, decorated with the deep blue of tiny sapphires, the greatest of which shone in the midst of its forehead like a third, unseeing eye. The horns themselves—swept back from that royal brow—were chased in silver.

It did not squint as it stepped into the light as did so many of its kind, but looked down on me in my nakedness like the avatar of some stygian god. "At last, you have come, honored kinsman." It spoke the standard perfectly, and stooping presented Prince Aranata's bloody ring on its palm. "Welcome to this . . . my home, my *Dharan-Tun*. I have been waiting for you for such a long time."

I found I could not speak. I could hardly think. It was as though my mind could not accept the reality of my situation. It was as if I'd awoken not merely *on* another world, but *in* another world, as if the universe I'd known—that of the Sollan Empire, of the Red Company, of Padmurak and Nessus, Forum and Vorgossos and Emesh—was gone. Severine had said the *Tamerlane* was destroyed, that all my people—all my friends—were dead. I could not accept that, could not even take it in. The thought that everyone I knew, everyone I loved, everyone I'd fought beside for so long . . . the thought that they were dead. Durand and Ilex; Koskinen and White; Elara, who had come up with me out of the pits of Emesh; and Lorian Aristedes—the whole Red Company. And Corvo and Crim. And Pallino . . . and Valka.

Valka . . .

Valka could not be dead. It simply wasn't possible. I would know.

"I would speak with you," the Prophet said, tilting its huge, horned head. Still offering Aranata's ring, it added, "Take it. Speak."

Quaking still from cold, I reached out and took the ring from Syriani's white hand. Not taking my eyes from its face, I fumbled the ring onto my right thumb, leaving the left to weep blood. "And say what?" I managed, swaying where I sat.

Syriani straightened, regained its full height. "You have taken two of my servants," it said. "Iubalu and Bahudde were dear to me. And you destroyed them." The Prince of Princes turned, robes fluttering in the slight gravity, and stalked to the edge of the pool of light. "What is more, kinsman, you have broken my armies, stymied my conquests, interfered in my efforts in your Commonwealth, murdered our kinsmen—though for this I should honor you, though it is not *namnaran*, not our way. What is more, your very existence is a blasphemy. You are *dunyasu*, accursed, and *attantar*, blessed. And you are *its* creature." The giant xenobite—slender as a saber—flexed narrow shoulders. Releasing the hem of its robe it turned. "Think you your trick on Berenike has unfanged me? Think you your god can prevail?" It tilted its head right—the Cielcin answer to a shake of the head. "*Veih.* No. Utannash is fickle. False. It will betray you. Abandon you."

"I don't understand," I said. "What is Utannash?"

The Prophet spoke as if it had not heard me. "When you call for it, it will be *Quiet.*"

"What do you want from me?" I asked, the question of every prisoner in every age.

Raising its white hand—still smeared with the blood from my ring—it pointed at me. "Twelve and four times twelve generations of my clan have passed since the days of Elu. Twelve and four times twelve generations of suffering. Of squalor." The hand dropped. "No more."

I looked on in silence, aching hands curling into fists. The other two rings—still on their cryoburned fingers—bit and tore the flesh. Hissing, I summoned all my strength . . . and stood. My head spun, but I am proud to say I did not fall. Feet apart for balance, I said, "That is nothing to do with us."

"You are in the way," Syriani Dorayaica said. "You. Your god. You must be swept aside. *My* empire shall stretch from star to farthest star, so that *they* might see me."

I took two steps forward, finding my strength at last. "Then kill me," I spat. A *nahute* hung strapped to the Prince's belt, a coil of bright silver. Dorayaica would have only to unspool it to end my life.

It did no such thing.

The Prince only smiled, its lipless mouth peeling back to reveal glassy teeth in black gums. I was struck by just how much there was redolent of the grave in the Cielcin species, as if Evolution in her caprice had crafted a species out of human nightmare and sent them against us. The Cielcin smile was a kind of snarl, not a smile at all.

"It is not enough that you should die, kinsman," the prince said. "You should die *well.*"

That said, it turned and—gathering up its robes once more—swept from the pool of light. Its braided queue vanished last of all, a white serpent slithering into the night. "Clean him up, doctor, and find a place for him. And fit him with a collar. We have a long way to travel."

And then it was gone. Somewhere in the dim distance, a door hissed. Severine plodded forward, rubber boots squelching in the slime and blood.

"Come, Lord Marlowe!" she said, gesturing. "Let us see to your poor hands."

I slapped her hand away, staggered, swore as the pain in my fingers worsened. The very air hurt. "Where are you taking me?"

She blinked at me through her mask. "To medica."

"Where is *it* taking me?" I snarled.

Severine only smiled.

CHAPTER 26

THE CAVE

SEVERINE WASHED ME AND taped correctives to my wounded hands and chest. The bruises and bruised bones from my beatings on Padmurak had not healed in fugue. She taped these as well—her ministrations watched by Cielcin guards in a medica that seemed tailored for human use, its instruments out of place in a chamber that appeared little more than a cave melted out of solid rock. I was fed as well, bland porridge made from bromos and a heel of brown bread. Better fare—somehow—than the Lothrians had offered me in their prison.

Though that was not to last.

These ministrations accomplished, the MINOS witch handed me over to the Pale, who beat me and held me down as the smallest among them fixed a metal collar about my neck. Something in the collar whined as it clamped shut, and a faint red light gleamed.

Dumb as I was and fugue-sick, I little remember the winding stairs and twisted corridors, the lifts and rattling chains of that horrid bastion. I am not Valka, and never was. My memory fails. Fades. Forgets.

For that, more than anything, I am grateful.

But I will not forget the *smell*, the stench of Dharan-Tun. Iron and sulfur. Blood and fire. Rot and death. For all the pandemonic glamour of the Prince of Princes, its dominion was a horror of iron and raw stone. It was a kingdom in exile, a kingdom on the move, rough-hewn and hideous in the hollows of a wandering moon. How vast it was I could never be sure, vaster than the moons of Emesh, vaster than some planets. Dharan-Tun was an entire world, a planet driven by engines huge as the empires of Old Earth and powerful as suns, and though its surface was dark and cold and rimed with frost, beneath its icy cap—in tunnels and in halls fit to outdo mythic Nidavellir in their scope—teemed millions, perhaps billions of the Cielcin and their thralls.

But where there were tunnels and halls there were caverns, too. Dungeons . . . and pits.

The door hissed and sealed shut behind me, its lock panel glowing a faint, ugly red. I had stopped shivering by then, but still I crossed my arms. Severine had given me a loose garment, a colorless kind of cassock, tight-sleeved but loose in the body so that it flapped about my ankles. Still bare-foot, I stepped into the darkness of my new home, squinting to see by the light of the door panel.

The dark stared back.

Slowly, advancing on bare and callused feet, I pressed forward into the gloom, testing the ground with my toes. The air felt warmer here than in the cubiculum where Severine had awakened me, warmer than the medica where she had bound my wounds. The air smelled of moist decay, fungal and earthy and strangely sweet.

Something splashed in the darkness.

"Who's there?" I called out, feeling my way along the wall with one bandaged hand. The stone felt glassy beneath my fingers, as if shaped with plasma or a cutting beam. After only a few steps I had to stop. Injured as I was, starving and fugue-sick, my head swam. Severine had kept me in medica—a drab stone room that beeped with instruments—for what felt like more than a day. I couldn't be sure. The lesser gravity, the darkness, and the sense of dislocation all mingled with the weight of the one thing I'd struggled with since the moment I crashed my chariot on the bridge.

Grief.

Another splash.

Shutting my eyes a moment and screwing grief to the back my mind, I shuffled forward. "Hello?" Absurdly, I almost expected to hear Brethren's chorus of voices rising from the darkness, almost expected to see its bloated arms waving through the gloom ahead. But there was nothing. Looking back, I saw the red glow of the door lock. Faint and far away as a star it seemed, though the short hall could not have been more than ten feet long. Ahead, the chamber opened to either side, its dimensions shrouded in dark. "Show yourself!"

Quiet.

The quiet stretched.

Another splash.

I'd made it perhaps a dozen paces from the end of the hall when my foot found water. A puddle? A pool . . . Hiking up my loose garment, I waded up to my knees, gritting my teeth against the cold. I was suddenly conscious of the throbbing of my injured hands and stopped, careful to keep the robe out of the water. Something brushed against my leg. I lurched backward, splashing back toward the shore. Whatever manner of sightless creature dwelt in those alien waters, I did not desire to meet it. I sank onto the shelf, my back against the rough wall just inside the hall. *It was just a fish,* I told myself. "Just a fish . . ."

Alone in the dark, I drew my damp legs close.

Alone at last.

At last the darkness closed in around me. The darkness and the reality of my imprisonment, the reality that the *Tamerlane* was lost, that Valka was dead. That everyone I knew and loved was gone. My Red Company. My people.

Hot tears fell, and I clenched my screaming fists, heedless of the pain that blossomed from beneath the black corrective tape. I wanted the pain, needed it . . . *deserved* it. I clenched my fists until the pain of those flayed fingers was enough to fill that pitch-dark cave with my ragged screams. Iovan's smile seemed to split the darkness, his evil, gray-skinned face leering at me, false eyes flashing. I understood a piece then of how Valka must feel, haunted as she was by Urbaine's specter. A sob escaped me, and its passage was like the falling of the first chips of stone that herald the breaking of a dam.

What was the last thing I'd said to her? I'd leaned in to kiss her before mounting the ladder to the roof of that evil van. Leaned in and said *I'll be back.* But I would never be back, could never go back. I had lied to her in the end—in a way. Valka was dead, had to be dead.

You don't know that.

Her voice, that bright Tavrosi voice, sounded so clear in the darkness of my cave that she might have been sitting across from me, sharing my cell as we had shared a cell in the dungeons of Kharn Sagara.

You don't know that.

They had been her last words to me, a reminder that I was not always right. I almost laughed—what better epitaph might there be for Valka Onderra Vhad Edda, once of Tavros? The memory pulled on another, and Iovan's smiling eyes seemed to shine at me from the shadows.

Your Tavrosi concubine, he'd said. *Her implants do pose a problem, one that . . .*

One that what?

I sat a little straighter. Iovan had not spoken of Valka as one dead. She'd been alive when I'd boarded the shuttle that brought me to this place. How long ago had that been? How long had I been frozen on my journey from Padmurak to Dharan-Tun? Hope and fury in me both, I stood and scraped my cheeks with the heels of my hands. I hurried back down the little hall away from the pool and pounded on the door, crying out for Severine, for Syriani—but no one came. I must have beaten on that portal for an hour before I staggered back against the wall, robe flapping about my heels. Focusing my vision, I peered across the vast infinitude of possibility, peering for a world where I opened the door and escaped.

There were none.

Reading this account, you might think my vision boundless, but it is hemmed in by what I know. In relying on my technician to power down the antimatter foundries on Eikana, I relied on his skills, only shepherding us along currents of time opened by his ability. I had no understanding of the mechanisms governing that Cielcin door, no knowledge whether the lock was electrical or mechanical, or where the controls might be. From my limited perspective, the door was as good as wall, and try as I might, the door as it presented itself to the limited prism of my consciousness would not open. I was Pandora's cat—neither living nor dead—and powerless to escape my prison.

Powerless to escape my collar, too. I dug my fingers beneath the lip of the collar and pulled, straining the hear the scrape of locking mechanisms. It wouldn't budge, not in mine or any universe. I could not see my way to choices I did not understand.

At length, I returned to the shelf by the black pool and listened to the trickle of water flowing over distant stone. How long I lay awake no man can say, for time itself dissolved in that darkness.

Days, I think, passed without event. By the end of the first day the inward gnawing of my stomach became difficult to ignore, and the desire for water drove me to drink from the pool. I had no way of knowing if the water was safe enough to drink, but the taste at least was not so evil. Bitter, yes, but not poisonous. I would know soon enough. If I had made some error, it would not be long before some waterborne animalcule turned my bowels to water and twisted my guts. I thought of Cat dying in her gutter.

What an end it would be if Hadrian Halfmortal, whom men said could not be killed, who caught highmatter in his hand, who had stood unburnt beneath the lance on Berenike, were struck down by some alien dysentery in a dungeon and the Dark.

But I would die of thirst elsewise.

The door opened, admitted a bloody flow of light.

"You look comfortable," came a drawling human voice. Two shadows stood in the arched portal. After what I guessed were days in darkness, even the dying-embers glow of Cielcin lighting was blinding. From the sneer I guessed that these were no thralls of Syriani's, no collared slaves, and as they drew nearer one kindled a lamp in the form of a slaved glowsphere that hung close to her shoulder.

That white light—harsher than the red by far—blinded me for true. But as my tortured eyes adjusted, I recognized the face of Doctor Severine, her gray eyes—the same as Iovan's—twinkling down at me. But it was her companion who had spoken. His voice and face were unfamiliar, though something of the ensemble spoke to me of old acquaintance. Milk-pale and hairless he was, tall and thin as if in imitation of his Cielcin masters, his eyes the familiar machine gray. He wore a knee-length brocade jacket cut Mandari fashion with high collar and knotted closures, so deep a purple it was almost charcoal with slippers to match, his legs sheathed in white hose.

Eyes aching from disuse, I cast my gaze around the chamber. Stalactites hung from above, spires of milky stone shot through with dark veins so like the stone of our necropolis beneath Devil's Rest on Delos far away. The rough floor of the shelf carved a crescent shape against the shore of the pool, which stretched perhaps two hundred feet to the far wall where the limestone rose in tumbled steps above the surface of the water. A narrow trough—perhaps six inches wide—ran along the far wall to a culvert of raw iron caked with grime. Water from the pool spilled down into it in a miserable trickle. A primitive latrine.

There were no other amenities, unless it were the iron rings hammered into the walls at intervals. Noting my interest in the rough toilet, the man said, "Oh, gave you one of the better cells, did they?" He glanced at Severine, who said nothing.

"What do you want?" I asked, voice hoarse. In the presence of other people, I was suddenly aware of how grimy I felt, of the oil on my face and hands. I felt an overwhelming urge to climb into that pool and scrub myself clean. But even my meager movements had set my stomach groaning.

The man exhaled. "To feed you. What else? The Prince asked us to keep his guest comfortable."

"Is that what you call it?"

"I am glad to find your experience with Iovan has not taken the temper out of your Imperial spine," the man said, coming from the hall onto the shelf proper. "That will make watching your time with the Prince all the more gratifying. He is an artist, you know." As he spoke, a crate floated in from the hall, carried by a gleaming drone held up on humming repulsors. It deposited the box and flew away, back out the open door. For a fleeting instant, I wondered if I might overpower the two sorcerers and make a dash for it.

I knew I could not.

The bald man sighed, massaged his neck. "It is a pity your bird men are not with you. One owes me a head."

My stomach turned over and knotted with old fury. "You're . . . Urbaine!"

"The very same." The MINOS sorcerer who crawled inside Valka's mind and crippled her bowed a mocking bow.

"I'd hoped you were dead," I said, though what a thin and feeble hope it proved.

Urbaine gave a thin-lipped smile. "You are not the only man in the galaxy to whom Death does not come easy." He looked me up and down. "I would love to test the limits of your legend, my lord. I understand some in the Empire believe you are some kind of god. Even the Prince—bless him—thinks you sent by one. But there are no gods. There is no magic, only mysteries we have not yet solved." As he spoke, he opened the lid of the crate and drew out a foil-wrapped packet. He tossed it at me with the air of a man tossing scraps at a dog. It slid across the floor.

It was a legion-style ration bar.

I did not move to take it. I would give neither Urbaine nor Severine the satisfaction of seeing me desperate. I would not beg or scramble for scraps as they so clearly hoped.

Severine spoke. "There should be enough to last you . . . about a standard year? Assuming you pace yourself." Her smile could have drawn blood. I matched it.

"How did you survive?" I asked Urbaine.

The sorcerer gestured to his heart with two fingers. "You missed my secondary transceiver. Broadcast an image of my daimon here while you were busy with poor Bahudde."

"I thought you needed a larger transmitter."

"Like the one on Arae?" He smiled and seated himself on the rations crate. "You missed us by *minutes* that time. No. On Arae we had to transmit several dozen daimon images about half a light-year, and we had to do it quickly. On Berenike there was only me . . . and I only needed to get to orbit." Urbaine's face grew sardonic. "You don't . . . know much about machines, do you?"

I shrugged and—using the rough wall for a handhold—pushed myself to my feet, my already grimy robe clinging about me. "Enough to know what you are."

Severine's smile had not faltered. "And what are we, Lord Marlowe?"

"Ghosts," I said. "You died with your original bodies."

The woman snorted, and laughing Urbaine said, "Primitive nonsense."

"It's not," I said, knowing too well the depth of the intrinsic linkage between consciousness and flesh. "You're just an image—to use your word—a shadow of . . . whoever you once were."

"We were shadows once," Severine said, cryptically. "We are more than human now."

I studied their faces. Severine appeared human enough, a Mandari woman, as I've said, but Urbaine had clearly left pieces of his humanity behind. His nose was flat and broad, not quite the slits of his Cielcin masters, and his ears—were they fused to the sides of his skull? "I met someone once who believed as you do. He was so abstracted from his humanity I think he could no longer even understand what he'd lost."

"Nonsense." Urbaine dismissed this with a hand.

"It's not," I said again. If it were nonsense, I felt sure I would have met one posthuman chimera not given to moral insanity. "You cannot become more than human by making yourself less human in the first place."

Urbaine stood smoothly. "There is no such thing as *human*. We are data. Genes. Thoughts. The form is irrelevant."

"The form creates the function," I said. "Change the body. Change the mind."

"We did not come here to debate philosophy!"

"No," I agreed. "You came to gloat." I spread my hands, fingers flexing without pain. The correctives had been hard at work while I languished in the dark, evidence that at least several days had passed. "Get on with it."

I had gained some semblance of solid footing despite my collar and my cage. Urbaine seemed to have noticed, for he snarled, "You're the one locked in here, Marlowe! You've lost!"

"I am," I said. "I have." I turned away, peered down into the water at my feet. In a distant voice—not really meaning to speak—I continued, "Your friend Iovan said you meant to destroy the Empire."

"To set humanity free," Urbaine replied, spreading pale, long-fingered hands.

"By enslaving them to the Cielcin?" I countered.

The sorcerers looked at one another. It was the woman who answered. "New paradigms," she said, "new growth. The Cielcin offer opportunities not . . . previously available."

I snapped my gaze back onto the two sorcerers. "Such as the dissolution of the Empire?"

"Such as," Severine said. "Humanity has grown fat in your Empire's care. When was the last great invention? The last industrial revolution? The last new idea? Your lords are perfectly willing to playact medieval darkness as though the Golden Age never ended."

I turned my back on the wizards and paced toward the shore of my pool. There were fish in it, whole shoals of little silver leapers no longer than my hand. "The Cielcin want to wipe us out."

"They want to wipe out the *yukajjimn*," Urbaine agreed. "*We* are not *yukajjimn*. *You* would not be *yukajjimn* if you but knelt."

My reflection stared back at me. "It's a caste?" I said, unable to scrub the shock from my voice. Long ago, when I'd met with Prince Aranata Otiolo, it had spoken of the human *yukajjimn* in such a way that seemed to refer exclusively to the Sollan Empire. Kharn Sagara had been exempt. I had not thought much of it at the time—there had been so much more to consider—but the distinction and the importance of it crystallized. Sagara had subordinated himself to that Prince in order to maintain a kind of peace and to trade with it. In doing so, he had signed himself onto the lowest rung of a ladder on whose highest stood the Prince itself. And no wonder—oaths were meaningless to the dark lord of Vorgossos, who served only himself. The Cielcin did not want to eradicate all of humanity . . . they wanted to eradicate every man who would not kneel to them.

"You are *Aeta* yourself," Urbaine said. "A human Aeta."

"A *yukajjimn* Aeta," Severine added.

"It's a caste . . ." I said again, dumbly, still looking out at the waters. "So you will force mankind to kneel to her conquerors?"

"We will force change," Urbaine replied. "Progress."

"Those are not the same thing."

"They are!" Urbaine countered, and I saw his shadow flickering on the wall across the water. "Under the Prophet's Hand, humanity will spread across the galaxy, across *galaxies*. We will fight in his armies, build his cities. We will *ascend*. We will *evolve*. Humanity will become *more*. We must."

I turned to look at the wizard, at the clear imitation of his alien masters styled on his flesh. Examining his inhuman face, I understood him. He craved power. All his talk of uplifting mankind he directed at himself. He would sell trillions into bondage and the abattoir if it brought him prestige. At minimum, he meant to serve as the vizier of a new and inhuman emperor. But it was more than that. Urbaine was a *believer*, whatever his protestations.

"You are a man of science, sorcerer," I said, sparing a glance for the other, who had gone strangely silent. "You say there are no gods. I say that religion and science are each journeys of faith. Each quests for something—the same *something*, in my experience."

Urbaine snorted. "You're a fool. We are building a better world."

"Paradise," I said to him. "Enlightenment? Call it what you will." The slap of that riposte wrongfooted the two sorcerers, and I pressed on. "Speaking only in terms of science: most change is evil. All change increases entropy, and all entropy is loss." As I spoke, I thought of my final, apocalyptic vision of the darkness at the end of time, of the last stars winking out like candles as dark energy sundered light from light. "The only good comes in preserving those things—peoples, institutions, whatever—which are good themselves."

Severine sniffed. "And who defines good? You?"

"There are *trillions* of people in the Empire. *Trillions* who will die defending it." I turned at last and glowered at Urbaine and Severine. "How many are you?" I felt the sting take hold.

Like the revolutionaries who penned the Lothriad, the magi of MINOS were doubtless few in number. Revolutionaries are always few, always forcing their vision on the disinterested masses, caring little for how those masses suffered in the execution of their dreams.

"Oh, we have people *everywhere*," Severine sneered.

"Not trillions, then?" I managed a derisive sniff of my own.

Urbaine's face had gone grave as stone. "I would not be so proud, if I were you," he said. "You think it is only the Commonwealth we've suborned? Our fingers are everywhere. In everything. The Principalities. The Republic. The Small Kingdoms. What's left of the Freeholds . . ."

"And the Empire itself, I don't doubt." I no longer had the energy to be surprised. "I should have killed you when I had the chance." I had no guarantee that carving the heart out of the wizard would have destroyed him for good. There was always the chance some backup of Urbaine's *image*, his *daimon*, remained on some faraway world. But it would not be the same *daimon*, not the same man.

How could one vanquish an enemy for whom Death meant so little?

Urbaine's smile revealed a set of entirely canine teeth. "And now you never will." He drew a step nearer. "It is a pity your woman was lost. I would have liked to have her as well. The things we might have done with those implants of hers." He cackled then, and licked his lips.

My vision went white, and I hurled myself at the sorcerer, aiming to knock those pointed teeth from his face. Weak though I was, my overhand still caught the magus on the side of his jaw, and he folded like paper, like a bundle of dry twigs. For an instant, I stood over the man whose worm had chewed through Valka's brain, the man who had crippled her for a time, had nearly killed her. For a moment, I stood triumphant, fist raised for the second blow.

Pain flooded my sensorium, as if lightning had struck every nerve ending and every synapse at once. It was as if I'd been encased in white-hot metal, as if my bones had been packed with glowing coals. I felt my skin blister and peel away, my cords snap and curl. If I screamed—and I must have screamed—I could not hear it over the pure liquid agony my universe had become. No acid, no poison, no virus—not even the vile *dispholide* of the Chantry priests—could burn with such heat.

And then it was done, switched off as smartly as a lamp.

When I recovered, I found I had fallen on my back, my rags and hair soaked by the water's edge. The pain had gone entirely, but its memory remained like a boot print on my heart. Severine and Urbaine were staring down at me. The latter was grinning his imitation Cielcin smile.

His teeth were red.

I pointed up at him. "Got you."

The pain flared again, brief and bright. When it passed, my throat was raw from screaming. I coughed, choked—would have retched if I had eaten the rations Urbaine had tossed my way. I only heaved instead.

"You think this is one of your stories," the sorcerer said. "You think yourself some kind of hero. You think you are fighting *evil*." He shook his head. "Your Empire has kept you simple. There are no heroes. There is no good or evil. Stories are for children . . . and children have to be made to grow up."

I understood what had happened then. "The collar . . ." I could still hardly speak without coughing. One of the sorcerers had activated the device by way of their implants. I couldn't have fought back if I tried.

"Nerve induction," Urbaine explained, touching the back of his own neck. "Applied directly to your spinal cord. Not pleasant, is it? I wrote the configuration myself. I've sampled every sensation the human brain is capable of feeling. . . . Believe me when I say it *can* get worse." He turned to go, and paused to kick the ration packet toward me with a pointed gesture. "Eat, Lord Marlowe. You will need your strength."

Severine followed in his wake, her hard shoes clacking after his Mandari slippers. The last thing I heard before the door squealed shut was her voice saying, "We'll leave the light."

CHAPTER 27

THE WHITE HAND

I MARKED TIME IN meals, starting from the moment Urbaine and Severine left me lying on the margins of the pool. The packet contained a humble ration bar with a pasty, chemical flavor and a texture equal parts rawhide and sand. One bar was not enough to satisfy, though the nutritional content was calculated to keep me alive and healthy on two a day. Urbaine had played a cruel joke giving the box to me. Not only had giving me control of my own eating prevented me gaining any sense of the passage of time a gaoler's visits might have engendered, it put me in charge of how quickly I ran out of food.

But I would not play their games, and held myself to two a day—or to what felt approximately like a day. With each meal I carved a notch on one wall with a bit of loose stone, crossed it to form an X as each *day* passed. The foil I carefully placed back into the crate, which was where I also placed my spent correctives when my cryoburn had healed, leaving raw, white scars.

Beneath the light of the solitary glowsphere—which I felt certain must also have been a camera through which MINOS and Syriani alike kept watch on my imprisonment—I explored the confines of my cell. It was by far the largest cell I'd ever been confined to, with the special exception of Maddalo House, but it was the most foul. Even the cell beneath the People's Palace in Vedatharad had had plumbing. In the dark beneath the surface of Dharan-Tun, I had no water but the bitter water of the pool that trickled down through cracks in the high ceiling, leaving stalactites like Cielcin fingers reaching down. My only company were the strange, extraterranic fish, eyeless and blind—the only sound their occasional splashing and the metronomic *drip, drip, drip* of water. I explored every crack, every corner, even dove into the icy waters of the pool in an attempt to find any means of escape.

There were none, and even if I could escape that chamber . . . where would I go? I was alone and as good as naked miles beneath the surface of an alien world. And Urbaine's collar yet hung about my neck. I entertained dreams of overpowering the guards, of using the mouth of a *nahute* to grind the collar down and make my escape into the bowels of that dark world as I had made my way along the tunnels beneath Vedatharad . . . but they were only dreams.

Guards never came.

A score of X marks marched along the wall. Two score. Three. No one came.

I talked to myself. Told stories, recounted tales of Simeon the Red, of Kasia Soulier and the Cid Arthur. I recited passages from *The Romance of Alexander*, from *Meditations* and *The Book of the Mind*, I sang songs I'd learned from Pallino and Switch in Colosso, even some of Valka's I'd learned by years of long exposure. Anything to pass the time, to fill the silence.

But the silence came on anyway, and though I could not be idle and paced the confines of my cage like the very tigers whose story I'd shared on Padmurak, I grew quiet in time, muttering to myself. Sleep came less and less, and though my wounds healed I felt a gray sickness settle upon me, mingling with the grief that all my friends were dead or captured and the last, terrible parcel of hope that denied that same grief.

But I would not accept it. I would not choose.

The door opened, its squeal hounding me from some lonely place between waking and dream.

"*Uimmaa o-tajun!*" came the rough voice of a Cielcin. I stirred slowly, sluggish from lack of sleep. Five of the Prophet's guards entered, striated black armor gleaming, the badge of the White Hand imprinted over their hearts. "*Ijanammaa o-tajun junne wo!*"

Hold him down.

The one whose deep blue surcoat marked it for an officer stood by while the others held my face to the stone floor and affixed binders to my wrists. I did not resist, and the soldiers hauled me roughly to my feet, their taloned hands carving shallow scratches into my flesh.

It took a measure of doing to find my tongue after I knew not how many days or weeks of disuse. "Where are you taking me?" I asked. The xenobites blinked at me—one shoved me by the head. I repeated the question in its own tongue.

The officer bared its glassy teeth, but gave no answer.

"You're sure the Great One said we can't have our play?" asked one of the guards before me, tilting its horned head.

"*Suja wo!*" barked the officer, shoving its underling away from me. "This one's for the Prince! You heard our orders! *Unharmed,* he said—and you ask about play!" The Cielcin's nose slits flared. "Can't you see it's the wrong *kind* anyhow? You'd kill it and lose your spawn. And then where'd we be, Gurana? The Great One'd grind us up for meal." It shoved its subordinate again.

"I'm carrying is all!" said the one called Gurana.

Its commander snarled, "Then you find somewhere else to shove it. This one's for the Prince!" Even after more than three centuries of life, my grasp of the xenobites' language was tenuous. Though I was undoubtedly by then one of the Imperium's premier experts, there was so much of the Cielcin culture we simply did not know. Without cities to plunder and libraries to raid—much of Cielcin tradition was oral, preserved by *baetayan* like Tanaran—the niceties remained mysterious even to me.

Still . . . I could guess the sort of play Gurana had in mind. *Carrying,* it had said. Starved and starved for sleep as I was, I looked on my captors with new horror. The Cielcin were hermaphrodites, mono-sexed but with twin roles: the *akaranta*, active, and *ietumna*, passive. Early in the war, we believed the Cielcin reproduced as we did, one impregnating the other, but it was not simple. The Cielcin were parthenogenetic, so that any one might conceive a child on its own, a genetic duplicate. Rather than impregnating a partner, the gravid Cielcin might implant its self-made embryo in another of the species, whereupon the genetic makeup of the host would change the developing fetus via something our magi called *conjugation,* so that the resulting child—which had begun as a genetic duplicate of the first parent—would take on the traits of both. What was more—provided it acted quickly—this second parent might avoid implantation and pass the child to another, so that the embryo was the product not of one parent or two, but three. Perhaps more.

I had never imagined that the host might not need to be a member of their own species.

I felt sick and said nothing as the officer frogmarched me from my cell.

The sound of screaming resonated up the hall as we hurried on, passing a Cielcin in an iron mask who led a column of human slaves chained collar to collar. In the dim, red light, I might have been forgiven for thinking I'd died and gone to hell. My guards were mostly silent as they marched me up a winding stair carved in the living rock, its pale walls gleaming orange in the light of low sconces. Higher and higher we climbed.

The nature of the corridors changed. Gone was the graven rock, the burrows and sealed tunnel-mouths. Reaching the top of another stair, we passed between two sculpted horrors, three-headed Cielcin figures with faces peering across the archway and in either direction, their black-glass eyes concealing cameras that watched all who came and went. Beyond, we stepped out into an echoing hall whose high, ribbed arches stretched above us like black bones. Other Cielcin paused in their business to watch us pass, or else hurried out of our way. Many wore the dark, organic-looking armor I'd grown accustomed to. These marched in units or stood sentinel, their white-masked faces and horned crests proud in the bloody light. Still more wore silken robes or sleeveless suits in whites or grays or blues, with here and there a green or violet. Among them—naked or dressed in rags— moved human slaves, hollow-eyed and underfed. A group of them carried one Cielcin master on a litter, while another—laden with a heavy pack like some bipedal mule—delivered goods from the mouth of one side passage to another.

It was a street.

I was on a Cielcin street.

The boy I'd been wanted to stop in wonder, but my guards would not allow it. They pushed me along, past a pack of staring human slaves. From their pallor, I took many of them for Lothrians, but there was one gray-haired man with clear, green eyes who might have been of the Imperium. I held his gaze a moment, long enough to see him mouth a single word.

Palatine.

I nodded. He averted his eyes.

Gurana and the other guards shoved me past a line of inhuman guards and through a passage that opened onto a truly massive space, vaster than any of the domes of Vedatharad, vaster than the hollow places of Vorgossos. I did stop in wonder then, and earned a beating from Gurana. Ahead of us stretched a narrow bridge across a vast pit, one of many like the spokes of a great wheel that converged on the far side before the gnarled edifice of the *Dhar-Iagon*, the fortress-palace at the heart of Dharan-Tun, whose tall and pointed gates yawned to admit me, lit by the molten gleam of magma from the exposed mantle far below.

A shrill cry went up as we approached within sight of the gate, and the mighty doors swung outward. Half-carried by the inhuman soldiers who held me, my callused feet scraping the smooth stone, we passed beneath the arch and along a mighty hall dominated left and right by monstrous carvings.

They were not carvings of Cielcin.

My escort raised their faces in gestures of submission—bearing their throats—as we passed beneath their monolithic shadows. I could not help but emulate them, turning my face to stare in horror and in awe. I did not mark the strangeness of the contrast then, that the Cielcin bowed their heads to signal a willingness to do violence, and raised their chins in submission where we men bow in deference and raise our chins to provoke. What was to them a gesture of reverence to the *things* carved on those mighty plinths was to me a last vain gesture of defiance to those dark gods whom my captors praised.

I caught sight of the shapes of curling tendrils, of membranous wings worked in stone, of faces folded and wrinkled as tonsils, of eyes and arms too numerous and misshapen to count. One had the shape of a mighty serpent, and another a form like a brain with many hands. Another, bat-like thing clung to a graven pillar, while a shapeless horror of rippling stone boiled beneath the next arch.

"Watchers . . ." I breathed, still looking on. But my escort did not speak the tongues of men, and paid me no mind.

Still more guards showed us to a lift, and we ascended to another hall, this one greater than the first and supported by arched and slanting columns. Throngs of the Pale watched from either side as my hosts shunted me along, my bare feet soiling rich carpets.

The scent of incense filled the air, and the crackle of burning. We ascended a shallow stair to a round arch where guards in black and white armed with polished glaives stood sentinel. Coming to the top of that stair, I beheld what I knew must be our final destination. Violet light fell through windows high above, and I recognized the fractal distortions of warp travel, the blurred and stretched stars ahead blueshifted by the speed of our travel. That distortion set ripples to playing on the jet-black floor. The unholy geometries of iron archways and pointed windows were like no human building, the floor ridged and uneven, the surfaces of the walls and pillars knurled like spurs of Cielcin bone.

Like a throne room it seemed to me, but there was no throne. Instead, a hemisphere of white stone dominated the space beneath the high and narrow windows, a round door in its front, its only approach a narrow span of naked stone that jutted out across a pit whose depths none had fathomed and survived.

Boom.

The moment I crossed the threshold into that black chamber, a deep drum sounded.

Boom-doom.

Beyond the arch, about incense braziers burning low and smoky to either side, a crowd of Cielcin retainers in silks of purest white gathered and lay one by one with their faces to the ground.

"*Teke!*" cried a herald, and the gathered retainers replied, "*Teke! Teke! Tekeli!*"

It was not a Cielcin word, though to the uninitiated it had the sound of their language. I puzzled over it, turning the sounds in my head as I turned my head from side to side. I had heard it before. On Berenike. But I did not know its meaning.

Boom-doom.

A Cielcin holding the heraldic spear rattled its silver chimes. "*Raka attantar Aeta ba-ajun, Ikurshu ba-Elu!*" it proclaimed. *Blessed be our Clan-Chief, Bloodshoot of Elu!*

"*Yaiya toh!*" came the reply.

"Blessed be our Clan Chief, who holds in his hands our world-fleet and blood-clan!"

"*Yaiya toh!*"

"Blessed be our Clan Chief! The White-Handed Godkiller!"

"*Yaiya toh!*"

"Blessed be the Prince of the Princes of Eue!"

"*Yaiya toh!*"

"Blessed be the Prince Syriani Dorayaica! Our Master! Our Keeper! Our Father! Our Mother!" The herald's mantra had reached some kind of crescendo, and with each pronouncement the crowd replied with the *yaiya toh*, each coming faster and faster with the drumbeats. The soldiers beat the butts of their glaives against the stone floor in time with that drumming until the whole of the palace of *Dhar-Iagon* shook with their thunder.

The black door in the white dome across the narrow bridge opened on a deeper darkness, and the *Shiomu* appeared. Dorayaica wore the same sculpted black armor it had worn on our first meeting, the same black and silver toga and cape. The same chased silver shone in its crown, and its long cord of braided white hair hung over one shoulder to its waist.

Unbidden, Gibson's ancient rebuke rose in my mind. *Must everything you say sound like it's straight out of a Eudoran melodrama?* Despite the horror of my circumstances, I almost laughed, but it was a nervous laughter, the laughter of the condemned. Syriani Dorayaica placed one foot in front of the other and crossed that narrow way. The bridge could not have been wider than the fingers of my outstretched hand, but the Prophet seemed not to mind. It raised its hands for silence, and silence fell.

"*Tekeli!*" it said, repeating the strange word, which the prostrate inhuman crowd echoed without raising their eyes. "I am the *Shiomu*, the Prophet Syriani who has brought you out of the darkness. I am the Prince whom Elu foretold, who will lead our people through that darkness to new life. I am the sword that will wipe clean the universe! I am the hand that will make it anew!"

"*Yaiya toh!*" the crowd intoned, rising to their knees. "*Yaiya toh!*"

I stood even straighter before this pronouncement, until the Prophet's eyes found me. "*Cielucin ba-koun!*" it proclaimed. "My People! The Fire is kindled! The Clan Chiefs of our Blood-Kin gather. An *Aetavanni* has been called for. I have called for it."

Aetavanni?

Vannuri was *to meet. Vanni* then was a *meeting. Aetavanni* a meeting of *Aeta*, of *Clan Chiefs*, of *War Princes*.

A kingsmoot.

Not for the first time, my blood ran cold.

Syriani's huge black eyes had not left my face throughout this entire monologue. I understood then why I was being kept alive. I was to be paraded in triumph before the princes of the Cielcin as I had paraded Iubalu's chimeric hulk before Caesar and the great houses of the Imperium. Eye for eye. Tooth for tooth. I wondered if the Cielcin had always practiced such public humiliations, or if it were another thing—like the toga it wore—that Syriani had acquired from its study of mankind.

"*Nietada Iubalu oyumn ekan ka'iri o-manasie,*" I said, raising my voice to challenge the Prophet's for that silent hall, speaking Cielcin so that those listening would understand. *Iubalu said I was to be a sacrifice.*

"You dare to speak her name!" a high voice wailed. Among the ribbed columns and kneeling suppliants, red light shone. I knew the voice at once; I had heard it before. On Eikana. The eye descended from the emptiness above, a red spark in a white metal sphere no more than a cubit in diameter. *"Okun ne?"* Hushansa—the true Hushansa, the mind and inhuman brain that controlled the iron puppets I had battled on Virdi Planum—peered down at me from within its floating chassis. In the rear of the room, statues moved.

Syriani raised a hand. "Quiet, *ushan belu. Onnanna.*" The Prophet drew near, one hand securing the drape of its garments. Switching from its native tongue to Galstani, Syriani Dorayaica said, "Without you, Marlowe, I could never be." It stooped over me, its breath a fetid poison in that place of sweet-smelling smoke. With one clawed hand it reached up and combed my knotted hair back behind one ear. "All that I do, I do through you. You are my soil. My bedrock. All I build, I build on you." It drew back, baring glass fangs. It gestured at the white dome and the black door. "Narrow is the way to rule! Narrower still the path which is ordained for me."

"Which path?" I asked.

"I shall become a god," the Prophet answered. "I shall make an offering of your people to the gods who dwell in the darkness beyond the farther suns, and in so doing I will destroy Utannash. I will destroy the *Lie.*"

"The Quiet?" I frowned in spite of myself, a pit forming in my chest. Syriani *had* some kind of vision, it seemed, for it seemed to know the Quiet dwelt among our possible futures, a creature whose creation depended on the survival of mankind.

Syriani hissed. "So you call it." It drew back, moving to within a few bare paces of the precipice. My head swam with fantasies of breaking free of the guards that held me, of making a last, desperate rush at the Prophet and sending us both to our deaths far below. But something of that thought must have written itself on my face, for no sooner had the thought entered my mind than a metallic ring as of spurs sounded and a white-armored figure appeared from behind a pillar. The *vayadan*-general Vati stood far to one side, but I knew the chimera could move fast as thinking.

I'd never make it, even if I could escape my guards, and an experimental effort to try earned me a sharp knee to my guts. Shackled, I knelt on the floor not a dozen paces from the dark lord. Syriani—perhaps eight feet tall and crowned in silver—said, "Utannash is the Lie, the author of this lying universe, this prison! It is false! Its powers will fail you, and when they do, you will see the Truth."

As it spoke, a giant shape moved in the shadows to one side. Turning my head, I saw a hulking shape crawling along the aisle beyond the nearest row of pillars behind the kneeling courtiers. Six-legged it was, like one of the walking tanks deployed by our legions. Its head swung like a turret, one-eyed as Hushansa, its white carapace lit red beneath in the gloom by the light of the incense braziers.

"There are no gods but ours," the Prophet said, raising its voice to the whole chamber.

"There are no gods but ours!" the court echoed, high voices scratching at the ribbed vaults.

Lowering its voice once more, speaking only to me, Syriani Dorayaica said, "I will destroy it, and you. And everything."

"Then kill me!" I said, and remembering my audience I raised my voice and said it again. *"Shuza biqqa o-koun wo!"*

The great prince made a gesture, and Gurana or one of the others cuffed me about the ears. I struck the stone floor face-first and lay there. In my weakened state, it was almost too much to contemplate standing. Still in my own language, the clan chief hissed, "You do not give the orders here, kinsman. Think you that I am a fool? Think you that you might goad me to error? No. Your death is appointed. It will occur. But it will occur in its time."

"At your moot," I said.

"The *Aetavanni.*" Syriani made the breathy sound that passed for an affirmative in its native tongue. "I see you understand me perfectly. Your time is running down."

"It's not hard to understand," I countered. "You mean to make a spectacle of me. To impress the other Aeta into kneeling before you." I was aware suddenly of how still was the congregation about us, the functionaries of Dorayaica's court all kneeling on the hard floor, unmoving as stone.

A high keening noise escaped the prince's throat. It was a Cielcin laugh. "Impress them? Yes. Yes, indeed."

A rush of wind battered the air, and looking up I saw a pale shape alight on a spar that stretched between two pillars. Its body was whip-slender, an articulate metal serpent with two thin legs and shoulders barely broader than a boy's. Its armored white head bore a horned crown like the ones on Hushansa's puppet bodies. As I watched, it folded huge, gossamer wings and slid down the column even as the spider-thing advanced on six legs to join Vati and Hushansa about their lord.

Four of them.

There had been six.

Counting them, I knew I beheld the four remaining fingers of the White Hand, the four surviving members of the Iedyr Yemani, the exalted holy slaves who served the Prophet. As I drank in this revelation, the winged creature shrilled, "This *yukajji* killed Bahudde!" The creature prostrated itself before its lord, wings folding into its back. "It killed Iubalu! We must have blood!"

"Silence, Aulamn!" Syriani said, sweeping its gaze over the throng. *"Rakayu uelacyr udantha."*

The time is not right.

We were on stage. The Prophet was performing for its court. I was the centerpiece in a pageant of tribal justice. The *vayadayan* of the Iedyr Yemani had entered in line with a script. Twice now the Prophet had silenced its Hand, twice it had refused to hear their pleas.

The huge six-legged *thing* swiveled its turret head, and a voice deep as the pit at Dorayaica's back said, "Iubalu and Bahudde were our sister-brothers. This creature must be punished. Its life is *dunyasu*, an affront! Each breath it takes it stole from your most holy slaves."

For a third time, Syriani Dorayaica said, "Silence!"

Then Vati knelt, and kneeling the chimera was almost as tall as its lord, its horned and feathered crest tipped back as the machine bared its throat in gesture of submission. It alone of the four fingers of the White Hand had not spoken. "Teyanu speaks truth, Great One. The *dunyasu* Marlowe has profaned the blood-clan! We are dishonored! Only blood may wash out blood."

"Life for life!" the winged one, Aulamn, exclaimed.

"Uja raka Aeta wo!" the Prophet replied. "It is *Aeta*, and an *Aetavanni* has been called. By the laws of Elu, it is protected."

The huge creature called Teyanu countered, "By the laws of Elu it is forsworn."

The Prophet and its Iedyr had reached some form of impasse. I thought I understood. By the ancient laws that governed Cielcin society, no prince might kill another under the flag of truce, and the act of calling for this *Aetavanni* had raised that flag. But those selfsame laws—and perhaps older laws, the laws of the jungle, of the cave tunnels, of the birds and fishes—decreed that any who attacked the *itani*, the blood-clan, and the *scianda*, the world-fleet, was forfeit. Honor demanded Dorayaica destroy me, and honor demanded it protect my life.

It was the tension between these two demands that had arranged this pageant, and it was likely the tension between these demands that had caused me to be kept in my cell for so long. The powers in Dorayaica's clan, its *vayadayan* and *baetayan*, its warriors and priests and close counselors must have deliberated over this moment for weeks to confect this performance.

Speaking for the gathered courtiers, its voice raised, the Prince of Princes said, "No Aeta may kill Aeta when the Fire is lit. We sail for Akterumu, where Elu the Great met the whispering gods! Would you have me break our sacred laws?"

"*Veih!*" the courtiers proclaimed, the Cielcin word for *no.*

Speaking for the Hand, Vati—still kneeling, still baring its throat— asked, "But this *dunyasu* has slain two of our sister-brothers! Two of our bond-mates and bed-mates! Should it be spared? Should we then break our sacred laws?"

"*Veih!*" the throng cried once more.

Speaking in its appointed time, Syriani asked, "What then is to be done?"

"It must be chastised!" answered Aulamn.

"It must be mortified!" replied Hushansa.

And Teyanu added, "It must be punished!"

I hardly heard any of this, for all my attention was given over to a single word.

Akterumu.

Syriani had said we were sailing for Akterumu. It was a word I'd heard but twice before, from Tanaran, the *baetan* of Prince Aranata Otiolo, who had said that it and the *ichakta* captain Uvanari had discovered the location of Emesh and its Quiet ruins from Akterumu; and again in my dreams, chanted beneath the shadow of the black dome.

Slowly, I eased myself back to my knees.

Speaking then in a stage whisper, in Galstani so that only I might hear and understand, Syriani said, "It grieves me that it must come to this, kinsman. But my slaves speak truly. You have assaulted my blood-clan, killed two of my mates. This I cannot abide. This I cannot forgive."

"Mates?" I could not help myself, and looked round at the iron horrors standing or fallen about their lord. Tall Vati, with its pale crest and banded armor. The winged terror, Aulamn, still prostrate before the Prophet. The hulking Teyanu, six-legged and larger than any groundcar. And Hushansa, Hushansa the Many-Handed, whose nucleus orbited the gathering like an evil satellite.

I had wondered how it was the Aeta kept its pet giants in thrall, why the chimeras did not simply slaughter their Prophet and each other in a mad scramble for the top. Could it truly be . . . love? Obedience out of devotion? Could the Cielcin feel such a thing? Stunned to silence, I watched the Aeta with its retainers, and despite everything I felt a glimmer of the hope I'd known as a boy, the hope that conciliation might be possible between their race and ours.

The spark blew out in the next instant.

There would be no conciliation between our two races. I am no conciliator.

At a gesture from the Prophet, my guards clamped clawed hands on my shoulders and held me fast. Syriani drew nearer, its huge face descending as it bowed toward me. "Give me your hands, kinsman."

I made no move, and Gurana seized me by the hair and tipped my head back, baring my throat in forced submission. I gritted my teeth and clenched my fists as the Prophet seized my right hand with its cold, damp ones, dragging the left along with it in its manacle. Slowly, inexorably, Syriani worked its clawed fingers around my own and forced my right hand to open. "We are Aeta, you and I," it said, still speaking my own tongue. Holding my right hand in its left, it displayed its right, fingers spread. "But you have taken two fingers from my hand." And curling one digit down and then another, it said, "Iubalu. Bahudde."

What it did next I have never forgotten. Syriani did not move quickly, but moved instead with deliberate strength to place the last two fingers of my right hand into its mouth. So stunned was I, so horrified, I forgot to react for an instant. An instant was long enough. The xenobite's jaw clenched as it clamped down and bit off my two fingers. Howling, I pulled my hand away, trying to rise, to run, to fall away from the monster that had taken half my good hand. I felt my heart beating in those wounded fingers, saw red blood dripping from the ruined stumps and down the Prophet's chin. For another single, obscene instant, I saw the red ends of my fingers still between Syriani's teeth. Then it tipped its head back and swallowed them whole.

For one of very few times in my life, I was struck speechless. I clutched the ruined appendage to my chest, blood soaking my robe. The Prophet smiled down at me, teeth red with my own blood. It laughed then, laughed the high wailing laughter of its kind. I felt shame rise in me. It was all a joke, all a hideous joke: fingers for fingers.

"*Taguttaa o-tajun wo!*" Syriani ordered. Gurana's hands seized the neck of my robe and rent the garment in two. Then raising its voice for the crowd, Syriani proclaimed, "*Shiabbaa! Ute Aeta ba-Yukajjimn!*"

Behold, the king of men!

I wanted to say that it was not true, that I was not the Emperor. But to be Aeta was not quite the same thing. The Aeta must be warriors, and our Caesar fought from the rear, commanding others to bloody their hands in his name. Syriani doubtless understood this fact, understood that to human eyes I was only a knight, but I had bested Aranata and Ulurani both. With my men I had bested Iubalu and Bahudde. I was Aeta, the only human to carry that title, and so I was—to the Cielcin—the Prince of the Princes of Men.

It was no wonder the Prophet wanted me for its triumph. Killing me before the *Aetavanni* in Akterumu would be a coup to end all coups. *All that I do,* Syriani had said, *I do through you.* Through me—through my death—it would solidify its claim to be the Aeta ba-Aetane, the Prince of Princes and High King of the Cielcin.

Syriani raised its white hand and gave a sign. I heard the whip snap before I felt it, the red pain burning my back. I felt hot blood well and run as skin tore and split. The whip snapped again, and I choked off my cry and slumped as my handlers propped me up. I would not scream. Gibson had not screamed. The lash fell a third time. A fourth. Blood soaked my torn gown and ran down my thighs, and I screwed my eyes shut.

What is pain? the teacher asked his student.

It is an illusion, the student answered.

The teacher struck his student across the face.

Urbaine had believed the phantom pain he'd administered to be a masterpiece of sadism, and perhaps it was. Perhaps the sensations he'd engineered were exquisite in their intricate cruelty. But nothing is worth the real thing. Pain, I have said, forms the basis of all morality, for no man who suffers pain doubts that it is evil. No one who experiences pain can even question it.

How many times did the lash fall? A dozen? Three?

When it was over, my gaolers released me, and I fell to the bloody floor at Syriani's feet.

"What I do to this," Syriani said, and from the shadow that fell across me where I lay I knew it pointed down at me, "I will do to every one of its kind." It gathered up its robes and pitched its voice to address my escort. "Take it to the wall and hang it!" it decreed. "Let the slaves see their king!"

CHAPTER 28

HADRIAN BOUND

THE PAIN DROWNED EVERYTHING, even itself. Every inch of me was numb, though with each subtle motion of my body the agony flared white hot and new within me. I opened my eyes. The world resolved slowly.

I wished it had not resolved at all.

Beneath and before me lay a cyclopean city of iron and black stone. Cruel towers rose beside rivers of glowing magma, or else hung like stalactites from the metal roof of the world thousands of feet above. Crude metal stacks carried the fumes of industry from evil mills and foundries fed by those same rivers, and the whole place stank of burning and of brimstone. As I watched, I could see the shapes of men in the distance hauling steel beams into place, laboring at the construction of some new tower or monument beneath the watchful eyes of their Pale masters. So vast was that subterranean space that it might have swallowed whole two of the great domes of Vedatharad and yet had room for a third, and from my high vantage I could see the openings of arched passages to other caverns and tunnels equally immense.

Never before had I seen so great and terrible a city of the enemy. Indeed, no greater city of the Cielcin was there in creation—save one, and that they did not build.

Only slowly did I recognize that I was in the same cavernous vaults through which I'd marched on my approach to the *Dhar-Iagon* and the Prophet's throne, the black city of Dharan-Tun.

I tried to crane my neck to see, and realized I was falling.

With a shout, I looked down to rough flagstones a hundred feet below, bare feet dangling over nothing. Movement sent a flaring agony up my arm to my throbbing hand, and full understanding came only steadily, as if reality would not fit itself—could not fit itself—into my brain.

I was hanging on a chain, strung up by my right arm, the other arm and both legs free. My sudden movement had set me swinging like the pendulum of an old clock, and I struck the wall, impact sending waves of pain shooting up my arm and across my tortured back. It was only then that I remembered the whipping, and looking down saw dried blood streaking my naked legs. They'd taken my gown from me, and I hung unclothed for all to see, my mutilated right hand permanently raised as a sign and warning to all who saw me.

I had defied the Prince of Princes, and all would see the consequences of that defiance.

How long I hung there I never knew, nor could guess how long I'd been unconscious. Cielcin passed in the plaza below, stopped and pointed. What human thralls there came averted their eyes and hurried past, chains rattling. It would not be until later that I realized precisely where I was, hanging from the wall beyond the arched outer entrance to the gates of the *Dhar-Iagon*.

When had I last tasted water? Last eaten?

With a titanic effort, I reached up with my free hand and seized the chain above the binder that held my wrist. Pulling upward, I managed to take the tension off my tortured arm, though I shut my eyes to block out the sight of my mangled hand and the memory of my fingers caught between Syriani's teeth. Blood welled up where the manacle cut flesh and dribbled down my arm. One pain traded for another, as the act of pulling lit up my tortured back even as my arm and shoulder cried with relief. Stunned, I let go of the chain, returning my weight entirely to the tortured limb. The short drop and sudden stop whited out my vision, and when I came to once more, it was to the sound of a winch, of rattling chains, and to the sensation of rough stone scraping my torn back.

Rough hands pulled me over the lip and into a close, low-ceilinged chamber whose open face looked down on the plaza below. Dazed as I was, mind blurred by the numb agony in my tormented arm and shoulder, I was only dimly aware of the foul-tasting rag my inhuman captors had shoved into my mouth. So parched was I that I sucked at the rag's contents without thinking, and gagged at the taste: foul, salty, and alkaline.

The hollow chamber filled with the harsh sound of alien laughter.

I recognized the taste of urine too late and coughed, spat the rag out on the floor.

"*Pitatonyu edediu!*" one of the gaolers barked.

"It don't know what's good for it!"

Pale hands held me down while they forced the foul rag back between my teeth and squeezed. I choked, tried in vain to fend the Cielcin off, but ultimately . . . I failed. They left me lying on the bare stone, still chained by my wrist. Alone. I fantasized about looping the chain about my neck and leaping from the open face of the chamber, but it took every effort, every ounce of energy left just to roll onto my side and spare my back.

That was how he found me.

The door opened some time later. I did not even try to move, not even when something cool burned my back. I smelled antiseptic. Alcohol.

An old man's face peered down at me, skin leathered by torment and by time. He had a plebeian's blunt features: dull eyes, flat nose, jug ears, and his jaw quavered as he went about his ministry, cleaning my wounds with a sponge and a bucket of what I took for antiseptic.

"Why bother?" I managed to grunt.

The old man did not answer, but produced a squeeze bottle and tipped clear water down my throat. I spit it out, expecting another trick. I could still taste the Cielcin urine, and eyed the fellow with suspicion. He shook his head, jowls quavering.

"Who are you?"

In answer, the man pointed to my collar, then to his own.

"You don't . . . speak standard?" I asked. The man shook his head, opened his mouth to reveal a black hole where tongue and teeth once had been. "I'm sorry."

He shrugged, then proffered the water again. I took it with my left hand and managed to drink, clenched my teeth as the alcohol burned the marks the lash had made. I lay there in silence, permitting the slave to do what he was ordered to do: to treat my wounds, to see that I survived for another day's torment.

His work finished on my back, he moved to my wrist and mangled hand. As he did so, I caught sight of the sunburst tattoo on his neck and the faded number opposite it. 111.

"You were a soldier?" I murmured, gesturing weakly at the mark. They were a legionnaire's tattoos. He had been taken in battle, or else taken in fugue. He would have been a young man when that happened, and so had lived his life in bondage. A knot twisted in my guts at the thought. "What's to be done with me?"

The man paused in his ministrations to point squarely at his ruined mouth again, eyes narrow. I felt shame and looked away. I felt a hand on mine a moment later and flinched away, but the fellow caught my arm and pressed his sponge to the stumps of my fingers. I almost whited out from the pain and cursed, trying to flinch away, but the soldier held me fast. I tried to pull my hand free, but he held me, and when I found his face again through tears, I found his eyes captured by something he saw on my hand.

It was the Emperor's ring.

The mute slave's eyes darted to my face, back to the ring. And as the poor slave in the street had done, the fellow mouthed the word *palatine*.

"Yes," I said roughly. "Hadrian. My name is Hadrian."

The slave nodded, eyes darting to my hand again. He seemed to be thinking about something. He sucked on the inside of his cheek. What that something was I realized too late. He seized the Emperor's ring and tugged it off my finger, and when I cried out he stood sharply, upsetting the bucket of disinfectant in his haste to be gone. I tried to rise, but my healer struck me with his heel, and I fell back stunned. The little man leaped on me, and before I could resist he seized the chain about my neck—the chain from which hung the Quiet's shell.

"No!" I hissed, and threw the man off me.

The chain snapped in his fingers, and the pendant rolled across the floor. Injured as I was, I could not stand, and the man found his feet before me. "Guard!" I shouted, and remembering just where I was shouted again, *"Shuindu!"* I had little hope of the Cielcin coming to save me. Now, the thought almost makes me laugh.

But it might have frightened the slave all the same. The little man scrabbled for the pendant and snatched it up. He glared down at me and made a cursing sign—first and last fingers extended—as he mouthed the word again. *Palatine*.

I tried to rise. I failed.

The mute slave's heel cracked out again, and the world went dark.

The Cielcin returned, the noise of their coming a thunder that shattered my fitful sleep. Before I could get a word out or get my bearings, they seized me wrist and ankle and tossed me over the ledge and out into the stinking air. I felt my shoulder pop as the chain went taut and the manacle tore my wrist. The pain was unbearable, and howling darkness like warm, black ink flooded my eyes.

It was the fourth time they'd suspended me from that chain, five counting that first experience. Five days, or what passed for days on

Dharan-Tun, and when each day was done, when I could scarcely breathe, they would haul me back into the cell, torment me, and leave me to another mute slave, a woman who salved my wounds and nursed me on clean water and porridge. What had befallen the man who had stolen the Emperor's ring I never knew, nor learned why he had not taken the others. The woman could not say. Her tongue had also been cut out.

All I suffered I shall not recount, for some things do not bear repeating.

I opened my eyes again, the pain in my shoulder louder than the unheard burning of the stars. The great city of the Cielcin lay before me. It didn't seem real. It was some nightmare out of Milton or Bosch or Chambers, a painting of hell.

"You're not going to die here, you know," a cool voice said. A shadow fell across my sight, and turning I saw my brother Crispin standing on the wall beside me as though it were the floor. He took a bite of an apple and grinned down at me, looking for all the world like he had when I'd left him on the floor at Haspida, a boy of fifteen. "You're going to die *there*."

"Shut up, Crispin," I groaned, but when I looked back, he was gone. I missed him at once, and felt myself begin to cry, stupidly, for a brother who had hated me and a home I'd never loved.

But he was right. I was not going to die here. I was going to Akterumu to die. This was only hell. Death came later.

"He's going mad!" the cool voice said. It took an effort of will to realize the voice had never been Crispin's. Urbaine was standing in the square below me, dressed in his violet Mandari silks, his bald and unnaturally tall crown hidden beneath a dome-shaped cap.

Beside him, Severine nodded. "That did not take long."

"I must say, I am disappointed, my Lord Marlowe!" Urbaine called out. "They say you are the Earth's Chosen. Surely the Chosen need not suffer so!" He laughed.

I had tried already. A thousand times I'd reached for my second sight, my vision of the collapsing waveform of potential, and a thousand times I'd failed. The vision would not come. Starved and tormented as I was, I could not reach the rivers of time any more than I could reach up with my left hand and lift myself to save my tortured right. Delirious, I could not summon the focus necessary to free myself.

In the distance, a gang of men dragged stones.

I could not free myself. Or fly. Whatever power I had, it was sundered from me. The Quiet had gone *quiet* indeed, just as Syriani had said it would.

"Come down, my lord!" Urbaine mocked. "Come down among us mortals. Will you not come down?"

"Come up instead!" I groaned, swaying on my chain and making the cords of my shoulder ache. "You're missing the view!"

Urbaine's laughter filled the square below. "I much prefer this one!"

"I will kill you!" I shouted, sending paroxysms racing up my arm. Against my best wishes, I cried out, turning the shriek into a threat. "By Earth, I *will* kill you!" Blood pounded in my ears, and I fantasized about tearing my own arm from its socket and falling on the black sorcerer.

Urbaine's pale face never stopped smiling. "I was sorry to miss your meeting with the Great One!" he called, meaning Prince Syriani. "I heard it was quite the performance." I said nothing. My scream had taken all my strength from me, and I hung there in a gray haze. Urbaine faded beneath me, and Severine with him. A warm wind buffeted my face, and looking up I saw a great bird stooping over me, its dark pinions spread.

"Udax?" I asked, reaching out with my left hand to clap the Irchtani on the shoulder. But Udax was dead, had died fighting Bahudde on the fields of Berenike. It was an eagle I saw, the very bird that Jove had set to torment Prometheus. It watched me with dark, reptilian eyes.

"They are going to kill him like this," said a woman's voice, far away. Valka? No, that was Severine. Valka was dead. Was Valka dead? She was not dead, she couldn't be. That was a lie Iovan and the other sorcerers had told me.

Prometheus had begged Heracles to slay him, and that bastard son of Jove had asked his father—the old titan's gaoler—to speed his arrow and release Prometheus from torment. But Jove, in his caprice, sent instead the eagle who tormented Prometheus to bear Heracles to the titan's side. But it was a trick Jove played, for not even Heracles could break the chain the father of the gods had used to bind Prometheus, and Jove laughed at him from the peak of Mount Caucasus. But Heracles was undaunted, and struck not the chain, but struck off the mad titan's arm and fled with him from the god's dark mountain. So it was by many trials that Heracles brought the maimed Prometheus to his son, Deucalion, in the days before Jove sent his flood to wash away the world. Jove's arrogance had been his undoing, for it came to pass that it was Prometheus's fire in the hands of Deucalion that delivered mankind from the waters Jove sent to unmake them.

But there was no Heracles, nor any eagle. The chain was torment enough in itself.

Like Urbaine had said, my story was no story at all. There was no hero coming to save me, no good to prevail. But there was evil. There is always evil—and the Cielcin *were* a flood come to wash mankind away.

I blinked.

There was no eagle. Only Urbaine and Severine looking up at me, one grinning, the other stone-faced. "They must cut him down," Severine was saying.

"Not yet," Urbaine said to her. "He's not done yet."

CHAPTER 29

MARKING TIME

TIME IS THE MERCY of Eternity, or so the poets say. But the mind makes Eternity of Time. When Milton's monster said the mind might make heaven of hell, it was the father of lies who spoke those words—the very devil whose image my ancestors took for their sign. Great though the mind may be, even in its capacity for self-deception, it has limits. No mind can make heaven of hell, not even mine. You cannot dream your way out of prison, not truly, nor think your way from the camps. No one would say to those suffering under the *Lothriad* that they could simply imagine a better world. It is one thing to tell the slaves of the Cielcin to shoulder their burdens and fight to survive, quite another to tell them to imagine they wear no chains.

I could not imagine I was free, or think my way out of pain.

The torment on the wall continued until I thought I must lose my arm, until I knew I must starve. The tortured appendage was blue from blood loss and contusion, and ached worse as the blood returned to it each night. The torments of my guards worsened, their laughter grown harsher and more cruel. The mute slaves visited less and less, and when the Cielcin returned and did not lower me down the wall, but draped my arms over their shoulders and marched me down through the *Dhar-Iagon* beneath the sculptures of the Watchers and out into that accursed city and down once more by several winding stairs and blind tunnels to the cave cell with its iron door, I did not resist them.

Alone again, I slept—and for how long?

No one came. Not even Death—though I heard her bony feet and the rustle of dark robes at the door to the hall many a time. Against my more rational parts, the animal in me staved her off; forced me to crawl on my belly like a worm first to the water's edge, then to the replenished stock of ration bars Urbaine had left for me.

I could not let myself die.

Valka was alive. I knew she must be. Urbaine . . . Severine . . . Iovan . . . I knew they all had lied.

I could not die.

Not again.

The pain ebbed by inches, wounds hardening to scars. In time I knelt, and stood, and cleaned myself in the waters, thereafter drinking only from the thin stream that ran down the limestone wall. In time, I began to carve my marks in the stone wall again, away from the first set I'd made.

I was sure I'd marked a standard year, and surer still that more time had passed, for I could not account for my time above the gates or the time I spent recovering on the floor. I might have lost months.

But I had recovered, though I had not recovered anything like my full strength. I could hardly stand, and though my limbs were wasting of muscle, they seemed heavier to me than ever they had before. It was a trial to walk from one end of my cell to the next, and so most often I sat with my back against the wall, staring at the shrinking shadows as Urbaine's watchful eye drifted lazily overhead.

I muttered to myself, and in time fell silent.

The ration crate emptied and stayed empty. Desperation drove me to catch the slimy things that swam in the waters of my pool, to eat them raw and spit out the bones. In time I forgot the foul taste of the creatures, as I had forgotten the taste of wine and the warm caress of the sun. I had healed, but I had not healed well, and the motion of my torn shoulder was awkward and unsteady. I could not raise that arm above my head no matter how I stretched it, nor could I raise it at all without pain. No matter. Though the three fingers left to me on that hand remained, that hand could never grasp a sword—not well. In the Empire they might grow the bones and flesh anew, might mend the poorly knit tissues of my shoulder, but I was not in the Empire.

I might never see the Empire again.

That was a strange thought. I had grown to love it, in its way. For all its faults and failings, it was home. I loved my Empire not for what it was, but for what it should be, what it must be. For whatever it was, it was not Dharan-Tun. It was not Padmurak. It was not Vorgossos. It was a place where humanity might live. Might live . . . and remain human.

But it was lost to me, as I was lost in the dungeons of the enemy.

Lost without a star, without the light of some other world to remind me that hell was *only* here, to remind me—as Gibson once had—that most of the universe was peaceful and quiet.

The only light I had my enemy had given me, and it illumined nothing save my cage.

CHAPTER 30

THE TRUTH AND THE LIE

THEY HAD TO DRAG me to my next audience. I tried to walk, but the muscles of my legs cramped before I had climbed twenty paces. They were not gentle, and my feet were bloody by the time we reached our destination.

Pale light illuminated the grotto not the customary low red, but bright enough it hurt my eyes. The rough stone walls had been carefully sculpted, depicting the circular anaglyphs of the Cielcin language: some symbols small as robin's eggs, some large as dinner plates. I recognized a symbol here and there, but their grammar remained mysterious to me. There were no sentences, no linear thoughts. The Cielcin looked at the runes and saw images, forming relationships and semantic meaning by the relative position and size of one symbol to the next, so that a cluster of marks might suggest several meanings at once. I knew enough to know that one cluster spoke of *virtues* and *princes*, another of *masters* and *slaves*, but the relationships between one and the next were blurred to me.

The guards dropped me on the uneven floor, and I remained there, chest heaving, knees bruised by the fall.

"*Ennallaa kounsur,*" ordered the familiar voice. *Leave us.*

The Cielcin did not argue with their lord. I was hardly in any condition to stand, much less fight—and my hands again were bound.

Syriani Dorayaica stood not ten paces away, its silver-crowned form framed in a round portal. Gone was the striated armor. In its place, the Prophet of the Cielcin wore sleeveless robes of *irinyr*, the heavy, glossy material that passed for silk. Its arms were sheathed in silver rings hung with fine chains that dripped with sapphires and lapis lazuli, and black filigree—carefully applied—decorated the flat, white face. It looked less the warrior and more the sybarite, its white hair carefully braided and musked with something smoky and unpleasant.

Aware that I was on my knees, I struggled to stand. I felt grubby before the Great One, dressed in nothing but rags cinched about my waist.

"Beautiful," the Prophet said in Galstani, huge black eyes studying me the way a gourmand studies his food. "There is a purity to suffering, do you not think?" Standing, I gave no answer, but leaned against the wall. "Your own philosophers and priests acknowledge this. It is no betrayal to agree." It drew nearer a step. "Your own quietude will not bring you closer to Utannash, kinsman. Speak."

It was only with great effort that I found my voice. I had not used it in a long time, and the sound was more alien to me than the voice of the Prophet. "The nobility is in how we bear suffering. Not in the pain itself."

Syriani's lower lip stretched, and it advanced toward me. "Think you that it is so?" It continued its study of me, eyes picking over the whip-scars that stood out white on my shoulders and flanks. "Pain purifies. It reminds us of the division between the *ouluu*, what you call the *atman*, the soul— and this." Reaching down, it pinched the soft flesh at the crease between arm and chest. "*Ujazayu*. The substance." One talon *snicked*, sliced into the flesh. I did not wince, but shut my eyes as a rivulet of blood ran down my side and stained the rags about my waist. "Better to accept the pain, to *escape* through it. To bear it only is to accept the Lie."

"The Lie?" I said. "Utannash."

The Prophet hissed. "It is the author of the Lie. We are not *this*." It pointed first at its chest, then my own. "Not *things*. None of this . . ." It pointed at the cave, at Dharan-Tun and the universe beyond. "None of this is real. It is the work of Utannash, who is false. Whose work is false. Pain brings us closer to *them*, closer to the truth."

"To your gods?" I asked. "To the Watchers?"

Syriani made the breathy *yes* sound. "You begin to see."

"So I'm being . . . purified?" I asked.

"Purity is the greatest sacrifice," Syriani intoned. "I wish for you to understand before you die." It drew back a pace, half-turning to contemplate the carvings on the walls. "The gods seek to free us from this prison. To destroy this world and set us free. Free to join them in *Iazyr Kulah*, the true world."

"Paradise," I said.

"Just so," the Prince of Princes said, affecting a human-seeming nod.

"Your Utannash built this world to punish us. We must destroy it, and so we must destroy *it*." Syriani paused and turned away, wandering a few paces up the hall toward the portal whence it had entered. "How do you survive so confusing a language?"

I said nothing for a long moment, stared at my host in confusion and disbelief. "You want to . . . destroy the universe?" I almost laughed. The thought was ludicrous on its very face. It simply wasn't possible. "You're insane."

Syriani Dorayaica turned and looked down at me. "With all you know, kinsman, you say this thing?" It made a negating gesture, tossing its head. It gestured at the portal and said, *"Wegga ush ti-koun."*

Walk with me.

Moving gingerly on raw feet, I limped to join the Prophet, all too aware of the rough scrape of callus and stick of raw flesh on the cold, damp stone. Shallow pools lined the path, sunk into the dark rock. There tiny, luminescent fish swam, their blue-white radiance illuminating the phosphorescent glyph carvings in the walls. Syriani did not speak for a moment, but picked its meditative way between the pools and over stepping stones nearly flush with the surface of the still, clear water.

"You surprised me at Berenike," it said at last, stopping beneath an arched and sloping wall thick with carved signs that glowed silver in the fish-light. "Clearly, you are more resourceful than I anticipated. You should have died."

"You were overconfident," I said, keeping my distance.

"I was not certain I would have such a chance again." Syriani had its back to me, its braided queue on full display where it sprouted from the base and back of its skull behind the flange of the epoccipital crest. "I acted hastily. A mistake I will not replicate." It looked back over its shoulder and amended. "*Have not* replicated."

I narrowed my eyes. "A chance to kill me?"

"To destroy a servant of Utannash, yes."

"I thought you wanted me for your Aetavanni."

"I was prepared to compromise," the Prophet answered, and shut its eyes. "But the gods reward their servants. Now I do not have to."

It turned back and continued walking along what I was starting to realize was a kind of garden path. Pale and glowing fungi grew from the walls and contributed to the tableau, and thin streams of water cascaded over rocks and into pools clear and black as space. I limped after the Prophet, whose bare feet clicked on the stonework. Evidently I had been summoned to accompany the Scourge of Earth on its walk through something like its palace gardens. I expected to see servants or collared slaves—human and Cielcin alike—but we were utterly alone.

At length, I asked, "Why do you call it that?" When Syriani did not answer, I added, "Utannash?"

"It is its name," Syriani answered, one clawed hand caressing the edge of a fan-like mushroom as it stopped to admire it. "*Utannash* is *That-Which-Lies*, or *the Deceiver*—you would say. That is the word?"

Unseen, I nodded, but said, "*Iugannan* is *liar* in Cielcin, is it not?"

"In Cielcin?" Syriani made a low clicking noise I took for disapproval. "Think you we have but one language?" It looked at me, nictitating membranes blinking across the surface of eyes large as eggs. "You understand less of us than I thought . . . I thought we were alike. I have read and studied so much of your history. Your art. Your philosophy. I sense you have not reciprocated as much as I had thought—though you speak well." There was a note of almost human sorrow in the xenobite's voice.

"As do you." Indeed, it spoke the standard better than most men I have known.

Dorayaica dismissed these words with a gesture. "*Utannash* is *the Lie* and *the Liar* both. It is an old word. An old word for an old enemy in a tongue little remembered by my people in these benighted times." Glass teeth—the very teeth that had maimed my right hand—flashed at me. "Do you not know that we too are a sunken race? Far fallen from our former glories?" The Prince of Princes crossed the surface of one black pool and stood before a glowing mural of interlocking circular runes. "Were Elu in my place . . . already our dominion would encompass this galaxy, and not a one of your kind would breathe free. Alas, I am not Elu, and the clans are not as they were in Eue after Se Vattayu."

"But why *Lie*?"

The Prophet's eyes drifted shut. "Because its world veils the truth of the *Caihanarin*."

"The Watchers?"

Again, Syriani made the sharp, breathy sound that meant *yes*. "They gave us *everything*. They made us. They taught us to fly, brought us out of Se Vattayu and gave us the stars, that we might cast down their enemies. Utannash would destroy them and make itself the only god, it would impose its lie—this universe—on all that is. It is *alatayu*. Nemesis, Destroyer . . . Devil, you would say."

I snorted. "So am I."

The joke evidently was not amusing to the Great One. Syriani Dorayaica gestured at the walls. "It took my *baetayan* several hundred of your years to create these gardens. To carve these *udaritani*. Can you read them?"

"Only a little," I admitted.

This seemed to impress the Cielcin lord. "They are a far subtler art than your primitive systems." It waved its hand at the arc of wall across the pool. "This is our story."

I imagined *baetayan* like Tanaran laboring for several times the life-age of a plebeian to complete the mural carvings. It must have taken a small army of them to complete the work, if the sheer scale and number of the tunnels was any indication.

"I thought the *baetayan* were oral historians of a kind."

"They are," Syriani said, "but stories should not live only on the tongue. Would you not agree?" It traced the perimeter of one gleaming mark with a clawed finger. "The *udaritanu* is not like your alphabet. They are a pictoral style. Like one of your blasphemous paintings."

I blinked. "Blasphemous?"

The Prophet acted as though it had not heard me, but marked a series of small circles with three triangles inscribed within each. "Here are our ships leaving Se Vattayu. And here the planet itself." It indicated a huge and convoluted glyph at the center of the image. Seeing it suddenly as an image and not a strange and unlinear sentence shifted my sense of it, and looking straight up along the curve of the wall I spied another equally convoluted glyph bound to the sign that represented the Cielcin homeworld by an almost helical chain of smaller signs. Clearly here was their destination, the world of their exile.

"But . . . blasphemous?"

Syriani turned its huge, horned head to peer down at me as though I were an unruly child. "You make images. Icons you would call them. Idols. To depict material things as they appear, as a part of Utannash and its Lie, is to deepen the Lie. It is an affront to the gods."

"But you have statues in your hall," I said. "Those . . . monsters."

"Monsters?" Syriani hissed again. "They are the gods, kinsman, and the gods alone are real."

I understood. Countless were the old traditions of men who turned against art and beauty. Who burned it, broke it, tore it down in the name of some transcendent principle. Their belief was that such images wrought by hands obscured or usurped the things they represented: that a flawed human icon of Beauty—failing to be beautiful—destroyed Beauty. Perverted it. Or that a great icon *replaced* Beauty—or Truth, or whichever virtue or ideal you cared to name—and became the thing itself. It is not so. Art, great art, serves as a reminder of invisible things and of their manifestation in things visible. The image, say, of our Radiant Emperor stamped upon the obverse of every hurasam serves not only to remind us who is Emperor, but of the virtues that make him Emperor. The sense of strength and dignity, the serene command.

"What then of your White Hand?" I asked.

Clasps fashioned in the shape of that hand secured the Prophet's robes. It fingered one before it replied. "I told you," it said. "I shall become a god."

"By conquering us?"

Syriani made the breathy *yes* sound again. "I shall make a sacrifice—not only of *you*, but of all your people. As Elu ascended, so shall I."

"Ascended?"

Glass teeth flashed. "You name your Emperors gods, do you not?"

"Only the first," I said tartly.

Syriani moved out beneath the great mural, one six-fingered hand spread as if to grasp the whole thing in its fingers. "Elu *was* the first. The gods spoke to him, taught him to build the ships that carried us from our dying world. It was Elu and his Twelve Aeta who left Se Vattayu, who made us *more* than the animals we were." Its outstretched hand traced the helical line from Se Vattayu to the next world. "As ants to wanton boys are we to the gods . . ."

"They kill us at their sport," I said, finishing the quotation.

"Ah, there is the Marlowe I expected."

"Shakespeare." I raised my chin.

"Just so," the Prophet said. "But my gods made us strong instead—though they might have smothered us in our infancy. Elu led those who would listen to a new world."

"Eue?" I asked, recalling the earlier name. I had heard it before. It was a part of one of the Prophet's titles . . . the Prince of the Princes of Eue.

The tall Cielcin bowed its head in what was for its kind a threatening gesture—it was a human nod. "It means *the gift*." Syriani turned away again and walked a few paces along the mural, raising its hand again to a cluster of *udaritanu* marks that spread out from the sign of the planet Eue. "It was on Eue we became *Cielcin*, became *godsborne*." When it saw the look of confusion on my face, Syriani added, "It is another old word."

"Urbaine seems to think humanity can become Cielcin," I said, and realizing my meaning might be vague, I added, "Become godsborne, that is."

Syriani's teeth flashed again. "Urbaine is a naked little climber, isn't he? He thinks putting on a body more like our own will win him some favor . . . and it may." The Prophet made a negatory gesture. "Urbaine believes humanity may be made to see the Truth, that in time your kind might serve the *Caihanarin* and aid in bringing about the end. I am not so sure. There is too much of the Lie about you. And you are weak."

"Weak?" I stood straight as I could, no easy task with my crabbed muscles and ruined shoulder. "We've held you off for centuries."

The expression on the Prophet's face might have been pitying. Even after so many years of familiarity with their kind, Cielcin faces were hard for me to read. "Is that what you've done?" Syriani Dorayaica began to move again, circling me as it had in our first meeting. "The stage is hardly even set, and already your Commonwealth is ours."

"They're not my Commonwealth."

"And yet your presence there suggests you need them, suggests that your Emperor is desperate."

I short *aah* escaped me, and I cast my gaze down at my bare and bloody feet. I understood then why I had been treated to this lecture on history and this walk through the Prince's grottoes. Screwing my eyes shut, I said, "It is customary to ask these questions *while* you torture a man, great Prince." My whole body ached with the memory of the pain I'd already suffered, and every sore and still-healing wound cried out at my obstinacy. "Not after."

The high wail of the inhuman laughter rebounded off the cave walls. "You are a brave one, my lord." It drew nearer as it spoke, hands clasped neatly before it. "But you *will* tell me what I want to know. I know your Emperor has left his home. I want to know where he is."

"Then you have the wrong man," I said simply. "I don't even know what year it is."

The Prince's White Hand rose up and slapped me full across the face with such force that I crashed sideways into a shallow pool. Glowing fish scattered, darting away from me where I lay. It took an effort simply to prop myself up on an elbow, and the binders on my wrist slowed me still more. "Think you that I am simple?" the Prince asked. It towered over me, clawed feet gripping the uneven stone. "Do not lie to me. I know you know his itinerary. I want the *list* of planets your Emperor intends to visit.

Names and catalog numbers. Coordinates." I managed to find my knees, and hunched over, eyes shut through the dull pain, my long and tangled hair hiding my face from the terrible *thing* before me. Syriani's cold, high voice filled my universe. "I *will* hurt you again, kinsman. Tell me what I want to know."

"I don't have it," I said. It wasn't strictly true. I was passingly familiar with the coordinates and star catalog numbers for the Nessus system, for Gododdin, and Aulos—perhaps some of the others. But there had been at least thirty names on the Imperial itinerary, and I was no navigator. It had been so long since we left Nessus, and so much had happened. I remembered a handful of names in the moment. Nessus. Vanaheim. Siraganon. Balanrot. Perfugium. "I don't know."

The Prophet crouched to bring itself nearer my level. "As I said, there is too much of the Lie about you. I want those names, *Utannashi,* and I will have them."

"Utannashi . . ." I translated. "Liar."

"Do you deny it?" Syriani asked, and the incredible stench of its breath filled my nostrils.

I managed a defensive little laugh. "Aranata Otiolo called me *Oimn Belu.*"

"The *Dark One,*" Syriani hissed. "I did not know Otiolo had such poetry in him." Reaching out, Syriani seized me by the hair and hauled me to my feet, forcing my face to look up into its own. "I had hoped your chastisement sufficient to purge the Lie from you. I was wrong. We have more work to do." It released its grip, and I slumped, scalp stinging where the skin had nearly torn.

Syriani turned away, jewelry rattling from arms and horns. It raised a hand in signal, two fingers outstretched. Some unseen eye or camera must have been on us, for in seconds a half dozen *scahari* warriors in armor and painted battle-masks appeared around a bend in the rocks. I felt myself tense reflexively as they drew near, their curved, white scimitars tucked in the crooks of their arms. What new devilry they portended I dared not guess, but stood stock-still as they laid hands on me.

"*Qattaa!*" Syriani barked an order, and the warriors all froze.

Switching back to the standard, Syriani said, "There is one other thing, kinsman." It paused, as if expecting me to ask some clarifying question or interrupt. "How did you survive on Berenike?"

The guards held me fast, and though I averted my gaze, one of the *scahari* seized me again by the hair and forced me to look, to bare my throat. When I did not speak at once, another slapped me with the flat of its sword, leaving a bright weal across my bare stomach and a thin line where the razor edge still cut. "You don't know?" I gasped.

Syriani Dorayaica studied me with inhuman focus, transparent membranes narrowing beneath hooded lids. "Your people say you do magic. That you perform miracles."

I did my best to shrug. "Perhaps Utannash's power is not so false as you claim."

The Prophet drew near again and placed clawed hands on my shoulders. It smiled down at me, teeth bared. "You can see the power of my gods all around us." With its eyes, it encompassed the whole of the grotto. "*We* are proof of their power. This world, this *Dharan-Tun,* is proof of their power. All you have are tricks."

"I turned your victory into a defeat," I said. "Not a bad trick."

Without any change in expression, the Prince of Princes dug its talons into my shoulders, blood welling up as the glassy claws dug into my flesh. I sensed the change in emotion behind the Prophet's eyes, sensed what I felt sure was anger. Frustration. I sensed that nothing would have made this enemy happier than tearing me apart then and there. Then—without warning—it released me. "Still you bluster!" it hissed, and turning crouched to cleanse its bloodied fingers in the water of the nearest pool. To my horror the little fish swam up and crowded about Syriani's hands and the water ran clearer. My guards did not move. Syriani had not dismissed them. "It brings me no pleasure to destroy you," it said, lowering its hands further into the water with exquisite slowness. "You are, I think, the only other creature in this *iugannan*—this universe, you would say— who can understand me." It lifted its cupped hands from the water, a single glowing fish in its grasp. Steadily, Syriani allowed the water to run out until it held the hungry little creature on its palm. It wriggled uselessly, gasping for air. Without preamble, Syriani crushed the helpless thing in its fist, water and some fluorescent liquid spilling back into the pool to the frenzied delight of the others, who swarmed to filter the water of their former compatriot's blood. "Certainly you are the only one of your kind who can. This war has often felt a contest between we two. After Berenike, I was certain." It dipped its gore-streaked hand into the water and allowed the little fish to feast. A moment later its eyes found mine again. "You're seen it, haven't you? My armies marching across the stars, burning your worlds? You've seen your death. You know I am the one who kills you—that you die at Akterumu. And you know that when you are gone, humanity falls. You know your people will be our slaves for a time, and when that time is done, they will be nothing."

It stood.

"I've seen it, too," the Prophet said.

"The rivers of time?" I found I could hardly speak.

I had held on to the possibility that Syriani was no prophet at all, that its *visions* were not the visions of a seer, but those of a visionary—that the future it predicted for its people was only a dream it had had. I had dared to hope the Prophet's visions were false.

But Syriani nodded.

"The Watchers see all," Syriani said, "and I have seen with their eyes. As you have seen with the eyes of Utannash." It half-turned, raising one hand in the same two-fingered gesture it had used to summon the guards. Halted. "And I have seen that you *will* tell me what I want to know. So I will give you one last chance to confess: tell me where you Emperor is."

"Don't you already know?" I ventured, suddenly not so sure.

Syriani made a slashing gesture with the hand not holding two fingers aloft, and again one of the *scahari* walloped me in the stomach with the flat of its blade. "Do you think this is a game we play?" it asked.

I took that for a *no*.

"Velenammaa jatti wo!" Syriani barked, lowering its two fingers. *Take it away!*

CHAPTER 31

PIECE OF MIND

SOMETHING DWELT IN THE waters below. It churned from time to time, disturbing the black surface, a surface close enough that if I reached down—*up*—with my free arm I might almost touch it.

Almost.

And what a blessing that would be. If my torment on the wall was worsened by the occasional reprieve, my torment in the pit was made worse by the lack of one. Without food, without water, they had bound my legs and one arm tight to my chest and hanged me by my ankles. I had started above the level of the pit, but inch by grievous inch I had descended half a hundred feet toward the water below. I should have lost consciousness long before, would have done so but for the careful incision they made along the hairline by my right temple. Thus the blood—which might have pooled in my head and so flooded my consciousness—dripped out instead.

It must have taken days to reach the bottom.

I hardly knew anymore.

It was the third time. Or was it the fourth?

They'd left the one arm free that I might signal my captors to haul me up, to signal that I was ready to surrender. To speak. I had signaled the first time, but when they had given me water, I spat in their faces and found myself on the chain again. I wasn't sure why they pulled me out the next time. Perhaps I was very nearly dead. Vague memories of a firm mat and the beep of medical machinery persist.

". . . lost too much blood," said a feminine voice. Severine?

"Why are palatines always AB positive?" a man asked.

The woman answered. "Old superstition. One of the corps that helped set up the old bloodlines was Nipponese."

"You were right about his neurological scans." Another woman. "Never seen anything like them. The Empire's still ahead of us in some ways."

"It's not Imperial work," the man said. It wasn't Urbaine.

"Could be random mutation?" the second woman suggested.

Severine replied. "Not likely."

The next time they lowered me into that dreadful hole, it was with one needle in my arm and another in my thigh, one to hydrate me and the other to constantly replenish my blood supply. I could not sleep. I could not die. At irregular intervals, one of the Cielcin would come to the lip of the pit above and rattle my chain.

"*Sikarra!*" the inhuman gaoler would cry. *Confess!*

When I did not, it would tug the chain so that I slammed into the wall and disturbed the *thing* that lived in the water. I would shut my eyes and feel the blood dripping from my wounded scalp, matting my overlong hair . . . and when I opened them, I would be somewhere else.

So much of my memory of Dharan-Tun is fragmented like this. Snatches remembered through delirium and pain. Periods of lucidity punctuating shiftless horror until eventually they dragged me back to my cave to heal before I would again confront the *Shiomu*, the Prophet.

I remember its face hanging in the dark above me where I lay on the floor of my cave, eyes narrow. "I weary of this game," it said. "Tell me where your Emperor is."

Candle smoke and the resinous scent of myrrh wafted from my dreams, the familiar, funereal smell of the Chantry. The Emperor knelt in prayer, alone and clad in white, his arms thrown wide. Above him on the dais the altar stood empty beneath the statue of the God Emperor and the dome frescoed with its image of Earth. Beyond the high, narrow windows, the city of Sananne rose.

Nessus.

"Tell me where your Emperor is."

The words floated unvoiced across the surface of my tongue. *Nessus. Gododdin. Vastauna. Siraganon. Perfugium.* I did not dare speak them.

I hung above black water, my heart beating in my head. Witch-lights sparked and shone in the depths below. I think now that some cousin to the fish that dwelt in the Prophet's grottoes must have lurked there, drinking the blood that dripped from my brow.

When I did not speak, they hurt me, hauled me from the pit and lashed me to a pole. They stripped me, whipped me until the blood ran hot down

my back, or peeled a strip of skin from my thigh and left the raw meat
exposed to dry and crack and scream.

"Tell me where your Emperor is."

The pain vanished, blotted out like a dream on waking. I felt . . . *nothing,* not even the cold. My mind went clear for the first time in . . . in I did
not know how long. Syriani Dorayaica stood at the edge of the pit above
which I hung, dressed once more in armorial black. It was not alone. Behind it stood Urbaine in a violet suit, his hands tucked into his sleeves, flaps
folded down from his Mandari cap to cover his flat ears. Three more
Cielcin stood to one side with the winch that operated the chain, and another MINOS operative in medical white stood at hand. Behind and above
them, the red-streaked ice walls gleamed like crystal, and I remembered
just how high up this new prison was. Great reservoirs of drinking water—
whole oceans of them—lay above the great caverns and warrens of Dharan-
Tun, trapped beneath layers of ice that shielded the Cielcin and their
human slaves from the predatory energies of space. My pit opened on one
such reservoir, high above before the waters filtered down through desali-
nating plants to be fed into the hellish city below. I could remember seeing
gangs of men and of Cielcin, too, laboring to maintain the pipes and locks
and the great lifts that carried ships and cargo up huge and airless shafts
toward the surface.

There could be nothing on the surface. Dharan-Tun was the size of a
planet, and nothing so large could possibly have the protection of shields—
even if Syriani had pillaged the technology of radiation shielding from
captured human vessels, as I guessed it might have. Anything unshielded
on the surface not trapped beneath the ice would be subject to the fierce
ion storms as particles got caught in the planet-sized vessel's warp envelope. I was so close to the sky in my pit, closer than I had been in what
must have been years . . . but it had never been farther away.

"Where is your Emperor going?" the Prophet inquired. Syriani Dorayaica had never before made an appearance at the pit. "Tell me, and this
ends now."

Blood dripped from my forehead with each passing heartbeat.

"I know you can hear me, kinsman," Syriani said. I had rotated on my
chain so that I looked out across the cavern yard to where a dozen other
pits waited with gallows and winches at the ready. "Names. Catalog numbers. Coordinates."

"I don't know them," I said.

The pain returned, switched on like a light. I felt the numb shock of the cold, the bone-deep ache from my hanging, the blood drumming in my head. I felt the hot line where my temple had been incised again and again with each subsequent hanging, and the raw, scabrous stripes where skin had been peeled from each thigh. I felt too the leathered tightness of the whip scars that had become my back.

"It's on," Urbaine said.

The collar.

I had almost forgotten about it. I'd worn it so long it had become a part of me, had chafed my neck until it bled. Evidently it didn't just cause pain. Urbaine had taken control of my spinal nerve and sensory cortex entirely.

"You are unusually resilient for one of your kind," Syriani said, circling into view. "But this has gone on too long. I will have my answer. And do not lie again. Urbaine will know." I had vague memories of having once given false planets to end my time in the pit. It had worked for a day. I guessed Syriani must have access to captured Imperial star charts or to MINOS's own database. "Where is your Emperor going?"

Perhaps you think I have undertaken this account in order to lionize my virtues, to paint a picture of Hadrian Marlowe, Hero of Mankind; or to illustrate my campaign and my victories against the enemy. That much perhaps is true, but I should say that when I started this account it was with the intention of telling the truth, a thing I have striven to do unflinchingly, though I have perhaps failed at times in this charge. But in setting my pen to this page and in spilling the scholiasts' vermilion ink I knew these moments must come.

I do not relish my memories of Dharan-Tun, of Syriani Dorayaica and its Iedyr. There is much I have not said. I have not stopped to tell you about the stacked human legs I saw in a barrow like cordwood, or dwelt upon the headless corpses that hung outside cave mouths, or on the gutters thick with red blood where those corpses had drained.

But I know this moment must be told, though it shames me.

"Perfugium!" I said, "Vanaheim! Balanrot! I don't know them all!" I cannot be sure which names I spoke, or if I spoke them all. Though I sat in on many a conference with the Emperor and the Magnarch discussing the details of His Radiance's tour of the Centaurine provinces, that had been years ago. I had spent seven years between Nessus and Gododdin before entering the freeze for the long haul to Padmurak. The names were all I had left.

But I am certain Perfugium was one.

"Perfugium!" I said again, and shut my eyes—and shut my mouth with shame.

The pain vanished, and at once I felt sick instead.

Urbaine was smiling his diseased smile, but Syriani was impassive. *"Su tutai wo,"* it said. "Very good." At this it made a sign, and the Cielcin at the winch lowered me back into my pit. The pain did not return; Urbaine kept the collar inhibiting sensation, so that I hung there, bound and bleeding, and could think about what I had done.

It was no mercy.

CHAPTER 32

WANDERING AND RELEASE

THERE CAME A TIME when I could no longer walk. Between torment and starvation, I had nothing left, and lay upon the stone floor of my cave cell. Half the skin of my thighs had been peeled away, and the nails of my left hand torn off. My universe had become one of damp agony, my only experience a dull, numb ache. The memory of my betrayal burned in me, a black shame deep as any pain.

Lying in the dark, I saw once more the titanic forms of the statues carved in the great hall of the *Dhar-Iagon*. The *Caihanarin*, the Watchers in all their supernatural horror. Syriani had said its gods were the only true things—the only truth. If it is so, then the truth is hideous. I heard the flap of their time-eaten wings about the fringes of my mind, felt the pressure of their obscene eyes questing, searching.

Kharn Sagara said there were other things in the dark of our universe, things greater than the Cielcin. Kharn had known, must have known just what monumental gods his Cielcin clients worshiped—and why. And Syriani had spoken of the Watchers like living things. Not gods such as Jupiter or Jehovah—stories told by our ancestors of old—but xenobites. In the darkness, I saw again the image of Syriani leading its army across the stars, just as I had seen it in Calagah when I was a boy. I saw a shadow fall and drown the stars, and knew what then had cast it.

I forgot to move, forgot almost to breathe, forgot even that I was a man. No stir of air was there in the lamplit dark of that cave, and the only sound save that of my ragged and shallow breathing was the distant splashing of the fish.

It was so quiet.

Nothing moved.

"Find us," came the familiar voice. "Find us in you."

I turned my head to look around, but there was no one there. That was just as well, for it had been my own voice . . . and a memory. I turned my head aside, looked toward the water. It was possible—almost possible—to imagine that it was the same water that pooled beneath the palace of the Undying on Vorgossos, the lost and sunless sea where Brethren dwelt imprisoned and enslaved. *Seek hardship,* the daimon had said to me, relying on its computational vision of the future.

I had found it, and it had broken me.

With a titanic effort I managed to roll onto my belly, and with my ruined hands I began to crawl toward the water. To drink? To drown? I cannot say, can only remember the dry scrape of stone on my naked skin. I was not a man anymore, but a rough beast, a crawling shadow. I collapsed, face pressed against the cool, pale stone. Not far. Not far enough. Grunting, I pushed myself up, feeling the torn nails tear again and weep blood and pus.

It was not a face that stared back at me from the surface of that black pool, only the rough impression of one made by an artist with only the faintest knowledge of who Hadrian Marlowe once had been. My hair fell in curtains, and might have reached my elbows if I stood, and though it had not fallen out, the shock and deprivation had bleached it white in places, in tangled and uneven streaks.

I touched the fierce white scar that ran across my temple from the forehead above my right eye almost to my ear, using my three-fingered right hand. The Emperor's ring was gone. When had I lost it?

I remembered only slowly. Even that first humiliation on the wall above the gates of the *Dhar-Iagon* was so remote a memory. Had I ever truly lived another life? Had Hadrian lived at all? I must have done. I shut my eyes and collapsed once more, rolling onto my back, my hair soaking in the freezing waters that ran through secret ways down from the caul of ice that englobed that frozen world.

"How far you've fallen."

The voice that spoke was cool, bright and feminine.

"Valka?" She'd come for me, somehow, just as I knew she would. But the face that hove into view above me was Mandari, not Tavrosi. My heart—which had absurdly swelled the moment before—deflated all at once. "You."

Severine's smooth face frowned. "I shudder to see you in such circumstances."

"Spare me," I rasped.

"No, I mean it." The MINOS woman looked down her nose at me. "You were great once. A hero to many."

I shut my eyes. I had to listen to her. I did not have to see. "Some hero."

To my astonishment, Severine did not rise to the bait. She was silent a long time, so long I thought she had left me, or else that she had been yet another hallucination, another figment of my fevered mind. "Hadrian Marlowe," she said at last, savoring the words. I cracked my eyes, found her sitting on the rations crate. "*Sir* Hadrian Marlowe. Royal Knight. Hero of Aptucca. Demon in White . . ." She rattled these monikers off with the air of a bored schoolteacher. They sounded hollow in the dead air, false.

False.

"They call you Halfmortal," she said. "They say you cannot be killed."

I did not say anything, and let the silence stretch on. It was a trick I'd learned from the Emperor, from Kharn Sagara, from my own father. Say nothing, and the other man says all.

"It is true?" Severine asked, right on cue. "The Prince seems to believe it." Still, I said nothing, permitting Severine to work herself up. I wish I could say I did it deliberately, that I was in control enough of myself to have any real agency in this conversation, but there was so little of me left. "I was not at Berenike, but I saw the footage. You should have been blown to atoms."

Her words hung in the air like smoke, but still I lay there, eyes fixed on the roof above my head, on the gnarled fingers of limestone descending drop by glacial drop like slow hands. One such drop struck the water near my head.

"Were you trying to drown yourself, my lord?"

My eyes flickered to her face. Her features were . . . wholly forgettable, lacking the Lothrian pallor and polish of Iovan or the inhuman qualities of Urbaine. She would have been totally at home in the retinue of some Wong-Hopper Director or similar executive. She picked at a spot on one pant leg and flicked it irritably away. I felt an indecent flush at the thought that I had irritated her. It had been so long since I'd struck any sort of blow for myself. It had begun to feel as if I did not exist at all, as if the *thing* called *Hadrian* were some eidolon, some phantasm without agency or voice.

"I am going to die," I said in answer.

"Yes," the Extrasolarian agreed. No denial, no comfort in that coldly feminine voice. "Dorayaica will offer you to the others as proof of its power. He will be *Aeta ba-Aetane*. King of Kings."

"I thought it already was."

Severine examined her nails, apparently bored by this line of questioning. "He has made his claim. Your death . . . *may* cement it." She let her hand fall, gray eyes flicking back to my face. "How did you survive that blast?"

"I *dodged* it," I said, steeping venom on my words. "How do you think?"

"Don't make me hurt you, my lord," she said, steel showing from beneath her velvet exterior.

I very nearly laughed. "It's a little late for that."

"On the contrary," she countered, "it is never too late." Severine stood and crossed the floor to stand over me, hard soles clacking on the limestone. "Now answer me."

I only stared at her.

The witch's eyebrows drew up and together, and she stepped over me and began pacing along the water's edge, her shadow flickering huge against the walls of the cave by the light of the lonely glowsphere. "I have been studying you ever since Lord Vati brought you here. Your genome, your . . . tissue samples, your neurological scans." She turned, luminous gray eyes peering down at me. "Certain parts of your brain fire faster than almost anything I've seen. I've seen slower computers."

"I don't understand . . ."

"What are you?" Severine asked. I could feel her flat, metallic eyes dissecting me, examining every inch of my torn body, as if she thought to read her answer written in my scars. "You're not a chimera—the only thing artificial about you are those bones. What then? Some . . . Imperial experiment? A homunculus?" When I did not answer her, she pressed on. "You're not Choir work. I'd recognize the Chantry's genetic markers anywhere. Who then? Vorgossos?"

I could only stare at her.

"Speak, damn you!"

"And say what? I don't—ah!" I had tried to sit up that I might better see her, and the effort sent a spasm of pain cascading along my back. Muscles seized, and I lay back against the stone, teeth clenched as I waited for the pain to pass.

It vanished instead, blotted out as Urbaine had blotted it out in the pit.

When I opened my eyes, I found Severine staring down at me, her head cocked to one side. I could still feel the tension in my back—the tightness of cord and sinew—but the pain gone, as if hidden beneath an inch of purest snow. In her sweetest voice, Severine said, "Answer my question. Please."

Moving with exquisite slowness, I forced myself to sit up, my long and sopping hair soaking through my grubby tunic. The pain gone for the moment, I became acutely aware of the meanness of my state: the layers of filth, the grease matting my hair, and the grotesque horror of my smell. The iron scent of blood mingled with the stench of fouler fluids and the musk of grime and unwashed flesh. I had hardly noticed it before. It had become a part of me, and a part invisible through the never-ending haze of pain.

"I am only what you see," I said.

Severine's eyes went glassy. "That is not an answer."

What could I say that she would accept? That I had met a god—or something like a god—in some abstract time upon a mountaintop that did not quite exist? That it had shown me a vision of naked time and charged me to ensure *its* time came to pass? "I . . ." The sight of my mutilated nails transfixed me, the scabrous beds oozing pus. I rubbed at the white band of cryoburn scar on my left thumb with the three fingers of my right hand. "I have nothing to say to you, witch. You said it yourself: I am a dead man."

Severine's sweet smile only sweetened. "Why do you think I'm here?" She reached into a pocket of her white smock and drew out a small, black object about the size of an eyeglass case. "The Great One will kill you—that cannot be stopped—but it does not mean that you have to die, my lord. I can offer you a path." She turned the black case over in her fingers. "Join us."

"Join you?" I blinked up at her. "Are you mad?"

"Do you know who Minos was?" she asked pointedly. "You're a student of antiquity, I understand."

The tangential nature of her question rocked me back, and I braced myself on my maimed hands. "He built the labyrinth on Crete."

"He was so much more," she countered. "Mannus to the Germans. Manu to the Hindus. Manes to the Lydians and the Romans. Menes in Egypt. Adam in Canaan. He was the first king, the man from whom we get the word *man* itself. We are his successors. Continuing his work."

"What work?" I asked incredulous. I was not aware of any connection between the mythical figures she'd named, though it was easy enough to hear the connection between the names themselves.

"Improving humanity," she said. "Dragging us forward, up. Minos built civilization to separate us from the animals. We will make men like gods."

"Iovan said the same," I said, following the witch as she paced back and forth before me, the black case in her hands. "Syriani will not share its power. It uses you to attack us. When you are no longer useful, it will kill you. Depend on it."

"Kill us?" Severine smiled. "Like you killed Urbaine?" I felt a damp coldness close over me. She'd scored a point, and she knew it. "We are not so easily destroyed!" She had stopped pacing and stood over me like a god. "You could live forever, never growing old. You could change your body, be what you always dreamed to be. And all this . . ." she gestured at the horrors her Cielcin masters had inflicted on me, ". . . all this could be washed away."

Severine knelt on the stone before me, set the case pointedly at her right hand as she took my hands in her own. She was wearing thin, membranous gloves, like those of a surgeon. "We have your blood. A new body can be made ready—just like the one you're wearing now. Syriani can have its sacrifice . . . and you can live again."

I averted my gaze and—shaking my head—smiled. "Does your master know you're here?"

"He doesn't have to," she said, fingers tightening over mine. "You are too valuable to waste. Your mutation . . . whatever it is . . . it changes everything." She cocked her head again, and asked, "What do you see?"

"What?"

"The way your brain processes information, you *must* perceive time differently. Maybe even at the Planck scale." Again, I could only stare. She was describing my vision of time. It made some sense: if what the Quiet had done to me was speed my perceptions of time, it might be that I saw time pass at a high enough resolution that I could see potential collapsing into reality as particles spun up or down. My silence had spoken for me, for Severine's face lit. "You can, can't you?" she paused, voice hushed. "That's how you did it. That's how you survived." She drew a breath. "You *did* dodge it."

She reached into another pocket of her smock and drew out a foil pack, which she opened and produced a sterile cloth. Reaching up, she dabbed at my forehead, washing off months of grime and dried blood. My skin stung from the alcohol, suddenly cold in the cool air. I didn't stop her, and she set the cloth aside to take up her case, which she opened and drew out the black tab of an electrode. Without preamble, she reached up to stick the tab to my forehead.

I seized her wrist with one hand. "And if I refuse?"

"Then you die," she said, her awe and smile faltering. "I have your blood. I don't *need* you. I am offering you a chance to escape death."

"Why?" I asked. "We're enemies."

"Petty morality!" Severine sneered. "We don't need to be. We're both fighting for the same thing. Fighting for humanity. For progress. You could join us. Live again."

She tried to pull her hand away, but I held it fast. "What's stopping you?" I asked, and looked away as if to hide my comprehension. She might have easily activated the collar again, subjected me to agony or crippled me to go about her work of stealing my mind. "Why offer me a choice?"

I could feel those flat, gray eyes searching my face. "The scan cannot be made if you resist it. If you fight it, you'll corrupt the transcription." She tried to free her hand and advance the electrode toward my face.

It took most of my remaining strength to shove her arm aside, but no thought, no consideration. "Go away."

Severine did not shout, she did not argue. She only narrowed her eyes. "You're making a mistake."

It took all my will not to fall over. "Let me ask you something, doctor. If I accepted your offer, would I still be in this cell?" She blinked at me, confused by the obvious nature of the question. "Will I still die?"

The witch of MINOS was silent then for a long moment, studying my face. "Nothing can stop that." She brandished the black case. "But if you let me map your brain, you *can* live again. I can do a complete synaptic scan and import the properties to a new host body. It will be as if you closed your eyes here and opened them . . . somewhere else."

Distantly, the faint drip and trickle of water could be heard running down the rocks and stalactites to the great pool at my back. Severine did not stand and retreat, but neither did she reach out again with her electrodes. "You're already dead," I said, voice hushed. "I killed you, too. Siran and me. On Arae. I saw your corpse. Delivered it to Legion Intelligence. They probably dissected it, mapped your implants, turned you over to the Inquisition for disposal." She was shaking her head as I spoke. "How many times have you died?" My own voice was raw in my ears. "I bet you've lost count." I swayed a little and steadied myself with my hands. "But I bet you don't remember any of them. Any of your deaths." Kharn Sagara could not remember his deaths, either. He had not seen the Howling Dark nor passed through it, and neither had this woman. "You've never *really* died."

I caught my voice trailing off, and I reflected on the face of the woman before me. She had the Mandari bronze coloring and the Mandari black hair, the Mandari high cheekbones with a touch of epicanthic folding about the eyes. Yet *Severine* was a Norman name, and many times I'd heard her curse in Jaddian. Had she been Jaddian once? Some immigrant girl in the Norman Expanse long ago? Was there anything left of the original girl in the woman before me?

"The Cielcin believe they are spirits trapped in this world," I said. "You believe that we are nothing but matter. Data. Information." I smiled up at her, realizing the game she was playing. "It's the same delusion."

She had nothing to say to that.

"You have no intention of saving me, even if you could," I said. "You've no intention of rebuilding me. The minute you have my mind you'll just . . . sift through it for what you want."

The woman's smile faltered. *False* indeed. I had no doubt that whatever model she might make of my consciousness she would keep only so long as it took for her to unravel the mystery of me. Far from saving me, she meant to keep a copy of me as a plaything, a slave, a puzzle to be solved.

"You want the truth?" I asked her, seeing no reason to lie. I looked her square in the face, finding renewed clarity in those moments free of pain. "Do you know of the Quiet, doctor?"

Severine's face split, several emotions appearing at once. Confusion. Surprise. Contempt. A number of Severines crouched before me like refractions viewed through a prism. I tried and failed to hold my breath.

After so long suffering, I had forgotten what it was like to *see*.

Her face collapsed into confusion, the possibility made real. "The xenobites?" she asked. "They're supposed to be extinct."

"It's not a xenobite," I said. "The Quiet is something else." The cold water splashed about me where I sat, ripples playing about the surface. "It *changed* me." And remembering something Jari the Seer had said, I said, "Gave me eyes." Though Jari's vision had destroyed Jari itself. The Exalted had drunk of the waters of the Deeps, and the alien animalcule had hollowed him out, altered his brain and body chemistry, mutated him until even his human components were not human anymore.

And then I did something I had not done on my own in I could not guess how long.

I stood.

Water splashed about me as I rose, the heady confusion of my second sight pitching about me. I squinted against the sudden rush of vertigo, unsteady on my torn feet, water running from my soaked tunic and hair.

Still crouching before me—almost kneeling—the witch Severine looked up with iron eyes wide. "You can stand?"

It took every erg of energy I had not to topple forward. My legs shook, burned where the Cielcin had peeled them. I had to shut my eyes.

There are certain creatures who came with us out of Earth—insects and spiders who secreted themselves aboard our first, slow ships—who could stride across the surface of a pool and not sink as men do. They accomplished this by relying upon the elastic tension that binds the molecules of a fluid together. It was possible—if not probable—that a creature heavier than those spiders might do the same, possible that the laws of nature and nature's God might stretch so far as to allow a man to stand upon the surface of the waters.

When first I returned out of the Dark beyond Death, I had seen the Quiet—walking in Gibson's shape—standing upon the water, standing above the chaos of our world.

I could see it then! Dancing flame-like on the fringes of my vision. I had only to step toward it, to step *up* upon the waters and *show* this witch of MINOS just what the Quiet was. I had but to take that step.

And so I did.

And the whole world came crashing down, white pain lanced through my tormented shoulder, and a cry more animal than human echoed off the fangy roof of the cavern. It did not sound like my voice at all, but it had come from my throat.

I had been so sure. So sure.

Severine's hands seized me, held my face from the water. "He'll kill me if you die now," she hissed, more to herself than to me. "What did you think you were doing?"

"Trying," I said with terrible effort. "Trying. To show . . . you."

"The Quiet," Severine said, nails biting my face. "Where did you find them? They're supposed to be extinct."

My vision blurred, smeared her face across the blackness above me, eyes like points of polished metal. I opened my mouth, tried to answer her, but only a groan escaped me.

Severine hissed.

The pain stopped, vanished in a trice the moment after. Even the pain from my fall vanished, and I guess the collar was blocking even that. My head went clear for the first time in what felt like lifetimes, leaving only the crushing sense of tiredness, a bone-deep weariness beyond mere sensation.

Severine was looking down at me. "Answer me and I will leave you like this," she said, fingers tracing the collar I wore. "Can you see the future?"

"The future?" I echoed her words, shook my head. "No. Not like you think. I *remember* time. Things that haven't happened, or won't. And things that *might* happen." I tried not to think about the water, about how I failed. The vision was gone completely then, no possibility flickered on the edge of human sight. "If I try, I can choose what happens. Just for a moment."

The witch blinked at me, gray eyes like the shutters of camera eyes. "The beam. On Berenike. You're saying you can perceive the possible world states and . . . collapse the waveform how you choose?"

I told her I did not know, but her eyes grew wide. I know now. The ancient mystes teach us that—unobserved—light acts like a wave, that it is the eye of the beholder that collapses light into coherent beams of energy. So it is with all things. So it is that all conscious observers collapse the potential universe, condense reality, make history with their eyes. It is only that my eyes—my mind—sees more than other men.

"The Quiet did this to you?" Severine asked. "Tell me where you found them!"

"*He* found me," I said at last, shaking my head.

That, evidently, was not the answer the witch desired, for the instant after I gave it, the pain returned. Not the numb ache of my countless injuries, not the bright fire from my fall, but the incandescent, roiling agony Urbaine had first inflicted on me. Through it all I felt her nails like talons on my face, heard her cold voice hiss. "Answer me, Marlowe!"

She let me fall then, let my face strike the water and the black stone beneath it. The water could not have been but inches deep, but lying on my face like I was, that was deep enough to kill me. Dimly I sensed a shape moving at my side, felt hands on me.

The pain had stopped, but the world was going dark. Through the splashing and the flood, I heard again the thunder of stamping feet and of truncheons hammering the ground.

"*Teke! Teke! Tekeli!*" cried inhuman voices, and "*Aeta! Aeta! Aeta!*"

I was lying on gray stone before an altar with iron rings fixed to it. At my back, the black dome rose, and in the distance I saw the gray-green blur of mountains, their faces sheer and smooth, angular as the fata morgana that castellate the sky.

"You knew it would come to this, kinsman," the Prophet said, and pointed at the sky and at the great ship descending on tangled ribbons of cloud. "Time runs down."

I screamed, coughed water and blood upon the stone.

"You are alive?" a rough voice asked me. I turned but slowly, found myself face to face with a human slave. One eye was missing, and his face was horribly scarred.

Severine was gone, and four Cielcin guards stood just inside the door.

"Severine . . ." I said, unsteadily. "Where?" I had to stop myself and coughed again, marking the signs of flaying in the ugly red stripes that decorated the man's wiry arms. No light shone in his dark eyes.

"Gone," the slave said. "She tried to kill you."

I looked from the slave to the inhuman guards at the door. They must have heard the sounds of my fall into the water and rushed in to find Severine standing over me.

"Tried to kill me?" I echoed, still disoriented. Thinking of her offer to help me escape, I said, "Something like that . . ."

CHAPTER 33

LIVING THE LIE

THE CHAIR'S WHEELS CREAKED as the slave pushed me along the ribbed and grotesque hall. It was the only sound save the padding of her bare feet on the naked rock. Clad in a new colorless tunic, I hung my head and stared at my mutilated hands: at the missing fingers and the ugly, red-white weals of cryoburn where my rings had peeled flesh from bone; at the regenerated fingernails and the older, fainter scars, relic of Irshan's sword. My body had become a mural, a temple whose reliefs spoke of pain.

I was not the only such monument.

There were always bodies in the city. I saw them when they carried me on a litter up the winding way from the prison in the deeps of that unholy place. Men, headless, hung on hooks above gutters thick with blood. No murmurous haunt of flies in that alien city, only the stink of corruption, of meat rotting for the Cielcin palate. They hung outside cave mouths like trophies, skinned and opened, the offal scooped out.

And then . . . there was the palace.

Each time when my torments had reached their end and I was brought before the Prophet to confess, I traveled through the corridors of the *Dhar-Iagon*, through the grottoes and high halls where inhuman soldiers stood sentinel and white-faced courtiers gnawed thighbones and gristle. More than once I saw the remains of human slaves lying on the stone floor, or saw only dark stains. Twice our guard halted to drag the bodies aside.

Before long, the slave girl pushed me through a pointed arch and into a narrow corridor. Many hands had ground the stone floor smooth, but the walls retained the unhewn roughness of the wandering planet's native rock, and the chair creaked only slightly as the slave pushed it forward, upsetting the saline bag on its staff beside my head. I craned my neck to see around the bend ahead, but was stopped by the heavy straps that held me above the knee and about the chest. I had not left the chair for days while Severine's correctives worked their subtle art of repair. I could sense the vastness of the chamber beyond only by the open quality of the air, the gentle breeze that wafted about the dark stone. It spoke of volumes, of emptiness.

We entered onto a kind of shelf, an open space several hundred feet long bounded by a sheer drop into abyssal dark ahead and on the left side. To the right, the raw stone rose to the cavern roof, from which huge glass lanterns hung, their round faces cutting the glare to a somber, demonic red. Somewhere in a corner, the hollow piping of a flute played, wailing and atonal, and before me—seated at the head of what seemed a kind of feasting table—sat the Prophet in its robes of imperial black.

Syriani Dorayaica stood as we approached and raised its arms as if to embrace me from the far end of that table. "Here he is!" it said in the standard. *"Shiabbaa o-tajun, cielucin ba-koun! Shiabbaa cahyr ute Aeta ba-Yukajjimn!* Behold my kinsman, my fellow clan-chief. Will you not all kneel?" It glanced sidelong about the chamber, moving its head snake-like from the wall to my right to the precipitous drop at my left. It was only then that I—who had had eyes but for my enemy—realized we were not alone. In the rusted shadows beneath the lanterns stood a congregation of inhuman persons. Soldiers dressed in glistening black, white-masked and white-crested. White-robed counselors and courtiers dressed in elaborate robes of blue or gray. Painted concubines clad in silver jewelry, naked and androgynous beside collared human slaves.

And all of them silent save the lonely minstrel whose flute suddenly stopped.

"Gasvaa!" the Prophet ordered, and stretched its iron claws.

As a single organism, the crowd sank to its knees about me, even the human slave girl who had pushed my chair. Above it all, the Prophet settled back in its high seat and smiled its alien smile, its glass teeth bared. Speaking once more in my own tongue, it said, "Are you well, kinsman?" It raised a hand to indicate my state.

I glanced down at the thick straps that bound my legs and chest and at the medical correctives taped over my flayed thighs, and once more at the ruin of my hands. All at once I was acutely aware of the medical bags hanging from the staff beside my head, and of the waste hoses socketed into my flesh beneath the long, drab garment I wore.

I was on display. Like so many captured lords of antiquity, I had been trotted out as a symbol. There were so few emotions that stood congruent

in the hearts of our two species, so few rituals held in common. But humiliation was one. And shame. These we had between us, man and Cielcin.
These we shared. *Ute Aeta ba-Yukajjimn,* Syriani had called me. *The True
King of Man.* I was not the Emperor, but I had slain two princes of the
tribes of Eue. I was a prince in their eyes, *elutanura ve ti-ikurrar,* to use the
Cielcin phrase. Crowned in blood. Yet I was no king, and no true Aeta—
for I was not Cielcin. I was a living blasphemy in the eyes of the xenobites,
and so I had been brought forth to be mocked.

"Your courtesies leave much to be desired," I said, and gesturing at my
state, at the wheelchair and the corrective taped to my hands and thighs,
asked, "Why am I being treated?"

The great prince leaned forward in its rough stone seat, claws splayed
on the corners of the long dining table between us. "You must walk where
we are going," it said, still in the standard, still for my ears alone. It rose to
its feet in a stirring of black and silver chains, the *udaritanu* embroidered on
its robes glittering like the constellations. Lifting its hands again it addressed the gathered throng, high, harsh voice raised. *"Raka Oranganyr
ba-Utannash!* The Champion of the Lie! He is *Ute Dunyasu,* the Great Affront, and *Oimn Belu!* The Dark One!" As it spoke Syriani tossed its head
from side to side, hurling its words like thunderbolts. It stepped to the
corner of the table, one hand trailing along the surface. "It was his hand
that slew Aranata Otiolo, his hand that cut down Venatimn Ulurani. He
took my Iubalu, my Bahudde from me. He is the greatest of their warriors!
The greatest enemy of all whose eyes are fixed upon *Iazyr Kulah!"*

As it spoke it proceeded along perhaps a third the length of the table,
dragging its claws on the polished stone. It was the strangest table I had
ever seen, not flat like the tables of men, but deeply furrowed, so that a
trench perhaps a cubit deep and three cubits wide ran down the length, its
walls slanted steeply from the wide lip.

And there were grates in the bottom.

The whole thing had the look of some vile feeding trough.

Syriani had not finished, and flashing shark's teeth at the still-kneeling
congregants, it said, "But he is broken now. He has been purified. He has
confessed! He has given us the location of the *Uganatai,* their false king!
Their *Emperor.*" It spoke this last word in the standard, pronouncing it with
carefully measured tones.

I hung my head, the memory of my shame washing over me like a tide.
How long had I endured the question? Endured my *purification,* my mor-
tification at the hands of the enemy? Not long enough. I should have died

before betraying the Emperor as I had. Others would have done so. I clenched my hands in my lap, feeling the absent fingers ache as the stumps moved. I had never been a great patriot, no true lover of Empire. As a boy, I had very nearly hated her: had I not marveled at her cruelty and reviled her for it? Had I not reviled my own father? Was he not avatar of the Imperium in my eyes?

And yet I loved her then—and love her now, who has wounded her more deeply than any man living or dead.

I loved the Empire not for the breadth of her dominion, nor admired her for the strength of her arms. I loved only that which she defended: mankind itself, palatine and patrician, plutocrat and plebe. I loved the Sollan Empire for the shield she was, the bulwark she built up against the darkness beyond the light of her suns.

And I had failed her, and failed the Emperor, and in so doing, failed every man, woman, and child the Emperor held in his charge.

My distress must have made itself plain on my face—and I sensed that Syriani had a better measure of human feeling than I had of Cielcin—for it addressed its court, saying, "Our journey is almost done. In twice twelve and nine watches we will reach Akterumu. There we will meet our brethren, and there take what is rightfully ours! Then we will burn the *yukajjimn* from our skies. We will find their *Uganatai* and I will drink his blood myself."

"*Teke teke tekeli!*" cried a white-robed Cielcin near the fore of the table, still kneeling on the stone.

"*Yaiya toh!*" the others replied, and one by one hurled themselves to the floor.

All fell about their lord and were still.

In the fresh silence, Syriani lifted its voice again and proclaimed, "Too long we have kept to the darkness. Have we forgotten that Elu bid us step into the light? That it was he who answered Miudanar's call and led us to the sky? Have we forgotten that the gods taught us to fly? That we are a chosen people? That we alone may join them in the next world when this *iugannan* is washed away and the Deceiver is cast down?"

It turned back, returned with loping strides to take its place before the high seat. "I am the prince whom Elu promised. I am the one to unite our people once again, to gather the thirteen tribes of Eue under one banner—to hold them in my Hand." It pointed at me where I sat bound and crippled at the opposite end of the table. "And it is *my* Hand that gives you this great gift, this great enemy. His capture is proof! The gods fight with us!"

"*Adiqasur Caihanarin ush ti-ajun wo! Adiqasur Caihanarin!*" the Cielcin echoed, many of them raising their faces. "The gods fight with us!"

"I am the prince who will wash away the Lie! I will give you the stars! I will lead you all to paradise!" And here the great prince clapped its ringed and taloned hands, bangles clattering like chains. "Take this as a token of what is to come."

Thereupon a door opened in the stone wall to my right, and a double line of human slaves emerged, chained to one another by the ankles and carrying heavy trays of black glass on bars between them. These they carried forward and lay across the table-trough.

But I could smell the meat before I saw it, and cursed as the slaves withdrew.

The Cielcin do not cook their meat. There had been little fuel in the tunnels and cave warrens of their native world. They would eat burned meat—I had seen charred bodies in the ruins of ships and of cities with strips of flesh removed—but it was not their preference. *Aging* passed for cookery among the Pale.

Rotting.

Still, I recognized the bare ribs, the stacked limbs, and there was no mistaking the heads that—eyeless—stared from the center of skinned and artfully arranged thighs. The nearest stared up at me, empty eyes black as pits, as coals. Black as the eyes of the enemy. The Pale had peeled the skin from the dead man's face and applied some greenish paste to the browned and marbled flesh of cheek and jowl. But it was not the face that most stirred my horror, nor the whorl of nestled limbs of which it formed the centerpiece. Nor was it the tray of mounded organs—fresher than the meat. It was the red cloth that lined the tray. No alien silk was this, but the dyed wool of a humble legionary tunic. The huge trays were lined with them, each requiring perhaps half a dozen to cover their black glass surfaces, each arranged so that the short sleeves draped over the sides and the epaulets of rank were on full display.

These were blank-plated legionnaires, or triasters with their single bar, and here and there I marked the double bar of a decurion. Ordinary men. Common soldiers. Once. But it was not even the tunics and the badges of rank that drew my eye. It was the insignia beneath the rank identifier, above the little embossed sunburst that was the mark of the Sollan Empire.

A pitchfork and a pentacle.

My pitchfork and pentacle.

My vision blurred, if only for a moment. Fury boiled my tears away.

"These were *my* men!" I shouted, and there was a strength in my voice I had not heard there for a very long time. About me, the other Cielcin had begun to find their feet, were rising like a gray and deathly chorus from the stone floor all around. I strained against the bonds that held me, but they would not yield. "My men!"

Syriani did not smile, but settled itself in its stone chair with almost pharaonic serenity to contrast the anguish and the rage coming off me in waves.

"How?" I demanded, shaking in my seat. "When?"

The Prince of Princes gave no answer, though its eyes—like sockets themselves—never left my face. *"Cielucin ba-koun!"* it said, voice still filling that high-vaulted place of rough stone. "My people! I give you a piece of this abomination's army! These *yukajjimn* would have burned these halls. They would have slaughtered you. Us! They would have destroyed our dreams of paradise. I have destroyed them." It raised a hand, three fingers extended like a *vate* offering benediction from atop his pillar. "This is but a foretaste of what is to come."

"Where are the others?" I demanded, speaking standard to avoid a scene. "Syriani, where are the others?"

The Cielcin to either side edged closer, communicating not with words but with the careful, teasing steps of the pack approaching its chief, chins raised, throats bared, lips parted, testing the great prince.

But the prince had eyes only for me. Leaning forward so that the fine chains that decorated its horned crown swayed and sparkled in the red lamplight, its gripped the corners of the table. "Where they have been all this time," it answered in perfect Galstani. "In my keeping."

One of the white-robed courtiers drew too near the table, and the Prophet snapped its attentions from me. It hissed, jaw distending to extend the black gums and glassy fangs forward from its otherwise flat face. The lesser creature recoiled and dropped to its knees.

For a moment, I felt as if I had come out of my seat—out of my body. "In your keeping?" I repeated, shaking my head. "Severine said the ship was lost with all hands." I never quite believed her, and yet . . .

"She is *yukajjimn*," the Prophet said. *"Yukajjimn* lie . . ." It trailed off then, turning to regard the kneeling creature. A furrow formed between the xenobite's hairless brows. "But her lie has served the Truth, because it has served me." All around us, the other Cielcin were shifting in hungry agitation. I could practically hear the saliva dripping from their fangs. They but waited for the bell, for their master's signal. "I wanted you to think you were alone. Because you *are* alone. Your people did not escape Padmurak. They will not escape their fate, as you will not escape yours." I shut my eyes to stop a fresh flood of tears. The Great One kept talking, voice smooth and sharp as glass. "No one knows you are here. No one is coming to save you."

"It won't matter," I said, and raised my voice then to stop it breaking. "My *death* won't matter. The Imperial fleet outnumbers yours ten thousand to one. You cannot hope to match their strength."

"Strength . . ." the Prophet said. "*Vandate . . .* Do you even know what *strength* is? What it is to have strength?" Opening my eyes again, I marked the Cielcin standing all about me, held from their feast by deference to the Prophet on its throne. Syriani was still speaking the standard, speaking for my ears only, and I had to remind myself that I, too, was *Aeta*, and that when *Aetamn* spoke, the Cielcin deferred, no matter their hunger. "You think it is *wallati*? Power? Numbers? Think you it is weapons?"

The great prince turned its attention on the prostrate member of its court. "*Okun-kih,*" it said, and the creature lifted its face. The Prince of Princes raised its hand and pointed. "*Iagga,*" it said. *Go.* The Cielcin stood, inky eyes following its master's taloned finger to the edge of the shelf on which we all stood. I followed that finger, too. The blackest abyss yawned below us. How deep it stretched or how wide it was defied my ability to know. There was only the dark—like the Dark of night, of space—except that here there were no stars, no light but the red glow of lanterns.

The doomed Cielcin jerked its head to one side, a nervous tic I had to remind myself was the Cielcin affirmative. It did not question, did not splutter or plead. The white-robed courtier shuffled back on padded feet, eyes wide, unblinking. It looked over its shoulder, and—finding itself mere paces from the edge—turned and faced oblivion. It hesitated only an instant before stepping out into open air.

It vanished in a silent rush of silk and hair.

Vanished. And was gone.

None of the others stirred or gave a cry. Some shuffled awkward from side to side, still more bared their throats in submission to their demon king. None challenged its actions, none questioned its supremacy. I said nothing, but waited for the great prince to speak. Syriani looked round at its gathered courtiers, translucent fangs bared in a snarling, inhuman smile. "*Vandate . . . strength* is not *strength*, kinsman," it said, speaking the standard still for my benefit. "Think you if all these wished me dead that I might defy them by my *strength*?" Syriani shook its head—the human gesture out of place and strangely obscene. "Know you what your Empire is?"

The question came at me seemingly from nowhere, and I could not help but ask, "What?"

"*Imperium*," the prince said, "means *command*. Order. It is a belief, a compulsion. Faith. A liar's faith, yes. But faith." And here it extended a clawed hand toward the abyss and the creature who had thrown itself into its maw. "There you see true faith. The faith of one who acts in the name of Truth. My new empire is a command, too, a command given me by Miudanar, great among the gods! My command, my faith, is truth. *Truth* is power. The gods' Truth. It was our faith, our *caiharu*, that broke your fleet at Berenike, or have you forgotten?"

I had not. How well I remembered the sky fires burning, the light of the annihilation cascade filling the sky like ten thousand setting suns. At Bahudde's command, the Cielcin fleet had penetrated the shield curtain of our own defensive fleet before destroying their own AM fuel stores. Titus Hauptmann had grouped the fleet too close together, and the result-ing wave of destruction tore our cordon apart. Our men had stood no chance, had died because the Cielcin berserkers cared nothing for their lives. How many Cielcin had died to make that sacrifice? How many hundreds? How many thousands?

We never knew. Their remains had all been blown to atoms.

"You're right," I said. "Truth is power. So let me tell you a little truth." I leaned forward so far as my restraints would allow, the stench of corrup-tion masked by exotic and sweet-smelling spices filling my nose. "You think you've already won, but . . ." I looked down at the rotting feast spread above the trench-table before me. The empty eye sockets of my men stared up at me, their gaze inescapable. "But this is not a victory. Do you know how many of us there are? How many trillions? And you think you can wipe us out? You think they won't fight you when I'm gone? Hunt you? Hound you to the last? You think the blood of Earth so thin that my destruction will be enough to break them? Do you really think we are a *sunken race*? We did not need your gods to pull us from the muck. We are not savages or thralls as you. You may triumph in battle after battle, but you will not win the war."

The Prophet's jaw snapped forward, every one of its more than a hun-dred pointed teeth exposed. It hissed, and I did not need to have studied the expressions of its kind for so many centuries to know that here was anger. For the first time since coming to Dharan-Tun, for the first time since my miracle on Berenike, I had rattled the old demon. Syriani's nictitating membranes flicked shut and open over those black pits it called eyes, and it raised two taloned fingers like a priest in benediction. Letting the hand fall, it said, "*Paqqaa.*"

Eat.

The Cielcin to either side of the table rushed forward, no ceremony, no decorum. The creatures only wore the dress of courtiers and aristocrats. They were beasts, and all pretense at civilization was in that instant stripped away. Ministers clambered over concubines to tear soft strips of meat from artfully arranged bones. One Cielcin in the white costume of a minister lashed out at another, talons tearing the creature's face. Paying the wounded Cielcin no mind, the minister stooped, flanged jaws extending, and tore at one of the platters. Not far off, I saw two of the concubines in brightly patterned silks seize one of the human slaves who'd carried in the meal. The boy cried out as one of the concubines bit down on his throat and tore.

I shut my eyes, but still I could see the Prophet's smile shining in the blackness. Still I could hear the noise of feasting. I might have vomited had I anything to lose.

"Not a victory, you say?" came Syriani's cold and glassy voice. The great prince leaned forward in its high-backed seat, pausing to survey its feasting, bestial courtiers. "But you forget: I need not kill each one of you *yukajjimn* to achieve dominion. I do not wish to." It spread its hands, indicating the rotting feast. "Your kind have their place at my table."

"You can't win," I said. "Kill me, and you'll give my people a hero. I'm as dangerous to you dead as alive."

"And your Emperor?" the great prince countered, and reaching out peeled a strip of flesh from the platter before it and—lifting it as some ancient pharaoh might a bunch of grapes—slid the morsel between opened jaws. "Will he be dangerous when he is dead?"

I had no response to that. The demon king's eyes went wide, and its leering smile returned. "I thought not," it said, and chewed savagely, dark juice running down its chin. At a gesture the nearest Cielcin courtier approached its master, throat bared. Syriani seized a strip of the concubine's fabric and dabbed at its chin before lashing the creature with one hand. The concubine went to its knees, clutching the stained fabric to its breast as it crawled away. The prince's eyes found mine again, and held my gaze until I broke and looked back down at my hands.

"Perfugium," it said at last, voice tinged with something like relish.

"Vanaheim. Balanrot." They were the names of the planets on the Emperor's itinerary. The names I had betrayed. I looked up, sick with horror and self-loathing. But the Great One was not finished. "Carteia," it said, "Aulos. Nessus. Ostrannas. Siraganon. Ibarnis. Thielbad. Kebren . . ." It rattled off an ever-growing number of worlds in precise sequence. Deliberate sequence. A dozen. Two. More than thirty planets distributed across the Centaurine provinces. Only slowly did I recognize them for what they were: the Emperor's complete itinerary.

"How did . . . ?" I felt as though a pit had opened beneath my feet. "I didn't . . ." I hadn't given Syriani *everything*. I hadn't remembered every name. I wasn't even sure I'd known them all.

"You really think you were the only one we questioned?" asked Syriani Doryaica. The great prince reached out one pale, six-fingered hand and seized an object from the heart of the platter nearest it. "It took some time to ascertain which of your people had the knowledge we sought . . . but what is that charming human expression? *He sang.*" The Great One lifted the object—the head—by its neat dark hair.

Despite the days of corruption and the gray-green spice paste plastered to the dead man's features, still I knew that nobile face: the proud palatine nose and hard jaw, the prominent brows and jutting chin. In life, Adric White had been the *Tamerlane*'s navigator, one of the officers who had joined us upon the occasion of my investiture, when His Radiance the Emperor named me to his Royal Victorian Knights. I had never grown to know Adric well, but he was—had been—a good officer. Quiet, efficient, competent to the last. Yet we were never friends, and so I hope you will forgive me when I report my initial response was not grief, but horror.

Adric had been aboard the *Tamerlane*, not on Padmurak at all.

It was true. All of it. The *Tamerlane* had been captured. The Red Company imprisoned. Somehow I'd dared to hope, even with my men skinned and separated on the banquet table and torn apart in feasting, that it was all some elaborate sham. So terrible was that banquet and so terrible the truth of it that my very mind rebelled, and I had sat there bound in my seat not with hope, but with denial. For until that moment, I felt that none of it was real. Syriani had tormented me, tortured me to separate me from my body—to prove the truth of its philosophy. To prove that this world—*the* world—was a lie.

The Lie.

I had not believed it, had not believed that all was lost, that all my people were taken prisoner, that Valka and Corvo, Pallino and Crim and the few survivors of the battle in Vedatharad could not have survived. I had denied reality ever since I'd awoken in the fugue creche in Severine's arms. I had believed, without knowing I believed, exactly what Syriani wanted. That the truth was lies.

Recognizing this, I stopped. I had to shut my eyes and clenched my fists against the grief that came then. The desolation. I had been tortured to no purpose but my own disgrace. "You knew," I managed to say. "The whole time. You knew the planets. Catalog numbers. Coordinates."

"Your ship's records were all we needed, that and your . . . friend's? Testimony." I opened my eyes in time to see Syriani toss poor Adric's head aside. Three of the courtiers chased after it, eager to eat a morsel discarded by their Aeta. My vision blurred with tears. "You begin to understand. All I did, I did to get that little truth from you. I wanted to see if it was possible." And here the Great One stood, leaned over the banquet table like a white and spreading shadow. "You will never be Cielcin, Lord Marlowe. You will never serve Truth." It raised its eyes to the red lamps hanging high above and ceased to move, the frozen center of that tableau of animalistic feasting, the fixed center of a roiling social order. "And you *will* die. You. Your Empire. Your god. Everything."

I was being dismissed.

Tears fell on my bandaged hands. Tears for Adric, whom I hardly knew. Tears for Koskinen and Pherrine. Tears for Ilex and Elara, for Lorian Aristedes. Tears for Durand and Halford and all the brave soldiers of my Red Company. Tears for Pallino. For Crim and Corvo. Tears for Valka, for Valka most of all. And tears for Hadrian Marlowe, whose end was coming fast.

Akterumu awaited.

CHAPTER 34

THE DESCENT

TWICE TWELVE AND NINE watches passed, or must have done. Severine and a pair of human medical technicians in drab gray visited me in my cell repeatedly, and it was after the third or fourth of these visits that I began to realize they were coming *daily*, and coming the same time every day. How I knew this I cannot say. Perhaps after so long adrift in unmarked time some antique and well-trained part of me recognized the ticking of a clock in their actions. Perhaps that was their intention, to reassert something like the regular ebb and flow of events, to prepare me and return me to sanity for what was yet to come. At length I was removed from my chair, my waste hoses and saline drip lines extracted, my medical correctives removed.

I was whole again—or whole as I could be.

My torn fingernails had fully regenerated, and where the Pale had flayed me there remained only flat, white scars. They did not restore my fingers—though they might have done—and the right shoulder still ached with old torment. They might have done more to heal me, but they had done what little was necessary. As Syriani had said, I had been made strong again for but one purpose.

To die.

How many times had I seen it in my dreams? The end? That last, long walk to Akterumu, the place of the rock? It was why I had been hunted since before the Battle of Berenike. Why I had been captured. Why I was still alive.

The door opened, and Severine entered, flanked not only by her customary medical technicians, but by two Cielcin soldiers in ribbed black armor. The xenobites carried a crate between them, a trunk of alien manufacture, which they placed on the ground just inside the tunnel that led from the cell door.

I stood—because I could stand—and faced them, chin raised in defiance. Remembering the gesture signaled submission to the inhumans, I ducked my head instead, stepped back as Severine bowed. "Gentle lord," she said, no trace of mockery in her tone.

"We've arrived," I said, sensing the pregnant quality of the air. "At Akterumu."

The doctor signaled her technicians, a white light pulsing at one corner of her jaw. She fixed those gray, metallic eyes on me, and not for the first time I shuddered at the absence of spark or humanity in those too-bright globes. The revenant woman gestured at the crate flanked by its Cielcin stevedores. "Your presence is required aboard the Great One's landing barge. I have been ordered to see that you dress yourself." And at her sign one of the Cielcin kicked the catch that secured the lid of the crate, revealing the contents within.

The old familiar sigil shone up at me, the pitchfork and pentacle embossed amidst its pattern of raven wings, black on black. I stared down at it, disbelieving, at the black tunic with its crimson-fringed labyrinth embroidery, at the leather-wrapped ceramic of the breastplate, the sculpted bracers and greaves, the pteruges decorated with images of faces and of stars.

I did not reach for it.

"Put it on," the MINOS witch said.

I could see the black armorweave of the skin-suit rolled in one corner, but did not move. I had thought never to see my armor again, had thought it abandoned on Padmurak, or else carried off as a trophy for the prince or by one of the sorcerers of MINOS. Instead, it looked as if it had been cleaned and impeccably repaired. No sign of the filth of Vedatharad remained, and the damage it had sustained in my flight and final stand upon the bridge had been mended by some careful artisan. It looked new as the day it was printed.

Tears in my eyes, I asked, "What's to be done with me?"

Severine's gray eyes narrowed. "You are to be presented to the *Aetavanni* in the city below. The other clan chiefs are arriving."

"The city?" I asked. The Cielcin did not build cities. Not on planets.

"Akterumu," she said.

"I thought Akterumu was the planet."

"Akterumu is the city," she said, half-turned to watch her inhuman guards. "Eue is the planet."

"Eue?" I froze. Hearing the sacred name in my verminous mouth, one of the Cielcin guards lunged and struck me in the jaw. Weak as I was, I folded like a paper house. "We're going to Eue?"

Eue.

The very name evoked a primitive darkness from beyond the borders of infinity. For all my contact with the Pale, it remained a black shape at the edge of comprehension, a myth to rival lost Atlantis or vanished Sarnath. It was to Eue that the Cielcin King Elu led the survivors of the doom that befell their homeworld. It was on Eue that the Cielcin ceased to be mere barbarians and learned to sail the stars. It was from Eue that the first Aeta launched their fleets into those same stars when Elu at last was gone.

It was the holiest site in all the Cielcin universe, as central to them as Earth was to us. I had never imagined—not in my deepest nightmares—that the place was still out there, still *real.*

"*Iukatta, qisabar-kih!*" Severine exclaimed, ordering the guard back. "*Biqunna o-tajun wo! Eza shuza netotebe ti-Shiomu!*" She crouched over me, dry fingers on my face. "Are you hurt?" I had no illusions. It was her own skin she cared for, not mine. It would be she who suffered if I came to harm. The Cielcin guards both retreated a step. Human Severine might have been, but she was not *yukajjimn.* She was Exalted, a posthuman servant of their dark master.

"We must not keep the Great One waiting," Severine said coolly. "Come now." With gentle hands, the witch-woman helped me to my feet and pulled the loose gown up over my head. Naked but beyond shame, I stood there as the two medtechs advanced and sprayed me with some antiseptic agent that foamed and boiled in the cool air, lifting the grime and sweat from my scarred and leathered flesh. At length, they helped me don the skin-suit and tighten the seals. The garment cinched tight about my starved frame, and for the first time I was acutely aware of the wastage of muscle and sinew. My shadow dancing on the floor looked half-Cielcin, so thin and skeletal the limbs, so hollow the belly.

I permitted the technicians to pull my tunic over my head. One held my waist-length hair while Severine assisted the other in fitting my breastplate.

"It won't go," the junior man said, indicating the fit about my neck. "We have to take the collar."

A light at Severine's jaw pulsed. Communicating with Urbaine, I guessed, or with some Cielcin authority. She nodded, and speaking neither to me or to the technician, said, "He won't be any trouble." She paused, listening perhaps. Dry fingers brushed my neck, and the witch's dead eyes stared into mine. "Isn't that right, gentle lord?" I did not answer her, and after another attentive pause, Severine said, "Understood."

The collar *clicked* open in her slim fingers, and she lifted the thing away. How long had I worn it? My neck felt thin and fragile without it, and the skin beneath was raw. It burned as they adjusted the skin-suit's neckline and attached the molded breastplate. Old servos whined as the armor tightened itself, and before long greaves and gauntlets went on.

"That's better," Severine said, and combed my lank and over-long hair back with her fingers. "You look almost yourself again." She held my tresses in her hand, as if weighing them. The once black hair was shot with white like veins in black marble. "Though you are old before your time." She smiled up at me, almost coy. A temptress's smile. "It is not too late to accept my offer."

Looking down on her, I smiled in spite of everything. "It was always too late for that, witch."

Severine let her hand fall, her unassuming face dark. *"Witch!"* she sneered. "You're a fool. And you'll die a fool."

I raised my wrists for her to cuff them. In the gauntlets, it was almost impossible to tell my two fingers were gone. "I'll die a man," I said.

Her smile—which had faltered at my refusal—flickered back into place, but there was a sadness in it now, a finality, and a strange kind of victory. "You'll die."

A green light suffused the access tube that led from the tunnels to the great prince's landing barge. I could see little of the vessel ahead, but I guessed it was of the broken-circle shape preferred by the xenobites for their smaller craft. Through the glassed walls of the tube glittered the icy surface of Dharan-Tun. The great shipyards and iron docks of the Prophet's legions had been carved into the walls of some crater or sinkhole to shelter them from the surface so that workers might move about even while the great worldship was at warp. Gantries and the mechanical arms of fuel injectors hung above and below, and in the green-lit distance I could make out the crescent shapes of other vessels, shuttles or lightercraft doubtless meant to escort the Prophet's barge.

My Cielcin escort held my arms with taloned hands and set the pace with their long strides, so that I half-jogged and was half-dragged along, chains rattling the while.

"Do you see it?" Severine called from behind me.

I did not have to ask what she meant.

The world above filled half the sky, its marshy face lit by a pale sun I could not see. Its watery greens and rust browns streaked with grayish cloud, sickly and putrefied, Eue stared down at us from the heavens from amid its parliament of moons. It loomed over the lip of the crater above like the face of some idiot god. I felt its presence like a vast and lidless eye, as though the planet itself were watching me.

And why not? If the legends were to be believed, it was to Eue that the Watchers had brought their inhuman thralls. Looking up, I felt almost as though it were *they* who watched me, and thinking of the awful statues in the halls of the *Dhar-Iagon*, I shuddered. But I had stopped too long, and stumbled as my guides urged me forward and jerked the chains that bound me.

Like a puppet on its strings, I followed.

Scahari warriors in suits of enameled black marked with the mirrored imprint of the six-fingered White Hand stood guard just inside, flanking squat pillars that bristled with cylindrical protrusions like blunt spines. More of the low, red lanterns hung in the spaces between them: glass spheres in which a radiant gas gleamed. The atrium might have been another room of the palace, so unlike a ship it seemed, worked all of metal and graven stone. Murals done in the *udaritanu* letters covered recesses in the walls, and ahead an iron door rose like the portcullis of some medieval castle to admit us.

My escort half-carried me up stairs higher and shallower than any human step. I heard Severine and her companions laboring behind. A herald in robes of snowy white and azure slammed the butt of its ceremonial spear against a metal plate in the floor as I entered and announced, *"Aeta Hadrian Marlowe wo! Ute Aeta ba-Yukajjimn! Beletaru ba-Uatanyr Thun-savadedim ba-Zahaka. Anabiqan ba-Otiolo. Ba-Ulurani. Elutanura tajun ve ti-Ikurrar!"*

Hearing my name and titles rendered in the Cielcin tongue turned my stomach to water, and I was glad of my armor. Absurdly, some ancient part of me—the part that had thrilled to meet with Uvanari and with Makisomn in the pits of Emesh—wondered if the Cielcin had always employed heralds and titles like our own, or if Syriani Dorayaica had changed the traditional practices to better resemble the style of our Imperial court, as had been the practice of human barbarians since Sargon came to Uruk.

The high hall resembled the greater one in the *Dhar-Iagon*, with knurled pillars and ribbed arches that made me think of flesh. Green light from the holy planet's hideous face streamed through the arched glass of the roof above and the wall behind the dais that rose before me. Looking up, I was struck by what a display of opulence and strength that glass roof was. No human vessel I had ever seen boasted so large a window. Most had no windows at all, preferring imitation windows, screens that often as not depicted false images of planets and of stars. Windows were weaknesses, places where hull integrity might fail. To build so large a window on so important a craft—the great prince's personal landing barge—was to project power to awe all who bore witness to its terrible splendor. Here, it said, is a prince without fear, a prince mightier than fear, a prince who has conquered fear.

And beneath that mighty roof, framed before a wall of glass almost as mighty and looking out upon its shipyards, stood the great prince itself. Syriani Dorayaica did not turn as I approached, but surveyed its dominion with hands clasped behind its back, flanked by its generals, Vati and the winged Aulamn. Of Hushansa and Teyanu there was no sign.

"*Yelnna, tanyr-do,*" the Prophet said, and gestured to a place at its side. "Join us. We ascend presently. I wished for you to see, scholar that you are." My guards marched me up the royal steps to stand with the Prophet. There was no throne, nor any semblance of one. The dais was bare but for a tracery of glyphs etched onto the floor. I could not read them. One hand raised to dismiss the guards, Syriani said, "*Ennallaa o-ajun.*"

The guards dropped to their knees and crawled back down the stairs, leaving me with the Prophet and its two holy slaves. Syriani Dorayaica spoke into the renewed quiet. "Do you know where we are?"

"Eue," I said.

Syriani hissed, and the two chimeras made low thrumming noises, more machine than organic. "I see . . ." It glanced to Severine, who along with her two associates knelt at once. "Do you know its meaning?"

"Its meaning?" I echoed, confused. Chained though I was, my armor made me *man* again, and I did not shrink from the Great One as I had in our previous meetings. "It's the planet Elu brought your ancestors to when Se Vattayu was lost."

"*Tuka qisaban!*" the winged general, Aulamn, snapped, red eyes flaring. Syriani raised one ringed and taloned hand to silence its slave. "Elu did not *bring* our people out of Se Vattayu. We are *Cielcin*. *Kielukishunna* in the old tongue. 'Those carried by the Gods.' *Godsborne,* you might say."

I blinked, understanding for the first time. "*They* brought you off-world? The Watchers?"

The Great One bared its teeth. "It was Miudanar, the Dreamer, who taught Elu the art of shipbuilding. He taught him to fashion the hull and split the atom. He showed Elu how to cross the darkness, and led our people here." With that said, the prince reached up with one white hand as if to scratch the face of the green world above us.

Eue. The gift.

Had I not often wondered how so vicious and primitive a people had won their way to the stars? A metallic clangor shook the vessel beneath us, and Vati turned its head away, as if listening. I found my vision pulled skyward yet again, and I traced the contours of the rusted mountains and mossy pools across the surface of the planet above. I saw no shape of canals or sign of cities, no great mark of industry or civilization. It was the day side that faced us, and so if there were any lights to see, they were invisible. About it moved its countless tiny moons in stately procession like a flock of logothetes about their lord.

"Your gods . . . the Watchers taught you everything?" I said, not taking my face away.

"*Cara,*" Syriani amended. *Much.* "Some things we found at Akterumu."

I felt my brows contract, and I brought my attention back to my demonic host. "Akterumu . . ." I said, and glanced back down the steps to where Severine stood among the pillars and the guards. "Doctor Severine said it was a city."

"It *is* a city, you would say," the Great One said. "The oldest city."

"How old?" I asked. I realized I did not know how old Cielcin civilization was. It was one of the great mysteries that surrounded their kind. On Forum and later, on Nessus, I had reviewed studies done by scholiasts and lay academics who'd pored over artifacts recovered from the various worldships captured in the fighting. Valka and I had assisted in some—Valka ever eager in those days to understand the connection between the Cielcin and the Quiet. Some of the smaller vessels we'd seized or destroyed had superstructures dating back five or six thousand years, but there had been certain artifacts—drinking vessels or stone monuments, tablets carved with *udaritani*—that experts guessed were nearer four or five times that number, dating back to before the Golden Age of Earth.

The Prophet turned at last from its contemplation of the holy world in

the sky above us and looked down at me, transparent membranes clicking over the ink-dark surfaces of its eyes. Silver chains swayed across its
bony forehead as it angled its crown in an almost didactic pose, as though
it were the scholiast and I the ignorant student. "It was old in Elu's day,"
it said.

Again, I blinked uncomprehending. "Old in . . . what?"

The *vayadan*-general Vati interrupted then, its high, cold voice scratching at the windowpanes. "All is made ready, *Aeta-Shiomu*," it said, using
the Cielcin title meaning *Lord Prophet.*

Syriani Dorayaica inclined its head and waved a royal gesture. *"Tutai
wo. Velenamma o-ajun junne, vayadan-kih."* It returned its attention to the
green planet in the sky. *Take us down.* The Prophet's nose-slits dilated as it
exhaled. "The *baetayan* sing that there is no time on Eue. That nothing
passes. Nothing changes. I do not know if it is truly so, but it is an ancient
world, and most ancient is Akterumu, whose towers were old when the
stars were young." Sparing a glance for my confused silence, the Prophet
said, "We did not build it. Elu did not build it."

"The Watchers?" I asked. "This . . . Miudanar?"

Placing a hand on its breast, Syriani answered, "We are slime. Filth.
Creatures of the Lie—as are you. But we do not have to be. In submission
to the gods, we receive our *ouluu*, our soul. Our spark. It is a pearl that
connects us to the gods, a gift. Like Eue!" Another clangor resounded
through the structure of the barge about us, and above and below alike there
roared to life a flat and ceaseless hum as the engines flared to life. Through
the windows before us, I marked several smaller crescent-shaped craft flaring up in the berths that studded the crater walls. Grand as the spectacle
was, it was as nothing next to the Prince's next words. "We are not the
only ones the gods bore up," it said.

We began to rise, though my stomach stayed where I had left it, and
my heart sank.

"You mean . . ." I could not speak. Snatches of the visions I had seen
atop the mountain rose from the tangle of memory, creatures defying de-
scription arrayed across the stars, nameless and numberless. The universe
teemed with life, had teemed with life before our time—would teem with
life when we were gone. "You're saying there were others? Other . . .
Cielcin? Other species that worshiped your gods?"

Aulamn laughed, and the noise of it made me start. *"Usayu u!"* it said.
Only one.

We were rising above the lip of the crater then, first in a grand and stately procession of black crescents. Through the windows to either side I could see the curving horns of the great prince's barge reaching out like arms to embrace the planet above.

"We are the Second. They are the *Enar*," Syriani said. "The First."

The implications of this revelation rocked me where I stood, and for a moment I forgot my torment, forgot that I was riding to my death, forgot even the two lethal chimeras that stood so near at hand. An ancient people, a civilization older than anything we had known, older than the oldest sites left by the Quiet.

"The Enar?" I repeated the strange word slowly, taking my time with each syllable. It was another ancient word. *First* was *udim* in the Cielcin tongue I knew, but like so many of the words the Prophet had taught me, I suspected *Enar* came from a language old as Elu, or older still.

"Utannash perverted all things, trapped them in these hideous forms— as we are trapped," Syriani said, and with a gesture indicated first its body, then my own. "The Enar sought escape, sought to free themselves from this world."

"They went extinct, you mean."

The prince's jaws snapped forward, jutting out past thin lips, fangs dripping as it snarled. "Do not jape with me," it hissed. "They *failed*. They could not destroy the Lie, though they burned a billion worlds."

Having lost too much to be cowed any longer, I asked, "What happened to them then?"

"They are gone." Syriani waved this question aside as though it were no more to it than a buzzing fly. "Destroyed perhaps by Utannash and his champions before they could complete their work. But what they left behind! Akterumu the Great! Akterumu of the Pillars! Akterumu of the Hundred Hundred Gates! This is their legacy! And *our* inheritance! Our *Eue*, our gift! Do you see?"

Even as it asked that question, we rose above the lip of the crater at last on slow repulsors. The Prophet's barge began to advance, drifting slowly up and forward. For the first time then I beheld the surface of its dark world. Like Vorgossos, Dharan-Tun lay sheathed in ice. Unlike Vorgossos, which had seemed lifeless and snowbound, Dharan-Tun's surface was a riddle of iron and of pits. Still more crater bays marched in file unto the shrinking horizon, where in the distance icy mountains stood crowned with the ugly stacks of industry and belched smoke into the airless sky. The greenish glow of Eue blotted out all but the brightest stars, and all was silent in that kingdom of death.

"Do you see?" Syriani asked again, and from its shift in tone I guessed it asked a new question. "For your kind . . . there can be no victory."

What could I say? Nothing.

So I said nothing.

It had been one thing to walk the tunnels below and to witness the demonic city in the deeps, but to see the surface of Dharan-Tun, to behold that vast and pitiless war machine unrolled beneath my feet was something else entirely. Vast though the resources of our Empire were and great our armies, I could not help but feel they were overmatched by the totalizing purity of the Cielcin effort. Everything on Dharan-Tun, *everything,* was bent to but one terrible purpose.

To the war.

To the annihilation of man.

What could we men do in the face of such resolve? Such *caiharu*? Such faith?

Beside me, Syriani Dorayaica lifted its face to the verdurous gloom, peering up with narrowed eyes through the glass roof toward Eue and the stars. "So many are here already!" Its translucent teeth flashed.

It took me a moment to understand what the Prince of Princes was seeing, and when I did I felt the last ounce of warmth in my blood run cold. It was not a parliament of moons that orbited the profane capital. Eue's attendants were not moons at all. The nearest of them shone in the skies above Dharan-Tun, large and bright as a silver kaspum, its left edge gutted and hollow, revealing the cyclopean engineering beneath: the halls and bays, the towers and silos and the great mechanism of the engines that propelled the *worldship* between the stars.

With spreading horror I comprehended the mass and charge, the cosmic scope of the *fleet* arrayed about the planet Eue. Each moon was a ship, and each ship was the core of its own fleet of lesser vessels. A thousand moons filled the sky about the planet, each the capital and flagship of a Cielcin clan. Some great, some small—but none greater than the Prophet's. Mighty though the fortresses of those other clan-chiefs seemed, none seemed to me so great or so terrible as the world I left behind.

Syriani had said the *Aetavanni* met at its command, and I believed it, for surely the clan Dorayaica might crush any one of these others at a whim as our Emperor might annihilate a petty lord.

Who could dare refuse such a summons?

"How long has it been since so many were gathered here?" Vati asked its lord and master.

"Twelve and seven generations," the prince answered its slave. "Not since Araxaika ended the Kinslaying." Turning to me and switching from its native tongue to mine, the Prophet said, "That was perhaps twenty of your chiliads ago."

"Millennia?" I asked.

Twenty thousand years. Nineteen generations. Not for the first time, I wondered just how long the Cielcin might live—and how old Syriani was. Twenty thousand years . . . as a boy, I would never have imagined the Cielcin heirs to a tradition and a history so long as our own. They seemed so primitive, so unsophisticated by comparison. Yet it made some sense. Long-lived as they were, they were perhaps slower to innovate, slower to discover or to change. And if what Syriani had told me was *literally* true, their greatest innovations had been given them by powers, creatures they believed were gods. What reason had they to innovate? To discover?

The Prophet and its creatures looked on, an emotion I could not name filling the air about them like smoke. In hushed tones, Syriani said, "This thing has not happened since antiquity." To my astonishment, the prince reached out and seized Vati by the wrist, as if to find comfort or give affection. That brush—that grasping hand—has haunted me more than any of the hollow-eyed slaves I had seen in the halls of Dharan-Tun, haunted me nearly so much as the corpses arrayed on their platters in the hall of that Pale King.

I do not know why.

CHAPTER 35

THE BROKEN CIRCLE

RISING FROM DHARAN-TUN, WE sank toward Eue, sailing over miles of endless bog and low hills. There were no mountains, no rivers, no seas. Syriani had said that time did not pass on Eue. It seemed geologically true, at least. From our great height, the planet seemed dead, unchanging and eternal. Nothing lived there, nothing grew—unless it was the slime molds that choked the waterways with yellow and deathly green. Above those strangled wastes stretched tablelands of gray sand, the flatness relieved only occasionally by broken ridges of stone.

"*Yukajji-kih!*" cried the *vayadan*-general Aulamn to me. "You will see a thing unseen by your degenerate kind! You should count yourself blessed."

I said nothing to it, but stood silent and in chains beside the great prince, who was silent as I. Our shadow heralded our coming, its broken-ring shape cast upon the wastes below. Looking back and up through the arched glass overhead, I could see the other ships of our train descending, not shocking the air but sliding neatly into Eue's atmosphere. And I could see Dharan-Tun above, its face white and deceptively shining. No sign was there of pits or foundries, or of the torments that lay beneath that frozen hell of a world.

"There's nothing . . ." I heard myself say, and shut my mouth to keep from saying more. The place reminded me—in its way—of Annica, formless and void.

Aulamn hissed, its metal pinions flexing dangerously. I feared the beast would strike me, as others of its kind had done for perceived blasphemies, but its master's presence stayed its hand.

"*Sim ejaan,*" my host replied. "Not nothing. Look!"

We were flying low then, the wind of our passage rippling the slimy pools and strangled waterways below. Ahead, the horizon shimmered, and above its shine a black shape arose. The marshlands fell away, and at last we came upon a great expanse of sand the color of charcoal. The dunes-cape stretched from horizon to horizon, black as shale, clogged here and there with a snot-like growth of fungus. So vast it was I thought it must have been the bed of some long-vanished sea.

A gift, indeed.

The black mass on the horizon reared higher and higher as we approached, seeming to grow with each passing instant, rising from a blur at the margin of the world to a dark line of hills. From hills to mountains. How tall those mountains were I dared not guess, for each time I tried I realized how *far* our ships had yet to go. So flat was that barren emptiness that distance collapsed, became meaningless. The mountains might have been ten miles away or two hundred. And so I could not guess, not until we came beneath their shadow.

Lower we flew above the sands until we raked tracks across the desert with our passage. The mountains rose above the level of the desert plain, miles high and dozens of miles across. The closer we came, the more certain I was of one thing and one thing only: the mountains could not be a natural part of the landscape. Still distant as we were, I could see how flat and featureless were their gray-green faces, rising sheer as castle walls from the sand. What was more, there was nothing on Eue to suggest the tectonic forces required to uplift such a mass of stone. Featureless as the planet's face was, I guessed its geologic heart was cold and dead as the creatures who once had built upon its surface.

They were impossible. The mountains could not be real.

How can I impress their size upon you with mere *words*? The weight and shadow of them, their soaring pinnacles and sheer faces hung over the world in a way that flattened all who beheld them. The very clouds of Eue bent at their presence and pooled about their crowns. Not even the Storm Wall on Berenike was so mighty.

"There!" the Prophet exclaimed, and pointed with an open hand. "There are gathered the princes of the blood-clans! See you their banners?"

I opened my mouth to respond but remained silent. I did not see, not at first. I had not looked low enough. "I do," I said at last. Tall and narrow banners rose on masts like the ceremonial spears carried by an Aeta's *cote-liho*, its herald. A sea of greens and blues, of whites and blacks arrayed themselves on the fields before the mountain wall, still so remote that each stood no taller than a grain of rice. And nowhere was there a hint of red, a shout of yellow gold. No spark of orange or splash of umber, but every

blue and violet the imagination might conjure was there in residence. I
fancied even some of the blacks were ultraviolet to Cielcin eyes.

They did not perceive color as we.

Reminded of this, I looked round at the blackness of that dark vessel.
Was it dark to them? Or were there hidden patterns, secret designs in subtle hues no human eye could see? That thought only heightened my sense
of alienation.

"How many clans are there?" I asked.

"Thousands!" answered Vati.

"Only thirteen," Dorayaica replied, its answer cowing the general to
quiet. By way of explanation, it added, "So many fractures, so many
branchings." There was a gravelly note in the creature's voice I was coming
to recognize as melancholy. As regret.

As shame.

That word, *uatanyya, branchings,* plucked a string in my memory. "Aranata Otiolo," I said, drawing glances from the Great One and its holy
slaves. "Aranata Otiolo called itself *the Lord of the Seventeenth Branching.*"

The Prophet's eyes closed slowly. Aulamn made a mechanical screeching, part cry and part curse. "Betrayer!" it shouted. "Deceiver! Otiolo
brought corrosion upon the blood-clans! It slew Utaiharo. It was *vayadan*
and should have known its place!" The chimera struck the column nearest
it with an iron pinion, sending a cascade of sparks showering down the side
of the dais. Severine and the other MINOS servants flinched. "You did
well to slaughter it!"

"The line of Utaiharo stretched back to before the time of Araxaika the
Almost-Blessed," Syriani said, apparently unaffected by the winged chimera's display. "It was an old line, only seventeen times broken by violence
since the days of Elu. Otiolo should have shown respect."

"I don't understand," I said.

Syriani's eyes opened sharply, and though I could not distinguish iris
from pupil I knew they fixed upon my face. "You are a student of your
own history, are you not? Know you not that when dynasties fall, they
fracture? Great empires becoming little kingdoms in the rubble, ruled by
those lieutenants and heirs who survive the chaos? That chaos is *uatanyr,* is
a *branching.*" It glanced to Vati and to brooding Aulamn. "*My vayadayan*
will die if they kill me. Your sorcerers have made it so."

"Never!" Vati hastened to say, and prostrated itself before its master.
"Never, Great One!"

Almost lovingly, Syriani Dorayaica *stepped* on the back of its subordinate's head. Keeping its foot there, it looked down at me, eyes narrowing. "Your conquest, Otiolo, was bound to Utaiharo as *vayadan*. Its betrayal was *dunyasu*. Blasphemy. Where Utaiharo had been, there were others. Otiolo, Prince of Sacrilege. Ajimma. Tuanolo. Raiazu." It counted these on its fingers. "A *branching*. Chaos." It hissed, and released Vati from beneath its foot.

I chewed on this revelation a moment, watching Vati rise—still bowing to its master. "Diadochi," I said at last.

The Great One cocked its head. "I do not know this word."

Smiling with the reversal, I said, "It is an old word." The irony was not lost on the Prophet, whose face betrayed no amusement. "It means *successor*, specifically the successors of a very ancient emperor. Alexander, we called him. Our Elu . . . in a sense. They were his generals, and divided his kingdom when he died."

Syriani twitched its head in that way which signaled *yes* among its kind, and brushed past Vati to look out the window once more. The sheer greenish faces of the mountains filled all our view, the colored banners snapping in the wind had grown large as fingers. "Each *itani*, each blood-clan may trace its lineage back through each *uatanyr* to one of Elu's first *Aetane*. To one of his *Diadochi*, you might say." The Greek word sounded foul in the xenobite's mouth. "You are *Aeta* of the Eighteenth Branching of the House of Zahaka, who was Aeta to Elu. Twice six and six." Switching to its native tongue then, Syriani spoke to Vati. "Give the order to land in line with the gates and have the others form a line to either side of us. Fan out. Show them our numbers. I would have the others understand why it is Dorayaica has the right to call them here."

The general bowed and—still bent—signaled the crew who piloted the shuttle via its implants. Or so I gathered, for at once our flight began to slow and circle to the right, sliding across the airs on droning repulsors, kicking up great black clouds of dust.

Without warning, a short laugh escaped my nose. I stifled it, but too late.

"Dein?" Syriani asked.

"Twice six and six!" I laughed, realizing I could never explain the importance of that number or its relation to the emblems of my house.

Eighteen. Three sixes.

"It is nothing," I said, amazed that I could still laugh, if only at so trifling a coincidence.

Or so strange an omen.

Taking me at my word, the Prophet almost shrugged as it turned away to address Aulamn. *"Iamarara o-scaharimn wananuri ti-jattin!"* it said, ordering the general to ready its guards. "We are here!"

No ramp.

Still in chains, I stood well behind Syriani Dorayaica on a lift platform in the bowels of the prince's landing barge. The generals Vati and Aulamn bracketed their master like a pair of unmatched chess pieces. Behind me, Severine stood silently by, surrounded by a half-dozen other MINOS personnel in suits of gray or black. About us stood assembled some two hundred of the Prophet's *scahari* warriors, their scimitars drawn, long handles tucked against the crooks of their right arms, their shining *nahute* coiled and ready on their hips.

Almost I felt as if I were crowded into the lift in the coliseum, sweating and muttering with the myrmidons before a fight. I looked round. No sign of Pallino and Elara, nor of Siran, of Ghen . . . of Switch. The only human faces were of Severine and her companions—and so there were no true human faces at all.

If I expected any great words or lordly remark, I was disappointed. The great clan-chief of the blood-clan Dorayaica was silent again. One of the lesser warriors let out a cry, and above us the low, red lights—which I guessed seemed bright and pale to the xenobites—cycled blue. The platform beneath lurched, and with a rattling clangor like the turning of some immeasurable clock, we descended, hurtling smoothly to the ground.

Stale wind rushed up about us, carrying black sand like cold cinders that stung my exposed face. I was surprised I could breathe, truth be told, and guessed the algaes and the expanses of lurid fungal molds we'd crossed to reach this place had something to do with it. The whole place stank of brimstone and decay, of the static bite of desolation.

Of the tomb.

A white-robed *coteliho* marched forward, brandishing its heraldic spear tipped with the broken circle motif common to all Cielcin heraldry, beneath it the White Hand in a ring worked in silver. Behind it went two *scahari*, MINOS-built chimeras, white-limbed and white-armored, each carrying a tall, slim sable banner with the device of the Hand painted between Cielcin glyphs.

I had no eyes for them, nor for the triple column of Pale warriors, black-armored and cloaked in the Dorayaica black and royal azure that followed.

I had eyes only for the mountains.

Unhampered now by the windows of the landing barge and unhindered by the low-hanging clouds, I could look up from where I stood inside the circling embrace of the shuttle's two horns to where the peaks of the mountains rose, strangely square and regular, to battle the thin, gray sky.

They were no peaks, nor any mountains.

They were ramparts.

What I had taken for the sheer faces of mountains rising near at right angles from the gray-black sand were nothing of the kind. They were walls. Five miles high they stood, crowned with square towers, their heights decorated with pillared arcades and trapezoidal arches hundreds of feet high. How thick they were and how wide the space they encircled might be I could hardly estimate, for they marched from horizon to horizon.

I could see so little of it from the ground that its full plan and form were obscure. I guessed—but could not then be certain—that the structure formed a great ring about a vast and desolate plain, or that the ring wall itself was the city of which Syriani and Severine had spoken. I could see only twin horns of that open circle—that broken circle—broken as the head of every staff carried by every herald of the Pale, as though that great ruin and wall were a thumb and forefinger held half an inch apart.

Between them there was only sand, and beyond—within the great circle of the wall—those lone and level sands stretched to the edge of vision. From the ground, the far side of the ring city could be seen only as a gray-green blur across the lower reaches of the sky.

"The Enar built this?" I asked in wonder, and froze in awe of the scale, the sheer Olympian magnitude of all that greenish stone. No one answered, but I knew it must be so. Humanity could scarce have built such a temple, and the Cielcin? The Cielcin did not build *up*.

It was not in the Quiet's shadow that the Cielcin had grown to maturity—in tunnels on Se Vattayu as I had once believed—but in the shadow of these *Enar*, these First servants of their dark gods. Here. On Eue. At Akterumu.

I was wrong.

A cry went up, high and thin and ululating, rising and falling from Earth only knew how many thousand inhuman throats. Beneath the banners ahead and to either side of the great opening, I saw the waving of white swords and the flash of lances. Blue banners fluttered in that universe of gray green. Thousands of the Pale stood massed to either side, waving their arms and their flags beneath the slim spires of drop towers and the indescribable shapes of shuttlecraft. Most wore the battle masks or black visored helmets common to their kind, but where the creatures who served Dorayaica wore their masks white and unadorned, these were garishly painted, striped and whorled with devices I could not understand, markers of clan allegiance that Valka and I might have spent a lifetime deciphering.

They watched us through eyeslits narrow as coin slots to guard against the sun. Others wore heavy goggles and bared glassy fangs while still more—the poorest, most downtrodden of the *ietumna*, I guessed—squinted in the thin light of Eue's weak sun.

Few—like Syriani—wore no mask or helmet. But the Prophet seemed unaffected by the light. I caught myself wondering if it wore some manner of lens beneath its nictitating membranes, or else if MINOS had lavished some of their art upon the dread lord.

At a gesture from the great prince, my honor guard of four still-fleshly warriors dragged me forward. They shoved me to my knees beside Prince Syriani, who spared me a moment's glance before turning to peer up at the twin towers rising from either side of the vast bulwark.

"Akterumu," the great prince said. "City of the Enar. See them there?" It gestured with its horned crown at huge, crude images hewn half a mile high on the face of the mighty walls.

How can I describe their shape? Those images worn down by the passage of so many aeons? Crab-like they were, bodies flat and squashed, supported by crooked limbs—four or six or eight—no two seemed alike. I saw no sign of eyes nor shape of head, and here and there they carried weapons in pincered hands. The bas-reliefs showed them conquering other creatures, things stranger and more hideous even than they. Rank upon rank of jagged writing ran along above and below the figures, no doubt describing the feats of those ancient conquerors in lurid detail.

"Why didn't you destroy their images?" I asked, thinking of the Prophet's own murals depicting the story of its people in abstract form. "Are they not of the Lie?"

"They are reminders, *Oimn Belu*," Syriani replied. "The Enar were unworthy to be anything but our heralds. Their failure reminds us to keep faith." It looked down on me, face strangely placid. Thoughtful? "Akterumu is a monument to their shame, their failure—and our glory."

The great prince stood still as stone a moment, face turned up in contemplation of those mighty sculptures. It seemed to be awaiting its place in the marching column, and that I was to accompany it in its time. "The *baetayan* say that Miudanar ordered the city protected, that Elu forbade the desecration himself. But the treasures of Akterumu! These he took for his own. Their weapons. Their machines. These made us strong."

I nodded, imagining those ancient Cielcin landing here, emerging from their ark into the dim but blinding sunlight. "Did Elu conquer them? The Enar, I mean."

The great prince gathered its black cloak about itself to shield against the wind. *"Veih,"* it answered me. "No. They were dead and gone to dust while my people yet gnawed bones in the dark beneath Se Vattayu."

"What happened to them?" I asked, still squinting up at the reliefs. The Enar's arms—legs, whatever—looked armored, segmented as the carapace of certain of the Exalted appeared. Before the prince could answer, I asked, "Were they machines?"

"I do not know," Syriani replied. "They are gone, and there are none now who know save the gods alone." I turned from my contemplation of the ruin and looked into Syriani's face. The great prince of the Cielcin shaded its delicate eyes with a hand as it studied the ruins. "When Elu first came here, it is said the halls were filled with wonders. Weapons. Machines. They are gone now. Destroyed. Taken by the tribes. But that was so long ago. So little remains. The blood clans destroyed much to build what you see." It jerked its head in the direction of space, at the consortium of moons that littered Eue's pale and bloodless sky.

Was that sorrow in the great prince's voice? Trying to understand Cielcin emotions was still like trying to discern shadows on a pool of ink. I felt a pang of sorrow myself, seeing in the Prophet a distorted image of my own reflection. It pined for lost antiquity as I did, and saw in the grandeur of that ancient pile of stone something worth understanding—Lie or no. I felt it too, as I'd felt it standing above the crag at Calagah, or in the yard outside Fort Din when the Irchtani first soared overhead. It was the same wonder that lit Valka's face when she first stepped into the Great Library at Colchis.

Almost I could imagine we might have been friends. In another life, in a world where perhaps our kinds could reconcile to one another. What tales we might have told, what things learned of one another had we spent our passage in talk and not in torment.

Torment.

The memory of my torment came rushing back, and the sorrow

curdled to scorn. Shutting my eyes, I turned from the Pale prince and back to the walls and the army of white demons clustered about their base. I opened them again, peering over the heads and the forest of swords and lances to the gray desert beyond that mighty gate.

"It is a loss," the prince lamented, and a rush of wind escaped its four nostrils like a sigh. "What wonders we might have learned had we not been so quick to grow."

"Those who wreak destruction and call it progress are ever enemies of eternity . . ." I said, and spared another glance for my host. "And truth."

The prince hissed and raised two clawed fingers to admonish me. "Have a care, kinsman. It is my people you speak of now."

Cold though my blood ran, I turned and faced the prince squarely. "You're a race of scavengers," I said, barely containing a sneer. "Thieves. Vandals. You've created nothing. Everything you have you *took* or were given. Your ships, your technology—this world. Your very faith." I almost spat at the prince's feet, so fey a mood was on me. "Even your Elu. What did Elu achieve save to stand upon this grave of a world and call itself tall?" I did spit then. "And you call *us* rats!"

I did not see the blow until it was too late. Syriani Dorayaica did not snarl, did not telegraph its motion in any way. One taloned hand lashed out and caught me across the face. The boy who once had snapped so at his father hit the sand with a crash and a rattle of chains.

The pain came a moment later, white and searing across the left side of my face. Hot blood ran down into my eye. Struggling to my knees, I blinked it back, feeling the torn flesh with my fingers—suddenly conscious of the missing ones as the empty part of my right glove flapped against my face. Pain flared red as my fingers found the wounds: five deep channels slashed across my left cheek and jaw. I tasted blood, and realized one of the talons had pierced clean through my cheek.

My eye had been spared by microns.

In further retaliation, the Prophet spurned me with its heel, and I fell back upon the sand gasping. Flat on my back, the Cielcin lord looked down on me. "Do not blaspheme in this holy place," it said. "I *will* have your tongue removed. You do not need it any longer. I have thus far permitted you to retain it as a courtesy. Do not try me again."

It held out a hand to one side, palm up. Expectant. Interpreting the gesture, one of my guards shuffled toward its master. Syriani barked an order, and the creature handed my chain into the prince's hand.

It turned and started walking without another word, following its

troops toward the mighty opening that stretched between those two towers of the gods. Dragged behind it, I managed to lurch and stumble my
way back to my feet. Blood sheeted down my torn cheek, and the stinging
sand caught in the wounds, making me wince. Long hair stuck to my face,
and so great were the tall creature's strides that I had to jog to keep up.

What a sight I must have been, bloodied and wild-eyed like some
chieftain of the Germans dragged to Rome. The Prophet's warriors
marched to either side, seeming almost to glide over the sands. The other
Cielcin tribes each kept their distance. Some dipped their pennons as the
great prince approached, others bellowed. In greeting? Or in challenge? I
was perversely glad of the columns of *scahari* marching to either side and
of the white-armored chimeras that marched at intervals among their still-
fleshy compatriots. The slavering horde—there were thousands of them—
seemed as though at any moment they might spill over whatever unseen
line of decorum or fear held them back and crush us. I felt as I had at Arae,
trapped in a column between the hammer and the anvil.

Ahead, the column bent right and made for the gates of the tower. A
huge portal stood open, with neither door nor portcullis. The foremost of
Syriani's soldiers had gained that doorway and vanished beyond up a huge
and arcing stair to the vast warren within. Still jogging on behind the tall
prince, it was easy to imagine those ancient Cielcin flowering here, in halls
and darkened galleries. How many stories were there? How many thousands of miles of corridors and of rooms? The ring-city was vaster than any
city of man. Once it might have been home to millions of the Pale. Now
it was empty, filled only when the blood-clans met in moot.

As we approached the level of the gate and turned, I was accorded at
last a view of the desert beyond the perimeter of the Enar ruins unob-
structed by the Pale horde. Chained though I was to the Prince of Princes,
I lingered, transfixed. So great was the circumference of that ruinous circle that I could not resolve its far side. The curve of Eue bent away, reducing the square-capped ramparts and inhuman crenellations that crowned
the wall to the flat gray of distant mountains, so that the forbidden lands
within that great ring seemed the bottom of some god's bowl roofed in
sky. Or like the floor of some immeasurable arena. Where the outside of
the wall was sheer and decorated with mighty reliefs of Enar conquest, the
interior was terraced, stepped and segmented, with lesser walls running
within parallel to the outer fastness, their faces dotted with trapezoidal
windows, betraying chambers within. Inner towers and bridges, colon-
nades and arched galleries marched along the inner circumference of the

ruin, as though the wall were some gutted beast whose urban innards spilled onto the plain.

I had lingered too long in wonderment, and Syriani pulled my chain. Surprised, wrongfooted, I lurched and fell a second time, sprawling in the black dust.

It didn't matter.

It didn't matter because I had seen it before. I had known I *must* see it, that I *must* come to it in the end. *My* end. I knew that before long I must cross that final threshold and the desert beyond.

The land within was dead and flat as glass, unrelieved by hill or gully. Nothing grew in that uttermost desolation—not even the slimes that colored the landscape outside. There was nothing there, nothing but a forest of slim pillars, each wrought of the same greenish stone as the great miles-high city itself. How short they seemed, though each was surely a thousand feet high, so dwarfed were they by the surrounding ringed city. At a glance, the pillars appeared placed without plan, not in rows or columns. Later, when I would look out upon that plain from a terrace on the lower reaches of the city rings above, I would learn the ancient builders had arranged their pillars in broad spirals which processed from the dome in the precise center of the plain.

And yet not one pillar stood between the great gates of the outer wall and the black dome at its heart. Careful planning had left an avenue from the level of the two towers all the way to the dome, so broad that an army might march half a hundred men abreast along its length. It had been wrought for creatures larger than we, larger than the Cielcin. I tried to picture those tank-like crabs stomping, scuttling over the fused flagstones to the dome and shrine more than a dozen miles away.

Still bleeding from my torn face, I half-rose as the great prince tugged on my chain, my ruined shoulder crying out with pain. Gasping, I found my knees, and fell again as Syriani tugged at me. Face in the dust. It took a measure of doing to get my hands under me, to shake off the jeering and the shouts of the xenobites all around.

"Aeta ba-Yukajjimn wo!" one shouted, mocking.

"Yukajji! Yukajji!"

"Aeta ba-Yukajjimn ne? Aeta ba-Gaunun!"

Warka shanatim madatim itteche en.

"Gau! Gau wo!"

"Gau wo! Psanete wo!"

Teche!

On my knees again, I turned slowly. In among the jeers and the animal babble were words I did not know. A voice deep and dark as space, whispering as if at my ear. I turned sharply, half-expecting to find one of my captors by me. But I was alone. Syriani had dragged me across perhaps a dozen feet of black sand, leaving a disturbed trench in my wake. I was alone.

Ana mahriya teche!

I turned my head sharply left, following the voice along the avenue to the dome and shrine about which the Enar had ordered their universe. As I looked, the distance seemed to contract, the shrine growing larger in my vision—in my mind—as if some fell art altered the focal length of my eye to magnify the fate that was coming to me. I could see the steps, could almost see the iron ring to which I would be chained and sacrificed. In the vision it was all I could ever see. I had never *truly* seen the place before, never seen it as any more than shadows in a dream.

I saw it then with eyes unclouded, saw the dome and the place where the Quiet showed me I must die again beneath the rounded entrance to that black temple.

The entrance . . . the *entrance!*

What I had always taken for a simple circular arch was no such thing. It was no arch at all, but the orbit of a single, monstrous *eye*. So too the dome was no dome, but the smooth crown of a massive *skull* a thousand feet or more in diameter, its substance rippled and shining as obsidian glass.

Akterumu was not *akumn ba-terun* as I had first thought so long ago. It was *akute ba-rumumn*. The Shrine of the Skull.

I began to shake.

That single, lifeless eye held my gaze, the yawning emptiness within it calling out to me across the desert and the sea of pillars: a sucking void that filled me with a crawling horror until I felt certain I must scream. I could not shut my eyes, even though the sand stung them and tears ran. Still kneeling, my hands shook, rattling my chains. I could not stop them. It was all I could do to curl my tortured hands into fists, but that only set my whole body shaking.

It was one of the Watchers—or had been once. Of that I was certain. Indeed, here was the very head of Miudanar, the Dreamer. That which summoned Elu across the vast emptiness of space to serve it, that which had taught its Cielcin thralls to fly.

Even dead, its malevolence lingered, and I felt its gaze pin me to the sands. These ancient Enar had built their city—their entire world—to consecrate and hallow the corpse of their terrific god. The whole of that ringed city—the whole of Eue, in a sense—was its tomb. How many aeons had it lain broken and rotting in the desert? Its flesh wasted away, bones picked clean with the scouring sands?

Teche!

The ungodly voice crashed over me like thunder, and though the language was strange and the meaning beyond all hope of human comprehension, I felt the black joy of its malice all the same. I would later spy its ribs and vertebrae rising from the dust of the plain and marvel at the cosmic scale of it. It must have stood a mile high once, if *stand* were the right word, for surely so vast a creature must ply the black waves of space, for any gravity must crush so weighty an organism.

Whence had it come? Syriani had said the creatures were older than the universe, that the Quiet—which the Prophet claimed was the author of creation itself—had trapped its dark gods in fleshly prisons, but surely that could not be. Yet though my mind rejected it, my eyes could not but believe. Here then was one of the vile creatures that had warred—would war—with the Quiet across eternity. Creature of an older universe it was, or of the boiling chaos beyond creation, terrible even in death.

Ammarka!

A white pain flared behind my eyes, and I felt a sensation of fingers—nematodes slithering across the white matter of my brain. Hands seized me. Cielcin hands. I hardly felt them.

I hardly felt anything.

CHAPTER 36

THE SUPPLIANTS

THE CAVERNOUS HALL THAT the Prophet had selected for its meeting echoed with the sounds of inhuman feet. How many thousand steps had we climbed to reach that dark and secret place? And how many times had I fallen, my muscles cramping from disuse before at last Dorayaica forced its men to carry me?

The great prince had not remained with the others, whose camps filled the lowest levels of the ringed city, or else flooded the sands about the gate. Too well now I remember the stink of peat fires in the low halls and the noise of evil laughter; the carnival excitement of it all. Dorayaica told me it had been generations since all the clans gathered in one place. I could scarce imagine. It must have been as though all the children of Earth were called home to haunt her wasted hills and dry riverbeds and reveled in the ashes of man. Well I recall the tables laden with bones in the open doors we passed and the wailing of inhuman voices raised in prayer and in song.

But Dorayaica had not joined its lesser brethren, had instead brought us higher—level by torturous level—until only the wind whispered in the halls of the Enar city. There I lay, half-forgotten, upon the dais to one side of the seat the servants had erected, shackled to it by a heavy iron chain.

I think that several days had passed since our arrival at Akterumu. I cannot be sure. The great prince had condescended to allow Severine to treat my wounded brow and cheek, but had forbidden her to bind the wounds, and so the dry air burned my raw flesh and my head throbbed. Time itself passed in a haze, lucidity coming only fitfully, when terror forced my mind to focus, as it focused on the sound of clawed feet on stone.

A party of Cielcin had appeared in the high, trapezoidal arch, led by a herald in priestly white. Blearily, I sat up, chains rattling dully in the still air, and felt Dorayaica's eyes on me.

The herald approached with mincing steps, leading six lesser priests—*baetayan* in wraparounds white as that of their leader—who carried a metal chest on poles between them. Two of Dorayaica's *scaharimn* stepped forward to meet them with hands outstretched, their hooked scimitars tucked neatly against the crooks of their right arms.

Taking the hint, the herald knelt before the guards and the Prophet's chair. A green banner hung from the herald's staff, embroidered with Cielcin calligraphy in black. It gathered this in its fingers, gripping the stave as it sank to its knees and raised its high, atonal voice. *"Anamnato qi-aqara o-Aeta ba-Aetane,"* it said in formal greeting, head raised to bare its throat in submission. "On behalf of my master, Aeta Gurima Peledanu, Lord of the Fiftieth Branching of the Line of Imnun, I—a slave—offer homage." It raised its clawed, free hand, gesturing to the lesser priests with their metal box.

Almost lazily, the Prophet raised an allowing hand.

The lesser *baetayan* approached and lowered the chest to the floor, swinging it to face the Prophet. It was large as a coffin, and indeed I took it for one at first, bleary as I was. Two of the servants lifted the lid, and the herald stood to present the contents to the Prince of Princes. "Weapons, Great Lord!" it said, lifting one for Dorayaica to see. "Swords taken from the *yukajjimn*! Six twelves by twelve and seven, each won in battle!"

The herald's fingers squeezed, and I felt my stomach lurch as understanding struck me like a wave. The highmatter blade flowered in the green gloom of the hall, casting its harsh, white radiance on relief carvings that showed the Enar—four-legged and six-legged, eight-legged and more—marching across the stars.

Six twelves by twelve and seven.

Wordlessly, I converted the figure best I could. It was nearly a thousand. My cheek ached as my jaw fell in shock, but it was not the staggering wealth such a number represented—the price of a world and more—but the tragedy of it. Each had belonged to a knight of the Sollan Empire, and for every knight that fell, I knew a legion fell with him.

"This is a worthy gift," Dorayaica said after a moment, and the herald let out a gasp of relief. "Put down that weapon, slave!" When it had done as the Prophet ordered, Dorayaica said, "Where is your master?"

"I am here, Dorayaica!" came a shout from the gate, and through it—flanked by *scahari* warriors of its own—came a Cielcin armored and robed in green to match the herald's banner. Silver caps sheathed its crown of horn, and silver chains draped its high forehead as though it were some courtesan of Jadd. Bits of jade pierced its brows and studded the sharp cheekbones, and jade rings flashed upon its fingers. "You called, and I came!"

Dorayaica rose as the lesser prince advanced toward us. Seeing this, Peledanu sank to its knees before the Prophet. "Your oracle!" it said, baring its throat. "The message you sent! Is it truly time?"

"Raka," Dorayaica said. "It is."

Peledanu shut its eyes, whispered something I could not hear.

The Prophet advanced until it stood upon the lip of the dais, its back toward me. It towered over Peledanu on the floor below. "Are you constant to the old ways?"

The lesser Aeta looked up at Dorayaica. It did not speak at once. "I am your slave," it said at last. "I have *ever* been your slave. But the others! They do not believe as I do. There have been talks! Before you arrived, I heard Iamndaina and the others! *Vanahita!*"

Dorayaica hissed, one hand snatching the trailing hem of the Imperial toga it wore over its fasciated armor. "Speak not to me of the others. They are shadows, Peledanu. Creatures of the Lie. Are you constant to the old ways?"

"Eka iyadar ba-osun," it said again. "Always! I have been! Ever since you drove the *Eta Vananari* from this place! By the Dreamer, I swear it: you are Elu come again!"

I pressed my forehead against the side of the Prophet's throne to stop my head swimming. "Eta Vananari?" I mumbled the words. They were more of Dorayaica's *old words*, of that I was certain, for I could not divine their meaning.

Peledanu had spoken of an oracle, a message Dorayaica had sent. On Dharan-Tun, the Prophet itself had said it had called this *Aetavanni*, this meeting of the clans. What had it said? What word, what message could summon so many disparate clans? Did Dorayaica have the power to compel their obedience? Might it have threatened to hound them each across the stars? I did not think so, though its horde was vast and pitiless as the sun.

"Caiharu ba-okun," Dorayaica began. "Your *faith* redeems you. You were wise to come in *peace.*" At the word *peace*, Peledanu bent and pressed its face to the rough green stone. A thrill went through me at that word. *Qilete. Peace.* It was the same word Aranata Otiolo had used in our failed negotiations so very long ago, and hearing it then in that place I understood its meaning more sharply than ever before.

You were wise to submit.

Taloned feet clicking on the stone of the steps, Syriani Dorayaica descended, one hand holding its toga neatly in place. Peledanu did not rise, nor did any of its servants. As though it had all been rehearsed, the Prophet lifted one foot and stepped on the lesser prince's shoulder, and I winced as an indrawn breath rasped my wounded cheek, chains rattling as I drew a hand to my face. Unbidden I remembered another hall, another ceremony: myself kneeling before the Emperor, the ancient iron sword laid upon my shoulder. But where my ascension to knighthood had ended with the Emperor ordering me to rise, presenting me as a knight to his court, uplifting me and dignifying *me*, there was none of that here. Just as the Cielcin *udaritanu* characters were perversions of the language of the gods, so too this ceremony was a demonic mockery of the very thing I had experienced myself.

I am a soldier of the Empire.

By the same token, Peledanu had become a soldier of something else. Often I had imagined the great game of empire played like labyrinth chess across the stars: white king, black king, red. Here then I watched some lesser piece—a centurion, perhaps, or a pawn—wander into the heart of the labyrinth and win itself a crown, albeit a crown of chains.

"You are mine," Dorayaica hissed, and at length withdrew its foot.

Peledanu did not rise as I had risen, but crawled backward, snuffling as it did, not lifting its face from the earth. How easy it was to see in the lesser the burrowing creatures the Cielcin must have been before Bloody-Handed Evolution granted them their minds.

"Eka ba-osun," Peledanu answered.

"Stand aside," Dorayaica ordered. "There will be others."

Still the lesser prince did not raise its eyes, but crawled backward a long way before returning to its knees. Dorayaica's own men advanced and took up the chest Peledanu's men had brought and carried it aside. I did not envy the soldiers whose task it would be to carry the weighty thing back down the thousands of steps to the ground and the shuttle.

I had just witnessed a Cielcin negotiation, if negotiation it could be called. There had been no negotiation, no terms. Peledanu's surrender had been unconditional, its humiliation total. The whole conversation couldn't have lasted more than a couple minutes, though my hazy mind stretched time almost to breaking.

As Dorayaica turned to resume its seat, it looked down at me, teeth bared. "See you now that faith is power?" it asked.

I said nothing, but moved away from the throne as it sat back down, dragging my chain with me. The Prophet had chosen for its audience a short, broad arcade that opened off an inner hall. Deep, slanting shafts in the wall behind opened on the sky, and the gray light of Eue's sun fell in at angles, illuminating patches of the rough relief carvings that seemed to cover every flat inch of the city's surface. They showed the strange Enar embattled, fighting a race of tentacled beings in a city of square towers.

Lines of Enar script accompanied the reliefs, scratched into the stone as with claws. The characters all stemmed from a central groove, rising or falling from it like the perturbations of a sound wave. I had never seen its like.

"Valka . . ." I murmured. What would Valka have thought of this place? Images—imagined or remembered from some undiscovered time—played like shadows across the interior of my skull. Somewhere in the *other* memory of my vision, had we come here together? Found the place abandoned, empty of foes?

But Valka was dead, *had to be* dead. Adric's severed head peered back out of my memory with hollow sockets from the Prophet's table. Valka could not have escaped from Padmurak. With the *Tamerlane* lost, there would have been nowhere for her to go.

I shut my eyes against the gloom of the high hall, but it did not stop me remembering. The great gates of Vedatharad slammed closed, their iron clangor shaking my very soul. Why had I gone after the chariots? Could I have not stayed in the transport with Valka and the others? We might at least have died together, and I might have been spared those hideous years on Dharan-Tun.

It didn't matter. It would be over soon.

"*Onnanna!*" The Prophet's voice cut across me as surely as its claws had done, and I realized I'd been crying. "Enough!" it said. I could not see its face, saw only the ringed white hand tighten on the armrest of its throne.

I'd not realized what I was doing, and realizing stopped, holding my breath to keep myself from sobbing.

All dead. The words kept replaying themselves, ever circling in my heart.

All dead. They're all dead. Dead. Dead. Dead.

Grief is deep water. Gibson's words drifted back, but I had drowned long before—should have drowned myself in the waters of my cell. But if I had—if everything Dorayaica had told me was true—then that would still have served its purposes. On Annica, the Quiet had showed me something of the part I was to play, had showed me the futures and the pasts that never were. I had seen myself burn the Cielcin from the sky, and seen myself sacrificed on an altar beneath a black dome above a sea of pillars in a desert of black sand.

I knew but one would come to pass, if not as I had seen it.

In the vision, I had not been alone.

Alone.

We were not alone. Others came one by one to offer gifts and debase themselves before the Prophet. One by one Dorayaica accepted them, and one by one it stepped on them, in doing so taking the lesser princes into its service or reaffirming some service already taken. At length I pushed myself so far from the throne as my chains would allow, scrabbling on my heels until I sat with my back to the roughly hewn stone of the outer wall. Through it all, the beam of gray sunlight through the shaft above my head tracked across the far wall, illuminating portions of the Enar carvings. In the inconstant light, the crab-like horrors seemed to move, their graven limbs flickering, as if the carvers had hoped to simulate motion by the passing of Eue's pale sun. Perhaps the images had once been painted or enameled, but the color had long since gone.

The princes who came lay gifts of spices and perfumed oils before the Prince of Princes, or else gems and precious metals. One presented an idol wrought of human bones, and another a basin of white stone carved with Cielcin runes. More than a dozen came, and in their turns took up their places alongside Peledanu to either side. Among them was Muzugara, whose fleet we had burned at Thagura when I was young. Time and again, I would catch black eyes staring at me, doubtless wondering who the human rat was, chained to their master's seat. Did any of them know? Did any of them guess?

"Twice twelve and one," said the general Vati Inamna, who stood at the Prophet's left hand, unmoving as a statue. "So few."

"It is more than Elu had," Dorayaica replied, raising a hand to quiet its protector.

"Dorayaica!"

The shout came from the heavy stone arch at the end of the hall and plunged the chamber into silence. All eyes turned to the door, where something huge and hulking lumbered into sight. How I had not heard it sooner I dared not guess, for it was easily the mass of a small groundcar. At first I took it for a chimera of the sort MINOS had wrought for the Prophet, but as it advanced—lurching forward on a dozen four-clawed metal feet—I recognized it for what it was.

It was a chair.

The Cielcin who rode upon it wore heavy armor enameled with cobalt blue as anything I'd seen. Its face was squarer than Dorayaica's, a block of white bone beneath a crown of shorter horns. Its braid was likewise short, falling just barely past its left shoulder, but there was fierce savagery in its bearing, which burned cold and lethally in its dead, black eyes. Without being told, I knew that here was one greater than the others, greater than any in the room save Dorayaica itself.

No herald went before it to announce its coming, nor any gift.

"Attavaisa!" the Prophet exclaimed, not rising from its seat. "I did not think to see you!"

The prince in blue drove its chair lurching forward, its many legs clicking scarab-like in the still air. In its wake, a dozen warriors with cloaks to match the prince's armor moved like blue shadows.

"I have found it, *tanyr*!" Attavaisa said, bringing its chair to a halt ten paces from the lowest step of the dais. "Many times twelve worlds I searched, but I found it!" As it spoke, it lifted a cloth-wrapped bundle from its lap and stood.

I had to suppress a moment of shock. I had thought the creature lame, its armor all for show, but it moved swiftly, dropping to one knee—not two—at the base of the stair to proffer the bundle like a platter with both hands.

Syriani Dorayaica did not speak at once. "It cannot be . . ." it said at last. "You found one? After all this time?" The Prophet stood and descended the stairs before its throne. Beside it, Vati advanced, ready to leap to its master's protection at the slightest provocation, the chimera's electronic reflexes faster than any mere mortal—human or Cielcin. Watched by all the others, Dorayaica tugged the cloth covering Attavaisa's burden away.

I craned my neck, the better to see. My face throbbed with the effort.

It was a tablet of gray stone, not so unlike the stone of Akterumu itself. Indeed, I thought Attavaisa might have taken a piece of the city itself, chiseled the tablet from the wall.

Dorayaica seized the tablet with both hands, held it up to better see. I could just make out the tracery of fine circles clustered like bubbles, just like the Cielcin *udaritanu*. Just like the anaglyphs that were a part of the Quiet's strange machines. But written around it in tight, scratched lines, were the marks of the strange Enari script, spiked and angular.

These Enar had been aware then of the Quiet, too.

"Have you checked this against the others?" the Prophet asked.

Attavaisa tilted its head to the right—a Cielcin nod. "There are new worlds. Perhaps some were known to Utaiharo. We will never know all Otiolo took or destroyed, and many here are known to us already, but there are some. Six, perhaps seven, that I have found on no other record."

At the name of Otiolo, Dorayaica hissed, and several of the others joined it, hissing. I remembered what Dorayaica had said of Otiolo, calling the dead prince *Betrayer* and *Deceiver*, and began to wonder if I had done the enemy a favor. It seemed small wonder, then, that Otiolo had been interested in any sort of alliance with us.

It had been desperate. Friendless. Alone.

Dorayaica and Utaiharo had shared some common purpose, that much was plain. The tablet in Dorayaica's hands was some kind of atlas, a map of sorts leading . . . where? To Enar colonies? To Quiet ruins? To some remnant of the Watchers themselves? Or to all three?

Suddenly I understood why Uvanari and Tanaran had brought their doomed ship to Emesh all those years ago. Their master, Otiolo, had found Emesh on just such a tablet. *Tamnikano,* that was what they'd called it. It had a Cielcin sound, but it was no Cielcin word at all, but a rendering in the Cielcin tongue of some older word. The Enar name for the planet. Had the Enar been on Emesh once? Had the Watchers?

The Quiet's city on Annica was rushing backward across time, defying entropy—growing, not crumbling—rushing across some dimension higher than human sense. Some piece of the vision I'd been granted clicked into place, and I understood. The Quiet was building its cities—his cities, his kingdom—upon the bones of these Enar, just as any conqueror might found his palace upon the site of his triumph.

On Annica, I had been granted a glimpse of the great struggle, dark against light, Watchers against Quiet, many against One. I knew my part in that struggle, knew also that I had failed. But I glimpsed in the dimness of that hall something of the other side, tasted the desperation of Dorayaica's cause. It was scrambling in the dark, scouring the black of space for pieces of its gods' dead dominion before all was washed away.

"After all is done here," Dorayaica said, "we must search these worlds." The Prophet stood there a long moment, staring at the tablet, holding it as though it were a newborn child. "Perhaps the gods are not all dead."

Those words washed away the clarity I'd felt a moment before, replaced it with a cold terror like a blade of ice between my shoulder blades, colder

than the bloody pits of Dharan-Tun. I was holding my breath, I realized,
and heard again the words I'd heard in my mind when we'd arrived.

Ammarka.

Perhaps the gods are not all dead.

Ana mahriya teche.

It was not just ruins the Prophet sought, not just pieces of its gods' dominion, but its gods themselves. I tried to wrap my arms about myself, but
the manacles prevented me. Miudanar's skull waited in the desert outside,
its presence like a black shadow on my mind.

Teche.

Was it a memory of the words I heard again in that moment? Or the
words themselves? Dead the Dreamer might have been, but it did not rest
quiet.

"*Vati-kih, yelnna,*" the Prophet said, summoning the general to its side.
The white knight went and accepted the Enar tablet with machine care-
fulness. "See that this is delivered to Dharan-Tun with all care. Do it
yourself." It whispered the words so that the lesser princes gathered below
the seat could not hear, but I did. Then Dorayaica turned back to face
Prince Attavaisa, and in a louder voice said, "Are you constant to the
old ways?"

CHAPTER 37

THE DREAMER

A METALLIC CRASH WOKE me, and I rose to find a tall, slim iron lamppost lying on the ground, its coals red and glowing on the greenish stone floor. I sat there a long moment, blinking at the embers. There was nothing to catch fire. The bed on which I lay—if bed it could be called—was only a stone bench cut into a shelf beneath a trapezoidal window unglassed and unbarred.

I was in a cell again, if a cell more like the writing cells of Nov Belgaer than like the caves I'd grown accustomed to in my long years on Dharan-Tun. Cold wind blew through that open window, and sitting up I peered out over the broad sill—it must have been two yards deep—and down over the interior of the ringed city. I guessed my cell at around two thousand feet above the level of the desert plain, and from that great height I was accorded a commanding view of the great plain and the black temple of the skull at its heart.

It was night, and the Watcher's skull glowed in the light of stars and of Eue's thousands of artificial moons. From that vantage I could see the spiral patterns of the columns marching from the inner ring about the black dome toward the gray-green ramparts, terraces, and towers that formed the borders of the world. From that altitude, I could clearly see the square-topped ramparts of the far side; could make out the orange gleam of fires and low-red shine of Cielcin lamps. Here and there I spied the glint of moonlight on metal, and guessed the Pale were at guard, standing sentinel on the high walls of their holy city.

Akterumu.

I could hardly believe it was real.

To accept that it *was* was to accept so many things. It was to accept the Enar were real, an ancient race of monsters who had conquered the stars before mankind had even learned to walk. I had accepted a species of that belief once, when I accepted the Quiet were real, but when I learned the Quiet were of the future—and that the Quiet was not a people, but a person, a singular entity acting across time to ensure its, *his,* birth—my native Imperial prejudices had begun to reconstruct themselves. I had begun believing again that mankind was eldest and in a sense alone, despite knowing better. Despite knowing the Umandh of Emesh, the Cavaraad of Sadal Suud, the Irchtani of Judecca . . . the Deeps, the Cielcin. To accept the Enar as well was to accept an ancient and *living* universe. A universe of deep time in which mankind—however chosen—is only a small part.

A small people.

Tawdry, treacherous, and cruel.

It was to accept that smallness, that ignorance. And worst of all, to accept all I had learned was to accept that the Watchers were real. Where before they had been only a part of my visions—visions I never truly doubted, though you might, Reader—now I had seen their bones. No one who has had all of infinity and infinite time poured through their head can doubt such experiences, having lived them. Even less could I doubt that giant skull or the tumbled vertebrae half-buried in the sands. I could not disbelieve the socket of that lonely eye open like a door above the steps of the temple.

It simply *was.*

A gust of wind blew through the aperture again, so hard I was pushed back and nearly fell onto the bench. Doubtless that was what had upended the iron lamp the Cielcin had brought to light and warm my prison. I should have thought the clangor of it would have drawn guards, but none came, not in five minutes, not in ten.

I was alone.

Grunting with the pain of lying on hard stone in my armor, I clambered up onto the deep sill, edging inch by careful inch toward the edge. The lights on the far side of the wall—miles away—twinkled almost remote as stars. I stood there a long while, taking in that tableau. As in my cell upon the walls of the *Dhar-Iagon,* I might have leaped at any point in quest of freedom. But where such a leap from that wretched cell would be only to resume my hanging, to leap from the window of that cyclopean chamber would mean certain death.

More lights moved on the terraces below, and once or twice I made out the horned shapes of Cielcin sentinels, their scimitars drawn, clan colors draped about their shoulders. One could almost chew the tension in the air. So many *itanimn*, so many blood-clans in one place, their masters snarling at one another in the halls and across the ramparts. Sensing it, one imagined the whole city might erupt in paroxysms of violence at any moment, that clan might turn on clan and Eue might become the site of a civil war the likes of which the galaxy had scarcely seen. Every prince was on its guard, each fearing each.

On the far wall, a light flashed once, twice, glimmered and blinked in a sequence I did not understand as one prince signaled another. I wondered what secret message that light carried, and to whom.

Putting it from my mind, I looked down again and shut my eyes.

I must have stood there a century.

The Quiet would save me—had saved me before. As I had died upon the *Demiurge* and awakened somewhere else, I could die here.

Yet even as that thought crossed my mind, a memory of that unheard voice resounded in my soul. *Time changes,* the Quiet had said. *Soon your time will go beyond our sight.*

I was alone.

Was I alone?

Cold wind stung my wounded face, and it was only steadily that I opened my eyes and peered down once more. There were no sentinels patrolling the terrace below, though further down and left I spied a reddish light moving. They might not find me till morning, or until sundown. I realized I had no way of knowing just when the Cielcin would arise—instinct taught they should be nocturnal, but then . . . there is no sun underground. I teetered a moment on the brink of the precipice, one foot raised for the final step.

Decisions.

Another gust chose that moment to blast its way across the face of the ringed city, caught me unbalanced. With a cry I toppled back and fell from the sill to the giant stone bench with a yell. I avoided hitting my head only by accident.

Against all sense, I laughed. Whatever knot of nerves had wound itself about my heart and pulled my foot up and out over the edge unspooled itself then, and relief washed through me. Relief. I did not want to die. Even after all I'd suffered. On Padmurak. On Dharan-Tun. On Eue.

What would killing myself accomplish? Syriani would parade my corpse instead of me, mock and mutilate my remains. But living, I could choose how I endured it. If I was to be a spectacle one last time, I would not give the Cielcin the satisfaction of deciding how I looked upon the platform. If I must die, I would die a man, not the creature Syriani had tried to make me.

Teche!

Lying on my back, I tried to pretend I had not heard what I knew I'd heard. The ceiling above was flat, cut of the same green stone as the rest of the mighty structure, and carved with more images of Enar conquest.

Arkam resham aktullu. Arkam amtatsur.

I sat up. The wind had died, and all the world was still. Carefully then, I clambered back onto the sill, looking out once more at the gray desert and the forest of slim columns. The words were strange to me, their sound a pressure on my mind. Though I could not comprehend the sound of them, I sensed their meaning plain enough. They were a salutation, a salute. A summons. A crooked finger beckoning to me, begging me to leap, to hurry to its source.

I stopped again at the edge of that cutting, feeling the dead air.

Ana mahriya teche!

My own breath caught. A pale light was shining from the lonely eye socket that formed the arched opening of the shrine on the sands below, casting its faint and grayish radiance far out across the sands.

Teche!

I felt a sensation as of many hands seizing me, arms and wrists and ankles. They pulled me forward, out into empty air. I screamed and toppled from the balcony, knowing as I fell that I did not want to die. The terrace hurtled up to meet me, graven pillars soaring past.

The thrill of impact smashed through me, and I felt my suit's gel-layer harden to take the blow. I expected that final darkness to come crashing in like the tide, but there was only moonlight. There wasn't even pain. I lay upon the terrace, dazed and—apparently—unharmed. Had I conjured up my vision? Used it unconsciously? I felt half a fool. I might have used it earlier and climbed down on purpose—had I not used it to survive so long a fall on Berenike?

My ruined shoulder spasmed as I pushed myself to my feet. Ahead, a set of shallow, uneven steps descended in an arc paralleling the general arc of the city as it followed the curve of the great wall. I took them two at a time, pausing at each level out of fear I might meet one of the sentries at its prowl. As I was, I felt sure I would stand no chance in a fight, certainly not with my maimed hand and ruined shoulder. Above, the pale face of Dharan-Tun itself shone ice-white in reflected sunlight, bathing the nightscape with a corpse-lit glow. Red canals ran chiseled across its face where water ice mingled with the rust of salts, giving the alien worldship the appearance of dried blood on bloated flesh.

Beneath the shadow of a viaduct I paused to catch my breath. How long had it been since I'd run? The night air was cold, and my breath rose in a white mist against the backdrop of that haunted city. Not far below, the black sands beckoned, ripples wind-tossed like a slow and wine-dark sea.

I do not remember crossing them, nor could guess how I got so far without drawing the eyes of the uncounted legions on the walls. Reading this, you wonder why I did not make a break for one of the shuttles, why I did not try to escape. But even if I might have seized control of a vessel, I could not have flown it. I am only a poor pilot, and not even the best aquilarius in the Imperium could have flown a Cielcin vessel alone. There was too much to learn, too little time.

And there were no ships in the temple.

Up close, the Watcher's skull dwarfed the world. The ringed city stood about the horizon like distant mountains, and without the walls for comparison, the incredible size of the dead leviathan impressed itself on the mind, as though it were the only thing in creation. The skull lay where it fell, with the gray-green masonry of the Enar shoring up the foundations, buttressed by pylons of graven stone. The greatest of these faced the main avenue that ran from the opening of the broken circle and the great landing fields. Looking back, I could see the tall standards of the blood-clans flapping, their blues and greens transmuted all to black in the thin light of the false moons.

Along the greatest pylon was cut a broad and shallow stair that narrowed as it ascended to a platform arrayed beneath the pit of the Watcher's once-great eye. Mounting those steps, I lingered on that platform. Of the low altar—more dais than table—and the iron rings I'd seen myself chained to in so many visions there was no sign. The platform was smooth and bare, without device or railing, and served only as a gathering space beneath the upper stair that led to the entrance and the great, unseeing cavern of the eye.

The presence of Enari structures about the skull confirmed my earlier suspicion. The Watcher had died long before the Cielcin ever came to Eue. If it was Miudanar—as I thought—the very one who had whispered to Elu, then it had whispered from beyond its grave. Even dead, the thing was a horror, a black god more evolved and more dangerous than anything in human experience.

And I trembled in its luminous shadow.

How many times had I stood there in dreams? Looking back I saw the twin towers that marked the entrance to the forbidden lands within the ringed city some dozen miles away. Though the air was still, it was not silent. A murmurous rasp of voices seemed ever present, distant and soft as flowing water. But there was no flowing water on Eue, only scum-choked pools. Tilting my head, I moved toward the inner stair that led to the lip of the great eye.

The substance of the dead Watcher's bone shimmered in the moonlight, glittering like crystal, like obsidian glass. So close, the witch-gleam from its interior was like the light of distant stars, fading even as I drew near. The whispering grew louder, drowning all quietude until I could hardly think, until each step was a trial requiring the utmost concentration. Dead as it was, something in that dread titan lived still. Some quantum ghost impressed upon the world.

"Te ka ke ku ta!"

I paused on the first step of the inner stair, sure that I had heard that voice with my ears and not my mind. The murmuring continued, but this was different. This was a voice, and unlike any voice—human or Cielcin—that I had ever heard. At first, I thought it one of the Irchtani, for a clicking sound accompanied it, each syllable clear and defined, separate from one another. But it was not the Irchtani language. How could it be? Nor was it Cielcin, sharp-edged and brutal. Neither was it the strange, half-forgotten tongue that had driven me unconscious when I'd first laid eyes upon the temple of the skull, the language—or so I guessed—of the Watchers themselves.

"E na ta te ta ka! Vi lu na!"

Crouching so low I almost crawled, I reached the top of the stair, my shadow cast miles long. The chamber within bulged all around, so that I had to clamber down a short flight of steps wrought of the familiar green Enari stone to a kind of raised aisle that ran along the floor of the dead behemoth's eye socket. Ahead, stairs built into a narrow, vertical slit led upward along a channel once intended for the optic nerve toward a chamber higher still.

The chamber where the monstrous god's brain once had been.

Huge stelai stood in rows to either side, Enari images rendered in delicate and extraordinary detail, depicting the crustacean creatures leading armies across the stars. Wide-eyed, I soaked the images in, not really processing them. I saw Enari kings leading war parties against three-legged giants and slithering, shapeless *things*. I saw them kneeling spider-like before the one-eyed figure of a leviathan with a hundred arms—and seeing it knew it to be the very creature in whose hollowed skull I stood.

Miudanar. The Dreamer.

"E ku la. Te ke la."

The chanting brought me back to myself, and I hurried forward, mounting the inner stair. You must think me mad to hurry on, but I do not recollect feeling as though I had a choice. I was a dead man already.

The inner sanctum resolved only slowly. The crystalline dome above showed faint ridges where the long-vanished brain had pressed against the underside of the cranium. There were no windows. Here again were great stelai carved with relief images of conquest—ten feet around and three hundred high—that rose to the distant roof. Huge stone panels placed against the wall continued this motif, displaying scenes of empire underwritten by descriptions in the notched Enari script. The panel dead ahead showed the hundred-armed serpent Miudanar in the fullness of its life and living terror, grasping entire planets in its fists, their orbed shapes cracked and splintering in its talons, its single eye ablaze.

But all this carven splendor was lost on me.

For I was not alone.

Still hidden in the shadows by the stairs, I froze and watched the creatures at their ritual. Washed out and gray they seemed to me, like a fading memory or the ancient phototypes of the Mericanii which Valka and I had examined in Gabriel's Archive, somehow unreal. And yet still they terrified.

The Enar stood perhaps chest high to a man, but were nearly three times as broad. Their bodies—heads—were all of chitinous gray plate, without eyes or any organ I could name save the mouth lost behind mandibles like grasping fingers. They could not have been blind—why build a city like Akterumu and cover it in art if they could not see it, after all? And yet none seemed to notice me, which seemed to me impossible. They stood on legs tipped with cloven talons that too closely resembled human hands, splayed fingers clicking as they moved. As in the case of their monuments, the number of leg-arms varied. Some had but four, others six, others eight. Different sexes, perhaps?

It didn't matter.

There must have been two thousand of them packed into the high chamber, shoulder to shoulder or else clambering over one another like crabs in a pot.

"*Zu ga ai ya te ka u!*" proclaimed one with silver limbs I took for machine replacements who stood beneath the huge relief of Miudanar.

"*Te ke li!*" the crowd replied. "*Te ke li! Te ke li!*" And in that reply I recognized the ritual chant the Cielcin employed themselves. The continuity chilled me.

The leader raised two arms, grasping in its skeletal talons an amphora of black glass, carved—I think—from the very bones of the god in whose corpse we all stood.

"*Ap su!*" the Enar declared and drank.

"*Ap su!*" the others replied.

Almost at once, the high priest began to change. A black corruption blossomed across its face, and it hunched over, wheezing. Wisps of smoke arose, and the xenobite's whole body shook and began to dissolve. The fast-corrupting flesh ran like wax along the floor, moving with a will of its own toward the others, who stooped and touched the fluid with the delicate feelers that encircled their mouths. Then they too began to smoke and dissolve and run out across the floor, even the chitinous armor of their shells dissolving to slime.

I drew back in horror as the puddle grew. The dark water expanded in perfect circles, each merging into each. Not sure what I was watching, or why, or how I'd come to see it, I remained silent, jaw clenched against the terrible murmuring noise of the temple. The Enar had died aeons before man parted ways with the apes, yet here they were, dying before my eyes.

As they lay dying, one of the Enar turned its face toward me, mandibles clicking, falling away. I could almost swear it saw me as it rotted to nothing. The black fluid began running down the steps, and I drew back, afraid to touch it.

In destroying their bodies, they had severed their connection with the material universe, I realized. With the Lie. The Enar had been servants of the Watchers, like the Cielcin after them. Failing to destroy creation, the *iugannan*, they had opted for suicide, opted to destroy themselves, to free themselves from this mortal coil.

Backing away down the steps, I shivered.

It made so little sense. They had been conquerors! A race of killers terrible in victory and majesty! They had ruled the stars and all the living things under them, and had done so with the blessing of monsters indistinguishable from gods. And they had sacrificed it all for . . . nothing, as though all they'd had and achieved meant nothing.

I turned to go, found myself facing not the steps down to the atrium, but steps down into limitless black. The whispering grew louder, but the black fluid was at my back, running down the steps in snaking tendrils. I had to move, and so descended.

And fell hurtling through naked space. The whispers turned to screaming, and I saw the many-legged *things* burn cities and worlds. The great empire of the Enar stretched across the galaxy, greenish obelisks and stelai rising under alien suns, decorated with the skins of their vanquished foes. I saw the armored conquerors standing over piles of bodies and of limbs, saw banners of striped hide still wet with gore and the dance of flames. They burned entire races, kingdoms and empires great and small. They sterilized planets, boiled seas, and torched green hills to glass. It was their hand, I saw—their conquests—that had left our galaxy so barren, so empty, so void of life when mankind arose to inherit the stars.

But they were gone, their worlds and armies were dust, and nothing of the Enar and their order and terror remained save old stones and ashes. And from those ashes new life arose, small and mean and stumbling.

Our forebears.

Cool stone pressed against my face, and I opened my eyes only slowly. I was lying on my belly in the chamber of the eye at the base of the stairs that ran down from the domed chamber and the remnants of the Enar sacrifice. Of the black fluid there was no sign.

"*Yumnae shaan, Avarra-kita!*" a rough voice cried out. The words were thick, strange, but strangely familiar, too.

This way, I interpreted. The language was *like* that of the Cielcin, but the vowels were strange, longer, with a curious atonal quality I had not heard in the xenobite's tongue before. Footsteps sounded on the steps outside, and I roused myself, scrabbling across the raised floor to the shadows of one of the stelai. Images of the Enar flowed beneath my fingers as I peered out and around the bas-relief that spiraled round the column.

Two figures staggered over the threshold, looking up in wonderment and in terror, their black eyes wide and huge as fists. They were Cielcin, but dressed unlike any Cielcin I had ever seen. They wore no blacks, no ceramic armor fashioned to evoke skinned muscle, no black hoses and exposed tubes. They carried no *nahute*, nor wore masks of any kind. A filigree of azure lines stood out tattooed across their jaws and cheeks, and their garments were gray and bulky, with thick rings at the joints like the ancient pressure suits of our first sailors. They wore no helmets, but I could see the huge ring-locks about their necks where I guessed huge domes must fit to enclose their horned heads.

But it was their cloaks that drew my attention most. Pale white were they and roughly sewn—as of hides stitched together. Here and there the white was touched with blue to match the tattoos on the two Cielcin's faces. They were Cielcin skins. I could see the shapes of arms and skinned hands—three and four—that, tied, held the garments in place.

Were they of another tribe? Another of the blood-clans I had not seen before? There had been differences in dress between the servants of Otiolo and those of Dorayaica, but nothing so extreme, nothing so brutal, so primitive and terrible.

The hindmost of the pair muttered something, and the leader hushed it.

"Shem nethta!" the other hissed, ordering its companion to silence. I found the language a little easier to understand now I knew what to expect. Raising its voice, the Cielcin said, "I have come, Miudanar! I have come as you asked!"

If the dead god answered the creature, I could not hear it.

"What must I do?" the Cielcin asked, and sank to its knees. "What must I do?"

A pause. An answer?

"Ba-yahiya ukoto," it said, and standing drew a knife. *By your will. Yaiya toh.*

"Avarra-kita," the Cielcin said, turning. "Come here."

The other Cielcin drew back, eyes wide, throat raised in submission and in fear. "Elu?" it said. *"Veiyu! Veiyu!"*

No! I translated. *No!*

But Elu, King of the Cielcin, did not hesitate in obedience. The bone-white knife flashed and bathed the sacred stones in ichor black as ink. Who had that other been? Its brother? Its companion? Its mate?

I was dreaming. I had to be. Elu had lived twenty thousand years ago, when man was young. As I watched, the great king knelt and took up the body of the Cielcin it had murdered. *"Irnasar!"* it cried out. *I sacrifice!* "I sacrifice to you, my god! Give me strength and the will to see your truth."

Sure then that I was dreaming, I stepped out from behind the pillar and followed Elu through the arch of the eye and out into the darkness where an army of Cielcin stood covering the sands, their white and grimy faces turned toward their master with its sacrifice in its hands. Elu lay the body of the Cielcin called Avarra at the foot of the great stair. Unbidden, several of the others mounted the lower steps and knelt. There were thirteen. None seemed to notice me where I stood in the mouth of the eye above them, though the wind tossed my hair.

Thirteen.

Certain I was looking at the original *aetane*, the thirteen *aeta* who were the closest servants of the dread king itself, I descended the shallow steps. Torches burned in the hands of the congregation below, and a bloodstained Elu raised its hands toward its most faithful servants and said, "Build an altar. Bring oil."

And Avarra burned, and the light of its burning filled the sky with fires to match the conquests of the Enar. How many peoples had they burned before finding us? Standing behind Elu above Avarra's funeral pyre, I could look out at the stars above the ramparts of Akterumu and see those ancient conquests. I saw Cielcin armies sack a city of drum towers whose primitive, six-legged inhabitants bellowed in grief at the smoking skies. Raiding parties returned to Akterumu laden with treasure. With lapis and sapphires and crates of silver. With rolls of alien skins and strange spices brought from distant worlds. These they laid at the feet of their great king, and the once-great city of the Enar was great again.

In the service of their dead, dark god the Cielcin spread across the stars, and when Elu was gone their dominion splintered, the thirteen *aetane* leading their clans to scavenge far and wide. Still they returned to offer sacrifice at the altar where Elu had burned Avarra. And though Miudanar lay dead, it was not alone. One of Elu's *aetane* strode across burning sands and knelt as tendrils hundreds of feet long crested from the dunes, segments stretching to reveal the vile flesh beneath. The *aeta* knelt and offered sacrifice.

The whispers grew louder, and the vision changed. Red desert collapsed into rosy cloud, and I glimpsed the shape of wings and heard a roar to deafen the very thunder. A shadow blotted out the sky. When light returned, I stood upon grassy lowlands beneath a clear blue sky. The shapes of what might have been men were it not for their tall scarlet crowns moved along the shore of a gray sea. The ocean boiled, and a great arm burst from its surface, hundreds of feet high. The army on the shore let out a cry of dismay as the arm slammed the surface of the water and cast a wave to drown them all. *"Caiyuz!"* they shouted. *"Caiyuz!"*

The wave broke.

"You're trying to frighten me," I heard myself say.

It was working. Not since the mountaintop on Annica had I felt so small and so alone.

I knew I was dreaming, knew that—unconscious—I had slid into the dream of Miudanar itself. Though dead, some spark of malice yet remained in the old bones.

You should fear, said a voice dead and dry as the dust of Eue.

I did not answer, but turned away. Tall grass swayed, green and beautiful. Behind me, the strange, red army died. Above me on the crest of a low hillock a black figure stood, horribly wrong beneath the limbs of trees.

Syriani Dorayaica advanced, azure cloak spreading behind it like wings. I could see the destruction reflected in its eyes. The Prophet moved toward me, pale face split in a glassy smile as it reached into the folds of its robe and drew out a wicked black object. Where it walked, the vision faded. Torc. Left only darkness.

It raised the black object—like a claw. Pale light blossomed, and a spike of crystal flowered in its fist. The highmatter sword crackled and sparked from some defect in the pentaquark matrix in the handle.

I reached down, forgetting that I had no sword. But my fingers—my five fingers—found the hilt. I was whole again, and armed, and drew my blade, highmatter flowering with a familiar and friendly hum. The alien shore and treeline vanished, and the Prophet and I stood facing one another beneath the stelai in the chamber of the eye. Syriani lunged like a tower falling, and I parried its blow with a groan. The blade circled round, whistling as the Prince of the Princes of Eue made to strike off my head.

Moving faster than I thought I had in me, I ducked the blow and thrust forward, forcing the giant beast to dodge. The alien weapon was longer than any human sword. Where had it gotten such a thing, and how? Had the sorcerers of MINOS wrought it for their Pale master? Or had the great prince captured and perverted the weapon of some doomed human knight? The blade hissed and spat like a live wire, and with each blow, each parry, my muscles cried out in pain. The giant rushed at me, blade falling like a mountain to crush me.

With desperation, I trapped the xenobite's imitation blade against the quillions of my own, teeth clenched and snarling at the terrible strength in those alien thews. The great prince hissed at me, and spat. "I shall become a god!" it rasped, voice thin with strain.

And yet my blade advanced. Though Syriani had the strength, I had the leverage, and pressed the point of Olorin's sword higher, angling it inward to kiss the demon's neck. How many times in visions had I seen this moment? Our contest played out across potential time. How many times had I seen Syriani strike off my head, as Aranata had done?

Too many.

But never—not once—had I taken the demon's head.

My blade sank into the dread prince's flesh. Blood welled up about the shining blue-white blade. Not black! Not black, but *silver*! Blood like mercury sheeted down the Prince's chest. I recoiled, and in doing so finished what I'd started.

The Prophet's severed head tumbled and hit the floor. I turned to follow it, remembering how the world had tumbled as my own head fell from its shoulders. The head looked up at me, eyes flat and empty. But its lips moved, mouthed words I could not hear, but read on those writhing lips.

You cannot win.

Headless, the Prophet's body did not fall. The silver blood that covered its chest was like a mirror. My own mangled face stared at me, deep gouges bright on my left cheek. A dry voice—the same dry voice that had issued soundless from the severed head—resounded in my chest, repeating the Prophet's earlier boast.

I shall become a god.

Then something *sprouted* from Syriani's severed neck, curled and flexed, bent hideously as talons bit into the Dullahan's chest to find leverage.

Fingers.

A moment passed, and thin arms long as those of a fully grown man pushed themselves hideously from the ruined husk that once had been Syriani Dorayaica. Something terrible turned its narrow head to face me, and opened one lonely, burning eye.

I was afraid then—and awoke with a start.

The iron brazier lay toppled at the base of the stone bench the Prophet's soldiers had given me for a bed. The coals still glowed cherry red on the greenish marble, and I understood that the thing had only just fallen down and awoken me. Everything that had just happened, everything I had seen, had happened in the space of a heartbeat, in the first gasping breath of sudden wakefulness. A chill wind squealed through the windows above, and looking up I found not the huge, deep window out of which I had fallen, but three narrow slits hardly a hand's span wide.

There had never been a window large enough to climb through.

There had never been a way out.

The iron door ground open a moment after, and a guard peered in. The Cielcin had one milky eye, a hideous scar disfiguring the left side of its face. Seeing the fallen brazier, it grunted in a satisfied sort of way and slammed the door without so much as a word.

"A dream . . ." I told myself, clutching at my chest. The empty two fingers of my gauntlet folded strangely against my chest, and I remembered where I was, and all that had been done to me. *A vision*. And a cruel one at that. For a fleeting moment, I had been as I was before Dharan-Tun. Before the wall and the pit and the knife. So young I'd been, and strong.

Unbroken.

I held my breath to stop the tears from falling.

CHAPTER 38

PRELUDE TO MADNESS

I SAW PALE KINGS and princes, too. Pale warriors—death-pale were they all.

So the poet wrote, and so I write, standing in memory within a shadow of the great arch that marked the opening of one of the two towers at the threshold of that inner desert and the sea of pillars about the shrine of Miudanar's skull. Severine and Urbaine stood near at hand in MINOS grays fringed with white. Rank upon rank of the demons of Arae stood opposite them, ten feet tall and armored in snowy white.

All stood with me watching the others march by. Pale blue banners went past, painted with runes in darkest jet. "Hasurumn," said my Cielcin escort, the creature whom Dorayaica had sent to accompany me.

The Aeta Elantani Hasurumn itself appeared behind its banner-bearers, riding a gray, eight-legged beast that shambled like a bear but had the scaled hide of a serpent. It held its horned crown high, chin tucked in the royal way, its armor not black but bronze, its surcoat and cape the same eggshell blue as its banners. Behind it followed an honor guard of two dozen bronze-clad *scahari* berserkers.

"Raka oyumn Aeta Ugin Attavaisa," said my escort, indicating the next chieftain in the parade. Prince Ugin Attavaisa rode no beast, but sat upon its iron throne that marched on a dozen mechanical legs. Of cobalt were its banners, and cobalt too the enamel of its flanged armor. Its face was squarer than the last, and its short braid hung just barely over its shoulder as it sat back and gripped the black orbs that capped the arms of its rough seat. Another two dozen soldiers followed it, armed with what appeared to be contraband Imperial energy-lances. To my astonishment, I marked a human woman marching with Attavaisa's heralds beneath the cobalt banners, a gilded collar about her neck.

Still more princes rode by: Iamndaina and Eluginore, Peledanu and
Koleritan, Onasira and Muzugara—whom I battled at Thagura long ago.
Some rode upon long-necked beasts with slick and blistered hide, while
others rode gray chariots or upon walking thrones like the seat of Attavaisa.

"How many are there?" I asked, hoping for a better answer than the
one Vati and the Prophet had given me on our descent.

My Cielcin escort blinked. "Some twelve and five hundreds at last
count. Maybe more."

Seventeen hundred princes.

Seventeen hundred blood-clans.

I looked down at my feet, at the Enar marble green and dark between
them. Half a minute passed before I realized I was holding my breath.

The day had come at last. The last day. Glancing sideways, I watched
the thin line of the princes where they emerged from the tower opposite.
One by one the princes and their escorts emerged from the far tower and
marched to the central avenue before turning inward toward the temple of
the skull. Only the Prophet's clan, only the Itani Dorayaica waited in the
shadow of the other stair. Syriani's place was to be last of all. A place of
honor and of fear. The wail of inhuman voices filled the distance, and what
little I could see of the parade route was lined with masked and armed
Cielcin waving the banners of their tribes.

I could not see the temple or the pillars that encircled it, but I knew
what awaited me.

I had walked that way before.

A sharp, cold voice sounded at my rear, and my attendant drew back,
folding itself neatly to the floor. The four guards that secured me snapped
to rigid attention, rattling the heavy chains that bound me waist and wrists.
A familiar metallic tread sounded on the steps behind me, and I turned my
head in time to see the slim, armored shoulders and tall, white crest of the
vayadan-general Vati heave into view.

"*Raka uelacyr jujia,*" it said, speaking to the chimeric soldiers that stood
to one side, ordering them to readiness. "*Yelnun.*"

He comes.

The general pivoted its turret of a head, surveying the demons, the
scahari, the MINOS personnel. "We move after Netanebo!" it said, doubtless the name of yet another clan chief.

"*Aya!*" the soldiers replied, and stamped their booted feet.

The great prince was to come up last of all, to arrive at the Temple of

Elu after all the others were in place, after all were present and ordered. Syriani wanted to be seen, wanted the gathered forces of the blood-clans to see it arrayed in all its majesty alongside its warriors and its witches.

The general made no speech, but turned to face me. It had no face, but I sensed the ghost of a smile in its words as it cycled from Cielcin to the standard. "You are to have a place of high honor, *Oimn Belu*."

"The roast always has a place of high honor at table," I said stiffly, looking past the giant to where the gray sunlight fell. "But the lamb would rather be at pasture, I think."

Under the general's shoulder, I saw Urbaine's teeth flash.

Vati cocked its head. "You are to be the last *aeta* to make pilgrimage before the Great One." It twitched its heavy white cape aside, revealing the azure beneath. With one claw-like hand it reached up and seized a packet tied beneath one arm and drew it out. "A gift from the Great One. *Sha ti-Aeta, ti-Aeta*."

From one Aeta to another.

The general put the packet into my hands.

It was light, and wrapped in black silk. For a mad instant, I thought the Prophet had given me back my sword. But there was nothing in it, I could feel it in my hands. The packet was empty, was only cloth. "What is it?"

The general gestured for me to unravel it, and I opened it in my shackled hands.

It was a cloak woven of *irinyr*, the finest Cielcin silk, a heavy weave black as midnight. It unrolled in my hands, flowing on the air and over the green marble slab at my feet. Its lining shone red in the pale light as arterial blood.

My colors. I looked up and into Vati's false and glowing eyes. The Cielcin could not see red. I glanced at Urbaine and Severine and the other magi. This was their doing.

Raising its voice so the Cielcin of the great prince's escort could hear, it proclaimed in their tongue, "A cloak for a king!" The noise of inhuman laughter filled those alien vaults, and I could almost feel the blood freezing in my heart.

Seizing the garment from me, Vati draped the royal cloak about my shoulders and pinned it in place. It was precisely such a mantle as Syriani wore itself, with a stiff, short collar standing at the neck and fitted to the shoulder. I shuddered, remembering: I had worn a Cielcin cloak when I walked that final road in my dream in the dungeons of the Grand Conclave.

The Cielcin gathered round rattled their scimitars and wailed their frigid amusement, hooting like demonic apes.

"*Aeta!*" one of them declared.

"*Aeta ba-Yukajjimn!*" another joined in.

The king of vermin, I translated.

"A king!" the mocking chorus came. "A king! A king!"

My vision and reality marched side by side, the future reaching back to meet me like the great cities of the Quiet. I hadn't long to wait. In just a few moments I would be ushered out to join the pilgrimage across that vast expanse of desert . . .

. . . to meet my vision.

"Where is your master, slave?" I asked the general.

Vati's metal arm flashed, one razored fingertip slicing just above the level of my eyes. A line of red pain flowered an instant after, and hot blood dripped into my eyes. The creature's machine-augmented brain had calculated the distance between us to the micron, had calibrated its strike with transhuman precision. A half inch nearer and it would have perforated my skull with that talon, half a foot nearer and it would have smashed my skull to pulp.

I hadn't even seen it coming. The speed of it had blurred the limb to invisibility, faster than my optic nerve could track. Still, I did not cower. I did not draw back. There had been no time for fear, and if it came now it would come too late. I had no desire to give the beast its satisfaction, and so—fresh blood on my forehead to match the dried blood on my cheek—I stepped forward. "Is it not time?"

"Soon," Vati answered. "The Great One will follow last of all. Once the others are in place." The chimera reached out and touched my bloody forehead with the back of its hand. The ceramic was cold as ice, as death itself. "You little understand the importance of this day. This place. This meeting."

"Your master means to make itself a king," I said, not flinching away at Vati's touch. "It isn't hard to understand."

The *vayadan*-general made a low, coughing noise that might have been a laugh. Vati turned its back—my blood red and bright on its hand. "He will become greater than any since Elu this day." It seemed to peer *through* the vaulted roof and the dark above, through the relief images of the Enar trampling their foes. Speaking the standard so that only I and the magi might understand, it said, "Perhaps greater than Elu."

"Is that not blasphemy?" I asked, thinking of Aulamn's violent reaction to Prince Aranata's impieties.

"It is Truth!" Vati countered. "He shall be set among the gods!"

My nightmare flashed before my eyes. The Prophet's head tumbling at my feet, the silver blood sheeting down its front, the terrible fingers digging their way out from within the prince's severed throat.

Beyond the open arch and the walls of the tower, the gathered Cielcin roared, pulling me back from my tumble into waking terror. The sun—gray and dim as it was—was still shining. I was not dreaming, I knew. I knew the difference, knew the pain in my forehead was real—and the aching in my bones.

"It is time, *vayadan-doh*," said one of the white-clad courtiers, crawling toward Vati where it stood in the center of the entrance hall. "The *yukajji* must go."

By way of acknowledgment, the *vayadan*-general spurned the creature with its toe, flipped it onto its back and pinned it with a foot. The courtier lay quiescent. Vati gestured to the chimeras nearest the door, but if it gave an order it did so via the praxis that bonded its mind to the metal it wore in place of discarded flesh.

Watching the creature move, I wondered if it viewed its alteration as a blessing, a casting off of the mortal and lying flesh it believed Utannash and the *iugannan* had given to it. Did it believe the less flesh remained to it, the more pure it was? Or was its state a sacrifice offered in service to its lord, as Avarra had sacrificed all for Elu?

My guards pulled at my chains, dragging me forward across the entrance hall. My sabatons rang on the tile as I staggered out after them, dragged hands-first. Urbaine leered at me as I passed. "You've never been prettier, my lord!" he jeered. "The blood suits you."

Beside him, Severine bowed her head and said nothing.

I spat at his feet. "I'd wear yours better."

Urbaine arched his brows as I went past and gestured at his companions. "We are immortals! You are only half!"

"Then why did your woman here want me so badly?" I countered, and nodded at Severine.

If my remark stung the magus, he did not rise to the bait. "You'll be with your people soon," he said, and smiled. The bloodless lips peeled back too far from his pointed teeth, a servant's imitation of his master's inhuman grin.

"I've no doubt," I said coolly. "I know what comes after, sorcerer. You have no idea."

"I think you'll find it is you who knows nothing of what comes next, my lord," Urbaine said, smile undimmed. "But you will."

My escort had found my place in the formation and was nearly ready to go. I was to follow a block of the chimeric soldiers led by the hulking behemoth Teyanu, who waited beyond the outer arch. Four dozen still-organic *scahari* fighters surrounded me, their scimitars drawn and crooked in the traditional way. After me would come another block of chimeras led by Hushansa in three separate bodies, then another four dozen of the Prophet's personal guard in black and silver, and the heralds with their tall, slim banners showing the image of the White Hand. Last of all would come the great prince itself, flanked by Aulamn and Vati.

But first came the slaves. Some thousand human slaves waited beyond the gates, not chained but hemmed in by guards just as the prisoners had been hemmed in by the douleters in my father's Colosso. At a sign, these minders drove the slaves before them like cattle, chivying them along the parade line toward the central avenue. Shrill horns filled the air with screaming.

My guards began to move, pulling me by my hands, chains and armor ringing like silver bells. I moved forward into the light and turned right toward the temple of the king. A wave of sound rushed over me, damp-ened and dimmed by all that Enari stonework just a moment before. The Cielcin who held my reins tugged me forward again, steering me right across the level sands toward the avenue. They laughed as I half-tumbled, half-jogged to keep from falling.

When I looked up, I saw the crowd for the first time.

All along the great road, held back by guards in the prophet's black and silver, were great throngs of the enemy. They lined the avenue six and seven deep, the ones in the rear craning their necks or else pressing forward and through to the line of the guards. They ran thus all the way to the dome, where even so far away I could see their ranks swelled to encircle Elu's Temple.

Twelve miles away.

Far gone were the days when captains and generals marched their armies upcountry by the thousand, or crossed the Granicus into Persia. I had no knowledge just how long it took to march an army on foot over so long a distance. I was not even sure I could make it so far as I was then.

I knew it would take hours.

Ahead, the line of march stretched all the way to the shrine itself, princes and their retinues shining in the flat and colorless sun. Their armor and their banners were the only color in that gray and green-black world. The huge *vayadan*-general Teyanu—hunched in its six-legged tank of a body like an inflated parody of the Enar—moved only slowly. A huge gap had opened in the line between it and the retinue ahead. A quarter mile, perhaps. Into this gap the Cielcin douleters drove their thousand human slaves, their spears spitting lightning that sparked and flashed in still air. The sound of their laughter and their cruel voices was an echo of the hells that ground beneath Dharan-Tun.

Unlike in my dream, where wind scoured the empty space in the circle of that stone city, the air was dead and still, the gray sun cold and very small in the cloudless sky. My Cielcin cloak fluttered about my shoulders as I walked, my too-long and matted hair a curtain that hid my eyes.

There was no denying who held the power here. Seventeen hundred princes there might have been, and seventeen hundred blood-clans, too. But each of the princes I had seen had brought a scant two or four dozen *scahari* with it for the great moot, the *Aetavanni* which was to be held within the shrine of Miudanar's skull. The Prophet had brought thousands, and by its fleet ensured the others complied. Oh, they had brought their worthies by the thousand to bear witness on the black sands beneath the topless pillars. Nor did I doubt that from every window and turret, every arcade and balcony in the ringed city encircling us tens of thousands more waited and watched. But they were unarmed, or carried scimitars only, and were held at bay by the legions of the Prophet and its demonic corps.

No other prince of the Cielcin wielded creatures such as those Syriani had in its train. The demons that MINOS had designed towered over the ordinary horn-crowned xenobites, and moved with a pantherish grace and threat of violence. As they and the titanic Teyanu marched past, I could feel the surrounding throng go still and hush.

There could be no question who ruled on Eue. The Princes of Princes was nominally but the first among equals, but only nominally. The gathered Cielcin bared their throats as the *Shiomu*'s forces passed—until they saw me.

"*Yukajji!*" they cried. "*Aeta ba-Yukajjimn!*" And "*Aeta! Aeta!*" And "*Oimn Belu!*"

Their mocking tones and frigid laughter pulled at me with iron hooks, peeling chunks of my soul away on unseen chains as the twin iron leads pulled me forward. They had fastened my leash to brackets in Teyanu's rear, and from time to time I had to jog to keep from falling as the Exalted Cielcin strode on. Once or twice I looked back and saw the crowned trio of Hushansa's bodies marching behind, black cloaks flowing from their shoulders, single red eyes scanning the crowds. Such curious glances cost me my footing and twice I fell, prompting hideous laughter from the crowd. The *scahari* who walked with me seized me roughly beneath my arms and hauled me to my feet, spurring me forward with their lances.

Ahead, the dome of the temple rose black as space, its strangely crystalline substance almost sparkling in the light. Each time I met the gaze of the dead god's sightless eye, I felt the weight of the Dreamer's ghostly presence like a pressure on my mind. The unquiet whispers sounded again, rushing beneath the booming of the crowd, and time and again I had to shake myself to be rid of them.

How long had it been since I had walked so far? Not since my last voyage aboard the *Tamerlane*, when oft as not I would take my morning exercise with Commander Halford, running segments of the battleship's promenade above the lighters chambered atop their mag tubes.

"Aeta! Aeta! Aeta ba-Yukajjimn!"

"Aeta eza dunyasu!"

"Dunyasu! Raka dunyasu ne!"

Something wet and stinking struck my face. It stuck a moment before its own weight peeled it free to splatter on the ground. It was a strip of rotting meat. Human meat. A strip of rotting flesh hurled by one of the onlookers. The dam broken, a rain of flesh and white and grayish filth spattered the green stones. A glass bottle shattered, prompting the guards warding the line to push the riotous crowd back. Whitish slime burst on the stones at my feet, splashing across the tops of my boots. The foul stench wrinkled my nose, and I knew without needing to be told that it was Cielcin filth.

I kept walking, kept my eyes fixed ahead, fixed on Teyanu's mighty piston-limbs as it advanced along the aisle. The rotten sun beat down, thickening the still air. My tongue felt thick and fuzzy, and I fumbled with my shackled hands for the water tube concealed in a pocket along the inside of the neck flange of my breastplate. It took a measure of doing to fish it out and work it up between my teeth, and when I pulled on it, it came up dry. Dorayaica may have ordered my armor cleaned and restored, but someone had cut the catch-tube.

Letting it swing free, I cursed. A gobbet of alien waste struck my side, marring the fine *irinyr* cloak with its mucus.

Perhaps two hours of the forced march had passed, and more than half the distance. My feet dragged, and my head pounded from heat and want of water. The shouting. The mockery. The jeers never ceased. Pale shit and rotting meat spattered the stones before my feet, clung to my cloak and trailing hair. My shoulders ached from where the chains kept pulling me, and the shackles chafed my wrists each time the general Teyanu took a step, its huge peds shaking the earth.

"Aeta! Aeta! Aeta!"

There was blood on the green stones.

Red blood. Human blood. Great pools of it and smears stretching left and right.

I missed a step, surprised to see it there—to see something so familiar and so horrible in so alien a clime. Teyanu did not stop, but—silent—took another lurching step. I stumbled forward, fell, struck my knee. It took all I had scrape back to my feet and hurry forward. I had not heard a change in the screams beneath the wail of alien horns and the exultation of the crowd. But one scream rose above the rest and pulled me back through my haze of exhaustion and pain.

It was a child's voice, high and clean and very much alone.

"No!" it said. A boy? A girl? I could not be sure. I could be sure of nothing save that word. That single, final, necessary word.

No.

The child's scream was cut off sharp as any electrical current. There should have been silence after such a note. But there was only more screaming. The inhuman douleters had driven the thousand or so slaves forward along the avenue, so far—so far that the crowd to either side stood now thirty ranks deep, white faces staring and hooting and slavering to either side. They had driven the captive humans far enough, it seemed, and their grim inclusion in the Prophet's march was explained at last.

They were party favors.

Peering round Teyanu's hideous bulk, I watched as four Cielcin fell upon a woman who had fallen in her haste to stay ahead of the great prince's train. With no hesitation their leader seized the woman by her hair and raked its scimitar across her throat. Dying—but not dead—they shoved her to one side . . . toward the crowd. White hands reached out to take her, and in an instant she was gone, dragged into the crush of inhuman bodies. I did not have to see her fate to know it, remembered the fate of

Raine Smythe and poor Sir William Crossflane. Dismembered. Devoured. Torn apart.

With each dozen or so steps the douleters would seize upon another victim and slay him or her, alternating left and right.

We have to show that we are not abstractions, my father told me once. *That we are tangible powers.* I fancied almost that old Lord Alistair walked beside me, that it was his shadow and not the shadow of the *scahari* fighter at my shoulder that fell across me as I plodded on after the hulking general. *If you are to rule, you must show your people* why *you rule. You must give them a reason to obey.*

"Gifts," I mumbled, looking round, almost expecting to see the old archon striding along in his robes of red and black velvet. "Bribes."

Law. Justice. Order. These people do not understand. These men do not value. But food? Shelter? Safety? These have value men cannot deny. These men will accept in place of justice, because they are greater than justice.

"I don't believe that," I said, still searching for my father's face in the ranks to either side. "They are *baser* than justice. Not greater."

Men are base creatures, my father countered. *What is justice compared to hunger? Compared to fear? Nothing.*

"I do *not* believe that," I said again, more forcibly.

Then you die a fool.

"Men are not beasts!"

The guard at my right hand kicked me in the back of my knee, dropping me to the pavement. On reflex, I seized the chains that held my wrists to take the pressure off, clenched my teeth as Teyanu's steady, ceaseless motion hauled me two yards across the blood-soaked flagstones. In the brief space before the titan's next step, I found my feet again, hurried ahead to put slack back into the leads that bound me to the *vayadan*-general.

Men were not beasts, I knew. But the Pale were. I gave up trying to find my father—he was only a memory—but I saw one of the Cielcin standing behind the line of guards that manned the parade rout. Red blood smeared its face, and it held a man's forearm in its fingers, the flesh torn near the elbow.

By such donations, Syriani showed the gathered masses who was greatest among the shattered clans of Eue. There could be no doubt who ruled.

And if there was, Syriani itself dispelled it.

We came at last within the shadow of the great skull, its jet and crystalline surface drinking the colorless light and radiating gloom upon the crowd gathered round. Teyanu drew aside, and the *scaharimn* that had dogged me all the way from the outer gates shunted me along after it to stand in the empty space that had been cordoned off amidst the crowd. An ocean of inhuman faces stretched out all around. Those who had lined the grand avenue had followed us as the parade drew to an end, so that thousands of Cielcin encircled the Temple of Elu—Miudanar's skull. The entourage of each prince stood at intervals around the stepped concentric rings of megalithic Enar stone that formed the foundation that propped up the dead Watcher's remains, banners oddly still in the dead air beneath the pylons that supported the skull. Beyond them, the first ring of pillars rose, taller even than the black dome itself, their faces adorned with Enari writing and more of the omnipresent reliefs of ancient violence.

And beyond those pillars the sea of alien faces stretched. Thousands gathered close about the temple and across the black sands. Tens of thousands. As a mass they stamped their feet and rattled sabers, their cries never fading, never dying down. Of the human slaves the Pale had driven before them there was no sign, and I knew that each man and woman and every child of their number lay distributed amongst that crowd of thousands, bodies broken like bread.

Last of all came Syriani itself, flanked by Vati in its white cloak and tall, plumed crown and by winged Aulamn. The Prince of Princes did not ride the scaled *sulan* or drive a walking platform. Nor was it carried—as our Emperor so often is—upon a gestatory throne. Syriani Dorayaica had made the pilgrimage from the outer gates upon its own two feet, just as Elu had done. In so doing, it showed its resolve, its strength of character, and its piety. It was a profound statement of power, that after its generous gift of human cattle and display of martial force—after its white-plated demons, after Teyanu and Hushansa, after Vati and Aulamn and the captive demon-prince Hadrian himself—that the prince who had summoned the entire Cielcin people home to roost arrayed itself not as an *aeta*, not as a prince, but as a conqueror. In place of the servants who carried the *flabella* before the Imperial person, there marched four heralds, *coteliho* carrying their heraldic spears topped with the image of the Hand and the broken circle.

The broken circle of Akterumu, I realized—the meaning of that symbol locking into place. The heralds rattled their spears as the Prophet approached, their high, cold voices raised in proclamation. *"Raka attantar Aeta ba-ajun, Ikurshu ba-Elu!"* they declared with one voice, chimes ringing on the still air with each declamation.

Blessed be our Clan-Chief, Bloodshoot of Elu!

"Raka attantar Aeta ba-ajun, ijanameu deni ve ti-iedyya ta-tajun ba-scianda eza ba-itani!"

Blessed be our Clan-Chief, who holds in his hands our world-fleet and blood-clan!

"Raka attantar Aeta ba-ajun! Ute Iedyrin Yemani Iugannan-Biqarin!"

Blessed be our Clan-Chief! The White-Handed Godkiller!

"Raka attantar Ute Aeta ba-Aetane ba-Eue!"

Blessed be the Prince of the Princes of Eue!

"Blessed be he in the sight of Miudanar!" the heralds cried out. "Blessed be his name in the ears of Iaqaram! Blessed be his life in the hands of the gods!"

"Yaiya toh! Yaiya toh! Yaiya toh!"

Syriani reached the end of the avenue and drew up to where I stood beside Teyanu. It looked down at me. It might have looked down its nose at me if it had one. The Prophet reached out with one silver-bangled hand, and two warriors came forward and detached my chains from the *vayadan-general* in accordance with some prearranged plan. They put my leash into their prince's hands and bowed as they drew away.

"I told you once that we are a sunken race. Do you remember?" I did not answer, but swayed on the spot, exhausted from the hours-long walk and the sun and the still air. Casually, the prince struck me with the back of its hand. It was not a hard blow, but it was still sufficient to stagger me, to turn my head and reopen the wounds its claws had placed the previous day. "I asked if you remembered, *kinsman.*"

Face stinging, I smiled up at the demon, my destroyer. "I do."

Syriani Dorayaica's lips flexed in amusement. It paused a moment, as if weighing its words, and wound my chain about its one hand. "Today we rise." It brushed past me, jerking the lead so that I stumbled after it as it moved toward the stairs and the platform where Elu had burned Avarra's body millennia ago.

CHAPTER 39

AETAVANNI

SYRIANI KNELT UPON THE highest step and, stooping, kissed the threshold at the orbital of Miudanar's eye. Still kneeling, it turned to look at me, fine silver chains swaying on its forehead and upon the lower reaches of its horned crown. "You must do the same," it said. "You are *aeta*. The least *aeta*, but even so you are accorded this respect." It pointed with open hand and claws extended at the lip of crystalline stone. "Here you see *Truth*, kinsman."

Si fueris Romae . . .

The great prince did not force me. I held its gaze a moment. It meant to honor me, to pay respect to a mighty enemy—or to the shadow of one long broken. I could refuse, *should* refuse. I was a dead man, and had nothing to lose. I was bleeding, aching, covered in shit and slime. To refuse would be only to bring death down sooner, would it not?

No. It would bring only more humiliation. Only more pain.

I knelt and kissed the old skull, imagining as I did so the tens of thousands of Cielcin mouths that had kissed that bone before me. I shuddered, and stood.

"Wait here," Syriani said to Aulamn and Vati, then, tugging on my chains, led me over the threshold and into that sacred, profane place, that place where no human had gone before—and where none has gone since. "Only the *aeta* may enter the temple," the prince said. "You are blessed."

The chamber of the eye was almost as I remembered it from my dream the night before. The ancient Enar had built a level floor into the otherwise organic shape of the chamber that once had housed the Watcher's eye. The narrow vertical slit in the back that had followed nerve channels to the emptied brain case lay dead ahead, narrow stairs built into its floor, just wide enough that three Cielcin—or two Enar—might climb abreast. The great stelai still ran in rows to either side, but where their faces once had showed proud scenes of Enar conquest in my vision, here they were chipped smooth, the images sanded down, the careful, claw-like runes of that ancient race wiped away and replaced with Cielcin circle-writing. Huge medallions hung on chains high up between the stelai, each with clusters of *udaritanu* script inlaid in silver upon their black surfaces.

"The inscriptions are gone," I said without thinking, looking up and around at the vile place.

Syriani stopped sharply and looked at me. "What?"

What once had been an Enar place was now a Cielcin one. Though the great pillars in the desert and much of the city beyond had been spared the iconoclasm, it seemed that within that most sacred place some ancient and pious prince of the Cielcin—Elu itself, perhaps, or this Araxaika Syriani had mentioned—had destroyed every line and image wrought by the elder race. The very air stank of *time*, of epochs measureless and without number. I felt as I think the French must have felt looking up at the dusty pillars at Karnak, relic of an age impossibly ancient to the mind and indisputably grand to the senses.

Grand, but terrible.

"What is the meaning of this, Dorayaica?" A harsh voice broke the hushed quietude of the temple, and shaken from my examination of the pillars, I looked round to find a number of Cielcin descending the narrow stair from the inner sanctum on the level above. Without being told, I knew they were all *aetane*, all princes. Each was dressed in armor variously black or white, no two styles precisely alike. The horned crowns of each were banded or tipped in silver, and silver chains whence hung lapis and sapphires and little bangles graven with runes hung draped across their foreheads. Some wore bits of onyx or lapis pierced through their brows or under their eyes, plating their faces like jewel-bright carapaces. Many wore capes of royal azure, or of cerulean, or sable. One even wore a milky cape of Cielcin hide in a style not so different than that I'd seen Elu itself wear in my vision of the past.

The creature who had spoken—who led the party down the narrow way—wore a similar cloak, but the skinned hands that hung from the dusky silver brooch at its throat had five fingers, not six. Its armor was dull white, colorless as the Euean sky, but decorated with bits of the jade-like Enari stone. Its face and horns were similarly adorned, accentuating the sharp jut of brow and of cheekbones, secured by pins that pierced the waxen flesh. What I took for bronze hoops hanging on its arms I recognized a moment later were the time-darkened jawbones of men. Half a dozen hung from each bicep like the segmented armor plates of a Sollan legionary.

Syriani did not turn at once to greet this newcomer, but squinted at me, still puzzled by my statement.

"Are you mad?" the newcomer demanded. "Bringing such filth to this sacred place?"

The Prophet threw up a hand to stop the bone-clad chieftain from reaching me. *"Lannu!"* it hissed. "The *yukajji* is *aeta*, Iamndaina! It is this that slew Otiolo and Ulurani."

The one called Iamndaina checked its advance, for whatever its station and strength, I guessed it did not like its chances in a battle with the self-styled Prince of Princes, whose army had forced this meeting and whose chimeric generals waited mere feet away at the threshold to the temple. Ancient law might hold that only the *aeta* could enter Elu's temple, but I sensed that if these here attacked the Prophet that ancient law would hold nothing at all.

Iamndaina drew up short and narrowed its ink-spot eyes. Behind it, the other princes stopped, too. I recognized the black-and-cobalt-clad Ugin Attavaisa among them, and Prince Gurima Peledanu from my escort's recitations early that morning. *"This* slew Ulurani?" it asked, examining me as a woman might a stain a dog left behind. *"This?"*

One of the others, a grim figure in a greenish cloak, said, "Ulurani was a great warrior. One of the finest of the old clans. And Otiolo—Otiolo was *dunyasu,* but Otiolo was a beast." It, too, looked me over with measuring eyes. "If what you say is true, Dorayaica, you bring a *susulataya* into our midst."

"The *yukajji* must be slain!" Iamndaina exclaimed, baring its fangs, its hand flying to the scimitar on its hip.

Syriani hissed in answer, interposing itself between Iamndaina and myself. "It is one of us, Avarrana!" It did not reach for any weapon—indeed it did not seem to have one. "Stay your hand! It is forbidden that *aeta* should slay *aeta* in this place! By Elu's word is it forbidden."

Avarrana Iamndaina's jaws hinged, teeth jutting out past thin lips, its round eyes narrowing.

"Peace, *kinsman,*" said Ugin Attavaisa, and lay a hand on Iamndaina's shoulder. "You know the laws. Who breaks them here will not know Truth."

Prince Iamndaina's white face darkened. "It cannot be permitted. This . . . *beast* must be destroyed. It profanes the very air it breathes!"

The one called Attavaisa moved its head in the curious clockwise way that signaled affirmation or assent. A Cielcin nod. "It will be, *kinsman*. It will be. But in its time! Dorayaica has called an Aetavanni, and if what Dorayaica says is true—if this *dunyasu ujin yukajji* is truly *aeta*, then it is *dunyasu* to kill it now." Saying this, it laid a clawed hand on Iamndaina's arm, forestalling any attempt to draw its blade. "It is forbidden. By Elu's word."

"*Yaiya toh,*" said Prince Peledanu in assent.

Attavaisa glanced from Iamndaina to Dorayaica, as if seeking approval from the Prince of Princes. Dorayaica gestured for the cobalt prince to release the bone-clad one, and Attavaisa obeyed.

Seeing this dynamic, Iamndaina sneered, jaws once again jutting out past its lips in that horribly serpentine way. "*Ti-nartu gin ba-Elu ne?*" it sneered, teeth clacking. "By Elu's word? By Dorayaica's, you mean?" It thrust a talon at Syriani. "You are not *him*, nor any sort of prophet. You and your *slaves*," it directed the word slaves, *kajadimn*, at Attavaisa and Peledanu, "may have the numbers to force this meeting, but no army can make you a second Elu. Nothing can!"

Syriani Dorayaica took this with a serenity that would not have been out of place on the face of our Emperor. Its four slit nostrils flared, the only hint at the unquiet boiling beneath the Pale prince's icy surface. "Think you it is by the sword I rule?"

"It is by the sword you compelled the blood-clans to this clans-moot!" Iamndaina countered.

"Is it?" Syriani cocked its head, addressing the question not to Iamndaina, but to the others. "Was it my sword that summoned you, Peledanu?"

Prince Gurima Peledanu bared its throat. "You know it was not, *Aeta ba-Aetane.*"

Ugin Attavaisa said, "It was the *Blood*, lord!"

"The blood!" Peledanu agreed, and two of the others. "*Izhkurrah! Izhkurrah!*"

At least, I thought it was *blood* they were saying. *Ikurran* was *blood*. But *izhkurrah*? It had the sound of that older Cielcin tongue I'd heard from the mouths of Elu and Avarra in my dream, muddier and atonal. What the significance of that older word was I could not guess. Were they saying that Dorayaica was in some way descended from Elu? There had been no reference to *uatanyya*, to *branchings* in its titles. Did these others obey out of some deference to heredity? Was Syriani Elu's direct descendant? Or was it something else?

"The signs could be falsified!" said another of the princes from near the rear.

"To falsify the signs is blasphemy!" Iamndaina agreed.

Syriani spread its hands. "Is that not why we are here? To see Truth?" Hands still spread. "I am Syriani ba-Izhkurrah, Syriani of the Blood."

Iamndaina's hand went to its scimitar again, prompting Syriani's loyalists—Attavaisa and Peledanu chief among them—to draw nearer. "Blasphemy!" the bone-clad prince said.

Rather than respond, Prince Syriani said, "Will you not come up with us, Avarrana Iamndaina, Lord of the Thirty-First Branching? Will you not join us?" With each question it took a step nearer the skeletal lord. "Will you not see Truth?"

Prince Avarrana Iamndaina hunched and bared its fangs, sensing it was cornered. "You blaspheme here? Within Elu's temple? Within the body of god itself?"

"It is only blasphemy to *lie*," Syriani said in answer. I expected it to strike Iamndaina down, to slash its face or break its neck. But Syriani did no such thing. Instead, it laid hands on the other prince's shoulders and—almost gently—forced Iamndaina to its knees. Knowing it was outnumbered and surrounded, Iamndaina allowed itself to be compelled, its knees bending only slowly. With a single hand, Syriani reached up and seized one of the great primary horns that rose and swept back from the corners above Iamndaina's eyes. Gripping this, Syriani forced Iamndaina's head back, baring its throat. For a horrible instant, I expected the greater prince to stoop and tear the throat from its antagonist, but it never did.

Instead, the great prince *spat* in the face of the lesser one. I recoiled, so perverse and vulgar was the instant, as though it were a scene from some dockside whorehouse and not some holy place. But these were the Cielcin, I reminded myself. They were not men.

Syriani released Iamndaina at once. The lesser prince did not wipe the slime from its face, but kept its throat bared. *"Junne,"* Syriani said, and pointed at the ground before its feet.

Apparently beaten, Iamndaina pressed its face to the Enari marble floor and permitted Syriani to step upon its face.

"Very good," the Prince of Princes said, stepping *over* its erstwhile opponent and acknowledging Peledanu and Attavaisa with a sharp movement of its horned crown. "Enough of that. The others are all inside?"

Attavaisa bowed low, head twisted to offer the side of its neck should Syriani have wished it. "Yes, lord. All are here."

"All?" Syriani cocked its head. "I was told Oralo and some thrice twelve others refused the call."

"Oralo has not come, it is true," Attavaisa said. "Balagarimn. Kutuanu, Loreganwa. Some others. Not thrice twelve. Twice twelve and six, perhaps."

Syriani Dorayaica continued walking until my chain ran taut, pulling me past the still-kneeling and thoroughly subordinated Iamndaina where it lay upon the stone. "They must be hunted down and killed. They are attainted and must be cleansed."

"Yaiya toh," Attavaisa said, swept along in Syriani's wake.

The great prince ensured that it was the last to mount that narrow stair. The last of its kind, that is. I might have been little more than a dog to it, bound in chains. Syriani held my chains in one hand, and I followed a half-dozen steps behind as we climbed up along the channel of the dead Watcher's optic nerve to the great domed hall that once had housed the monster's brain.

My skin crawled, and with each passing step I heard the faint whispering of my vision growing louder, and half-expected to find a rotting Enar scuttling down the steps to meet us, dripping black slime and smoking as its organic components dissolved and ran over its machine parts.

No such beast appeared.

The stair did not ascend in a straight line, but bent slightly, following some crooked imperfection in the leviathan's bone structure, so that one could not see the top from the bottom until one rounded a slight bend and the stairs ran nearly straight for some two hundred feet to the summit. The whispering grew louder, and with each passing step I expected to hear the black voice of the undead god ringing in my ears.

"Ute tajun ti-saem gi ne?"

"Dein velenamuri mnu darya?"

"Dein tsuarunbe Iamndaina ne?"

The sound of the name *Iamndaina* brought the whispering into focus. It was not the endless murmur of the undead god I heard at all, but Cielcin muttering, a confluence of voices chattering and rolling over one another.

In the dream, what little light had been in that awful chamber had come from the augmented bodies of the Enar themselves, echoing and rebounding off the deep ridges in the black crystal where the Watcher's brain had shaped the interior of the alien skull. As below, so here the Cielcin had made their mark, plastering over the huge monoliths on which the Enar had depicted themselves and sanding the stelai smooth. As below, they replaced these images with their delicate, soap-bubble writing, doubt-less attesting to Cielcin conquest and history precisely as the Enar had done, albeit in a form more palatable to the afterling race that now claimed Eue and Akterumu for its own.

But the relief carving of Miudanar itself was untouched. Images of the god were not of the Lie, but reflections of Truth, and so had been spared the chisel. It was that image that appeared first as we climbed the stairs, lit hellishly by the red Cielcin lamps. The great serpent coiled across green stone, its thousand arms gathering planets to itself, its thousand hands grasping or crushing them to powder. The Dreamer's solitary eye presided over that dim and smoky chamber . . .

. . . and the congress of demons gathered for their rite.

There was no trumpet, no herald to announce our coming. Gone was the splendor of the parade, gone the noise and the raucous, bloody theater of the crowd outside. Attavaisa, Peledanu, and the others—including the slumped and beaten Iamndaina—all stepped hurriedly aside to permit Syr-iani Dorayaica command of the entrance.

Seventeen hundred Cielcin faces turned to face us and were silent. It was an imperfect silence, one punctuated by the faint jangling of silver jewelry and the rustling of robes. The various *aetane* of the blood-clans stood gathered in the center of the great chamber in tight clusters, heads having previously been together in discussion. These little knots untied themselves as we entered, sentences cut short. A few bared their throats in proskynesis. Others lowered their horns in threat. But the greatest part of the congregation simply stood and waited, expectant.

"*Ba-tanyya-do*," Syriani said. "Kinsmen. Brothers. Lords. Welcome *home*. Welcome to this . . . holy place. How many generations has it been since so many were gathered here? Since we *all* were gathered here?" It paused then, allowing the audience time to reflect on the answer. Syriani did not shout. Indeed it spoke barely above a whisper, drawing the listen-ers to it. "Not since Araxaika ended the Kinslaying—and *never* have so many been gathered, for never have we been so many." Once more it paused and let its arms fall to its side, my chain ringing against the marble floor. "Thirteen," it said. "Twelve and one were we when Elu left us his kingdom. How many are we now?"

Syriani did not answer this question. Its answer was evident, after all, written in the faces of each and every one of the war princes there gathered. "Are we greater than we were in Elu's day?" This elicited a chorus of murmurs and outraged whispers, but none challenged the question as Iamndaina had in the hall below. "Which of you could stand with Dumann or Zahaka without shame? Which of you could look Umna, Avarra's own blood, in the eye unblinking?" Letting my chain stretch to its full length, the great prince advanced one measured step at a time into the throng.

"Utannashi!" cried one voice, harsh and unpleasant and rebounding in that stony place. "Deceiver! You believe it is you who can do these things!"

Some unseen dam had bottled the anger and the pride of the clan-chiefs until that moment, and unstoppered by that shout all spilled forth at once. Hissing and spitting filled the air, and some animal part of me tightened with fear, as if the tiny, tree-dwelling beast in me recalled the serpent, our predator, and shivered in its sight.

"You are not Elu!" another voice decried. "You are false!"

"False!" the cry went up. "False!"

My eyes found Iamndaina, who mere minutes before had been so strident an opponent of the Prophet. The bone-clad prince made no sound, but stood with hunched shoulders to one side, the Prophet's spittle still on its face. How deep, how instantaneous was the Cielcin instinct for subordination. Humiliated, it might be years before that prince recovered its dignity.

Syriani did not give answer to these charges, not with words. Half-turning, the great prince adjusted its grip on my line and pulled. The chains tugged at me, and I stumbled forward, wrong-footed by the sudden violence of the gesture. I fell, crushing my bad shoulder on the way down. Pain white as lightning blotted out my vision, and I felt myself groan and gather my limbs beneath myself.

What a sight I must have been. The great hero—the great villain—smeared with shit and gore, a pathetic bundle of flesh and raw nerves dressed in armor too grand for his station and an alien cloak, his unwashed hair a vile tangle of white and black.

The roil of inhuman voices died down, faded from hysterics to a quiet hissing as of steam vents. Confusion. I gritted my teeth as the white flash of pain began bleeding to dull red. The *aetane* circled all around me, peering down at me with round, black-eyes.

"Shiabbaa o-Oranganyr ba-Utannash wo!" Dorayaica said. "You call me *Utannashi*. Me!" It jerked its head in the alien negative. "*This. This* is

Utannashi. This *filth* killed Ulurani. This killed Otiolo. By the laws of Elu, this *yukajji* is *aeta*."

"*Dunyasu!*" exclaimed one of the others. "Blasphemy!"

"It is!" Syriani agreed, its black-armored feet clicking into view on the tile beside my head. I made no effort to rise, sensing that to do so would only serve to have me knocked down again. "But it is so—and I ask you: who but Elu's heir could bring low so great an enemy?"

An aeta armored in bronze shouldered its way to the front of the crowd, its *irinyr* cloak an obscene, almost child-like shade of pale blue. I recognized Prince Elentani Hasurumn, who raised its voice in challenge to Dorayaica. "Who says this beast is *Utannashi*?"

"It is Truth!" Syriani replied, its clawed feet scratching the stone inches from my nose. "This is the one called Hadrian Marlowe."

I was absurdly pleased at the hush that fell at this revelation, this connection of points—of stories like stars in a constellation—in the minds of Dorayaica's audience. The wave of shock and redoubled interest that moved through the inhuman congregation was almost enough to bring a smile to my face.

They knew me.

"Marlowe?" said Prince Hasurumn. "This . . . is Marlowe?"

In answer, Syriani Dorayaica placed one clawed foot on my shoulder and laid me flat on my back, allowing the various *aetane* a better look at me. Only then did I begin to rise, but the great prince stomped down on my breastplate, pinning me there.

Hasurumn peered down at me. "This?" it said again. "*This* bested Ulurani?"

Another Pale face appeared at Hasurumn's shoulder. "You should not have brought it," it said. "It is forbidden."

Syriani's eyes flicked to Iamndaina, still slouched and silent on the edge of the crowd. "So I have been told." The implicit threat made, Syriani Dorayaica took its foot from my chest and stepped away. "But by the laws of Elu, it is one of us. It belongs here." Glassy teeth flashed. "Besides, it amuses me."

"Amuses you?" said another of the princes, gray-armored and black-robed, its suit etched with runes and augmented with human bones. "If this truly is the Marlowe, it is no pet, Dorayaica. It should be killed at once!" The creature's brows contracted, a motion accentuated by the bits of man-ivory pinned to the flesh above its eyes.

In answer, Syriani Dorayaica lifted its splayed and taloned foot from my chest and drew back, my leash rattling in its fingers. "It is no threat to you, Onasira. Nor to any of us. I have pulled its fangs." Moving with spider-like precision, the great prince stamped down on my right wrist, as if to highlight my maimed hand, the hand that could hardly have wielded a sword. The effect of this point was lost somewhat, spoiled by the gauntlet and glove I wore, which hid the absent fingers. "It will never again be a threat to our kind." As if to underscore this remark, Dorayaica let the chains drop from its hand and backed away.

"It should be sacrificed!" said Hasurumn, stepping nearer.

I did not rise at once, sensing that to do so would be to provoke these others to frenzied reply, and instead rolled onto my belly, the better to get my hands under me. I could not hope to fight back, to defend myself. Not against so many. Not even if I had been whole.

And I knew I would never be whole again.

Dorayaica walked past me, so that its back and braided hair—white as chalk—were on full display. Mad fantasies of strangling the monster with my free chain flowered in my mind. Iamndaina would surely thank me for it, and Hasurumn and Onasira. But they were only fantasies. "All in time," the great prince agreed. "But we have more pressing concerns, ba-tanyya-do. The yukajjimn are building new fleets. Their Uganatai, their Emperor is on the move. Now is the time for action."

"And so you waste time gathering us here?" Onasira demanded. "How many cycles have we lost crossing the emptiness to return here? I was raiding the hakurani beyond the core when your oracle came. Nearly five times twelve cycles lost to answer your call! Five twelves, Syriani! How many battles might I have won for my itani, for my people, in all that time?"

"Your people?" Three loping strides were all it took to close the space between Syriani and Onasira, and Syriani took them. "Your people, Onasira?" Inches apart, Syriani stood nearly a foot taller than the lesser prince. "Are we not one people, kinsman? Not all children of Elu? If you were out raiding the hakurani, then you were no good to us at all! What are the hakurani compared to the yukajjimn? Our war is with the yukajjimn! Miudanar's war is with the yukajjimn! The gods' war is with the yukajjimn!"

Onasira's jaw unhinged, teeth folding out as it snarled microns from the great prince's face. In answer, Syriani raised one clawed, beringed hand so that its talons drifted near the lesser lordling's huge, black eyes.

Watching this, I pushed myself slowly back to my knees and—standing—gathered my chains to myself, coiled them in my good left hand. I felt my jaw hanging open and closed it. What was Prince Onasira talking about? *Hakurani?* Beyond the core? Was there another race of xenobites in the galaxy? One great among the stars and not confined to its homeworld like the *coloni* races of Emesh and Judecca and the rest? Despite the horror of my circumstances, my mind raced at the implications. Humanity had only explored perhaps a third of the galactic volume. So little. I felt in that moment as I thought the ancient Mandari must have felt to learn that Rome lay beyond the deserts of Asia, at the end of the world.

How little we know!

But I had little time to contemplate this revelation.

"You presume to speak for the gods?" Onasira demanded through its snarl, black tongue writhing with obscene threat, snake-like behind those fangs.

Syriani curled its fingers into a fist until it pointed with two claws at Onasira's eyes. "The gods presumed to speak *to* me."

"Again you blaspheme!" shouted one of the others.

Syriani rounded on this other, stalking about the perimeter of the crowded princes like a wolf bounding its territory. "It is not blasphemy to speak Truth, Ajimma!"

"Truth?" the one called Ajimma echoed the word. "*Kulan?* You speak of *Kulan,* but what proof have you given us?"

"Did you not see the Blood?" Peledanu asked, using that old word for blood again: *izhkurrah,* not *ikurran.*

But Prince Ajimma was unconvinced, and narrowed its huge eyes in the bloody light. "The oracle was not proof. It is deception! Dorayaica means only to win power for himself! He deceives you, Attavaisa! And you, Peledanu! He shows us images! Projections! These are not proof!"

"It is for proof that we have come!" cried another of the princes, and this set up a chorus of voices crying out *Datorete! Datorete!*

Proof! Proof!

White hands thrust into the air in imprecation and salute. Prince Ajimma turned its head, surveying the congregation with a light like satisfaction in its smooth face, nodding in the unbalanced way of its kind. Looking on, I remembered why the name of Ajimma should sound familiar to me. It was one of the princes who had absconded with a portion of Utaiharo's clan when Aranata Otiolo had killed its former master. Syriani had mentioned its name when discussing Prince Aranata's blasphemous murder. I studied Ajimma's face. We were relatives, in a sense, cousins in a lineage of conquest. "You may make claims all you wish, Syriani. You may present this *susulatayu* of yours as a *gift.* What matter these things if they are lies?"

"What do they matter?" Syriani asked. "Tell me, Ajimma. Tell me, *all of you:* What have *you* mattered? What have you achieved?" It thrust a hand back toward its previous quarry. "Onasira here has raided the *hakurani.* The *hakurani!* The rest of you have pillaged the *yukajjimn.* Burned worlds, it is so! Burned hundreds of worlds! But to what purpose? To what end? Are we not *Cielcin?* Are we not a chosen people? Is it not in our hands to un- make the Lie? To tear down this *iugannan* and lead our people to the next world?" It spat upon the stone floor in the midst of the congregation, its fangs on full display as its sneered, voice high and cold as the peaks of dis- tant mountains. "And you talk of *raiding!*"

Not one to be so easily cowed, Onasira's nostrils flared. "Did not Elu himself order the Thirteen to pillage the lesser worlds and bring their spoils here? To Akterumu? Did not Dumann burn the cities of the *Azh-Hakkai?* Were not the Enar themselves conquerors who bent the stars to kneel?"

"And the Enar are dead!" Syriani roared at Onasira. "They were not *righteous!* And Miudanar destroyed them!"

"*Veih,*" a quiet voice said. "*No.* They took their own lives. Drank poison."

Seventeen hundred pairs of black eyes moved to me, and it was only after three seconds of silence—real silence—that I realized it was I who had spoken.

"*Dein marereu ne?*" Syriani asked, turning to face me. *What did you say?*

I stood alone nearest the mouth of the stairs. The congregation—the *Aetavanni*—stretched about me in a broad arc, rank upon rank of alien faces running backward toward the smoothed-over Enari pillars. Above them, the icon of Miudanar looked down with its single, hollow eye. All eyes were on me, all ears bent to my word.

"I saw them," I said simply, speaking so my inhuman audience would understand. "The Enar were not destroyed by an act of god. They failed to destroy our universe, so they destroyed themselves."

One might have heard the dropping of a pin on the Enari marble.

"You . . . saw them?" Syriani asked, speaking for the first time since we'd arrived at the temple in my own language.

Refusing to follow its example, I pointed at the floor of the temple between us and said—still in the Cielcin language to be sure the others understood me—"Here." The great prince shifted, arms slack at its sides, fingers reaching nearly to its knees. "They died right here . . . and all across their empire. They *surrendered.* They could not achieve what their gods demanded of them, and so they killed themselves." I kept my eyes locked on the xenobite who called itself *the Prophet*. "You'll die, too. Before the end. You'll *fail*."

Before Syriani Dorayaica could respond, strong hands seized me by the hair and tugged my head back with such force that I thought my scalp might tear. Another hand snaked round, a white knife flashed at my throat, and I felt my veins constrict, chest tightening as my body forced adrenaline into every fiber, eyes and nostrils stretched wide. I seized that hand with both my own—dropping my chain in the process.

"Nieton kushanar!" came the slithering, reptilian voice above my ear. *It speaks poison.*

Hard fingers released my hair and snaked round, clutching me by the forehead to hold back my chin. Earth and Emperor! The strength in those inhuman fingers. Even with both hands on the creature's gauntleted arm, it was all I could do to hold that knife at bay. I could feel the edge cold against my skin, clenched my teeth.

"Release it, Hasurumn!" Attavaisa snarled, leaping toward me. "It is not for you!"

"Its lying tongue has profaned this holy place!" the voice behind me hissed. Hot breath wafted over me, moist and stinking of decay. "It should never have been allowed to pass the god's eye!"

I felt a burning sensation just above my suit collar and winced as I felt a thin dribble of blood spill out and run down my neck. I gasped, swore in my native tongue. I could feel my muscles giving way, their malnourished fibers cramping and crying out with strain.

"Put it down!" Attavaisa hissed again, and its cry was taken up by several of the others.

Did I dare attack the prince holding me? Stamp its foot or hurl my weight upon it? I could not strike it in the face with my head as I might a human opponent, so much taller than me it was . . .

I did not get a chance to decide.

A huge weight slammed into Prince Hasurumn and myself from the left, and we both went skidding wildly across the greenish marble. A blow caught me in the stomach and sent me sliding across the floor while Hasurumn wrestled with the prince who had tackled us to the ground. I saw a blur of black mingled with Hasurumn's pale blue, and recognized one of the princes who had come downstairs to help check Iamndaina. One of Syriani's toadies.

Chains rattled, and before I could stand I found myself being dragged clear of the fighting *aetamn*. Clawed hands seized me, touched the blood on my neck. "I'm fine!" I nearly shouted, forgetting to use the xenobite tongue. *"Eka udata! Eka udata!"*

"Ikurra!" my savior exclaimed. Turning my head, I saw Prince Ugin Attavaisa towering behind me, its pale hand outstretched, my red blood black in the low light of the hall. "Blood has been spilled!"

The whole hall erupted into a furor of inhuman voices. Shouts and hurled insults flew like arrows from prince to prince, words rebounding off the whorled and ridged surface of the dome above.

"Ikurra!"

"Ikurra pa ba-ikurra!" one voice rang out, louder than the rest.

Attavaisa raised its voice in agreement. *"Ikurra pa ba ikurra!"* it said. "Blood for blood!"

On the floor, the other *aeta* had successfully wrested away Hasurumn's dagger and threw it skittering across the floor, where it vanished—snatched up by one of the other princes. Peledanu had joined it in restraining Hasurumn, and together they held my would-be assassin down.

"You defend *yukajjimn* now, Dorayaica?" Hasurumn demanded, voice cracking as it strained against its oppressors.

"Svassa!" Peledanu hissed, holding Hasurumn by the horns whilst the other grappled with it. *Surrender!*

Syriani Dorayaica towered above this chaos, so still it might have been a piece of Enar sculpture. The peculiarities of my statement and its heresy momentarily forgotten, it studied Hasurumn, transparent membranes flicking vertically across its black and glassy eyes.

"Iugah!" Hasurumn shrieked. "You are false, Dorayaica. You are Utannash himself!"

The room again was nearly silent as the Prince of Princes advanced on Hasurumn, head cocked to the left in a subtle negative. "You have drawn blood in Elu's Temple, Elentani Hasurumn," it said, half-turned to regard Attavaisa's still-outstretched hand. In writing this, I realize that my blood doubtless appeared black to the Cielcin as well—that it appeared black in any condition, under any circumstance, any light—black as their own. "You have done violence against one of your *tanyya*, against an *aeta ba-itanimn*. Against a prince of the clans." It was standing above Hasurumn by then, its horned crown cutting a shadow across the lesser prince's face.

As it had spat on Iamndaina, it spat on Hasurumn. "Your line is ended. Your clan attainted. Does any object?"

Not a single prince in the chamber raised its voice, not Ajimma or Onasira, nor any of the others who had opposed Dorayaica. Whatever their feelings toward the great prince, all were of a party with regard to this single point of tradition.

When no voice spoke in Hasurumn's defense, Hasurumn spoke for itself. "I did not harm an *aeta* of the clans! You defend vermin, Dorayaica! One of the *yukajjimn!*"

Syriani turned its back. "Attavaisa, Peledanu. Take who you need and escort Prince Hasurumn outside. Tell them it has profaned the god's holy corpse and blasphemed against the will of Elu."

"*Yaiya toh!*" Prince Attavaisa said, stepping out from behind me and leaving me alone, again, near to the stair. It approached Syriani and bowed, twisting its head as it did so to expose its throat to its master.

To its *Imperial* master, I realized. Syriani had little control over most of the seventeen hundred, but there were some—a radical minority, I guessed no more than a hundred of those gathered beneath the dome of Miudanar's skull—who obeyed the prince utterly. The rest had come for fear of its armies, or out of curiosity.

Hasurumn hissed as Peledanu and four others wrestled it to its feet. Attavaisa made a sign to several others, and to my astonishment some five or six dozen of the princes stepped forward to escort Hasurumn from the chamber.

"So many?" I could not help but mumble, though none within earshot heard or understood. I reached down, scrambled to pull my chain out of the way as the mob advanced and hoisted Prince Elentani Hasurumn into the air, clawed fingers piercing the flesh of arms and legs as they carried it aloft and passed down the stairs and the channel of the optic nerve, feet clicking and echoing on the cold, dead stone.

Watching them go, I could not help but feel the prince's escort excessive. Six others would have been amply sufficient to remove the prince, but sixty? I touched my throat. The fingers came away wet.

"Only a scratch."

Looking on, I could not shake the feeling that some sort of quorum had been reached, or else that some manner of ritual begun. Syriani was not looking at me—had forgotten about my interjection, had forgotten about me entirely. It stood as a man carrying some great weight. Not a physical weight, but a weight of time, of *moment*. It seemed to me then like nothing less than Anubis holding the all of a man in its hands.

It was the future it held, of itself, of its empire, of its species.

What was I next to that? Only what it had said: an amusement.

The prince turned to what remained of the congregation. "You asked for signs," it said, bowing its head, its shoulder back and squared. "For proof. I have brought you all the spoils of an empire! The slaves I offered your people this day are a but a foretaste of what is to come! I have burned their armies; attacked their foundries, their fortresses; crippled their fleets. They are weak, defensive. All this I have done in the name of Truth! In the name of the gods! In the names of Miudanar and Iaqaram. Of Pthamaru and Shamazha, of Usathlam and Shetebo and Nazhtenah and all those who dwell beneath the stars, dead and deathless!" The Prophet's hands vanished beneath its dark cloak. "And I have bested our greatest enemy! The Champion of Utannash himself! Are these not proof enough of the gods' favor?"

The princes muttered to one another, horned heads moving back and forth in consultation like a forest of bare trees swaying in an unfelt wind.

"Veih!" one voice dared to venture, and the sound of it was like a spark kindling the conflagration, and before long the majority of those remaining voices were shouting along with that first. *"Veih! Veih! Veih!"*

No. No. No.

I looked on, searching for a face not shouting the Prophet down. I found none, and felt a sudden sharp sense of foreboding. Had all the princes who supported Syriani gone to slaughter Hasurumn? I took a step nearer the great prince, eyes narrowing. I was no idle amusement. I had been brought deliberately, brought to provoke precisely the response I had. Had it not been from Hasurumn, it would have been from another. A more prudent, patient Iamndaina, or Onasira or Ajimma or any of the others.

Syriani had deployed me like a chess piece, like bait.

"Show us the Blood!" exclaimed one of the others, using the old word again.

Taroretta Izhkurrah!

The Prince of Princes rounded on the speaker, and it was only as they froze in place before it that I realized the right flank of the princes had been advancing on Syriani inch by careful inch. A sudden thrill of terror for it and for myself filled me. We were horribly outnumbered, and only ceremony and religious law kept that crowd of hundreds at bay. I sensed they would gladly have killed Syriani and myself and restored balance and normalcy to their lives, sensed too that it was only Elu's ancient commands that held them back. That, curiosity, and holy fear.

Seeing this motion, Syriani reached into its belt and drew forth a short, crooked blade. Milk-white it was and hooked as one of the Cielcin's own claws. Syriani held it in reverse grip, its first finger threaded through a loop in the pommel. It was a pitiful small thing compared to the advancing horde, that blade shorter than a hand's span.

Syriani raised the knife for all to see, standing with left arm thrown wide, the right clutching the knife above its head. "Behold me, *kinsmen!*" it said, voice high and cold enough to scratch the dome above us all.

What happened next I have never forgotten.

It closed the fingers of its left hand over the knife above its head and pulled, slashing the palm and fingers just as Irshan's blade had cut my hand in the Grand Colosseum of the Eternal City. The great prince did not wince. It offered no expression or made any sign it felt pain. It only opened its hand and showed the blood on it to the congregation.

Not black it was, but silver.

Just as it had been in my dream.

My mind went blank then, silent with pure horror as I recalled the monstrous fingers that had pried their way from the Prophet's severed neck. "Do you believe me now?" it asked, raking fathomless eyes across its subject-brethren.

No one spoke, but stood in frozen apprehension of this sign.

"The Blood of Elu flows in my veins anew," Syriani said, and clenched its fist until the blood welled like quicksilver between its fingers.

Ajimma stepped forward and fell to its knees. "Dorayaica . . ." it moaned, pressing its face to the stone at the great prince's feet.

Syriani stepped forward and placed its foot on Ajimma's head. "I am not Dorayaica," it said. "Dorayaica is dead. I am *Shiomu*. Prophet. And *Elusha*." It lifted its clawed foot so that the pointed heel aimed down and stamped on Ajimma's skull in the soft place behind the horned crest. Gore spattering its black-armored boot and the hem of its cloak, Dorayaica glowered at the others. "King."

"It is forbidden!" one of the others objected, voice breaking. "You killed Ajimma! You have done . . . violence here."

"It is forbidden that aeta should slay aeta," came a shout from one of the others.

"I told you, Vanahita," the creature once called Syriani Dorayaica said. "I am not *aeta*." It shook Ajimma's brains from its foot as it answered and drew back a step. "And neither are you."

As if on cue, blood began to run from Prince Vanahita's nostrils. Four black lines that broke over its mouth. The princes all began to cough and choke. One fell to its knees, gasping like a stranded fish. Another toppled like a tower shorn of its foundation. Still more seemed to understand what was happening, and began moving at once, some stumbling, others running for the exit. Some among them stopped and retched, spilling gray bile on the ancient stones.

"*Kurshanan!*" one exclaimed, lurching toward Syriani. "You've poisoned us!"

Syriani jerked its head in the negative. "It is the will of the gods. You had your chance. You chose the Lie."

The staggering prince raised a clawed finger. "You . . . arranged this."

Gas. The word leaped into my head, and I stumbled backward for the door and the stairs. Dorayaica had administered some species of nerve agent, doubtless one designed by Urbaine or Severine or another of its pet magi. Reaching up, I fumbled with the controls to don my helmet. If I could just close my helmet, I might survive. An indicator on the suit's wrist-terminal blinked red. My hair! Suit sensors had detected my hair was in the way and would not deploy the helmet. Cursing, fearing that at any moment my own gorge would rise and my blood with it, I reached the top of the stair, stumbled against the pillar nearest the opening, its surface chipped smooth, defaced by some antique Cielcin chisel. Numb fingers wrestled with the elastic coif tucked into the collar of the suit, nearly dislodged the conduction patch behind my right ear.

No good.

I couldn't do it. Not with my wrists bound.

I coughed, and imagined I felt a thin pain in my chest. I almost fell onto the first step, threw out hands to steady myself against the wall. Before I could make it another step down, my chains went taut and pulled me backward. My head struck stone, and looking back with burning eyes I saw Syriani standing amid the carnage like a pillar itself, my chains secure in one hand.

"You have nothing to fear," it said, speaking my language. "The poison kills only Cielcin."

What are you? I wanted to ask, but the words caught in my throat. About me, a scant few of the clan-princes still moved, crawling toward where I lay upon the topmost stair. Vision gray and blurring, I saw their grasping hands, coughed as whatever poison MINOS had engineered filled my lungs. It might not be lethal, but it was not without pain.

White hands reached toward me, pawing to get past me. A shadow blocked one of the red Cielcin lamps, and looking up—eyes misty and lungs choking for air—I saw Syriani flip the nearest prince on its back and pin it there, almost gently. The Prophet held its dying kinsman's gaze until

it ceased to move. There was no feeling in the Pale King's face. No re-
morse, no delight. Dorayaica's face was empty, as expressionless as a funeral
mask.

Another fit of coughing seized me, and I rolled to my stomach, pushed
myself to hands and knees and spat upon the stone.

"I can't . . . can't breathe," I managed to say, chest heaving.

"Quiet," Syriani ordered. "Stop your groveling. This is not the way
you die."

CHAPTER 40

WHAT GREEN ALTAR

I WAS A LONG time recovering my breath. For a while, I could focus only on the feeling of it: the raw, red pain and the gray blurring of my vision. Each breath threatened to cause another fit of spasms and coughing, and once I retched upon the floor. Through my haze I saw Syriani kneeling in the midst of its destruction, arms spread wide before the graven image of its black god. Miudanar looked down on the carnage, its image betraying no sense of approval or condemnation.

"You killed them," I managed to say at last, and shaking found my feet. I could hardly remember feeling so weak. I was sure I must have in the pits of Dharan-Tun, in the throes of my torment, but time and pain have blunted those memories, and the exhaustion I felt standing beneath that rippled dome was an exhaustion not just of body, but of mind. It was a minor miracle I could stand at all, so thirsty was I, so wrung dry of water and of tears.

"Yes," Syriani Dorayaica replied. It spoke in standard. There was no Cielcin word for *yes*.

"All of them," I said, more slowly still.

"Yes."

My chain lay strung across the floor, and I gathered it slowly, links slithering across the cracked and immeasurably ancient marble. "It was not your gods' doing," I said. I did not ask.

"No." My head swam, and so I leaned against the nearest pillar. The Pale King did not turn. "Your magi have their uses."

"How was it done?"

The creature now calling itself Shiomu Elusha turned and stared at me. "What you said. About the Enar and their end. What did you mean?"

"Ah . . ." I had wondered if that would come up again. I looked around at the carnage in the alien sanctum, at the mingled blood and filth and vomit. It did not take much to imagine it was the Enar's death I saw again about me, their ruined bodies rotting as if on holograph recordings played back at a thousand times the speed. "I saw them. Here. They made their end here, cowering in this chamber. They drank some . . . substance. Some potion or praxis. It dissolved them. Turned them to dust." I felt a bout of coughing coming and screwed shut my eyes to better clamp down on my breathing. "They weren't judged by your gods. They didn't attain your paradise. They'd conquered the galaxy, but it wasn't enough." With each word, I felt a little better, a little stronger. "You really think you can destroy *everything*?"

The Shiomu Elusha's huge eyes eyes narrowed, but it did not stand. "Do you doubt it?"

"Not your convictions," I said, "only your power."

The former prince's face split into a huge inhuman grin. "You forget . . . or perhaps you do not understand. I do not have to destroy everything. I have to destroy *you*. Without you . . . your kind will fail. Without your kind, Utannash will never be."

"I . . ." I *had* forgotten.

"And if Utannash is never born, this universe will have never been." It stood slowly, swaying. I sensed the king was as exhausted as I was, and reminded myself that it, too, had made the long walk from the ringed city that morning. "Think you that I have exaggerated in calling your master the author of this . . . ?" It spread its hands as if to encapsulate the cosmos. "Utannash made the world. You would call it *god*, but it is not. It is beyond time, but it was born within it. Begotten here. Destroying you and your kind will break the cycle, will end this flawed creation and free my masters—the true gods—the gods of the nothing that was *before*." It showed me its hand, the silver blood still wet and bright on the palm. "That is why they made me this way."

Silence stretched between us then, and for the first time I could hear the distant furor of the crowd outside. The Elusha crossed half the distance between us in three strides, began circling me. "We are the same, you know. Each touched by higher powers."

"Do you dream the future?" I asked, slashing this line of conversation.

The Pale King stopped its orbit, cocked its head. Again the black-rimmed smile broke its smooth face. "There is no future. Soon we will be free."

The sound of armored feet rang on the stairs, and turning I was surprised to see the *vayadan*-general Vati emerge from the narrow arch,

Attavaisa and Peledanu in pursuit. All three knelt and pressed their faces to the floor. *"Elusha ba-koarin,"* they said in unison. *My King.*

Vati raised its head, red eyes taking in the mounded corpses. "It is done, then."

"It is done," the Elusha replied. Was that a note of sorrow in the great demon's voice? "But it is not over. We have conquered . . . now we must rule. Are the others in place?"

Vati rose without breaking its bow—no mean feat that, and one aided by its machine body. "The ship is being brought down as we speak. The crowd has already spotted it. They ask *what has our king brought for us?"*

"You flatter me, Vati," the Shiomu Elusha replied. "They do not call me *king.*"

"They will, *ushan belu!"* Prince Attavaisa said, still kneeling.

Ushan belu? I looked from Attavaisa to Dorayaica and back. The term meant *beloved.* It was a name reserved between an *aeta* and its *vayadayan,* its slaves and mates. Attavaisa raised its face to its new king, eyes wide and open. I wondered . . . were Attavaisa and Peledanu *vayadayan* now? Replacements for Iubalu and Bahudde? Concubines and consorts for the new king?

The Shiomu Elusha dismissed this further flattery with a gesture. "Summon the *kalupanari.* Have them fetch these bodies down and give them to the soldiers. Let them see what becomes of those who challenge my dominion." *Kalupanari* meant the chimeras, the demons of Arae.

It had directed these words to Vati, who raised its chin in salute and stood. *"Yaiya toh."*

"Ushan belu, what will you tell the people happened?" the former prince, the *vayadan* Peledanu asked its lover and master. It knelt still and did not rise.

The Shiomu Elusha blinked membranes and lids alike. *"Ejaan,"* it replied. "Nothing. Let them see what is true. Let them believe." It raised its silver hand to underscore this response.

"And those who do not believe?" Attavaisa asked. "What of them, Dorayaica?"

The Pale King snarled. "There is no *Dorayaica,"* it hissed. "No more. I am *Shiomu Elusha.* Do not forget it, Attavaisa, or you will fast find yourself with these." It raised its still-dripping hand to encompass the slaughter in the temple.

Attavaisa said nothing, but angled its head where it knelt to signal submission.

"Those who will not believe and submit are *Utannashimn* and will be destroyed. But they *will* submit," it said, eyes turning to me. "I have brought them a mighty gift." These words hung upon the air then, thick as the poison that had killed the other princes. For a moment, the only noise was my faint coughing and the dim thunder of the crowd outside. Then more metal feet sounded on the stairs to herald the corpse-bearers who would carry the *aetane* to their final resting place in the stomachs and at the hands of their former subjects.

"We must go down," the great king said at last. *"Raka ute uelacyr."*

It is time.

The bodies of the princes lay stacked like cordwood beneath the stelai in the chamber of the eye. The sun had swollen to a lurid orange and hung low on the horizon, threatening the tops of the distant towers that marked the gate and opening of the ringed city. The chimeras had made short work of ordering the bodies, had readied them for the new-made king's display.

I could sense the restiveness of the crowd even through the walls of the great skull, could hear them roil and bicker. The princes had been inside a long while, and but for the group that had carried Hasurumn forth and the disappearance of the chimeras inside there had been no sign of an end to the *Aetavanni*.

But it *had* ended, and the Cielcin world had been forever changed.

I sat with my back against one of the stelai, staring at nothing. A chimera held my chain, stood inert as a statue to one side.

"It will be over soon," said a cold but human voice.

Looking up I saw the magus Urbaine standing over me, his crossed arms tucked into flowing gray sleeves. Severine stood beside him, alongside another woman, each in suits to match the more senior sorcerer.

"What are we waiting for?" I asked.

Urbaine only smiled, and the third woman asked, "Are you so eager to die?"

"How long have I been a prisoner?" I asked in response.

Severine and Urbaine exchanged glances. It was Severine who answered. "Since Vati brought you to Dharan-Tun? Seven standard years. Three months. Twenty-seven days." From the flattened, clinical nature of her response, I guessed she was consulting some feature of her neural implants.

I felt sick. Had I anything left in my stomach to lose, I would have lost it then. How many times had I asked that question since I awoke in slime and in cold? How many hundred times without an answer? "Seven years . . ." I managed at last, and held the gaze of the other MINOS woman. "Seven years . . . and you ask if I am eager to die?" I dropped my gaze, for merely to look at the sorcerers kindled a sick fury that I knew I would never satisfy. "I knew this day was coming. I've known it all along. Known there was no escape. But no . . ." I shook my head fiercely, and shook away a fresh fall of tears. "I am not eager to die."

In truth, I was not sure I could die—not really. That was the most terrible part. Perhaps if I could, death might have been a comfort after all I had endured. But I had died before, and death had been no release. What would happen if Dorayaica—if the Elusha, I corrected myself—sacrificed me, but I endured? Would I then be condemned to live in captivity and die a thousand deaths for the amusement of the Pale King?

"Have you any water?" I asked, without hope.

To my astonishment, Urbaine produced a half-emptied flask concealed beneath his robe. "A final courtesy," he said.

I drank it greedily, spilled some of it down my chin in my haste to drink it down. It was not urine, as it had so often been at the hands of my Cielcin tormentors. Such a small mercy. "Thank you," I said, voice breaking just a little.

By the time I finished, alien trumpets began to sound, and a torrent of inhuman voices welled up to greet them. Looking up, I saw Syriani Dorayaica, the Shiomu Elusha, the heir of Elu and High King of the Cielcin, emerge from the upper stair. It did not stop, did not turn its head to either side, but passed the mounds of bodies and the troops gathered in that lower hall, passed its chimeras and human magi, passed the surviving princes who had named themselves its slaves. Passed me and the soldiers who stood guard over me and out beneath the arch of its dead god's eye and into the light of that setting sun.

"*Cielcin ba-kousun!*" it cried, voice magnified by some unseen instrument, booming from speakers embedded in the bodies of the chimeric soldiers who stood at the front of the crowd. "My Cielcin!" it decreed. "My people!" *Mine.* The storming crowd broke and fell to silence, and into that silence the great king exclaimed, "The princes are dead!" The silence grew deeper still; confusion—and not Dorayaica—was king in that instant. About me, the chimeric soldiers began hoisting corpses in their too-long, articulated limbs. I recognized the body of Iamndaina among them, and heard the shouts and indrawn breath as the first soldiers carried those first corpses outside.

"For the first time since the time of Elu, the blood-clans stand united!" the Pale King proclaimed. "I am *Elusha! Shiomu Elusha!* I have spoken with the very gods! With Miudanar who dreams here in death! I am he whom Elu foretold. I am the one who will lead our people through the darkness to new life. I am the sword that will wipe clean the universe! I am the hand that will make it anew!"

Craning my neck, I could just see the Prophet's crowned silhouette on the stair that led down to Elu's altar. At the word *iedyr*, hand, the Elusha thrust its slashed hand skyward, displaying the Blood for the crowd to see. The Pale King was silent, waiting for the crowd to draw its own conclusions.

The signs were known.

While the Pale King spoke, the chimeric warriors hurled the bodies of the dead *aetane* into the crowd the way great princes of the Imperium tossed coins to beggars on parade. If I expected the crowd to hesitate out of deference to the dead, I was disappointed. The Cielcin mob seized upon their dead princes like vultures, stripping rings from fingers and fingers from bones. There would be poor soldiers sporting gems in the halls of Akterumu that night, and slaves killed by masters for trinkets and bits of cloth.

"*Izhkurrah!*" one of the throng cried out, and an instant later the word was taken up by those around it until the whole desert was shouting along with it. "*Izhkurrah! Izhkurrah! Elusha ba-Izhkurrah! Elusha ba-Cielcin!*"

"King of the Blood," Urbaine said softly, a wicked smile pulling at his lips.

"King of the Cielcin," Severine added.

"A new age begins!" The king's voice shook dust from the stelai and the roof above. "Elu brought us out of Se Vattayu! Brought us here! Miudanar gave us wings! Gave us ships and the will to build them! It was Umna, Elu's own, who freed Usathlam from his chains beneath the waters of the Baikosi! It was Dumann, and Zahaka, and Inumgalu—the first *aetane*—who made slaves of the *Azh-Hakkai*, who are no more! By Elu's word did they do these things. It was Elu who built our first ships. Elu who built our first kingdom over the stars." Here it drew its hands down, fists clenched before its eyes like a boxer. As it spoke, it descended the short flight of stairs to approach the green altar. "It is *Elusha* who will reclaim those stars. It is Elusha who will make slaves of the *yukajjimn*! It is Elusha who has brought you their great champion. Their *aeta*!"

Clawed hands spread wide, as if the one-time Prince of Princes might gather all the Pale unto itself. Responding to some silent cue, the chimera that held my chains advanced, prodding me with its free hand.

I stood unsteadily, braced myself against the defaced stele.

Urbaine grinned at me, and reaching up cupped my cheek with one damp hand. "I am so going to enjoy our time together," it said. Seeing the confusion on my face, he patted me with his hand. "The Great One has promised us your head."

And with that, I lurched forward—half-pulled like a dog—into the lurid orange light. I froze upon the top step, looking out upon the crowd. Entering the temple, I had not occasion to marvel at its number. Hundreds of thousands of Cielcin clustered on the level sands before the shrine of the skull. A veritable ocean of faces and of blue and violet banners stretched and spread among the pillars. Some Cielcin had even climbed the nearer pillars and clung from their sculpted faces, the better to see above the horned heads of their compatriots. In the distance, more banners from terraces and from the balconies of the distant city of Akterumu, and I guessed that for every creature standing on the sand, half a hundred gathered in the city. The whole Cielcin race—save those clans who had refused the Pale King's call—was gathered at Akterumu, on Eue, or in the fleet above it.

There must have been billions of them.

"Behold it!" the Shiomu Elusha said. "Behold the Champion of Utannash, who defied me in battle and is brought low!" As the creature spoke, it raised its silver hand again for the throng to see. "Here is the greatest of them! Let it be a sacrifice to mark the kindling of this new age! As Avarra sacrificed itself for Elu, let us sacrifice this great king of our enemy to the Dreamer and the Watchers who are with us even now!" The great prince turned and made a slashing gesture with its good hand.

My guard shoved me, and I tumbled down the steps to land sprawling at the Pale King's feet. I looked up and saw the Prophet had climbed the dais to stand behind the altar on the spot where its forebear and namesake had burned the body of its mate. "As I offer this creature to Miudanar the Great in Elu's name, let this be an offering to you—*my people*—as a promise of all that is to come!"

That said, it took its slashed and bloody hand and reached across its face, smearing the silver blood across cheeks and lips and jaw before raising the hand once more to the heavens, pointing at the sun. The eyes of the congregation followed, and somewhere below us huge drums began to sound.

A shadow fell across the sun, and even as I regained my feet, my heart fell and shattered.

"No!" I said, voice crushed and small. "No!"

Hearing me, the King of the Cielcin turned, black robes snapping about its heels, eyes dead and cold and far away. Over its shoulders, the chimeras tossed another salvo of dead princes to the crowd, who stood waiting, pulsing, jumping with hands outstretched. Silver blood framed the Elusha's glassy teeth, but still it pointed to the heavens and said the words I knew I would hear. "You knew it would come to this, *kinsman*," it said, and from the blackness of its eyes I knew it knew that I had seen this moment, too. "Time runs down."

Dharan-Tun had not blocked the sun as it had on Berenike, but something had. Her black shape slid above the towers and the great wall of Akterumu, moving like a thunderhead still higher than any cloud. The putrefying sunlight caught on the polished hull and on the huge, alien vessels that buoyed her. Great towers and spires hung from her belly, a city inverted to the alien city that rose from those gray-black sands. The mouths of her guns stood lonely and quiet, and the ports from which lightercraft were fired gleamed silver-bright beneath the glowing line of her equator. She came lower, and almost I felt in my bones the creaking of her superstructure in the grip of Eue's deadly gravity. She had been built for space, and no ship her size could bear to land and survive. As she cleared walls she turned, the convex arc of her drive cluster cutting a slice out of the sky.

The great spire that hung down near the aft like an inverse castle was *gone*, blasted or shorn off, but still I knew her—I would have known her anywhere.

The *Tamerlane* swung low over the battlements of the ringed city, suspended by four huge Cielcin lifters on blue-glowing repulsors. The air groaned and shook with the complaints of twisted metal and a rushing like never-ending thunder. I looked on, frozen, petrified, tears streaming freely down my face.

Never before had the sight of her inspired such grief and such terror.

Dorayaica, the Elusha, meant to *land* the *Tamerlane* within the circle of Akterumu. It meant to offer the ship—and the ninety thousand slumbering aboard—as spoils to unite its newly minted army and empire.

"No . . ." I could only say. But it was there. How many times had I borne witness to this moment in my dreams? How many times had my unconscious mind shown me this very moment—like a traumatic memory—and urged me to do all I could to avoid it?

But it had come in its time, in its way.

I had not escaped Fate.

The great horde had already turned its back on the temple to watch the battleship descend. Many in the rear had already spread out, eager to come nearer the ship, but a line of the king's chimeras turned them back and worked to secure a landing space. The music of the drums and the terrible trumpets played louder, and the war cries of the Cielcin filled the air and challenged the burning of the lifter rockets for supremacy. I caught the words *Elusha* and *Izhkurrah* on the wind many times.

When at last the groaning vessel cleared the walls, soldiers on the ground fired primitive flares, trailing columns of green and azure smoke painting columns against the gloomy sky, guiding the vessel to ground. Never before had I seen the *Tamerlane* so close while standing on my own two feet. The *Eriel*-class battleship dwarfed us all, dwarfed even the head of the Watcher enshrined in the heart of that dead land. Beneath its dripping shadow, the white-armored chimeras appeared no larger than ants. As I watched, the vessel sank lower still, its battlements and bay doors pitted and scarred from so long in space without care.

It must have lain somewhere on the surface of Dharan-Tun for all the years of my imprisonment, or else in the holds of some lesser worldship of Vati's ferried all this way from Padmurak. The signs of battle and of looting were evident, even from a mile off: the heavy armor of the dorsal hull showed the deep, geometric cracks where the long-chain molecules in the adamant had shattered under titanic assault. Cielcin boarding craft still studded the lower decks like poisoned arrowheads in the flank of an iron giant.

She hung a thousand feet above the desert then, lower than the tops of the columns of bright smoke. I could make out white-crowned Hushansa directing the troops managing the landing. Five hundred feet. Greenish flares marked her descent, taller, less permanent than the pillars of the Enar. Three hundred feet. Two hundred. The black towers that like stalactites hung from the bottom of the dying vessel brushed the tops of the Enar columns. The great ship swayed as the lifters burned brighter, hotter, bluer in the sunset. A conning spire struck one of the antique pillars. How long had it stood sentinel there? How many millions of years had passed since its vile builders set it in place?

It fell in seconds.

And the *Tamerlane* fell atop it. A hundred feet from ground, the lifters cut their lines. How many pillars she broke in that final fall I never knew, and the noise of her impact shamed the drums and every clap of thunder on every world, for it was the ending of mine. Huge clouds of gray sand rose into the sky, washing over the chimeric landing team and halting the rioting horde in its tracks.

Silence fell.

I knew what came next.

The *Tamerlane*'s nearest side—her port—stood a mere mile from the temple steps, and the thunder of her final fall had thrown the Cielcin horde into chaos. Following silent orders relayed over their implants, the chimeras scrambled to assert control over the masses of the Pale. I heard the crack of gunfire as the iron demons fired on the crowd, hurling the bodies of rioters aside as examples to terrify the others into line.

The instinct for obedience ran deep in their race, and in mere minutes the chimeras had corralled the horde and re-established a central aisle along the paved avenue from the temple toward the outer gates to where the *Tamerlane* lay shattered and broken on the path.

I wanted to protest, to stop the great king, to break my chains. But I knew . . . knew that even if I did, even if I could, I would face the king itself, its White Hand, its sworn *aeta*, the chimeras, the *scahari*, and half a million screaming Cielcin.

What could I do but die?

The first human shapes that emerged from the wreck of my world brought me to my knees. My vision blurred with tears to see the red and the black of them, the officers in their undress blacks and the men in their maroon fatigues. Syriani had emptied the *Tamerlane*'s cubicula, had thawed out what must have been at least half of the mighty vessel's ninety thousand. Perhaps it had awakened them all.

They came without armor, some of them stumbling and clearly still fugue-sick, clutching one another and shrinking from the fell beasts at either side. The Pale King's guards did not hurry them, did not snap at their heels and crack the whip as they had done with the poor slaves that started our parade. Syriani had planned the event with masterful precision. One could practically smell the saliva dripping from alien fangs, could almost taste the anticipation mounting as the moment stretched.

I saw Ilex first. Her green skin and mossy hair stood out against all those pale faces and the dark. My heart broke to see her, to see any familiar and friendly face after all my years alone.

"Ilex!" I stood and hurried toward the altar, heedless of my chains, planning to vault the vile stone and hurry down the steps to join my people. As I did, I spied the knot of black-clad officers about her. I could just make out Commander Halford's bald pate and prominent ears, and that tiny form! That was Lorian!

My chain went taut, choking me. My feet kept going, spun out beneath me, and I struck my head as I fell. "Why?" I hissed to no one. "Why like this?"

A cold, dead voice replied, *"Dajaggaa o-tajun junne!"* It was not an answer. Was not a reply at all, and so numb was I and confused and overwhelmed with joy and terror and grief at once that I did not understand the words until iron hands seized me and dragged me back to my feet. Before I could breathe—before I could blink—the soldiers holding me slammed my face into the altar and held it there, fingers tight in my hair. Only a chance turn of my head spared my nose. My vision swam. The sound of the crowd blurred, dulled—as though I heard it through water. I was a boy again, alone and friendless in the dark night of Borosevo, and caught.

"Not like this . . ." I groaned, or thought I did.

Through my ringing mind I discerned the rattle of chains. The chain that bound my wrists they pulled down and looped through an iron bracket beneath the slab of the altar on the far side, so that I had no choice but to bend my neck above the altar, where there was a trough—not so unlike the trough that formed the centerpiece of the feasting table in the halls of Dharan-Tun. I knew how it would end, had seen it a thousand times. Syriani Dorayaica, the Scourge of Earth, the Shiomu Elusha, King of the Cielcin, would seize me by the hair and torque back my head. Using its crooked knife, the Elusha would lay open my throat from ear to ear. My blood would spill out into the trough, the only red in all that place.

But it would not do so yet.

My suffering was not yet done.

The other victims had drawn nearer by then, were gathered at the base of the stair. I remember I could not stop looking at them. I could not stop smiling—that was the worst part. After so long in solitude, so long in torment without a succor or friend, I was truly, perversely, overjoyed to see them. My tears flowed freely, and I was glad of the awful curtains of my hair.

The Cielcin guards at the base of the stair checked their march, crossed scimitars to keep them from coming any further forward. In the rear, men were still climbing out of the ruined *Tamerlane*, goaded on by douleters with scimitars of their own and wicked pikes. The Red Company crowded into an ever-widening space between shoals of Cielcin, held back only by the threat of the chimeras that held the line to either side. My people made a great wedge before me.

Twenty or so men stood shoulder to shoulder at the base of the steps below me, each garbed in an officer's undress blacks: Ilex still stood out the sharpest, the dryad with her high cheekbones and bare arms, blinking up at me with amber eyes. Beside her, Elara stood—the last of my myrmidons, for surely Pallino was dead. She met my gaze and nodded, but said no word. Her big, brown eyes shimmered with tears. There again was Halford, the night captain, and beside him Koskinen and Pherrine and the junior officers, men I little knew. I did not recognize Tor Varro at first. The scholiast had donned an officer's blacks. I had never seen him dressed in anything but the green suits of a Chalcenterite scholiast. His bronze face was impassive, empty as ever of feeling—like his own monument. At his right—near the center—stood Lorian Aristedes, barely elbow-high to the scholiast, his too-long white hair crudely tied at one shoulder to keep it from blowing across his face. Without his cane or his silver braces, he looked half a child. Indeed, he might have been a child were it not for the pain in his bloodless face. His colorless, pale eyes found mine, and he nodded.

It was telling of the gravity of the situation that Lorian said nothing at all.

"Had!" Elara called out. I could barely hear her beneath the tumult of the inhuman crowd, but understood her by the shape her lips made. "Where's Pallino?"

I could only shake my head. I did not know whether to be glad or devastated by the old man's absence. Pallino was nowhere to be seen. Nor Crim, nor Otavia . . .

. . . nor Valka.

"Had!" Elara's motherly face flushed with anger and with fear. "What happened to him?"

Eyes shut, I pressed my forehead to the cold stone. *Dead,* I wanted to say. *Dead and buried.*

The Scourge of Earth rounded the altar and stood at the top of the stairs, turning its head slowly as it surveyed the humanity gathered between the twin shoals of its new-made horde.

Not like this . . .

The doom-drums began to beat again, and the Pale King thrust its silver hand skyward, the right thrown wide to admit the torrent of cheers and the raucous chant of *Izhkurrah! Izhkurrah! Izhkurrah!*

The Elusha dropped its hand, and when the riot fell back a bit it spoke—not to the crowd, but to the humans gathered before it. "Which of you is captain here?" it asked, speaking the standard so that its captives might understand.

The officers stirred, none answering, each turning from side to side, checking to see how the others would answer first. I could only imagine what this world was like for them. For better or worse, I had lived among the Pale for years. For the others, it must have been like awakening in hell, or else like not awakening at all, but rising to a dream and a kind of waking terror from which there was no escape.

When no one answered, the king asked again, "Which of you is captain?" It tilted its head, jeweled chains and bangles swaying with the motion. Its cloak and the Imperial-style toga it wore over its organic-looking armor shifted as it moved, looking in every way the opposite number to our Emperor. Behind it, Vati and Aulamn and the floating sphere that housed Hushansa's brain looked on with glowing eyes. The giant Teyanu loomed over the officers, flanking the base of the stairs. White-armored chimeras and *scahari* in black and blue held tall, slim banners of the White Hand waving in their hands . . . and in the distance? The ramparts and ugly towers of Akterumu—of Pandaemonium itself—rose green and gray and encircled the world and ruined *Tamerlane*.

At a gesture from the king, Aulamn leaped forward, spreading huge, membranous wings. The *vayadan* leaped down among the officers, seizing one by the shoulders with its clawed feet. The winged monster flapped its wings once, rocketing skyward with a gust of wind. A thousand feet above the desert, it let the man fall. He screamed and struck the sands amidst the Cielcin horde, which closed in over him in a frenzy like sharks in bloody water. Its feat accomplished, Aulamn settled back to roost beside Vati on the upper stairs before the cavernous eye of Miudanar.

"Answer me!" Syriani said, not raising its voice. "Which of you is captain?" It raised its hand, threatening to loose its winged lover and slave again.

"I am!" came a tired, reedy voice.

Looking down, I saw a thin, narrow-shouldered man push his way to the front of the line. "I am!" he said again, throwing up a hand. He wore an officer's legionary blacks, but his head was shaved like any common soldier. Bastien Durand had always been a quiet, unassuming man, a dour, officious bookkeeper forever lost in Corvo's Amazonian shadow. I had never liked him, finding him cold and curiously formal for a mercenary, and we had butted heads in the past. I had always thought him a man of little personal courage, if a dutiful enough officer.

Had he been hiding behind the others?

It did not matter. He was not hiding anymore. Stepping forth, the scholarly soldier adjusted his purely cosmetic spectacles and exhaled sharply. "I am captain here," he said, lifting his chin—a gesture of defiance, not defeat. He approached the guards at the base of the stairs, who checked his advance with crossed swords.

"*Ujjaa nevasari,*" the great king said, ordering its men to let Bastien by. The scimitars uncrossed, and when Durand hesitated, one of the *scahari* seized him above the elbow and frogmarched him up the steps. The xenobite forced him to kneel on the green marble before the altar. Before the Elusha.

Ever the student of human customs, the Shiomu Elusha offered a ringed hand for the commander to kiss. Bastien glanced to me, eyes narrowing. But he had hesitated too long. The Cielcin ruler lashed Bastien across the face, tearing a line from his cheek cousin to my own. Still, the blow had not been hard, and to his credit Bastien squared his shoulders. I nodded at him, granting my approval—but I cannot be sure he saw me.

He kissed the ring all the same, shuddering as he grasped the alien hand. When he was done, the Elusha wrapped too-long fingers around the nape of Bastien's neck, and said, "I want you to confirm for me and for your people that this is Hadrian Marlowe." It jerked its head in my direction. "I want them to know that what they see is not a *Lie*. That it is no trick. That they are not dreaming. Will you do this?"

"You want me to . . ."

"Confirm that *this*," it pointed at me with two fingers, talons slowly extruding from their sheaths, "is your master." The Pale King's gesture softened as it opened its bloody hand, inviting Bastien to approach the altar. Below, the Red Company craned its collective neck to see their captain—their First Officer, in truth—and the Pale King. Even in hell, human curiosity was endless. About them, the Cielcin tide grew higher, swelling like an ocean of blackness, white-capped, to either side.

Bastien Durand nodded and accepted the Pale King's invitation. Moving with his customary stiffness, the Norman officer approached the altar. "Lord Marlowe, sir?" he asked.

"Bastien," I replied, looking up as best I could, chained as I was at the edge of the altar.

At the sound of my voice, the younger man snapped to salute, beating his breast before extending his right arm in the Imperial fashion. "My lord." He glanced up at the skull of the dead god and the chimeric generals on the steps above us. "Hideous place to die, isn't it?"

"It is," I agreed.

"Otavia, sir . . ." Bastien's voice broke. He couldn't bring himself to ask the terrible question: *Is she dead?*

I shook my head. "Lost. On Padmurak. Her and . . ." Then it was my turn to be unable to finish my sentence. I could not say the words: . . . *and Valka.*

Bastien shut his eyes, massaged them with his fingers, upsetting his glasses. It was the most feeling I'd ever seen from the man, and it was gone as quickly as it had appeared.

"You agree this is no deception?" The xenobite's voice intruded on our grief, cold, brittle, and terrible.

Bastien Durand inhaled sharply, and turning back to face the Shiomu Elusha replied, "It's him."

The bleeding silver hand gestured at the humans penned in between the shoals of the enemy. "Tell them."

Before he did, Durand looked at me one last time, and I marked a solitary tear where it traced a line down his dark face. For me? For Otavia? For himself? Durand's face darkened. "I thought you were supposed to be the Chosen," he said, bitterness flooding his tone.

The words fell like blows, and cut deeper than any knife or lash I'd suffered. I lowered my eyes, pressed my forehead to the cool stone of the altar. It was my fault. Had I been more vigilant, I would have sensed the trap on Padmurak before it was too late. Had I not leaped to destroy the charioteers in Vedatharad, I might have been with Valka and Otavia, Pallino and Crim when their doom came. I might have saved them, and we might have saved the *Tamerlane.* None of this would have happened, and the Empire would know the Commonwealth had betrayed mankind to the Cielcin.

I did not look up as Bastien confirmed for the human onlookers that I really was myself. I felt—more than I heard or saw—the indrawn breath and the cries of despair from my Red Company. My universe consisted of my bound hands shackled beneath the slab of the altar. I tried to focus, to blink back tears and clench my jaw, tried to see a place where those fetters

broke and I won free. I pictured myself leaping over the altar and strangling the monarch with my chains there before its army and my own,
pictured us winning free in a desperate brawl against the armies of the
Cielcin . . .

Fantasies.

I had no illusions left. Even if I could summon my vanished power and
free myself, I knew I would not make it over the altar. If the Iedyr and its
guards did not stop me, the king itself would. Even at my full strength, the
xenobite king was stronger—and I had not been at my full strength in
years. And even if I could overpower the Elusha, even if we humans won
the day—outnumbered five or six to one though we were—we had nowhere to go. Akterumu was filled with millions more of the Pale, and
orbited by billions. The worldships of seventeen hundred blood-clans
waited for us.

We were finished.

Screams broke through the walls of my little universe. Shock and raw
dismay.

I looked up, and saw a headless man in undress blacks standing where
Bastien Durand had been, right at the top of the lower stair. The body
swayed a moment and tumbled down the stairs toward the crowd. The
king who had been Syriani Dorayaica stood beside it, grasping in its hand
a gleaming sword. Not white ceramic, not a scimitar of the kind wielded
by the Pale.

The highmatter blade looked small in its hand, like little more than a
knife in its long and spidery fingers. It was not the crackling monstrosity
Carax had spoken of in his address to the Emperor so long ago, not the
weapon I'd seen in my vision of the night before. The blade was bright and
smooth as crystal, as moonlight, its rippling length offset by quillions of
liquid metal that shielded the hand. Its fittings were of silver, the grip
wrapped in wine-colored leather. It was a Jaddian blade. Olorin's blade.
My blade.

All this time I had thought it lost on Padmurak, in Iovan's possession,
perhaps, or a trophy kept by Lorth Talleg. But the Lothrians had given it
to Vati, and Vati—ever faithful—had given it to its master.

And Syriani had used it to kill Bastien Durand.

The commander's head had tumbled to the base of the stairs, lay now
in the narrow stripe of empty ground between the guards who held the
stair and my officers who stood before them. No one spoke, and almost I
thought that not a one of the humans drew breath, so solemn and still were

they, cowed by the sight of what had happened, and by what they knew was yet to come.

The Elusha raised its voice again, cold tones artificially magnified as it spoke once more to all my captured men. "On your knees, humanity!" it proclaimed, and thrust my sword out like a statue of Justice challenging the throng. Slowly, steadily, the Red Company—all ninety thousand men—sank to their knees. The monarch let its arm drop, and in hushed tones continued, "I am Cielcin. *The Cielcin*. I have bested your master, your prince." It waved its bloody hand in my direction. "Your Hadrian dies today, and your Emperor will follow. Your people shall be a nation of slaves. Of cattle. But take heart! You have fought well. Your deaths will be swift." My own sword flashed in my direction. Slowly, I raised my eyes, squared my shoulders. The Shiomu Elusha pointed my Jaddian weapon at my eyes, and in a voice not magnified for the crowd, it said, "But first: you must choose."

I met the Prophet's eyes, but did not speak. Behind it, the ruined *Tamerlane* smoked, black tongues rising above the ramparts of Akterumu unto heaven. Above it all, the countless Cielcin moons looked on.

"You must choose one," Syriani said. "One of your people must go to your Emperor, and tell him you are dead. I shall permit you your choice."

The officers had all heard, and the first several ranks of men shifted awkwardly where they knelt. Bastien's body lay between them and me, his blood violently red in that place of gray and green. His head lay on its side not five paces from where Halford and Koskinen knelt. I met Koskinen's eye a moment, and Halford's—recalling how the latter had saved the Red Company and the *Tamerlane* at Nagapur. He had grown into a fine officer. I looked at Elara, but she shook her head and averted her eyes. I understood her well enough.

Don't you dare.

"I . . ." Was it a final courtesy? A boon offered a worthy adversary? Or was it a curse? A final act of cruelty? Beneath the altar, I pulled my chains tight, stretched my wrists as far apart as they would go. Ilex looked up at me, nearly so blank-faced as Varro. Pherrine was crying quietly, her shoulders slumped. Commander Aristedes knelt beside her, shrunken in defeat, his thin hand on hers, a fleeting, final moment of humanity in that alien waste.

Only one.

I could save only one.

It wasn't really a choice. A righteous anger burned in me, searing through the pain and the indignities I had endured. Clearing the clot in my throat, I said, "Lorian." He was the ranking officer, after all, with Bastien and Otavia dead.

The intus cursed foully and stood. "I won't go!"

"You must!" I said.

"And leave you to die?" he said, advancing to within striking distance of the crossed scimitars. At a sign from the great king, the guards permitted Lorian to pass. He limped in his awkward way up the bloody stairs—skirting poor Bastien's body. He did not cower as he drew near the Prophet, who stood nearly twice his height, but tucked his chin like a boxer and said nothing.

"What an amusing little creature," Syriani said, looking to me. "Your lords keep such pets, do they not? What does it do?" Long used to such abuse, Lorian chewed his lip, but to my astonishment said nothing.

Syriani sniffed, four nostrils flaring. "Take him."

Footsteps sounded on the tile behind, and twisting in my bonds I turned and saw Severine advance with one of the chimeras. The guard seized Lorian by the neck and dragged him along the terrace that encircled Miudanar's skull. A dull wind blew, and I beheld the gray shape of a shuttle—a man-made shuttle, to judge by its harsh, plain lines—descend.

"Lorian!" I called after the retreating backs. Severine halted, permitted Lorian to look back. I met the junior man's pale eyes, and only then did I mark the first sign of tears in the man. He blinked them back.

"Avenge us!"

CHAPTER 41

THE BLACK FEAST

BLACK WINGS CUT THE gloaming air, and a gust of wind slashed the terrace before the dome of the skull. The Cielcin king had wasted no time sending forth its messenger. I wondered at that. Even after all my education—all my experience—the ways of the Cielcin were strange to me. Had it but waited, Dorayaica might have sent the Emperor my head. Yet it seemed other demands and concerns governed the great king's attentions. Perhaps it feared chaos in the city as the various factions, the generals and servants, ministers and *vayadayan* that served the murdered princes scrambled in the aftermath of the Elusha's regicide. Perhaps Lorian had some part to play in the next phase of its plans, a part that would not wait.

Or perhaps it only wanted me to watch as the shuttle vanished into the darkening sky.

Again, I pressed my forehead to the lip of the altar, staring down at my hands while Syriani spoke, addressing its own people once again. A light blinked on my wrist-terminal, a power indicator, I guessed, some sensor warning of damage to my suit. The cut water lines, perhaps. *"Cielucin ba-koun!"* it said, "My people! Behold *my* victory! The *yukajjimn* on their knees." I looked up in time to see the Elusha raise its bleeding hand once more. "Fight for me, and we shall bend their every world!" Behind me, the chimeras began distributing the bodies of the dead princes yet again, tossing the corpses unceremoniously from the terrace to the Cielcin below. *"Ti-koun!"* the Prophet proclaimed. "In me the Blood of Elu—the Blood of the Gods—flows anew!"

Hand still raised, blade outstretched, Syriani turned and faced the skull of the dead giant, looming over me from across the altar. "Miudanar! Dreamer! Watcher! God! I am your servant, as Elu was before me!"

Again the doom-drums began to sound, low and deep to shake the bones and rattle the teeth of all who gathered in that hideous place. I tried to meet Syriani's eyes, but the sinking sun had fallen almost to where its bloated orange disc shone through its horned crown, transmuting the Pale King to a dark silhouette. "I have brought you one who serves Utannash, the Deceiver! A Champion of the Lie! May his life sever the chains that bind you in Death! With this sacrifice I strike against the *Lie* itself! I am your instrument! I am the Truth of God!"

A roar went up from the chimeras and from the army of the great king. Scimitars and banners flashed and fluttered above the vast ocean of alien bodies.

Stowing my blade, Syriani wheeled about. Still in its own tongue, it said, "Here Avarra offered its life that Elu might prove his devotion! As Elu made sacrifice, so I offer this creature to the gods—and offer these!" And here the Prophet spread its arms, highlighting the kneeling humans on the plains before the stair. "To you, my people!"

I knew what must come next, had seen it—as I had seen so much of that terrible day—a thousand times in my dreams.

But I was not dreaming.

A thousand times I'd seen the Prophet raise those glittering hands. A thousand times I'd heard their dry slap, the sound reverberating throughout my visions and backward across time.

It clapped its hands, and said that single, terrible word—that final, horrible command: *"Paqqaa."*

Eat.

The chimeras who had held back the crowd put up their arms, and like black water the Cielcin rushed in, leaping on the kneeling and defenseless Red Company from either side. Ninety thousand men and women howled and scrambled to their feet in terror as hundreds of thousands of the Pale pressed in. One lunged at Pherrine in the front line, but Koskinen leaped in front of her, striking the monster across its face with his elbow. The Cielcin staggered back, and the palatine helmsman leaped atop it, knocking it to the ground. I had a brief image of the junior officer hammering the xenobite with his fists before two more Cielcin seized him by the arms and—planting a clawed foot on his chest—tore his arms from him.

I never heard Koskinen's cry of pain.

My scream drowned my universe, and I slammed my forehead against the altar and tried to stand, to pull the iron chain from its ring beneath the altar and free myself. The little light kept sparking on my gauntlet, warning me of the failure in my suit.

Not like this.

Screwing up my eyes, I clamped down on my breathing. The only noise then—louder than the distant shrieks and shouts of terror—was the thunderous tympani of my heart. Syriani turned to me, and said—voice even and smooth as glass, "You see? Your legend is a lie. Your god cannot save you."

I ignored it. Focusing on my chains. Surely the old iron loop must break. I tried to focus, to find the quiet place within me. *Grief is deep water,* I told myself. *Rage is blindness.* But every stoic aphorism, every lecture of Gibson's, every scrap of philosophy or poetry I had ever learned fell flat and hollow in that windless hell. It all meant nothing before that horror. Behind it all the *Tamerlane* smoked, her ruin blackening the sky. And above all, a shadow slashed the bottom of the sun, and the very air turned gray with false twilight. Looking up, I understood.

Dharan-Tun had moved to occult the sun. Syriani had ordered its captain and its sailors to darken the sky just as they had at Berenike. It was a crude bit of theater, of melodrama, and melodrama was the lowest form of art. But had I not learned that the lowest things are closest to the ground and truth?

I pressed my forehead to the altar stone, willing the chain to break as I strained with all my sinews, boots planted on the Enari marble, knees and back bent. My wrists ached where the manacles chewed into them despite the gauntlets I wore.

"No," I hissed. "No!"

Rough hands seized me, slammed my face into the stone. Dazed, I permitted those hands to turn my vision upward. "Watch!" Syriani hissed in my ear. "I want you to *see*. I want you to know your god deceived you, deserted you. I want you to know *Truth*."

Somehow, Ilex and Elara both had wrested scimitars from the *scaharimn*, and behind them other knots of men had drawn together. Ninety thousand was no small number. They would be a long time dying.

"See how they struggle?" the Prophet asked. "We have not had a festival such as this since before the Scattering." Claws dug into my scalp, blood welling from new wounds where the great king held me. I winced, sagged back against the altar, knees striking stone.

"Why don't you just kill me?" I mumbled.

The Elusha released my bleeding head, and I slumped back against the altar. I could do nothing while my people died. Nothing.

The gray air grew darker, and the sounds of feasting and wicked laughter rose from the sands below. And screaming. And tears.

"Your time is not yet done," Syriani said, gesturing at the sun and the false moon eclipsing it. "Utannash has forsaken you. Admit it."

Hot blood ran down my face. I blinked it back, bent my face away, pressed my forehead back against the altar. I could not look anymore, could not stand to see the suffering I had failed to prevent. The suffering I caused. I could not stop *hearing*, however—could not stop *listening* to the sounds of tearing flesh and terror.

"Admit that what you did at Berenike was a lie," Dorayaica said, standing over me. Beneath that black sun, it cast no shadow, for its shadow fell on all the world. "You have no power. You never did. You are as false as your false master. You cheated me."

I glanced up at the great king in its black armor and robes, at its Imperial-styled toga, at the silver jewelry that decorated hands and horns. I shook with rage, with grief, with remembered pain.

I turned my face away.

"You are alone," the great king said. "Your people are alone. They have lived like kings. But they will die like rats. I will step over your body and onto every one of your worlds. Your people I will root out. Enslave. Work to the last man. And when you are gone, your future will never be. Utannash will die, and the gods will be free at last. Free from this false universe. Free to build a better one."

True darkness fell.

Light.

Blue-white and clear as moonlight.

A Jaddian blade. My blade.

"Die now and forever," Syriani said, and lifted that blade.

The world went silent and still as stone, as if Time herself faltered. Severine had said she thought that I could perceive time differently than ordinary men, that my brain processed it in higher resolution, in smaller increments. Small enough to perceive the quantum branchings of possibility, small enough that instants seemed like hours.

I listened, heard nothing.

I saw.

I might have wept, if weeping were possible in such a state and space of time. My vision had returned, and I turned with eyes unclouded to look upon myself arrayed across the infinite *now*. Countless Hadrians knelt in chains, or crouched, or stood defiant, each representing a line of possibility that had not happened. Reading this, you imagine that there were—that there are—an infinity of other worlds. You think that what we do does not matter, because we have done everything once somewhere. Some*when*.

It is not so.

Only what does happen has happened. But the universe remembers what does not. The alternate pasts are not lost. Nothing is lost. Not matter. Not energy. Nor possibility either. I turned my eye to see those other selves, to peer into that abyss of uncounted possibilities, events so remote and so unlikely they could never have occurred at all.

The other Hadrians stared back, and met my vision eye to eye.

In the Alcaz du Badr, the great palace of the Princes of Jadd, there is a hall of mirrors. In its center lies a silver fountain and a pool whose fish—so the porphyrogeneticists say—can never die. Beneath the light of that fountain's crystal lamps, the hall appears reflected, refracted, in infinite variation in the polished walls. Sitting on the marble rail, the prince in meditation might feel himself the center of the universe, and look out upon himself and his undying fountain echoing forever in those perfect mirrors.

So it was with me.

I blinked, and in the space of that eyeblink my vision changed. No longer was I a line stretched across the potential present, but the focus of a kaleidoscopic vision whose every facet reflected another version of me.

Something had changed in me, brought on by the crisis. I was awake as though for the first time, and clear. Not without pain or grief, but past both. Past everything. My torment and the final horror of that place had pushed me to some windswept place in my soul where not even my own passions could reach. I was *clean*, and clean I saw everything.

Though still aware I slumped with my head upon the altar—I could feel the cold, dry stone against my face—I saw with a kind of double vision the abyssal Dark beyond death.

Find us, a familiar, polished voice resounded in my ears. *Find us in you.*

Hadrian Marlowe stood over me, just as I had seen him in the dungeons of the Conclave. His matted hair—striped and shocked with white—fell to his waist. His ribs showed through skin translucent as ivory. His eyes shone sunken deep in their holes. Huge scars covered his arms and bare thighs, and his face bore the marks of tooth and claw.

Was I dead already?

When I had died aboard the *Demiurge*, my own image had greeted me—garbed in finery of deepest black. I had changed so much. Suffered so much. Lost . . . so much. I looked up at myself, ragged and torn. He lifted a hand, offered me the thing he held in three fingers.

With three fingers, I took it.

For a moment, we locked eyes, that other Hadrian and me.

"Avenge us," he said, as I had said to Lorian.

I nodded, and understood. He was one of the might-have-beens, a Hadrian that never was. A Hadrian that failed, a Hadrian who—in his final moments—had reached out across time from his time. A time that never happened. A past that never happened, a time now lost to time. He had failed, that I . . . and *we*, might not.

"I will."

Beneath the altar, a weight came into my hands. Bound in chains, I gripped the object, feeling the smooth play of leather beneath my gloved fingers. The vision faded, and I tightened my grip, feeling the familiar shape of the emitter and the rain guard. I pointed it down, shut my eyes, and taking the hilt in both hands, I squeezed the trigger and drew the blade with the press of twin buttons. Highmatter flowered above those desert sands, and with a single stroke I severed the chain that bound me and sheared through the altar to catch the blade falling toward my neck. When the blow struck, I felt my blade bend, and feared for a moment that my own sword might take my life.

But I heard a grunt, a gasp of pain, and—freed from my bonds—I rolled with my back to the altar to face my enemy.

Silver blood spilled from a wound in the great king's side, and it pressed its slashed palm to the spot, staggered back. As it faded back I stood, using my left hand to steady myself against the cracked altar, sword held out before me with my ruined right. The Elusha glared at me, eyes wide. With fear? With fury?

"How?" it asked.

I was quiet.

For a solitary instant, the world was still, though the slaughter churned below us. We stared at one another, two matched chess pieces squared off at the center of the board, each holding an identical sword.

The same sword.

Holding an unsteady guard with my maimed hand, I fumbled with my shield-belt, found the long-unused catch that triggered the energy curtain. I half-expected it to fail. After so long a period of neglect, it *should* have failed, but the graphene battery in the belt pack had held its charge since Padmurak. The fractal curtain sprang up and closed about me, air shimmering a moment before it faded to invisibility. Thus shielded, I put both hands back on my sword and pressed forward, hoping to catch the great king on the defensive. On the steps above, Vati leaped to its master's defense, but the Prophet threw up a hand to halt its servant in its tracks. The general froze, one hand on the ceramic blade sheathed at its hip.

As we stood facing one another, I heard a distant cry boil from the plain at the foot of the stairs. "Halfmortal!" that fragile human voice rang out. "Halfmortal!"

They had seen me, and soon the cry rose up from a thousand different throats. "Halfmortal!" they shouted, and rallied to their last defense. "Halfmortal!" I lunged, sweeping my blade up to catch the king of the monsters on its hip.

Still clutching its side, the Elusha parried with my own blade, forcing my weapon down. Even injured, the Cielcin lord loomed over me like a breaking wave, its glassy teeth a snarling tangle. "You will not take . . . my victory from me," it hissed, and slammed its forehead down into my face.

I managed to tuck my chin in the last instant so that the king's bony brows struck the top of my head and not my nose. The force of it still flattened me, knees buckling like old timbers. I bit my tongue as I struck tile.

I was not the man I was. However resolute, however righteous in my fury, I was not strong enough. My time in the dungeon of Dharan-Tun, on the walls and in the pits and under the knife, had taken so much from me. I could stand, but it was nearly all I could do to stand.

"Another trick!" the Prophet hissed, eyeing my weapon. "Concealed in your suit somehow?" It raised its sword to strike, grunting as the movement stretched the wound in its flank. That instant's hesitation bought me all the time I needed. I rolled sideways, passing under Elu's altar, and stumbled back to my feet. The light was still blinking on my gauntlet as I brought the sword back to guard, mindful of the Cielcin grappling with my men at the base of the stair. If I could slay Dorayaica, it might be enough to turn the tide, to break its newly welded-together Cielcin empire back into seventeen hundred little factions. Without a clear leader, they would tear one another apart in their desperation to get at us.

"Hadrian!" Elara yelled. "The *Tamerlane*! We have to get to the *Tamerlane*!"

I ignored her. The *Tamerlane* was no good. Anyone with eyes to see knew that. She would never fly again, could never fly again. That final fall had broken her, and the black smoke heralded huge internal fires. Soon they would spill forth and drink deep of Eue's airs.

The ship was lost.

The Elusha moved around the altar, bleeding hand pressed to its wounded side. It swept its blade at me. I raised my sword just in time so that wild blow bounced off, skipping like a stone across the surface of still water. The blade circled round, and Syriani slashed downward with all the finality of an executioner.

My left arm saved me, as it had in Colosso so long ago. Kharn Sagara's printed adamantine bones held fast, and the highmatter caught against my elbow, shearing through suit and skin alike. The force of that blow still staggered me, and I collapsed against the altar. In a blind panic, I seized Syriani by the wrist, stopping its sword's descent with my good left hand. Before I could slash at it with my own blade, the Elusha's bloody hand shot down and pinned my arm to the altar beside me. Its teeth flashed.

"Why prolong your struggle?" the monster snarled, voice thick with strain. "You will die!" The Elusha's blade inched nearer and nearer my face, its rippling edge gleaming like moonlight. Sharp as highmatter was, it would take no force to press through skin and bone and brain. Micron by micron it drew nearer. I tried to free my sword arm, but the monster's talons clamped down the harder. "You *must* . . . die."

I was trapped. I could not even raise my sword again to get it between Syriani's weapon and my face. The blade was caught pointed down, and my opponent leaned all its terrible weight on my wrist, trapping the weapon beside me, my arm at full spread. The other hand barely held the highmatter from my face then. Saliva dripped from the vampire's fangs, so near my face I half-expected the creature's jaws to unhinge and snap forward. I could smell its fetid breath, and the stench of raw meat and corruption mingled with the metallic tang of the blood smeared across its face washed over me.

My tormented shoulder screamed white fire, and I knew I would not last long. The Prophet's slit nostils flared, and as I turned my face away, I saw it: a faint stirring below. My eyes flickered down to the monster's wounded side. Blood like mercury dribbled down its flank, staining the beast's stygian robes. I had struck it a mighty blow, but my weapon had not bitten near deep enough to kill. Still, the injury should have put down any ordinary foe.

I hung there a moment, straining against the Prophet's inhuman strength, transfixed by the sight of its open side. Had I imagined it? My eyes went back to Syriani's face, to its teeth bared in a snarl of triumph. Triumph, and comprehension. It knew what I had seen.

Again I looked down, and saw what I could not have seen.

Something pale and wicked slithered beneath the Prophet's skin, like a fish just beneath the surface of a clouded pool. I felt my eyes stretch wide, remembering the nightmare of my vision in my cell, the pale fingers stretching from the Prophet's severed neck. Miudanar's skull loomed over the Prophet's shoulder, its single, evil eye dead and empty and full of deathless malice.

"What *are* you?" asked Hadrian Marlowe, voice so terribly small.

"I told you," the Prophet answered. "I shall become a god!"

It leaned against me with all its weight. My shoulder screamed. I was going to die after all. Even my miracle had been for nothing. The high-matter would pierce my flesh without force, without resistance.

Without resistance.

I had forgotten the very thing Crispin had forgotten so much when we were boys together.

I had forgotten that highmatter was *not* steel.

The edge needed no force to cut, needed no room to accelerate.

Inches were enough.

Inches were all I had.

And so I stopped trying to free my wrist, stopped trying to raise my sword. I dragged it *in* instead, angling the point so that I struck the demon king's leg behind the ankle. Limited though my range of movement was, the weapon notched black armor and severed cloth, bit perhaps halfway through the bone.

Syriani hissed and fell on top of me, its sword falling wide. I slid free, drawing up my sword to make the final strike, to end the Prophet there upon its own altar.

Something huge and solid as stone struck me then, and I went flying through the air, over the heads of the guards battling at the foot of the stairs and into the crowd of men and bodies below. I struggled to sit up, blood clinging to the *irinyr* cape from the bodies beneath my hands, but it was no good.

The *vayadan*-general Vati stood atop the steps, its white cloak abandoned, its skeletal form standing tall between its master and me. The beast had flashed toward me with all the speed its augmented body could muster. My shield had insulated me, but the mass of it and the sheer kinetic force of that impact had been enough to hurl me almost a hundred feet from the altar platform.

Something soft had broken my fall, and for an instant I lay there, dazed.

The sounds of chaos churned about me, and the world spun and would not still. I turned my head, experienced the sensation of falling. Then my vision cleared, and I found myself staring into what once had been a woman's face. I could not recognize her. Both eyes were gone, and the flesh of one cheek hung down from her jaw, baring bloodied teeth. I yelled and tied to stand, but the softness beneath me shifted, and I staggered, found I lay on damp red sand amid a carpet of ruined bodies. Fatigues torn apart like parchment paper, strips of skin and meat, offal spilled and stinking clung to my armor.

With a terrible effort, I forced myself to sit up among the carnage.

Men and women warred about me, many of them armed with stolen spears or scimitars. As I looked round, Teyanu squashed one fleeing man beneath its feet, and one of the chimeras lifted a woman above its head and—seizing her by the ankles and under the arms—tore her in two pieces, hurling the pieces over its shoulder to the hungry crowd. The sounds of laughter and fey hooting and of the evil drums filled the circle of Akterumu.

Above me, Vati helped its lord to stand. Syriani still held my sword—my original sword—and glared down at me with narrowed eyes. It favored its right leg, and the left bled furiously before the altar of sacrifice, mingling with the dregs of Bastien's. To look at it, I had half-severed the royal foot, and knew that ever after the dark lord would walk with a limp.

But it was impossible to take satisfaction in that small victory. The memory of my vision and of the pale *thing* moving beneath the alien flesh turned my already emptied stomach.

It was all I could do not to fall back and join the dead.

Rough hands seized me. Human hands, I realized, and looking round saw Elara and Ilex and one of the lesser chiliarchs. Petros, that was his name. "On your feet!" Ilex said, trying to lift me. "We have to move!"

"*Biqqaa!*" Syriani was shouting, pointing with my stolen sword. "*Biqqaa totajun wo!*"

But the Prophet's words were lost. Drowned out in the instant that followed.

The light came first, white and angry as the sun until the day shone brighter beneath the Prophet's eclipse than any day had ever on Eue. The explosion followed a moment after, as air boiled and alien flesh, and before my hearing returned, I felt—rather than heard—the deep concussive booming of guns.

"Impossible." I felt the word in my bones, and turning looked back.

The *Tamerlane* had opened fire. Though she lay broken and flightless, doomed as a stranded whale, her every bank and battery glowed red and smoked with fury. Standing among my final friends in all the universe, I raised my sword and laughed.

"Earth!" I shouted, and hurled the word at the Shiomu Elusha, at Syriani Dorayaica and its court of devils. "Earth! Earth and Emperor!" And though my throat was ragged and my ears rang, I heard the words arise in the throats of the defenders gathered nearest me.

"Earth! Earth and Emperor!" they sang, and "Halfmortal! Halfmortal!"

In the shadow of its dead and deathless god, the Prophet staggered, frozen in shock and confusion. I looked round, sharing the beast's astonishment. My first thought was that it was Lorian, that the little man had overpowered Severine and her guard and done . . . *something*. But it wasn't possible. I raised a hand to shade my eyes—for surely that flash had been one of the *Tamerlane's* terawatt lasers—and froze.

I was looking at the light on my gauntlet, the light I'd kept seeing on my wrist-terminal throughout my botched execution. It wasn't a failed sensor or fuel indicator.

It was the comms.

How had I not realized?

Numb, I checked the conduction patch in the collar of my suit just below my ear with my left hand. It was still there. Stupidly, I prodded at the terminal switch on the gauntlet, blade still bright in my hands.

I almost dropped it.

"'Tis about time!" came the bright, familiar voice. "I thought I was going to have to come out there and drag you here myself."

My heart caught in my throat. "Val . . . Valka?"

"Of course 'tis me, *anaryan!*" her own voice broke, and I choked to hear it. "Get to the *Tamerlane!*"

"But!" I could hardly think. I looked back up at the Elusha and its generals. We would never again have such a chance.

"'Tis no time! You have to run! Get Elara and everyone you can!"

My hands went to my side, and I turned, looking from the temple steps to the ruined battleship, torn in two. About me lay strewn the bodies of dead men and Cielcin, red blood and black thickening the sands.

"Run, damn you! Run!"

CHAPTER 42

SACRIFICE

VALKA IS ALIVE.

I was still reeling. I had lived so long with so little hope that I had all but abandoned the feeling. To experience it again after so long was a torment terrible as the pit, a desperate joy that ached as redly as the lash.

Alive.

Elara was still at my side, and I seized her by the shoulder. "We have to move!"

About us, the carnage crashed like a sea in storm. We had been accorded our brief island of calm only by the breadth of humanity about us and the new terror of the guns. The Cielcin horde had fractured a bit, those farthest from the temple turning and running for the distant walls of Akterumu. They stood little chance of reaching the wedge of humanity that stretched from the *Tamerlane* to the shrine of Miudanar's skull, and so had no reason to remain.

"Valka!" I practically screamed into my comm. "Target the temple! Target the temple! Dorayaica is here!"

Even as I spoke, I felt a blast of wind rush over me, and looking up I saw the crescent shapes of Cielcin lighters wing overhead, repulsors shaking the air as they slewed into a sliding orbit about the Watcher's skull.

Another voice, rough and tense with focus, answered me. "You're too close! If I point one of the T-watts your way, it'll take out the whole building."

"Corvo?" I could hardly believe it, and wondered if the soaring in my chest was what Lin and Pallino and Valka had felt seeing me return from the dead. "You're alive!"

"Aye, but not for long if you don't move. I'm on the bridge. The doctor's firing up the *Ascalon*. You have to hurry." The captain bit each word off. Too clearly I could picture her hunched over the holography well on the *Tamerlane*'s bridge, desperately directing the action.

"The *Ascalon*!" I almost laughed for joy. I had forgotten the little Challis-class interceptor. Evidently, so had the Cielcin. Hope blossomed for true. There was a way out. Turning about, I began staggering away from the temple, sword flashing in my hand. Elara and Ilex moved beside me, pushing the men before us. But hope is a delicate thing, and rotted through to horror in the next instant. I missed a step, and the chiliarch, Petros, caught me and kept me on my feet. "Otavia," I said, voice gone ragged, "what about the others? The *Ascalon* can't take even a hundred men!"

There wasn't any answer.

"Otavia!"

When the Norman captain's reply came, it was tight as monofilament wire. "I know."

"There are ninety thousand men out here!" I shouted, throat raw.

"I know!" she shouted back. "There's nothing I can do!"

"The shuttles!" I said, still moving to stay clear of the carnage. "The lighters!"

The captain snapped, "None of those can make the jump to warp, even if we could field them all." A pit opened in my bowels, devouring all light. They would be destroyed before they could breach the atmosphere, and they could not hide on Eue, not for the years or decades it would take for reinforcements to come. If any of our people escaped the circle of Akterumu, they would be hunted, hounded for sport across the wastes and choking pits of slime that passed for open spaces and seas on that ruin of a world.

A hundred people. Maybe less.

That was all we could save.

I felt the old Imperial iron straighten my spine, felt jaw clench and sinews stiffen. There was nothing to do but run and fight and save however many we could. But I was not going to die in that terrible place. Not anymore. Not when Valka had come back to me and the fortunes of the world had turned. And yet I knew if any should stay and fight it should be me, knew if any should die that day in the fighting, it should be me.

Pushing that choice aside for the time being, I said, "Elara! Ilex! We have to go!" I pointed my sword toward the hulking ruin of the *Tamerlane*, heart rising from the ashes of my soul. Valka was alive, and Corvo, too. And if they were alive—then surely Pallino and Crim had made it, too.

Elara's reply was lost beneath the rolling of the guns. Clouds of vapor and black sand burst in the middle distance, and I saw Cielcin bodies hurled skyward, torn limbs twisted, falling like rain. The Cielcin horde was a chaos, with whole parties peeling away and sprinting across the sands, eager to escape Otavia's cannons.

"Earth!" someone was shouting.

"To the ship!" I roared, trying to rally the men.

Light drowned the world, blinding the eyes and filling all with a terrible silence. A moment after, a thunder shook creation as the terawatt laser tore through the horde, vaporizing a whole swath of the Cielcin's right flank. Half-blind but still moving forward, I fell—sword punching a hole in the slick Enari road beneath my feet. As my blurred vision began to clear, I saw what it was I'd tripped over: the torn and headless trunk of a man. Shutting my eyes, I crawled free, scrabbling to my feet. Gunfire shook the desert, and about me all was blood and screaming.

"To the ship!" I yelled again, and shoved a poor, young soldier back in the right direction. Wide-eyed, the boy ran on about twenty feet, buffeted by the passage of the other soldiers alongside. I watched him go, his shaved legionnaire's head bobbing pale in that sea of black and burgundy. Then one of the demons of Arae leaped ape-like from the sidelines, plowing through our route like a combine through wheat, mowing men beneath it. The creature turned its featureless mask of a face in my direction, white armor streaked with gore. It straightened, drawing itself up to its full height, and barred my path.

Beside me, Ilex swore.

Nowhere to run, I raised my sword high, ready for the attack I knew must come. Memories of the battle with Hushansa on Eikana came back to me, the *vayadan*'s charge, my vision striking true, the chimera falling in two pieces. Even with the impossible sword in my hand, I was not sure I could do that thing again, and I would need every miracle to defeat such a monster as I was.

It bounded at me on all fours, galloping like a tiger preparing to leap upon a deer.

Though my cry was lost in the noise of the *Tamerlane*'s cannons firing a mile off, I roared and started forward.

The chimera exploded in the next instant, a thousand tiny pieces spattering the sands about me. Its head struck the roadway at my feet, and I checked my advance, looking up in wonder. Had Corvo made that shot?

"I told you waving that sword around won't do you much good, boss!"

The voice over my comm almost laughed, and a black shape fell out of the clear sky with a roar of engines and a rush of air. Great wings scooped, repulsors firing as the shuttle plunged out of the blackened sky. I threw an arm across my face as waves of grit and dust kicked up all around. The Cielcin nearest the ship drew back as it sank lower, fearing a salvo like the one that had killed the chimera. Through the grayed alumglass of the cockpit, I could see Crim's toothy grin, a set grimace offset by the glint of determination in his eyes. He raised a hand in salute as he brought the shuttle in to float inches off the ground. I returned the gesture, spurred Elara forward as Crim worked to turn the shuttle gently round.

Realizing their prey had found escape, the nearest Cielcin closed in.

A hail of plasma fire tore from the open hatch in the shuttle's starboard side, accompanied by a yell louder almost than the *Tamerlane*'s distant guns. The spray of violet fire cut the Cielcin charge off at its knees, and smoking bodies fell in ruins, their flesh and armor fused or burned to carbon, cinders torn off by the wind. The shuttle completed its half-turn so that the clamshell side door stood open dead ahead, and there, seated on the lip of the hatchway, with one leg dangling off the side, a heavy plasma rifle tucked against his shoulder, was Pallino.

"Move your tight asses! We haven't got all day!" the old soldier barked, shifting in the gunner's seat. The chiliarch still wore the black and red Red Company plate he'd worn during that last, final scramble from Vedatharad, more scratched and worn perhaps, as though he'd gone through hell himself to come to that terrible place, and a short, stiff beard—more gray than black—covered his rough face. But the light in his blue eyes was bright and fierce as ever it had been. He grinned savagely, sighted down the barrel, and fired into the horde. "Now!"

"Pallino!" Elara broke away from me and started toward the shuttle, thrusting up her hand. All around, the crush of humanity started in toward the little ship, each desperate man and wide-eyed woman hoping to get aboard.

I slowed down, safe for a moment with so many between me and the enemy. It was an *Ibis*-class lander. The *Ibis*es were rated for thirty men, maybe forty—once we accounted for the fact that none of the men on the field were armed or armored.

There was a choice to make.

Whoever climbed aboard that shuttle—like as not—would alone escape that terrible plain. Fewer than a hundred men . . . of ninety thousand. Did I have any right to be one of them? If not for me, they would not have been there. In Akterumu. On Eue. Beneath Dharan-Tun.

"Ilex!" Pallino shouted at the green-faced woman. "Get his lordship and come on!"

The dryad seized me by the arm, and I shook her off. "You go," I said. "I can make it on foot."

The one-time engineering officer blinked at me. "You can hardly stand."

"I can do it," I said. "Take someone else. No one's dying in my place."

"We can't save them all!" Pallino said, standing in the door of the shuttle. To my horror, the old soldier aimed his weapon down at his fellow humans as they drew near. "That's far enough! We can't take all of you. You all need to keep moving to the *Tamerlane*. I'm here for his lordship!"

All eyes turned to me, and before I could object, a dozen hands reached out and seized me, dragging me forward.

"Lord Marlowe," one man said, clapping my shoulder.

"Let him through!" another man bellowed, clearing the path before me. Hands stretched toward me, not to hinder me, but just to touch my arms, my cloak, my soiled hair.

"What happened to him?"

"Is that really him?"

"What did they do to him?"

"Black planet!"

"Shit!"

There were tears thick in my eyes then, and I hardly walked straight. The desperate crowd parted, and Ilex and I were shunted forward. I kept my sword held high so as not to harm anyone, and after a moment I stowed the blade. Screams broke out behind, and looking back I saw the flashing scimitars of the Pale not two hundred feet behind. A wall of humanity held them back, men armed or else defenseless grappling with xenobites nearly twice their size, a tide of oil striking water.

We hadn't long.

Somehow, I made it to the shuttle before Elara, and Pallino stooped—one hand on a bracket inside the door—and offered me his hand. I practically fell onto the shuttle floor, and my old friend helped me to my feet. "You look like hell, Had," he said, and sniffed. "Smell worse."

"You've looked better."

He grunted, turned back outside. "We can take thirty-five if you pack in! Move, you dogs!"

I leaned against the bulkhead, chest heaving. Finding that moment of stillness, the tunnel vision of battle faded, and looking out past Pallino where he stood helping the first men onto the shuttle, I beheld the churning sea of flesh behind, the crumbling wall of men hemmed in by the horned and hollow-eyed faces.

They came on like the tide, Cielcin clambering over mounds of bodies and broken limbs. Above it all, a black crescent sailed, winging above the carnage toward the clear air beyond the battlements of Akterumu. Seeing it, I knew Syriani was aboard. The wounded king of monsters would live—if indeed it could be killed at all. Blood like mercury stained my right hand where the Elusha had pinned me, half-dried and chalky. I stared down at it, heedless for a moment to the chaos and the carnage. I kept seeing Syriani's death in my dreams, the pale fingers snaking out from the severed neck, the alien *something* struggling to be born.

I shall become a god, the Prophet had said.

The limn of Miudanar's giant skull shone darkly through the open hatch, its bulk concealed by the shuttle. I could not see its eye. Syriani had said the Watcher *whispered* to it, that it had heard the dark god's call. Had I not also heard it? Howling from its place beyond death?

I thought I understood the vision then.

The beast longed for resurrection, and Syriani was its instrument. Or— a worse thought occurred to me. Syriani had been *changed* in some way, rebuilt from its cells up. Perhaps it was changing still, transforming into something more Watcher than Cielcin, or some unholy hybrid of the two, as though it were Miudanar's byblow. Its *child.*

It was suddenly very, very cold.

"Ilex, Elara!" Pallino's shout shocked me back into my body. "Petros, you too—double quick!" The chiliarch waved furiously to the others, and he thrust his rifle up again to bar the crush of men clustered just below the gate. "Back, you lot!"

Something changed then. I couldn't put my finger on it at first. The air *thickened*, and the strangled noise of distant screams took on a heightened, fevered pitch. Pallino looked at me, a horror mounting in his rejuvenated eyes. Understanding came to him a moment before me—I saw it in his eyes. But the word went up from some poor man on the ground, and if my blood were ice already, those three syllables plunged my heart to absolute zero.

"Nahute!"

The thickened quality of the air took on new dimension, and I understood that what I sensed—what I felt rather than heard—was the buzzing drone of the xenobites' most vicious weapon. Over the heads of the onrushing hordes they came, thick as locusts, a swarm of iron serpents seeking flesh. Why the Cielcin had not used them sooner was any man's guess. Until the shuttle's coming, there had been a hideous, almost carnival atmosphere to the carnage. We were so outnumbered, so outmatched, unarmed and penned in like sheep. Knowing this, the Cielcin wall that encircled the human knot had advanced with casual violence, tearing men apart in taloned hands—breaking them like bread. Red blood smeared their faces, dripped from wagging tongues, and the air was thick with the noise of jeering and hideous laughter. Yet with the shuttle's appearance, the pitch of the combat changed, and the revelry and black feast of the Pale turned from festival to fury, fury that any of their prey might challenge them and escape.

In the instant before the cloud of *nahute* struck the group clambering into the shuttle, I had a clear impression of one of the inhuman banner-bearers, a *coteliho* hoisting its slim flag high on its lance. A human head topped that banner, its open throat pierced by the metal shaft so that blood stained the black silks. Shave-pated as it was, it might have been any of the common soldiery, but I knew it must be young Halford. I thought I recognized the prominent ears, even so far off.

Ilex accepted Pallino's hand up even as the *nahute* tore into the desperate men, drill mouths whirring, whining high and sharp in counterpoint to the deep hum of their repulsors. The primitive things tracked heat and motion, their spinning maws chewing flesh and bone to pulp to reach center mass. Men struck by those awful projectiles shrieked, clawed at the flying serpents with desperate fingers as carbon teeth bit deep and pulped their tender flesh. Unshielded, unarmored, the men on the ground never stood a chance.

Roaring, Pallino threaded the air above the panicking men with plasma, and dozens of the evil things fell upon the survivors in smoking, half-molten heaps, but it did no good. For every one the myrmidon felled, three more got through and latched like leeches to the meat of some poor bastard below. Men stumbled and fell, frantic hands trying in vain to tug the slithering iron eels from bellies and from under ribs.

"Elara!" Pallino thrust out his arm.

She'd gotten separated from Ilex and from me in the crush of bodies and the scramble to reach the ship. Indeed, the same crowd which had parted to spur me on had pushed her aside, blocked her approach. Ilex staggered against the bulkhead beside me, banged open the inner hatch to join Crim. I heard the Norman assassin's voice sharp as killing steel. "Pall-ino, we have to go!"

But the old myrmidon ignored him, let his rifle drop and swing from its shoulder strap as he reached further out. "Slew to starboard, Crim, you Norman bastard!"

I could almost feel the tension in Crim's jaw as he torqued the yoke sideways. Repulsors twisted in their fixtures in the *Ibis's* short wings, and the whole shuttle plowed right, knocking down men and women like blades of grass. I wanted to turn away—so horrible was that sight—but found I could no longer move. I gripped an overhead bar instead, ignored the eyes of the men nearest me, stared fixedly at Pallino, his hand out-stretched.

Thirty feet separated the chiliarch from his woman. Elara raised her own hand in answer, her dark eyes white and wild in her terror among the survivors yet stranded on the ground. Miudanar's massive skull loomed a thousand feet behind, and looking into its eye I felt again its whispers slithering across my mind.

"Come on!" Pallino yelled.

One man caught the lip of the shuttle hatch, tried to climb in, but it was no good. He slipped, leaving bloody handprints on the metal floor, and struck his chin as he tumbled back. The Cielcin were in among the survivors then—where once had been a wall of ragged defenders, there was running mayhem as the odd survivors darted every which way, des-perate to join the greater mass of humanity running toward the *Tamerlane* a mile off.

Elara's hand flew above the gathered heads like a banner. Pallino crouched lower, hanging onto the handle just inside the hatchway, face stretched in a desperate grimace. Hand reached for hand.

"I've got you!" Pallino grunted, arm shaking as he tried to pull his woman one-handed from the throng below. The shuttle swayed, but Elara rose, feet leaving the ground. Another man leaped and tried to claw his way through the hatch. Those crowded into the *Ibis's* compartment crouched and tried to help Elara and the other man into the ship, while those behind them held the men in front, so that all the men in the shuttle compartment were linked together: a single, defiant organism.

"Go, Crim!" Ilex shouted, slapping the bulkhead behind the pilot's chair.

The Norman mercenary wasted no time, flicked a series of controls.

The wings extended, cupping the air, and the humming whine of repulsors intensified. The shuttle began to rise. A red sea spread beneath us, the field strewn with corpses. Some of the bodies still moved, twitching as *nahute* burrowed through them, darting from man to man. About the fringes, Cielcin stooped, vampire-like, and tore flesh from bone with teeth like knives. Here and there I saw naked men and women pinned—still struggling—each against two or three of the Pale. Seeing the way they moved, I thought of Gurana, and was very nearly sick.

"God of Fire, she's heavy!" Crim swore.

"Pull me up!" Elara said, strain evident in her voice.

Pallino's reply was fierce. "I'm trying!"

Two of the men scrambled to help the chiliarch, one holding the other's belt as he leaned out to seize the myrmidon by the wrist. "Drop your sword, ma'am!" one of the others shouted. Beside her, the other man had half-climbed through the hatch edge.

Elara hesitated only a moment, released the scimitar. It tumbled down into the abbatoir below the shuttle. I was useless, crushed against the bulkhead by the mass of humanity crammed into that narrow compartment. The air stank of iron and musk. The fellow seized Elara's hand, and between him and Pallino they pulled her high enough that she planted her knees on the lip of the hatchway.

Something struck Elara in the back, slamming her into Pallino's arms. She opened her mouth to scream, but blood ran out instead. A high, grinding wail resounded through the cabin.

"No!" Pallino's hands slapped at her back, trying to find the tail of the evil machine that had bored its way into his lover's back. Elara sagged against him. Pallino closed his fist around the braided metal of the *nahute*, and with a yell like the breaking of the world—which I supposed it was— he pulled the evil thing from Elara's back. The *nahute*'s head still spun, spraying blood and bits of gore across Pallino's face and the open hatch beside him. The old soldier stared down Elara's murderer, half in fury, half in disbelief, and smashed its head and carbon teeth against the bulkhead. "No!" he said again, dropping the busted weapon out the open hatch. "No no no no no no no!" He cradled her head in his hands. "Just when I'd found you again." He kissed her, but her head lolled back.

It was too late. Elara was already dead.

The other man was hoisted to safety a moment later, and Crim turned the shuttle around, fat and sluggish on the air. Though we moved, all were still. A *nahute*'s wounds were always traumatic, teeth grinding organ and bone, leaving a gaping hole an inch across. Never straight like the wound of knife or sword, but winding through the body like a worm through fruit. Pallino had stopped the drone entering Elara completely, but there was no telling how severe the internal damage had been.

There had never been any saving her.

"You've got to let her go, Pal," Ilex said, voice gentle as could be. "We can't take her with us." She was right: packed as we were into the *Ibis*, there was no room to lay a body down.

Pallino turned to look at her—to look at me. I had never seen the rough old soldier so bereft, face an open of empty, jaw trembling for want of words. "I . . ." Tears filled those piercing blue eyes for the first time I could remember. "I . . . we can put her in a creche."

He wasn't wrong. If we could get her to the *Tamerlane*, to the *Ascalon*, if we could pack her into fugue fast enough, it might arrest brain death long enough to get her to a surgeon. Damaged organs could be regrown.

"There isn't time, sir," said one of the others near the back, a thin woman with the green star of a medical technician on her upper arm. "We'd have to get her prepped inside ten minutes. We don't have a field kit." As if to emphasize this point, the *Ibis* rocked beneath us, and the noise of killing and death wafted through the open hatchway.

"We can't carry her," Ilex said. "You can't. We need you."

"Pallino," came a dry, far-off voice, "I'm sorry." Only when the words were spoken did I realize they were my own.

The chiliarch blinked at me, blue eyes blacker and more hollow than the eyes of any Cielcin. "I . . ." He shut those eyes, nodded, and kept nodding, as if he were trying to persuade himself. "I'm sorry," he rasped, and let Elara go.

She tipped backward, fell almost gracefully from the lip of the hatch and out into the clear air. Eyes still shut, Pallino pounded the hatch control with his fist and slumped against the bulkhead.

There would be time to mourn Elara later.

"Lord Marlowe?" I looked round, found a round-faced young legionary looking at me, hairless and pale. "What is this place?"

I blinked at him. A plebeian, the lad couldn't have been older than twenty years standard, nearly so young as I had been when I left Delos. Looking past him, I marked the other faces watching me. Pallino did not look up. A shadow lay on him, obscuring his eyes.

Why, this is hell, I thought, but did not say. *Nor are we out of it.*

But I said, "It's their home, soldier. Or as near to one as they have." The color drained from several faces, and I marked that the other chiliarch, Petros, was not among them. The officer had been left on the ground.

The shuttle shook beneath us, and I turned—clutching my Cielcin cloak about my shoulders—and pressed through the inner hatch to where Ilex leaned over Crim in the pilot's seat. The *Tamerlane* lay dead ahead, a veritable mountain of steel.

"Are we hit?" I asked.

Ilex gripped Crim's shoulder, and the assassin replied, "If you climb out of this shuttle too, boss, I'll kill you."

I did not laugh.

"They *are* firing on us. It's those damned chimeras," Crim said. "Shields are holding." He banked the shuttle, steering right along the broken length of the *Tamerlane* toward the great vessel's stern.

Valka's voice sounded over mine and the shuttle's comms, broadcasting on all channels. "Crim. Where are you?"

"Above the ship. Port side. About three miles out."

"You cleared the landing zone?"

"Aye, doctor," the Norman replied.

"And Hadrian?"

"I'm here!" I shouted over the din of the guns firing away a thousand feet beneath us. Crim had tipped the *Ibis* into a steep climb that brought us up and over the crumbling hull, clear of the swarming *nahute*, clear of the chimera's weapons.

"We lost Elara," Ilex said, words raw and rough-edged. "And Bastien."

"We're *losing* everyone," I said, slumped against the hatchway door. Ilex's words struck me as pitifully inadequate, almost insane. Below us, the entire Red Company was dying. And I should have been dying with them, should almost have died upon the altar.

"*Khun!*" Valka swore in her native tongue. I pictured her hunched over a console aboard the *Ascalon*, knuckles white. "I'm almost ready here. Hurry!"

"Fast as we can," came Crim's terse reply.

The shuttle sped through a pillar of smoke black as hell, and beyond the walls of Akterumu loomed high as mountains. Really seeing them for the first time, Ilex gasped. "They built all this?" she breathed.

"They didn't build anything," I said, drawing looks even from Crim, who arched his eyebrows.

An explosion rocked the *Ibis* then, and the Norman cursed and banked left, pitching the shuttle into a dive that brought the *Tamerlane* hurtling up to meet us. Ilex staggered into me, and I caught her, braced as I was in the door. The men behind us shouted and stumbled, rattling like loose coins in a box. Crim tweaked the yoke back, leveling off a mere dozen yards from the black surface. I cannot recall ever having seen the hull from so close before. The adamant was not truly black, but the deep gray of charcoal, ridged with an almost fibrous texture. It slanted up and away to our left, a megalithic plane rising toward the darkened sky. Huge rents showed in its surface where the substance had fractured along the seams between hull segments. Each segment was itself a single molecule, thousands of feet long and hundreds wide and bonded to the battleship's carbon and titanium frame.

She was collapsing under her own weight.

Red light streamed through the alumglass canopy, and the shuttle rattled as another blast sounded.

"*Noyn jitat!*" Crim hissed. "That was close!"

"What's firing on us?"

A horrible noise flooded the air—sounded even over the shuttle's comms system—a wailing screech so high and so thin I thought it must scratch the very glass above us.

"It's the Hand," I said, and I was shocked to hear just how quiet my voice was.

As if to answer the question no one had time to ask, a thin, white shape landed on the canopy of shuttle, gripping the frame with slender hands. Membranous huge wings spread wide, filling our vision and the air. Aulamn's red eyes pierced the canopy and locked onto my face. It did not speak, but offered that horrid cry again as a short appendage flicked up over its left shoulder like the tail of scorpion. I recognized the energy-lance an instant before it fired, and shoved Ilex roughly to the ground to shield her with my body. The invisible beam struck the canopy, made it glow. It softened where the weapon beam had struck, red as the monster's eyes.

"Get it off!" I yelled, hearing the confused shouts of men in the compartment behind.

Crim jerked the yoke up and to one side, tipping the shuttle into a spin that carried us over the *Tamerlane*'s meridian and along her sloping far side, away from the carnage toward the side that faced the greater desert and the gates of Akterumu.

Aulamn braced itself, but held fast. Its eyes never left my face, not for a second. Even as the shuttle spiraled and the horizon flipped behind it, the *vayadan*-general drew back its hand—bladed finger held flat like a blade—and stabbed at the glass just above the gleaming point the beast's lance beam had made. Aulamn's hand bounced off the canopy with a metallic *ping*. Undeterred, the general punched again, and the ceramic cracked. Crim cut his spin and slammed the air brake, repulsors kicking back to bleed momentum and force the giant off.

It didn't work.

The *vayadan*-general hammered again, wielding its fingers like a mattock, forearm spiking with more force than cannon fire. "Do something!" Ilex screamed.

"I'm all ears!"

The alumglass withstood one blow, then a second. A third.

But four was one too many. Four—so the Nipponese say—is Death.

The winged general's hand smashed the ceramic canopy to flinders, and I threw my cape across Ilex to save her from the spray of shattered glass.

It was a small mercy. It spared her one final sight of Crim.

The Norman did not cry out as white fingers seized him and tore him—straps and all, from his seat. Crim—Karim Garone—did not curse or flail. His hands went to his belt, to the bandoleer that housed his countless knives. His Jaddian kaftan—striped red and white—fluttered like wings of his own as he plunged one of the vibrating blades deep into Aulamn's eye. He moved fast as any man I'd ever seen, but it wasn't fast enough. That blow, which would have felled any man or any Cielcin, would not fell the chimera. Knife still in its socket, Aulamn squeezed. Fingers tightening about his throat, Crim groaned.

"Crim! No!" Ilex shouted. It was Pallino and Elara all over again.

I had to hold Ilex down—kept my cloak over her eyes. The shuttle was starting to spin, was held aloft by its repulsors, but drifted without course, spiraling along its trajectory with what scarce remained of its momentum. An alarm beeped violently, shouting over the wind and the whine of the half-machine *thing* that grasped my dying friend and servant.

I raised my sword and moved forward, but Crim raised a hand and with his last strength shoved me toward the rear compartment. "Get her out of here!" he grunted, and as Aulamn clenched its fingers, Crim raised a hand in defiance, first and final fingers raised to curse his killer.

The devil's horns.

The *vayadan*'s fingers tightened, squeezed Crim's head from his shoulders as though he were a clay mommet in the fist of an angry boy. Flesh pulped and tore, blood ran . . . and it was only after that final moment that I understood the assassin's gesture.

It was not an alarm I heard beeping.

The charges exploded in the next instant. Three sharp bursts. Staccato. Two on Aulamn's arm, a third on its chest. When had Crim placed them? The little magnetic mines blew the Iedyr's arm apart, and the third blasted Aulamn back and out of the compartment. The shuttle jerked wildly, and I guessed it struck a wing on its way out and down.

An alarm did start then for true, and I lurched to the console—trying not to look at the pulped remains of my friend—and seized the yoke. I tried desperately to level off, but the *Ibis* was beyond help.

"Get in back!" I howled at Ilex, then to the shuttle at large, "Brace yourselves!"

We struck the hull an instant later, metal grinding on adamant with a noise almost so terrible as Aulamn's battle cry. Valka shouted in my ear, but I ignored her. There wasn't time. We were down, and I killed power to the repulsors. There was nothing to do. No brakes to be had, and to deploy the landing peds in that moment would have been worse than useless. I'd bitten my tongue on impact, and the taste of iron filled my mouth.

I spat.

"Pallino!" I said. "We need to move!"

Someone opened the side hatches in the rear compartment. I saw gray light streaming in. Dharan-Tun had begun passing away from the face of Eue's sun, and the air had a dense, chalky quality. Not hesitating to stand on ceremony we could not afford, I tugged Crim's bloodstained pistol from its holster and handed it to Ilex by the barrel. "I need you with me," I said, standing as best I could between her and her dead man.

There were tears in the dryad's amber eyes, but they had yet to fall. "He saved our lives," I said, hand shaking as I held out the gun and ashamed that she had seen it. "Let's not waste them."

Ilex reached out to take the gun. Her own hands were still, and the tears in her eyes held to their place as she said, "You could have saved him."

"What?" I blinked at her.

"You could have saved him," she said again, more sharply.

I found I was shaking my head. "I couldn't have."

"Don't bullshit me, Marlowe," she said, tearing the gun from my trembling fingers. Not *Hadrian*, I have always remembered that, but *Marlowe*. "You could have made that thing's arm break against the window or made it pass right through him . . ." she glared past me to where Crim's body lay pulped and dripping in the pilot's seat, ". . . but you didn't."

I wanted to tell her there was nothing I could have done, wanted to tell her how weak I was, how tenuous was my grasp of the vision. I wanted to tell her I hadn't had enough time, that I hadn't been fast enough—couldn't have been fast enough. But it didn't matter. None of it would have mattered. Like Pallino, she was in pain, and nothing I could have said would reach her in that dread kingdom.

So I shook my head instead. The dryad's pointed face twisted in disgust, and she turned and stormed out of the cockpit.

I lingered only long enough to tug one of Crim's knives free from his bandoleer. I am not a religious man, and even if I were, Crim was of the Jaddian faith, and I did not know what words might best convey his *fravashi* spirit to his lord of light. I bowed my head instead, and was quiet.

CHAPTER 43

THE SON OF FORTITUDE

THE MEN WERE ALREADY pouring out of the shuttle and onto the *Tamerlane*'s great expanse of hull. We must have been a mile or more above the desert, so far were we toward the *Tamerlane*'s stern, where the great mass of the engines and the drained fuel tanks swelled beneath the smooth arc of the dorsal hull. However high we were, it was high enough that a dry wind scoured the almost limitless curve of adamant beneath our feet, pulling at my long hair and cloak like dead fingers hoping to drag me back down to hell upon those black sands.

I leaped down after the men, eyes following the carbon black scar the Ibis had made upon the *Tamerlane*. For more than a thousand feet it ran, following the slope of the enormous vessel down toward the sands and the temple. Behind us, the *Tamerlane*'s bow lay crumpled and broken. Ahead, the engine clusters and the ridge towers above the line of the stern rose in human challenge to the distant, square towers of the Enar's ringed city. Looking back, I could see the dome of Miudanar's skull below, could feel the pressure of its solitary and empty eye pressing on us all.

From so privileged a vantage point, I could see the tightening red spot of our army between twin shoals of black. The Cielcin had circled round behind the rear of the human column, cutting them off from retreat. So high above the carnage, the noise of slaughter was reduced to a thin and distant wail beneath the thunder of the *Tamerlane*'s guns. But Corvo could not fire on the Pale nearest the survivors, not without killing them. She could only drive off the outermost members of the horde. I saw little knots of Cielcin hurrying out across the sands, blue and green banners snapping or hurled down.

"Where do we go, lord?" asked one of the soldiers, a square-faced young woman, bald as any of the men. She was bleeding from twin gashes on her scalp, relic of some near brush with the Pale on the sands below.

"Inside," I said, and looked about. "Pallino?"

The old chiliarch grunted as he emerged from the shuttle, red-eyed pain plain on his face. He checked the huge plasma rifle, ejected the tungsten core of the main heat sink before slotting another into place. "Should be a hatch somewhere near."

Old habit brought a finger to the contact patch behind my ear. "Corvo," I said, "are you tracking us?"

The captain's response came a second later. "You and Pal, yes. There's a service hatch about half a mile from you. Toward the stern and starboard."

"Understood," I said.

"What did she say?" Ilex asked. She had no comms unit. None of the others had, save Pallino.

"There's a way in," I said, scanning in the horizon for the right direction. I pointed with Crim's knife. "That way."

Ilex didn't wait, but turned sharply, shouting to the men. "We have to move! Come on!" Then she was gone, leading the charge across the desolate hull of the wrecked ship, a green figure in legionary black.

"There isn't much time," Corvo said in my ear. "I won't be able to keep them out of the ship for long."

I hardly heard her. I had turned my gaze outward to the gates of Akterumu. The two towers rose higher than the setting sun, half-emerged by then from behind the limn of Dharan-Tun. Beneath that umber radiance, a great cloud was rising, gray dust kicked up by the passage of a new menace.

"The hell is that?" Pallino asked, seeming to stir from the fog Elara's death had laid on him.

Not for the first time that day, I cursed my hair for keeping me from wearing my helmet. Without magnification, the cloud was just that.

"Corvo?" I said. "I think we have company."

The Norman officer swore an oath that curdled even my well-seasoned ears. Her next words painted pictures, sketches white against the black pages of my mind. Outriders on skiffs kicking up great clouds of sand, xenobites clambering into low-flying shuttles bent to intercept and join the fray, and behind them? A second horde ravening on foot to slam shut our book of souls.

The port-side guns began to fire, and the outriders and the shuttles spread out, weaving, threading Corvo's guns. Mighty as her defense was, Otavia Corvo was but one woman, and no mortal man or woman could fight so many. And yet she tried—like old Horatius at the bridge—she tried to hold back the tide of the enemy.

"Run!" someone yelled, and looking round I found that nearly all the men had fled with Ilex, were hurrying up the slope of the hull toward the engines. A mere four remained with myself and Pallino.

The old myrmidon had not moved.

"It's not far now," I said, pushing one of the men on and moving toward Pallino. "Half a mile, Corvo said. Then down to the *Ascalon*, eh?"

Pallino didn't seem to hear me. He kept looking down at the churning mass of humanity and Cielcin, at the red blood—the great spreading patch of it visible even from this height—and at the skull of the vile god presiding over all. "This is it," he said at last. "Isn't it?"

"Not yet," I said, and seized him by the shoulders.

"I used to think evil didn't exist," he said, not taking his eyes from the bloodletting. "That it was just dog-eat-dog, that everyone was a bastard just because it's bastards as get to eat." His hands tightened on the rifle slung over his shoulder. "But this . . . what can we do against this?"

Empty cup that I was, cracked and broken, I poured what little feeling I had left—what little energy—into that man who was then my oldest friend in all the universe. "Whatever we can."

"*This* is evil, Hadrian," he said, tears rising in red eyes again. "She's gone."

"I know," I said. "I'm sorry." I tried to move him, but he shook me off. Ilex's words still stung me. *You could have saved him.* They had all died because of me. Elara had died because of me. Crim had died because of me. Bastien and Halford, Koskinen and Pherrine and all the others . . . dead because of me.

"It should have been me," the myrmidon said. "Why wasn't it me?" I could not argue with him. Had I not felt the same? Asked myself the same? "How can we stop this? We can't stop this."

I had not released the fellow's arm. "We live. We fight. We die if we have to."

"But she's dead! They're all dead!"

Before I could think, my fist slammed into the side of Pallino's face. The myrmidon staggered back, cursing. He went to one knee—I was shocked and privately pleased to find such force remained in my arms. "*We* are *not* dead!" I screamed.

The old soldier blinked up at me with the eye his service had earned him, one hand on his bearded cheek.

"You're right," he said. "You're right. Shit. Where's that dumb pup from Colosso I used to know?"

"He *died*," I said pointedly, and offered Pallino my hand.

Pallino slapped my hand aside. "I can stand, you asshole."

"Then come on."

We hadn't far to go. Ilex and the others had already found the hatchway—to judge from the way they were clustered about a narrow round that swelled from the surface of the hull like the barrow of some ancient king. The mound rose gently, with a steep drop toward the *Tamerlane*'s stern that—precisely like those barrows—housed the narrow door.

"It won't open!" Ilex shouted. Five men clustered about the doorway, pried at it with their hands.

"Stand back!" I said, pushing past the men clustered about the mound. The short run had cost me dearly, and I doubled over coughing. One man steadied me as I spat phlegm upon the ground at my feet, pink with blood.

The man at my arm asked, "Are you all right, my lord?"

"Poison," I said, patting the fellow on the back as I straightened. "In the lungs." Seeing his eyes grow wide, I shook my head. "It isn't fatal." I coughed again, gestured mutely at the men standing between me and the door, my sword unkindled in my fist. They got the message and stood clear. I tightened my grip, and the blade shone forth. The hull was adamant, but the hatch was common metal. I plunged the point through the metal of the gate, felt hot air rush out from where the blade tore its hole. Fire on the inside? I leaned against the pommel, pressing down to carve a slit from lintel to threshold, then adjusted my grip to drag the blade across the bottom of the door.

That was when we heard it again, high and cold and terrible as the moons that filled the sky above. Aulamn's cry split the evening air, and high up I heard the beat of monstrous wings. Looking up, I saw the winged terror falling from heaven like the devil itself, wings tucked, clawed feet extended. Crim's explosives had not killed it, had only maimed its arm and armor. A mere hundred feet separated those talons from me, and I raised my sword in mute defiance.

A dry *boom* shook the air around us, and a burst of violet flame caught the falling titan and blasted it aside.

"Got you, you bastard!" Pallino sighted along his rifle, watched the giant fall. Aulamn struck the hull several hundred feet away with a clatter of tangled limbs. The arm wasn't all Crim's bombs had seen to, it seemed. The *vayadan* had no shield. "Had!" the chiliarch shouted. "Get that fucking door open!"

"What happened?" Valka asked, voice chiming in over the comm.

"White Hand!" was all I managed in answer, returning to my work on the door. Pallino's gun fired, and in the distance I heard the whine of engines.

Corvo's voice came in then, crackling in my ear. "Those shuttles will be on you in about two minutes. You're like a raw nerve up there!"

Why couldn't they stop talking? Why couldn't they all stop talking?

The hatch was three inches of titanium plate, and even highmatter took its time shearing through it. I pulled with all my weight, carving a notch in the top of the hatch with the sword. A heavy shot smote the air, and red blood splashed across the door and the back of my head. Another shot, and a man screamed and fell beside me, clutching a ragged mess where his legs had been. A third shot broke against my shield, and whirling I saw Aulamn had recovered its feet then, spread membranous red wings. Its remaining arm had opened like a flower, exposing a short-barreled MAG weapon. The grainy red point of a targeting laser fingered my chest, and I raised an arm to shield my face.

The tungsten ball struck my shield at several times the speed of sound, shocking the very air. Only the Royse effect saved me, meeting the shot with its own kinetic energy. The pellet shattered into powder, and my shield curtain flickered blue-white. Pallino replied, opening fire on the demon, but Aulamn leaped skyward, shot twice more. Two of the men nearest me fell, their heads bursting apart as the MAG rounds tore through them.

"Door!" Pallino shouted, sprinting toward us.

I turned back to my charge, jammed the point of the Jaddian sword back through the metal door, dragging the molecule-fine edge down through the common metal. That done, I hurled my weight upon it, but the door would not budge. Men shouted behind me, and I heard the whine of engines, sensed the shuttles were drawing near. Ilex shouted something, and I heard the *spat* of plasma fire as she and Pallino battled Aulamn on the hull at my back. Again I threw my weight against the door, felt something buckle in the old metal.

Again Pallino shouted, "Door!"

"It's stuck!" I growled, throwing my good left shoulder at the hatch.

One of the legionnaires joined me, his hands smearing blood on the bright metal. "On three, sir!" he said, counting down. On three we two threw our shoulders against the door. Something snapped behind the hatchway, and the heavy door fell inward on a lozenge-shaped airlock whose inner door opened by a lever striped yellow and black.

"We're in!" I called back to Pallino as the other man moved to open the inner door. "Move!"

By then Aulamn had landed among a knot of the others, and with a sweep of one mighty wing it cuffed three men to the ground. With one clawed and bladed foot, the *vayadan* crushed one of the fallen, carving her into neat pieces as it took aim again at Pallino. The myrmidon got a shot off faster, and a bolt of violet plasma washed over the creature, tearing a chunk from the base of its left wing. Unfeeling, the Iedyr fired its weapon, and the tungsten round struck true. Pallino cursed blue lightning and dropped his smoking rifle. Shielded though he was, the muzzle of the huge plasma gun protruded farther than the Royse curtain could protect. Aulamn's daimon-assisted mind had found its mark with laser-fine precision.

"You think you can escape *him*?" Aulamn's voice came flat and cold, wholly without the strain of any living voice, so casual it might have been speaking across the banquet table. "You think you can defy fate?" The beast looked from me to Pallino, assessing threats. Crim's knife still vibrated in its face.

A shot pinged off its head, knocked it back a step. Aulamn turned that head and found its attacker. Ilex stood not ten paces from it, Crim's gun in her hands. She was impossibly steady. Cold. Tough as old roots. She did not say a word. The general had taken Crim from her. What words were there to say?

She shot Aulamn again, and the plasma tore a hole in one crimson wing.

Aulamn rounded on her. "Miserable insect," it said. It raised its one remaining hand, the fingers clicking back into place, plates sliding to hide the MAG weapon away. With jagged motions, it reached up and plucked the dagger from its sparking eye. Ilex fired, and this time Aulamn pulled its wing across its face to weather the blow. Ilex fired again, three quick shots until the weapon hissed and ejected its heat sink. The smoking blank bounced away, and Aulamn turned, folding its wings back.

I saw Ilex's eyes go wide. She did not have another heat sink. She ought not to have pushed the gun so hard. The Iedyr made a satisfied grunting sound, arm blurring as it hurled the knife. The blade caught Ilex point-first in the eye, the left eye, the same eye Crim had put out. The force of the impact snapped her head back, and she bent back, folding like a paper castle. I let out a stunned little gasp—too late. She was dead before she hit the deck.

But she had not died in vain. The wing Aulamn had used to shield itself flapped now in tatters from its adamantine frame. This it threw from its shoulder like the cape of a matador entering the coliseum before his opening bow. One-eyed, one-winged, Aulamn of the White Hand rounded on me.

"Run!" I said to the men about me. "Get to the ship!"

"Durem ne?" Aulamn echoed. "Ship?" It snarled, staring at me across a hundred feet of open deck. "My master should have killed you years ago, *yukajji*. You are poison!"

"My lord?" the man nearest me asked, and it was only then that I recognized the ensign, Leon, who had served with me on Eikana.

Lifting my sword, I leveled its point at the *vayadan*, my torn shoulder flashing with pain. Still I held the blade in line, arm shaking from the strain. My lungs burned from the MINOS toxin that had killed the *Aetavanni*, and my head pounded where the Elusha's claws had opened my scalp. "Go!" I said, and tried to focus my vision. Years of inability marred my sight, and the pain stretched my faculties almost to breaking. Still, I saw Aulamn as through a prism, its image multiplied across the breadth of time.

One strike. One strike was I all needed. All I could manage.

One strike, as I had used to slay Hushansa's puppet on the sands of Virdi Planum. Aulamn crouched, preparing to strike. No word came to me then. No quotation. No cutting remark. A scream escaped instead—beneath language and beyond it—a roar of fury and of seven years of pain. The soldiers fled past me, clambering over the torn door and into the airlock. The first man had already opened the inner door and had gone inside. I little heeded them. My world collapsed then, narrowed into a slim corridor, a line connecting the demon and me.

Bladed talons scraping the deck, Aulamn pounced.

Roaring like the demon himself, Pallino barreled in from the side, caught Aulamn about the midsection and knocked the monster to the ground. Tall as it was, Aulamn's body was mostly ceramic, and weighed little—weighed less, in fact, than the old myrmidon. Pallino wrestled the monster to the ground, threw his weight across its body and its one remaining arm. Before the monster could reply, Pallino had drawn his own knife and plunged the tip into the tangle of pistons and cords that passed for the chimera's neck. Jerking the knife horribly, Pallino dragged the vibrating blade through wires and struts, severing them like tendon and sinew. White hydraulic fluid sprayed out, and Pallino grunted as a stream grazed his cheek and sliced it open. Still he torqued the knife, twisted until Aulamn's red eye went dark and the white armored head lolled, more than half-severed from its body. I stood there, stunned, still braced for the blow that never came, mouth open in shock and mingled awe.

Pallino had beaten the demon nearly bare-handed.

But the demon had not died.

Aulamn tore its lone remaining hand free and clocked the myrmidon on the side of his head. It was a glancing blow, and a relatively weak one due to the weight of Pallino's body on its shoulder, but it was sufficient to send the man rolling a dozen feet across the gray deck. Headless, blind, Aulamn lashed about, using its huge wingspan to sweep the space around it.

"Into the ship!" I shouted to the lone dozen or so survivors still outside. "Find Captain Corvo on the bridge and bring her to the *Ascalon!*"

"But sir!" The ensign, Leon, was still there.

"Damn your eyes, go!" I roared, inching nearer the wounded *vayadan*. "You're no use here!" I raised my sword to parry a flailing wingtip, but the thing's skeleton was adamant, and my blade was batted aside. Sensing me, blind Aulamn wheeled about and hurled its whole body in my direction. Only a desperate leap saved me from its claws, and I landed badly on my ruined shoulder and cried out. That noise brought the blind demon about, and—crawling with its one hand, feeling its way with its pinions, the torn crimson membranes of its wings fluttering in the stale breeze—Aulamn closed on me.

Again Pallino hurled himself at the monster, knife singing in his hand. Relying more on his weight than on strength alone, Pallino forced the demon down, rammed the point of his knife between the adamant plates at his enemy's shoulder and into the metal beneath. "Had, you bastard! Go!" he said, voice thick with strain.

"I won't leave you!" I said, and hewed at the exposed back of one iron knee. Aulamn kicked like a mule, a blow that caught me in the hip.

"You don't get it, do you?" the old myrmidon groaned, holding the Iedyr's chassis tight, trapping its lone arm to keep the bladed fingers from his exposed face. "It's all worthless if you die! You're the one that matters!"

Those words dealt a blow worse than the kick had, worse than any of the lashings I'd received. "I'm not leaving you!"

The Iedyr's head wobbled on its few remaining connectors. It writhed beneath Pallino's weight, scrabbling for a foothold in that smooth and barren place. Without warning, a hatch opened in its shoulder, and a short muzzle emerged, swiveled like a black eye toward Pallino. The myrmidon ducked as the shot caromed off his shield, bullet blown to splinters. The distraction was all Aulamn needed. Pallino's knife slipped, and his hold on the blind monster's arm slipped with it. The *vayadan* slammed its elbow into Pallino's chest, and he flew three yards and struck his head against the hull plates. He lay there, stunned.

Still blind and nearly headless, Aulamn thrashed about, wielding its wings liked scythes. I parried one swipe, drawing the creature's ire. One wing whipped out—I tried to parry it, but a lance of pain spiked up my arm, and I fell short. It caught me on the side of the head, and I fell, one adamantine pinion pinning me to the deck. I slashed at it, shredding a segment of the membrane, but skeleton would not cut. Holding me in place, the *vayadan* felt around with its arm, feeling for Pallino, crawling in his direction while still holding me down. When I turned my head, I could see the gauntleted hand seize my friend by the ankle.

"No!" Not again. It could not happen again! I tried to rise, but Aulamn tightened the crook of its wing, trapping me in place.

Aulamn dragged Pallino nearer, then lifted him from the ground as easily as a child lifts an unloved doll. Pallino seemed to come to all at once, and waved his arms, tried to right himself. I caught his eye then, and his brows contracted.

Then the *vayadan* slammed Pallino in the ground, slapped him against the hull as a fishmonger beats his prize against the pier. Pallino made no sound, even when Aulamn lifted him up and slapped him against the hull again. After the third time, Pallino lay still, bleeding from his head. My vision blurred again with tears, and I hammered on the pinion that held me, slicing through feet of wing membrane in my desperation to be free.

"*Suja wo!*" Aulamn said, voice coming from speakers embedded in its chest. "Enough of this!" Releasing Pallino's ankle, it felt its way up his body, seeking his head, fingers groping their unseeing way ever upward. Its torn shoulder sparked as it drew up, looming over the other man.

Pallino turned his head. He was still alive! His lips moved, mouthed words I understood sharp as anything. *Should have . . . run.*

We were alone at the last. Leon and the others had run, gone to find Corvo and bring her to Valka. How often had we two been in such straits? In Colosso and after?

One last time.

"Pallino!" I said, and did the only thing I could.

I threw away my sword.

The blade vanished in a tongue of bluish vapor as it skittered across the deck and came to rest against the other man's side. Pallino had seen it coming, and his fingers found the triggers. A second passed while the pentaquark core in the hilt cycled from one state to the next. An instant later, blue crystal sprang forth and flowed upward.

Pallino's aim was true, and Aulamn's arm fell from its shoulder and writhed upon the hull plates like a snake. Without its arm, the *vayadan* toppled, though its wing squeezed tighter, not letting me rise. I had a clear view of Pallino, however, standing with sword in hand. And then Pallino of Trieste, son of Auberno, did the single bravest thing I think I have ever seen.

He stood up.

Blood ran from the back of his head. His eyes were glassy and dull, and every fiber of him gave the impression that here was a man held together by nothing but sheer force of will. That, and pure—if righteous—rage.

"I have had . . . it up to here," he said, words slurred. He paused, spat blood upon the deck. ". . . with you damned Pale bastards." Aulamn half-righted itself and made to stand, its shoulder gun swiveling to find its target. But in doing so, the Iedyr succeeded only in offering the hole of its severed neck to Pallino's blade.

My old friend wasted no time. He slammed the point of Sir Olorin's sword downward, down along the chimera's spinal column and into the chest cavity where doubtless lay the brain. In a final, desperate act, Aulamn released me and wrapped its pinions around Pallino's hands, using what was left of its wings as surrogate arms. It had no fingers, but the adamant bars squeezed tight as pincers. I swore I heard the bones in Pallino's hands break, saw blue sparks crackle from the sword hilt.

Pallino winced, but did not blink or pull away. The sword smoked in his hands, but he gritted his teeth and drove the point in further.

Another moment passed, and it was over.

Aulamn fell dead, and Pallino sagged atop it, coughing. Free at last, I rolled him over and propped him up against the dead monster's corpse. Phosphorescent blue fluid dribbled from the severed neck, mingled with the milky hydraulic discharge. Pallino had struck true and scrambled Aulamn's brain in its armored chassis.

"Dead?" he asked, grinning with bloody teeth.

I went to one knee before him, hands on his shoulders. "Dead," I confirmed. "We haven't far to go. Can you walk?"

"Shit!" the myrmidon almost laughed. "Can't fucking stand, Had. Bastard broke damn near . . . every rib I've got, I reckon." His breathing was shallow, ragged, came in desperate gasps. "Fucked your sword," he said.

The hilt lay in his lap along with his broken hands. Azure smoke rose in lazy coils from the emitter. The wine-dark Jaddian leather was torn, and the metal beneath had more in common with a dinted rations can than a work of art. I took it from him with great care, slotted it into its hasp at my belt. "Doesn't matter."

"No wonder you think you're so good, eh?" He nodded to indicate the ruined weapon. "Shit makes it all too easy." I laughed. He laughed, and both of us descended into coughing and gasps of pain. When Pallino opened his eyes again—his pupils uneven and unfocused—he said, "The fuck they do to you?"

"About everything you can imagine," I said.

"I'm sorry," he said, and his chest burbled as he breathed. "I'm sorry."

"You don't have to be sorry," I said. "I can carry you."

"No good!" Pallino tried to shake his head, but failed. "Won't be long now."

My own head started shaking before I knew it. It was all too much, too terrible. A stale wind raked over us, carrying with it the scent of smoke and the sound of distant slaughter. Far below, the red patch of humanity had shrunk almost to naught. I realized I had not heard the thunder of the *Tamerlane*'s guns for several minutes. Where were the shuttles and the army spilling in from Akterumu's outer gates? I could not see them.

The sun had sunk very low.

"It's all right," the other man said. "Was old when we met. You gave me a second life. Only right I give it back." Another bout of coughing took him, and he cursed the pain. "You have to go."

"I won't leave you."

"You dumb-ass, pig-headed bastard," Pallino said, speaking over me. "You can't die here. Not after all you've done." Blue eyes settled on my face and seemed to find their focus. "You're too important. These things you can do . . . you kill the bastard for me, eh? Tell them I sent you."

"You tell them yourself," I said. "You're the Son of Fortitude, remember?"

"The Son of Fortitude!" Pallino snorted, regretted it at once. The man was silent for an instant, and very still, but it was only a prelude to the final stillness settling over his limbs. "I would have gone with you to the end, Had," he said. "The very end."

My fingers—five and three—tightened on his armored shoulders. "I know."

"Tell me one thing, before . . ." His words failed to silence. "Before." Pallino's head lolled backward, and I had to steady it with my own. The back of his skull felt soft. "This ain't it, right? This ain't . . . all? I mean . . ."

I knew what he meant. "It's not," I told him, breathing sharply to hold back the tears.

Absurdly, Pallino smiled. "Then I'll be . . . be seeing . . . be seeing Elara sooner than I thought. See Ghen, too, and Switch and the rest. I'll tell them, tell them Hadrian said hello." His eyes focused on some point beyond my shoulder, and his lips hardly moved. "You give them hell now," he said.

And then his eyes focused on no point at all.

Stiffly, I stood, cloak billowing about me. There was no time to build a monument or say a few words. I had lingered too long already. So late, I turned and heeded my dead friend's words: drying my eyes as best I could, I ran toward the gate and ducked into the dying *Tamerlane*.

The day and its horrors were not quite done.

CHAPTER 44

FLIGHT OF THE ASCALON

"NOT FAR," I SAID, not speaking to any of the others in particular as we hurried along the busted tramway. Stumbling, I leaned against the tunnel wall, gloves leaving bloody handprints on the raw metal. "Not far."

Most of the others had hurried on as I had ordered, had gone to retrieve Corvo from the bridge, or else gone on ahead directly to the *Ascalon* where it waited in one of the rear holds. I coughed again, both from the residual effects of the MINOS toxin and from the thin layer of smoke that filled the tunnel. Blood pounded in my ears with the strain of running, and thirst thickened my tongue.

"Forget the horse . . ." I murmured, doubtless sounding mad to the few men who'd remained—the ensign, Leon, among them. *My kingdom for a drink.*

Otavia's voice sounded in my ear, relayed through the patch in my suit's collar. "They've landed those shuttles on the dorsal hull. The ship is breached."

"Is the *Ascalon* still clear?" I asked, and spurred myself to motion.

"For now."

"I sent a few of the men to get you." My bootheels rang on the metal decking, accompanied by the dry snap of the others' bare feet. The whole hall sloped upward toward the stern, so that by every step we climbed higher. Everything was askew, canted, lending a sense of imbalance to the world.

And the world *was* off its axis.

Pallino was dead. And Ilex. And Crim. Elara, Durand, Koskinen, Pherrine, Halford . . . the whole Red Company. Dead. Gone. "What about the main force?" I asked, climbing past the opening of a cross tunnel, a juncture where the *Tamerlane*'s defunct tram network branched, traveling across the ship rather than longitudinally. Somewhere up ahead there was a guard station, one of the reinforced holdouts ship's security used. There'd be weapons there, and a new charge pack for my shield.

Corvo's words stumbled over the line. "They're . . . almost finished outside."

Almost finished. The words had an ominous ring, cover that they were on the truth: that what the Cielcin were almost finished with was the wholesale slaughter of ninety thousand human souls. Unable to help myself, I pounded my fist on the bulkhead, sending a spasm of pain lancing up my right arm. Before long, the halls of the *Tamerlane* would be lousy with Cielcin warriors, and our mad dash would become a wild hunt.

"Lord Marlowe!" Leon's voice rang back from two dozen paces ahead. "It's here!"

The guard station door was dead, and required three men to prise it open. I'd tried my sword, but the Jaddian blade only smoked and hissed, spitting sparks. Closer inspection confirmed my worst fears: the reservoir that held the blade's pentaquark highmatter had cracked in Aulamn's grasp, allowing the exotic matter to escape confinement.

The old thing was dead.

But there was no time to grieve over the loss of the weapon, just as there was no time to grieve over so much loss of life. Leon and the other survivors found phase disruptors in a wall safe and shield belts on a rack. They kitted up with shaky efficiency—two were limping badly from foot or leg injuries, and all wore a grave mask to hide the horror in their souls. I struggled to remind myself that I was not alone anymore, not alone in my suffering.

It was hard.

"Here, sir." Leon extended his arm. I looked at the phase disruptor in my left hand—I could hold it with the right, but not well—and checked the new power pack on my shield belt.

"Phase disruptor won't stop Cielcin on a single shot," I told him, and told them all. The myelin-like substance that insulated the xenobites' nerves was thicker than our own, more resistant to the disruptor's energies. "You see one, you fire until it drops." Leon and the others nodded and made curt, affirmative sounds. "All systems blue?" I asked, sweeping my eyes over the others, battered and dead-eyed. A scant dozen, maybe less.

One woman—a shaved-pate conscript with the Red Company sigil tattooed on her neck—checked her weapon and said, "Sir."

"Let's move."

We left the guard station and the tramway platform, hurried instead into an ordinary hall lit only by the red glow of emergency lighting. That light evoked memories of the dungeons of Dharan-Tun, and I felt my chest constrict. *Fear is a poison,* I told myself, but the aphorism did little to admonish my tortured nerves. *Fear is a poison.*

The smoke grew thicker as we climbed. Not far ahead, a bank of lift tubes ran the height of the great ship. Those lifts were sure to be dead. While the weapons systems still operated under emergency power, it was all but certain the fall had damaged the lift tubes and bent them beyond all hope of repair or function. We would have to climb down the access stairs, relying on maintenance corridors to reach the launch bay that housed the *Ascalon.*

Without warning, the deck beneath our feet gave way, buckled and dropped half a cubit before juddering to a halt. "Earth and Emperor!" one of the men shouted, leaping toward the wall.

"Keep moving!" I said, and led the way in stepping up onto the next segment of the hall. The whole ship was crumbling, collapsing under its own weight like some delicate sea creature cast upon the land. The metal corridor had sheared, split along a weld line, the metal tearing like paper. The low screeching of tortured alloy chased us up the hall.

Again Corvo sounded in my ear, "They're in the ship. I've locked down all the emergency doors I could, but they'll get in."

We hadn't far to go, another half mile up the corridor to the lift lobby, and then down the stairs several flights to the launch bays. "Are the others there for you yet?"

"Not yet," she answered.

"Damn them, then," I said. "You get out of there. We're nearly to the lifts."

Valka's voice chimed in, bright but tense as piano wire. "Where are you?"

"G-Level, about half a mile forward of the lifts."

"G-Level?" the dismay in Valka's voice was an almost solid thing. A thing with mass, with volume. "You're eighty-four levels up."

That news only gave me a moment's pause, and I watched Leon and the bald woman hurry past me, disruptors at the ready. I'd known it was something like that. "At least we're going down," I said, and added, "This whole place is falling apart."

"She was never meant to land," Valka replied. Then, in a quieter voice, as if to herself, she continued. "The Cielcin purged the main fuel tanks, but they missed the *Ascalon.*"

Corvo chimed in, "They must have thought it was a shuttle. Didn't look too close."

"Corvo, you need to move. You're farther from the launch bay than we are."

"I'm also faster than you," came the captain's retort. "You need to hurry. They found that hatch you cut open. How many are with you?"

I counted. "Eleven."

"Eleven?" I could almost picture Corvo's horrified face. Then she asked the next, terrible question. "Crim? Pallino?"

My eyes slid closed, but I kept moving, the motion of my screaming legs made mechanical by sheer and desperate necessity. "They didn't make it."

Both women's silence deafened me, and so I barely heard the first shots fired by the men ahead of me. But their oaths grabbed my attention.

"Earth and Emperor!"

"How'd they get ahead of us?"

"Back!" one yelled, and I recognized the voice of the bald woman. "Back!"

Their bare feet slapped on the metal flooring, and their eyes were wide as they barreled back down the hall toward me, slowing only so long as it took to half-turn and fire back up the hall. Pale faces emerged from the dark behind, white-horned Cielcin faces with eyes like the black of space, teeth flashing, black and glossy in the dim red glow of the emergency sconces. They must have cut their way through another of the hatches on the dorsal hull and found the stairs.

Now they stood between us and the *Ascalon*. Between Valka and me.

"Back!" I called along with the others, then seeing a branching ahead, said, "Left! Back to the tramway!" My breath burned in my lungs, but I ran anyway, raw flames where my legs should have been. I felt half a corpse running, and half-lost my footing rounding that corner. Hexagonal portals stood shut to either side, the doors to what once had been the cabins of junior officers. We were running toward the *Tamerlane*'s port side through the dormitory grid. Not far ahead would be a tram line that ran along the battleship's central spin, connecting the officers' quarters with the main bridge, which lay at the vessel's extreme front end. The tram line itself was almost certainly broken, snapped when the ship had crashed. But the surrounding tunnel was still intact enough—we had traveled up it to reach the guard station.

The ship's trams had not only traveled the length of the vessel, but moved vertically as well, or along sloping shafts that connected to lower decks and connected several of the *Tamerlane*'s more critical zones. If the stairs were barred to us, we might take the tramway down several layers—even without a car—and so find our way to one of the other lift carousels and another stair.

We hadn't far to go.

At the end of the side hall, I turned right. Several of the others had outpaced me, though Leon stayed ever just two or three paces ahead. A rectangular opening in the left wall led out onto another tram platform, and the foremost of our company had reached the platform's striped black and yellow edge. There he waited, disruptor raised to fire. At his back one of the cars waited, its running lights all dead.

"Onto the track!" I shouted, waving for the man to leap ahead.

He fired instead, and I heard an alien groan and—looking back over my shoulder—saw a Cielcin stagger and catch itself on the door. It couldn't have been more than thirty feet behind.

"I'll cover you," he said, then said to one of the others, "Garan, the door!" He fired again, caught the Cielcin in the face. The second shot felled the creature, and it fell to the ground, scimitar clattering.

One of the others followed the gunman's finger to the control panel that ran the great sliding door to the hall. "No!" I shouted, knowing the panel was dead. "No time!" I shoved the gunman toward the track. But the man on the door did not stop, and slammed the emergency switch. As I expected, the door did not move. It was dead, just as I'd suspected. "Go!" I slid down the steep metal slope to the electromagnetic rail, boots clattering on the corrugated flooring. Leon and the bald woman skidded down just ahead of me, along with a handful of the others. The one called Garan and the gunman were still above, and an instant later I heard the electric *hiss* of disruptor fire and more Cielcin shouting.

Not far . . . I told myself. *Not far.*

More shouting from the deck above, then a human cry, and the gunman shouting, "Garan!"

A Cielcin voice rose above the din behind. *"Bayarraa o-totajun! Bayarraa o-totajun!"*

Cut them off.

"Corvo!" I shouted, pressing fingers to my collar. "Get to the *Ascalon*! There isn't any time to waste!"

"I can still keep the main force from boarding," came the captain's firm reply.

"Otavia, run!" Valka said.

The whole ship shook under us, and distantly I heard the screech of tortured metal. The ground shook, and gouts of black smoke billowed in from a side passage up ahead, red–lit from beneath.

"This whole place is falling apart!" Leon said at my side.

Rather than reply, I said, "There should be a down shaft up ahead! Maintenance stair on the right."

"Are you sure?"

"Just move!"

All my years of solitude and slow wandering aboard the sleeping *Tamerlane* had paid for themselves. I knew I was right. The tram shaft did not penetrate all the way down to the level of the bays. We would have to find our way by a different road, but it would free us from our pursuers.

Not far . . .

The hall sloped upward, and ahead the red lights shone brighter. Perhaps two hundred paces from us, the tramway widened. The shaft! My boots clattered on the metal floor, multiplying the sound of our flight to the noise of a platoon. The dry clatter of Cielcin talons shook the hall behind.

"*Kiannaa!*" their fell voices cried. "*Kiannaa, yukajjimn-kih! Kiannaa eza ujarraa!*"

Run! Run!

Their shrill and hooting laughter spurred us on like whips, and I fired blindly over my shoulder . . . and stopped, frozen with dismay.

Black shapes appeared on the slope above us, white scimitars gleaming redly in their hands. The Cielcin formed a wall, filling the tunnel ahead.

Cut them off, they'd said.

They had.

"We have you!" their captain called. "*Svassaa!*"

"Hadrian?" Valka's voice sounded in my ear. "Hadrian, what's happening?"

I did not answer her.

It was over. All of it. All . . . over. I had lost. *We* had lost. Humanity had lost. I had dared to hope, had produced a miracle. But my sword was broken, and my hopes had proved in vain.

Lies.

The deck shook beneath us, and I turned back, saw the pursuers hurrying up the ramps to fill in behind. There was no side passage. No way out.

"Svassaa!" the Cielcin captain called. *Surrender.*

"Wemayu udim!" I shouted. A black spirit lay on me, and I spread my hands, throwing back my *irinyr* cape. "Death first!" I would not be taken alive, would not return to slavery and torment in the bowels of Dharan-Tun. I would follow Pallino, as Pallino had followed Elara. And Valka would follow me.

Valka . . .

I would never see Valka again, I knew. And she was so close. After so long, after seven years in the dungeons of the Prophet, I was minutes from her side.

It may as well have been millennia.

The captain cocked its head, and behind its white and featureless mask, I guessed it must have smiled. "Death?" it said. "You are dead already! You are ours! You are *his!"*

About me, Leon and the others shuddered and drew close, disruptors raised and primed, their slit muzzles glowing more red than the emergency lights.

"Hadrian!" Valka chimed in my ear.

"It's over," I said to her.

"What's going on?"

"I love you."

She didn't answer. I knew what she must say.

Well, you're not wrong.

I said nothing to the Pale. I would not give them a choice. I raised the disruptor, leveled its maw at the captain. It wore no pilfered shield, no spoil stolen from human victims.

I fired.

The bolt struck the captain full in the face. It went to one knee, cursing. Futile though I knew resistance was, I would not die a coward. Broken though I was, I would not die in pieces. I shot again, pulled the trigger a third time. The captain fell dead, smoking from where the disruptor had at last fried its hardened nerves. Training the gun on the next target, I ran forward, firing, meant to run straight into their line. I had no sword, and would be hacked to pieces.

But the deck beneath my feet buckled, black smoke rising all about. All froze where they stood, and about us metal screamed and bent, and the whole shaft *buckled* like rotting wood. I yelled, and heard Valka scream in my ear. The whole horrible iron labyrinth collapsed around me, blue sparks flying where wires tore. The world tumbled about me, and I caught confused snatches of men and of monsters falling all around, and of flames rushing past.

"Hadrian!" I heard Valka scream again.

I was falling, falling through open air. Pain flared as I struck the deck below with my bad shoulder, and I tumbled farther still. My last impression was of dark metal rushing up to meet me, then darkness fell like a hammer blow.

"Hadrian!" a familiar voice kept calling, bright and sharp as glass. "Hadrian Anaxander Marlowe, you bastard! Wake up!"

Anaxander, I remembered thinking. *What sort of name is Anaxander? Greek.*

It was Greek.

"Damn your purple fucking eyes, are you there?"

"Valka?"

Valka let out a relieved breath. I could almost see her eyes close, chest empty of tension and of air. "I thought you were dead."

I felt dead. My head rang, and every muscle ached as though tenderized with a wooden mallet. I was lying on the floor atop a heap of ruined metal, broken struts and torn wires and bent slabs of floor. "Where am I?"

I was alone, and reminded myself that Valka was aboard the *Ascalon.* I had to find the *Ascalon.* My arms shook as I heaved myself to my feet. Only chance had kept me from being buried. When I'd landed in this new hall, I must have rolled forward of the greater part of the crash, for looking round I saw the snarled mass of the cave in at my back, ruined metal and bodies tangled, filling up the space behind. Those few steps I'd taken toward the Cielcin army, my suicidal final charge, had—by perverse act of providence—saved my life.

"Leon?" I said, casting about for any sign of life from the others. "Leon?"

"Who's Leon?" Valka asked.

I did not answer her. It took all my concentration and every ounce of strength just to stand, just to contemplate the need to carry on. My arms trembled as I heaved myself to a kneeling position. "How long have I been out?"

"Ten minutes," she said. "Otavia said there was a cave-in."

I nodded, said nothing. Ten minutes. Not long, but long enough to know that I was reasonably safe. Were there still Cielcin about, they would have been on me long before then. I'd been lucky, in a perverse sort of way. The dense black smoke of electrical fires dotted the hill of ruined metal at my back, lit from beneath by oily red flame. The scent of burnt plastic and burning hair filled the corridor, and I choked. I took a step. My ankle lit up with pain. I tested it. It was not broken. Still, it flared with every odd step.

"They're all dead," I said, and a broken laugh escaped me then. "Every one."

"We're running out of time, Hadrian!" Valka said. "They must be all over the ship by now!"

Leaning against a damaged bulkhead, I pressed begrimed gauntlets to my eyes, hoping the pressure would relieve some of the pain splitting my head apart. Somehow, it made me cough instead, and I doubled over, tried to spit. So dehydrated was I—I had had no water since before the great march and pilgrimage of the Cielcin. Had that really only been that morning? How long were the days on that accursed planet?

"I know . . ." I managed at last. "I'm coming . . ."

A pair of dead Cielcin lay not far ahead, one crushed by a heavy beam, the other half-buried where the corridor wall buckled along the right side. From the way the soft part of the monster's skull behind and beneath the crest had caved in, I guessed the beast had died in the fall, and was glad of my recharged shield, which I felt certain had saved my life. The hilt of the inhuman warrior's scimitar stuck out from beneath it.

I had no weapon. I'd lost the phase disruptor in the fall.

Stooping, I tugged the hooked and milky blade from beneath the dead creature. Point to pommel, the blade came nearly to my chin, making it longer than any rapier or longsword, and so heavy—next to highmatter— that I knew I would need two hands to wield it. That was just as well; my right was as good as useless on its own. I used the blade as a cane instead, rested my weight against the zirconium point. The shaft should still have been just ahead, up the slope of the ruined corridor and under the snapped cross-beam where the roof above had buckled, nearly blocking the passage. The only way forward lay through a narrow wedge of space against the left side—a slit just wide enough for a man to pass.

I made a step toward it, leaning gingerly on my twisted ankle.

Something made me pause, and I looked back down at the body of the Cielcin I'd despoiled. There was something out of place. My vision and sense of balance still hazy, I sank to one knee beside the corpse—pausing long enough to prod the body with the sword to ensure it was *truly* dead.

My eyes settled on the thing that had bothered me after just a moment. There was a fine silver chain strung about its neck. That was not remarkable in itself—the Cielcin were always wearing silver—but the chain was clearly of human make, its links fashioned of fine, interlinking squares in a style wholly alien to the xenobites.

A style I knew all too well.

"No . . ." I said, raising shaking fingers to tug the chain out from beneath the fallen warrior. It wasn't possible. It simply wasn't possible. And yet . . .

Numb fingers found the pendant a moment after, and I held it in my fingers, astonishment washing over me like a wave.

White as white and whiter still the Quiet's shell shone, set neatly within its silver ring and held in place by delicate pins. I looked at it for what felt like lifetimes, stunned by the mere fact of its presence. Looking at it, I felt a deep and overriding sense of weight, of purpose, as though that chain held not a necklace, but the world. I closed my fingers about the medallion, reassuring myself that it was real.

It was.

What improbable journey had it undertaken to return to me from the hands of the slave who had taken it? Had this Cielcin taken it from the poor, aglossal bastard who had robbed me when I hung from the walls of the Dhar-Iagon? Or had it come by some road longer and stranger still?

I opened my fingers, and stared down at the shard of shell as though it were a holy relic—which I suppose it was. Syriani claimed that Utannash, the Quiet, had created our world—our entire universe. Was it not then a god, if not one begotten of its own creation? It was a relic, as was I, and looking at it then—in that place, that hell, of all places—I believed. The Quiet had placed it there that I might find it. It, *he,* had placed the sword that I might be drawn to it. He had saved me when all the others had fallen, preserved me as he had delivered me from death beneath Aranata's sword.

Clutching the relic tight, I stood, and—leaning on my pilfered sword for support—I moved on.

The shaft was where I had hoped to find it, and the stair. My boots rang on the powdered metal, and I tried not to look down. The shaft plunged some sixty levels down, and only a steel grill separated the maintenance stair from the tram shaft, and a fear of falling gripped me. It was a miracle the stair was still intact, but I was growing not to question such things. Smoke rose from side passages, vented up the shaft toward the dorsal hull.

I knew where I was. From the bottom of the shaft, I had only to follow the tramway along the spine of the ship for perhaps a quarter of a mile. There would be another platform, another security station, and beyond that a simple corridor to the original stair alongside the lift tubes with access to the launch bays, the *Ascalon*, and Valka.

The stair sawtoothed back and forth. Down a dozen steps, turn, down a dozen more. Turn. Down. Turn. Down. Again. Again. Again.

"Is Otavia with you yet?" I asked Vulka.

The captain answered herself. "I'm still on the bridge. I managed to divert emergency power to the dorsal gun, cleaned up some of those landing shuttles."

"Don't be a hero!" I said. "They're already in the ship, Corvo! Get to the . . ." I paused to catch my breath, leaned against the rail. "Get to the launch bay, now!"

Corvo hesitated. "That mob from outside is already into some of the lower holds. I can do some damage. Thin them out."

"Everyone else is dead!" I almost shouted, heard my words rebound off the walls of the tram shaft. *Dead. Dead. Dead.* Afraid I'd call the Cielcin down on myself, I hissed, "I won't lose you, too. Move, damn you!"

I could practically see Corvo shaking her head. "No good. If they get out of those holds, they'll be right between you and the ship."

"They'll be right between *you* and the ship, Corvo, if you don't move *now*." I slammed a fist against the grille separating me from the main shaft. Some twenty levels left to go.

Silence on the line. I kept moving, nearly tripping over myself in my exhaustion as I scrambled down the stairs, wielding my borrowed scimitar like a cane in my left hand. The bit of the Quiet's shell I'd shoved into a pouch at my belt for safekeeping, leaving my maimed right hand free to steady me on the rail.

"Corvo!"

I felt her jump at the harshness in my tone, even over the comm. "I'm going."

My eyes flickered shut with relief. "Good. I'll see you soon."

"Where are you?" Valka asked. I could hear the tension in her voice, edging toward panic.

"Nearly at the bottom of one of the tram down-shafts," I said. "Almost there."

I was a dead man walking, but a dead man walking across the bottom of the shaft, along the ruined tram line that ran the length of the *Tamerlane*'s spine. Somewhere behind me, Otavia Corvo was moving along just such a tunnel. The bridge lay on G-level, sixty floors above and all the way at the rear of the ship, perhaps ten miles back. At my very best, it had taken me a little over an hour to run from one end of the ship to the other. Corvo could do it faster, though how much faster was any man's guess. As I stumped along the tunnel, practically dragging the zircon sword, I was remembering the fight in the Imperial Embassy, the way Corvo had torn through the Conclave Guard with her bare hands. I willed her to move faster.

The platform was right where I expected to find it. I threw my sword up over the edge and succeeded in climbing the short ladder to retrieve it. The emergency lights flickered here, and white-hot sparks flashed from torn panels on the wall. The air stank of corruption, and old stains colored the walls. Blood, I guessed. Relics of the battle to take the *Tamerlane* at Padmurak. I saw no bodies, and could guess where they had gone.

Plasma burns marred the walls, and here and there a patch of metal or warped plastic showed where the fighting had been thickest. Huge scratches ran along the floor, and I guessed that these were the markings left by the demons of Arae, the chimeras in their haste.

"Corvo, where are you?" I asked. "I'm nearly there."

No answer.

"Corvo?"

"I'm moving as fast as I can," she said after another silence. "Keep going!"

Something in the way the old ship groaned as its struts stretched and decks collapsed reminded me of whale song. How often had I heard that baleful music in the night at Devil's Rest, carried on the winds from the great bay and the Apollan Ocean below our acropolis? I limped as quickly as my wounds would allow, the tip of my scimitar *pinging* off the deck beneath my feet. Elara's dead eyes kept flashing before my own, and the way Crim's head had sloughed off in Aulamn's fingers. The tears flowed freely, but I did not slow. I could not. Pallino's words kept pushing me, and my own words to Lorian.

You give them hell now.

Avenge us.

"Avenge us," I muttered. "I will. I will."

I dried my eyes upon my cape, trying not the think of the refuse smeared on it. The lift carousel lay dead ahead, and I could see the red-painted door that accessed the stair. The sight of it bled energy back into my flagging limbs, and I trotted toward it. The handle turned, and the bolts thudded out of alignment.

"*Iukatta!*"

I turned my head.

A solitary Cielcin stood at the end of a corridor perpendicular to the one I'd come up. Not one of Syriani's, this one wore a rubberized suit of slick gray-green, reminding me more of the primitive suits Otiolo's servants had worn on the Emesh expedition. We stared at one another for a long moment—I wasn't sure it recognized me, though it knew that I was human. The xenobite's nictitating membranes flicked once over its flat and soulless eyes. If only I'd not lost my phase disruptor. I could have shot it, simple as.

Instead, the Cielcin turned its head and shouted, "*Yukajjimn! Shuga o-yukajjimn!*"

The door banged as I shoved it fully open and tore down the stairs. These were broader, flatter, and spiraled gently where the others had zagged back and forth. I almost fell down them.

"I've been seen!" I said into the comm. "Corvo, where are you? I've been seen!"

"Just hurry!" came Valka's reply. "The reactor's primed. We can leave any time!"

The door banged open above me once again, and I heard the clatter of taloned feet on the stairs behind. I almost fell down the stairs then, caught myself on the rail with my bad hand. Cursing the pain in my ankle, I staggered on, trying desperately to keep ahead and out of sight of my pursuers. There must have been half a dozen of them, to judge by the clamor they made. Once, perhaps, I could engage six *scahari* berserkers. Shielded and armed with highmatter, they would not have proven a great challenge, but as I was? Those six were as good as the half a million who had gathered about the black temple outside. At least they had no *nahute*, or if they did, they did not use them.

The decks below G-level were numbered, not lettered, in Mandari numerals stenciled red against the gray metal, with the conventional numbers just beneath. *70. Eighty-four.*

The lever squealed as I leaned my weight upon it, and I banged my shin as I pulled the door inward. My sculpted greave saved me, and I leaped over the threshold, ungraceful as I cursed my damned limbs. As I left the stair, I fancied I caught a blur of motion on the stairs behind.

"Uimmaa o-tajun!" an inhuman voice called out. *"Kisurraa! Qita! Qita! Qita!"*

The door swung shut behind, momentarily cutting off their voices. The corridor ran left and right, the opposite wall slanting up and away from the floor, studded with trapezoidal windows.

Was it right or left?

I went left, watched the sloped windows on my right, seeing the vast armatures that housed the magnetic clamps that held the ship in its hold.

They were empty.

"Shit!"

I turned around, hurried back in the opposite direction. The door to the stairs opened, and the first of the Cielcin rushed out. I screamed, raised the scimitar in both hands and swung. No art behind that blow, not an instant of all my centuries of training. But the blade struck true, cleaved into the joint at the base of the monster's neck, and *stuck* there. Ichor black as ink spilled out, and the Cielcin buckled like wet clay.

The other Cielcin spilled into the corridor a moment after, but by then I was a hundred feet down the hall. I could see the *Ascalon* through the portals at my left, its knife-like body safely nestled in the clamp armatures. The last orange light of day filtered in from the open doors of the launch bay. I dared not even begin to guess how Valka had opened them under emergency power, but my heart soared to see them, and my limbs felt lighter as I skidded round that final corner and galloped toward the gangway.

"Valka!"

She stood in the circular mouth of the airlock, jaw set, golden eyes narrowed with resolve. My heart swelled at the sight of her, and I thought I would stumble from shock and the sheer weight of feeling that rushed to fill the hollows of my soul. Tears flooded my eyes, but for the first time that day they were tears of joy.

Valka wore no armor save a shield-belt, was dressed simply in the skin-tight underlayment every legionnaire wore beneath his kit. Her hair was long—longer than I had ever seen it—and hung at her shoulder in a thick braid.

"Look out!" I cried, looking back to see the Cielcin filling the gangway behind.

Without a word, Valka raised her Tavrosi service repeater and sighted along it, one eye drifting closed. I ducked. She fired. A wedge of violet flame split the air of the gangway with a noise like lightning. Valka fired again, and a strangled cry issued from one of my pursuers as it hit the deck. A buzzing, grinding sound filled the air then. I recognized the sound of *nahute* and hurled myself forward, keeping low as Valka fired a third time.

"Get in!" she shouted, firing again. Throwing myself against the right wall of the umbilical, I threw myself the last few feet, turned so that I hit the deck inside the *Ascalon*'s forward airlock on my left side. Valka fired thrice more, felling the last of my pursuers. Three *nahute* winged toward her, lamprey mouths spinning like sawblades. Valka raised a hand as if to catch one in her fist, and an instant later the drones fell dead and clattered to the gangway.

"Are you all right?" Valka asked, punching the button that sealed the outer door on the ruined *Tamerlane*. She only glanced at me, but for Valka that glance told all.

I lay upon the floor, gasping. "I'll live." Valka was already moving, boots clomping on the deck plates as she hurried toward the bridge. I watched her go upside-down, my chest heaving, and rolled to follow, exhausted and absurdly conscious of the blood and filth that covered me. I was shaking badly by then, muscles cramped and sore, but I found my knees and called after her. "Where's Corvo?" I looked around, half-expecting to see the tall, bronze captain standing in a doorway or to emerge from one of the supply crates and throw back a hood.

But understanding hit me an instant before Valka said, "She isn't coming."

"What?" I lurched back to my feet, chased Valka toward the bridge. "No! No, where is she?"

Valka was already clambering into the pilot's chair. "The minute I fire the main reactor, they'll know we're here," she said, keying the controls that slid the pilot's chair out on tracks in the glass geodesic that fronted the *Ascalon*. "All those little ships will be shooting at us. Otavia volunteered to stay and cover our retreat."

"She can't!" I said. Corvo had lied to me. Valka had lied to me.

"'Twas always the plan." Valka did not stop to look at me, but threw a series of switches and seized the yoke in both hands. Far behind, a faint, humming roar rose up, filling the ship and shaking the very ground on which I stood. "Strap yourself in, or find something to hang onto." There was an edge to Valka's tone, sharper even than highmatter. I identified it at once: she was holding herself together by a spider's thread of brittle rage.

Growling, I turned my back on the cockpit, pressed fingers to my collar. "Corvo, explain yourself."

Unlike before, the captain answered at once. "Easy choice to make," she said simply. "Especially when I thought I was trading my life for as many as could fit on the *Ascalon*."

"You're not!" I hissed. "It's just Valka and me."

"It's still an easy choice." She sounded almost calm. "I know what you are."

"That makes one of us." I half fell against the rounded arch of the door.

Corvo laughed. "If anyone can kill these bastards, it's you." I wanted to tell her she was wrong, but I couldn't do it. Pallino and Elara, Ilex and Crim, and all the others had given their lives in that same belief. Ninety thousand men had died in that light, for that reason. In my mind's eye, I saw the great captain leaning over the holography well, hair floating about her head like a halo, shoulders bunched like Atlas holding up the world. Clear as day in my mind, I saw her raise her eyes and say, "It was a privilege fighting for you, Hadrian."

I punched the bulkhead, punched it until my hand went numb and I thought the knuckles must break. Screwing my eyes shut, I tipped my head back, stared through eyelids at the ceiling. "The privilege was mine."

Was.

"I'll fight on," she said. "Take a few thousand of them with me. Go!"

"Hadrian, strap in!" Valka exclaimed. "We're going!"

Silent, shaking, I sank into the navigator's chair and tugged the restraints into place. Valka was just as silent. I could sense the whiteness of her knuckles beneath her gloves. The *Ascalon* thrummed beneath us, shaking dust from the rafters of the *Tamerlane*'s great hold. A series of heavy metal thuds resounded as the clamp armatures disengaged, and we were floating on repulsors.

"They heard that!" Corvo's voice played over the ship's loudspeakers. "Their air support's coming round."

"Understood," Valka said, every atom the old Tavrosi guard captain then. "We're off."

That said, Valka punched the engines. Not the slow-burn ion drives. The primary fusion torch. A torrent of red and violet flame burst from the back of the ship and engulfed us, filling the hold with fire. The *Ascalon* kicked, and even with the suppression field engaged I was slammed back into my seat as we lanced forward and up. An instant later, we'd cleared the flame and were rising, sailing above the black sand between the

Tamerlane and the outer wall. I saw the ring and the twin towers of the gates of Akterumu rising ahead. A Cielcin gunship—a lance of blackened steel, or so it seemed—flew toward us.

From below, the *Tamerlane* answered, all guns blazing. Unshielded, the Cielcin vessel blew apart, fragments showering on the sands.

"We'll never make it out past their fleet!" I said, catching sight of the gleaming false moons that filled the sky beyond the ringed city.

Valka did not blink. "We will."

One of the terawatt lasers flashed, its radiance polarized by the window glass. Still I turned my head away at the glow, watched two ships fall to pieces. Valka pulled the yoke back, tipping the interceptor almost straight up like one of the rockets of yore.

"Otavia," she said, "we're clear to jump."

"Clear to jump?" I said, aghast. "Inside the atmosphere?" Ordinarily, making the jump to warp inside a planet's atmosphere was extraordinarily dangerous. The process of warping space to form the spatial envelope that surrounded the vessel itself was hugely destructive to whatever was caught in its manifold. The curvature of space and gravity are—so the scholiasts teach us—one and the same. To bend space is to increase local gravity. Thus to make the jump to warp speed was to expose the surrounding space to extraordinary tidal stresses. For this reason, ships always accelerated beyond a planet's gravity well before the jump to warp. It was safer for those left behind.

On Eue, that hardly mattered.

Corvo's answer overrode my objection. She cleared her throat. "See it done," she said.

Valka pushed the lever forward.

The sky stretched, towers and moons alike retreating as if someone were playing a trick with the focal length of my eyes. The *Tamerlane*'s guns tore through another trio of on-rushing shuttles. They burst in glowing nimbuses, like fireworks at a triumph. I sank back into my chair, and an instant later the towers of Akterumu and the moons of the Cielcin fleet vanished, and the bruised orange sky melted away to total darkness and silence.

Neither of us moved.

We were free.

CHAPTER 45

A MAN MUST BELONG

"WATER," I SAID, SPEAKING into the stiff silence. Valka had not spoken, had not stirred from the pilot's chair in minutes. Perhaps in hours, for I felt that surely I had passed in and out of consciousness strapped in the navigator's chair. The ultramarine lights of warp coruscated beyond the forward windows, smeared and spiraling across the ship's warp envelope. I watched them a long time, sure I must have passed out again. My vision swam, and when at last I focused my eyes I saw Valka peering down at me. Gloved hands pressed a cup to my lips.

The water might have been ambrosia, and I drank greedily, the clean taste of it seeming to swell in my chest. My wounded temples throbbed. "Where?" I spluttered, coughed, spilled water all down my front. Valka pulled the cup away. "Where are we going?"

Those familiar golden eyes slid away from my face. "Nowhere," she said. "Anywhere. I set a randomized course, ten light-years out. I'm fairly confident they didn't put any kind of tracer on board, but I'm not certain yet. I want be sure."

"You won't find one," I said, leaning my head back against the seat. "Dorayaica wasn't expecting . . ." I raised my hand. "You."

"I want to be sure," she said again, standing back.

I did not like the way she looked at me, brows contracted with pity and horror both, nose wrinkled against the stink of me—which I felt sure must be hideous, but I had long since ceased to smell it. "How?" I asked at length, head still swimming. "How are you here? How did you . . . ?"

"Escape?" Valka took a step back, neither wanting to flee nor to get too close. "Survive?" She looked left, studying the instrument panels along the starboard control bank. Satisfied that all was well, she looked up. "'Twas not easy. The Lothrians had destroyed our shuttle. We hijacked a . . . an in-system freighter, managed to get to orbit, but the *Tamerlane* was already lost. I guess Durand was taken by surprise."

Stupidly, I said, "Durand's dead." I could still see him standing defiant before the altar where Elu had burned its lover's corpse, still see the way his head tumbled from his shoulders—just as my head once had done. Only Durand had not come back.

Valka looked at me as though I were headless myself. "I know," she said, and resumed her narration. "We tracked the *Tamerlane*'s telegraph. Managed to join a Lothrian convoy supplying the Cielcin fleet. Stowed away in a crater on one of those worldships. Slept in shifts for four years before we got to Dharan-Tun."

"Four years . . ." That must have been Vati's ship, the same that had carried me from Padmurak to Dharan-Tun. So it had been more than a decade since my last stand upon the bridge. "Why did you wait?"

"There were *four* of us, Hadrian," Valka said, incredulous, "against a planet full of *them*!" She turned her back. "And we were trapped. We couldn't leave our ship, not at warp."

A tiny *ah* of understanding escaped me, and I felt a fool, felt like the stupid boy I'd been when we first met in Borosevo. Highly charged particles and cosmic radiation had a tendency to catch inside the warp envelope. That was why ships relied on ray shielding and on dense hull materials—like adamant or the huge cauls of ice that coated Cielcin vessels—to protect their delicate passengers. Anyone caught on the surface in little more than an environment suit was sure to risk damage and maybe even death.

"We did everything we could," she said. "We knew we couldn't save everyone, not with the *Tamerlane* as it was. You should have seen the state of it."

"I saw some of it," I said.

Valka shrugged. "Otavia came up with the plan. She volunteered to . . . to stay behind. I'd pilot the *Ascalon*, Crim and Pallino would find you and everyone they could." She shook her head, still standing with her back to me, hands twisting about the empty water cup as though she hoped to strangle it. "We couldn't save everyone. We never could. But you? Elara? Ilex? Lorian?"

Seeing a ray of hope, I leaped at it. "Lorian's alive." Valka's shoulders drew up and together, and she flinched as though struck, but she said nothing. "At least . . . I think he might be. Dorayaica sent him away as an emissary."

"Why would it do that?" Valka asked. "Why not wait until you were dead?"

"I don't know," I wiped at my eyes. "I don't know, Valka." A dry sob shook me, and I doubled over, shaking like a peasant struck by palsy. "Maybe it just wanted Lorian out of the way. Maybe it was going to send him later. You didn't see what it was like down there. It was a charnel house, Valka. They tore our people *apart*." I tried not to think of the piles of limbs, or of poor Adric White carved upon his platter—tried not to think what fate awaited Lorian now we had escaped. Would Dorayaica send him on to the Emperor anyway and claim that I was dead? Lorian would know no different. Or would Dorayaica instead exact its vengeance on the only man of my company still alive?

Seeing me as I was, she drew nearer. She knelt and took my right hand in hers, pausing only so long as it took to set the cup aside. "'Tis all right," she said, sharp voice gone soft.

"It's not all right!" I said. "Everyone is dead! They're all dead! Pallino! Elara! Crim! Ilex and Durand! Halford, Pherrine, Koskinen . . . they carved White into pieces and served him to me at table." The shaking was getting worse, and Valka's fingers tightened over mine.

I felt her stiffen, draw back a moment later. "What did they do to your hand?" She worked at the seals that held the gauntlet in place. I did not answer her. She would discover the truth soon enough. The seals clicked and hissed faintly as she removed the vambrace and the gauntlet beneath. My flesh stank of sweat, adding a new, fresher element to the horrific odor rising from me. Valka moved slowly, as if peeling the funeral mask from the face of a corpse. She gasped when she saw my hand: the cryoburn scars, the missing fingers. *"Forfehdri . . ."* she swore, and drew the hand to her lips. "What happened?"

"I . . ." I wanted to tell her everything. About the pit, about the wall and the chains, about the peeling, the lash, the hundred depredations. But tears were shimmering in Valka's eyes already, and I shook my head. "Please help me get this armor off." I wanted to be clean, wanted nothing more in all the universe.

Nodding, Valka stood and pulled my arm over her shoulders. I winced as my bad shoulder pulled painfully, but stood all the same. "We need to clean your wounds," she said, and I could feel her gaze on my wounded scalp. "You've lost a lot of blood."

The crew showers were one deck below, beside the *Ascalon*'s dead hydroponics section. The air stank of algae and rotting fish, but the lights sprang on at our presence, and I permitted Valka to undress me. I could not stop shaking, nor still the inconstant sobs that racked me. In time, she'd removed the bloodstained armor and stinking cape. "We'll have to clean all this," she said, looking at the stains. "What did you get into?"

"Blood and shit," I said. "They threw shit at me, and bits of . . ." I could not bring myself to say *people,* but remembered the way the crowd of Cielcin had tossed scraps of the dead slaves at me like rotten produce. Nor did I tell her how my guards had forced me to drink piss and beat me. I shut my eyes, flinched as Valka relaxed the seals that held the skin-suit tight, and when she put her hands on the collar of the suit to tug it down I yelled and tumbled to the floor, a tangle of limbs and hair. How long I lay there, quaking like a leaf in storm, curled up and coughing, shoveling air and panic into my shredded lungs, I cannot say.

"Do you want me to go?" she asked at length. Dimly, I was aware that she'd been sitting with her back against the bulkhead for a long time, knees drawn to her chin.

Something in her voice uncoiled the serpent that had tightened its noose about me, and fiber by fiber I unclenched. Gingerly, I reached out with my maimed hand and touched the only part of her I could reach. Her toe. We stayed that way a long time, neither speaking. That simple contact between us spoke for me, and for us both. I was acutely aware of the foul snarl of hair that draped over my face, and in time peeled my face from the floor, leaving brownish spots where the dried blood sloughed off. Fresh blood dribbled down my face, and I struggled to tug my left arm free of the clinging, rubbery garment. It came loose, turning the suit sleeve inside out in the process, exposing the sweat-wicking surfaces beneath.

The right arm gave me more trouble. I panted, teeth clenched as the shoulder ached bright and red behind my eyes. Seeing my struggle, Valka came off the wall and helped to free me. I heard her indrawn breath. "Your back." I felt her hands on the thick scars there and shuddered.

"Seven years," I said, as though this were an answer. "Seven years."

"What did they do?" Valka asked, more rhetorically than not.

More than you can imagine, I wanted to say, but said nothing.

"Come on," she said, urging me to stand. I tripped over the raised threshold into the shower stall, landed on hands and knees with a curse.

Valka made to step in after me, but I raised a hand to stop her. "I can do it," I said, and reached up to key the controls. A shower was a monstrous luxury aboard a starship, and so in the name of conservation the jets blasted me with a fine mist while the sonic scrubbers squealed higher than human hearing. Valka sealed the door behind me, and—still on the ground—I stretched my legs out so far as they would go. Sweat and blood and filth began to run like ink from my face and hair, and the mist flattened my hair to my body.

Beneath the silence, I felt and heard the humming of the engines, and reality began to sink in, its weight and substance a smothering blanket.

I was alive. Alive . . . and free.

Was it another vision? A waking dream? Would I awake in the next instant, upside down in the pit, blood running from a gash behind my ear? "No," I whispered. A denial? A prayer? Raising my eyes, I saw my reflection in the glass of the shower door. Our eyes met, just as I had met the gaze of the other Hadrian in the cell beneath the People's Palace, just as I had met the gaze of every Hadrian in the fullness of my vision; violet and violet.

From the glass, a corpse contemplated me.

My hair: black, white-streaked like night split by lightning. My eyes: hooded, shadowed, deep-sunken, twin sparks shining as from the depth of a well. My ribs shone through skin like parchment paper, my flesh a tapestry of scars and burns ill-healed.

I had not seen myself—not truly—since Vedatharad.

I did not know me.

Movement beyond the glass drew my eye, and I refocused, found Valka looking at me, tears running silent down her face. A faint spasm tugged at the left corner of her mouth, pulled me back from the depths of myself. There were Urbaine's fingerprints. There stood Valka, and not a dream.

"I told them *everything*," I said at last. "Dorayaica tortured me, and I told it *everything*." I raised my scarred and ruinous hands to hide my face. "Perfugium. Vanaheim. Balanrot. Thielbad. Ostrannas." It was important she understand, but I knew I wasn't making sense. "Aulos. Carteia. Ibarnis. Siraganon."

"Hush, now," she said.

"Kebren," I said, and screwed my eyes shut. "Nessus."

The door cycled, and I sensed a warm, dark presence looming over me. Smoke and sandalwood, though there could not have been either. She could not have had her soaps crouched aboard a Lothrian freighter for eleven years. Was I going mad? Or were memory and affection stronger than truth?

The shower beeped, and an instant later a torrent of warm water fell on both of us as Valka knelt and embraced me. She did not speak. Did not stir. But held me fast and close and did not let me go.

I was alive. *We* were alive.

"They tore them apart, Valka," I said. "Every one of them. I couldn't save them. I couldn't . . . it's all my fault. All my fault. None of them would have been here if it hadn't been for me."

"You know 'tis not true," she said. "We were betrayed."

"But I shouldn't be alive," I said. "They should be alive. Pallino. Elara. Everyone. Not me. Not me." I opened my eyes then, held her at arm's length, heedless of the water thudding down over us both. She was still fully clad, had paused only to unseal the gloves on her skin-suit, red-black hair plastered to her face. "I'm not worth all their lives."

If Valka yet wept, her tears were lost in the flow. She put a hand on my cheek and smiled lopsidedly. Her smile had never been quite the same after Urbaine's virus, after our visit to Edda to crush the serpent in her mind. It looked almost like mine. "You mustn't think like that," she said.

Yet I could not help but think such things, and so said nothing.

When at last the filth was washed from me and Valka bathed herself, she emerged dripping on the rubber mat, strangely shrunken without her suit. She studied me a long time, where I sat naked upon the bench. After a great while, she said, "We should do something about your hair."

I looked up at her, then past her to my reflection in one of the washroom's many mirrors. The effect was worse than the shower door had been. Starker, harder to deny. Thin but ragged red lines marred the left side of my face, fresher cousins to the white stripes on back and legs. The hair in question was a heavy curtain, its own white stripes a sober reminder of the toll my torment had taken from me. I could not remember when last it had been properly clean, though it must have been when I accompanied the Lothrians and toured Everfrost Station.

So I submitted myself to Valka's scissors and her shears, and the quiet noise of them filled the deeper quiet between us. An ordinary thing, an ordinary moment against all that we had each endured. Locks of hair longer than my arm fell about me like heavy smoke, and when she was done I looked half myself again, though I fancied there was nearly so much white as black in my shortened mane.

Look how old you are, I told my reflection. I was nearly three and half centuries from the birthing vat by then, and it had been a hard road. All the same, I allowed myself to be lulled by Valka's sober presence, by her altered smile and the careful touch of her dry, smooth fingers as she applied beta gels and corrective tapes.

I cannot remember sleeping, nor indeed remember much of those first days. I think I slept the greater part of them. Weeks, I think. Perhaps a month. Dim memories are all that remain. Meals. Sleep. Valka's arms about me in the night. The steady drone of the engines. I can remember Valka cursing in her native Panthai as she mucked about the ruined hydroponics section, packing cartons of rotten plant matter and fish bones to follow my hair out the vacuum disposal. I remember fussing over my armor, dismantling it and scrubbing the individual components.

But all of it, I remember as through a haze.

Days later, or weeks, Valka found me in the utility room beside hydroponics, contemplating the disposal tube. The lights above shone stark and white, almost loud in the quiet of the lonely ship.

"What are you doing?"

The *irinyr* cloak lay cleaned and folded on the counter beside the vacuum tube's aperture. I had been thinking of throwing the inhuman thing into the tube and blasting it into space, but I could not quite make myself do it. All my life I had amassed such relics, trappings of my life. I could not decide if the cloak should join them, or if it should be cast into the darkness.

"Just thinking," I said. "It's quiet in here. You can't really hear the drives." I looked round, uncrossed my arms. A few of the crates we'd packed from Maddalo House had remained aboard the *Ascalon*, by some miracle, and so I wore my own tunic and trousers.

Valka pursed her lips in thought. "I hadn't noticed."

"I spent a lot of time in a cave," I said—I had told her everything. "You don't realize how loud everything is until it's gone." I had known true silence—and true darkness—for so long that the gray solitude of the *Ascalon* was almost too much. "Are you all right?"

She was holding a rag, I realized, was polishing her hands absently. "Fine. I've got clean water in hydroponics at last. New algae cultures should be in full bloom in a day or two."

"That's good," I said, hugging myself. New algae meant clean air.

"I think some of the seeds are still good. I'll need your help getting them going."

"Of course."

Valka stopped rubbing her hands. "I wish I could help you," she said.

"I know."

"I miss them, too," she said. I shut my eyes, blotting out the cloak and the disposal tube and the choice—for the moment—with them. "We're coming up on reversion in a couple of days."

It was the third randomized jump she'd taken us on in the weeks since we'd escaped Eue. We'd swept the ship for beacons, and after the second jump, we'd even suited up to check the exterior. Found nothing.

"We need a destination."

I did not even hesitate. "Colchis," I said, and turned fully to face Valka, opening my eyes. "Siran's on Colchis. She's the only one still . . . still . . ." I could not get the word out. The weight of too many ghosts sat on my chest. "She's the only one left."

The pity—the terrible pity—sharpened once more in Valka's eyes. I realized my mistake the instant before she spoke it into being. "Hadrian, we've been gone from Colchis for *centuries*. For more than four hundred years. Siran is . . . long dead. You know that, yes?"

I was nodding then, as if the movement of my head might dull her words, might stop me hearing them. Some part of me had known the truth, even as the words escaped my lips. *Siran is long dead.* Still, my tongue felt thick and useless in my mouth. At length, I croaked, "I know. I should have known." Then something in Valka's voice clicked into place for me, and I said, "I'm not mad, Valka."

Silence fell so deeply then that I could hear the faint thrum of the drives, not silenced after all. Valka did not speak. The both of us just stood there together, alone in the silence.

"I wasn't thinking," I said, trying to explain. I had been so long without time, so long in the cave and the pits, that I had forgotten how swift was its flight.

May Time, Ever-Fleeting, forgive us . . .

"We're not the only ones left," Valka said, and tried to smile in her way. I could hear it in her voice, risked a glance her way. "You said they sent Lorian to Nessus." Those golden eyes slid across my face. How old she looked then! As old as I felt, her braid frayed by the day's labor, eyes sunken with care and strain.

"I only *think* they sent Lorian to Nessus," I said, and held my maimed hand to my face, mouth hanging open between thoughts. "After the battle? I don't know. He could be dead, too."

"I wouldn't bet against him," Valka said.

"I still want to go to Colchis," I said, speaking over Lorian's ghost. "If only to find Siran's . . . grave. And Gibson's." I did not say that Gibson would not have a grave. The scholiasts burned their dead and scattered the ashes on the wind. But he was surely dead himself, who had been ancient when I was young—and I was ancient then. That we had met at all on Colchis was a fluke of cosmic justice, a chance thin and sharp as highmatter. But I could not stand the thought of grieving alone. Colchis was the closest place to home in all the human universe, for Gibson, and Siran, and the Red Company *were* home, and that home was lost forever.

Alone.

But I was not alone, not truly. Valka was with me. But Valka was as much a part of me—and I of her. A man needs more. A man must have a people, must *belong* somewhere. To someone. A man must have a family, born, chosen, or made.

I needed mine.

But they were gone.

"Colchis, then," Valka agreed.

It was as good a place as any. We would have to return to the Imperium, have to sound the alarm. Doryaica had sent Lorian to herald its coming, to proclaim its dominion over all the armies of the Pale. *If* Lorian reached Nessus, it would be with those tidings, and more: he would proclaim that Valka and I were dead. And what of the Commonwealth? Did Lorian know of their betrayal? He must guess, surely. But he had been aboard the *Tamerlane*. Had he even been conscious when Vati and its troops attacked?

We *had* to return.

"Do you know how long the journey will be?"

CHAPTER 46

TO COLCHIS

"HOW LONG WILL IT take?" I asked.

Valka's words hung in the bridge's air like fading thunder. I knew I could not have heard her properly. The silent stars hung in blackness beyond the *Ascalon*'s forward windows. We had come out of warp while we slept, alone in the dead Dark light-years from any star, safely lost. Valka had spent the better part of an hour working the navigation system, getting our bearings and charting a course to Colchis.

"Twenty-eight years, five months, thirteen days," she said, hands between her knees.

Perfectly precise. The machine in her brain had answered for her, I did not doubt, and held her glowing eyes with mine. The revelation moved me to near-catatonic stillness. I should not have been surprised by the figure—wherever Eue was in all the black galaxy, it could not have been near to any human world. Whatever journey we might make was bound to be a long one, but to hear the figure spoken plain, stated so flatly by the iron part of Valka's brain, was a kind of horror and fresh torment.

Twenty-eight years.

A lifetime for many, and four times the time I languished in the dungeons of Dharan-Tun.

Twenty-eight years alone, just the two of us, in that metal prison of a ship.

After a stretched minute, I found my tongue. "Can we make it?"

Valka thought about her answer for several seconds—never a good sign. Her neural lace processed faster, far faster—if less flexibly—than her ordinary neurons. She was seldom slow to reply, save when tact checked her tongue, and that was rare enough. "We have the fuel," she said. "Containment held all those years, and Corvo kept her full. Some of the comms are damaged—in the escape, maybe. The tightbeam maser's gone. I'm not sure about the radio. Couple of the antenna clusters got knocked off."

"So no datanet access?"

"'Twould do us little good in any case," Valka said. "We're so far out, the nearest datanet relay must be a thousand light-years out, maybe more." She turned the navigator's seat, fiddled with the starboard-side console a moment. "We could telegraph the Imperium. The QET's undamaged. They might have a scout ship somewhere not far. We could sit and wait for—"

"No!" The vehemence in my tone surprised even me, and raised Valka's eyebrows. I put a hand on the circular arch that led back into the ship's main cabin, fingers gripping the padded wall. I could feel my heart pounding in my chest. Why should I be so afraid? Valka did not interrupt, waited me out instead. I was a while finding my words. "If we wave the Empire, they'll never let us go to Colchis."

The wooded halls and dark greenery of Maddalo House rose up in my mind, the wind in the pencil cypresses whistling as through the bars in the door of my cell. With my maimed hand, I tugged the knit blanket I'd draped over my shoulders tight about myself. *Another prison,* I thought. "Just another prison."

Valka seemed to understand. "'Tis the rations I'm worried about," she said, and massaged her temples with long fingers.

I shuffled onto the bridge, lowered myself into the copilot's seat opposite her, turned the bucket to face her across the empty space beneath the black bubble of the holography well embedded in the ceiling.

"We have enough *bromos* protein to get us through . . . about half that time. Some of the bars went bad, but the bouillon . . ."

"Will outlast the stars, yes." I drew one knee to my chin, gasping as the taut muscles cried out at the stretch. I did not fancy the prospect of boiling protein paste with salt water and seaweed from hydroponics for years and decades, but I didn't see that we had any other choice. Even if we did telegraph the Imperium, there was no guarantee they could reach us in any reasonable amount of time. It behooved us to make for Imperial space in any case. "What about hydroponics?"

"You saw what 'tis like," Valka answered. "We'll have to purge the beds. Everything's rotten. Some of the seed banks are still good. We can salvage it. Some of it."

"But the algae's good?"

"We're not running out of air if that's what you mean," Valka said. "Those systems run themselves, more or less. But they should be cleaned, and we'll need to replant the vegetable beds. I can't do it all alone."

My ruined hands twisted in my lap, scars shining in the console light. I did not answer her, but turned to look out the window.

What good was I? I asked myself, flexing my back until my shoulder squealed white fire. If the pale stars beyond the glass had an answer, it was in some language strange to me. The pain was a kind of answer, a brutal, wordless one.

No good. No use.

The thin sound of exhalation escaped Valka's nose then, and she said, "I need your help, Hadrian."

"I know." I shut my eyes to drown out the pitiless stars. That was a mistake, for without the stars to distract my mind, I saw once more the plain of Akterumu all too clearly, felt the torn bodies and chewed limbs of my men give beneath me as I struggled to rise from the charnel heap at the base of the temple stairs. Syriani Dorayaica—the Shiomu-Elusha—loomed over me, its face painted silver with its own blood, its glass teeth bared in a rictus of inhuman delight. Shaking myself, I opened my eyes. "I know."

I had wallowed long enough. Too long. For all that I had suffered, I had not died. Quiet though the ship was, it was not the quiet of the tomb. I was alive, and Valka was alive, and living meant *work*. The *Ascalon* might run with only one man awake to maintain her, but that was when she was in top working order—and a crew of at least three was preferable even at the best of times.

Ours were not the best of times. Valka needed me. The algae tanks needed to be flushed, she'd said, and the food beds replanted. No doubt there were other troubles aboard our long-neglected vessel. The *Ascalon* had languished in the *Tamerlane*'s holds for eleven years, forgotten for the entire journey from Padmurak to Eue. It was a miracle the damn thing had flown at all.

"Hadrian?"

I blinked around at Valka, found her standing over me, looking down at me with such pity in her yellow eyes I could hardly stand it. I did not want her pity. I wanted never to have needed her pity. "I know," I said a third time, and looked away.

She caught my maimed hand and raised it to her lips.

"Eleven years," she breathed, not letting go. Again she kissed my fingers, pressed my palm to her face. "It took eleven years to get you back. I *need* you now."

Were those tears?

I brushed them away with my thumb. Though she had not suffered the pits and the lash as I had, she had suffered. I tried to imagine what it must have been like, trapped in some Lothrian starship, her and Corvo, Pallino and Crim—sleeping in shifts, praying the Cielcin would not find them, unable to move with their ships at warp.

"I need you, too," I said, and smiled that broken—twice broken—Marlowe smile.

She gripped my ruined hand, and leaning down kissed my brow. I wrapped my arms around her, and there we remained a countless moment.

"I should set course," she mumbled. "If we're going to go, there's no sense waiting. 'Tis a long way to Colchis."

Aching, I let her go, watched her swing back into the navigator's seat. As she tapped at the controls, I pulled myself to my feet and crossed the short distance between us, steadied myself against the back of her seat. "Where are we, exactly?"

Voice husky with emotion, Valka replied, "About fifteen thousand light-years north-northwest of the core, as far up the Sagittarius as it gets."

"North of the Commonwealth," I said. We were well beyond the limits of human-settled space then, at the headwaters of the Sagittarius Arm, at the joint where its spiral met the throbbing heart of our galaxy. We would have to cross back through Lothrian space and the Rasan Belt to reach the Upper Sagittarius and the nearest Imperial frontier.

"More than twenty-five kilolights," Valka said. "This ship'll do just over a thousand C, but 'tis a long way." She continued ministering to the controls.

"Sagittarius . . ." I rolled the word on my tongue, shook my head. Human civilization had expanded to fill most of the southern half of the galaxy, had pressed forward until the Cielcin pressed back, pushing at us from the east in the Norman Expanse—which was lost and overrun. But the arm of Sagittarius spiraled west around the core—whose stars and dark stars are too numerous and close to risk warp travel through. My fingers tightened on the back of Valka's chair as I imagined the new-made Prophet-King's legions pouring around the core of the galaxy east and west to pincer all mankind. "They must control half the galaxy."

Valka stopped keying in our course. "They don't control anything. You know that. They just go where they please. Our ships and colonies must have been passing them in the Dark for centuries before Cressgard. Space is big, Hadrian."

I knew she was right. Have I not said the map of the human universe is one filled with inner edges? Though our worlds are strung across half the galactic volume, we could never claim every star—only those worlds kind or kind enough to human life were ours, and certain places we could not do without: trade posts along strategic routes, lifeless systems rich in mineral wealth. The Cielcin might cover half the galaxy, but they did so with as thin a blanket as we. Perhaps thinner.

"That doesn't change what's coming," I said, darkly. "Did you see how many ships there were in orbit above Eue? There must be *thousands*—tens of *thousands*! How many trillion Cielcin do you think there are?"

"I don't know," Valka said, sitting very still.

After a moment's silence, she stiffly stood and brushed past me for the copilot's seat, leaned over the console, her braid hanging from her shoulder—another reminder of the long years she'd spent herself in solitude. I heard the ticking of switches. "They'll come for Forum, if they can. If they have the coordinates. Avalon. Nessus. Goddodin. Earth, if they're able." At the thought of Earth burned again, annihilated by those demons, I choked, pulled my blanket hard about my shoulders. I was not a religious man, but the thought was still a blow and a blasphemy.

Distantly, I felt the warp core thrum to life, felt it through my feet and in the way the air seemed suddenly charged. It was always strange watching a ship prepare for warp. We were not moving, unless it was to drift across the trackless void. The sublight engines did not fire—they did not have to. It it is not the ship that moves at warp, but the space around it, an envelope of night against the night. We would go from still darkness one moment, to violet lambency the next.

Valka ignored my words—or perhaps she only had no reply for them. "You'll want to hold onto something. There may be a shock." The suppression field ought to minimize any shock from the jump to warp, but she was right. I resumed my seat in the copilot's chair. We were both silent then as Valka finalized the sequence that would take us to warp. Far behind us, at the very rear of the slim vessel, an oscillating hum intensified. I gripped the stumps of my missing fingers, bowed my head, and waited.

How many times had I stood upon the *Tamerlane*'s bridge and listened as Koskinen and White prepared for warp? As Corvo and Durand barked their orders, and Lorian and Pherrine relayed their information?

The memory of Corvo's last words on the comm echoed in my mind.

See it done.

Valka's hand gripped the yoke then—course set—and pressed it forward. The *Ascalon* whined, and for a moment I imagined we rode upon the point of an arrow loosed across the stars. Numberless sparks turned to smears, turned from white to azure, from azure to indigo. To violet.

We were on our way.

CHAPTER 47

THE LONG DARK

THOSE FIRST DAYS OF our journey to Colchis passed in a gray haze. Until that point, Valka had been content to leave me be, and I had sat— swaddled in my blanket—upon the empty bridge or in the cargo hold, listening to the drives or watching the stars twist and stretch across infinity. I had been as one dead, as though I were not aboard the *Ascalon* at all, but Charon's ferry, slouching not to Colchis, but to the afterlife.

But Valka was right, we were not dead, and at her patient insistence throughout the days that followed, I dragged myself after her, forced myself to dress and to set about helping her to repair our critical systems.

We hardly spoke in all that time. Despite all our years apart, there was nothing to say, and each of us had been so long in isolation that neither knew how to speak to the other. But we did not need to. There are older, deeper languages than language, and love has little need of words. It was enough that she was there, and would not let me be alone.

With the algae vats purged and running properly and most of the rotten plant matter and dead fish gone from the aquaculture systems, it was only a matter of time to rewater and replant the beds, and it was not long after that the foul smell of the air abated. Through it all, Valka moved with a quiet, diligent efficiency. It had been easy, for so long, to forget that she had been a sailor once. So easy to forget that she had fled her home on Edda not once, but twice: once when they tried to *cure* her of Urbaine's virus, and once so long ago, when she had used the credit she accrued from her military service to buy passage from the Demarchy to see the galaxy and the ruins she so loved.

Old natures, it seemed, died hard.

"You know we can't both go under the ice," Valka said, putting her foot within striking distance of the issue coiled between us. "The ship won't fly itself—and even if it could, hydroponics would be right back to where we started, and worse."

I said nothing. I had known this conversation was coming—had been coming for days . . . or was it weeks? But I hadn't wanted to face it. There was only one reasonable outcome, and I was not yet ready to be alone.

Irked by my silence, Valka's voice sharpened, and she said, "We could put in somewhere nearer. Resupply. Once we cross the Rasan Belt, there must be some outpost where we could—"

"No!" I said, turning from the crate row of squash seedlings beneath their heat lamps, surprising myself with the vehemence in my voice. "Valka, the minute we're flagged on Imperial systems, they'll impound us. We can't hit a fuel depot, or put into port to take on a couple spacers—and we couldn't pay them, anyway. We'll never get to Colchis."

Valka looked up from the test kit she'd been using to check the minerality of the water beds, brows knitting. She held the testing rod frozen in two fingers, as if she'd forgotten her arm. "Why do you want to go to Colchis so badly?" she asked. "Hadrian, Siran is dead. Gibson is dead. You know that."

"I know that," I agreed, unable to mask the bitterness in my voice. "It's just . . ." My mouth had gone dry, and I had to screw my eyes shut to find the words again. "We have to get back to Nessus eventually. Or to Forum. But we can't go there directly. They're too far away. We have to go somewhere, and that may as well be Colchis." I wiped my hands on the gray rag I'd hung over the lip of the bed, pushed myself back on my rolling seat, and listened to the misting armatures hiss for a minute. "If we put in at the nearest outpost—wherever that is—there's no telling who'll come for us: it *might* be the Emperor's men, if we're lucky. And whatever happens, Legion Intelligence will want its way with us. But it might be the Inquisition."

Valka let her hand fall. "I didn't think of that."

"If we go to Colchis, we can control how we make contact. We can use the athenaeum, make it official. That way the Chantry can't make us . . . disappear." I smiled to keep the memory of the Chantry's assassin on Thermon from my mind. "And the *Ascalon* can bypass orbital defense and find . . . whatever's left of Siran."

"Her grave, you mean?"

"Of course I mean her grave!" I said. "Do you have to make me say it?"

I bit my tongue to stop the bitterness from catching. In a voice crushed to smallness, I carried on. "But she's the only one who has one. The only one I can visit. I *have* to do that first. Then we'll go to the athenaeum and hand ourselves over to the Imperium."

I hung my head and said no more. Perhaps Valka was right to worry about me. Maybe I had gone mad, but some part of me felt that I would find her there, and Gibson. Nearly five hundred years had passed since we left Colchis on our fateful voyage to Annica, but Colchis was another world, and it seemed to me that I should have left it standing still when I departed. After all, I had found Gibson there once centuries after I thought he must have died. My father's vindictive nature alone had ensured that meeting. He had shipped Gibson to Colchis among the freight, on the slowest ship he could find. Thus it is in the nature of things that ugliness and evil bend to good in time. Gibson had arrived on Colchis a mere handful of years before I, and so we had been allowed our reunion. We would not be allowed another.

I knew that.

I had left a letter for him when we journeyed past Colchis on our way to Padmurak. There had been no reply, would be no reply. And yet I knew that to stand in the grottoes beneath the Great Library and to walk those halls once more would do me good. Simply to walk where Gibson had walked, and to return and tarry once again upon the sands of Thessa, was in a sense to return to that earlier time. How I longed to swim in those waters where once—however briefly—I had been happy and free. Still some part of me knew that what I really longed for was to hear once more the shouts and laughter of my men, and to feel that sense of family that is what we truly call *home*.

And I knew also that I would never feel it. Not ever again.

"You should be the one to sleep," Valka said, meaning fugue. "Your injuries . . . you need to recover."

I shook my head violently, rebelling against the pity in her tone. "We both know I can't do that on ice. I need time to . . . to take care of myself." My left hand gripped my ruined shoulder. No amount of exercise would set the joint to rights. I needed a doctor. We both knew it.

"You *need* to rest," Valka said, putting her tools down, the better to survey me across the water bed between us. "When we get to Colchis, they can do something for your poor hand and the . . . the rest of it."

Suddenly self-conscious, I turned my slashed face away, all too aware of the corrective tape she had laid over the marks of Syriani's talons. I could half-see them in the polished white of the hydroponics room: black seams on pale flesh, like the solder in Jinan's shattered water basin.

"You should be the one to go under," I said. "Nothing is going to happen to us. We're safe at warp. I can watch the ship."

"Can you?" There was no venom in Valka's voice—only doubt—and that was the far more terrible thing.

I cursed myself in that moment. My weakness. A shadow had crawled up from the pits of Dharan-Tun, a shadow and worm that wore my name. I had spent those first weeks of our voyage shattered and worthless. Forgivable? Perhaps. Understandable? Certainly. But misery was a thing we could ill afford. I sucked in a deep breath, nodding all the while, and felt as I felt the holograph image of a crumbling statue must feel when played in reverse, my every part and particle struggling to force itself back together. "I don't like the thought of leaving you alone," I said. It took every ounce of self-control I had not to glance at her left hand, remembering the way it had squeezed her throat under the sway of Urbaine's worm. I could not leave her to watch the ship alone, and besides . . . Valka was a clansman of Tavros. She did not have twenty-eight years to waste.

I was palatine—*am* palatine.

I had twenty-eight years to give. For her.

"I can do it," I said.

"You're not a sailor, Hadrian," she said, looking at me with sorrow in her sharp and lovely face.

"And you don't have the time," I said. "Twenty-eight years is a long time."

"'Tis too long for anyone to spend alone," she replied. "You can't seriously be proposing that I leave you here by yourself." She gestured round at the *Ascalon*. "I'm not so old as that yet. We Tavrosi don't live so long as you palatines, but I have time. We have the supplies for a few years, at least."

I seized the damp, gray towel to have something to do with my hands, squeezed it in my fists until my hands ached, and chewed my tongue. "A few years, fine. No one has to go under the ice yet. But when someone does, you and I both know it should be you."

For once, she did not argue. "We need to get the ship back in full working order," she said after another long pause, all business. But in a soft voice—more to herself than to me—she whispered, "We can do this. We can do this."

Thus the first years of our journey passed by. With the ship at warp, we busied ourselves repairing hydroponics and seeing to the growth of the vegetables meant to supplement our steady diet of porridge made from rehydrated bromos bouillon. I knew next to nothing of aquaculture, and so relied on Valka—whose mind, naturally, contained volumes on the subject encoded in her neural lace. But I learned steadily, and she learned, too—for the knowledge she held was no more a part of her than a book at my disposal was a part of me. Often she'd described it to me like a library, a psychic palace of near infinite, interlocking rooms through which she moved—knowing always the contents of each chamber as she entered.

The scholiasts employed a similar technique—without the use of machines such as those Valka employed—to ensure that they forgot nothing. It was said that a master scholiast could perform as well as such machines, but it took a man a lifetime to master such techniques. Valka been born with such mastery. It had been built into her. And though even after all our years her powers frightened me, I thanked whatever gods there are— the Quiet, I guessed—for them. And for her.

It was months before the first harvest was ready, and we feasted such as we could: on squash and onions, potatoes, tomatoes, and beans to complement the omnipresent porridge. There were even herbs in seed storage: rosemary, sage, and thyme, and so it seemed a feast indeed, despite the lack of meat. In truth, I did not long for it, who had so often eaten raw fish in the lake of my cell and whatever foul, stinking flesh—I dared not guess what kind—that my guards had fed me when the ration bars ran out.

I am ashamed to say I wept at the first bite, though in my heart I dreamed of bread and cheese and wine. Still, it was a return to civilization, to the human world.

But we had not yet come to civilization. Valka and I were alone, and many were the days—gray and numberless—that I dreamed of music, of crowded streets, and the wind through the trees of the English Garden at Maddalo House. How much less a prison it seemed than that cold and quiet ship.

And yet it was not so bad as that, for though Valka and I were alone— we were alone together. I have said before that in love the universe contracts, its horizons shrinking until you and the other fill the universe entire. For Valka and me, then, it was almost literally true. As we had come together in the dungeons of Vorgossos, shivering in the dark and cold, so we faced the long night of that voyage together.

Years passed, and as they passed the memory of Akterumu and Dharan-Tun retreated a pace. The scars on my face and body dulled from red fire to dull embers to white ash, and though still my shoulder pained me and my missing fingers woke me burning in the night, I found I lived each day better than the last. I never would be like I was—even if we reached the Imperium, even if they mended my shoulder and regenerated my hand—I knew a part of me would forever lie on black sands beneath the Dreamer's hollow eye.

There are endings, Reader, for all things.

And before long, one such ending came.

"I don't like this," Valka said for what seemed the thousandth time.

It was not yet cold in the cubiculum. Not a one of the ship's forty fugue creches was active—that was the worst part. Each one belonged to a man we might have saved. Corvo might have slept in the one to Valka's left, Pallino and Crim further down. Ilex and Elara and young Leon might have joined us—and the men whose names I did not know who had survived Aulamn's attack and made it to the *Tamerlane*.

Each stood empty, instead.

"I know," I said. "I'll be all right. I promise."

Valka did not answer, but turned away, bent to examine the connections that fitted her creche to the coolant supply and circulation system, a job that—properly—should have been the role of a fugue technician, but we had none. It was no great matter. Of all the systems on board a starship, the ones that ran the fugue creches were the most automated, the most insulated from error.

Presently, she straightened, turned to look me in the face. "I still think we could take it in shifts. The TX-9 supply is low, but there should be enough to run a fresh creche once or twice."

"I know that, too," I said, using an old scholiast technique to clamp down on my breathing. "Let's get you ready."

"We can wait another day," Valka said, not moving to undress herself.

"We've been saying that for weeks." I tucked my chin, crossed my arms, studied the polished floor between us and the pointed toes of Valka's boots. "It's time."

She sniffed, and though I did not look up I knew she nodded. "All right." Risking a glance, I caught her staring up at the ceiling, at the lamp crawling along its track at the vertex of the arched ceiling. We were on the *Ascalon's* highest level, right below the dorsal hull, and the weight of all the emptiness and of the whorling stars beyond oppressed my mind. She didn't move, and in her stillness I recognized the hollow ache of a woman fighting tears.

"I can't help but feel like you won't . . . won't be here when I wake up," she said at last, and sniffed again, pressing her eyes shut.

I went to her, crushed her to me, and gritted my teeth as my torn shoulder wailed. "I'm not going anywhere. I'll be right here."

Her hands came up, held me with the delicateness of disbelief. "Promise me," she murmured, breath on my neck, "promise me you'll wake me. When you have to."

"*If* I have to."

"I know what I said."

Letting her go, I stepped back, did my best to smile. "I will," I said, knowing I would not. As Valka had said, our supply of cryonic fluid was low. Corvo had not kept the *Ascalon* supplied during the voyage to Padmurak. There had been no cause for it, and what little maintenance the *Tamerlane's* crew had performed on the lesser vessel, it had been just that: maintenance.

Valka let out a ragged sigh, clenched her jaw as she pulled her shirt up over her head. She was naked beneath, and I caught myself remembering the first time I'd undressed for the freeze aboard Demetri's *Eurynasir.* How cold it had been, and how unforgiving the universe. We had been six years sailing from Eue by then. There were twenty-two to go.

"I'll take the clothes," I said, watching Valka lean against the console to tug her boots free. She didn't answer except to toss the boots onto the floor with her striped shirt.

Before long she wore nothing at all. Nothing save the tarnished half-moon pendant that hung about her neck on its fine silver chain. The black lines of her clan *saylash* drank the light, so black was it against her skin, the dense fractal lines spiraling up her arm and down her flank to one swelling hip. She looked so small in the stark light of the cubiculum—but then, I guessed we all did in our turn. She raised her left hand to the medallion and tugged it free, then proffered it to me, holding it by the chain.

"Watch this for me," she said, letting it drop into my palm.

An absurd thrill of shame washed through me then. My own

phylactery—the one containing Valka's cells—remained in Maddalo House where I had left it. I closed my fingers round the metal before putting the thing safely into a pocket of my tunic.

"I'll keep it safe," I said, doing my best to smile. "And you."

Hands behind her back, she crossed the short space between us, raised herself on her toes to kiss me on the cheek. "I mean it," she said. "You wake me when 'tis time." She drew back a step, squinted up at me. "I don't want you playing the hero anymore."

"No more playing," I said, and to this day I cannot tell you how I meant it.

She kissed me properly then, and when we were done, she drew back and turned to step into the creche. I watched her a long moment, then stepped in to help her with the blood line and the cuffs to keep her in place. Urbaine's worm would not threaten her in the deep dream beneath the ice, and that—at least—was a comfort. I'm sure some other word or honest nothing passed between us, some idle phrase mouthed a million times in darkness or in day. But when all was done I drew back and pressed the controls to drop the lid. Metal and glass shut like a blossom at the end of day, and I hit the switch on the console to start the process.

She was asleep before the cryonic fluid filled the tank.

And I was as alone as I had ever been.

Wake me. When you have to.

In the end, I never did. Not after five years, nor ten, nor twenty—though I needed her back at once. I escaped the kingdoms of death and returned to that great empire of silence, and in silence lived for years. Routine made me sane again—at first. Then solitude drove me mad. We are not meant to live alone, and many were the days I spent in the dark cold of the cubiculum, regarding Valka's sleeping face through the glass of her creche, like the prince in those oldest tales, finding his princess in death.

How peaceful she seemed to me, so nearly dead. She had come so far, through so much.

For me.

Not for the first time—nor for the last—I endeavored to put my life to paper. Lacking parchment and pen, I wrote volumes on my terminal, and wrote as well on other subjects. I wrote of Pallino, of Corvo and the others we had lost, and of the torments I suffered in Dharan-Tun. In writing

I dissolved my madness and my sorrow both, for it is the peculiar nature of words to trap feelings larger than themselves, and so reduce those forces and passions which might overthrow us to objects we can handle and name.

Sorrow. Grief. Fear. Pain.

I called them each by name.

There in the silence of the ship, for silent years, I set myself in order once again. Not whole, not healed, and though I think I spent years in a state close to dreaming or to coma, lying on my bed, in time I rose and began to live again, and to speak with myself. I began as well to try to strengthen my body once again—so much as my tortured limbs and aching shoulder would allow. I hoped that when we returned to civilization there might be help or healing to be found. New fingers, as Pallino once had won a new eye. That was something remarkable: I *hoped*. So, hoping, I counted the days until reversion.

Until Valka woke from sleep.

CHAPTER 48

THE FAR SHORE

THE FIRST BREATH OF air that wafted up the *Ascalon*'s ramp carried with it sunlight and the smell of salt, heralding the nearby sea. Valka and I blinked, and I confess my eyes brimmed with tears. I'd spent most of the twenty-eight year journey aboard the *Ascalon* alone, tending Valka's creche and the vegetables in the water gardens, and though Valka had been awake again for nearly a year and though her presence had restored a piece of my humanity and my soul, I wept to see and to experience anything beyond the confines of that wretched ship and to feel the proper weight of a world pulling at my feet.

Colchis.

I nearly went to my knees at the base of the ramp, would have gladly squeezed the sandy earth in my fingers. I felt almost *numb* with longing, so overwhelmed was I, as a condemned man laughs at the sunlight on his walk to the scaffold after so long in his cell. I turned about, eyes drinking in the vista: the *Ascalon* perched upon a rocky shelf above the blue-green sea, the waters filling the bowl of the world unto the horizon. The pale sky shone, the orange eye of the gas giant Atlas glimmered in the sun, and the distant cry of terranic gulls dragged my soul all the way to childhood and the beach beneath our acropolis. I laughed then, and leaving Valka and the ramp ran along the hillside toward the shore: a man alive again.

I had not seen the villagers approaching, shouting and pointing, laughing themselves in wonder at the approach of a ship from the sea beyond the skies. We had been to Racha, to the island village, only once before, on a fishing trip with the natives when we enjoyed our time at Thessa. Not much had changed in the decades we'd been away. The wooden houses still stood on stone pilings on the ridge above the shore, pitched roofs and narrow chimneys small and quaint against the alien sky. Here and there a white banner flew, the red Imperial sun shining bright, a prideful declaration that the peasants here claimed no lord save the Emperor himself, who—on account of the Great Library in Aea far across the sea—claimed Colchis as one of his many demesnes.

Valka called after me, and turning I saw her standing in the shadow of the *Ascalon*'s tall rear fin, shading her eyes. "No pursuers," she said, and tapped her temple. "Nothing on the general comm. I think we slipped customs and patrol."

"Good!" I looked round, still smiling like a fool, and took in the salt air. I was alive. *We* were alive. The words had a different sound beside the water, under the pale sky. If we had managed to evade detection, we would have the time we wanted, time to find Siran—or her grave. Time to tell her what had happened. Though so much time had passed for me, the solitude had kept the wounds fresh, and though I could walk and act like a man, I felt more ghost than living. Hadrian's Marlowe's shade—not Hadrian Marlowe himself.

"Ho there!" a voice called, drawing both Valka's and my attention from one another. The villagers had drawn near then, a group of twenty-some, young and old, each dressed in clothing of dun homespun with spiral patterns blue and red embroidered on. The speaker was an older woman, pale-faced, sun-spotted, and smiling. "What brings you to Racha, sailorman? Are you traders?"

I shook my head, raised my whole left hand in greeting—ashamed of the right. "No, madam! We are travelers. I seek Siran of Emesh, who wedded Lem, your eolderman."

The woman's hand fell at once, and her eyes narrowed. "None here by that name, sailor!"

I felt my heart sink, and Valka said, "'Twould have been long ago!"

"Then surely she's dead!" the peasant woman said.

"Lem were eolderman in my granda's day!" said a man. "And he was patrician! Lived to be three hundred, he did!"

"We know!" Valka answered him. "We seek her tomb—her children, if she had any. Or their children."

The crowd muttered amongst itself then, and a woman in a plaid apron had to rein in a straying child. While they deliberated, chewing over this piece of information, I returned up the gentle slope to join Valka. I had found one of my long coats during the long voyage from Eue, and its tails snapped about my calves. My roughly shorn hair—never recovered from my torments and still shocked with white—blew across my face. An old man peered at me from the back of the throng, eyes an almost colorless blue that reminded me of Lorian, and he said, "Who are you, lad?"

Did I dare tell them? I looked to Valka, but her face was unreadable. I doubted word would leave the island with any speed. Like most Imperial subjects, the Rachan villagers lived simple lives. They would have but little technology: ice chests, electric lighting, climate control for the houses, the odd holograph projector or two, maybe a groundcar—though Racha had few roads suitable for such—or a skiff. They would have radios and datasphere uplinks to receive the planetary broadcast service and to communicate with Aea and the rest of Colchis's settlements, but I did not think it likely word would get out that we were present. Racha was very isolated, a little village on an archipelago whose remoteness was its greatest claim to fame.

But I was spared by the decision by an even older man who said, "You're Hadrian Marlowe, ain't you?" When I did not at once answer, the fellow stepped forward, removing his salt-stained felt cap. "I thought it was you. Only the white in your hair spoiled my guess. But your voice, lordship. No mistaking it. Silver as the Emperor's own tongue, if you'll pardon my saying so." He bobbed his head. "An' I recog your woman, lord. 'Member her markings, sure as sunrise. Meaning no disrespect." When still I did not speak, he came forward and bowed stiffly, if as low as he could go. "You won't remember me, but I was prentice to old Lem, sire. Name of Ejaz. That was centuries ago. Did my time as a sailor an' come home, but I recog you."

"Ejaz?" I said, studying the old fellow's face. I thought I recalled a lad of that name who had fished with Siran's Lem. At once I felt foolish. We should never have come to Colchis. Siran was dead, and Gibson was certainly dead. Five hundred years was enough to turn even most palatines to dust, and neither Siran nor Gibson had been young when we left them. I told myself that Colchis had been on our way.

"I remember you, Ejaz," I said, though it was not quite true, and shut my eyes. "I did not expect to find anyone still living from those days."

Ejaz's jowls quivered, and he said, "It is you, then?"

"It is," I said, and raising my voice so all could better hear, I said, "I am Hadrian Marlowe. I come seeking the grave of my friend, Siran, who lived among you."

Old Ejaz bowed more deeply still. "Knew it was you, lord."

"Marlowe!" the woman who'd first addressed us exclaimed. "You're the Halfmortal?"

"So they say, madam," I said. "Please, tell me where my friend is buried."

The old woman shook her head, but the blue-eyed man said, "We should take them to see Imrah!"

"Imrah!" Ejaz said.

"She's Keeper, ain't she?" the old woman said. "She'll know what's best."

Taking a step forward, I drew level with Ejaz and—stooping so that I met the old woman at eye level—I asked, "Keeper?" It was not a title I recognized. "Keeper of what?"

"Of the tombs, lord!" the woman answered. "Of the isle of the dead!"

I looked around at Valka, who shrugged and smoothed the collar of her shirt.

I cannot say why, but I had expected Imrah to be another crone. Perhaps it was because the villagers who had met and spoken with us on the strand were all older themselves. But the Keeper was a young woman, comely and well-built, with oiled black hair neatly combed and painstakingly twisted into a knot secured by crossed wooden pins.

"You really are Hadrian and Valka?" she asked, looking from my face to Valka and back again. She smiled. "Grandmother always told me stories . . ."

A gentle wind blew in through the open shutters, tousled a wooden chime that hung just outside. Imrah glanced toward it, and I followed her gaze to where I could see the *Ascalon*'s fin rising above the low rooftops, and to the sea beyond. One of the squat gray shapes on the horizon, I knew, was Thessa, the island where the Red Company once had stayed. I was not sure which it was.

"Siran was your grandmother?" I asked.

"What?" Imrah shook her head. "No, no. She was Grandmother's grandmother. I never knew her." The Keeper of Thessa poured cups of something green and steaming from a ceramic pot, turned the service tray on its spindle so that cups faced Valka and myself. Valka drank at once, but I studied Imrah's face. I thought I could detect traces of Siran there. In the slightly darker tint of her skin, yes, in the almond shape of the eyes, in the way her jaw worked as she spoke. How strange it was, the passage of Time. Ever-Fleeting, indeed. "I suppose I've you to thank for my patrician standing."

I shook my head. "You have her to thank," I said with feeling. "Siran was . . . a good friend. A good fighter. She saved my life many times."

"She always thought you'd come back." Imrah set her cup down on the table, cradled it in her hands. "But I never thought it would happen in my time. Never thought I'd be the one."

"The one to what?"

Imrah blinked. "You don't know?" She looked from me to Valka again, eyes narrowing. "Then why are you here?"

Without thinking, I said, "They're all dead."

Valka laid a hand on mine where it lay on the tabletop. "We lost people. We did not know where else to go." I sat silently by then as Valka recounted—in the broadest possible terms—the capture and destruction of the Red Company. I stared fixedly into my cup of greenish broth, not quite meeting my reflection's eye. The chimes sounded again beyond the open window, and I glanced out to sea, counted the sea stacks where they rose gray against the horizon.

"I'm sorry," Imrah said, horror plain on her face. "For your loss. So you came seeking . . . refuge?"

"Quiet," I said. An answer, not a command.

"Peace," Valka translated, and there was a brokenness in her voice that I had but seldom heard, and reminded myself that she had spent more than a decade holed up on a freighter beneath the snows of Dharan-Tun with Corvo, Crim, and Pallino. That she had suffered—if suffered differently than I had done.

I cleared my throat, set my cup back down untouched. "We have nowhere else to go."

Imrah accepted this with arched eyebrows. "Why not go back to where you came from?" She cast about for the name. "Nessus?"

"Because everyone is dead! Don't you understand?" I half-rose from the seat, hands shaking. I clenched them into fists. "Don't you know what they'll do on Nessus? What they'll *ask*?"

I could not relive what had happened, could not so much as bear the thought of enduring a debrief or writing a report. I have stopped many, many times in recording this account. Lingered over no more than a sentence in a day, limped through Dharan-Tun and the ruins of Akterumu.

Even after so long . . . there is no true healing. There are only scars, wounds not even my writing and my art could heal.

"I can't do it," I heard myself whisper, "I can't . . ."

I had been so long alone, and it was too much—far too much—just to sit there with Valka and this woman, this echo of the friend whom I had lost. I had thought my time alone aboard the *Ascalon* had been curative, but I sensed then that it had only hollowed me out. While we had fought across the stars and suffered, time had flowed by. Why had we come to that place? What had I hoped to find? Siran alive? Surely not. And though this girl was Siran's blood, she was not Siran. There was no family, no *belonging* here.

Valka stood and steadied me with gentle hands. "Forgive us."

Imrah shook her head. "There's nothing to forgive." I looked away as soon as she finished speaking. I could not bear the pity in her eyes. After a moment's silence, she carried on. "So then . . . you don't know about the island?"

I was as yet in no fit state to reply, and so it was left to Valka to ask, "The island of the dead?" Valka still held my shoulders, but kept her attention squarely on the young lady across the table. Outside, the wooden chimes sparkled on the air. "What is it?"

Again the Keeper shook her head. "I always thought you would know. Grandmother always thought you would know."

"Know what?"

"Your father," Imrah said, inclining her head at me. "Your father is there."

I blinked, sneered, "My *father* is an old man on Delos, woman." Brushing Valka's hands away, I fell back into my seat, leaned over the table. "Do not play games with me."

Siran's twice-great-granddaughter blanched and leaned back. "He said you would return here one day, and that he wanted to be here when you did. He ordered a fugue pod sent to Thessa."

I hid my hands beneath the tabletop, shut my eyes. "My *father* is the Lord Archon of Devil's Rest!"

"Siran helped him!" Imrah said.

"Liar!"

Imrah's voice came out choked, and I realized I'd been shouting. "My family has maintained the pod for nearly five hundred years!" Valka's hands settled on my shoulders, held me in place as I snarled and rose to leave.

We should never have come.

"Siran first, then her daughter, Elara. Then my grandmother, my father, now me." She was speaking very fast by then, clearly frightened of me. I didn't care. I did not even feel the blow of discovering Siran had named a child after Elara, did not stop to remember her namesake's final fall from the shuttle hatch. "Ever since he left the college! I swear, lord—I do not lie!"

Whatever rage I had felt a moment earlier dissolved like dewfall in the sun. "The college?" I said, aghast, and let my hands unclench. "You mean . . . the athenaeum?" I glanced at Valka, eyes suddenly wide. The Keeper spoke not of my father at all, but of . . .

"Gibson," Valka said. "Tor Gibson?"

"He was a scholiast, yes?" Imrah asked.

"Was?" I turned from Valka to the Keeper, blinking back emotions I cannot rightly describe. "What do you mean?" One could not simply cease to be a scholiast. One might be disbarred or anathematized, his research collected and buried or destroyed, but a vow to embrace Stricture was for life.

The young lady looked at Valka and me, confused. "You really don't know anything about it?"

My anger flared again, and I said, "We don't, damn your eyes."

Imrah pressed her lips together. "He's not your father, then?"

"He's as good as," interjected Valka. "You're saying Tor Gibson is on Thessa? In cryonic fugue?"

I sat stunned, trying to take in this revelation. Gibson . . . alive? Again I shut my eyes and held my face in my hands. Imrah shifted in her seat, the wood creaking. "My great-great-grandmother, she helped set him up. Promised to watch over him. For you." She paused, and the distant cries of the gulls rushed in through the open window.

Pawns again, I thought, and touched the Quiet's shell through my shirt. *Always forward.*

My regrets and anger at having come to that backwater place vanished in a trice. "How did he get out of the athenaeum?"

Imrah blinked at the question. "I . . . don't know?"

I rubbed my face, willed myself to be human again. "I'm sorry," I said, and did my best to smile at the young woman seated across from me. I saw again the echoes of Siran in her face, the traces of my old friend. I felt suddenly very old. Old and lonely. She was so young, perhaps not even thirty! I was more than ten times her age, had spent nearly so long as she'd been alive locked aboard the *Ascalon*, alone. Nearly a thousand years of human history had passed since the High College spun my genome on the breeding looms and Tor Ada had pulled me from the vats. Could this woman, this *girl*, even conceive of such a span of years? I was not sure I could, who had lived so much and so awfully. "You cannot know what this means," I said at last. "Can you take us to him?"

The Keeper brightened then, and laid her hand on the table. "Of course."

CHAPTER 49

THE ISLE OF THE DEAD

THESSA ROSE FROM THE waves like the worn-down fang of a giant. That thought put me in mind of Miudanar's massive skull, and of the vision I had seen of the red-crowned creatures standing by as a colossus erupted from the waves, and despite the warmth of the Colchean sun, I shivered and hugged myself, letting the spray scour my face. Turning, I saw Valka standing at the rear of the boat, talking with one of Imrah's cousins—another of Siran's descendants—a man called Ginoh. Imrah herself sat in the control cabin with her brother, Alvar, who manned the controls.

Our prow broke one of the waves, and a fine mist blew across the deck and sparkled in the noonday sun. Turning my face to the water, I shut my eyes and let the rime wash over me. Opening them again, I thought I could see the low, white shapes of the old prefabricated modules we'd brought down to the island to house the Red Company for our shore leave during our previous stay on Colchis, like lime-washed sepulchers. A deep, hollow melancholy filled me at the sight, and I gripped the rail with my maimed hand, the remaining knuckles turning white.

"Are you all right?"

Imrah had come out of the cabin, leaving Alvar at the controls. She wore a hydrophobic cape of dun homespun embroidered with the angular red serpent designs so beloved of the natives.

I looked down at her—she was more than a head shorter than I—and did my best to smile. It must have looked something frightful, for Imrah drew back a step. Turning my face up to the clear, gray sky, I said, "I was just wishing for rain."

"For rain?" the Keeper echoed.

"I haven't seen rain in more than forty years," I told her, and realized only as I spoke the words that they were true. Forty years since Severine awakened me from the creche. A lifetime. Looking up, I imagined the gray sky was the gray of clouds, and that a rain might come and wash me clean. I could still feel the dull ache in my shoulder, and knew then I would never find a water pure enough to make me clean again.

The young woman squinted at the sky, marked a couple distant clouds scudding over the horizon. "Won't be any rain today, I think," she said. "But you stay long enough, you're sure to find some."

Remembering the look my previous smile had put on Imrah's face, I kept my own face still and said, "I am sorry. I've been alone a long time. I did not mean to frighten you."

The Keeper drew her cape about herself and moved to look out from the rail beside me. Thessa was drawing ever closer, and the white shapes of the barracks modules shone brightly in the sun. Even at this distance, I could see where the locals had run lines between them laden with banners, and that stone foundations had been packed in beneath the landing peds.

"Your doctor said you spent the passage alone."

I held her gaze then. Not wanting to talk about my voyage, I moved my head in the direction of the shore. "Are people living in the camp now?"

"Oh no," Imrah said, clearly glad of the easier line of conversation. "Grandmother's mother had those foundations put in. Them and those dikes along the shoreline. There." She pointed.

Someone had built a pier as well, a narrow stone strand atop cement piles, thick with barnacles and a reddish, coraline growth that I guessed was native to the watery moon. As we drew nearer, Imrah's cousin Ginoh leaped ashore and tied us off. As I mounted the steps onto the pier, the man stuck out his hand. I shook it on reflex, acutely aware of my phantom fingers as the stout fisherman's hand gripped mine.

"Just wanted to say I'd done it, sir," he said, and stepped back to give me space. Valka grinned wryly up at me, clearly amused as she clambered onto the pier. Imrah came last of all, cape fluttering about her slim shoulders.

"I'll mind the boat, Imrah!" Alvar said, cracking open an icebox and drawing out a dark bottle.

"Mind you do!" she shot back. "Don't get too deep in that chest now!"

Her brother grinned and raised the drink in salute.

All was as I had seen it from the boat: Imrah and her family had put stone foundations under the old barracks pods and laid huge paving stones on the beach. Painted flags flew from lines hung overhead, filling the air with a sound like soft wings. Ginoh went on ahead, Imrah not far behind.

I flagged, stared up past the protected beach to where the dark stone of the cliffs rose, tall trees swaying in the sea wind. The whole of the world was hushed, as if in Chantry, and the waves crashed gentle at our backs.

Pointing to a barren patch of sand, I said, "That's where the lads were boxing, do you remember?"

"Yes," Valka said simply. I remembered a step too late that she forgot nothing, that for her memory was sharp as sight. Her hand found mine, and she pointed up at the promontory overlooking the bay. "And there's our spot. Remember when Otavia found us that first day?"

"I do!" I said, squeezing her fingers with my good left hand.

An oily melancholy hung on me, and with each halting step I thought I heard a man's shout or a woman's laughter. Thought I saw young Aristedes sneak off toward the officers' quarters, a local girl leading him by the hand. Fancied I heard Pallino's rough voice raised above all. *"Right, so there I was!"*

If I had come to build a marker, to raise a monument to our honored dead, I had found one ready made and tended by the Keepers of Racha. Siran's kin. A place had been made ready long before.

"Lord Marlowe!" Imrah called from the path ahead, waving. "This way!"

I shook myself from the grasp of memory and climbed the path after Imrah and her cousin. Beyond the last row of low, white lozenge buildings the rocky shelf of the island rose steeply, and we followed a path Valka and I knew well up the cliff toward the promontory.

"Siran had the hospital pod set up on the ridge to keep it clear of the storms!" the Keeper exclaimed, throwing her words back over her shoulder as she led us on our hike.

We turned left at the top of the path, turning our backs on the spur of stone that looked out over the bay that Valka and I had enjoyed so long ago. Ahead, the path curved left, following the crescent shape of the island, and rose slightly to a kind of plateau overlooking the sea, the center of which was dominated by a solitary dome of scuffed white tile, like some strange, scaled fungus. Once, the structure had stood upon three huge landing peds, mighty columns bent like the legs of dogs. As with the housing pods in our ancient camp below, Imrah's family—Siran's family—had shored up the foundation with rough masonry. The dome itself had a distinct Consortium look to it, belied by the Mandari writing stenciled to the right of the door in faded indigo. Like the pods below, the dome clearly had been lowered from space, and I fancied still I could see the black marks of burnt stone where fusion flame had left its mark when the pod came in to land.

Seeing all this, I did not see the cairns at once, and so it fell to Imrah to point to the row of stone mounds. They ran along the right side of the path; hunched, rounded things with man-high pillars at the end facing the roads. Cords of some imperishable fiber wove through the tight-packed stones, red and white, their lengths hung with charms. Prayer cards, I realized.

"The other Keepers," Imrah said proudly, and placed her hands on her hips. Bowing slightly to the nearest, she said, "This is my father's. He was shipwrecked about ten years back. He's the only one not buried here."

Valka spoke for us both. "I'm sorry."

Imrah smiled and adjusted one of the fine plastic placards that hung from the knotted cord. *BAGOS,* it read. The man's name. "It's all right," Imrah said. "He is with me still. The soul lives on in the heart. In the memory. No one is ever truly dead."

No one is ever truly dead.

She looked up at me, still smiling sweetly, and asked, "If I may, lord: they say you died." She did not ask the question.

I did not answer her at once, but turned to look beyond the funeral markers to the gray-tossed sea below. A salt wind rushed over us, pulling my hair and setting the prayer cards bound to the cairns to rattling. Looking round, I envisioned an army of lesser monuments laid out across the bluffs, rank and file hung with cards or carved with half-forgotten names.

Ninety thousand names.

"It's true," I said at length, not saying more.

"Then surely, you know better than any of us." She looked round at Valka, who yet stood beside me, and for Ginoh, who had moved toward the hatch that opened the domed structure ahead. "Are not the dead still with us?"

Corvo and Durand.

My eyes slipped from the girl's face to the path behind her. I had not spoken of the Howling Dark to any save Valka in any detail, though many had asked. I shook my head, tried to find the words to capture that experience. I had not seen any but myself in the Dark, and yet. . . . "It was Dark," I said roughly, simply, spreading my free hand. "I was worn to tatters, thin as smoke, and crawled. Dark as it was, I knew there was light beneath and ahead. I never saw a face or heard a word in all that silence, but I wasn't alone."

How had I forgotten?

Like fish in dark water I had thought them, those other presences, each of us moving forward and ever down toward the light beneath that divine darkness, crawling as a serf must crawl to reach the throne. Not alone.

Ilex and Crim.

I inhaled sharply to stay the tears. "Not alone."

Imrah brightened. "I knew it. It is said we will meet again on Earth."

"On the Earth," I echoed, doubting. "Or elsewhere."

Imrah indicated the next cairn. "This is my grandmother's. She was Keeper for more than a hundred fifty years." Briefly, she touched the placard hung from this cairn's braided cord. I read the name *AMARTA*. Imrah touched the name plate of the third cairn too. "And her mother."

ELARA.

The familiar name caught in me like a spark, and I jerked my head away. I knew without Imrah's saying a word whose name was on that last monument.

She spoke anyway. "Here she is."

SIRAN.

My knees went out from under me, and I released Valka's hand. Turning my face up to take in the gravestone, I found rain in that cloudless sky. Water fell upon my face—fell *from* my face. "She thought I would stop her staying," I said at last, the fingers of my ruined hand scrabbling in the stony earth at my side. "She was right. I wanted to. I wanted to."

Valka's hand settled on my shoulder. I pawed at it, held it fast.

"If I'd . . . stopped her . . . stopped her leaving, I mean, she'd be dead, too." Of course, she was dead anyway. But dead with honor, buried with love. Better Thessa than Akterumu, better Colchis than Eue. I did not shake or sob, but neither could I stop the flow of tears from reddening eyes. "How many of the others would be in places like this if not for me?"

Valka's hand trembled, then clenched my shoulder with sublime force. "None."

None?

I looked up at her, and for a moment Imrah and Ginoh—the whole of the great plateau and the ancient hospital pod—were only shadows. "She would be ashes in the coliseum incinerator were it not for you. You brought her here."

"And brought the rest to Akterumu," I groaned, thinking of the coliseum.

Pallino and Elara.

Pallino and Elara should have been here at least, buried next to Siran.

Valka traced her thumb along my collarbone, back and forth. "Siran chose to leave. They chose to follow. You did not know where our path would lead. You're not Fate, Hadrian—or Death herself."

"I should be dead," I said. "They should each have a place like this." Taking up a pebble from the soil, I tossed it at Siran's cairn, resolving then—in that moment—to raise monuments for the others, for as many of the others as I could name.

Valka's fingers tightened. "They died for you. So that you could keep fighting. Because they believed in you."

"And what did their faith earn them?" I asked. "They should have stayed home." I found another flat piece of rock and placed it on the cairn. "My father was right. I should have listened. Gone to Vesperad. Become a torturer—I would have done less harm."

"And less *good*," Valka said, and kissed the top of my head. "How many millions have you saved? At Berenike? Senuessa? Mettina? Arae? Aptucca? How many?" When I did not move at once, she shook me, held my gaze as though pinning me to a board. "Your *father* is here, remember? Let's go to him."

Gibson, I reminded myself, and blew out a long breath. *Gibson is alive.*

Cold air greeted us once we passed the airlock and entered the cubiculum. The whole dome was not large, and but for the airlock itself comprised only a single chamber half a hundred feet in diameter. Every surface was the same white plastic and ceramic tile as the exterior, with consoles and counters surfaced in black glass. A dozen fugue creches lay flat at waist height, radiating from the center console like the spokes of a wheel. Their glass lids all stood open, raised like the petals of a flower.

All but one.

"How've you kept it powered?" Valka asked, chafing her arms.

"There's a small reactor underwater on the far side of the island," Ginoh said, tapping a console to turn up the cold, white lights. "Breaks the water down for fuel."

Advancing on the pod whose lid was shut, Imrah added, "It doesn't draw much power with just the one pod running."

"Siran couldn't possibly afford all this," I said, turning on the spot. The cold air stung my damp cheeks, and I rubbed my face in my hands. She'd left the Red Company with nothing but the clothes on her back, and the men of Racha were not likely ever to afford such a thing. It must have cost half a million marks at least. Perhaps more. There was a stamp of fine craftsmanship about every component in the chamber, not the cheap and fragile plastic work one commonly associated with Wong-Hopper materials.

Imrah stopped beside the casket and looked up, face clearly puzzled, "She didn't. He did." When I only blinked at her and turned to Valka, she continued, "You are lords, are you not?"

I was speechless. Gibson was a scholiast. He had nothing. Owned nothing. The scholiasts renounced all worldly possessions save their robes, the better to give their lives to their service and their pursuits. He had nothing, no assets, no holdings, no money to speak of.

It wasn't possible. It didn't make sense.

And yet . . . there he was. I drew level with Imrah beside the sealed creche, looked down through frosted glass and violet fluid at the beloved face. Gibson looked—if anything—younger in the freeze, not dead, not corpse-like at all. The thinning mane and leonine whiskers were right where they had ever been, and the notch that marred his left nostril where Sir Felix's knife had cut was unchanged.

"It's really him," I said, voice barely more than a whisper. "What is he doing here? How can this be?" The reality of what I was seeing, of Gibson's presence, was only just sinking in. Some part of me had felt as though I were dreaming ever since we clattered down the ramp onto the beach. Seldom had my interplanetary wanderings come at such a cost. So many of my friends and companions, so many of the fixtures of the Imperium— the Magnarch, the various officers, the Imperial Council, and the Emperor himself—either traveled with me or were palatine, and so long-lived they had not vanished to be replaced by their grandchildren.

In the Golden Age, men told tales of sailors adrift in time, sailors who—traveling so near the speed of light—outstripped the flow of Time itself and sailed fast into the future. Such men returned to Earth in distant ages to find only smoking ruins, or an empire of apes, or machines. Warp travel bypasses the relativistic flow of Time, but the distances between stars are so vast—and in fugue the processes of life are so suspended—that the effect is not so different. Though I fought to save the Empire, no more was it the Empire I'd begun my fight to save. That Empire was in the past, and would never be again. And its people were in the past, and in the ground.

But not all of them.

"What are you doing here?" I breathed, laying my hand on the glass surface of the casket, smiling in disbelief at the beloved face within. Lifting my eyes to the Keeper, I said, "Can you wake him up?"

Imrah's dark eyes widened. She glanced at Ginoh, and said in hushed tones, "I . . . we've never done it before."

"No matter. 'Tis simple," Valka said. "I'll do it." Without further ceremony, my Tavrosi witch brushed the young Keeper aside and tapped a couple of the controls, nails drumming the glass surface as she waited on some unseen mechanism. Using the blade of my hand, I wiped away at the frost coating the lid of Gibson's creche. Beneath the glass, he looked like the graven image of a king laid down upon his tomb.

The faint whir of a centrifuge spun up within the center console, and a temperature gauge began to climb. *77 Kelvin. 78.* While in fugue, a constant flow of TX-9 is supplied to the sleeper's bloodstream, always in motion to keep the tissues from freezing solid and developing cryoburn. The first phase of resurrection required the temperature of that intravenous flow be increased, warming the body from the core outward in preparation for the reintroduction of blood and the purgation of the remaining cryonic fluids. Only then would the tank be drained and current applied through the electrodes fixed to the chest to restart the latent heart and brain.

Done properly, the window in which the sleeper is susceptible to brain damage is less than a minute long.

"Core temperature's rising," Valka noted. I checked the gauge. *137 K.*

"What can we do?" Imrah asked.

I gestured toward the lockers surrounding the low dome. "Are there blankets?" Both Imrah and Ginoh paused, wheels in their minds turning. Presently the man leaped into action, moving off toward a bank of compartments lining a far stretch of wall. Leaning in beside Valka, I asked, "Is he all right?"

She nodded. "You know so well as I the process mostly drives itself." As if to give the lie to this statement, Valka reached down and tapped an indicator. "Ninety seconds to saline flush."

I moved back to stand beside the sarcophagus. There was no reason to fear—extracting a sleeper from fugue was as routine as anything—and yet I could not stop my hands from sweating.

219 K.

At *300* the TX-9 would be exchanged for the saline solution, and the process would enter its final phase. Ginoh came hurrying back with a heavy white blanket in his arms. I stayed him with a raised hand. Beneath the fingers of the other, the frost on Gibson's casket began to drip and run onto the rubberized floor.

"Thirty seconds." Valka's eyes met mine across the console, and she smiled. For the first time since I leaped from the chariot in Vedatharad, I felt a warmth well up in my chest. I returned her smile. "Mark."

The instant the saline flush started, the tank began to drain, violet fluid retreating through openings in the base of the creche to be boiled and returned to the tank. A pneumatic hiss followed an instant later, and I drew back as the clamshell lid began to rise. Gibson lay naked on a padded white slab, his arms—spotted and time-eaten—at his sides. A hose ran from his mouth to siphon the fluid from his lungs, and a braided cable ran into his arm. As I watched, hot blood flowed red as dull fire up the line and into Gibson's veins.

"Stay clear!" Valka said, hand reaching for the switch to arm the electrodes.

My eyes found the heart rate monitor, its line flat and dead.

A bright note sounded, strangely cheerful, and Gibson convulsed on the slab, hair soaked and flesh damp from the creche. I marked a thin scar on his chest, as from a sword. I had never seen it before—had never had occasion to see it before, and wondered at it. On the monitor, the line jumped. Jumped again. His heart was beating. Brain activity showed on panels of black glass, but even after decades of familiarity with the readings, I little understood them.

"Blanket!" I said to Ginoh. The native man handed the cloth to me, and I draped it over Gibson to hide his grubby nakedness. It was not right that I had seen him so. Still, I gripped his hand in mine. The old man wheezed, coughed gently, and his thin fingers tightened reflexively on my own. Looking to Valka, I asked, "Should I pull the tube?"

She made a gesture in the affirmative.

With smooth but firm motion, I reached up and tugged the siphon free. Gibson coughed again, rolled blindly to his side and retched. A thin stream of purplish fluid ran out. Cryonic rebirth—for all its high art and science—was just as undignified as birth itself. Releasing Gibson's hand, I held his shoulders, kept the blanket in place. At once, I found myself remembering another bedside. Another world. Another life.

What in Earth's name were you doing in the city alone?

"What in Earth's name are you doing here?" I asked, unable to keep from grinning.

The old scholiast's gray eyes raked over my face, unseeing. That was no surprise. Fugue blindness was so common it was nearly inevitable. "Livy?" he croaked, turning his head in an effort to find the source of my voice. "Livy? Is that you?"

Livy? There was an ancient historian named Livy. A Greek? A Roman? Was this Livy then a scholiast? "No, Gibson," I said, bringing my face closer to his ear. He had been deafening as long as I'd known him. "No. No, it's Hadrian."

A warm smile split the scholiast's face. "Hadrian!" He raised a hand, upsetting the weighted blanket. Fresh from fugue, Gibson's scholiast rigor had yet to assert itself, and his emotions ran free and wild across the seamed face. "Hadrian!" The bony fingers found my face, and the sightless eyes turned toward me. "You found my . . . letter."

"What letter?" I didn't understand. Scholiasts didn't send letters, not from athenaeum. The colleges were meant to be a retreat from the wider world, places of isolated contemplation and study, places nearer the abstract realm of form and theory. But of course, Gibson was not *at* athenaeum. Had some letter come to Nessus and been blocked by Venantian's people? "What letter?" I asked again, shaking my head.

"Doesn't matter," he murmured, voice barely more than a whisper. "You're here."

It didn't matter. Unable to restrain myself, I stooped and took the old man in my arms, embracing him as a son should embrace his father.

"I am."

CHAPTER 50

MEMORY AND HISTORY

TWO DAYS PASSED BEFORE Gibson was fully conscious again. Old as he was, fugue had taken its toll. Once Valka was certain his condition was stable, I carried him down the cliff path to the old camp, gritting my teeth through the pain in my shoulder all the way. We did not return to Racha—I did not wish to take Gibson too far from the hospital module on the off chance his condition worsened—and instead set up in one of the blocks which once had served as accommodations for the officers.

The old lights still functioned, but it took Ginoh and Imrah the better part of that first day to get the water and sanitary facilities back online with Valka's help. Gibson muttered the while, slipping in and out of consciousness and dream. Snatches of scholastic English burbled forth, and from time to time he would call out for me, or for his *Livy*, or for Sister Carina, who had been his caretaker in the archivists' grotto beneath the Great Library. Once or twice, he even called for my father. This I found most distressing of all. Gibson had been my father's tutor when Lord Alistair had been a boy, and had counseled him through the Orin Rebellion and the attack on Linon. I did not like remembering that fact. It brought my father and me too close together.

How old he was! I stayed by his side while he recovered and tended him, and studied the familiar face. His skin was like wrinkled parchment, so folded and spotted it was impossible to imagine the young man he once had been. Rebirth had shrunk him, and beneath the heavy coverlets he was a construction of paper skin and wooden bones. For all I had suffered carrying him down from the plateau above, he was not heavy.

"Have you not slept?" His first coherent words in days, the first whose tone suggested awareness of his place or my presence.

I had been sleeping, in fact, or in a state so like sleep it made no difference. Smiling down at him, I said, "I don't really sleep anymore."

"Some things never change, I see," the scholiast said. "Melodramatic as ever."

"I've perhaps earned it by now," I told him.

Gibson turned his head and peered out the window. I was not sure how much he could see, but we had chosen a room for him that overlooked the water. After a minute's amiable silence, the old man asked, "What year is it?"

"ISD 17089," I said shortly.

The scholiast accepted this with a scant inclination of his head. "Nearly five hundred years. May Time, Ever-Fleeting, forgive me . . ." His gaze wandered half-seeing over the rounded square of the window panes. "I never thought I'd live so long. To so remote a time . . . but it worked." He looked at me and smiled. "I got to see you again."

"But how?" I asked, leaning toward the old man.

"I assume your friend Siran is dead," Gibson said, not directly answering.

"Yes," I said. "Her great-great-granddaughter was watching over you." Unable to stop myself smiling a little, I said, "They went and turned this island into a proper monument. You should see it." The old man smiled himself, but old habit asserted itself and he banished the expression, shut his eyes to better take in the pale sunlight falling through the great window.

Eyes still shut, Gibson said, "Her great-great-granddaughter. Earth and Emperor, they live such short lives."

Unable to help myself, I asked the question burning its hole in my tongue. "How?" I said, stumbling. "How is any of this possible? How did you leave the athenaeum? Where did you get the money for that hospital module?"

Gibson opened gray eyes and turned from the light. He studied me a long while, beetling brows contracted with studious concern. "What happened to you?" he said, seeing me then for the first time, the scars on my face, the white shocks in my hair. "Your face . . ."

"Later," I said. I could spoil our reunion with talk of Dharan-Tun, of Eue, and the Prophet-made-King. But I would not. "Valka will want to see you, too. She's here—but come! Please! Tell me how. How did you do all this?"

"It took a measure of doing," Gibson said at last. "Your friend, Siran, petitioned the college for an archivist. It took her years."

That didn't make any sense. "The colleges don't grant scholiasts to peasant eolderman."

"They don't," Gibson agreed, and tried to sit up. I lurched forward to assist him, adjusted the pillows beneath his head and shoulders. "But they have been known to evoke one of us to document local populations. The Sevrastene—the islanders, that is—the Rachans and so on . . . have a unique local language and culture. Siran and her husband wanted their traditions written down. I convinced the primate to allow me to be the one to do it." He suppressed another grin. "All my plan, of course. After we had the medica installed and I was sleeping, Siran sent word that I'd . . . passed away." From the unsteadiness in his tone, I guessed talk of his own demise discomforted my old tutor.

"They didn't come looking for you?" I asked in disbelief.

"Siran took them an urn—at least I assume she did. No one from Aea ventures this far south. There's nothing out here but fishermen."

I shook my head, disbelief still king in me. "But the fugue creches? The medica?"

"I was not always a scholiast, Hadrian." Gibson smiled sadly, and this time his scholiast's training did not wipe that sorrow away. "When you left here, I knew . . . I knew you would be coming back one day. Call it a scholiast's computation, or an old man's intuition, if you prefer." He raised his shoulders, hands still beneath the coverlet. "I did not wish to leave you alone."

My own shoulders shook, and I hunched over in my seat, unable to speak or articulate the wash of feelings that warred and roiled in me. Not able to name them, I could not dismiss them in stoic fashion, but then, for all my education—the aphorisms, the breathing exercises, the antique literature—I have always been a poor stoic.

"Hadrian?" Gibson sat up straighter, reached out with a gnarled hand and gripped my knee. "Dear boy, are you all right?"

I seized that hand with my three-fingered one, an answer in itself. Evil had a piece of me, and always would. Part of me was with Syriani Dorayaica forever. "No," I said, honestly. I was not sure I would ever be all right again. "No, I'm not." I did not tell him all then, though I would in the coming days. It was enough that he was there, enough that he was living.

We would spend years on Colchis, most of it in solitude on Thessa: Valka, Gibson, and I. Much of what transpired and what we talked about I shall not here record. They are quiet moments, private moments, moments which belong to us and to memory, not to history and you. Valka and I had each suffered, and such wounds do not ever really heal. Scars are not the flesh that was before the wound was made, and Time—as I have so oft lamented—flows in but one direction.

Years passed, and though the galaxy turned about us, we did not care. Time and again we would return with Imrah and Ginoh to join Alvar and the rest of Siran's clan on Racha. Often I would go out with the fishermen and help them to collect their catch—leastways so much as my injuries permitted me. Thus I fell in love with Colchis and the sea, just as Siran had done so long ago. Many were the evenings I would sit and listen while Gibson lectured the children of the village, or told them some story of the ancient world, just as he once had entertained me as a boy. Valka would rest her head upon my shoulder whilst he spoke of Simeon the Red and Kasia Soulier, of Alexander and Arthur, and of the God Emperor himself. Many were the days I would spend with Gibson, walking along the paths of Thessa, speaking about what I had endured. He kept me company as I raised cairn after little cairn upon the crown of the island, first for Pallino, then for Elara, for Corvo and Durand, Ilex and Crim, Halford and Koskinen and poor Adric White. I painted their names on the hard plastic of prayer cards, sprayed them to resist the wind and rain. They are there still, there alongside ninety unmarked piles that line the path back down to the beach and our old camp.

One for each of my thousands.

All the while, Gibson would listen—at first with tears in his eyes—as I spoke of our battles, of Nessus and Padmurak, Eue and Dharan-Tun. Many and long were our days, and many, too, were the nights I spent with Valka, and those were more sweet and as healing. As Thessa once had been a place apart from the war and the horror of the universe, so it was again, and though my scars remained, their luster dimmed, and the ugliness of the world was far away.

"How long do you mean to stay here?" Gibson asked, seating himself on the trunk of a fallen tree. "Let me rest a moment." The wind blew about us, crisp and cool with the threat of winter. We had been on Colchis then for four standard years, and the weather was growing cold at last. The gray sun shone thinly on the upland trees, and beyond the cliff's edge the sea rolled gray and white-capped. Gone were the rich blues of summer, and the world was fading. Even the gas giant Atlas seemed gray, its vibrant oranges gone to umber.

It was not the first time Gibson had asked that question, and I answered him in the usual way. "Are you so eager to be rid of me?" I did not want to tell him the truth: that I did not want to leave Colchis, that I still woke sweating and sobbing in the night.

He knew.

"I am too old to be eager for anything at all," Gibson answered me, and laid his cane across his knees. "But you cannot stay here forever, dear boy."

"Can I not?" I asked sourly, probing the spot in my mouth where a new tooth was sprouting to replace one of the ones I'd lost. New teeth were always strange, discomforting reminders of the artificiality of the palatine caste. Grown men were not meant to grow new teeth.

The scholiast did not answer at once. "I told you once about the ugliness of the world. Do you remember?"

"That was the day Father banished you."

"It was."

Voice sharply bitter, I asked, "How could I forget?" But then another, more pressing question came to me, and I added, "Did you know?"

"Did I know Sir Felix was going to arrest me?" Gibson fixed me with gray eyes. He looked strange out of his scholiast's green. The robes had not survived his long internment, and so he wore my own blacks. The tunic and trousers hung on him as loosely as on a scarecrow. "Yes. Alcuin told me. A professional courtesy. He knew how much you meant to me, and wanted me to have a chance to say goodbye."

I blinked at him. "What? Why would he do that?" I had not thought about Tor Alcuin in years, in decades probably. I wondered if Father's favorite scholiast were still alive. It was possible. Alcuin had been palatine himself, and Father was still alive, preserved—or so I understood it—by several long trips back and forth in fugue to the Consortium offices at Arcturus.

"Because he knew that I was innocent," Gibson said. "Your father knew you were behind your escape attempt, not I. He wanted you punished, but it would not have done for him to harm you."

Because it couldn't be you, Father had said when I'd asked why he'd done what he'd done. I looked away from Gibson in his outsized blacks, stared out across the sea. From our height, the dim shape of Racha was visible, and the sparse fingers of the sea stacks that rose like columns from the water were like the tops of sunken towers. "Damn him." After so many centuries, my hatred of Lord Alistair Marlowe had cooled, transformed from a white-hot coal to something oily and dead, not gone, but rotten and cold. "I wish I knew how he found out about the plan." That had always bothered me. I had been so careful—or thought I had been careful.

"Alistair has borne much of the world's ugliness, Hadrian," Gibson said. "He is a harsh man. The pursuit of power calls for harsh men, as does its exercise. I believe Alistair thinks greater harshness will earn him greater power, and he may be right. Times of calamity like ours are ever opportunities for such men." He twisted his cane in his lap. "But you should not despise him for what he is. We are all shaped by our suffering. That we are only what we are is ever our chiefest sin."

I raised my eyebrows. "You would have me forgive him?"

"Him," Gibson said, "and yourself."

"I don't deserve forgiveness," I said, remaining agnostic on the question of my father.

"*Kwatz!*" Gibson exclaimed, his verbal slap. "Be grateful we do not get what we deserve, dear boy. If we did, paradise would be empty, and this life would be even darker and more difficult than it is." He studied me then a long time with his fading eyes. "You are not your father. But you are his son."

"You have said that before as well."

"And it is no less true," Gibson replied stiffly. "Alistair was not always as you knew him. His father's death. The Orin Rebellion. Your mother. Most of all: his office. These forged him." There was a sadness in Gibson's voice then I had seldom heard there, a sadness his scholiast's training did not arise to check. I wondered just what my father had been like in his youth, and if Gibson mourned the loss of that man. "Pity him his trials, and have mercy. On him, and yourself."

We each were silent then. Nothing spoke but the wind. Coat flapping about my legs, I moved toward the treeline, looking down over the bay, the white lozenge-shapes of the old camp lining the shore like gravestones. "I led all those people to their deaths, Gibson."

"*Kwatz!*" Once more I heard the sound of Gibson's cane striking the earth. "Are you this Syriani Dorayaica?" I turned back to look at Gibson. The old man had planted his cane in the dirt between his feet, hands folded on the brass knob. "You did not kill those people."

"I as good as," I said.

Gibson rejected this with another *thump* of his cane. Into the fresh quiet, he said, "You take too much on yourself. You cannot carry the universe."

"And yet the universe is what is asked of me!" I said, thinking of the Quiet. "Gibson, the things I've seen! The things I can do!"

"I know." The scholiast clamped his jaw shut, fixed his eyes on some point on the twiggy ground between us. "Hadrian, have you considered it is not your survival that so haunts you? That it is your time here you cannot forgive?"

My mouth opened to reply, but no words came out. I shut it again. My last words to Lorian rattled in my mind. *Avenge us. Avenge us.* I was alive, and that charge fell upon my shoulders. What right had I to languish on Thessa in comfort and in peace? To wallow in misery and pain when so much *wrong* had happened?

None.

"Am I a coward?" I asked, echoing Prince Hamlet.

"No," Gibson answered flatly.

The white sails of fishing boats stood tall against the sea, signs that the universe went on in spite of all. I watched them then, not knowing what to say. The air tasted of salt—like tears—but the music of gulls was brighter than the sun. How could the Cielcin believe all creation a lie? Beauty is Truth, wrote Keats, and the world was beautiful.

"Only the past is written," Gibson said. "You are not dead, Hadrian. This island is not your tomb." I nodded along, still watching the ships, the birds and the fishes. Again I probed the spot where the new tooth was coming in. "Nothing is finished."

Nothing is finished.

"You're right," I said. "I only wish it weren't so hard."

"So do I," Gibson said, "and so do we all, each with our own burdens. We are each Sisyphos in our way, pushing our rocks up our hills." He groaned, stood unsteadily. I hurried to his side. "One of us will reach the top eventually." Leaning on his cane, Gibson gripped my shoulder. "This is not the life I hoped for you, my boy."

I laughed. "Nor I."

But there was something then in Gibson's eyes, a sharpness I had scarcely seen. "I hoped to spare you the whip," he said, and I knew his fingers sensed the thick scars on my shoulders. "I'm sorry."

"It wasn't your doing," I said, thinking of the scars that covered both our backs, testimony to the burdens we each had borne.

Those gray eyes grew sharper still, and I understood the point he'd scored on me. The old man smiled painfully. "Got you."

Grimacing, Gibson and I went down from the plateau, passing by the cairns that housed Siran and her descendants. On our way, we passed the point overlooking the sheltered bay where Valka and I had kissed that first day on Thessa so very long ago. Gibson pointed at it with his cane. "When we were having the medica prepared, I used to sit out there and watch the sun come up," he said. "Siran would tell me stories about you."

"Did she?" I asked.

Gibson stopped walking and looked me in the eyes again. "She used to say she wished she'd gone with you. That she should have."

I turned away. "I'm glad she didn't."

The old man leaned less heavily on his cane. "I am proud of you, Hadrian," he said. "Of the man you've become."

"Some man," I said, unable to hide the derision in my voice.

"Some man indeed," he said. "I do not pretend to understand what is happening to you, to understand this business of the Cielcin and the Quiet, but I know Siran was proud of you, too. Your friends loved you, as I do— as your Valka does. That is why they saved you. And that love, I told you, is a mighty thing! That's worth fighting for, even after those who loved us are gone."

"He thinks we should go," I said, taking the wine Valka offered. I sipped it speculatively. The wines the islanders produced were all too sweet for my taste, loud and unsophisticated, so white they were almost green. Still, it was wine, and I would not abuse Imrah's kindness by complaining. I could see Gibson below, seated among the children by the bonfire, the brass head of his cane winking in the orange light. I could just barely hear him from the porch, his deep and rasping voice reciting:

> *Ye sons (he cried) of Ithaca, give ear;*
> *Hear all! but chiefly you, O rivals! hear.*
> *Destruction sure o'er all your heads impends;*
> *Ulysses comes, and death his step attends.*

Ignoring my words, Valka asked, "What is it tonight?" She bobbed her head in Gibson's direction, settling onto the low couch beside me. Though the nights were growing cold, she was warm, and the tall silvered column-heater warmed the veranda that encircled Imrah's house. Siran's house, I supposed, and guessed that she and her fisherman had sat on the nearly the same spot so many hundred years before.

Drawing Valka close beneath my arm, I said, "Homer. The *Odyssey*. He's giving them a right classical education." I could not help but smile.

"He used to recite these to me when I was a boy. Made me memorize some."

"'Twould explain a lot," Valka said, and drank her wine. I swatted her, and she laughed. "I don't know this one."

I let Gibson go on a moment before responding. "It's about a man—a soldier, a king—who can't go home. He's won a great victory, but he mocked the gods . . . and for that he's doomed to wander." I paused and drank my own wine, grimacing at the taste. "His son's at home, and in his father's absence suitors have all moved in to claim his mother and his father's throne." I felt Valka squirm at the word *claim*, and understood her perfectly. Had I not twice been so claimed by lords for their daughters? By Balian Mataro for Anaïs, and again by the Emperor for Selene?

"Does he make it home?" she asked.

"He does," I said, and placed my cup on the table at my elbow. "But it's not the same. Neither is he." I told her how brave Ulysses returned with the help of his son and slaughtered his wife's suitors, doing violence in his own home, and how he and Penelope were at last reconciled. "I suppose, in a sense, you never can go home. Because it's never the same home."

Below, Gibson spread his hands as he continued his recitation. He was recounting the scene in which Telemachus reproached his people for not driving the suitors from his father's house and—finding little sympathy— begs for a ship to sail to Pylos that he might seek his father, Ulysses. The circle of children listened intently, leaning in. Gibson delivered his lyric translation in a rolling, thunderous voice so much stronger than his usual tones, as though he were a man many centuries younger, a father reading to his sons.

> O prince, in early youth divinely wise,
> Born, the Ulysses of thy age to rise
> If to the son the father's worth descends,
> O'er the wide wave success thy ways attends.
> To tread the walks of death he stood prepared;
> And what he greatly thought, he nobly dared.

"He's so good with the children," Valka said, drawing closer, her head nestled against my chest.

Fingers smoothing her hair, I said, "He always was."

"'Tis strange, no?" she began softly. "Almost all the children down there are Siran's, five or six generations removed. Amazing how much impact one person can have." She drew closer. "'Tis almost enough to make me want children."

I did not say anything, but pressed my lips to the top of Valka's head.

And lo, with speed we plough the watery way;
My power shall guard thee, and my hand convey:
The winged vessel studious I prepare,
Through seas and realms companion of thy care.

CHAPTER 51

THE GLORY OF THE WORLD

DESPITE OUR TALK OF leaving, neither Valka nor I was in any hurry to depart. We had grown comfortable with Imrah's family, and the villagers gave no sign of wanting us gone. The years went by, and the children in the village grew older and began to accompany the men out to sea. More and more I went with them, and tried to content myself with the little actions of ordinary life. Day by day the torments of Dharan-Tun slipped further away, and the stars shone a little brighter.

But still I waited. What I waited for I could not say, though it lurked in the corners of my mind like a spider. Thoughts of the war burning across the stars haunted my dreams, but not a wisp of smoke from all that burning darkened the Colchean sky. Though the stars called and my own words hounded me at night—*Avenge us! Avenge us!*—I was content. I was not healed, I told myself—not whole—though I knew the only healing I might find for my body lay in an Imperial hospital.

It was only an excuse.

My sign came in the ninth year of our sojourn amongst the Sevrastene. I returned to Thessa with Ginoh and Alvar and with fresh supplies to find Valka waiting on the strand. From the way her chest heaved, I knew she had run out to meet us the moment our sails had appeared on the horizon. From the dread whiteness of her face, I knew.

I had been waiting for Gibson to die.

"What is it?" I asked, leaping from the deck, feeling the answer like an ax head deep in my chest.

Wordless, Valka wrapped her arms around me and drew me close. "You have to see him."

He lay in the same bed I'd put him in after we extracted him from fugue, the one with a view of the bay. The room stank in that stale way all death-beds do, and the very light that fell through the window seemed muted and colorless. He did not move as I entered, but lay as one dead.

"What happened?" I asked through stinging eyes.

"Fell," Valka said, and rubbed her left arm self-consciously. I pushed past her, heedless of Ginoh, who had followed me from the dock.

I lay a hand on Gibson's forehead, found it dry and cool. He did not respond. I checked his breathing, found it steady. "Where did you find him?"

"Just out front," Valka answered, seating herself at the foot of the bed.

"We should get him up to the medica," I said, looking round. "Ginoh! Do you have something we can use to carry him?"

The young fisherman's eyes rolled up into his head as he thought. "Could use one of the nets, make a hammock."

Valka caught my wrist. "What are you thinking?"

"We can freeze him," I said, shaking her off. "We can freeze him and transfer him to the *Ascalon*. Take him to Aea. Get help."

Not letting go of my wrist, Valka said, "We don't know what's wrong with him. The trauma of the freeze might do more harm than good."

I sank to my knees at Gibson's bedside, pressed my forehead against the edge of the mattress. Still Valka did not let me go. After a moment's silence, I said, "I can't do nothing, Valka." In a voice smaller still, I added, "I can't lose him." And yet I knew at the same time that I had been wait-ing *to* lose him. Gibson—and Gibson alone—had kept me in that place, in those islands. I was like one waking from a dream, a dream in which Valka and I had been man and wife, caring for our aging father in his final years.

"It might be stroke," Valka said.

"We have to move him," I said. "There are med-scanners in the hos-pital pod."

Valka ran her thumb back and forth along my hand. Without looking, I could feel the pity in those golden eyes. "Maybe there's a field scanner. I can go look."

"There's one on the *Ascalon*," I said, and turning to Ginoh I asked, "There's a doctor in the village, isn't there?"

The fisherman shook his head. "Always send to Egris for the doc,"

Ginoh said. Egris was one of the larger settlements in the southern wilds, away east on the mainland. "We can wave for him though, have him fly out. There's an uplink at the caravansary in town."

"Will you go?" I asked, directing my words to Valka.

"Me?" Valka blinked, surprised that I would ask her to leave me.

"You can get the scanner from the ship," I said.

Valka looked down, eyes not really fixed on anything as she mulled this over. "Hadrian," she said at last, "if we go for the doctor, they'll know we're here."

We both knew she was right. Using the village uplink to communicate with Egris would certainly alert the governor-general's office in Aea. Whatever doctor there was in the city was sure to be on the Imperial dole, and a palatine lord and his Tavrosi companion were sure to raise eyebrows. It didn't matter.

I squeezed her hand. "It's all right," I said. "It's time."

In the end, Valka left with Ginoh in pursuit of the scanner. I watched the little fishing boat go, back across the water to Racha, and seated myself on a wooden chair beside the bed of the man who made me what I am. There was no strength in Gibson's fingers, and the warmth of his hand was sparse as the cinders of a dying fire.

"I never said I was sorry," I said, speaking to no one, really, for I was sure Gibson could not hear. "I never wanted you to suffer on my account. It's strange, when I left home, I never planned on coming back. I never wanted to see Father again, or Crispin. Or any of the others. I knew I wasn't going to be like one of the heroes in the old stories: there and home again. My story was going to be different." I looked up at the white plastic of the roof above us both, not really seeing it. I saw instead the looming heavens, black and pregnant with the threat of all that was out there in the watchful Dark. "I thought I could *be* different, thought I could make peace." As I spoke, I massaged the stumps of my fingers, remembering Syriani's fangs. In the silence of the chamber, I heard once more the screaming of men and the cold laughter of the feasting Pale beneath the greenish shadows of Akterumu. "I was wrong."

There was no peace. Not with the Cielcin, nor with their dark gods.

"And I was wrong about going home," I said, and heard my own voice break.

Still Gibson did not move, unless it was to breathe softly beneath white linen. Beyond the window, the waves and the gulls made no sound.

"That's twice now I thought I'd never see you again," I said. "But you were always there. Even now. After everything." Again I looked round the spartan apartment, white-on-white. Little touches had made a home of the place in the last several years. Curtains hung on the windows, decorated with the red right-angle patterns of the natives. The very chair on which I sat had been carved on Racha, as had the table set in one corner. The rug beneath it was woven of the same dun stuff as the curtains, showing similar geometric designs. "I don't even know how you did it."

Colchis was not the farthest place from Delos in the universe. I had come from places farther still, and yet we were so far and so long removed from that day at the whipping post before the steps of the great keep at Devil's Rest that to meet at all—much less twice—was itself a form of miracle.

"I guess I did come home, in a way," I said, still sure he could not hear me. "Thank you, Gibson. If you can hear me. Thank you."

Valka was gone a long time, and the sky without grew dark. From time to time Gibson shivered on the bed. Once or twice his lips moved, but no sound came out. It took about an hour and a half to cross the water to Racha. That meant about four hours for her to collect the scanner, make the call, and return. Longer, if she had to explain herself to Imrah, longer still if she had to explain what was happening to the authorities.

It was absurd to me that, in a universe where messages might cross light-years in an instant via quantum telegraph, communication should be so slow. But there was nothing on Thessa to connect to Colchis's anemic datasphere. Valka might have used her implants, but to do so would have been to invite Chantry scrutiny, and the last thing we needed was to have an inquisitor prying into the nature of Valka's Tavrosi implants. Better to use the official channels.

"I'm sorry." Gibson's voice roused me, small and thin as it was. "I'm so sorry . . ."

I shook myself. Night had fallen, and Valka had not returned. There were no lights, no signs of boat or starship on the horizon, only the dim umber glow of Atlas suffusing the night air. Gibson had shifted in his sleep, rolled onto his side so that he faced me, his white hair disheveled.

"Gibson?" I sat forward, laid a hand on his shoulder.

"I'm sorry," he said again, words muddy and slurred. I realized with horror that he was weeping. I had never seen him weep before. He was a scholiast, and scholiasts do not weep. "Livy, I was wrong."

Still gripping the old man's shoulder, I said, "Who is Livy?"

Gibson moved his head strangely, eyes trying to find my face. "Hadrian?"

I moved my hand to grip his own. "Yes, Gibson, it's me." The thin fingers did not close. Valka's diagnosis of stroke seemed more and more likely by the minute. Where was she? What had taken so long? "Valka's gone for the doctor. We're going to get help."

The old man tried to shake his head. His jaw trembled. "Too late," he said. "Too late."

"It's not," I said, forced my eyes shut. "Don't say that."

Neither of us moved then. I cannot say what held Gibson's tongue, but I could find no words for the gray howling in my soul. No words, except *no* and *please*. I had my answer the next instant. The gray eyes were closed.

Twice more he awoke in the night, and still Valka did not return. Without my terminal, I had no way of contacting her, nothing to do but wait. It was possible that Ginoh had not wanted to sail by night, that they would wait for the doctor to arrive from Egris by flier and return. Or so I told myself. There was nothing I could do, nothing anyone could do. Gibson was palatine, and the oldest man—save Kharn Sagara alone—that I had ever known. And for palatines, when the end came, it came swiftly.

I tried to make him comfortable, adjusted his cushions, propped him up to afford a vision of the waves, of the world and the glory of it. Atlas's orange glow cast fiery highlights on the wine-dark sea, and what stars were visible shone untouchable in the heavens.

On earth, an old man shivered and groaned. "Livy . . ." Gibson said again, cresting like a whale from the ocean of sleep, "tell Livy I was wrong."

"Who is Livy?" I asked. I had asked him before, a dozen times in the long years we'd shared on the island together.

A brother scholiast, Gibson had always said, and only said. *An old friend.*

"Damn him!" Gibson hissed, more venom in the man than I had ever heard. I started, hurried back to his bedside from where I'd been sitting with my head on the table. "Where is he?"

Resuming my seat, I took Gibson's hand again. "Who?"

Gibson did not seem to hear me. "He should be here!" His words were still blurred and imprecise things, and his eyes flickered across my face, half-seeing. One pupil was larger than the other, and I had a horrible memory of Valka's face after Urbaine's worm had chewed through her neural circuitry. I had to shut my eyes. "He put me here!"

Gone was every vestige of the scholiast's calm. The stroke—if stroke it was—had cracked Gibson's centuries of composure. The *apatheia* had never been farther away. His other hand gripped mine with a fierceness I little expected. "Alois!" he said. "Where is my son?"

"Your son?" I stood, tearing myself from Gibson's grasp in the process. The wooden chair toppled to the floor, and I stumbled back. "Is Livy . . . your son?"

Never once in all the years I'd known him had Gibson referenced family. He was palatine, and so he must have married, must have had his offspring approved by the High College. Why then had he become a scholiast, renounced family and titles?

Who had he been, *before*?

The gray eyes sharpened, found my face. "Alois!" he said, not recognizing me. He looked around, blinking. "What is this place?"

"Colchis, Gibson," I said, blinking back tears. It was one thing to face the old man's death—quite another to face his forgetting me. "Gibson, it's Hadrian."

The one-time scholiast raised a spotted hand and swatted my words away. "I don't like it. Where are we?"

Not righting my seat, I knelt by the old man's bedside, took his paralytic hand in both my own. "We're in the islands. At Thessa. On Colchis. Do you remember?" I squeezed his hand, willing him to recall. "It's me. It's Hadrian."

"Hadrian?" Again the fog on his vision seemed to clear, and he looked around at the apartment as if he were seeing it for the first time. Still blinking, his head lolled back against the cushions. "This . . ." he began, a frown creasing his face, "this is not Belusha?"

"Belusha?" I blinked myself. I could hardly get the word out, so great was my shock. "Belusha?" Belusha was the greatest of the Emperor's prison planets, a place for banished lords and Imperial embarrassments. Sir Lorcan Breathnach, the erstwhile Director of Legion Intelligence who had plotted with the Empress and the Old Lions to assassinate me on Forum, had been sent there, or so I was told. I assumed he must be dead. "Who are you?"

Gibson shut his eyes, leaned his head back against the cushions. "Thessa," he said. "Ill name. Thessalus, son of Jason. Murdered." He shook his head, did not open his eyes. Something of what he said sparked another thought in him, and he said, "My son should be here."

"I *am* here, damn it!"

"Livy . . ." Gibson murmured, voice little more then than a whisper. "I'm sorry. Forgive me. Forgive . . ." He sucked in a long, rattling breath. "I betrayed you. Betrayed . . . our house. Wanted to rule. Wanted . . ." He fell silent then, and lay a long time still as death. I did not leave his side, did not release his hand. More silent still, a voice began to whisper what I already knew. Gibson would not live until Valka returned. Death stood in the doorway, dressed in the same black veil my grandmother's corpse had worn when Crispin and I saw her lying in the porphyry chamber, a shapeless darkness come at the end of life. She carried no scythe, but stood with open hands.

Gibson did not go all at once, but awoke one final time, and seeing me seated beside him, said, "Alistair." He thought I was my father, and he smiled. "Dear boy. Where have you been?"

"I am not my father," I said, clutching the beloved hand. "Gibson, it's Hadrian."

"Hadrian!" The misty eyes cleared. "Hadrian."

"Yes," I said, latching onto that last, tenuous connection.

"Do you remember the Forms of Obedience?" he asked. I told him that I did. My hands still clutched his paralytic one, and Gibson placed his other hand atop them as in benediction. "Remember which is highest."

"Obedience out of devotion," I said, reflexively, as though I were a boy in lecture.

A smile creased that too-creased face. "Love, yes. Do not forget it. Do not make the mistake I made."

"What mistake?" I asked.

"Power is nothing. Power . . ." But his voice had gone thin as old smoke. His lips moved without sound. Stopped.

"Gibson?" My own voice sounded just as thin.

I squeezed his hand, willed his fingers to close on mine. But his eyes closed instead, and I knew that Gibson was gone.

How long I sat still by the dead man's bedside I could not say. The sun had risen again, and a new shadow stood in the door. Not Death. Only Valka with Ginoh and an older woman I did not know. The doctor from Egris. Too late.

Wordless, Valka hurried to my side and wrapped me in her arms. I was not weeping any longer, though I had been for hours. She held me a long time, and Ginoh and the doctor withdrew.

When at last I could manage words again, I said, "I should bury him."

Whatever Valka said, I cannot remember. I can remember only the look on her face, the hurt and pity in her eyes—and the fear. I did not recognize it for what it was at the time. What should she have feared? Not me. I realized later that she feared *for* me. We had come fleeing death and horror, and found death here, too. And yet—as I carried Gibson back up the mountain path toward the plateau and the cairns which housed the Keepers—I found no horror in Gibson's death. There was sorrow, yes, but joy as well, for he had died an ordinary death. The world, my world, had not ended on Eue, at Akterumu.

"Nothing is finished," I said over the body.

I laid him to rest—not with the Keepers along the path to the medica dome—but upon the heights overlooking the bay. Valka stood some distance off, Ginoh and Imrah behind. Thus it was I stood with Gibson one last time, as we had stood together upon the sea wall of Devil's Rest, overlooking the ocean. How far we had come to arrive in the same place.

I was a long time finding the stones for Gibson's cairn. I had taken so many to build the funeral markers for the others that more than once I was forced to trek down to the level of the water to find stones large enough and flat enough to pile on Gibson's bones. Though my hands bled and my ruined shoulder ached, I would not let the others approach, would not let them place stones of their own upon the mound. "He was my father," I said. "I should be the one to bury him."

The sun was going down again by the time I finished my work, and a low, squat pile of stones stood over Gibson's body. It was not so graceful as the others, nor so tall, but it was mine, and in the years to come Imrah and her children would in turn straighten the stones that I had laid, on Gibson's mound and on all the others. On them would fall the honor and the charge of tending the paths and tombs of Thessa, of keeping the Isle of the Dead.

He is there still. Travel from Aea across the sea to where the Sevrast Islands rise from gray waters. Climb the stony paths of Thessa and walk the cliffs overlooking the sea, and you will find him there. There his body will remain until the stars go out, or that gray isle crumbles into the ocean. Find him, if you wish, and know that all I have said is true.

Valka came up beside me, and stood silent a long while, arms crossed against the chill wind. We both stared at the cairn that I had built, neither moving.

"How did he know?" I asked, the one question of all the questions that burned the brightest. "How did he know that we were coming back?"

Valka did not answer.

"I don't know what to do," I said. "He was always there. Even when I thought he was dead all those years, I hoped. I would ask myself what he would do, what he would think. But now he's gone. Now I *know* he's gone." I shook my head, wiped my face with grimy hands. "How did he know? How did he know I'd need him? Need . . . *this*."

I did not have to look to know that Valka smiled. "He didn't," she said. "He told me. He only hoped."

I smiled. "It's beautiful here," I said, and put an arm around her shoulders, drew her close. "But we can't stay, can we?"

"No," she said. "They're sure to come for us now. They know we're here."

"Then we should go," I said.

"To Aea?" Valka asked.

I chewed my lip. "To the Library. There are some questions I want answered."

"We should go, then," Valka said. "If we hand ourselves over to your people, they may spare the villagers the inquiry."

She was probably right. I did not like the thought of the Inquisition or Legion Intelligence sweeping into Racha to question poor Imrah and her family about our long presence. They had been generous hosts, and in any case I did not want Siran's family to suffer for my sake. Still, I drew Valka in a little more tightly. "Just a moment longer," I said, smiling at the grave.

Now hear this. The old words seemed to drift back to me on the wind, carried by the ocean airs from world to world. *Here's a lesson no tor or primate of the college will ever teach you, if it even can be taught. The world's soft the way the ocean is. Ask any sailor what I mean. But even when it is at its most violent, Hadrian . . . focus on the beauty of it.*

"I will," I murmured to the old man's shade, and did not heed Valka's confusion at my side. "I promise." And reaching down I drew a weight I had carried every day on Colchis from a pocket of my coat. The ruined sword hilt weighed heavy in my hands, its cracked reservoir empty, its fittings tarnished and broken. How much heavier than a feather was its weight? How many souls hung in its balance?

Turning, I hurled the ruined weapon out into the sea.

I did not see where it landed, nor did I hear a splash.

There are endings, Reader, and this is one. A part of me will forever lie within that broken ring of green stone, amid the blood and sacrifice before the ruin of that dreaming god of night. But a part, too, rests now and always on a sunlit cliff above the waters of Colchis, under a sunlit sky. There is pain always, and ugliness, but the light and beauty of the world shine always above and beyond the powers of darkness to destroy.

I was alive, had come like Orpheus out of Hades—but unlike Orpheus, I had not come out alone. But I had come out wounded, scarred. More wounds and worse awaited me, wounds that would leave no mark. If what I have suffered—if what I have done—disturbs you, Reader, I do not blame you. If you would read no further, I understand. You have the luxury of foresight. You know where this ends.

I shall go on alone.

Dramatis Personae

THE MEIDUA RED COMPANY

FORMALLY CONSTITUTED AS AN Imperial special company after Hadrian Marlowe's defeat of the Cielcin Prince Aranata Otiolo in ISD 16227, the Meidua Red Company served at the front of more than a dozen major engagements during the Cielcin Wars, from Thagura, to Arae, to Aptucca, to the famous Battle of the Beast on the road to Nemavand and the legendary Battle of Berenike. After a sojourn to the Demarchy of Tavros on a private mission, the Red Company returned to battle several times, most notably at the horrific siege of Senuessa, and later at Sybaris, where Lord Hadrian Marlowe was arrested by the Holy Office of the Inquisition and taken to Thermon for trial. Marlowe's famous trial was inconclusive, and after twelve years the Chantry simply tried to assassinate the man, but Marlowe survived, and the Emperor—intervening to save the life of his servant—had Hadrian put under guard in a country manor on Nessus, where Lord Marlowe served as advisor to the Magnarch Karol Venantian on all things relating to the Cielcin. Lord Marlowe remained on Nessus until ISD 17006, when an attack on the fuelworks at Eikana prompted the Emperor to order the Red Company back into combat for the first time in over century.

Here follows a list of those members of the Red Company mentioned in this volume of Lord Marlowe's account:

LORD HADRIAN ANAXANDER MARLOWE, Royal Knight Victorian, Lord Commandant of the Red Company, Hero of Aptucca. The Halfmortal, the Sun Eater, Starbreaker, Palekiller, Deathless. Notorious genocide responsible for the death of the entire Cielcin species.

—His paramour, **VALKA ONDERRA VHAD EDDA,** a Tavrosi demarchist and xenologist interested in the Quiet phenomenon, afflicted by an Extrasolarian mind virus.

—His myrmidons, friends and former coliseum fighters from Emesh:

—**PALLINO OF TRIESTE,** chiliarch and HADRIAN's bound arms-man. A veteran of the Cielcin Wars, raised to the patrician class. Origi-nally lost his eye in the Battle of Argissa.

—His paramour, **ELARA OF EMESH,** quartermaster for the *ISV Tamerlane* and HADRIAN's bound armsman. Raised to the patrician class.

OTAVIA CORVO, captain of the *ISV Tamerlane*, former Norman mercenary recruited during the Pharos Affair. Possibly a homunculus.

—Her First Officer, **BASTIEN DURAND,** commander, former Norman mercenary from Algernon recruited during the Pharos Affair.

—Her officers:

—**RODERICK HALFORD,** commander, the so-called *night captain*, in charge of running the *Tamerlane* while the rest of the crew rests in cryonic fugue, the seventh son of a minor palatine lord.

—**LORIAN ARISTEDES,** commander and tactical officer for the *ISV Tamerlane*. The bastard son of the Grand Duke of Patmos and one of his knights, a palatine intus plagued by idiosyncratic pain and connective tissue disorders.

—**KARIM GARONE,** called **CRIM,** lieutenant commander and se-curity officer for the *ISV Tamerlane*, former Norman mercenary recruited during the Pharos affair.

—His paramour, **ILEX,** lieutenant commander, ship's engineer. A dryad homunculus recruited on Monmara.

—**FELIX KOSKINEN,** lieutenant and ship's helmsman. A young pal-atine officer.

—**ADRIC WHITE,** lieutenant and ship's navigator. A young palatine officer.

—**JULIANA PHERRINE,** lieutenant and ship's communications offi-cer. A young palatine officer.

—**LUANA OKOYO,** lieutenant commander and ship's chief medical officer. Former Norman mercenary recruited during the Pharos affair.

—**TOR VARRO,** Chalcenterite scholiast and scientific advisor.

LEON, an ensign newly assigned to the Red Company.

GALBA, OTHO, BARO, and **GARAN,** enlisted men.

{UDAX OF JUDECCA}, an Irchtani xenobite and First Centurion of the Irchtani Auxiliary Unit attached to the Red Company, killed at the Battle of Berenike.

—His commander, **BARDA OF JUDECCA.**

THE IMPERIAL COURT

Dating back to the House of Windsor and Earth's Golden Age, the Aventine Dynasty has ruled over the Sollan Empire and mankind since the defeat of the Mericanii in antiquity. The reigning Emperor of Lord Marlowe's day, William XXIII, took the throne as a young man in ISD 15826 after the passing of his mother, the Empress Titania Augusta, and ruled for an unprecedented thousand-year reign—spending much of his time in transit around the Imperium, unlike most of his predecessors. He began one such tour in ISD 16989, sailing with a Legion fleet from Forum to Gododdin to Nessus, and then in a circuit about the Centaurine provinces to assess the damage dealt by Cielcin invasions and the general warreadiness of the provinces. This tour required the uprooting of much of the Imperial court, as well as an escort of several Martian Legions.

Here follows a list of those members of the Imperial Court mentioned in this volume of Lord Marlowe's account:

His Imperial Radiance, the **EMPEROR WILLIAM THE TWENTY-THIRD OF THE HOUSE AVENT;** Firstborn Son of the Earth; Guardian of the Solar System; King of Avalon; Lord Sovereign of the Kingdom of Windsor-in-Exile; Prince Imperator of the Arms of Orion, of Sagittarius, of Perseus, and Centaurus; Magnarch of Orion; Conqueror of Norma; Grand Strategos of the Legions of the Sun; Supreme Lord of the Cities of Forum; North Star of the

Constellations of the Blood Palatine; Defender of the Children of Men; and Servant of the Servants of Earth.

—His wife, **EMPRESS MARIA AGRIPPINA AVENT,** Princess of Avalon, Archduchess of Shakespeare, and Mother of Light.

—Their children:

—**AURELIAN,** Crown Prince and firstborn child.

—**SELENE,** ninety-ninth-born child, potentially betrothed to HADRIAN MARLOWE.

—**ALEXANDER,** one hundred seventh–born child and former squire to Sir HADRIAN MARLOWE.

—**VIVIENNE,** one hundred twenty-sixth–born child.

—His ancestor, {**KING WILLIAM VII WINDSOR**}, called **WILLIAM THE ADVENT,** the God Emperor, Emperor of Avalon and Eden, Last King of the United Kingdom of Great Britain, King-in-Avalon, and Lord Sovereign of the Kingdom of Windsor-in-Exile. The first Sollan Emperor, deified by the Chantry.

—His predecessor and mother, {**TITANIA AUGUSTA III**}, whose reign first brought humanity into contact with the Cielcin. Fondly remembered for her hawkish response to the crisis.

The Imperial Council:

—**PRINCE HECTOR AVENT,** Supreme Chancellor of the Imperial Council, Prince of Aeolus, a brother of the EMPEROR.

—**LORD RAND MAHIDOL,** Minister of War, a member of the Lion Party.

—His subordinate, **SIR GRAY RINEHART,** a logothete in the Legion Intelligence Office.

—**LORD ALLANDER PEAKE,** Minister of Justice, a member of the Lion Party.

—**LORD PETER HABSBURG,** Minister of Works, a member of the Lion Party.

—**LADY LEDA ASCANIA,** Minister of Public Enlightenment, a member of the Lion Party.

—**LORD HAREN BULSARA,** Director of the Colonial Office, a member of the Lion Party.

—**LADY MIANA HARTNELL,** Minister of Welfare.

—**LORD NOLAN CORDWAINER,** Minister of Revenue.

—**LORD CASSIAN POWERS,** Special Advisor on the Cielcin Question and Baron of Ashbless. The so-called Avenger of Cressgard, formerly a strategos in the Legions who led humanity to their first victory against the Cielcin in the Second Battle of Cressgard. A member of the Lion Party.

—His Holy Wisdom, **VERGILIAN XIII,** Synarch of the Holy Terran Chantry, First-Among-Equals of the Synod and the Choir, Grand Prior of Forum, Metropolitan High Priest of the Eternal City, and Speaker for the Vanished Earth.

Unnamed members of the Council:

    —The **LORD MINISTER OF RITES**.

    —The **DIRECTOR OF THE HOME OFFICE,** a member of the Lion Party.

{**LORD AUGUSTIN BOURBON**}, former Minister of War and member of the Lion Party. Son of the late Prince Philippe Bourbon. Killed on HADRIAN MARLOWE's orders in retribution for his role in a failed attempt to assassinate Lord MARLOWE.

    —His ally, **SIR LORCAN BREATHNACH,** former Director of the Legion Intelligence Office. Convicted for conspiracy to murder HADRIAN MARLOWE and sentenced to life on the prison planet Belusha.

LEONORA, an Archprior of the Holy Terran Chantry. The EMPEROR's personal confessor.

NICEPHORUS, the EMPEROR's butler, an androgyn homunculus.

THE LEGIONS

There are thousands of legions constituted under the Imperial banner, broadly divided by geography, with the various Perseid, Orionid, Sagittarine, and Centaurine Legions comprising the bulk of the force, in addition to the Norman Legions (greatly reduced in number due to the fighting with the Cielcin) and the Martian Legions tasked with the protection of Forum, Avalon, and the various other estates of the Aventine House itself. The smallest legion may number as few as thirty thousand men—naval officers, flight crewmen, and troopers—or as many as three hundred thousand. These legions are loyal to the Emperor, and are composed primarily of recruits raised on direct Imperial holdings (those with Governor-Generals and not under the auspices of a feudal lord), although in wartime levies have been extracted from feudal demesnes. The Legions are not to be confused with the private armies of said lords, who are not answerable to the Emperor in themselves.

Here follows a list of those members of the Imperial Legions mentioned in this volume of Lord Marlowe's account:

{LORD TITUS HAUPTMANN}, Duke of Andernach and former First Strategos of the Legions of Centaurus, killed in action at the Battle of Berenike.

SIR LEONID BARTOSZ, strategos and military advisor to the EMPEROR. Former legate of the 437th Centaurine Legion.

SENDHIL MASSA, Legate of the 409th Centaurine Legion.

BASSANDER LIN, a tribune in the 409th Centaurine Legion and captain of the *ISV Tempest*, formerly attached to the 437th Legion. A longtime associate of HADRIAN MARLOWE, present at his death in the battle against ARANATA OTIOLO.

> —His former commander, **{DAME RAINE SMYTHE}**, a tribune of the 437th Centaurine Legion, killed in action by Prince ARANATA OTIOLO.

IN THE SOLLAN EMPIRE

By the dawn of the seventeenth millennium ISD, the Sollan Empire stretched across much of four of the galaxy's spiral arms, half a billion habitable worlds, and billions of airless moons and station outposts. Comprising innumerable ethnic groups, countless religions, hundreds of thousands of nobile families—palatine and patrician—and tens of millions of soldiers, its total population cannot be counted, but the best estimates put the number at more than one quintillion human souls.

Founded approximately two thousand years after the development of space travel, the Sollan Empire began when William, King of Avalon, defeated the last bastion of the Mericanii Empire at Earth. Crowning himself Emperor of Man on the Aventine Hill in Rome, William Windsor launched the greatest dynasty in human history. The renamed Aventine House has ruled for sixteen thousand years in line unbroken, maintaining its control of the lesser nobility through a careful breeding program that has wrested reproductive control from the nobile houses and placed it in the hands of the Imperial Office. His line and Empire have endured several threats throughout its long history, none greater than the invasion of the Cielcin.

Here follows a list of those people appearing in various settings throughout the Sollan Empire mentioned in this volume of Lord Marlowe's account:

ON NESSUS:

Conquered by the Sollan Empire late in the ninth millennium, the planet Nessus has remained under the direct control of the Imperial House through the person of the Magnarch, an appointed representative of the Emperor. A pastoral world, Nessus was originally settled by the ancestors of the Normans, among them a devout Cid Arthurian community, who trained warrior monks in the highlands. Since falling into Imperial hands, it has been an agricultural and industrial center, producing starships and provisions, as well as a training ground for legionnaires in the region. Through Nessus and the Magnarch of Centaurus, the Emperor has exerted his control over the far provinces, and even pressed into the Norman Expanse, but that control has for centuries been jeopardized by the arrival of the Cielcin.

LORD KAROL MARCUS VENANTIAN, Magnarch of the Centaurine Provinces, Viceroy of Alicante Province, Governor-General of Nessus, Archon of Sananne Prefecture, appointed by His Radiance, the EMPEROR.

—His subordinates:

—**SIR ANDERS LYNCH,** Commandant of Alden Station in orbit above Nessus.

—**SIR DAVETH KARTZINEL,** Commandant of Fort Horn on Nessus.

ANJU, chief of HADRIAN MARLOWE's domestic staff at Maddalo House.

ON COLCHIS:

The primary moon of the planet SAG-8813D, called Atlas by the locals, Colchis was settled in the fifth millennium ISD, then the furthest settled world from Earth. Following the Hundred Year Terror of Boniface Grael, Emperor Gabriel II ordered the Imperial Archives moved from Avalon for safekeeping. Despite this critical function, Colchis is largely underdeveloped, with the majority of its population—primarily members of the Legions and Imperial civil service—living in the capital city of Aea. The remaining locals are primarily fisherfolk descended from the original colonists.

LORD VELAN DORR, Governor-General of Colchis, an Imperial appointee.

TOR ARRIAN, formerly **LORD MARCUS AVENT,** a cousin of the EMPEROR. Primate of Nov Belgaer athenaeum and master of the Imperial Library.

{SIRAN OF EMESH}, formerly a companion of HADRIAN MARLOWE, one of his myrmidon companions. Retired to Colchis. First Keeper of Thessa. Deceased.

—Her husband, **{LEM OF COLCHIS},** once eolderman of the village of Racha, a native Sevrastene.

—His former apprentice, **EJAZ,** an elderly fisherman.

—Their descendants:

—{**ELARA OF COLCHIS**}, Second Keeper of Thessa, named for ELARA OF EMESH.

—{**AMARTA OF COLCHIS**}, Third Keeper of Thessa.

—{**BAGOS OF COLCHIS**}, Fourth Keeper of Thessa.

—His children:

—**IMRAH OF COLCHIS**, Fifth Keeper of Thessa.

—**ALVAR OF COLCHIS.**

—Their cousin, **GINOH.**

TOR GIBSON OF SYRACUSE, a scholiast. Former tutor to House Marlowe of Delos and something of a father figure to HADRIAN. Banished from Delos for abetting HADRIAN's escape from his father.

THE CIELCIN

According to this account and their own legends, the Cielcin were delivered from their homeworld, Se Vattayu, to the planet Eue by the High King, Elu, who with its adherents, the thirteen Aeta, constituted a kind of Cielcin Empire on the far side of the galaxy. After Elu's death, the various Aeta turned on one another, their armies fracturing into tribes. Each *Aeta*, or clan-chief, could at one time trace its lineage by blood or conquest back to one of the original thirteen. By Hadrian's day, those thirteen had fractured to more than a thousand different clans, each calling home a fleet of interstellar ships, some large as moons, and all distributed across the galactic volume in the Norman Expanse and the farther regions beyond the galactic core.

Here follows a list of those Cielcin mentioned in this volume of Lord Marlowe's account:

SYRIANI DORAYAICA, the Prophet of the Cielcin and Prince of Princes. Shiomu. Aeta-ba-Aetane and Aeta-Prince of the Itani Dorayaica. Supreme Ruler of Dharan-Tun. Blood of Elu. Blessed of Miudanar. Master of the Thirteen Tribes of Eue. Called the Scourge of Earth by the humans.

—Its Generals, the **IEDYR YEMANI,** or White Hand:

—**VATI INAMNA,** the First Sword. Closest companion of the Prophet. One of SYRIANI's vayadan, its servant and concubine. Converted into a half-machine chimera with the aid of MINOS. Chief Admiral of the Prophet's forces.

—Its lieutenant, **GORRE**.

—**HUSHANSA,** the Many-Handed. One of SYRIANI's vayadan, its servant and concubine. Converted into a half-machine chimera with the aid of MINOS. Capable of occupying several bodies at once.

—**TEYANU,** the Unbreakable. One of SYRIANI's vayadan, its servant and concubine. Converted into a half-machine chimera with the aid of MINOS.

—**AULAMN,** the Wings of Despair. One of SYRIANI's vayadan, its servant and concubine. Converted into a half-machine chimera with the aid of MINOS.

—**{IUBALU},** the Four-Handed. One of SYRIANI's vayadan, its servant and concubine. Converted into a half-machine chimera with the aid of MINOS. Slain at the Battle of the Beast.

—**{BAHUDDE},** the Giant. One of SYRIANI's vayadan, its servant and concubine. Converted into a half-machine chimera with the aid of MINOS. Slain at the Battle of Berenike.

—Its slave, **GURANA,** a common soldier.

—Its allies:

—**UGIN ATTAVAISA,** the Blue. Aeta-Prince of the Itani Attavaisa. Commander of the fleet at the Battle of Perfugium.

—**GURIMA PELEDANU,** Aeta-Prince of the Itani Peledanu, Lord of the Fiftieth Branching of the Line of Imnun. Commander of the Fleet at the Battle of Ganelon.

The Lesser Princes:

—**AVARRANA IAMNDAINA,** Aeta-Prince of the Itani Iamndaina, an opponent of DORAYAICA.

—**ELENTANI HASURUMN,** Aeta-Prince of the Itani Hasurumn, an opponent of DORAYAICA.

—**AJIMMA,** Lord of the Seventeenth Branching of the Line of ZAHAKA, formerly vayadan to UTAIHARO. An opponent of DORAYAICA.

—**RAIAZU** and **TUANOLO,** Lords of the Seventeenth Branching of the Line of ZAHAKA, both formerly vayadan to UTAIHARO.

—**ONASIRA,** a prince from far away. Noted for raiding the *hakurani* beyond the core.

—**MUZUGARA,** once battled HADRIAN MARLOWE at the Battle of Thagura.

—**VANAHITA,** an opponent of DORAYAICA.

—**KOLERITAN, ELUGINORE,** and **NETANEBO.**

HEIUN ORALO, Aeta-Prince of the Itani Oralo, Lord of the Thirty-First Branching of the Line of Dumann. Principle Cielcin chief of the approximately forty to reject DORAYAICA's summons to the Aetavanni on Eue. An opponent of DORAYAICA.

—Its fellow exiles, **BALAGARIMN, KUTUANU,** and **LOREGANWA,** each the chiefs of their own clans. Opponents of DORAYAICA.

{**ARANATA OTIOLO**}, Viudihom, Aeta-Prince of the Itani Otiolo, Lord of the Seventeenth Branching of the Line of ZAHAKA. Slayer of and former vayadan to UTAIHARO. Once supreme ruler of the worldship *Bahali imnal Akura*. Killed by HADRIAN MARLOWE in the battle aboard the *Demiurge*.

—Its child, **{NOBUTA OTIOLO}**, killed by HADRIAN MARLOWE in the battle aboard the *Demiurge*.

—Its former master, **{UMNA UTAIHARO}**, last scion of the Line of UTAIHARO, a branch of the Line of ZAHAKA.

—Its servants:

   —**{CASANTORA TANARAN IAKATO}**, a baetan, priest-historian of its clan.

   —**{ITANA UVANARI AYATOMN}**, ichakta, captain of the ill-fated Cielcin expedition to Emesh.

{VENATIMN ULURANI}, former Aeta of the ULURANI clan, killed by HADRIAN MARLOWE in single combat at the Battle of Aptucca, allowing a nearly bloodless human victory.

{ELU}, a mythical figure. According to legend, the Cielcin High King who brought its tribe through space to the planet Eue. Blessed of MIUDANAR.

—Its mate, **{AVARRA}**, sacrificed to MIUDANAR according to Cielcin legend.

   —Their offspring, **{UMNA}**, the First Aeta.

—Its followers, **{DUMANN}**, **{IMNUN}**, **{ZAHAKA}**, and **{IN-UMGALU}**, among the first Aeta, and the progenitors of various lines of Cielcin succession.

{ARAXAIKA}, the Almost-Blessed, another mythical figure. Brought an end to the Kinslaying, a civil war between the Cielcin clans attested to in this account. Failed to unite the tribes.

THE EXTRASOLARIANS

For as long as the Sollan Empire has existed, there have been those eager to escape it. Tracing their descent back to survivors of the Mericanii and of the Mandari corporate clans, the Extrasolarians are not truly a people.

The term is rather an umbrella capturing innumerable disparate factions dwelling in the spaces between the stars, on asteroids and rogue planets, on black-site stations and on huge migratory starships called Sojourners. They may be part of microstates or planetary kingdoms, or part of no state at all, many being anarchists and economic adventurers. They are united only in their opposition to the Sollan Empire and in their willingness to use technologies forbidden by the Chantry.

Multiple factions and agencies among the Extras are referenced in Lord Marlowe's account; here follows a list of those described:

ON VORGOSSOS:

According to legend, the planet Vorgossos was settled in ancient times by the ancestors of the Extrasolarians fleeing the early Empire. Lord Marlowe's account indicates that the settlement of the planet may go back even further, and that the city he visited may have been an outpost of the Mericanii Empire during the Foundation War. What is more, Marlowe's account insists on there being some truth to the legend of Kharn Sagara, insisting that the ancient warlord found a manner of immortality by relying on abandoned Mericanii technology and has ruled the planet since antiquity, providing a hideaway for pirates, mercenaries, and for all manner of unsavory activity, notably the black-market genetics and cybernetics trades.

KHARN SAGARA, called the **UNDYING,** King of Vorgossos. Presumably the same Kharn Sagara from ancient legend, a man more than fifteen thousand years old. Last seen divided into two bodies.

—His children: **{SUZUHA}** and **{REN},** both clones. Dead, the mind and personality of KHARN SAGARA has possessed both of them.

—His servants:

—**BRETHREN,** a Mericanii artificial intelligence composed of human tissue confined to the underground sea beneath Vorgossos.

—**CALVERT,** Exalted magus in charge of the cloning program and body farms of Vorgossos.

—**YUME,** a golem or android.

OF MINOS:

Virtually no reference to an Extrasolarian organization called MINOS exists in the Imperial record outside Lord Marlowe's account, casting some doubt as to whether or not they are another of his inventions. It is the case that the Cielcin Prince Syriani Dorayaica contracted various Extrasolarian agencies during the wars to construct equipment and soldiers for its armies, but Marlowe's claims of an order of magi capable of traveling between bodies and across light-years cannot be corroborated.

The Elect-Masters of MINOS, comprising several magi, their total number unknown:

—**URBAINE,** Elect-Master of MINOS, nominally an advisor to Prince SYRIANI DORAYAICA. Infected VALKA ONDERRA with a dangerous mind virus at the Battle of Berenike.

—**SEVERINE,** Elect-Master of MINOS, nominally an advisor to Prince SYRIANI DORAYAICA. Encountered HADRIAN MARLOWE at the Battle of Arae.

—**IOVAN,** Elect-Master of MINOS, serving as an agent among the Lothrians, disguised as the man in the NINTH CHAIR.

THE LOTHRIAN COMMONWEALTH

The origins of the Lothrian Commonwealth are little understood. Believed to have been settled by Extrasolarians in the late fifth or early sixth millennium, the planet Padmurak has always been an inhospitable place. Some historians believe the settlement goes back even further, that the Lothrians can trace their descent to Mericanii refugees fleeing the Foundation War, but this has never been successfully demonstrated. A hermit state for much of its early existence, the teachings of the *Lothriad* book of laws and its partisans certainly dates back to the sixth millennium, but it wasn't until the tenth millennium that the Lothrians began to stir and expand from beyond their isolated star cluster in the Upper Sagittarius. Radically totalitarian and collectivist, the Lothrian language has abolished all means of personal reference in an effort to fundamentally alter the nature of human society, and if Lord Marlowe's account is to be believed, human biology as well. They have been stalwart opponents of both the Sollan Empire and the Jaddian Principalities on the galactic stage, especially with regard to territory in the Upper Perseus near the outer rim.

Here follows a list of those members of the Lothrian Commonwealth mentioned in this volume of Lord Marlowe's account:

THE LOTHRIAD, the central legal text of the Lothrian Commonwealth, comprising two volumes: the first containing the laws of the Commonwealth, the second a collection of all approved words and phrases, constantly revised. Nominally, the text is the supreme authority in the Lothrian state.

—The Lothrian Grand Conclave, comprising thirty-four ministers, called **CHAIRS**:

—**FIRST CHAIR,** the nominal head of the Conclave.

—**THIRD CHAIR.**

—**SIXTH CHAIR.**

—**NINTH CHAIR,** the leader of a radical pro-Lothriad faction on the Conclave. In reality the Extrasolarian magus **IOVAN,** an Elect-Master of MINOS.

—His ally, **THIRTEENTH CHAIR,** another MINOS plant.

—**SEVENTEENTH CHAIR,** a scholiast-trained man named **LORTH TALLEG,** head of the more moderate wing of the Conclave.

—**TWENTY-FIFTH CHAIR.**

LORD DAMON ARGYRIS, Chief Consul and Director of the Sollan Imperial Consulate on Padmurak, a member of House Argyrisof Anxia.

CARRY, a scavenger and boatman dwelling in the tunnels beneath Vedatharad.

—His child, **LOOKER,** an androgyn. One of the Lothrian *new men.*

MAGDA, a physician and Museum Catholic convert.

—Her mentor, **{FATHER DIAS},** a Museum Catholic priest and missionary, dead for several years.

THE WIDER WORLD

A small number of the persons mentioned in Lord Marlowe's account are difficult to group with the others due to their remoteness from the events he describes.

Here follows a list of all those persons mentioned in this volume of Lord Marlowe's account:

LORD ALISTAIR DIOMEDES FRIEDRICH MARLOWE, Archon of Meidua Prefecture and Lord of Devil's Rest, former Lord Executor of Delos System, and Butcher of Linon. HADRIAN's father.

    —His wife, **{LILIANA KEPHALOS-MARLOWE},** a celebrated librettist and filmmaker, deceased.

    —Their other children:

        —**CRISPIN ORESTES MARLOWE,** presumptive heir to Devil's Rest.

        —**SABINE DORYSSA MARLOWE,** a daughter born to replace HADRIAN after his exile.

    —His castellan, **SIR FELIX MARTYN,** Commander of the House Guard and Master-at-Arms in charge of instructing the Marlowe children.

    —His counselor, **TOR ALCUIN,** a scholiast.

EDOUARD ALBÉ, an Imperial intelligence officer.

THOSE BEYOND

Lord Marlowe's account makes frequent references to entities not attested to by science or the historical record. These may be broadly divided into two groups: the Quiet, previously described as an extinct race of xenobites of great antiquity, and the Watchers, initially assumed by Lord Marlowe to be the pagan idols of the Cielcin people. Lord Marlowe's account claims both these groups are real, and that their reality is common knowledge among the Cielcin. It is impossible—from studies of Cielcin writings and artifacts—to conclude that both the Quiet and Watchers are anything but religious fetishes promulgated by the Cielcin faith. That there are the ruins of many ancient races across the galaxy is not disputed in athenaeum. The ruins on Emesh, for instance, exist as Lord Marlowe describes. That these ruins are related to sites on other worlds—such as the Marching Towers of Sadal Suud—has never been corroborated by scholiast research, though I grant this may be the result of Chantry interference in our work. The so-called *Quiet* hypothesis has existed for thousands of years, but cannot be examined due to Inquisition censors and oversight of our colleges. In any case, Lord Marlowe's claims that the Quiet is a singular entity, and that the ruins on these worlds are anti-entropic structures traveling backward through time, likewise cannot be corroborated. Further investigation is needed.

As for the Watchers, the names of these various deities do appear in numerous Cielcin sources captured during the war, but no artifacts have been positively identified as confirming the existence of these creatures. The planet Eue, attested to in this account, has—to the knowledge of the Imperial Library—never been located, nor the bones of Miudanar found. These Watchers are therefore, in the opinion of the translator, wholly fictional, and Marlowe's account is to be regarded as highly fanciful and mythologized. Nevertheless, their names and roles are recorded here:

THE QUIET, called **UTANNASH,** the **LIAR,** by the Cielcin, believed by them to be the author of the universe itself and eternal enemy of the Watchers. An entity of pure will aligned with humanity, protector of HADRIAN MARLOWE. Previously assumed to be an extinct species of ancient xenobites.

MIUDANAR, the **DREAMER,** chief god of the Cielcin pantheon, a massive one-eyed serpent with many arms, once worshiped by the Enar. Gave technology to the Cielcin and brought Elu to Eue. Apparently dead.

—The other Watchers:

—**IAQARAM,** who it is said hears all things. Occupies a place of honor in Cielcin worship second only to dead MIUDANAR.

—**SHAMAZHA,** Father of Giants.

—**NAZHTENAH, PTHAMARU, SHETEBO,** and **USATHLAM,** of whom little is known.

INDEX OF WORLDS

HEREIN IS APPENDED A list of all those worlds referenced by Lord Marlowe in this volume of his account. The purpose of this list is simply to remind the reader which world is which. For detailed notes regarding astrography and planetology, please refer the Vandenberg Catalog. What information I have provided here is sufficient to understand Lord Marlowe's text.

—*Tor Paulos of Nov Belgaer*

Annica   An airless world orbiting a red dwarf somewhere on the far side of the galactic core, apparently connected to the Quiet.

Aptucca   An Imperial colony in the Veil, site of the defeat of the Cielcin Prince Ulurani in single combat by Hadrian Marlowe.

Arae   Site of a battle in the Cielcin Wars where Hadrian Marlowe discovered evidence of an alliance between the Cielcin and Extrasolarian humans.

Atlas   The gas giant in the Colchis system about which Colchis orbits.

Aulos   An Imperial colony in the Centaurine Provinces, one of the sites on Emperor William XXIII's tour of the frontier.

Avalon   One of the original human colonies, site of heavy European colonization by generation ark. Birthplace of the Sollan Empire.

Belusha   The most famous of the Imperial prison planets, the last destination of many political prisoners. A dismal, cold world.

Berenike   A former trading hub and mining colony on the Centaurine frontier on the border with the Veil of Marinus, site of a major battle in the Cielcin Wars.

Carcassone   Originally settled by Museum Catholic missions, now an Imperial core world, Carcassone is temperate and a paradise world for terranic life. Famed for its wines.

Carteia   An icy world in the Centaurine provinces, devastated by the Cielcin in the war. One of the sites on Emperor William XXIII's tour of the frontier.

Centaurus Arm   The innermost and farthest of the four arms of the galaxy colonized by the Sollan Empire, north of Sagittarius, Orion, and Perseus. Most Centaurine provinces are clustered near the heart of the galaxy, just south of the Veil of Marinus and the galactic core.

Colchis   The first Imperial colony in the Centaurus Arm, named for the garden at the end of the world, a moon of the gas giant Atlas. Never an important colony (it was eclipsed quickly by its neighbors), it is known for the massive Scholiast athenaeum of Nov Belgaer.

Comum   A Centaurine demesne, site of the Battle of Comum, one of Lord Marlowe's many battles.

Delos   Birthplace of Hadrian Marlowe and seat of the Duchy of House Kephalos in the Spur of Orion, a temperate world with wan sunlight, famed for its uranium deposits, which made it extremely wealthy.

Dharan-Tun   A Cielcin worldship larger than some moons, the seat of Prince Syriani Dorayaica.

Eikana   An airless, desert world in the central Centaurine provinces, noted for its antimatter fuel manufactory, operated by Yamato Interstellar. The primary fuel supplier for Nessus.

Elos   A world renowned for its particle foundries.

Emesh   A watery world in the Veil of Marinus, seat of House Mataro. Home of the coloni Umandh and the subterranean ruins at Calagah. Originally a Norman colony.

Eue	A planet belonging to the Enar and later to the Cielcin, the site of Cielcin migration from Se Vattayu and the seat of their early empire. Resting place of the Watcher Miudanar.
Forum	The capital of the Sollan Empire. A gas giant with a breathable atmosphere in whose cloud belt are several flying palace cities that serve as the administrative hub of the Imperium.
Gododdin	A system between the Centaurus and Sagittarius Arms of the galaxy, famously destroyed by Hadrian Marlowe during the final battle in the Crusade.
Ibarnis	An Imperial colony in the Centaurine provinces, one of the sites on Emperor William XXIII's tour of the frontier.
Judecca	A frigid, mountainous world in the Sagittarius Arm. Famously the site of the Temple of Athten Var and birthplace of the Irchtani species. Site of Simeon the Red's struggle against the mutineers, a famous story.
Kebren	An Imperial colony in the Centaurine Provinces, one of the sites on Emperor William XXIII's tour of the frontier.
Linon	Moon of a gas giant in Delos system, formerly the demesne of the exsul House Orin and site of the Battle of Linon in ISD 5863, in which Alistair Marlowe killed the entire house.
Marinus	The first Norman Freehold seized by the Imperium and amongst their first colonies in the Expanse. The Imperial capital in the Veil of Marinus.
Mettina	A Centaurine demesne. Site of the Battle of Mettina, one of Lord Marlowe's many battles.
Nagapur	A trading hub on the old core-roads from the Orion provinces out toward Centaurus and the Veil.
Nemavand	An Imperial colony in Rammanu Province on the Centaurine frontier.
Nessus	Seat of the Centaurine Magnarchate, famously the site of Hadrian Marlowe's nearly 100-year exile following his arrest and near assassination by the Holy Terran Chantry.
Norman Expanse	See VEIL OF MARINUS. The terms are used interchangeably, though the Veil moniker is more common in the Empire, while the Normans refer to it as the Expanse.
Old Earth	Birthplace of the human species. A nuclear ruin and victim of environmental collapse, she is protected by the Chantry Wardens and none may walk there.
Ostrannas	An Imperial colony in the Centaurine Provinces, one of the sites on Emperor William XXIII's tour of the frontier.
Oxiana	The site of a minor battle in the Cielcin Wars.
Padmurak	Capital of the Lothrian Commonwealth, a frigid, airless world in the Upper Sagittarius, on the far side of the Rasan Belt.
Pagus Minor	One of the Sollan Empire's prison planets.

Perfugium A colonial distribution center in the Centaurine provinces, the home of billions of sleeping human colonists. The site of a major battle in the Cielcin Wars.

Perseus Arm The outermost of the four settled arms of the galaxy, comprising most of the outer-rim territories. Variously settled by the Sollan Empire, the Principalities of Jadd, the Durantine Republic, and various freeholder colonies and smaller states not annexed or allied with a greater power.

Pharos A Norman freehold ruled for a time by Marius Whent, an ex-Imperial legate defeated by Hadrian Marlowe during his time as a mercenary.

Rammanu An Imperial colony on the Centaurine frontier, right on the border with the Veil of Marinus.

Rasan Belt A broad swath of unsettled space, one hundred light-years across, that stretches across the Upper Sagittarius between the Sollan Empire and the Lothrian Commonwealth.

Sadal Suud A wild world in the Spur of Orion, kept mostly untrammeled. Home to the Cavaraad Giants, a huge species of xenobite, as well as to the Marching Towers, one of the Ninety-Nine Wonders of the Universe. Ruled by House Rodolfo.

Sagittarius Arm The second arm of the galaxy colonized by humanity, north of Orion but south of Centaurus. Comprises the core of the Sollan Empire—along with Orion—but the Lothrian Commonwealth constitutes a large portion of its western frontier.

Second Gulf The vast emptiness between the arms of Sagittarius and Centaurus.

Se Vattayu The mythical homeworld of the Cielcin, its surface apparently honeycombed with labyrinthine tunnels like those the Quiet dug at Calagah on Emesh.

Senuessa A Sagittarine world, site of the Battle of Senuessa, one of the bloodiest in the entirety of the Cielcin Wars.

Sete An Imperial colony on the inner reaches of the Norman Expanse.

Teukros A desert world in the Imperium, notably the site of the scholiasts' athenaeum at Nov Senber.

Thermon A Chantry stronghold in the Sagittarine Provinces, famously the site of Hadrian Marlowe's twelve-year-long trial for witchcraft.

Thielbad An Imperial colony in the Centaurine Provinces, one of the sites on Emperor William XXIII's tour of the frontier.

Vanaheim An Imperial colony in the Centaurine Provinces, one of the sites on Emperor William XXIII's tour of the frontier.

Veil of Marinus The region of space at the base of the Norma Arm of the galaxy where it joins the galactic core. Formerly a colonial expansion region dominated by the Sollan Empire and Norman Freeholders, it is also the site of most Cielcin incursions into human space.

Vesperad A moon orbiting the gas giant Ius. The oldest Chantry-controlled planet, boasting its largest seminary complex.

Vorgossos   A mythical Extrasolarian world orbiting a brown dwarf, said to be a mecca for the black-market genetics trade. Formerly a hideout for the Exalted, presided over now by a warlord known as the Undying.

Zigana   An Imperial planet along the inner edge of the Sagittarius Arm, a Legion training and production center. Its harsh environs provide an excellent place to train legionnaires.

LEXICON

HEREIN IS APPENDED AN index of those terms appearing in this fourth volume of Lord Marlowe's manuscript which are not easily translated into the Classical English, or which bear a specific technical or cultural definition requiring clarification in the opinion of the translator. For a more complete explanation of the methodology employed in devising these coinages for this translation, please refer to the appendices in volume one.

—*Tor Paulos of Nov Belgaer*

adamant   Any of the various long-chain carbon materials used for starship hulls and body armor.

adorator   A member of any antique religious cult maintained by the Empire and tolerated by the Chantry.

Aeta   A Cielcin prince-chieftain. Appears to have ownership rights over its subjects and their property.

alumglass   A transparent, ceramic form of aluminum, stronger than glass, which is commonly used in windows, particularly in ship design.

androgyn   A homunculus exhibiting either, neither, or both male and female sex characteristics.

apostol   An ambassador, usually one from the Sollan Empire, especially one sent for a limited time or to achieve a limited goal. An emissary.

aquilarius   A fighter pilot.

Archprior   Within the Chantry clergy, a senior prior, usually one entrenched in the Chantry bureaucracy.

armsman   Any individual—usually patrician—sworn to serve the person of a palatine lord or his/her house in perpetuity.

athenaeum   Any of the research compounds/monasteries of the scholiastic orders.

auctor   An office appointed by the Emperor to serve as his proxy, to speak with his voice and authority in matters where the Emperor cannot be present.

Azh-Hakkai   According to Lord Marlowe's account, possibly a species of xenobite or faction of xenobite hunted to extinction by the Cielcin.

baetan   In Cielcin culture, a sort of priest-historian of the scianda.

bastille   Any Chantry judicial and penal center, usually attached to a temple sanctum.

Bench   The assembly of thirty-four grand ministers presiding over the Lothrian Grand Conclave. In charge of Lothrian governmental policy, especially revisions to the Lothriad.

beta   An extracellular matrix applied as a paste or foam to accelerate the healing process, especially following surgery or in the case of traumatic injury.

bromos   A protein-rich strain of engineered hyper-oat that serves as the basis for ration bars and as protein base for artificial meat production.

cathar   A surgeon-torturer employed by the Holy Terran Chantry.

Cavaraad   A species of giant xenobite native to the planet Sadal Suud. May grow up to forty feet tall and nominally immortal. Enslaved by the Sollan Empire.

centurion   A rank in the Imperial Legions, commands one hundred men.

Chair	Any of the thirty-four men and women seated on the Bench in the Lothrian Grand Conclave. Technically refers to the seat on the Conclave occupied by the person and not the person him or herself.
chariot	A flying personal vehicle in which the pilot stands vertical and changes directions by leaning and via the hand controls.
chiliarch	A rank in the Imperial Legions, commands one thousand men.
chimera	Any genetically altered or artificially created animal, usually by blending the genetic code of two or more animals.
Choir	The Chantry's clandestine research and intelligence division.
Cid Arthurianism	A syncretic religion founded late in the fourth millennium as an offshoot of Buddhism recognizing the British King Arthur as a Buddha, emphasizing chivalric virtue as a means of pursuing enlightenment.
Cielcin	Spacefaring alien species. Humanoid and carnivorous.
coloni	Any intelligent, pre-industrial race of xenobites on a human-occupied world, particularly in the Sollan Empire.
commissar	A Party officer in the Lothrian Commonwealth, usually an officer of the Conclave Guard, considered equivalent to the rank of knight in the Sollan Empire.
Consortium	The Wong-Hopper Consortium. The largest of the Mandari interstellar corporations, specializing in terraforming technologies.
consul	A type of Imperial apostol formally installed in a consulate among foreign powers, a permanent ambassador.
cryoburn	Burns incurred as a side effect of improper cryonic freezing.
cubiculum	A chamber where persons are kept in cryonic fugue, usually aboard a starship.
daimon	An artificial intelligence. Sometimes erroneously applied to non-intelligent computer systems.
datanet	The loose association of all planetary dataspheres connected by quantum telegraphs and inter-space satellite relays.
datasphere	Any planetary data network. In the Empire, access is strictly restricted to the patrician and palatine caste.
Deeps	A species of possibly artificial and intelligent microorganisms found on several worlds, capable of digesting and altering other living creatures.
Demarchy of Tavros	A small interstellar polity far from Imperial control. Radically open to technology, the people vote on all measures using neural lace implants.
dispholide	A rare hemotoxic poison, likely of Chantry design and manufacture, that disables the coagulation process and dissolves collagen and even bone at an astonishing rate, effectively liquefying the victim.

douleter	A slave overseer or trader.
Doxe	The supreme executive authority of the Durantine Republic, elected to a fifty-year term by the assembly per the Durantine constitution.
dryad	Any of a species of green-skinned homunculi capable of photosynthesis, designed for work in outer space.
duplication	One of the Twelve Abominations. The copying of an individual's genetics, likeness, personality, or memories through cloning or related practices.
Durantine Republic	An interstellar republic of some three thousand worlds. Pays tribute to the Empire.
eali	The Jaddian ruling caste, product of intense eugenic development. Practically superhuman.
Elusha	The Cielcin word for "king," a title granted to Syriani Dorayaica, previously held by the semi-mythical Cielcin ruler Elu, whence comes the word.
Emperor	The supreme ruler of the Sollan Empire, considered a god and the reincarnation of his/her predecessor. Holds absolute power.
Enar	An ancient and extinct species of xenobite who, according to Lord Marlowe's account, ruled much of the galaxy and destroyed millions of planets and races several million years ago, and whose legacy explains the relative emptiness of the universe. Not attested to in the fossil record.
entoptics	Augmented reality device where images are projected directly onto the retina.
eolderman	The elected head of a plebeian community. Typically seen in more rural regions on Imperial planets.
Exalted	A faction among the Extrasolarians noted for their extreme cybernetic augmentations.
Excubitor	The innermost circle of the Emperor's guard, comprising 108 of the finest knights and fighters in the Empire.
Extrasolarian	Any of the barbarians living outside Imperial control, often possessing illegal praxis.
extraterranic	In terraforming and ecology, refers to any organism not of Old Earth extraction. Extraterrestrial.
fravashi	In the Zoroastrian religion of Jadd, the spirit of a person, specifically the part of one's spirit who remains with their God in the spirit world.
Galstani	The common language of the Sollan Empire, descended from Classical English, with heavy Hindi and Franco-Germanic influences.
Grand Conclave	The ruling bureaucratic organization of the Lothrian Commonwealth, led by the thirty-four members of the Bench, but containing several hundred functionaries and Party members.

Great Charters   Ancient collection of legal codes imposed on the Empire by a coalition of the houses palatine. Maintains the balance among the houses and between the houses and the Emperor.

groundcar   An automobile, usually powered by solar or by internal combustion.

Hakurani   According to Lord Marlowe's account, an interstellar race or polity in the unexplored regions of the galaxy.

highmatter   A form of exotic matter produced by alchemists. Used to make the swords of Imperial knights, which can cut almost anything.

Holy Terran Chantry   State religion of the Empire. Functions as the judicial arm of the state, especially where the use of forbidden technology is involved.

homunculus   Any artificial human or near-human, especially those grown for a task, or for aesthetic purposes.

hoplite   A shielded foot soldier. Heavy infantry.

hurasam   Gold coin used among the Imperial peasant classes, worth its mark-weight in gold. Print notes for various denominations exist.

Iazyr Kulah   In the Cielcin religion, the universe of pure thought or spirit that existed before the Big Bang, and which is obscured by the material universe. Paradise.

ichakta   A Cielcin title, referring to the captain of a ship.

Iedyr Yemani   The six *vayadan*-generals sworn in fanatic servitude to Syriani Dorayaica. The so-called White Hand.

Imperial Council   The ruling and advisory board of the Sollan Empire, headed by the Chancellor and comprising the lords of the various ministries, the Synarch of the Chantry, various legionary strategoi, and certain special advisors. Advises the Emperor, but also runs the various executive offices of the Imperium.

Imperium   See SOLLAN EMPIRE.

Inquisition   The judicial branch of the Chantry, primarily concerned with the use of illegal technologies.

intus   A palatine born outside the oversight of the High College, usually possessing several physical or psychological defects; a bastard.

Irchtani   Species of coloni xenobite native to the planet Judecca. Bird-like with massive wings. Considered an exemplar of coloni assimilation.

irinyr   A silk-like fabric used by the Cielcin, the byproduct of a many-legged aquatic bottom-feeding worm.

Jaddian   The official language of the Principalities of Jadd, a patois of ancient Romance and Semitic languages with some Greek influences.

legate   A rank in the Imperial Legions, commands an entire Legion.

Legion Intelligence Office   The Empire's military intelligence, espionage, and foreign intervention agency.

legionnaire   Any soldier in the Imperial Legions, especially the common foot soldier.

liberalist   Democratic insurgents in the Lothrian Commonwealth, possibly fictional.

lictor   A bodyguard for a nobile or other dignitary. Usually a knight.

lighter   Any starship small enough to make landfall on a planet.

logothete   A minister in any of the governmental agencies of any palatine house, used colloquially of any civil servant.

Lothriad   The legal text of the Lothrian Commonwealth, in two volumes: the first containing the laws of the Commonwealth, the second a dictionary of all approved words and phrases, constantly revised.

**Lothrian
    Commonwealth**   The second largest human polity in the galaxy, a totalitarian collectivist state. Longtime antagonist of the Empire.

Magnarch   The chief Imperial Viceroy in each arm of the galaxy: Orion, Sagittarius, Perseus, and Centaurus. Essentially co-Emperors.

Magnarchate   Region of the Empire ruled by a Magnarch, comprising several provinces.

magus   An intellectual, most especially a scientist or natural philosopher.

mamluk   Any homunculus slave-soldier of the Jaddian Principalities.

Mandari   An ethnic group semi-detached from Imperial society, most commonly found staffing the massive interstellar trading corporations.

Martian Guard   The Emperor's palace guard, an elite corps of soldiers raised from the population on Earth's nearest neighbor, Mars.

medica   A hospital, typically aboard a starship.

Mericanii   The ancient first interstellar colonists. A hyper-advanced technologic civilization run by artificial intelligences. Destroyed by the Empire.

MINOS   An Extrasolarian organization or order specializing in biomechanics and technological research and development, apparently aligned with the Cielcin Prophet.

nahute   A Cielcin weapon. Resembles a flying metal snake. Seeks out targets and drills into them.

Nipponese   The descendants of the Japanese colonists who fled Old Earth system in the Third Peregrination.

nobile   Blanket term referring to any member of the palatine and patrician castes in the Sollan Empire.

Norman   Anyone native to one of the planets of the Norman Expanse, particularly those not under Imperial control. A so-called Freeholder.

Norman Expanse   The frontier of human settlement in the Norma Arm of the Milky Way, near to the galactic core.

palatine	The Imperial aristocracy, descended from those free humans who opposed the Mericanii. Genetically enhanced, they may live for several centuries.
Pale	The Cielcin. Slang, considered offensive by xenophiles.
Panthai	A Tavrosi language descended from the Thai, Lao, and Khmer-speaking peoples who settled the Wisp alongside the Nordei.
Party	The government of the Lothrian Commonwealth, composed of adherents to the two books of the Lothriad, including the Grand Conclave on Padmurak, the lesser conclaves on the other planets of the Commonwealth, and the lesser government institutions.
patrician	Any plebeian or plutocrat awarded with genetic augmentations at the behest of the palatine caste as a reward for services rendered.
pentaquark	Refers to a class of particles composed of five quarks, as opposed to the more typical three-quark particles comprising most matter. Highmatter is a pentaquark material.
Persean Wars	A series of conflicts fought between the Sollan Empire and their Jaddian allies against the Lothrian Commonwealth in the thirteenth millennium.
phylactery	A device for storing the genetic and epigenetic information of an individual for the purposes of artificial reproduction.
pitrasnuk	Any member of the Lothrian Party, especially those involved directly in the government apparatus.
plebeian	The Imperial peasantry, descended from unaltered human stock seeded on the oldest colony ships. Forbidden to use high technology.
posthuman	A catch-all term referring to anyone so heavily augmented or modified—either genetically or through praxis—as to no longer be conventionally recognizable as human to the Imperial observer.
praetor	In the Chantry's Inquisition, a judge, especially one actually presiding over a trial or sentencing.
prefecture	In the Empire, any administrative district ruled by an Archon.
primate	The highest administrative office of a scholiasts' athenaeum, akin to a university chancellor.
Principalities of Jadd	Nation of eighty former Imperial provinces in Perseus that revolted over palatine reproductive rights. Heavily militaristic and caste-driven.
repulsor	A device which makes use of the Royse Effect to allow objects to float without disturbing the air or environment.
rugyeh	The Lothrian word for the Cielcin. Literally *"the others."*
satrap	A planetary governor in the Principalities of Jadd, subordinate to one of the regional Princes.

scholiast   Any member of the monastic order of researchers, academics, and theoreticians tracing their origins to the Mericanii scientists captured at the end of the Foundation War.

Shiomu   The Cielcin word for *Prophet*, a title granted to Syriani Dorayaica.

Sojourner   Any of a class of massive Extrasolarian starship, often hundreds of miles long, especially those crewed by the Exalted.

Solar Throne   The Imperial throne. Sometimes used as a synonym for the Imperial Presence or Office.

Sollan Empire   The largest and oldest single polity in human-controlled space, comprising some half a billion habitable planets.

static field   A highly permeable variant of the Royse Field used in climate control to keep conditioned air inside buildings.

strategos   An admiral in the Imperial Legions, responsible for the command of an entire fleet, comprising several legions.

Stricture   The formal rules governing the lifestyle and behavior of those members of the scholiast order as outlined in *The Book of the Mind* and the rest of Imore's writings.

sulan   An ancient predator native to the Cielcin homeworld.

Synarch   The highest ecclesiastic office of the Imperial Chantry. Their most important function is the coronation of new Emperors.

Synod   The ruling body of the Holy Terran Chantry, a college of Archpriors presided over by the Synarch.

Tavrosi   Any of the languages from the Demarchy of Tavros. Typically refers to Nordei.

Telegraph/QET   A device which uses entangled quantum particles to communicate instantly over vast distances.

terranic   In terraforming and ecology, refers to any organism of Old Earth extraction. Not extraterrestrial.

trias   A unit of three legionnaires, usually two peltasts and one hoplite.

tribune   A Legion officer in command of a cohort (four to a legion). Commands both ground forces and naval officers.

Twelve Abominations   The twelve most grievous sins according to the Chantry. Legal privileges do not apply in such cases.

Umandh   A coloni species native to the planet Emesh. Amphibious and tripedal, they have an intelligence comparable to that of dolphins.

vate   Any preacher or holy man not formally a part of the Chantry clergy.

vayadan   In Cielcin culture, the bound mates and bodyguards of an Aeta.

verrox   A powerful pseudoamphetamine derived from the leaves of the verroca plant. It is taken by ingesting the leaves, which are usually candied.

Watchers	According to this account, a species or collection of powerful xenobites, possibly worshiped as gods by the Cielcin and other alien races.
worldship	Any of the massive Cielcin vessels—some as large as moons—which make up the core of their fleets.
xenobite	Any life form not originating in terranic or human stock, especially those life forms which are considered intelligent; an alien.
xenologist	A scholiast or lay magus specializing in the study of inhuman beings, especially those rising to the level of sentience.
Yamato Interstellar	An interstellar manufacturing company owned by House Yamato and based out of Nichibotsu.
zuk	Any of the working class of the Lothrian Commonwealth.